PLAYING THE JACK

Once again the mist cleared momentarily and I saw a horseman, a darker shape against the backdrop of the forest. For a moment I thought I must be mistaken – a tree stump perhaps – then that it might be Jack, come back for us, but as the vapour closed round us again I realized with a dreadful sinking of the heart that Jack was not wearing a three-cornered hat when he left us, nor was he riding a black horse with a white blaze to its forehead. . . . A trickle of fear ran down my spine and I found I was praying aloud that I might have been mistaken.

But I wasn't. A masked figure rode out from under the trees, into the suddenly clear night, and I was already pulling back on the bridle of my horse as the pistols swung in my direction and the dread words rang out: 'Stand and deliver! Your money or your life!'

Playing the Jack

MARY BROWN

THE SHERIDAN
BOOK COMPANY

This edition published in 1995 by
The Sheridan Book Company

First published in Great Britain by
Hutchinson & Co. (Publishers) Ltd 1984
Random House, 20 Vauxhall Bridge Road, London SW1V 2SA
Arrow edition 1986

Phototypeset in Linotron Baskerville
by Input Typesetting Limited, London

Printed and bound in Great Britain by
Cox & Wyman Ltd, Reading, Berkshire

ISBN 1–85501–705–9

For my children, David and 'Berta, with love

My thanks to:

My patient and loving husband, Peter;

My typist, Anne Pitt, who gave generously of her free
  time;

The erudite and helpful librarians at Rickmansworth;

My editor, Paul Sidey, and his assistant, Ingrid von
  Essen;

And 'Wellington', who shared the long hours of
  composition.

BOOK ONE
Sprat

1

On the thirteenth of April in the year 1785 I was sitting in a ditch in Derbyshire, convinced I was dying.

The ditch was unremarkable: a straggly hawthorn hedge behind, a damp, stony bottom full of the usual crawly things, a fringe of grass in front and beyond that the rutted road. I was not particularly remarkable either: I suppose I looked then like any undersized lad who was both starving and cold. In fact the only thing that made us of note was that our temporary and unsought association seemed about to become a permanence: the ditch would soon be elevated to the distinction of a grave whilst I should be reduced to the provision of the corpse.

The precise moment when this would take place was still a matter for conjecture, but the time could not be too far ahead. I only hoped dying didn't hurt too much. I remembered being told once that our five senses deserted us one by one as death approached, the last coward being our hearing. If that were so I still had some way to go, for as far as I could tell I was functioning with all five: I could feel the discomfort of hunger and cold, though my extremities were growing numb; I supposed I could taste, though all I had had in my mouth for hours were my tongue and my teeth; I could smell crushed grass and my damp clothes; my eyes still worked, although their focus wavered a little; and I clearly heard a robin sing above me. Perhaps the thread of his song would be the last filament to break in that thin link between being and unbeing. . . .

On a hawthorn twig above my head the robin, careless of my probable fate, sang his song to the patch of blue sky that showed between the heavy clouds moving away to the east. Whimpering, I shifted my cramped legs, and he stopped singing to put his head on one side and consider me with a sharp, black eye, then gave an impatient chirp and fluffed up his feathers. There was no point in both of us starving and automatically I felt in my pouch for a piece of bread, remembering too late there was none, had been none for the past two days. With numb fingers I upturned the pouch I knew was empty, but a few crumbs fell out. My stomach contracted with hunger and I curled up again, hands to gnawing belly, hunched against the damp and cold, but the robin was more easily satisfied. Through half-closed lids I watched him land confidently on the turf, sure beak dealing efficiently with the scattered fragments. Feast finished he flew back to his perch, wiped his beak on a twig, and tried out his song again, the vibration making the optimistic bunches of green on his tree seem to quiver invitingly before my eyes. 'Bread and butter' we called those first shoots of hawthorn and many times as a child I had picked and eaten them in early April, but trying similar leaves yesterday had left me sick and gasping, my empty stomach revolting.

Sprouting leaves like those had been the encouragement that had made those first few easy miles five days ago seem like the road to a golden future: surely spring is here, they had said. The sun had shone with a deceptive warmth, lambs were already past their first wobbling steps, coltsfoot glowed at my feet and that first night I had found the remains of a winter rick in which to curl up, but the very next day April had shown how fickle she could be. It had started to rain, rain backed by a blustering northwesterly that sought every seam in my jacket and snapped at my close-cropped head until my ears tingled. I hadn't realized, either, how hungry the cold and unaccustomed walking would make me. I had packed enough bread, cheese and cold bacon to last me for a week, or so I thought, but it was all gone in two days. The few coins in my pocket were lost when I had been idiot enough to ignore a roughly scrawled notice pinned to a gate: the words looked old and faded enough to disregard, but the bull was real and

I had regained the road minus money and my second pack, containing blanket, waterbottle, spare shoes with brass buckles, and three pocket handkerchiefs. I dared not try to retrieve them, and indeed the last glimpse showed one shoe impaled on a fearsome horn and my blanket well and truly trampled into the muddy ground.

I had trudged on, lighter in weight but heavier at heart: at least I still had the important parcel, and to save my remaining shoes I would go barefoot, grateful for my stepfather's insistence that children were better without footwear. This had resulted in economy for him and a pair of hardy thick-soled feet for me, well capable of walking the paths and fields I had chosen in preference to the high road. That those same feet were now too cut, bruised and swollen for me to resume my shoes was due to a further mishap yesterday – or was it the day before? Time had ceased to have much meaning, merging as it did into a wet, cold, hungry succession of days and nights; I remembered leaving the house before it was light all those days ago and creeping through the deserted streets till I was clear of civilization, then turning south, keeping the distant hills to my left and using the byways, not only for fear of pursuit but also because of the tales I had heard of travellers being waylaid by bands of robbers who watched the roads for the unprotected. Unlikely that they would have harmed a skinny boy with only the clothes to his back, but they might have knocked me on the head for my parcel of books. As it was I had slipped aside whenever I heard anyone nearby and the attack, when it came, was from an entirely unexpected quarter. By yesterday morning I was so desperately hungry I forgot my customary caution and begged a coin from a well-dressed lady out riding with her groom.

She had stared at me down her long nose, then asked abruptly: 'Can you run, boy?'

'A–a little, ma'am,' I had faltered.

'Then we shall have some sport: a coin, Jarvey!' She

11

had held it up for me to see. 'A silver coin, boy. Worth running for, eh? Well then, off you go!'

They had let me reach the far hedge before they took up pursuit and it wasn't till I felt her whip across my shoulders and heard her 'Tally-ho!' that I realized what my role was meant to be. They had pursued me up slippery slopes, across streams and down lanes where the sharp stones had cut my feet, until at last I sought refuge in a small wood, careless of the tough brambles that pierced my skin and made the flesh of my calves burn with scratches. Even then they would not let me go: I heard her exhorting her groom to flush me out. 'Can't have the beggar go to earth . . . .' Besides being terrified and hurt, I was bewildered; I knew some people were thoughtless and unkind but I had never envisaged this sort of savage game where people were cruel for the sake of it.

Half-dead though I was I had to escape, so I struggled through the wood to the other side and kept on running, now through unfamiliar countryside with hills on all sides, moorland crossed by innumerable streams and peopled by ragged, yellow-eyed sheep who regarded me with antagonism. On into the night I stumbled, all sense of direction gone, till finally I found a road and collapsed into the ditch where I was now lying.

I think I was unconscious for a while, for my struggle back to reality took a long time and I was completely disorientated, the more so as there was no sun and I had no idea of north, south or of any landmarks. The hills appeared to be behind me now, and from what I could see I was surrounded by a softer landscape. Even the weather looked as if it might be changing for the better, but it was too late for me. I knew I could travel no further and I also knew that if I did not eat soon I should never move again, for a deadly lethargy was stealing over me and I was not even sure whether I woke or slept.

I supposed that if I were really dying I ought to say a prayer, so I struggled to my knees, folded hands and closed my eyes. It was no use, I could not concentrate:

the robin above my head was singing too loud, and surely he was off key? I glanced up, for his song was becoming even more discordant, but even as I looked he flicked his tail and flew away, leaving his song, however, still in my muddled brain. It seemed to grow louder, accompanied by a thudding like the beating of my heart —

Not my heart: horses' hooves. I saw their feathers only a foot or so from my retreat and they were followed by large, impossibly painted wheels. Raising my eyes I saw a decorated caravan approaching, followed by two others and a cart. Gone now was the fear, the instinct to avoid human contact, all that mattered was my hunger, cold, and despair. I opened my mouth and called out but any sound I made was drowned by the hooves, squeaking axles, rumbling wheels, and an errant shrill piping that seemed to come out of the air. The first horse was past me now: I had to make the effort. Desperately I crawled out of the ditch, pulled myself upright and tottered forward to catch at the step of the caravan as it passed, but the impetus of the vehicle, slowly though it was travelling, was enough to throw me off balance and I landed in a heap in the road, aware that the wheels were dangerously near.

There was a shouted curse, then the wheels, creaks, and hooves stopped. Levering myself to my feet again I gazed up at the very angry driver, reins in one hand and wooden flute in the other, who scowled down at me.

'Hell and damnation, boy! What do you mean by jumping out like some petty hedge-creeper? Don't you realize you might have been killed?'

'Please, sir,' I faltered. 'I didn't mean . . . I just wanted . . . .'

'I don't need any other hands and especially not youngsters who look as if they have slept out all night and not eaten for days — '

'Please, sir,' I said again. 'I have . . . and I haven't, and I didn't want . . . only . . . .' It was absurd; I was standing quite still yet the whole world was slowly revolving round me. Only the dark, saturnine visage above me stayed still, mouthing rejection, whilst all around little dwarves jumped up and down and round, chattering in words I could not understand. Surely I had indeed died and been consigned to hell for running away, and the devil did not want me either and was organizing his imps to throw me out. I needed an angel, and luckily for me there was one at hand.

'Now what's all this then – waking a lady from her beauty sleep?'

The voice was comfortable, North Country, and as she put her hands under my elbows to steady me, my vision cleared and I stared up at the largest woman I had ever seen. Fat billowed out in generous curves, falls, rounds, cushions and pillows from all over this well-endowed lady and I stared at her in wonder, my plight temporarily forgotten. There was a sudden alarming creak of stays as she bent closer, her question for my ears only.

'Run away and not eaten for a couple of days?' Upon my nod she raised her voice, addressing the dark man. 'Nowt to worry about, Jack lad. The boy lost his road, that's all: could do with a bite to eat and a lift partways. Here, you,' she addressed one of the little men, 'fetch a crust and that jug of milk . . . .'

Moments later I was tearing at fresh bread and sipping still-warm milk while my large angel exhorted me to: 'Eat slow now, or you'll heave the lot up again!' My stomach reacted warningly to this good advice so I heeded it and consequently felt a hundred times better by the time the sun had arrived to warm my shivering body.

'Thank you, ma'am; thank you, sir,' I said politely, remembering to add a respectful duck of the head to each.

'Feel better, love?' asked my angel. 'Nice manners, Jack: better than some I could call to mind.'

'If you've finished playing Good Samaritan and giving away our hard-earned victuals, perhaps we may continue to take advantage of the road ahead – that is, if you are sure there are no more like him lurking in the ditch to delay us?' said the dark man in a bored, nasal drawl. He addressed the air about two feet above my head. 'If you want a lift you can hop up on the wagon at the back, but don't dirty anything. Where are you bound?'

'Gloucester,' I ventured.

'Well, we're on the road to Shrewsbury. We camp tonight not far from the highroad. You'll make a few miles on from there if your feet will stand it.' Shaking the reins, he set his caravan moving forward. My angel was already seated in the second one and the dwarves were climbing aboard the third. One of them was already at the reins of the wagon and he jerked his thumb at the strapped load behind. I needed no second invitation: grabbing my parcel from the hedge I hauled myself up by way of one of the wheels and lay back on the sacking. Whatever lay underneath was hard and unyielding, but with the sun warm on my body, the bread and milk comfortable in my belly, and the rocking motion of the wagon, I soon closed my eyes and slept, safe for the moment from anxieties. The last thing I heard was the creaking of the wheels and a faint discordant piping from the lead caravan.

I awoke as the wagon jolted on uneven ground. A red sun was sinking behind low hills to the west and the air had chilled again. We were drawn to a halt on a piece of heath, a couple of hundred yards from a well-made road. The caravans and wagon were drawn up in a semicircle and everyone seemed busy: uncoupling the horses, shaking out palliasses, gathering firewood. Slipping down from my perch and skirting the dark man, who was rubbing down some tack, I made my way to where the fat lady was peeling onions and mending a new-lit fire.

'Sleep well, love? Bet you're hungry again, ain't you? Well, we've boiled potatoes tonight and I've a couple of beefbones to put with these onions . . . . Now, you make yourself useful and we'll see if we can't get round him,' and she nodded in the direction of the dark man. 'Jack's all right when you gets to know his style. Barks a bit at

15

first, but that's just his way. A full stomach and a drink'll work wonders, you'll see . . . . Speak to him fair and easy and polite and show willing, that's best. Got your story right?'

'S–story?' I stuttered.

'Well, it's plain as the little nose on your face as you've runned away – no, don't say nothing till you've sorted yourself out – and he'll want to be sure you ain't done nothing bad. Not but what I'm sure you're a good boy,' she hastened to add, shredding some cabbage, 'but if you ain't, he's sure to find out. My second brother ran away once: younger than you though. Got as far as Preston before he decided home was best. Travelled far?'

'From Chester way. And I haven't got a home, not a proper one. My parents are dead.'

She gave me a quick, oniony hug. 'Poor lamb . . . nothing worse than them charity places. Never mind, Annie'll take care of you! Now, just you take this pail and fill it at the stream in the wood over there. And put on your shoes: there's thorns about.'

Luckily the swelling of my feet had gone down considerably, so I did as I was bid and filled three buckets at her direction. By the time I returned with the last the fire was drawing well, its welcome flames bringing the dusk closer.

'Dinner's on. Let's have a look at those feet of yours . . . . Can't see much for the muck. Best have a dip in that stream, and not just the feet. You look as if you've been up chimney! Got a clean shirt in that parcel of yours? And a bit of soap? Go get a wash, then, and I'll put your things in the tub with mine when you get back. You can clean off a bit of that mud from your breeches and jacket while you're about it: take this brush. Well, now: what you waiting for? You haven't got all night!'

Returning from the stream I could have found my way by my nose alone, quite without the firelight flickering ruddily through the trees. A delicious smell of food drifted past my nostrils, filling my mouth with saliva and setting my stomach to rumbling again. My fat lady was washing

16

what at first I took to be a pair of sheets, but found to my confusion were two enormous flounced petticoats. Handing me a pot of salve for my feet, she added my grubby shirt to the tub and it was soon spread on a nearby bush to dry, looking like a baby's ghost against her more substantial stuff.

Having done, she waddled across to the fire, added a pinch of some herb to the pot, and tasted the result from a large iron ladle.

'Five minutes more . . . . Got a comb? Nay, lad, let me do it . . . .' Expertly she dealt with my coiffure. 'Looks as if rats have been at it —' my collar '— that button needs tightening —' and my jacket '— get it off'n a scarecrow, did you?' All with a kindness and good humour that took any sting from the words. 'Now perhaps your friends might recognize you again!'

She tasted supper once more, and nodded. 'Two minutes.' Handing me a large loaf and a knife she had me dividing it into a dozen equal portions, while she stirred the pot. 'Perhaps you didn't realize we're fair folk, travellers of the road, strolling players? Jack, now, he's the boss, owns us all. Bought me and the dwarves from a man as wanted to retire. Nottingham Fair it was, two years back. Don't know what he did before that, but I reckon there's a spot of the military there and more than a touch of the gentleman . . . . No, he's all right, is Jack, but those dwarves, now I never did seem to get on with them: tricky little beggars as keeps themselves to themselves and quarrels all the time in that foreign lingo, but'll gang up on any that interferes . . . . Clever, though; just watch, they're practising now . . . .'

In the firelight they built a pyramid of bodies, dissolved in a tumbling heap, juggled, clowned, somersaulted, all the while keeping up a falsetto chatter of directions and abuse in a language that sounded as though it had its roots in Italian, or some other Latin-based variation. They changed positions so quickly I never quite managed to number them all; I counted to seven twice, then suddenly

17

saw two more – or was it three? – who I was sure I had not reckoned. Although their antics fascinated me I didn't think I should ever find them friendly: the only glances I had received so far had been contemptuous, but that was probably because I looked so ragged and clumsy.

'But what do *you* do, ma'am?' I asked curiously.

Throwing back her head she laughed till the tears squeezed out of the corners of her eyes and she had to dab them away with the corner of her vast apron.

'Do? Do! Why, bless your heart, nothing! I don't do nothing at all! I just sits and they pays money to see me do just that! Didn't you see what was writ on my van? Not that I can write or read, you understand, but I can tell you those words by heart. "Fat Annie, The Largest Woman on Earth!" it says on one side, and underneath "By Appointment". On the other side there's a picture of me, all dressed in pink with me sleeves rolled up, me skirts up round me knees, airing the dairy . . . . Wasn't sure I liked that bit at first, but Jack says as it Titillates the Imagination, and I suppose he's right, seeing as it's me boobs he's talking about.'

'Who is the "By Appointment" to?' I asked admiringly.

'Crowned Heads, my dear, Crowned Heads! Not that they've been that thick on the ground lately, but one day –'

She broke off as the dark man strode over from his caravan to warm his hands by the fire, and I shrank back into the shadows.

'Supper, Annie? My stomach thinks my throat's cut.'

She took a final taste. 'Ready as it'll ever be.' She banged on one of the pots with a spoon and the dwarves ceased their clowning and scrambled forward, pushing and shoving to be first served. She laid about her with the ladle, good-naturedly enough. 'Wait your turn, you little freaks, or you'll go without!' She scooped out a generous helping into a wooden bowl, and turned to me. 'Go give this to Jack,' she whispered, indicating where he had seated himself away to my right. 'And a couple of pieces of bread.'

I hesitated.

'Go on – he'll not bite, and it'll show you can be useful.'

'Potatoes?' I whispered back.

'Not keen on 'em, lessen we've nowt else: generally keep them for filling up these little beggars. And I've got something special for Jack later.'

He took the food with a nod and a rather disconcerting gaze that took in my tidied appearance without comment; I crept back to Annie and thoroughly enjoyed my stew and bread: I noticed there were even a few shreds of meat with my vegetables.

To my surprise she ate very little. 'Won't you go thinner if you don't eat more?'

'My weight's nowt to do with me diet – wish it were. No, a doctor told me once there was something working away inside of me that would keep me fat whatever I did, just as some people are always thin as a lath however much they stuff themselves.' She sighed. 'I wasn't as fat as this when I were a girl: had to watch my weight a bit, mind, but it wasn't till I lost my second child that I found I couldn't stop the fat . . . . My husband, may he rot in hell, ran off with some fly-by-night down Freckleton Marsh way – not that it did him much good: got drunk one night, fell in Lytham Creek and were drowned – but I were left on my own with both our children lying in the churchyard up the hill . . . . After that I don't suppose I cared much what became of me, and I just swelled up all over. Then I met this man at the fair: he told me to put on a bit more and he'd come back for me the next year. He told me I was worth me weight in gold: to him, maybe.' She chuckled, chasing the last drop of gravy round the bowl with her finger. 'I've found it's taken a fair number of years to get even a bit put by for when I retire.'

'Will that be soon?'

'Well, love, fat ladies don't go on forever. The body gets tired of carrying around all that extra, and it's a strain on the heart, they say. You wouldn't guess it, but I'm not thirty yet; no, in another couple of years or so I'll happen go look after my eldest brother and his children – his wife died in childbirth a couple of years back, and they need a woman's care . . . . Ah, now them's done to a turn!'

Fishing out a couple of large marrowbones from the remains of the stew, she put them on a large platter and I could see the juice trickling out invitingly. She added a piece of bread.

'For him?' I nodded over to the dark man.

'That's his treat; perhaps if you hadn't turned up I'd've kept 'em for another day.' She gave me a little push. 'Off you go!'

This time as I handed him the platter he detained me with a hand on my sleeve.

'Sit down, boy. I want to talk to you.'

This sounded ominous, but obediently I seated myself cross-legged on the grass as far away as I thought prudent. At first I kept my gaze on the fire, but as he seemed to be ignoring me, I ventured a glance or two in his direction. He was using a travelling knife, fork and spoon set, which even contained tiny salt and pepper pots, and he made great play with the handle of the spoon, scooping out the marrow. Not to waste any he even tipped back the bones and let the remaining substances trickle down his throat; some spilled over on to his chin, which he wiped with a rather grubby napkin. Finished, he wiped his cutlery with the same cloth, replacing it in its leather case in his pocket, tossed the bones in the general direction of the fire, knotted platter and bowl in the napkin and threw the bundle over to Annie; belched, drew a long pipe from his sleeve, tamped down the tobacco and lit it with a glowing twig. That done, he sighed contentedly and lay back on the grass, blowing smoke rings.

Judging the moment to be opportune I started to slide away towards safety, but immediately his free hand shot out and grabbed my wrist.

'Patience, boy! I haven't finished with you yet. I thought

20

I said I wanted to talk to you . . . . Hey, Nob!' he shouted, making me jump nervously. 'Fetch my flask – it's on the bed. And no sly nips, or I'll have your guts for a hammock!'

One of the dwarves trotted away to reappear with a silver hipflask which he tossed from hand to hand as though it were a juggling toy. 'Keep your tricks for the paying customers,' growled my jailor. Obediently the dwarf dropped the flask at his feet, then skipped away, thumbing his nose when he was out of reach. 'A week or two of real work'll knock the cockiness out of you,' muttered the dark man, releasing me and transferring his attention to the brandy. A couple of good swallows and he lay back again, apparently at peace with the world.

For the second time I thought I had escaped, and was contemplating retreat when he spoke, ostensibly to the sky.

'Run away, have you?'

Now it must not be supposed that I had not anticipated this question, even before I had committed myself to the act, and I had decided on the answer long ago, even rehearsed replies to all the possible alternatives I might be faced with, but somehow this inquisitor was different: I should have to be very careful.

'No.' The answer was such a squeak that I had to clear my throat and start again. 'No; I'm on my way to visit my uncle –'

I lay on my back, gazing at the sudden multitude of stars that disappeared as soon as they flashed across, and nursed a tingling cheek. As I raised myself I saw from the corner of an eye Annie make an involuntary movement towards us, then recall herself.

'That was for lying, boy. Never lie to me, it doesn't pay. Now, sit up properly and we'll start again.' His voice was quiet, dispassionate, and I obeyed, gulping back the astonished tears. Now he too was sitting up, elbows on knees, the firelight making strange shadows of his long nose and the sinister elflocks that framed his dark face. He turned his pipe between his fingers and said, not

21

looking at me: 'I don't like liars and I don't like runaways and I don't much like small boys, either . . . . How old are you?'

'Fifteen,' I answered, surprised by the switch into truth.

'You look younger – and are behaving like half your age. Now, where are you from?'

'I lived with my parents at Leebeck, in Derbyshire, but they are both dead. I've come from Chester way, where I lived with my aunt. She wasn't my real aunt, only a relation of my stepfather's by marriage, and she didn't really want me – so I ran away.' That wasn't all, but as far as it went it was truthful.

'And what was all that about going to Gloucester?'

I explained about the bookseller friend of my stepfather's with whom he had corresponded for years, and how I was hoping to make my way down to the cathedral town to see if he could find work for me. All the while I was explaining I kept my eyes on my interrogator's face, for the very word 'Gloucester' had brought vividly to mind the picture of Richard III, one-time Duke of Gloucester, in the volume of Shakespeare that had belonged to my stepfather. It was an etching of Richard supposedly anticipating the murder of his nephews, and there he was in my mind's eye: thin, crooked body, face a vulpine snarl, eyes gleaming, tattered hair down to his chin – and here, in the firelight of this country common, was the very same Richard, all but humpback and gilded crown.

He caught my stare. 'What's the matter? You look like a scared rabbit!'

'Who are – what are you, sir?' I blurted out, thinking of nothing but the horrid resemblance to the picture, and feeling, I suppose, very much as the royal captives must have felt, waiting for their doom.

'Who am I? Who – am – I?' he repeated slowly, then suddenly everything – the mood, the man, the night – changed, and I was his audience of tomorrow, next week, next fair. Leaping to his feet he threw a branch on the fire so that it sparked and flared and the flames licked high, turning the clearing into a stage.

'Who am I?' said the tall thin man of the dark clothes and wild hair, pretending to consider, long finger to long nose. 'Why, I'm – Jack! That's who I am!' He gave the words all the excitement of finding buried treasure, but that was not enough: he would not just be plain Jack, he had to be them all . . . . 'Jack! Jack o' Lent? Nay, Jack Sauce maybe and certain Jack o' Legs and now Jack-out-of-doors! A Jack of all trades and mayhap Jack-in-the-pulpit and perhaps Jack at a Pinch but never Jack Straw nor Jack on the Cheap . . . . You may think me Jack Brag but I could also be your Cousin Jack –' With each Jack he changed his voice to suit: loud, soft, boastful, wheedling. His posture, too: cringing, confident, awkward, graceful. His face reflected the different characters, solemn, sly, vacant, or merry as the role demanded. Suddenly he dropped to his knees, then shot up like a puff of black smoke. 'Jack-in-the-Box I am too, if it's illusion you want, and as Jack Frost I can chill you to the marrow with strange tales . . . . Like Jack o' Lantern I will lead you astray for always I can Play the Jack, and especially for the ladies . . . .' Now he was a lecher: 'So beware, gentlemen, for every Jack must have his Jill and his Jenny, too, so lock up your wives and sweethearts lest this Jack in the Orchard should storm Jack's Castle one dark night . . . .'

This was the first time of hundreds I was to hear his patter but for me this time always held a special magic, perhaps because it was so unexpected, perhaps because of my recent relief from hunger and cold, perhaps because it was to become so much part of my life for the next eighteen months, but probably most of all because I suddenly stopped being afraid of the man who looked like Richard III, realizing how much of what he did and said was just another act.

No time to think: now I was part of that act, for he danced forward and chucked me under the chin. 'How are you tonight, my pretty maid?' Momentarily uneasy, I luckily realized I was merely fuel to his fire and murmured some shyness which he turned to his use. In turn I was yokel with suitably rustic answer, woman on her way to market, old gentleman with stick, and young soldier; he made me see them all and laugh when he scored a verbal trick from the one I was supposed to be. This must have continued for some twenty minutes, until he decided to bring reality into the game.

'And now you – yes, you, lad, there at the back. Come up beside me now; I see from your clothes that you are a travelling man like myself . . . .' There was a sudden giggle from Annie who, like the dwarves, had abandoned pretence of anything but listening.

'Ah, I see you have brought your little sister with you, too . . . .' He gestured at Annie. 'And whither are you bound?'

Trying not to be too distracted by his improvisation – a gift I was to see so much of in the coming weeks – I stepped forward and answered pertly: 'Bound for to apprentice myself, Sir Jack, and find a suitable position for my sister.'

'I fear me your sister looks fit for but one position, lad, and that one you are too young to appreciate.' He winked broadly at his imaginary audience. 'And what is your chosen profession?'

'I had hoped to become a showman like you, sir.'

'What?' said he, pretending displeasure. 'Hope, a miserable boy like you, to emulate the Great Jack?'

'Nay,' said I, 'for I am but a sprat to the mackerel-backed Jack – but yet a sprat may grow to be a mackerel, so may I not be Jack's Sprat?'

It was clumsy enough repartee, but I could see he was impressed. Dropping the patter he grinned at me quizzically.

'There's more to you than meets the eye . . . . What say you, Annie?'

24

'I'd say it were a pity not to let the lad learn a little – with you to teach him.'

He considered me for a moment.

'We shall be going Gloucester way eventually – want to travel with us and make yourself generally useful? You'll have to work damned hard, and I'll expect you to learn some of the travelling language, the cant, the grafters' slang. I'll pay you what you're worth, and that won't be much, but shelter's free and food depends on what we make. It'll save your feet: what do you say?'

I nodded. What alternative was there? At best, if on my own, I would be hungry and penniless when – and if – I reached Gloucester, and once I arrived there was no guarantee that my stepfather's friend would give me a job, much less a home. Running away had been a far more perilous venture than I had envisaged and it had nearly proved fatal. With these new acquaintances I should be fed and housed for a while, and Annie at least was my friend. Jack was still a largely unknown quantity but I was sure that knowing him would add to my store of human knowledge, if nothing else. There remained other problems, but I could now see a week or two ahead and provided I kept my head and my wits about me, I thought I could manage.

'Shake hands on it, then,' said Jack and, all unsuspecting, I held out my hand. A moment later I measured my length on the grass once more, my ears ringing.

'And that,' he said, 'is your first lesson. Learn to duck, boy, or at least to ride a blow. There'll be plenty coming your way, I have no doubt, and by your speech you've led a sheltered life – so far!' Hauling me to my feet by the scruff of my neck, he dusted me down. 'Besides,' he added, shaking me playfully, 'you deserved it for your far too clever backchat: I'm the clever one, remember that!'

This time I was booted several feet across the grass, to land in a heap at Annie's feet.

'Second lesson,' said Jack. 'Never turn your back on

Sailor Jack – pretty boys get into trouble that way, and next time it may not be just a boot you get up your arse!'

'He's not really a Jesuit,' whispered Annie comfortingly as she led me off to find a spare palliasse and blanket. 'Just warning you that, specially 'mongst artistes like ourselves, there are men who like boys better'n girls. He's one for the women, always has been.'

Which, under the circumstances, was small comfort.

When I woke it was quite dark outside and I lay for a moment listening to the sounds of the night: faint rustlings, the yap of a dog fox, a faraway screech owl – sounds that merely seemed a pleasant background from the safety of a palliasse on the floor of a caravan. Last night, from the ditch, they had sounded more sinister.

Jack had offered me a few feet of space by the door of his van and I had been asleep as soon as I lay down, my head on my rolled-up jacket and a rough blanket pulled up to my chin. When I had gone to bed the door had been open but now the bottom half was closed. Even so the night air was chill and I turned over to discover Jack on a rickety stool by the table, reading by the light of a couple of candles. For a moment I watched silently, the flickering light fragmenting into splintered rays through my lowered lashes, then suddenly I had a horrid thought and reached for the pack of books that should be at my head. The Bible was there, but the other book had gone! I sat up in a panic.

'Please, sir, please, Jack . . . . Isn't that my book you're reading?'

'Why, yes, I believe it is.' He made no apology, merely turned his head to regard me. 'Your father's, I suppose?'

'My stepfather's: he left it to me.'

'It is a very fine copy,' and he smoothed the white vellum cover. He must have sensed my dismay, though I said nothing, for he laughed and spread his hands wide. 'Don't worry: I did wash my hands after supper. I would

26

not dream of handling something like this with greasy fingers. Have faith, child!'

I knew he was mocking me, but was surprised how quickly he had guessed my anxiety. Surprised, too, at the quiet confidential way he was talking, almost as though, without a larger audience, there was quite an ordinary, reasonable man under the veneer.

'You can read?' he asked.

'My stepfather was the village schoolmaster.'

'That explains a lot . . . . I never asked your name, boy.'

'No,' I said. 'You didn't.'

He moved impatiently. 'Well?'

I hesitated, and he noticed.

'Remember what I told you about lying.'

'It's . . . it's Zo-Zo-Zoroaster Mortimer,' I stammered.

He laughed. 'Well, Zo-Zo-Zoroaster,' he mimicked, 'I can understand your hesitation. No one could possibly be called that!'

'It's Persian,' I said, offended.

'I don't care if it is High German or double Dutch, I am *not* yelling Zo-ro-as-ter all over the place if I need you. No, a shorter name is best. Zoro? That sounds too miserable.'

' "Boy" is all right: I'll know who you mean.'

'Any idea how many boys would answer to that between here and Gloucester? And we'll have no Tom or Dick, either: too many of them.' He thought for a moment, then chuckled. 'Nay, you christened yourself earlier this evening, as I recall.' He snuffed one of the candles. 'It is past midnight: go to sleep – Sprat!'

We were up before dawn and broke our fast only after all was packed and we were on the road. For the first mile or so I trotted alongside the vans, munching a breakfast of bread and cheese, but after a while I was glad enough to jump up on the step of Annie's conveyance. She let me take the reins for a while and in my imagination her docile nag became by turns one of a team of six pulling a stagecoach and when that palled one of a pair racing a Roman chariot to victory . . . . These dreams were always interrupted, sooner or later, by Jack's infernal screeching on the wooden pipe he tried to play. The sound was so shrill it rose above all others, and at last I covered my ears, to Annie's amusement.

'Nay, lad: you'll get used to it, and he'll improve. Why, he can do anything once he sets his mind to it. Last year he learned to juggle three balls in the air at once – took all summer to get it right, mind, but he did it in the end. Year before that it was a look at the crystal ball and a bit of cardsharping; says you never know when those sort of things could come in useful.'

'He's a man of many parts,' I said, remembering the way he had read my Shakespeare.

'Aye, and I'm right glad as he's taken to you!' and she gave me a sudden bone-cracking hug that left me breathless. 'It'll be nice to have a bit of company – it gets a bit lonely sometimes, hidden away in a caravan all day when I'm not performing. Can't go walking around giving folk free peeps, otherwise they won't come and pay when the show's on. It's all right when we're alone, like last night, and when we're on the road like this, but soon as it gets busier near the town I'll disappear inside and one of the manikins'll drive the van in.'

Sure enough, as we came in sight of the first houses on the outskirts of town, the road suddenly became busier as it met another. There were cattle being driven into market, dogs snapping at their heels, drover's children running beside our vans, their eyes wide with curiosity, and Annie withdrew to the obscurity of her curtained interior. A dwarf took over the driving – they could not be hidden for they were needed to erect the stage, and it was their tumbling, not their size, folks came to watch – and I slipped on ahead to see what I could see. The road had widened but the traffic had increased as well. There were a couple of vans like ours, wagons in plenty, mostly loaded with skins or wood, carts full of sacks with families perched on top, and lots of folk coming in loaded with some basket or bundle or riding two, and sometimes three, astride plough-horses. We passed a pedlar, box strapped to his back, and Jack pulled up. Apparently they knew each other and the pedlar obviously exchanged gossip for a lift, for as I passed I heard talk of the Frenchies and the price of tea. I couldn't stand the slow pace we were now going, due to the increasing congestion ahead, and I started to push my way past the traffic, but Jack called me back.

'Time enough for sightseeing later, Sprat! Keep by Annie till I need you, otherwise you'll get lost. Anyway, by the time I've finished you will be too tired to do anything other than sleep.'

I laughed – I didn't believe him.

2

But he was right, of course.

We were a day early for the fair proper but even so the streets were packed with a shouting, shoving, scrofulous crowd of tinkers, farmers, shopkeepers, vagabonds, pedlars, beggars, sightseers, children, cattle and dogs in profusion; an occasional wealthy citizen could be seen, nosegay in hand, employing a convenience of servants to clear a way through the crowds. It was the largest town I had ever seen, for although my aunt lived on the outskirts of Chester I had never had occasion to visit it myself, and I gazed around me with a lively anticipation. At first the streets were narrow, with tall houses squashed tight together, their timbering black with age. Some were leaning almost to touch their opposite numbers across, and all so close; not just for company, it would seem, like our comfortable cottages at home, but more as an expedient, for some of them were so tumbledown and crooked that they would surely have descended into the gutter without their bolstering neighbours either side. And, once down there, they would have been crushed to powder in a moment by the innumerable feet, wheels, and hooves, or else carried away on the flood of garbage and scum that filled the running sewer that made me pinch my nostrils till I grew used to the smell.

The streets widened as we approached the market square but as we emerged by the Cross the confusion was, if possible, worse. Over on one side were pens for cattle and a few sheep and round the other three sides of the square were platforms, stalls, booths, and tables in various stages of erection, and what with the lowing of the little black Welsh cattle, barking of dogs, hammering, swearing and shouting, my head quite ached. It appeared we were not setting up our attractions in the square itself – which was just as well, there not being a foot to spare – for Jack led the vans under a low arch into the cobbled yard of an inn. On the right were the stables, to the left a covered walkway to the kitchens and eating rooms and opposite the arch the galleried bedrooms.

We backed the vans into the spaces on either side of the arch and Jack led the horses off to the stables while the dwarves produced the boards and planks of the stage from the underside of their van. With Jack's help and the unheeded advice of several loafers they erected a platform some ten feet square and two feet high; the bottom was boxed in and with the aid of stout poles at the corners a tarpaulin was stretched round, about three feet high. On it was painted, in lurid primary colours, optimistic balancing feats by countless smiling little men and across the front the legend: 'Jack's Daring Dwarves and Mighty Midgets! Special Presentation for 1785!' I noticed that the last numeral was freshly painted: underneath one could still see the faint ghost of a 4, but once the flares were fixed in front for the performance it would not be so noticeable.

The innkeeper came out to us, wiping his hands on an

apron almost as vast as Annie's, and Jack broke off to greet him. From where I was sitting on the step of the van polishing the buttons on a green velvet waistcoat, I could hear their conversation.

'You're punctual – your man has been asking for you.'

'Where've you put him?'

'Same room as last time.' The innkeeper nodded towards the upper gallery.

'How much for the pitch?'

'Three days?'

'Probably.'

'I regret the price is up this year: taxes, more call for your place – '

'All right, all right . . . .'

There was the chink of coin passing and Jack swung away, scowling. Catching sight of me, mouth open, cleaning suspended, his frown deepened and, snatching up a handy clod, he hurled it in my direction.

'When you've finished that, go draw some water from the pump: I'm not hiring you to sit on your backside all day.'

And after that there were shoes to polish, panels and wheels on the vans to wash free of travelling grime, leather to soap, cobbles to sweep, errands to run, torches to set up in their brackets – indeed it was time to light the first by the time we had Annie's stall ready. In order that none should see unless they had paid their pennies, her booth was built as an extension to her caravan; canvas-roofed, a set of wooden, leather-hinged panels folded around her like a small room. Inside, the van steps were converted into a makeshift throne with purple velvet curtains and cushions and a gold-fringed footstool. The space before would probably hold a dozen people at one time and any who wanted to touch, prod, or probe were to be discouraged, except on payment of another penny. Further favours – Jack didn't specify what these were – were at the discretion of Annie and after hours.

'And now go and wash yourself, disreputable urchin,'

said Jack, looking with disfavour at my necessarily grubby hands, face, and feet. 'You will be taking Annie's money tonight; don't argue, it's easy enough and it'll leave one of the dwarves to play straight to me.'

I ran off to the pump, dowsed my head and rinsed my hands and legs as best I could, drying my face on my sleeve. Jack beckoned me into our van and handed me a red cloth tabard with a cross-eyed lion embroidered on it in yellow wool.

'A little large for you –' it fitted like a smock '– but it will have to do. These stockings –' green, and well-darned '– are better than bare legs. Now, a cap . . . .' The one he found was faded blue velvet and came right down over my ears. He stood back and surveyed me. 'You look terrible!'

I agreed, having caught a glimpse of myself in the mirror that hung over his dressing chest.

'Never mind, there are plenty of odds and ends in the wardrobe box and we'll get Annie busy with needle and thread tomorrow. For tonight you will just have to use your imagination . . . . No good you using the drum, you've had no practice: just take the box,' and he handed me a gaily painted one with a long handle. 'The slot will take pennies only and it's a close fit: so if the coin slips through too easily, look for halfpennies or counters – some people will try anything on, especially if you're busy. Now, when we're ready let them through a dozen at a time, no more. If there's only a small crowd you can take a smaller number rather than waiting, but don't give them as long to gawp. And keep up the patter: don't lose their interest or they'll find another attraction. Remember, you have a commodity to sell: Annie!'

Outside it was dusk and the torches were smoking and flaring. We had an audience already, it seemed: customers from the inn were hanging around, ale in hand, eyeing us speculatively. The flickering lights made the paintings on Annie's van seem to have a life of their own, jumping and quivering in a multitude of flesh tints till it seemed as though Annie herself were laughing soundlessly down at us, the fat under her chin, on her arms, her bosom, shaking in time to her chuckles. Not that the painting looked very like her; it was almost a caricature of any fat lady and was really rather coarse. The phrase she had used earlier about 'airing the dairy' made sense to me now, for the creature in the representation had lost any pretence to modesty as far as her front was concerned and two great breasts like inflated bladders stuck out in a most unlikely fashion.

'Right,' said Jack. 'Off you go!'

Not having the slightest idea how to begin, I gaped helplessly at Jack, the bystanders, and back to Jack. Apart from anything else, my stomach was rumbling loud enough to be heard, for I had not eaten since breakfast, and my costume itched, tickled, and made me perspire uncomfortably.

'What are you waiting for?'

'Is – is Annie ready?'

'Why don't you go and see?'

Slipping in through the curtained doorway I found Annie seated on her 'throne', dressed in pink silk petticoat and yellow taffeta dress, her hair a mass of ringlets, a lace cap, slightly askew, atop the lot. She was nibbling at a plate of almond comfits, and my mouth watered.

'Hullo, love! Are we ready then?' She glanced curiously at my costume, then shook her head. 'Those won't do, dear: make you look a fright!'

'Oh, Annie!' I wailed. 'Jack wants me to do the collecting and introduce you and I don't know how!'

'Have a sweetie, and don't worry,' she said comfortingly. 'It's easy, really. All you has to do is shake the box a little when you've got some money in it and call out: "Roll up! Roll up! See the fattest lady in the world!" and then describe me a bit –'

'What's going on?' hissed Jack, putting his head round the curtain.

'Just telling him what *you* ought to have,' she said

33

accusingly. 'How you expect the poor lad to manage when he's never done the like before, I just don't know!' She put an arm round me and popped a sugared almond in my mouth. 'Boy's hungry, too: can hear his belly growling like thunder –'

'He'll eat,' said Jack through his teeth, 'when we all do. And that won't be till somebody has earned enough to pay for it. And that won't be till –'

'Till you teach him the spiel,' interrupted Annie. 'Be a good lad, Jack, and go through it once first, just to show how it's done. I'll wager he takes to it like a duck to water once he sees how . . . .'

Jack shot me a furious glance; he was angry, not only with me but with himself as well, I guessed, for misjudging my abilities. Perhaps he had genuinely forgotten I had never done anything like this before until it was too late and then had taken a chance; be that as it may, he calmed down and sighed.

'I'll show you how it's done once, and once only. After that you're on your own; I can't be in two places at once.'

Pulling me out behind him he stood and faced the audience.

'Ladies and gentlemen, lads and lassies, boys and girls! Little do you realize the treat in store for you! Maybe you just came here out of curiosity, but I can promise that you will stay to marvel! But what has Jack got for you, you ask yourselves, what has he got that you will pay to see? What is there in this world that we have not already seen, have not already been surfeited with? For we are canny citizens, and we are not going to throw away our pennies on something of no account, of no merit . . . . Quite right, my friends, quite right! And honest Jack would be the last person to ask you to dig into your pockets for something less than the best. But, ladies and gentlemen, but, I say, Jack *has* got the best! Here, fresh from her triumphs in the Frozen North (where, there being so much more of her to freeze, she had the largest and rosiest – cheeks, shall we say – I have ever seen), here, I say, for the only time this

34

year, at great expense and by special invitation, is that gorgeous fruit of womanhood, that juicy pear just ripe for plucking (and talking of a pair, you'll not believe – but no, you must see for yourselves), here is that bounteous harvest of feminity, that pulchritudinous personification of plenty, the one and only Antipodean Annie! If beauty were skin-tight instead of skin-deep I would swear she had the measure by yards of the most handsome women in history! But she must be seen to be believed, a sight to tell your children and your grandchildren, for never, I predict, will there be one to rival, let alone surpass, her vast charms!

'Here, pretty lass –' He broke off to chuck a giggling chambermaid under the chin, then tweaked a ribbon from her bodice and held it stretched tight between his fingers. 'See this ribbon? But a moment ago it nestled sweetly on your bosom and by my eye it would circle your trim waist to a nicety: am I right? But this same ribbon, some twenty inches round, believe it or not, this ribbon is not long enough to circle so much as one – one, ladies and gentlemen – of Fat Annie's wrists! I see you all still look disbelieving: well, I shall put it to the test. I should like a volunteer – you, my dear, for it is your ribbon we shall put to the test, you I shall give a free peep. All for nothing you shall experience that which will leave you gasping.' He indicated the gangling stableboy at her side. 'Your beau will lend you for a moment?' Not waiting for the answer he slipped an arm around her waist and drew her towards the entrance. 'And you can tell these disbelievers, after, that Jack has not lied . . . .'

With a wink in my direction he disappeared into the booth, accompanied only too willingly by the gullible girl.

A moment later there was an audible gasp from within, a muffled: 'Oh, sir! You didn't –', cut off in midsentence, then a low murmur from Jack and Annie's throaty chuckle. I had an idea what had initiated the girl's sudden reaction and a glance at her flushed face and downcast eyes as they emerged confirmed it.

But Jack had got what he wanted. 'Tell 'em, lass: was it worth it?'

She nodded, glancing slyly at her sweetheart.

'You were amazed, were you not?' Jack persisted.

'Aye, sir, that I was!'

'Worth a penny?'

'Worth double, sir, I should say . . . .'

That did it. Jack thrust the box into my hand. 'Take their money, then listen.'

Once in the booth with a captive audience he expounded on Annie's charms, using comparisons I was sure would be bound to offend her, but to my surprise she blossomed like an overblown rose under his blandishments. Willingly she rolled up her sleeves to let him pinch and poke her flabby upper arms, happily she raised her skirt to snap the frilly garter that would have compassed my chest with ease. She seemed to grow in girth before my eyes, actually swelling like rising dough in the warmth of her audience's approval. Glancing first at her and then at Jack, whose mercurial verbosity lit his dark saturnine face like the glow of his proverbial namesake, Jack-o'-Lantern, I began to understand how these showpeople needed an audience, however small, to come to life. All at once, I too, became infected with their feverish gaiety, spread by the smell of the spluttering torches, the feel of painted cloth, the gesticulations of Jack, the murmur of applause, the taste of success in my mouth like indigestion.

Jack snapped his fingers under my nose.

'Back to earth, greenhorn! They've all gone. I'm going to introduce my dwarves: as soon as they finish it's you and her ladyship again.'

Left alone I glanced at Annie. Her face was glazed with sweat and her bosom heaved as if she had been running.

'Annie . . . .'

'Yes, love?'

'You all right?'

' 'Course . . . exciting, ain't it?'

36

'What made that young lady so appreciative?' I had to ask.

'Well, it weren't the dimples in me knees, dearie! Jack pinched her arse and then stopped her mouth with a juicy one! Right kissing-man he is, too: no girl's going to split on that one. Turns 'em on, he does.'

'I can't see how –'

' 'Cos you're a lad, that's why. Were I meself ten, nay, five years younger and half a ton lighter, I'd've had a go long since. Even though he loves 'em and leaves 'em there are those as would say it were worth it!'

I watched Jack go into his patter to introduce the dwarves, one of them beating a drum to gain attention. By now this was an essential, for though Jack stood under the arch leading into the courtyard to attract custom, he had now to compete with all the other showmen, later perhaps in starting but making up for that with a perfect din of shouts, hails, yells, flutes, fiddles, and even the drone of a bladder-pipe, all filling the square outside with a perfect cacophony of sound. Being Jack, however, he merely shouted louder than them all and soon managed to gather an appreciable audience. The dwarves started with a foursome, then suddenly they were six, then nine, then reversed the process, leaving me as mystified as any and only to be disillusioned five days later when I helped to dismantle the stage and found the sprung trap door. This spoiled the magic, but I could still appreciate the skill, for I never saw the door open or close once, hard as I looked.

When they finished their turn Jack nodded to me and I realized I was to hold those already there while he went to tout for the next customers. The first time I was hopeless because I tried to use the same words as Jack and couldn't remember them; once I realized that I should be seeing Annie through a boy's eyes instead of a man's, I did much better. By this time I was so hungry she became subconsciously equated in my mind with food and all my verbal comparisons were of hams and pies and loaves and cheese, ballooning into the vast repast my stomach craved.

Suddenly there were no more customers, and Jack was holding out his hand for the money box.

'That'll do for tonight: it's past ten.' He weighed the box calculatingly. 'Not bad, but we'll do better tomorrow. Now, help Annie pack up and then go to bed,' and turning on his heel he disappeared before I had the chance to ask about supper. Annie was already in her van, from the sounds preparing for bed. Alone, I packed the cushions and drapes into their box, then knocked on her closed door.

'Annie?'

'Yes, love?' She sounded half-asleep already.

'Do you . . . Do you want any supper?'

'I sent out for a pie earlier – My word, I'd quite forgot you'd had none. Go find Jack, he'll give you some money. Probably in the bar parlour by now . . . . Goodnight, lad, see you in the morning, and then we'll do summat about your clothes . . . .'

Jack had vanished; the dwarves, from the sound of it, were locked in furious argument in their van; and there were few customers left in the inn. Glancing out into the square I saw that torches were being extinguished, booths curtained, tables stacked, and there were some youngsters asleep already under a wagon, their parents piling unsold hides and skins. I crossed the yard towards the bar but halted at a shout from above.

'Hey, Sprat!' He was on the upper gallery outside the sleeping-rooms. 'Fetch my satchel – it's under the bed. We're in the third room along.' He had gone before I had the chance to ask how to reach the gallery.

Clutching the satchel, I eventually located the steep, twisting stairs and climbed, in darkness most of the way, to the second floor. Counting the doors from the stairwell I knocked on the third and, receiving no reply, walked in to find an elderly gentleman entertaining two ladies of the town. I don't know who was the more embarrassed, he or

I, but my entrance provoked a stream of abuse from the two women, one of whom was in the act of rifling the man's pockets, the other's task obviously having been that of distraction, judging from her undress. Even as I hastily closed the door again I realized their stratagem had been divined, for I retreated to the sound of shouts, slaps and screams.

Pausing before the next door I was more wary, and applied my ear to the panels. A deep, rumbling snore: no Jack. Behind me the two harlots came running out in some disorder and hurried towards the stairs, each blaming the other and both cursing me for their loss of earnings. I shrank back into the shadows by the following door and as I waited for them to pull on their stockings and adjust their dresses before descending, I tried to listen for any sounds from the room. There was a murmur of voices, men's voices; I did not want to make another mistake, so I bent closer to listen, and what I heard, after the two women had gone, was enough to keep me still to hear more. I knew it was wrong to eavesdrop, but I was also determined to learn more about the enigmatic Jack, and curiosity won.

'. . . afraid no change: probably worse, if anything.' Not Jack's, that voice; it had a dry, crumbly sound, well-educated but with a hint of servility. 'And of course the other is deeper in than ever . . . .'

Jack swore. 'How much this time?'

'All of five thousand, but if I may advise –'

'You may not. I'll give you a draft to patch up the cracks, but no more: let him sweat a little.' There was the scratch of a pen. 'You have the receipts for the other? Good.' There was the scrape of a chair. 'Where the hell is that damned boy? Ten minutes is long enough to hang a man, let alone bring him to the gallows . . . .'

I backed away from the door, ready to effect a sudden entrance, but the other man was speaking again, and I hovered indecisively.

'. . . at least go and see her.'

'No,' said Jack. 'Not till – never mind. Tell Lady Jestyn that although my business keeps me abroad a while longer, I send her my fond remembrances and will see her as soon as I can. As for George . . . . Tell him nothing. Nothing at all: you understand?'

There was a silence, a shuffling of papers, and I judged it time to appear. Retreating a little, I then trod loudly back to the door and knocked.

'Come in,' came Jack's impatient voice. 'You've been long enough.'

'It was dark . . . I got the wrong door,' I faltered.

'I said the third from the end. Can't you count?'

'It's the fifth –'

'From the other end, you idiot. I suppose you came up the wrong stair? Never mind that now: give me the satchel. You haven't opened it?'

I shook my head, too weary to be indignant.

'Wait a moment, then, while I check if all is here.'

He tipped the contents onto a table already crowded with papers. While he checked the documents I had time to study his companion. A small man, middle-aged, in a snuff-coloured coat and black breeches, an old-fashioned wig and silver-buckled shoes. He stared back at me with a curl to his nostrils as if I smelt, which I probably did after all the running round I had had to do that day.

'All seems in order,' said Jack. 'Go to bed. Leave the van door on the latch and don't wait up for me.'

I hesitated, then plucked up courage. 'Annie said you would give me something to buy some supper.'

'Supper? Haven't you had any yet?' He made it sound as if it was all my own fault. Rummaging under the papers on the table, he brought forth a corner of pie and tossed it to me. 'There you are: nice bit of game left in that. Now, begone, you miserable child, or I shall turn you into a toad!'

I escaped thankfully, cramming the pie into my mouth as I stumbled down the ill-lit stairs. Back in the van I lay on my palliasse and composed myself for sleep, but that was a long time coming; the pie lay heavy and indigestible in my stomach, and tired though I was my mind kept remembering the conversation I had half heard upstairs, and tried to make sense of the pieces. In the end all I could be sure of was that Jack was paying someone's debts (but five thousand sounded so much I was sure I had misheard), there was one woman he was trying to avoid, a Lady Something-or-other he liked, and someone called George whom he hated. Not much to go on but my mind kept chasing round like a mouse on a wheel until what with that and the disagreeing pie I heard the first cock's crow before I slept.

And Jack must have been later still, for he had still not come to bed by the time I dozed off.

By noon of that next day the market and fair were in full swing. The former was mainly for the Welshmen bringing in their little dark cattle from over the hills to the west, but as it was one of the first gatherings of the year there were many other travelling people like ourselves trying out their acts after the laying-up of the winter. There was a strong man who bent iron bars and lifted great weights to the accompaniment of grunts and groans more fascinating than the feats themselves, jugglers, two-headed or six-legged creatures in jars, a bearded lady, two fortune-tellers, and even a fire-eater, his exploits, especially after dark, drawing huge crowds. Added to these were ribbon- and trinket-sellers, balladmongers, pie-men and toy-pedlars, and so when Jack gave me a whole shilling for my part in last night's work I behaved like any other gullible sightseer and spent it as if there were no tomorrow. In less than an hour my hard-earned pennies were gone on some of the sights, a honey cake and a tinselled ribbon for Annie. She kissed me lovingly, declared it was the prettiest one she had ever seen, and promptly gave me another shilling.

'Now go and spend that wisely, love, not on sights you

will come to see as commonplace or fairings for your old Annie! Jack expects us to buy our own clothes, you know, and to look respectable at all times. Now, you've a button missing on your shirt and a coloured neckerchief would brighten you up for high days and holidays. Your shoes are stout enough but you've no stockings and a working smock or two would keep the rest clean for best. Let me see . . . .' She ticked off the items on her fingers. 'You want half a dozen – nay, a full dozen's best – of bone buttons; two pairs of stockings, one white, one brown; a cotton neckerchief, red or green would be nice; two and a half yards of worsted for smocks; some brown linen thread and a couple of strong needles. Your breeches won't last for ever either . . . . Oh dear, 'tis a good job Jack's off for an hour or two!' She reached in her money box again. 'A shilling won't go near: here's five more. Now you go and –'

'But I can't!' I interrupted. 'However could I pay you back?'

'A little at a time,' she said firmly. 'No hurry. In a good week you'll get fifteen, twenty shillings. Jack's fair, he shares it out equal. If we do well, we live well: a bad couple of weeks and we all pulls our belts in.' I smiled involuntarily, to think of Annie managing to pull in her stays even a quarter inch. 'Now, do you go and find Charlie Ribton's stall – he were over by the Fox and Goose last year – and give him this message: tell him Annie from Kirkham's in town, and he's to remember what he owes. It'll take all the six shilling, but he'll give fair measure. Hurry, there's a dear, and we'll get you measured for them smocks afore Jack gets back!'

'Where's he gone?'

'When Jack disappears you don't ask where; soon as he's back we'll have to work double hard, so hurry!'

I found Charlie Ribton's stall near where Annie had prophesied. He was a small, spare, sly-looking man with a habit of rubbing his nose as though it itched and a manner of speech that varied between the ingratiating and the obscene, depending on his clientele. At first he was offhand, but as soon as I mentioned Annie his manner changed and, his eyes gleaming, he set to rubbing his hooked nose into a shine.

'So-o-o: the fat old sow has found herself a little piglet, has she? No offence, pretty lad, no offence! God's wounds, is she still as fetching as ever? I remember Annie, God blast me if I don't, when she were as plump and juicy a young dell as ever set a man's jack a-twitching . . . but no more of that. So, she reminds old Charlie of his debt, do she? May God strike me blind, but she's a cool 'un, after all these years . . . . And what did she send you to buy, eh?'

I didn't like the familiar way he was referring to my benefactress, so I added a pair of breeches and a cap to Annie's list, looked him straight in the eye, and gave him five of the six shillings.

'What, my God, what does she expect me to do with five shilling? Five bloody shilling and the lad to be clothed like a prince; not possible, not possible, scratch me if it is! The old hag would beggar me if she could, and, rot me! all for a runt as wouldn't know how to lift a lady's skirt, I'll be bound . . . .' He went on in this manner for some time, but when I offered to take back the money and return to Annie empty-handed, he rubbed his nose again and appeared to reconsider. 'Well, at that price there's nothing new . . . but there again there might be something in the secondhand line . . . .' He gestured to the back of the stall. 'Have a look.'

I found a couple of pairs of stockings and a nice brown cap, and a rummage in a box of buttons soon produced twelve of a size. Further back I saw a scarce-worn pair of velveteen breeches, golden-brown with a smart short jacket to match. There was an off cut of brown linen some three yards in length on another shelf, and I decided this would be more practical for the warmer months than the worsted Annie had recommended. A green silk neckerchief looked more refined than the coarser cotton ones on display, so I piled everything up and returned to Charlie.

'These will do for the moment,' I said. 'And now some needles and thread, please.'

'Needles and –! Do you realize how much that lot you've got comes to? There's a couple of guineas' worth you got there . . . . Why, that jacket and breeches I got off a lady only last week, her son never wore them but the once! No, a joke's a joke and a debt's a debt, but you can tell that old turd enough is enough,' and he made as if to snatch the clothes away.

But I hung on tight. 'If you feel like that about an old friend after all these years, there's no more to be said. Forget about the needles and thread, then; but before I go, I'll just step across and pay my respects – and Annie's – to your good lady,' and I nodded across to where a thin shrewish-looking woman sat knitting furiously, on guard behind the ladies' stall.

I knew the gamble had paid off when he started, let go my bundle, and started to rub his nose crimson.

'Nay, lad, I was but joking: Charlie may have his little joke, mayn't he? Can't have Annie's pretty boy going off half provided for, now can we?' The placating words were accompanied by a glance of such pure malevolence that I recoiled. Muttering under his breath he went off to hunt on the haberdashery stall, to return with two hanks of thread and a packet of needles. 'Now be off, and tell that – that Annie of yours that the debt's paid in full, and over . . . .' And I left him rubbing his nose harder than ever.

Annie was surprised and pleased at the quality of the goods I returned with. 'Must be going soft in his old age,' she mused, turning over the clothes. 'And a shilling to the good . . . . Well done, lad: now, let's measure you for those smocks.'

While I was on my errand she had taken in the red tabard I wore for performances and found yellow stockings and a better-fitting red cap with a long black feather. She also insisted on trimming my hair.

'At the moment it sticks out all which ways like a flue-

44

brush, and though it's short, it'll grow better if we get it all the same length.' She snipped away busily. 'I've seen a better job on a sheep: who cut it for you last, lad?'

'My aunt.'

'Well, either she's cross-eyed or was in a bate with you . . . . Hey, keep still a minute.' She glanced at me sharply. 'Turn your face to the light.' Cupping my chin in her vast palm, she gazed at me steadily. 'To think I never noticed: odd-eyed as well. Some says it's lucky . . . .' She didn't sound convinced. 'Never mind, they're not too noticeable and you've nice long lashes to cover 'em. Why is it young lads always has the curly hair, too?' Turning to the shelf behind her, she handed me a large piece of fruit cake. 'Eat that up quick, I think I hear Jack now.'

Thus tidied and better dressed than for days, with neater hair and a half-full stomach, I did much better that second day and had the satisfaction of a nearly full money box at the end; and so the next day, and the next. By the end of the week I was able to repay Annie her five shillings and put a bit by, for, as she explained, we could only earn during the eight or nine months of the season and needed to put by keep for the winter. She even found me a little box for my earnings and kept it under the bed with her own, hidden away behind the large rose-patterned chamber pot.

We left Shrewsbury on the Sunday morning, to the sound of church bells. Already others were packing, some to strike east to the Midlands, others, like us, to skirt the Welsh marches on our gradual way south. For us the next stop was Ludlow, and I asked Annie why we didn't wait and travel with some of the other vans going our way.

'Sometimes Jack just ain't sociable: in the main he likes to travel in his own company, then he doesn't have to make excuses if he decides to turn off the way for a night or two to visit some out o' the way place. 'Sides, it's easier to find food that road: farm that's got enough for a dozen couldn't feed fifty. And there's no quarrelling over pitches if we travel fast and get there first; I travelled with a large

45

group once, some couple of dozen vans, and while it was good fun and fine company it seemed to take us twice as long to get anywhere, and there was more temptations on the way, as you might say. No, in the main I likes it better this way. 'Sides, I'm the only female around, and that ain't bad anytime!'

Be that as it may, our troupe was augmented by an extra act that same night. Jack had insisted on camping early, turning off the main highway down a rutted track that led to nothing but a deserted cottage, doors and windows gone, sentinelled by three Scots pines stark and grim in the greening of an April twilight. Water had to be fetched from a rather stagnant pond a quarter mile across broken ground for the well nearby was choked with rubbish. It was a chill evening and we lit a fire in the yard – one glance in the cottage and even the dwarves preferred the open. Many people had spent the night there in the past it was evident from the blackened hearth, scattered bones, and broken crocks, but the place had a dank, acrid stench and there was a scuttling of rats in the rafters.

We soon built up a roaring blaze in the open and because the week's takings had been good there was a fine cut of lamb sizzling on the travelling spit, turned by one of the dwarf women (for females there were also in that troupe, that kept usually to their van and were shared by all, according to Annie), and the usual bread, cheese and ale. There was even a pan of water coming to the boil for a precious cup of tea, a treat I was looking forward to especially as I had had little opportunity to indulge when I was younger and I liked the taste. So it was with relief that I turned from the pond with the last two buckets of water and headed back towards the glow of the fire and supper. It was almost dark now, with only a sliver of moon to light me back across the uneven ground; a thin mist curled at shoulder height and somewhere a curlew cried loneliness to the night.

I was nearly halfway to safety when I saw the unicorn.

It came stepping out of the mist some ten yards to my left, shining silver in the faint glow from moon and marshlight. The fabulous creature had but a small horn, and it picked its way delicately among the tussocks of grass to the accompaniment of faery bells; it was not even a particularly large unicorn, its head perhaps as high as my shoulder, but it would have made no difference had it been half as small or twice as big, my reaction would have been the same. I stood rigid, unable to move, my limbs locked in terror, my teeth chattering, my shaking hands slopping water from the buckets on to my ankles, adding an icy discomfort to the awfulness of the scene. The creature sensed my presence – indeed, it probably heard my teeth chattering – for it halted and turned its head in my direction, large, dark eyes considering. At the same moment the hair on the back of my neck rose, for something – *blew* – hot on my nape! That was too much: both buckets went and I swear my feet were winged as I went flying back to the safety of Annie's skirt and the firelight.

'Why, whatever's the matter, love?'

'It's – it's a unicorn!' I gasped. 'There, over there! And there's a great dragon breathing fire that nearly had me – !'

Jack hauled me to my feet. 'What's all this nonsense, boy?'

I pointed in the direction from whence I had come. 'Look! You can see it now . . . .' But my voice faltered and died away for, as the capricious mist thinned, there into the firelight stepped the daintiest white pony, drawing a wicker carriage. A small white plume topped the headpiece of its decorated bridle and from the cheekpieces silver bells tinkled.

Jack threw back his head and laughed. 'Welcome, Tom Fallon, you and your unicorn!' and walking behind the little carriage came a slight, soft-stepping man in a caped coat, leading a tall, iron-grey horse.

'Evening, Master,' said the man, in a quiet, country

47

voice. 'We'd have been here sooner but for Hannibal here casting a shoe some miles back, wouldn't we, my beauty?' and he patted the great horse, who had his gaze fixed on Jack, his ears pricked. Jack moved forwards and put his hands on either side of the fine jaw and spoke for the horse alone. Hannibal whickered and blew lovingly down his nostrils. So much for my dragon.

Properly ashamed, I crept away to retrieve the buckets.

When I returned Jack had evidently explained my terrors for the newcomer stepped forward and took me by the hand.

'Reckon you scared us near as much as we scared you, young 'un: 'twas an easy enough mistake to make. Now, do you come and be introduced to my Daisy, proper-like,' and he led me over to the white pony. 'Now, Daisy, here be a friend!' She snuffed gently at my hand and lipped my sleeve. 'Stroke her neck, my dear, she likes that . . . . Now, Daisy, do you say "hello" like the lady you are,' and to my astonishment she nodded her head once or twice, then bowed.

'She does tricks!' I exclaimed, delighted, and bowing back.

' 'Deed she does: most intelligent pony in England, ain't you, my beauty? Counts up to ten, she does, no trouble, and adds and subtracts better'n most boys I know.' And he grinned at me. 'Dances, too, she does, and dies for her country: you wait and see, eh, Daisy?'

'Are you coming with us then?'

'Been with the troupe last couple of years. Look after his horse when he's away, and bring up ol' Hannibal to meet him where he says. Fine riding horse, that one.'

'When he's away?' I questioned. 'Where does he go?'

'Now that I don't know,' said Tom evasively. 'Don't ask, don't get told . . . . Like to help get the pony unharnessed and comfortable?'

The wicker carriage, I now saw, was really a miniature caravan; it could be roofed over with tarpaulin stretched over thin hoops and inside there was room for a palliasse, a wooden chest, and a box of tack: different coloured bridles, a small saddle, brushes, and a horse blanket. This last he threw over Daisy, filling her a nosebag from a sack under the step.

'There you are, my beauty, all snug as a flea in a wig. Do you enjoy your supper while I get mine.'

'Aren't you going to hobble her?'

'Gracious, no! No need of that. She'll not stray far from my side.'

I was famished by the time we finally sat down to supper, but Annie rewarded me with the knucklebone and I chewed on it happily, watching Jack across the fire with Tom, the two talking away like old friends, the questions mostly coming from Jack. I could hear none of the content, what with the dwarves quarrelling over their meat on either side and the fire crackling between, but I did notice that Tom spoke with unusual deference, almost as though he were servant to Jack's master.

'Have they known each other long?' I asked Annie.

'Ever since I been with them; before that I wouldn't know. Allus seems thick as thieves together and Jack trusts him with that horse, come winter.'

'But why doesn't he take the horse with him? Where does he go?'

'Don't know, never asked. Maybe he goes abroad, over to those Frenchies, or maybe the Eyetalians, catching a bit of sun while we freeze. Always seems to keep a bit o' the sun on his skin, anyways . . . . Now, you go get that little teapot from my cupboard and three cups and we'll have a brew.'

After letting the tea infuse, she handed me a fine porcelain cup with pink roses and a gold rim and showed how to sip the fragrant liquid, with a word or two of caution.

'It's hot, so blow on it a little, like this.' She demonstrated. Copying her carefully, I held the handle daintily between finger and thumb, my little finger extended as far as it could, my elbow at right angles, and blew heartily.

Jack came over for his cup.

'Nay, Annie, if you let the lad sup like that they'll mistake him for a lass! 'Tis fine for you,' he added hastily, seeing her frown, 'but he should drink straight, like this –' and, holding the cup with his fingers round the rim, he tipped it back and drank in one swallow, burning his mouth and letting go the cup with an anguished howl. I caught it as it fell and handed it back to Annie.

'Some more?' she asked sweetly.

He scowled, hand to mouth, and I couldn't help adding: 'I don't mind blowing on it for you . . . .' For which impertinence I received a clip on the ear.

'Little boys who still believe in fairies and dragons should keep their breath where it belongs, lest it escape in the night and fly over the moon to join the wind!'

Regrettably, I stuck out my tongue at his retreating back and Annie clipped the other ear: she reckoned she could say what she liked, but that I must be respectful to my elders.

It seemed boys couldn't win.

Next morning I woke at dawn, scratching furiously, and caught and cracked a couple of fleas: I suspected they came from the empty cottage, for though the dwarves never seemed to wash, Jack was clean and so, within her limits, was Annie. Fortifying myself with the remembrance of what Lord Chesterfield had written in his famous letters about cleanliness and with memories of my stepfather's cold baths, I determined to catch up on a good wash while everyone still slept. Collecting the precious bar of soap I had bought – tax had gone up to two pence – my dirty shirt and the new smock Annie had found time to make, I tiptoed through the camp and made for the pond. Daisy whickered as I passed, and, sure enough, she was only a few feet from her master's van. I whispered a promise of a piece of bread later, and made my way across the field. This morning the pond looked less savoury than ever and, recalling a glint of water in the distance yesterday, I crossed a couple more fields and was lucky enough to find a stream, not much more than a straddle wide, but clean and fast-running. Stripping, I washed thoroughly, using the dirty shirt as a flannel, till I tingled all over with goose pimples and was tolerably clean. There was no one about, birds were waking, sheep calling in the hills, an occasional fly buzzed and the shadows lay long over the dew-heavy grass. The water was icy cold but the air heavy: rain later, probably. Half dry, I resumed my breeches and slipped the smock over my head, just in case, then finished washing my shirt and spread it out to dry. The smock was cool and comfortable and could be worn without a shirt; the sleeves were short and it had a round collar with a drawstring at the neck and fell just over my behind. I had wanted it a little longer but Annie had explained that at that length she could get three smocks instead of two from the piece of material I had bought from Charlie Ribton.

It was still early and I doubted whether the others would be up yet as nothing had been said about an early start the night before, so I lay for a while and watched the sun begin his climb. Rolling over, I saw I was being regarded watchfully by a hare some hundred yards distant; haunch-sitting, black-tipped ears erect, nose twitching for my scent, one paw straight, the other bent. I kept very still, and at last it dropped to all fours and lolloped off towards the distant hedge.

Deciding it must be time for breakfast, I set off for the camp, damp shirt flapping over my arm: it could finish drying hanging from the back of the van, high up enough to escape the dust. Stooping to pick some celandine for Annie I saw, tucked safe in a tussock of grass, still and self-possessed, a very small brown leveret, twitching nose and watchful eyes the only sign of life. Kneeling down, I marvelled at the instinct which kept it so still through the long day, so trustful that no harm would come nigh and that its dam would come to feed it again at dusk. So still it was no hawk would see movement; at that age it would

have little scent for a questing dog and it was only my
search for flowers that had revealed its hiding place. I
stretched out my hand to touch, to caress, to stroke the
little warm body, for suddenly I was filled with an
overwhelming urge to hold it, to hold something –
anything – warm and responsive in my arms, to kiss and
cuddle this lovable creature; in time I remembered that
should its dam smell humankind she could well abandon
it: even now she was probably near at hand, ready to
provide a diversion should real danger threaten her young.
Guiltily I drew back, my eyes alone left to embrace, my
hunger unsatiated.

There was the soft thud of hooves behind me and
turning, I saw Jack, riding on Hannibal, obviously out for
a canter before breakfast.

'Something for the pot?' he asked good-humouredly.

'No, no! It's a baby hare – look – and you mustn't touch
it or its mother may not come back.'

'Just the tasty morsel for a man like me,' he said
teasingly, and he made as though to dismount. 'Spitted
over a slow fire, or in a mess of onion and carrot . . . .'

'You wouldn't!' I expostulated, practically pushing him
back in the saddle, not sure whether he was joking or no.
'It's only tiny: it was meant to grow and enjoy life and
run free! You wouldn't want to hurt it . . . .'

'You're a strange lad,' he mused. 'Too soft-hearted by
far . . . . Jump up and I'll give you a lift back. It's past
seven.'

Glad he was not pursuing his former line of talk, I
stretched out my hand and he pulled me up to sit in front,
uncomfortably, on Hannibal's withers.

He slipped an arm around my waist to hold me steady.
'You smell of soap, Sprat,' he said, sniffing at my hair.

'I had a bath,' I said. 'In the stream.'

'I've said it once and I'll say it again: you're a strange
lad.'

And I knew better than to deny it.

3

The weather stayed kind that last week of April and pickings were good, except in Ironbridge where wages in the factories were so low that many people existed in a poverty I could not have imagined. Some even lived in caves carved out of the hillside, the children naked into their teens, the women scarce better, wearing rags that would have disgraced a scarecrow. One each of Jack's shirts and Annie's petticoats went missing from the drying bush one morning and I remembered some starved-looking children hanging around earlier; when I told Annie she frowned at first, then sighed, and finally smiled.

'Well, there's one thing: Jack's shirt may fit their dad, but I'll wager my petticoat'll make drawers for the lot, twice over!'

April took care of Ludlow, Ironbridge and Church Stretton, and as the days grew longer and warmer we zigzagged down through Leominster, Hereford (where I grew quite dizzy deciding just where the nave of the cathedral took its left-hand kink), and across to Worcester by the end of May. There we had a wet week and Annie caught a cold, so Jack decided to pull off the road for a few days and rest up before going on to Tewkesbury.

Annie's cold was a heavyweight affair that fitted her appearance: she was afflicted with sneezes like the spouting of a whale, used handkerchiefs like small sheets, coughed like a cow with croup and shook with agues that moved her flesh like an ill-set jelly. I ministered as best I could, trying to remember the correct proportions of honey and aniseed and preparing hot oatmeal packs the size of pillowcases to bind across her front. The aroma of onions and mint tea made the horses sneeze, but in the end mulled ale and gin seemed to have the best effect – at least she looked much happier after a quart or two of the first and a cup or so of the second.

'Resting up' as far as I was concerned meant quite the opposite. Jack decided that I would appear with Daisy; he had tried her out with one of the younger dwarves but he was impatient and surly and she didn't take to him at all, shying away and tossing her head, losing the concentration necessary to follow Tom Fallon's hand signals. Of course she could not really do arithmetic, but she was adept at reading her master's instructions, tapping her hoof on a drum for half a dozen answers, then finishing, when he deliberately asked a hard question, by shaking her head and nosing him gently over the dwarves' stage we used to show her off to the best advantage. Then she would kick up her heels and do a little dance, as if to say 'That's got rid of him!'

That was where I came in. I played the part of a vagrant lad (not difficult) asleep under a hedge; the pony had to find me, nudge me awake, then offer me a lift on her back. She also pulled paste apples from an artificial tree for us to pretend to eat, repulsed my wicked stepfather (another of the ubiquitous dwarves) and finally did a pirouette on her hind legs to make money for us both. Children loved all this when we finally came to try it out and begged for rides on the magic pony, for which of course their parents had to pay extra.

Jack was the storyteller for this little drama and even played a vastly improved tune on the wooden pipe for Daisy to dance to; Tom, who guided her discreetly with voice and hand at the side, showed him how to fit the music to her steps, not the other way round. As he explained to me, one did not train animals to do just what we wanted, it was we who adapted to what they did naturally, and nothing that Daisy did was in any way alien to the actions a pony did by instinct. Plucking the apples was an illustration of the way horses pulled down new tree shoots to nibble, counting was a disguise for pawing through the snow to find winter grass, and even

54

the prancing was an extension of her natural high spirits. It was in fitting the actions together and coaxing a sequence that Tom was a genius, allied to his acute observation and infinite patience, and there was a rewards system that kept Daisy perfectly happy.

Some actions she appeared to think out for herself, with both a sense of the dramatic and the humorous: one day, when the disguised dwarf was supposed to creep up and abduct me, instead of just baring her teeth and rearing when he sneaked up, as she had been taught, she took it into her head to improve matters a little. The dwarf had taken to jeering at her when at a safe distance, then turning his back and strutting away – implying, I suppose, that he found it beneath his dignity to perform with a mere animal – and on this night Daisy waited till his back was turned, then lowered her head and charged. The dwarf went flying head over heels into the audience; being a tumbler he did not hurt himself, but the crowd were delighted with his discomfiture and applauded loudly. Jack was all for keeping this episode in the act, but was overruled by Tom, who thought he detected a touch of temper in Daisy's antics. He took over the dwarf's part himself to prove his point, and not only did Daisy have to be retaught to bare her teeth but it was a struggle for her even to pretend any antagonism towards Tom.

I loved working with Daisy, but one thing I could not master was to ride standing on her back. Jack cursed me up hill and down dale but I just did not have the necessary balancing skills and I am sure Daisy got very tired of me tumbling off round her feet. I could manage to ride seated facing her tail, which always got a laugh, but I had to find a proper bareback rider at a fair and bribe her to explain to Jack that she had had to learn from the age of three to be upstanding and still practised every day before he let me off. I think it helped that she was very pretty . . . .

With all the caring for Annie's cold, rehearsing with Daisy, and the usual repairs, polishing, painting, and chores that were a normal by-product of our life, I was more than ready to agree when Jack suggested a holiday a couple of days before we were due to move on again. It was a beautiful morning in early June, with that slight early morning mist that betokens later heat, and Jack saddled Hannibal and put a saddlecloth and bridle on one of the van horses, a placid, one-paced nag with the patched, gipsy colouring.

'I need some more tobacco and a couple of pipes and I know a small shop up in Malvern; so, if you fancy a ride, Sprat, look lively and pack up some cheese and bread and a couple of onions.'

I felt highly honoured to be chosen as his companion, but my pride received a distinct dip as he explained why he had picked me.

Casually slinging a couple of sacks over my horse's withers he remarked: 'We need more potatoes and a side of pork wouldn't come amiss: they'll come cheaper further up. There's more straw for the palliasses too and Hannibal doesn't like being strung alongside a packhorse, so you'll come in useful: you're light and won't be missed for a few hours. Keep as close as you can, I don't want to have to stop every couple of miles for you to catch up.'

But it was too lovely a day to take umbrage and as we worked our way through the narrow rutted lanes up to the hills my heart soared with the bird song and rejoiced at the roses and honeysuckle just opening in the hedges, and Jack, once we had left the encampment behind, seemed to throw off all his cares and whistled merrily. We approached the hills from the northeast and as we curved round to begin the steep ascent to the town I could see them stretch away south like a bony, sleeping dragon, their lower slopes thickly wooded and the higher slopes dotted with sheep.

The last couple of miles up from the plain were hard going and my mount was definitely lagging as we dismounted in the inn yard. After ordering the stable-lad to rub both horses down and water them, Jack led the way to the tobacconist's, halfway along the street that sidled across the side of the hill. But the shop was shuttered, and the town seemed deserted.

'Damn! I forgot it was Sunday – they'll all be in church.' He pulled out his pocket watch. 'Should be out soon; come on, Sprat, a prayer or two won't do you any harm.'

He led the way a little down the hill to the right where the abbey church stood, squat and comfortable, its graves sheltered by great yews. As we approached, a clap of wings heralded a cloud of pigeons swooping from the tower as the clock chimed a half-hour. I could hear chanting from within and as we passed under the stone arch the coolness soothed like a benediction. It was a satisfying church, not pretentious but nicely proportioned, with the massy Norman pillars stretching up the nave and the great east and west windows letting in light to every corner. Jack stood easily at the back, unconscious perhaps of his somewhat outlandish appearance. I had grown used to the shabby green greatcoat with the huge poacher's pockets, to his red neckerchief and cord breeches, but a glance round this sober, respectable congregation made me realize how easily I had forgotten the social niceties and accepted standards of dress I had known so long: in my patched breeches, tight jacket and bare legs I looked like a vagrant, yet if truth were known I felt far more at home in them – except in church. The life I had been leading for the last eight weeks was more real to me now than that which the people around me would consider normal. In a way I was ashamed of being ashamed, and Jack's apparent unconcern made me feel worse. But somehow he looked right and more real than those around: whilst they merely seemed to exist, he was alive.

I crept away to the southern aisle and knelt on the cold stone, light from the stained-glass windows falling in medieval patterns on my folded hands, transient dyes dependent on the sun: thunder-purple, poppy-red and Madonna-blue. I prayed in a confused, muddled way for those dead I had loved, for the living who shared my life now, and for the future of the unsure seeker that was myself. I prayed for guidance, for a way out of my difficulties, for security both material and emotional, and for grace. The flagstone on which I knelt left a red mark on my knee but the prayers soothed my mind and gave me a determination to let things take their own course for a while: no more rebellion, no more running away and, as soon as possible, no more deception –

'What do boys pray for?' asked Jack, startling me into an unreligious squeak. 'Pies, sunshine, and every day a holiday?'

'Something like that . . . . But I did remember to pray for Annie and Tom and Daisy. And you,' I added, hastily.

'I am glad to hear you have your priorities right,' he said sarcastically. 'Keeping the most important till last . . . . Amuse yourself for five minutes, I have someone to see.'

I wandered up towards the altar, the bars of sunlight I crossed dancing with atoms of dust stirred by the departing congregation. The choir stalls were empty and I squatted down to examine the grotesque carvings on the underside of the seats: imps, demons, weird faces and fabled creatures, so well chiselled they seemed ready to crawl from the wood as soon as my back was turned. Strange, secular sculptures for surroundings of such sanctity; perhaps it was thought that to round them up and place them under the backsides of the choir was both to keep them safe and show them where they belonged: beneath contempt. Funny thing, though: they were far more vivid and real than the stone angels and glass saints, but perhaps it was always easier to make bad things lifelike, there being so much copy to hand.

As I straightened up I saw the vicar blessing someone in the side chapel and to my amazement realized it was Jack, arrogant head bowed, tangled elflocks humble on his brown cheeks. He would not have wished me to see him in what he would have been sure I should have considered a moment of weakness, so I slipped out by the eastern door, and when he came to find me I was jumping over a tempting tombstone.

'Off, you vandal!' he said, seizing me by an ear. 'We'll find Mr Snuff-and-Tobacco back behind his counter now, I shouldn't wonder.'

The tiny shop, dark with brown shelves and boxes, sepia packets, blue paper and grey string, was tickly with the exotic fragrance of the leaf and the pepper of snuff and I sneezed six times straight off before Jack booted me out, creeping back when I had composed myself to find the tobacconist wrapping the purchases and Jack asking directions to a likely farm to pick up our stores.

'Why, sir, my wife's sister's husband has a tidy place down the hill and I'm sure they can oblige. If you gave me an order I'd have my eldest run down there straightaway, and we could have it ready at the inn in an hour or so – say, four o'clock?'

Jack frowned, obviously weighing the advantage of saving a shilling or two by seeking the best bargain himself against the temptation of an idle afternoon in the sun, then shrugged his shoulders.

'Very well, but I'm not paying over the odds. Here's the list, and if you can throw in a couple of chickens and some eggs they would not go amiss.' He turned to me. 'Go fetch that packet of bread and cheese, and ask the landlord for a jug of his best ale: I'll settle with him later. Then, my lad, we'll find a view to dine off.'

He led the way, climbing fast with those long legs of his, and clumsy with bread, cheese, and onions clasped to my chest, I had much ado to keep up with him, especially as he unfairly lightened the jug of some of its contents before he reached the top. The hill climbed steeply, the grass dry and skiddy under the smooth soles of my shoes. Taking them off I did better, curling my toes into the ground to gain a purchase, but I was still a good couple of minutes behind Jack in reaching the summit.

I collapsed thankfully but he stood, slowly pivoting on his heels, coat a careless heap at his feet, the soft breeze lifting the untidy hair from his forehead and fingering his loosened neckerchief.

'Stand up, Sprat: this is a sight every man should see once in his life.'

Dragging myself to unwilling feet I surveyed a landscape that spread for miles around till it melted into the haze of June.

'You can see more counties of England and Wales from the top of the Malverns than anywhere else in the country,' he continued, and taking me by the shoulders, he turned me slowly full circle. 'There, to the northeast is Worcester; north is Evesham – the way we came – and to the west the hills of Wales. Directly south of us is the Beacon, and beyond that Tewkesbury, Gloucester, Bristol; to the southeast is the Severn, Bredon Hill and –' He broke off abruptly. 'And so back to Worcester. Where's that bread and cheese?'

We shared out the food and Jack drank most of the rest of the ale, rather warm and cloudy from its climb up the hill, then he lay back on the short grass, arms behind his head.

'My pocket watch is in my coat . . . . What time does it say?'

'Ten minutes before two o'clock.'

'Wake me at three,' and promptly he went to sleep.

Rolling over on to my stomach I stared for a while out over the valley of the Severn, conscious, without isolating the sounds, of the sweet ascending of larks, the scream of invisible swifts, bleat of sheep, rasping of grasshoppers. I heard the abbey church strike the quarter, then I too was asleep.

When I woke it was to see Jack, elbows on the turf, folding spyglass to his eye, staring out to the east.

'You're a fine watchdog,' he said. 'It's past three already.'

I sat up. 'What can you see?'

'Just this side of Bredon Hill there is a house whose western windows look to these hills; the green lawn slopes to the river, and on that river the swans glide . . . .' He was speaking as if to himself, not an explanation to me but a reminder to himself. 'There are spotted deer in the park and banks of lavender on the terrace . . . .'

I knew better than to interrupt, though I should dearly have liked to ask of whose house he spoke: his own, his lady friend's, just somewhere he had visited, but he sighed and snapped the spyglass shut.

'Well, Sprat – enjoyed your day out?'

'Yes, thank you,' I said. 'I've just remembered: what date is it?'

'Fifth – no, sixth, of June. I think. Why?'

'It's my birthday.'

'I *knew* you were lying! You weren't fifteen when we picked you out of that ditch – just splitting hairs, in your fifteenth year you were –' He laughed abruptly, then reached over, pulled my hair and rolled me over and over like Annie rolled a dumpling till I was tousled, covered with grass and gasping for air. How then could I possibly insist that indeed I was now sixteen, without him waxing sarcastic about my lack of inches and brawn? So I just went on playing the scarecrow lad he wanted, and grinned placatingly.

'You deserve a spanking for the untruth – remember what I said about lying?'

I gambled. 'You just said it was only splitting hairs . . . .'

Turning quickly he pressed my shoulders back on the turf and held me pinned by the upper arms, his weight across my thighs and stomach, his face a snarl.

'Don't quibble with me, child!' A wolf, teeth bared to snatch at my throat? The snarl became a scowl. 'Still, as you said, it was not an outright lie, just an evasion of the truth . . . .' King Richard, about to strangle his nephew? The scowl slowly faded to be replaced by an expression I had no name for. 'You know . . . you're far too pretty for a lad . . . .'

Suddenly he hauled me upright and turned my face to the sun.

'Good God! The child's odd-eyed: one green, the other hazel – What *are* you, Sprat? In my book the ones with eyes like yours are either witch's brat or village idiot – which, lad?'

'I don't think I am the latter and my mother was the parson's daughter,' I answered primly.

'Lord above! Offspring of a slate-and-pencil and the Book of Common Prayer! No wonder! No: I'll not believe it. You must be either changeling or by-blow . . . .'

I knew he only teased, but he was nearer to truth than he realized. 'Perhaps if the Little Folk left me it was to bring good luck?'

'Not that I've noticed . . . . But of course it would have to be here! You've kept those eyes hidden till –'

'You never looked –'

'Quiet! You kept them hidden, I say, till we are in the place where magic abounds, where Piers Plowman saw his Field of Fair Folk . . . .'

' "Wo-weary and wet-shod: went I forth after
As a reckless renk: that recketh not of sorrow
And yede forth as a lorel: all my lifetime
Til I wex weary of this world: and wilned eft to sleep . . . ." '

If he was surprised that I had ever heard of a fairly obscure piece of medieval writing, let alone that I could quote from it, he did not show it. Perhaps he thought that all village schoolmasters taught their children so, but more probably he was too caught up in his own kind of verbal magic to notice it except as a feed to his next words.

'Tis Will's country too: sleep . . . .

"To sleep! perchance to dream: aye, there's the rub;
For in that sleep of death what dreams may come
When we have shuffled off this mortal coil,
Must give us pause . . . ."

'Yes, lad, pause now and think – you've given me an idea. Why shouldn't we? Yes! Come on, we'll be late!' And picking up his coat he ran down the hill, leaping from tussock to tussock with precarious agility. I followed as best I could, snatches of the 'To be or not to be' speech floating back to me, punctuated in unusual places by his leaps and bounds. Once I nearly dropped the flagon in my haste to follow, and was well behind by the time he reached the inn.

Impatiently he loaded up – everything we had asked for had been provided at a reasonable price, and they had even found a basket of mushrooms – and turning Hannibal for home, he set off at a pace my poor nag could not hope to emulate. I pushed him on as fast as I could, jolting up and down painfully on his bony spine, but I was forced to call on Jack to wait. He halted reluctantly, Hannibal dancing impatiently on his toes, caught by his master's urgency.

'Can't you hurry that thing along? No, I suppose you can't. Never mind, we can go over some of the speeches together as we ride; come to think of it, I could probably use you, too.'

'As one of the little princes?' I asked, light beginning to dawn.

'Yes – no, stupid! Richard's soliloquys are just that: soliloquys. And why you've got this fixation about him, I don't know . . . . And yet, innocence at the side of the stage, caged canary in hand, symbolic of his own golden promise confined by the bars of his uncle's ambition . . . . Yes, it's possible. You're quicker than I thought. But Hamlet; that speech stands without distraction, save for a skull – yes, I know that comes later but most people won't know or care – and a dagger, good and sharp, winking in the torchlight . . . . What say you?'

Not much, for the uncomfortable gait of my horse and the provisions banging and flapping before and behind. 'You mean – scenes – from the – plays?'

'Oh, do stop jigging up and down, boy – no, not scenes; not full ones anyway. Performing of plays outside London is strictly forbidden. Extracts we could probably get away

with, and the most famous speeches: think you could play
Fool to my Lear, lad?'

'And – Desdemona – to Othello – Ouch!' I had fallen
off.

He looked down to where I lay in the ditch.

'It's possible, with a wig. After all, boys played women's
parts at the Globe Theatre. That's a thought: play it in
the manner of that time – no, cost too much for authentic
costume.'

I remounted. 'I was only joking.'

'Well, I wasn't. We'll have a look at your Shakespeare
as soon as we get back.'

'Oh, hell!' I said. 'And damnation, too!'

'Don't swear.'

'You do!'

'And don't argue. I dislike argumentative children. But
come to think of it,' he added maliciously, 'at fifteen you
aren't a child any more. So be your age!' and he gave my
horse such a smack on its rump that out of sheer surprise
it went careering off down the lane at a good ten miles an
hour with me hanging on for dear life, leaving a trail of
potatoes and mushrooms bouncing between the ruts.
Perhaps it was just as well Jack and Hannibal were
carrying the eggs.

It was past eight when we arrived back, but Annie, up
and about now, had put aside some meat. Jack folded his
between two pieces of bread, bade me to do the same and,
leaving the unpacking of the provisions to the dwarves,
dragged me up into the van to discuss Shakespeare. We
were at an immediate disadvantage, for the meat was
greasy so we could not easily turn the pages of my book
and had to rely largely on memory. It was agreed to try
Richard and Shylock, they both being villains and strong
drink to inflame an audience, but Jack had this moth in
his drawers about Othello. Misliking the thought of

wearing a wig and having to pad out my front, I suggested Henry V.

'You could do the "Once more into the breach" piece riding onto the stage on Hannibal . . . but the armour might be a problem.'

'Pasteboard – and there's an old sword in the props basket.'

'Then there's Brutus' speech from *Julius Caesar* . . . .'

'Mmmm . . . .' Jack put finger to nose. 'Psychological stuff, that: doubt it would go down. Remember your audience, Sprat: give 'em someone to love or someone to hate, strong action or plenty of humour, and preferably all four. If you are only presenting an excerpt, you can't spend half an hour explaining a five-minute speech; it's got to be short, snappy, and to the point. There are some speeches in Shakespeare that stand on their own – Jaques' Seven Ages, "The quality of mercy," the Queen Mab one, John of Gaunt's dying speech; but they are all static. Beautiful to listen to, better to read and ponder upon, but our audiences want us to move, to act. Still, plenty to think about, haven't we? Now, get you to bed. We're off to Tewkesbury in the morning, so you need a good night's sleep. I think I'll just slip down the road for a pint or two . . . .'

He was asleep when I brought his shaving water in the morning, stinking of stale beer, still dressed, and lying where he had fallen across the bed in a drunken stupor. From one of his pockets dangled a lady's white stocking; I shook him awake and retreated hastily, to help Annie with breakfast.

After everything had been packed up and we were ready to move, he called me over to the van and pointed to a paper parcel on his dressing chest.

'I bought a second-hand copy of Shakespeare last night: we can work from that rather than spoiling yours. Oh, by the way,' and he reached into his pocket, 'I thought you should have a small gift to mark your birthday. It's the sort of thing I treasured as a boy,' and he handed me a horn-handled pocket knife in a leather sheath. 'It's sharp, so don't go cutting your fingers off.'

I stared at the knife as it lay in the palm of my hand and tried to find words to express what I felt. 'It's – it's just what I wanted; so – useful.'

He nodded. 'Knew you would like it. In spite of your soft ways, I'm sure you are a true lad at heart. Thought it might encourage you to, well, you know . . . whittle away at something, as I used to. I was always, er, whittling away at bits of wood when I was your age. Good for you. Make you interested in doing things with your hands, er . . . .'

'Healthy, masculine occupation . . . .'

'Exactly. Make a – boat, or something.'

'Yes, Jack. I'll start – whittling away at something this very morning.'

He glanced at me sharply. 'Don't go carving away at anything that matters. No mutilating the vans or cutting lumps out of things . . . .'

'No, Jack.'

'Why are you laughing?'

'I'm not – yes, I suppose I am. I'm happy, that's all. I haven't had a present for ages. And certainly nothing as – as useful as this. When's *your* birthday?'

'Mine? March twenty-first: first day of spring.'

'Aries and Gemini . . . .'

'You read the stars, perhaps, to add to your other accomplishments?'

'Not really. Just guesswork.'

'Well, let's see just how good your "guessing" really is – how old am I?'

'I couldn't –'

'Guess!'

I glanced round wildly for inspiration and, finding none, decided to fall back on flattery.

'Thirty-one?'

By the time he had booted me down the van steps I

had it firmly fixed in my memory that he was only twenty-eight . . . .

We reached Tewkesbury two days later and Jack was lucky enough to secure a pitch in the main street, where it widened just before the abbey. The place was clean, there being plenty of straw down, people were in a spending mood and the weather stayed fine, so we had a good week. I was kept busy all day; firstly with chores: wood, water and food; secondly with my introduction of Annie; thirdly my act with Daisy; and lastly, and far hardest of all, on into candlelight hearing Jack's lines and looking out props and clothes for Annie to alter in her spare time.

Jack had decided to do a cameo of Crookback's life, all Shakespeare of course, but with amendments. He started with a speech from *Henry VI*: 'Would Edward were wasted' going on to his later speech from the same play, after the killing of Henry: 'See how my sword weeps', then to the opening of *Richard III* with 'Now is the winter of our discontent' and so to his speech on his betrothal to the Lady Anne, finishing with a combination of his speeches before the Battle of Bosworth: 'Give me another horse', the last words of all being 'hand in hand to hell!' It was a lot to learn and, I thought privately, a lot for the audience to digest, but Jack condensed some of the speeches and we had the advantage of performing scarce two hundred yards from the battlefield where the usurper was reputed to have killed the young Prince of Wales, to ensure his own brother Edward's accession. In order that the audience could follow the sequence easily Jack had me speak a short linking commentary behind a screen.

His only props were a crude throne, a gold-paper crown, and the ubiquitous sword, used later for *Henry V* and *Lear*. There was no need to use padding to suggest deformity, he hunched himself like a raven beneath an old black cloak and the only make-up was a whitened face and

blackened teeth. There was one concession to sensationalism: the performances took place at night, lit by as many
torches as there were speeches; at the end of each of the
latter I stepped out, dressed in a tabard bearing the
embroidered white boar of Gloucester, and bore one of
the lights away to signify the deepening gloom of evil;
when the final words of the playlet were spoken Jack
himself seized the last torch and threw it down onto a pile
of saltpetre and escaped to hell behind a screen, leaving
his audience choking and blinded by smoke and flare.

In our rehearsals the torches had fallen over and the
saltpetre had been damp, but the actual performances
went surprisingly well, the audiences increasing every
night, those who had seen it once returning two or three
times; in the end Tom Fallon had scarce time to get from
one end of the crowd to the other with the collection box.
I suppose the only real difficulty I had had was to get
Annie to imagine a white boar to embroider on my tabard.
We unpicked the yellow wool lion, but then she was stuck.
In the end I had to borrow a piglet from one of the traders
and we held him by ear and tail whilst she considered him
from all angles. The end result looked a little like a sheep
with fangs, but Jack's histrionics more than made up for
any minor artistic deficiencies in my appearance.

By the end of two weeks at Tewkesbury my box of
savings jingled very satisfactorily; I had enough for a pair
of strong shoes, a shirt for best, and another neckerchief,
blue this time. Jack seemed to suffer from anticlimax
every night when his performance was over and took to
wandering about like the ghost of Richard, shoulders
still hunched and muttering to himself; his restlessness
communicated itself to me and consequently I earned
more than a few cuffs and threats for carelessness and
inattention, so it was with a sense of relief that I learned
we were to pack up and move on.

That night we found a village ten miles further south
but it took Annie and me by surprise when Jack announced
before supper: 'We'll stay here two nights: do what

business you can without me,' and disappeared into the van. I thought he might be sick, but he reappeared half an hour later dressed immaculately in buckskin breeches, black riding boots, mulberry coat and three-cornered hat, unruly hair tied back neatly. Tom had Hannibal saddled ready and Jack swung himself up, scowled down at us all and muttered: 'I shan't be back till tomorrow night, maybe the following morning,' and cantered off back the way we had come.

'Well I never!' said Annie. 'He's keen . . . .'

'What on?' I asked, puzzled.

'Some female, I reckon. Only thing as would send a man off like that.'

'Maybe; and then again, maybe not,' said Tom, watching the road down which Jack had disappeared. 'One thing you can be sure of though: that one will come back like a bear with a sore head.'

There was another thing I was sure of before very long: without Jack we all fell down like a pack of cards. Much as I resented his dictatorial manner and continual harrying, at least it kept us together as a team, but even that first night, freed from continual reminders of the time and checks on equipment, we dined later than our usual six o'clock; I forgot the water, Annie burned the stew, and the dwarves refused to help with the clearing up – in fact, they refused to put a show on at all that night and spent the evening quarrelling more violently than usual amongst themselves and drinking in the little alehouse down the road. I muffed my introduction of Annie, who hadn't bothered to put on her best gown, and Tom, reliable Tom, was obviously miles away when he was supposed to be directing Daisy. Altogether it was a very poor show, and we were lucky to have only a couple of dozen uncritical villagers to entertain.

The van seemed very empty that night without Jack, and I tossed and turned on my palliasse, unused to being alone. After a while I dozed off, to dream of my childhood truckle bed under the lattice window and recall the old pear tree that used to tap-tap at my window when the wind rose. I remembered how I used to open my eyes for reassurance and gaze up at the moon as she rode at anchor among the racing waves of cloud. This night there was no wind, yet there was a scratching at the window as if the pear tree was asking to come in – but it couldn't be the tree for there was a mumbling like a boggart out there – and I awoke in a sudden panic, not even sure where I was, and looked up at the moon for reassurance. There it was, dangling above the open half of the van door, but it had great holes for eyes and nose and a mouth with no teeth but a great slobbering tongue and it smelled like a charnel house and it stretched out a nubbed gnarled hand and clawed at my hair –

I screamed and screamed, beating away the hands and face above me, and a long moment later there was blessed light and relief as Tom came running with hastily lit lantern and reassuring words to take the intruder by the arm and speak gently to us both. By the lantern's flickering light I saw it was only some poor idiot fellow, in his twenties maybe and dressed like a scarecrow, and the face I had thought the moon was deformed by some disease that had eaten away at the soft tissues of the face, leaving him half-blind and noseless. Some old crone came after him about five minutes later in her night attire, having found his bed empty, and she led him away, scolding him and apologizing to us in the same breath, as Annie arrived on the scene dressed in a vast wrapper that would have done duty as a tent.

'What was all that about, then? What with you a-screaming your head off and those dwarves yelling and bumping about in their van, I declare I haven't had a wink of sleep and it must be well past midnight . . . .' And she yawned cavernously.

' 'Twas nothing,' said Tom soothingly. 'Nothing but a poor lad a little touched in the head who wandered off from home seeking company. You should fasten that van

70

door properly at nights,' he added, turning to me. 'Specially when you are alone, like now.'

'But his *face*, Tom . . . .'

'Nay, young 'un, have you never seen one with the clap before? If they gets it young enough and bad enough it's a race a'tween softening of the brain and corruption of the body – 'tis death either way. That's why every grown man and woman should be sure they don't lie with one as is afflicted, for though there are cures if 'tis taken soon enough, these be a long and painful business, don't always work, and can even affect an unborn child.' He sighed. 'There's many a tragedy could have been avoided with a little care. So, be afraid of the disease itself but not the carriers: they need your prayers, as do all that've been corrupted,' and he gave me a strange significant look, as if his words meant more than they seemed.

'Well,' said Annie, after a little silence. 'Clap's the only bad thing my old man didn't give me, and our boy here's a little young to be lifting skirts as yet, so what do you say as we poke up that old fire a bit and has a brew of tea afore we goes back to bed? Best thing there is for the nerves, a nice cup of tea . . . .'

It seemed a long day, waiting for Jack's return. I soaped all the leather Tom hadn't already dealt with and had my usual rehearsal with Daisy, for, as Tom explained, if animals are to perform you must run through their routine each day till performing comes as naturally as breathing. Annie washed all her things and mine, and, greatly daring, ventured into Jack's van to sort out his. While she was laundering these, she gave me his shoes to polish, coats and waistcoats to sponge, and the interior of the van to dust and tidy.

'Not that he'll notice, mind,' she said, 'but we've done a good job, I reckon, and no moths or bugs to be seen. He may dress like a care-nothing himself, but he's a noticing man when it comes to others, right enough. You forget to sew on a ribbon or mend a tear in your lace and he's down like a 'venging angel! Not so particular about his girls, though: pretty they may be, but they're mostly trash. He wants to watch he don't get poxed by one of those doxies one of these days . . . .'

For a vivid instant I had a picture before my eyes of Jack, face eaten away by disease, mind unhinged, stumbling through life with a begging bowl and a stick, mumbling through broken, blackened teeth for alms –

I shivered. 'But he's careful, ain't he, Annie?'

'What man's ever careful when his jack's a-twitching? 'Tis fine if you've one woman only to turn to and can trust her not to lend it out when you're not looking, but he goes anywhere as takes his fancy, and one day . . . .'

I spent the rest of that afternoon remembering the poor idiot the night before, and wondering how to wean Jack from his indiscrimination. I knew Annie would consider it none of her business, or mine either if it came to that, but I thought perhaps he might listen to me; stupidly, in my do-good ignorance, putting him in my place: remembering how often I listened to his advice to me, and heeded it, too, knowing he was giving it for my betterment. I wondered if perhaps there was a leaflet or paper on the subject I could leave where he would find it: he would perhaps find that more tactful and it would spare my blushes.

We gave no performance that evening for the villagers had spent their few pence the night before, and Tom and I used the spare time to pack all up ready for an early start in the morning, were it needed.

'He may not come back tonight,' I said at supper, my mouth full of stew. 'This is really good, Annie . . . .'

'I believe he will,' said Tom. ' 'Tis not far he's travelling, not for him, and there's not much to keep a man, once there.'

'You know where he's gone, then?'

'Just an idea,' he said, leaning forward to put another branch on the fire. 'And if I'm right it were better any questions are forgot as soon as thought of: there's some things best left alone.'

He came cantering through the dusk just as we were finishing our meal and by the look of it he had ridden hard. Dismounting without a word he flung Hannibal's reins to Tom, who, equally silent, led the horse away. The dwarves had gone back to their van as soon as they had eaten, and Annie and I stared up at a scowling Jack slapping his riding whip against his dusty breeches, venturing nothing.

'Some stew, my dear?' she said affably. 'We saved you a bowlful and Sprat here says —'

'I'm not hungry,' he interrupted and, swinging on his heel, went off to the van, leaving Annie and me looking at each other like leftovers.

She shrugged. 'No point in letting it go to waste, then,' and she divided the stew into two equal portions, handing one to me and taking the other over to Tom, who was rubbing down Hannibal. 'Bread'll keep till morning,' she said, coming back. 'I suppose we shall be off at first light . . . like to go and ask him, love?'

There was a candle burning on the chest near the bed and by its light I saw Jack lying back on the bed in shirtsleeves. One hand was over his eyes and the other held a bottle of brandy.

'Jack,' I said timidly. 'They want to know what time we start tomorrow.'

He took his hand away from his eyes and to my horror they were red, as if he had been weeping.

'Never trust anyone, Sprat,' he said. 'And especially not a woman. You should thank whatever star you were born under that you have no relatives and no one to care for . . . . Stay away from all entanglements, don't get involved.'

'I don't intend to,' I said sincerely. 'I'm lucky, I suppose, to have you and Tom and Annie to —'

73

'You haven't got me or Tom or Annie or anyone and it's time you learned that it's better that way. I care for no one, and never will again –'

'One day you will settle down and –'

'Settle down nothing!' He tipped the bottle to his mouth and drank deep. 'I am Jack of all trades and master of none save myself, and that's enough!'

I picked his coat up from the floor, and held it, smoothing the collar. 'That's also an excuse,' I said, as steadily and calmly as I could, 'for carousing and wenching and becoming untidier and more careless of yourself every day.'

'What is it to you?' he said aggressively.

'Nothing, nothing at all – except that I hate to see waste.'

'Fine talk, boy; wait till you grow a little and then let's see you when the nights are hot and the thirst is heavy . . . . Let's see whether you will resist the lusts of the flesh when you are old enough to know temptation – until then, keep your mouth *shut*! You talk like all virgins: just wait till you find another use for your prick than to piss through! Then, and only then, will you have the right to cant and criticize –' He took another gulp of brandy and swung himself into a sitting position on the edge of the bunk. 'And even then it would be none of your business.'

' "No man is an island –" '

'And don't quote that parson to me.'

'John Donne was a rake once, but *he* repented.'

'I'm no Jack-in-the-pulpit.' He tossed the empty bottle out of the door, narrowly missing my head. 'If you want to preach, go for a priest – this is no life for you. Didn't you say your grandfather was a vicar, or something?' He groaned, head in hands. 'Is there no peace for me, even here? I say again: leave my way of life to me or I'll give you a whipping your backside will remember!'

His coat smelled of lavender: it *had* been a woman . . . .

'At least,' I said, laying it carefully across the chest, 'I shall know enough not to catch the clap –'

In a blur of movement he was on his feet and a fist crashed into the side of my mouth followed by another in the pit of my stomach. I tumbled against the side of the van, only to be hauled to my feet and shaken unmercifully. I could not breathe, my head was spinning, my mouth full of blood, and he was shouting and swearing, but a moment later I heard Tom's voice.

'That'll be enough, Master: it's only a child,' and hands took me and led me down the steps and laid me down on the grass. I could see Annie's face floating above me, her eyes full of concern, and behind her Jack swaying on top of the van steps, Tom talking to him urgently, his hand flat on Jack's chest, then I was very sick all over Annie's shoes.

Helping me back to her van, she washed my cut lip and put a cold cloth to my bitten tongue.

'Drink this, love: 'twill sting, but you'll feel better.'

I gulped down the neat gin and wiped the tears from my cheeks.

'Why did he behave like that, Annie?'

'Don't know, dearie – it must have been something you said on top of all that drink he had. Never mind; you shall sleep here tonight. I'll fetch your blanket, and in the morning I'll give him a piece of my mind. Knocking my poor lad about like that!'

'No, no!' I struggled to my feet, wincing from the pain to my bruised stomach muscles. 'He didn't mean it . . . . He's unhappy, Annie, and I was thoughtless and impertinent. Thank you for the offer, but I must go back,' and I stumbled down the steps and walked towards our van.

Tom's soft voice halted me.

'Where are you going?'

'Back to Jack.'

'Don't expect too much then, youngster,' and he put a comforting hand on my shoulder. 'He hit out at you without thinking and he's sorry, but you lit on a touchy subject. For a moment he forgot who you were, and who

75

he is. Go easy with him . . . perhaps it would be better to keep out of the way till morning.'

I shook my head. 'Thanks, Tom, but I'll chance it.' I wondered what words he had used to calm Jack down.

I ascended the steps of the van slowly. The candle still burned on the chest, beside the folded coat, and he was sitting back again on the edge of the bunk, head in hands once more.

I went forward, hesitated, and touched his shoulder. 'Jack?' He did not answer, so I tried again. 'Jack – I'm sorry.'

He looked up at that, and his face was haggard.

'Sorry?'

'Yes.'

'For what?'

'For – for upsetting you, saying the wrong thing, whatever it was . . . .'

'What's the matter with your voice – you're lisping!'

'I bit my tongue.'

He laughed a little then, but it was soberly enough.

'How many times have I told you to duck? How the hell can you speak Shakespeare with a tongue like a sponge! I had thought to start rehearsing soon for *The Merchant* with your Portia to my Shylock . . . .'

I gathered all was forgiven.

Not entirely forgotten, however. As I was drifting off to sleep at last, bruised mouth away from the pillow, a voice came out of the darkness.

'Remind me to show you tomorrow how to ride a blow; it's quite easy, really, rather like catching a hard-thrown ball. The theory is just the same: you anticipate speed and direction and move away in the . . . . Never mind, I'll show you in the morning.'

And as apologies go, it was better than most.

4

Bishops Cleeve and Churchtown provided good weeks and suddenly, almost before I realized it, we were nearing Gloucester.

'This is as far as we go this trip,' said Jack at Sherdingham. 'You'll have to make your own way from here. I can give you three days: say, noon on Wednesday. It should be enough if you can manage to get a lift part way.'

'Give me three days?' I said, stupidly.

'In case it's no good. You've nowhere else to go, have you?'

'I suppose not.' To tell the truth Gloucester had retreated so far to the back of my mind that I wasn't at all sure now that I wanted to find Matthew Brown, bookseller, let alone settle down with him even if he would have me. Somehow Jack and Annie and Tom were so much more real and exciting than the idea of life in a bookshop that, despite all the handicaps, I felt I would far rather stay with them.

'Well, get along, then; and don't get picked up as a vagrant, or it'll be the House of Correction!' He hesitated. 'You have some money?'

I nodded.

'Well, I probably owe you some: here's a guinea. Then we can call it quits,' and he turned away.

I caught him by the sleeve. 'Jack —'

'Haven't you gone yet?'

'What about the bits I do with Daisy and Annie? And the Shakespeare?'

'You're not indispensable, you know.'

'Yes, but —'

'You mean "No, but" . . . . Go. Vanish. Disappear.' He

made as if to cuff me, but by now I knew the difference between that and the real thing, and stood my ground.

'Thanks for everything.'

'None needed. Now, get along before I decide to hold you to your indentures!' and he turned and strode away without a backward glance.

I knew I hadn't signed any, but at that moment I almost wished I had.

I changed into the brown velveteen breeches and waistcoat and packed the bread and cheese Annie had provided round my stockings, best shoes and jacket, tying all neatly with twine – so neatly I had a job to get it undone when I wanted the food later: that was the first time Jack's knife came in really handy, because I couldn't whittle to save my life. . . .

Annie kissed me on both cheeks, cried a little, then hugged me.

'You're going to miss your old Annie. . . . I don't see why you want to go and leave us, anyways; just look at all that money you made – Oh, my saints! You've forgotten it! I'll just go get it –'

'No, I haven't!' I said, laughing. 'I've left it on purpose. If I do decide to stay in Gloucester I'm coming back first to say my goodbyes properly.' And spend Jack's guinea on you all, I added mentally. 'So keep my bits and pieces safe till I come back, won't you?'

'Of course, my lamb. They'll be safe as – as mine are, while you come back, and I can't say fairer than that!'

I kissed Daisy's soft nose and gave her a candy I had been saving, and shook Tom's hand. He and Annie saw me to the road but the dwarves ignored me and Jack was nowhere to be seen so it was with a slight sense of disappointment that I reached the signpost that said 'Worcester', 'Gloucester', and 'Cirencester' and took the right-hand fork.

The weather was chilly for early July and I trudged, barefoot to save the shoes, against a rising wind that rattled the branches in the copses I passed until I began to half-imagine robbers lurking behind every tree and was glad for the knife I carried. Very little traffic came from Gloucester: a couple of haycarts and a parson on a pony, singing a very secular song, and I was unluckier with anything going my way: it seemed Sunday was spent at home in Gloucestershire.

I spent the night in a barn a little way back from the road, waking with a start of terror when a screech owl uttered his bloodcurdling cry as he swept from his perch in the rafters above – it took me all my time not to scream out loud myself, and some of the old fear of being alone in the dark that had haunted me since I was a child now sneaked up on me. As then, it was no use being rational and sensible about it, and it took a long time to get to sleep again.

Next morning it rained early, but by the time I took to the road I was happy to hail a farmer carrying hides to town, and he was equally glad enough of an audience, for I found he rattled away inconsequentially, but in high good humour, about his farm, his family, his politics, and his friends all the way to the New Inn, just across from the cathedral.

As it was past noon and I had not eaten since bread and cheese the night before, I bought a plate of meat and dumplings at the inn, and enjoyed unaccustomed leisure watching the customers, coaches and carts. Gloucester seemed a fine place, in a valley with wooded hills around and the great tower of the cathedral dominating all. I found I had enough spare pence to pay for the meal and have a penny over, which I tossed with a grand air to the beggar at the gate, then strolled over to the cathedral, a full stomach and the warm sunshine tempting me to do a little sightseeing before I sought Matthew Brown: I remembered my stepfather telling me his shop was near the close, so I was headed in the right direction as well.

Inside, the cathedral was cool and beautiful, the great arches flying to the roof like the swept-back wings of angels. I wandered down the cloister, running my fingers round the monks' stone laving-bowls, and stepped for a moment into the abbot's garden, bright with sunshine and prayer-pure white roses whose blown petals petitioned the wind before drifting into the stone corridors behind to die. A peacock butterfly, glowing in purple, rested two Argus eyes on a stone arch nearby, its fragility more ephemeral than ever against the permanence of grey stone. It was easy to pray in such surroundings.

Matthew Brown's shop was the first down the alleyway leading from the close, its bow-fronted window full of dusty books. I tried the latch on the oaken door but the bolt was fast behind it; looking back at the window I saw a little black-edged card propped against the books at the front: 'Closed due to Bereavement' it said and a horrible presentiment squeezed my chest. I asked at the cake shop next door but the old crone was deaf and tried to sell me some jam tarts, and the next shop down was empty. I wandered back to the bookshop, sat on the step and wondered what to do next. A window over my head opened and the slops narrowly missed as I jumped to my feet; a disappointed voice that sounded as if it came through a pinched nose ordered me to be gone before she fetched the authorities.

'I'm no vagrant, ma'am: I am seeking Mister Brown –'

'You'll have a long wait, then! They're not back till tomorrow, and it's no use hanging around!' and the window slammed shut so hard I was surprised not to find the panes about my feet.

At least there was someone coming to the shop tomorrow and my spirits began to rise. There remained tonight to get through and I didn't want to break into Jack's guinea unnecessarily; I decided to chance the stables at the inn and, slipping in when no one was looking, climbed to the loft and curled up behind a bale of straw. I was hungry, yes, but then I had been hungry before and was tired enough to doze off fairly quickly in spite of the comings and goings in the inn yard. I woke a couple of times during the night but they had left a lantern in the doorway and its comforting beams shone up through the slats in the floor of the loft; from below the warm smell of horses rose like a breath and the occasional stamp of hooves were as soothing as the more regular chimes from the tower opposite . . . .

'Wot the 'ell d'yer think yer doin' up there?'

I fled, for with the dawn came the ostler for fresh straw, and I spent the next three hours wandering through the streets, hungry and cold, for the morning air was chill. I was perversely determined not to spend the guinea except as a last resort, hoping against hope that once the bookshop opened all my problems would be solved, starting with breakfast . . . .

As soon as the cathedral clock struck eight, the chimes falling from the great height of the tower like stricken doves, each clear and distinct yet dying with every yard they fell, I made my way to the shop but there was no one there, only the books, a little dustier, and two dead flies decorating the spaces between. I returned at nine, at ten, and at eleven but the shop stayed locked and deserted. By noon my stomach was rumbling loud enough to drown the chimes and by two o'clock I was dizzy with hunger and spent the next hour dozing under a tree in the churchyard till a clerkly-looking fellow came hurrying over and told me to clear off, looking me up and down as if he would dearly have liked to arrest me on suspicion of something or other. I supposed two nights sleeping rough had not improved my appearance but as I had no mirror and had forgotten my comb the best I could do was to go and wash my hands under the pump and run damp, conciliatory fingers through my tousled hair, hoping I looked better than I felt.

I decided to have one last try at the shop before making my way back to the security of Jack, and as I rounded the corner of the alleyway I saw, Glory be! that the door of the shop was open. Stumbling up the steps I blinked in the sudden gloom and finally made out the figures of a man and woman behind the counter.

'M – Mister Matthew Brown?'

The woman leaned across; she was dressed in black and she was frowning.

'Are you a stranger to these parts not to know my father has been dead these past two months and helpless from a stroke the six before? And what would you have had to do with him anyway, a rough-looking lad like you? Hoping for a hand-out, I suppose! Well, he was always too soft with scavengers, but you can rest assured I'm a different sort altogether. Now, be off with you!'

I burst into tears.

'I'm – I'm sorry, I didn't know he was dead, truly I didn't. I came to – to see whether . . . . He was a friend of my stepfather's, you see. They were at college together. I had hoped – but it doesn't matter now.'

The man moved forward.

'Come far, have you?'

'From – from Derbyshire . . . .' I rubbed at my eyes with my sleeve.

The man turned to his companion. 'He may look rough, but his speech is gentle enough.' He turned to me. 'What is your stepfather's name?'

'He's dead, too: he died last year.' I heard the woman give a little snort of disbelief, but hurried on. 'His name was Zoroaster Mortimer – perhaps your father mentioned him? They had corresponded for years.'

The man started. 'Why, there's that parcel up on the shelf the old man made up just before he became sick: never got sent, remember, Phoebe? I'll swear there was some such outlandish name writ on the paper.' He reached behind him to the highest shelf and brought down a sealed packet, which the woman took from him, glancing at the superscription.

'Whereabouts in Derbyshire did you say you came from?'

'Leebeck. That is –'

82

'Well, this is addressed to your stepfather right enough; however, if you say he's dead . . . .' She hesitated.

'It's only another book,' said the man. 'Shop's sold and stock with it. Don't think this was on the inventory, anyway, and nobody would miss it. I'm sure the lad would like it, as a memento of his stepfather's friend – go on, Phoebe.'

She hesitated again, then thrust the parcel into my hands as though she were afraid she might change her mind if she thought longer.

'There you are, then. I hope as how you can read?'

'Yes, ma'am, thank you.'

She moved to the door. 'Well, off you go then. We've a might of packing to finish before we drop the keys off at the lawyer's.'

I walked out into the late afternoon sunshine and as the door of the shop was shut firmly behind me it was as if another door had closed in my life. There was no returning that way: in fact, there was only one way ahead that I could see, and I wasn't quite sure whether I was glad or sorry.

I was by now so hungry that as I reckoned I had no hope of getting back to the others tonight, even with a lift, there was nothing for it but to spend some of Jack's guinea on food, and then perhaps buy my way back to them with a small gift each. Accordingly I took off my jacket, stockings and shoes and wrapped them into a bundle again, tucking my knife under the waistband of my breeches ready for dividing the large pie I intended to eat on the way. Thus equipped for a long trudge back, I followed my nose to the nearest food. This proved to be a pie stall down a side street near the inn where the stallholder was busy setting out a fresh batch of pies, warm from some oven. His stall was shaded by an old oak, and there was a bench to relax on whilst one ate. The smell of hot, gravy-soaked pastry was almost as acute as a pain and I hurried forward, already fumbling in my pocket for the guinea. It wasn't in the pocket I had thought it would be, so I tucked the book parcel in my waistcoat and put down my bundle of clothes. Out of the corner of my eye I saw a couple of boys, who had been kicking a pig's jawbone aimlessly around, abandon their game and walk towards the stall, but I suspected nothing. Just as I pulled out the guinea and the stallholder was straightening up with the last of the fresh pies from his basket, I received a violent push in the small of the back which sent me headlong into the stall, scattering pies and winding me.

A voice yelled: 'He's stealing your pies, mister!' and as I got to my feet I saw the boys disappearing round the corner of the street, clutching a pie apiece and my bundle of clothes tossed from one to the other, but even as I set off in pursuit I cannoned into a portly gentleman walking briskly past, which hurt us both.

He recovered first, and grabbed me by the arm. 'Hey! Why don't you look where you are going – why in such a hurry?' He peered closer. 'Haven't I seen you somewhere before?'

'Let me go!' I gasped. 'Those boys: they've stolen my bundle!' and I tried to wriggle from his grasp.

'Not so fast,' said he, his nose a mere inch from mine. 'I know you now: you're the vagabond I chased from the churchyard this morning for loitering about . . . . What's he been doing, Seth? Stealing your pies, I shouldn't wonder!'

'More'n likely,' said the pie-seller, gloomily surveying the ruin of his stall. 'There's three pies spoiled and as many missing, but whether it was this lad or another . . . .' Picking up a pie from the gutter, he blew the dirt off the top. 'Can only charge a penny for this one now . . . .'

With a sudden effort I twisted free of my captor and set off at a run down the road in the direction the boys had disappeared and I was no longer the hunter but the hunted, and I reckoned I would be lucky to get clear in one piece. But the aforesaid luck was out: as I rounded the corner my way was blocked by a half-dozen or so cattle being driven in for market tomorrow. I turned to run the other way, but it was no use: suddenly there seemed to be at least fifty good citizens responding to the cries of 'Stop thief!' from my original captor and the pie-seller.

By the time they had found a couple of responsible citizens to commit me to prison for the night, I had a fine black eye and was bruised all over. It seemed that all the citizens of Gloucester had been waiting for something to brighten the monotony of a dull Tuesday in July, and I was as good as a bear-baiting. After the first buffets and the knowledge that I was held fast, all fear left me: it was almost as though I had gained a protective shell through which, mercifully, I was aware, yet felt nothing. I saw their faces: curious, apprehensive, and some sympathetic; I suffered their pinches and blows; I heard the archaic words that committed me to custody and would bring me in front of the magistrates the following day, but it was all happening to someone else. Even the dark cell with the damp straw did not seem real: I heard the heavy door clang shut and the ringing of iron stayed in my ears like the sound of a great bell . . . .

I must have slept deeply, or indeed been unconscious, for some hours, for when I came to myself again it was pitch dark. All unreality had vanished, and I was perfectly lucid and utterly miserable. I was cold, one side was damp where I had been lying on wet, smelly straw, and I was so hungry that the thought of food practically drove away all the other discomforts. Stretching out my hand I could feel the rough stone of one of the walls, and I inched my way round the cell on hands and knees, hoping against hope, as I suppose all prisoners do, for a way of escape. Even as I searched for a way out part of my mind told me that most prisons were extremely efficient at keeping people in, and I think the action was merely a reflex. I had felt round two sides of my cell when I came upon the door; thick-planked and iron-studded, it had a cold, iron lock-plate that must have needed the biggest key in the world, for my index finger waggled about in the keyhole with room to spare. Rising to my feet, I felt for the grille above, and my hands had just grasped the bars when I heard it: a rustling, scratching, squeaking, chattering sound from the far corner of the cell. The hair crawled at the back of my neck and the blackness of my prison was instantly peopled with darker shapes of demon, bat, witch and rat. I told myself that I was mistaken, and that even if I weren't I was sixteen years old and that boys weren't afraid of the dark, but just faced facts and took everything in their stride; if danger threatened they took out the knife which I still kept tucked under my waistband and went into the attack.

My heart was pounding like a drum in my ears but the noises advanced, and all at once there was a sound like the scrape of a scaly tail on the stone floor. I regret that I lost my presence of mind at that point and yelled. I yelled for help, for light, for company. I yelled till I grew hoarse, till my hands were numb from gripping the bars of the grille, and my knees knotted with the effort to stay upright, and still the fear would not leave me. At long last I thought I saw a flicker of light, high up like a star, that wavered and dipped towards me and, thank God! there was someone coming down a flight of stairs towards the cell. My cries had faded into a hoarse rasp and I could clearly hear the shuffle of slippered feet, the clank of keys, and a grumbling monologue that accompanied the blessed candlelight.

'Such a commotion, such a noise! How can a man expect to sleep with all that hubbub? Only a lad, yet he screeches like a banshee! Wake the dead, he would, even though they lie a good quarter mile away; but then again, there's some of those that'd need the trumpet of the angel Gabriel himself to rouse 'em .... But there's the living here and they needs their rest, too, not to listen to the howlings and ravings of a young ne'er-do-well with nothing to do save kick his heels and wait till morning ....'

By this time he had reached the door, and held up the candlestick to the grille. We stared at one another: he was gap-toothed and stubble-chinned with a greasy stocking cap hanging over one ear, and, to judge from his expression, I wasn't making much impression either.

There was a long silence.

I expected him to do something without being asked, he obviously thought I would say something without being prompted, and there I suppose we might have stayed like statues till the candle burned out, but that suddenly that awful squeaking and squealing started up again and I found my tongue.

'Rats! There are rats in here!'

He rubbed his chin. 'Could be, could be . . . . Ain't had any complaints lately, though. Last lot in here was drunks, and mebbe they'd not notice. Gets through that bitty hole in the corner, there where the sewer runs.'

'But, please!' I begged. 'Can't you get rid of them? I can't stay in here with rats – they might eat me!'

'Old woman's tale, that. Still, you never know, I s'pose: once heard of an old fellow who went to sleep in a London jail and woke up with no toes . . . think they made that one up, but you never can tell. Tell you what: I'll fetch Thomas,' and he padded away up the stairs again, unfortunately taking the candle with him. It seemed an age before he reappeared, apparently without the person he had gone to fetch.

'They ain't after your supper, are they?' he asked.

'I haven't had any.'

'Bless me, neither you have! It's still here on the step. Must have forgotten. Should have asked, you know: still, you chew on this crust and have a swallow of the water, and Thomas'll get rid of them nasty creatures for you'.

He handed me a very dry and musty heel of loaf through the grille, but I was too hungry to quibble and down it went, followed by a sip of stale water.

'Now, step aside from that door a moment and we'll give Thomas a sight of the action,' and he set the candle down on the steps and proceeded to light an ancient and very smelly churchwarden that sent clouds of evil smoke drifting up the stairs. He drew to his satisfaction, then glanced up at me. 'What you waiting for?'

I had not moved and was staring up the stairs expectantly. 'Your friend.'

'Which friend?'

'Thomas?'

The old man laughed, a wheezy, bubbling reaction that had him coughing and spluttering and spitting on the floor in an instant.

'Just do as I says and step back from that door . . . . That's it. Up you go, Thomas my lad, and fetch your supper!'

A huge tabby cat suddenly appeared at the grille, squeezed himself through, dropped down to my side and disappeared. A moment later the sounds from the corner intensified; rushes, scurries, louder squeaks, and the unmistakeable hunting growl of a happy feline. After a while there was silence, followed by the delicate scrunch of bone.

'Ah, he's got 'un,' said my jailor. 'Good ratter, that. Don't eat 'em all, just the heads. Brains is good for him, or so he thinks. Rest of 'em makes him sick. Indigestible old things, is rats. He ate a whole one once, afore he had sense, and sicked the whole lot up a half-hour later. All of a piece it came out, too, but somehow it had all got mixed up in his stomach: old thing had got the pieces all which ways and it came out with head and tail in the middle and t'other bits at the ends . . . . You feeling all right, lad?'

The bread and water nearly went to join the rats, but I took several deep breaths and managed to keep them down.

The cat came and rubbed round my legs, and I bent to stroke the blunt old tom's head with the fight-folded ears. 'Thanks,' I whispered, and heard the deep rumbling purr of response.

'Well, I'm for my bed,' said the old man. 'You'll sleep easy, now.'

'Wait!' I cried, suddenly aware that with him would go light and companionship. 'Couldn't you leave the light?'

'Not allowed to do that . . . .'

'The cat, then: can Thomas stay?'

'How do I know you won't hurt 'im? No, come to think of it 'e's quicker 'n you and sees better in the dark. 'Sides, he's got claws. Still, up to him, not me. I'll leave the door open top of the stairs, case he wants out.'

He shuffled away and the candle bobbed unsteadily up the stairs. I bent and stroked Thomas.

'Please stay,' I whispered. 'You can curl up on my lap.'

For a moment I thought he wouldn't, but when I sat down on the damp straw my thighs were suddenly heavy with cat, purring deeply and rhythmically, sharp bits kneading happily on all four corners. But I didn't care: punctured knees were a small price to pay for his company.

And there he stayed till a grey dawnlight filtered through the small barred window to the street and my jailor came down with a bowl of gruel for my breakfast.

Apparently it took some time to assemble my accusers, for it was past noon before they were ready for me. I spent the morning with my nose pressed against the barred window to the street, standing on tiptoe, my vigil rewarded by more feet than I could ever remember. My cell was below street level at the corner of one of the thoroughfares and it was only by squinting sideways that I could see anything at all – except feet. I could hear: people, horses, birds, squeaks, bellows, rumbles and rolls, but usually not see their source. But, as I said, I saw feet: large feet, small feet; shod feet, bare feet; shoes, boots, slippers, pattens; new shoes, old ones, clean ones, dirty ones; plain ones, patterned ones, buckled ones, heeled ones, and flat ones. And all going somewhere, all busy, all with a purpose, even if that purpose was only a stroll in the sunshine. There were animals too: paws and hooves; walking, trotting, loping and lumbering across my line of vision. I wondered if anyone had ever painted a picture of feet, a proper picture in a gilded frame that one could hang over the mantelpiece. I reckoned one could have fun with a picture like that, just imagining the rest of the person or animal; did the pretty red-heeled slippers have as pretty a face above them? Did the dusty old riding boots have a dusty, down-at-heel owner? Did the white-feathered carthorse have a white streak down his forehead and the dog with big paws have a long tail? Only parts of things were infuriating and engrossing, too, and I found the morning passed quicker than I would have thought, and without the inevitable worry becoming too overwhelming. I had no illusions as to what would happen when I was dragged before the magistrates, even without remembering Jack's prophetic words about being picked up as a vagrant.

At last I heard steps coming down the stairs behind and I turned reluctantly to meet my fate. First came a beadle, done up in purple velvet and gold braid; very hot he looked, too, and if the heat and his uniform had made him as bad-tempered as he appeared, then I was in for a rough handling. Then there were two gentlemen in dark clothes, one of whom I recognized as my captor of the day before; following them came the pie-man and lastly a tight-lipped lady in faded brown pelisse and large bonnet, who held her nose in an exaggerated fashion as she approached the cell and peered at me through the grille.

'That's him: that's the one, no doubt of it. I knew he was up to no good!'

I had never seen her before, but I recognized the tight, pinched voice as that of the slops-thrower: she had audacity, accusing me of wrongdoing when she had transgressed by emptying her waste onto the pavement! I glared at her and she stepped back hastily.

'Nasty, vicious-looking boy! A lady wouldn't be safe . . . .'

'*Quite* safe with me 'ere,' said the beadle, in a deep, wheezy voice. 'But we'll put a tie on him, just to make sure.'

'No call to do that, surely,' said the milder of the two

men in black. 'Boy can't escape if you keep a firm hand on his shoulder and we walk on the other side. It's only a short step to the inn.'

'Not the court, then?' asked my jailor.

'For the likes of him?' said the cross man. 'No point in convening a full court for a quick decision like this: shouldn't take more'n five minutes.'

'He must have a fair hearing,' said the mild man.

'Of course, of course,' said the other irritably. 'But the sooner we start, the sooner we finish. Beadle! Lead the way with the prisoner!'

It was not a very impressive procession, at least if the central character was anything to go by. I caught a glimpse of twenty mes in the panes of a milliner's as we paused before crossing the street, and a sorry sight I looked: clothing torn, hair tangled, and if the state of my bare legs and hands were anything to go by, my face must have been filthy too. We were followed along the short journey by an increasing crowd, eager for diversion. I do not suppose they meant to be unkind or were more than merely curious at first, but their faces held for me the quality of a nightmare. Wherever I looked they were grinning, pointing, peering, and catcalling until I felt I was alone in a country of savages. Once I stumbled and fell and there was an anticipatory 'Ahhh . . . !' from the crowd as if they were waiting for the lions. The beadle jerked me to my feet with a vicious wrench and hissed in my ear: 'Stand up, you little bastard! Time enough to lie down when they've finished with you!'

No wonder that by the time we reached the improvised court in the front parlour of the Lion Inn I felt as though I had already been charged, tried and condemned before a word had been spoken. The surplus furniture had been pushed back; the floor freshly sanded, and a table set facing the door. There were three chairs: two for the gentlemen in black, one for their clerk. The beadle pulled and pushed me into a position facing my inquisitors, and the trial began.

They began with my name, and the clerk had to ask me how to spell it.

'Where are you from?' This from the sharp man.

'I've travelled from Leebeck, Derbyshire, but –'

'Ah! Not of this parish! You see!' he said, to no one in particular. 'That simplifies it.'

'I don't see how –' from the mild gentleman.

'Removal, removal,' said the first irritably. 'But first: the matter of the theft –'

'Alleged theft.'

'Oh, I have no doubt it was certain . . . . Now, where are the boy's accusers?'

There was a shuffling behind me and I became aware that the small room was as full as it was ever likely to be with the curious citizens of Gloucester: so full in fact that the pie-seller had to push hard to gain a space before the table.

'Now then, Seth Pruitt, tell us what happened yesterday afternoon when that young rapscallion stole your pies,' he prompted.

'But I didn't –' I began, and was promptly shut up by the beadle's hand across my mouth.

'Boy's entitled to defend himself,' said the mild man. 'Magna Carta and all that . . . .'

'He shall have his say later,' said the sharp man, dismissing my defence with a wave of the hand.

And so it went on: the pie-man told his story, then the woman above Matthew Brown's shop and the church-warden himself; even the ostler from the inn recounted how he had disturbed me in the act of stealing a horse from the stable, and every time I opened my mouth to deny, explain, question, I was either pinched, punched, or told to keep my mouth shut. The evidence of my guilt lay on the table before me: an unopened parcel, a guinea, and a dusty stale pie. Matthew Brown's daughter had given me the book, but I could not call on her, for I had no idea where she lived. Jack had given me the guinea, but I had no idea where he was either. Two boys had

92

stole the pies, but how persuade two small boys to stand up and confess their guilt? They had probably forgotten about it already. The more I heard the evidence pile up against me, the more hopeless my situation became; if I had been a dispassionate spectator to the proceedings I should have believed in my own guilt without hesitation. I *had* been loitering in the churchyard, I *had* been hanging about outside the bookshop, I *was* discovered in possession of a golden guinea but could not produce the donor . . . .

Outside the cathedral clock struck three, and all at once I remembered Jack's words: he would wait for me till noon on Wednesday. Three hours past: I could imagine him pulling out his pocket watch and frowning, pacing restlessly up and down beside the vans; Tom shaking his head and patting Daisy; Annie perhaps trying to delay as much as she could, out of the kindness of her heart. By now they would be well on the road to – where? I hadn't the faintest idea. For me our travels together had all been one great big adventure and I never bothered to ask about our destinations.

So, when they at last gave me a chance to defend myself, what could I say? That somewhere on the road to God knows where was a man called Jack who could vouch for me? And how did I know that they would take his word for anything – he was a wanderer, they could think him gipsy or charlatan and might investigate to see whether I had a true apprenticeship: I was not even sure that their profession as fair-people was a legitimate one. No, I could not involve them; not that I thought the citizens of Gloucester would be eager to finance an expedition round the countryside to find a tall, dark man who bore a passing resemblance to Richard III, a fat lady, and a magical white pony. Even if they believed me . . . .

So I was silent, and the prickling tears made a screen like bottle glass through which the faces about me floated and swam; one moment I saw the lugubrius pie-man, then the beadle, the ostler, the pinched lady and almost, for an instant, Jack –

'Nothing to say,' noted the sharp man with satisfaction. 'Put that down, clerk. Now, as to sentence. We find the case proven insofar as the boy is obviously a vagrant, with no visible means of support. We also find that he stole some pies, number unspecified, with or without accomplices and in front of witnesses. He was also found in possession of a guinea and a parcel, both probably stolen also. On the first count the punishment is a whipping, and on the second I shall invoke the Poor Law.' Taking an impressive document from the table, he began to read, much as a hungry parson with a small congregation will race through the set prayers. 'County of Gloucester: to wit. Complaint being made by the Church Wardens and Overseers of the Poor of the City of Gloucester . . . .' It went on; the said Zoroaster Mortimer was 'a poor Person and liable to become Chargeable', and he was to be 'removed and Conveyed out of the said City to –'

'*Where* did you say you came from?'

'Leebeck in Derbyshire,' I faltered.

'Expensive,' murmured the mild man. 'Couldn't we just give him a few shillings and evict him . . . ?'

'Hanging 'ud be cheaper,' growled the beadle.

'I was coming to that,' said the sharp man. 'Depends on the value of that parcel, and the ownership of same, and of the guinea. We shall have to make further investigations . . . . In the meantime we can carry out the first part of the sentence, and if he survives he can spend another day or two in jail. Beadle: do your duty!'

There was a murmur of satisfaction from the crowd. At last some action: there had been enough talking for one day, I heard someone say. The beadle seized me by the collar, half-strangling me and almost lifting my feet from the floor, and marched me out into the late afternoon sun. Down the main street I was paraded, the parcel tied about my neck with a piece of string, bumping uncomfortably against my chest. We came to the market place, and there in the middle were the stocks and the whipping post and it was only the sight of these that made me realize at last where circumstances and my folly had led me. Before, a whipping had merely meant the dozen or so cuts my aunt had inflicted now and again, but the wormholed wooden stake with the new crosspiece and the leather straps hanging from the ends filled me with terror. As I came nearer I could see the stains on the old post, marks where the wood had been torn away . . . .

The area around had been strewn with fresh sawdust and a bucket of water stood nearby. I saw a brown hound detach itself from the crowd, wander up to the post and give it a good sniff before relieving itself. A man with a whip chased it away: the whip had a frayed end and the man drew it lovingly through his fingers. His shirtsleeves were rolled up and he had taken off his neckerchief. Oh God! he must be the one to administer the punishment, and already my flesh cringed in anticipation of the blows. Too late I began to struggle, but the beadle held me tightly and the crowd pressed close. There were some sympathetic glances, yes, but the majority were only too happy to know there was to be an entertainment, and laughed and jeered at my discomfiture; the sorry part was that they would have been equally eager to applaud the dwarves, goggle at Annie, or marvel at Daisy, had they been available, and at that inappropriate moment I began to realize the value of showmen like Jack who channelled mob restlessness into safer waters. People like him were necessary to cater for the increasing leisure of the mindless and the sensation seekers: just as there had always been prostitutes, so there had also been ballad singers, freaks, and magicians: they were necessary.

The beadle grabbed me by the shirt whilst the magistrate's clerk read out the list of my crimes. My back was to the whipping post, the crowd in a large semicircle before us, and as the clerk finished and folded his paper, the cathedral clock chimed the three-quarters. At the same time came the faint tinkling of a bell, almost as if the smallest chime had got stuck.

The tinkling persisted, even above the anticipatory

murmurs of the crowd, and suddenly there came an eerie, ululating cry that would have frozen any of my blood not already ice. All heads swung in the direction of the sound and I could see the fringe of the crowd sway this way and that and hear a buzz of questioning; then like a scythe in ripe corn a sudden way was cleared right up to where the beadle and I were standing. Up that path, like a figure in a nightmare, came stooping and swaying a tall grotesque horror clad in a dirty white shift, bandages about the head and hands and even wrapped about the bulbous feet. In this – thing's – hand was a handbell that rang at every step.

'Way, make way for the afflicted! In the name of pity have mercy! Alas, alas, for the unclean! I seek my son, my poor son, afflicted as I am with a dread disease, branded with pain and suffering . . . . In him the illness has not yet eaten away at his face, his limbs, his hands and feet, and in him you still see the graceful lineaments of youth . . . . Help a poor man to find his crutch, his stay: my eyes are all but gone, and it was this same lad that led me by the hand, that nightly bound these running sores and crumbling limbs that must be hid from your eyes lest you faint from the sheer horror and your children fall into nightmare . . . .'

The horrid figure came to a stop in front of me and the one eye visible behind the grimy bandages rolled up into his head like a bloodstained pebble. He swayed and stumbled like a man drunk towards the crowd and they gave way, some crossing themselves, others with their hands or sleeves across their mouths against the contagion, whilst a thin frightened murmur ran back and forth like a trapped thing: 'Leper! Leper . . . .'

The beadle released his hold on me and took an uncertain pace forward.

'Now look here, my – man, you didn't ought –'

The figure darted forward at his words, and one filthy mummified hand grasped at the beadle's sleeve.

'A friend, a friend in my need . . . .'

96

He got no further for the beadle tore from his grasp and backed away, his face white and perspiring, hand brushing at his sleeve as if he would rid it of a swarm of bees, cursing horribly.

'No need to mock the afflicted, the blind, the leprous, who only – But what is this?' This time it was my arm that was gripped in a vice and the creature waved his bell before my face with his other hand. 'The Lord be praised! I have found my ewe lamb, my sheep that was lost . . . . Take the bell, my son, and clear a way through these good people that we may hasten to remove our deadly disease from this fair city . . . .'

Utterly bemused by his mistaking me for someone else, I took the bell and waved it like an automaton and, propelled by jabs from the leper behind, we walked through the shrinking crowd and away from the marketplace. No one tried to stop us and no one followed for the moment and we kept the same shuffling pace: to tell the truth I was too paralysed to move any faster, only too aware that I had escaped a mere beating only to be condemned to a more terrible death in life.

Of a sudden a woman darted from a side street.

'Stop thief! Stop, I say! That's my husband's nightshirt he stole, not ten minutes past!'

'Damn!' said Jack. 'I thought we had got clear – Run like hell, Sprat!'

5

And, after a moment's disbelief, run like hell I did, following Jack's extraordinary figure as he dodged down another side turning, shedding bandages, turban, false toes, and finally the grimy shift itself, leaving him in shirt and breeches. We ran through a cobbled yard, scattering a troop of squawking hens, and up and over the low wall at the end.

Jack hesitated. 'I think I've lost the way . . . .'

Behind us came shouts, running footsteps, the beginnings of a chase.

'Damn, damn, *damn*!' said Jack. 'Right or left?'

I was no help; after that run I was still gasping for breath, but a moment later I thought I recognized a street from my wanderings the day before. I pointed.

'We'll risk it – Come on, boy!' and grabbing my hand he pulled me in the direction I had indicated. We were lucky: round the next corner was Hannibal, tethered to a bench, happily munching daisies from someone's garden, and beyond him was the road out of the city. Jack pulled loose the tether, vaulted into the saddle, pulled me up behind him and, yelling at me to hang on, kicked Hannibal into a gallop down the twisty road. Someone ran out, waving his arms and calling on us to stop, but we swerved round him, the horse's hooves striking sparks from the stones, and in a couple of minutes we had left the houses behind and were on the open road. I glanced back, but what with the bumping up and down on Hannibal's rump, the dust we had kicked up, and the necessity to hold on to Jack's belt with both hands, there was very little I could see.

'Hold on tight!' called Jack. 'I'm taking a short cut.'

This entailed a hazardous jump over a wide ditch and a rash canter over some of the bumpiest and most uneven fields in England. Three or four miles later we stopped by a large pond and I slid gratefully to the ground, to crumple up as my legs gave way beneath me. Jack took a careful look around and leaving Hannibal to wander over to the water and drink his fill, joined me.

'Poof! What a day!' He stretched out on the grass, hands behind his head. 'Hungry? Silly question, really: when aren't you? There's cheese and bread in the saddle-bags. Fetch some, there's a good lad! Oh, one of them has all your belongings in as well: you'd better bring them and get changed. You look slightly less respectable than a scarecrow at the moment – and you've still got that parcel hanging round your neck . . . .'

'Jack, why –'

'Food.'

'But –'

'Food!'

He made me finish half a pound of cheese and a small loaf before I was allowed to speak again.

'Jack –'

'Any soap in your pack?'

Scrabbling among the carefully packed clothes – I thought I detected Annie's hand in the sprig of lavender nestling in my shirts – I found the oilskin pack.

'Yes, it's here, but –'

'It's that damned flour I daubed myself with: sticks like glue. I'm going to wash it off.' Discarding shirt, shoes and stockings he sauntered over to the pond with my soap.

A couple of persistent bluebottles buzzed around me and I looked down at my best clothes, which would be best no more. Sadly I decided they should be dumped as soon as possible, together with the grime that covered me from head to foot. Jack came back from the pond, clean and dripping, and flicked water on my upturned face.

'What are you waiting for? God, you smell like a sewer! Where did they keep you: down a drain?'

'But Jack –'

'I'll throw you in that water myself . . . .'

Grabbing soap, clean smock and second-best breeches I fled from the threat.

'And don't come back till you're absolutely clean; Hannibal doesn't like grubby passengers.'

I undressed hurriedly behind a bush, burying my filthy discards under a large stone. Glancing back, I saw that Jack was busy unwrapping the parcel I had carried round my neck, so I slid into the water and soaped till there was only a small sliver left. Something live wriggled away from between my toes and a disgusted newt paddled away from the contamination, long tail undulating him like a snake through the water. Hurriedly I pulled the clean clothes on over my wet skin and returned, clean but damp, back to Jack.

He was reading. 'You'll enjoy this – you've got pondweed in your hair, by the way – at least I think you should. I read part of it when I was your age.' He held up the book so that I could see the title: *Tom Jones*, by Henry Fielding.

'What's it about?'

'Oh, a young gallows-cheater like yourself . . . what *did* you do to get yourself in that pickle?'

I told him what had happened. 'I thought I saw you once: in the court?'

He nodded. 'I wanted to keep in the background till I knew what they had in mind for you.'

'But why didn't you say something then – about the guinea, anyway?'

'I couldn't be sure how much you had said – or done. For all I knew you were guilty as hell of everything else they accused you of: especially as you didn't mention us, or try to defend yourself.'

'I – I didn't know whether you wanted me to involve you; I didn't know whether I was ever legally working for you, and I didn't think they would believe me anyway. And I didn't do any of the things they said, except sleep in the loft . . . .'

'Excuses, excuses . . . .'

'No, they *aren't*!'

'No one but you could have got in such a mess . . . .'

'You're laughing! It wasn't funny –'

'Oh yes, it was! Don't be so parsonical: you'll laugh too, boy, when you recall it a week or two hence! I wish you could have seen your face when the leper claimed you as his own – it was worth all that running round for the costume . . . .' And in his turn he explained how he had slipped away from the trial, once he had seen how it was going, seeking inspiration, and had found it through an open window of a house near the court; had climbed in, stolen the discarded nightshirt and a sheet and 'borrowed' a handbell from a shop counter, together with some flour. Remembering the ghastly figure he had made I could not but marvel at his speed and ingenuity but I still thought it would have been easier if he had spoken up for me at the trial, and said so.

'Easier, yes; costlier too, in time and bribes – but not half so much fun!' He rose to his feet. 'Up and away, Sprat: the sun's near setting and we've a mile or three to go before we catch up with the others, even cross-country.'

He retrieved Hannibal, restrapped the saddlebags and pulled me up behind him. We jogged off into the sunset, but there was one more question I had to ask.

'Why did you come looking for me in the first place?'

'You were past time for returning, Daisy pined and Annie nagged: she saw your demise in cracked mirrors, crossed knives, and tea leaves all day and I became heartily sick of reminders of my duty as your employer. So I came just to get away from it all. It was a nice day for the ride and Hannibal needed the exercise, so I told them that although you were probably happy and settled and had forgotten us all, I would drop off your gear. That's all: satisfied?'

Hannibal pecked at a rabbit hole and I clasped at Jack to stay on. After that it seemed simpler to slip my arms round his waist and lay my cheek against his back.

'Yes,' I said. 'Thank you for coming.' We rode on in silence for a while and a waxing moon rose in the deepening sky.

'Jack . . . .'

'Bless the boy! I thought you had nodded off.'

'Not quite. Hannibal's not exactly soporific. Jack . . . .'

'You've said that once.'

I hesitated. 'You could have just dumped my stuff and gone back and told them I was all right . . . .'

'Stop snivelling.'

'But –'

101

'What do you want me to say?' He sounded half amused, half exasperated. 'I don't have to explain every action I take . . . . All right, then. It wasn't because you are indispensable, because you're not. Oh, you're not bad at your job, but there are others could do it as well. So, it wasn't that. And it wasn't that I fancied you, pretty boy though you are . . . .' He chuckled in the gloom. 'Though if we had been shipmates it might have been different. Still, I've never been faced by that problem, so I don't know. So it wasn't that either . . . . Then, what was it? There must have been something . . . .'

I could feel him laughing under my cheek. 'You need someone to play Fool to your Lear,' I suggested helpfully.

'Mmm . . . could be, though I am beginning to wonder just who is the fool . . . . No, it wasn't that either. I could always manage a soliloquy.' Suddenly he came up with a solution. 'I have it! During those three days you were away I missed having you around and I only realized it when I was shouting into thin air and swinging into empty space. I needed someone to boot around, that was it! You know how you talk to a pup when you're lonely, pat it if you're happy, shout at it if it piddles over your boots, heave a brick at it if you're really angry; don't notice it most of the time but miss it if it strays – Sprat! Are you snivelling again?'

'N–no, Jack. Honest.'

'Snivellers,' said Jack firmly, 'walk. All the way. So you'd better not.'

I wiped the grateful tears surreptitiously with my sleeve, and decided that Jack was the kindest, most wonderful man in the world.

Nearly always, anyway.

We continued our journey south by way of Stroud, Cirencester and Stratton St Mary, and so on into Wiltshire. The wild countryside with its rolling hills and wide valleys, its fields where the corn poppy, Demeter's bane, straggled

102

impudently into the grain, its grey, dusty roads and strange monuments, all made a deep impression on me. It seemed as though every corner turned might reveal a secret, but it never quite did; the very ground had a strange tingling effect on us all. Annie laughed louder, then stopped abruptly and glanced over her shoulder as if someone were watching; I felt more reckless and alive than I could remember and Jack's leaps and bounds became more histrionic and his rendering of King Lear had me feared for his wits at times. Even Daisy was more temperamental and Tom had to exercise all his patience when rehearsing her. She would suddenly throw up her head and neigh for no reason at all, then stand as though listening for an answer we could not hear.

'She'm hearing the silver bugles,' said Tom one day. 'Fairy bugles calling her to leave the trappings of man and join her wild brethren running free along the bones of the hill . . . .'

I remember we came one day upon a ring of huge stones, some standing, some lying among the long grass as though asleep, and we all felt uneasy. We were on our way to Marlborough and Jack decided at first that a meadow near the ring would be a good place to stop for the night, but after one then the other of us had walked round the outside of the deep ditch that surrounded it, then climbed to the middle of the circle and stood looking down an avenue of smaller stones that marched away over a hump of down, we all voted to go on a few miles. Not that the place, Avebury it was called, seemed evil; rather it felt as though we might disturb something stronger and older than all the books to be read, something that it were better to let lie. Indeed, my body felt intolerably heavy, yet tingled all over like my hair when I brushed it too hard and it crackled, standing up and yet clinging like butterfly's feet. In the centre of that circle I felt disorientated; if any had called I should have run in the wrong direction. Outside, looking in like a spectator waiting for a pageant, was not so bad, but I noticed even the sheep preferred the perimeter. Something there both drew and repelled me, and I think I was glad to leave. Not sure, because something uneasy in me wanted to find out more, but at the same time I knew that that same knowledge could change me. Tom said it was 'best left alone'; Annie tried singing a hymn tune and lost the melody, but Jack looked thoughtful, then echoed what I had felt, putting it much better.

'There are some places that hold memories longer than most, as though the essence of experience had somehow impregnated the very stones; this place was used for pagan rites at one time, I believe,' and he shivered involuntarily, then laughed. 'I could make a fortune if I could bottle and label an atmosphere like this: release it at a tea party and all the old tabbies would have the vapours!'

That was the night we lost the dwarves.

For weeks now they had become more and more surly and argumentative and no longer seemed to take heed of even Jack, who before had been more or less able to exact obedience. At nights we could hear them quarrelling angrily amongst themselves, but no one liked to interfere; their performances were becoming more ragged, and they no longer practised as they used to do. I had noticed that there seemed to be a change in their act and, while I could never be sure of counting them correctly during the show, I was sure they were one performer short; I supposed one of them was ill, but as no one else said anything I kept my thoughts to myself.

That night we pulled off the road into a clearing near a wood. The weather had changed and it felt more like January than late July; the sun went down early behind a bank of grey, menacing cloud and the wind rose, forcing Annie to take down her hopeful washing and blowing dust from the road onto our plates, making the meat taste gritty. Inside the vans the doors blew shut when we opened them, candles would not stay alight, and in the end we were all abed before nine. I glanced out before I fastened up for the night and the horses were standing in a huddle, heads down, tails to the wind, looking miserable. We had to close even the top of the half-doors and this, with the wind buffeting the vans every now and again like a giant's child kicking its toys, was probably why we heard nothing untoward.

I slept badly, and before dawn was up for a drink and to relieve myself. Once up I decided to fill the buckets with water and get them heated for washing and shaving, so I picked one up and headed for the pond in the wood. The wind had abated somewhat during the night, but here in the half-light of the trees it was still strong enough to rustle the branches menacingly overhead and scurry last year's leaves around my feet. I found the pool and dipped my bucket, but it caught on some obstruction: I tugged, but it stuck fast. Rolling up my sleeve I plunged my arm in down to the shoulder, feeling round for the snag. Suddenly my fingers encountered something soft, something familiar, yet terrible in its misplacement: I screamed, and leaped back. What my questing fingers had found was a face, a face under the water!

Then there was the comforting figure of Tom Fallon beside me, and I hurled myself against him and hung on, babbling out my terror.

'Easy now, my dear, easy!' he soothed. 'Take a deep breath, calm down and don't be afeared. Tom's here, and we'll have a look together.'

Taking my damp hand in his comforting clasp, he drew me back to the pool. It was getting lighter now, and we both stared down at the water; there, obscenely roped together in an embrace of death, were a naked male and female dwarf, floating free from whatever obstruction had held them down. They were bound inward to each other, and not only that, the man's head was between the woman's legs, and vice versa. Together they formed a lewd double-backed creature that bobbed on the dark water like some gross, pale spider.

Tom whistled softly. 'Never thought it would come to that, not after last time . . . . They've gone, rest of 'em.'

'Gone?' I echoed stupidly.

'Aye; van, horse, baggage: the lot. Sneaked off about two o'clock this morning, I reckon. Daisy heard 'em, but I thought she was whickering at them fairies again and took no notice. Still, reckon it's best they've gone this way, means we needn't get involved. They'll be away to the coast, Bristol most likely, sell up and cross to the Continent.'

'But why – this?'

He shrugged. 'Who can tell for sure? There were two families there, the Tartinis and the Schwartzes, and there was always friction; the Italians wanted the Germans' woman, and I reckoned they got her in the end. Remember that night Jack was away and that loony young fellow got to wandering about?' I nodded. 'Well, that morning I found one of the Germans with a knife in his back under a pile of leaves beyond the village. Did you never notice how the act had changed? Their top pyramid man, Franz, he was missing . . . .'

I shook my head. 'Sometimes I thought – but I could never be sure. Did Jack realize?'

'There was no need to worry him. He had enough to think of, what with one thing and another, that next night; afterwards, as usual, he'd leave the manikins to work out their own routines, reckoning they knew their own business best. I buried that last body where it wouldn't be found, and that's what we've got to do again. Run back and get that spade near my van, and if you sees Jack tell him I want it 'cos I got the gripes. He'll know by now they've gone if he's awake, so get him to ride off towards Marlborough a mile or so – say I thought I heard them go that way; and keep Annie out of the way. No point in more people knowing than necessary; it'll be our secret, yours and mine.'

'But why shouldn't we tell them?'

'Because that's part of growing up and making decisions,

and they ain't always pleasant things. It relieves one to share the burden, 'cos then you make someone else take on your troubles, but there are times when it just ain't kind or practical. Can you imagine what Annie would do – and say – if she knew that there'd been a murder on her doorstep? She'd just have to tell someone else and that someone might be in touch with the authorities and afore you knew it we'd all be in jail on suspicion. And why tell Jack? He's got enough to do planning how to keep the rest of us together and earning . . . . So, they must be buried deep, and quick, and not only in the earth but in our minds also, so that they may rest in peace.'

When I returned with the spade I was able to tell him there was no one else stirring.

'Good. Mebbe we can finish this quick.'

During my absence he had dragged them from the water and cut the ropes that bound them, and I could see where the cord had bitten deep to the bone.

'Tom . . . .' I hesitated. 'Why – why did they tie them up in that fashion?'

'Adultery; their way of pointing to the crime. Poor creatures were garroted first then fastened in the sinners' tie of death, facing not the heavens but the evil they had preferred on earth . . . . Hard, but that's their way: Romany justice.

'Come, we'll find some soft earth.'

We buried them side by side and though I was thoroughly warm by the time we finished, I shivered as I gazed down at the trampled earth.

Tom covered all traces with moss and leaves, using a branch to brush the earth smooth and work out our tracks, then he stood for a moment looking at the concealed grave.

'May you find the good Lord merciful, and so rest in peace.' He turned to me. 'Go pick up your bucket, young 'un, and fill it at the pool.' He must have seen my distaste, for he put an arm comfortingly round my shoulders. 'First lot'll do for the horses; after that it'll clear pretty quick.

You've drunk worse than that in your time, I'll be bound, without knowing it!'

We never heard from, or of, them again, though for some time afterwards I had nightmares in which they figured, dead and alive. Tom and I kept our secret; Annie was frankly glad to be rid of them, and so was I, though it meant extra work fetching and carrying, cleaning and currying. Jack was furious: they had taken the best van horse and the platform which had also been used for my act with Daisy and for Jack's playlets, and he had shrunk from an impresario with four acts to a mere showman with three, which didn't suit his ego.

Luckily for all of us Jack managed to pick up an extra act in Marlborough, a remarkably silent turbanned gentleman from the East who did the most amazing juggling and conjuring tricks. Unlike many 'foreign' performers, he was genuine, and we could only converse in sign language. He didn't wash at all, merely kept adding another layer of ointment to his already oily body, and carried all his belongings in a pack on his back, no horse, no van, sleeping in the open rain or shine and cooking his own food, which seemed to consist mainly of vegetables and sweet things; he said his prayers several times a day, kneeling on a pretty patterned mat. He bowed and smiled to us all in turn every morning, touching his heart, his lips and his forehead, and muttered something that sounded like 'Sa-am Alley-Come'. Annie decided that was his name, so from then on he was Sam. He was greatly taken with her, and would roll his eyes and describe her curves with his hands, grinning all the while like a great slice of cheese; he took to leaving little messes of sticky sweets on her van steps, wrapped in pink or blue paper, and these she would invariably pass on to me till I was surfeited, when Daisy profited.

We stayed in Marlborough over the week, for we needed another platform to replace the one the dwarves had taken with them, this time made to Jack's own specifications; larger, with removable poles at the corners that could be strung with ropes to hold curtains or backdrop.

During this time, too, Jack renewed acquaintance with an old friend.

She was pretty, plump and blonde, and her husband was in jail for the umpteenth time on some petty charge. They had a herb farm about two miles out of town but kept a stall in the marketplace, selling sachets of sweet lavender, bunches of herbs, and powdered concoctions for gripe, gout, constipation, and the ague. The first night Jack was missing I flew to Annie in a panic.

'He'll be with that Chlöe. Don't worry, my dear: she's a good enough lass in her way, and he did the same thing last year when we was here. Her husband was away that time, and he spent most of his nights with her, seemingly. She's no sleep-around, apart from Jack, and they'll do each other good. He'll come back looking like a cat that's been in the dairy, and not a cross word for a week: you'll see. He's safe enough in that orchard: there's apples and to spare . . . .'

True enough, Jack looked sleek and contented when he returned, and Chlöe came to see us off when we were ready to move on, bringing a basket of herbs for Annie and some coltsfoot rock for me. The two women had a good gossip together, no doubt discussing Jack, but I was excluded, being a lad, so I sat in the sunshine and chewed the candy, wondering on the strange lusts that could make a wife bed a stranger one night and her husband the next, apparently without preference or reproach. And it seemed men were even less choosy: I remembered something Annie had had to say on the subject when Jack had been missing once before. 'Their minds tell 'em one thing and their jacks another and when they've had a couple of drinks the two starts argufying, so to quiet them there's another drink and the jack wins and he becomes so cocky he's got to find somewheres to bury his head and get rid of it all and all burrows look alike to a rabbit in the dark . . . .'

Candy and all taken into consideration, I decided I liked Chlöe, if only for making Jack happy, for he was all smiles as we got under way, playing away merrily on his pipe, more or less tunefully too. We swung away south to skirt the great forest of Savernake; the trees were very old, some dead and collapsed and grey with lichen but most tall and thick and fat with the still leaves of summer. Jack wanted us to press on as fast as possible, for he had suddenly realized there were only about six weeks till the great September Fair of St Bartholomew, in London town itself, but everything conspired to delay us. First the wagon with the beautiful new platform strapped to it lost a wheel in the rutted road, and we wasted a whole morning while Tom went back the way we had come to find a wheelwright. Then we found that in the upheaval three of the curtain poles for the stage had snapped and one of the planks had split.

I learned very quickly that day the difference between young sappy wood, old brittle wood, and the seasoned timber Jack wanted, and was amazed at the ease with which little white blisters on one's hand ran together into one painful mass after an hour or so chopping down unsuitable replacement poles. Finally I got it right and Jack chose two of his and one of mine. Then they had to be shaped and smoothed, and in the end Annie was the only satisfied one, for as she said when she greased and bound my sore hands: 'Now you two have finished playing woodcutters, I reckon we've enough kindling to last a month of Sundays,' and, looking at the stack waiting for me to bundle, tie, and stow at my convenience in the wagon, I was inclined to agree.

Tom was back early the next morning with new wheel, pin, and the wheelwright, and we were ready to harness up by midday. It was then that the third of our troubles manifested itself. It had been my job the previous day to hobble the horses so they didn't stray too far, but apparently my mind must have been on other things for when we came to round them up, two were missing. We were on the fringes of the forest, but there were clumps of trees all around and heavy undergrowth, and no sign of the truants. I was roundly cursed by Jack and sent off to find both, on pain of a beating, so disappeared into the nearest part of the forest, as eager to get away from his anger as anything else.

It was a hot, sticky day, more so under the deceptive shade of the trees for there was no breath of wind here, only the stinging whine of insects and the drowsy moan of wood pigeons. I became hotter and tireder the further I penetrated into the wood and it was only when I stopped to rest for a moment after forcing my way through some particularly dense thicket, to be baulked further by a huge fallen trunk, that common sense reasserted itself. No horse would walk into a mess like this, they would wander in the open; I had been searching in entirely the wrong direction. Using some of Jack's choicest oaths, happy only in the knowledge that he could not hear me, I set off back to our encampment.

An hour later I had to admit I was lost. I had headed back the way I had come, or so I thought, and found, as I expected, that the trees gradually thinned out, followed a well-defined path, but ended up at a deserted charcoal-burner's hut. I backtracked along the path to find it led to a clearing, where there had been tree-felling earlier in the year. Dispiritedly I sat down on a stump and tried to get my bearings. The camp was on the western edge of the forest, so if I just went the way of the setting sun . . . .
It took another hour to find our camp, guided in the end by the iron pots Annie banged at regular intervals with her ladle. Of course the horses had been found, some quarter-hour after I had left, grazing peacefully behind a thick clump of hazel not far from the camp, so when I reappeared I got a couple of cuffs from Jack and no supper; that was until his back was turned, for of course Annie

had kept me some cold meat and bread, which she slipped to me surreptitiously as we went on into the dusk.

Jack had decided that as we had lost nearly two days, one way and another, we should travel on for at least a couple of hours so that we would be well on our way towards the plain of Salisbury by morning. The night was cool after the heat of the day, and while the moon lasted we made good progress, for the way was clearly marked and the trees lessened as we started a slow swing away from the forest. But after a while a mist started to curl around our ankles, for the ground was flat and marshy to our right, and inevitably we slowed down, the horses keeping to the track more by instinct than sight. Jack ordered me to the head of the lead van with a lantern and we made better going. After a while, though, he grew impatient and, tossing me the reins, bade me lead the procession, so I took our horse's bridle and plodded on, to be passed by Jack on Hannibal a moment later.

'There's an inn at the crossroads a mile or so further on: I'll wait for you there,' and he trotted away into the mist and was hidden. For a while I could hear the soft thud of Hannibal's hooves, then they, too, faded into the night.

'Where's he going?' called Annie from the van behind.

'For a jar or two of ale,' I answered gloomily. 'And at the rate we're going he'll have drunk the place dry before we get there.'

I heard a chuckle from Tom, then silence as we all concentrated on reaching our destination in one piece. The moon had gone behind hazy cloud and the mist was around my shoulders, ribbons of smoke that drifted out from the trees that swung forward to our path again as we approached the final spur of the forest. Every now and again the mist parted like water before me so I could gaze a hundred yards ahead, then closed in again capriciously and I could see scarce further than my next step, lantern or no lantern. Once again the mist cleared momentarily and I saw a horseman, a darker shape against the backdrop

112

of the forest. For a moment I thought I must be mistaken –
a tree stump perhaps – then that it might be Jack, come
back for us, but as the vapour closed round us again I
realized with a dreadful sinking of the heart that Jack was
not wearing a three-cornered hat when he left us, nor
was he riding a black horse with a white blaze to its
forehead . . . . A trickle of fear ran down my spine and I
found I was praying aloud that I might have been
mistaken.

But I wasn't. A masked figure rode out from under the
trees, into the suddenly clear night, and I was already
pulling back on the bridle of my horse as the pistols swung
in my direction and the dread words rang out: 'Stand and
deliver! Your money or your life!'

6

For a moment everything – we, the highwayman, time
itself – seemed to stand still; then like a violent belch a lot
happened at once. Simultaneously there was a clatter as
the horseman dropped one of his pistols, a scream from
Annie, a frightened neigh from one of the horses, and
a swift and silent wraith that passed along the blind side
of the van and disappeared. I heard Annie sobbing and
Tom soothing her and a muffled curse from the highwayman as, one-handed, he tried to keep his steed's head
straight. The other hand was still clutching a pistol that
wavered and ducked as his horse danced erratically on its
toes.

'Be still, blast your eyes! Demme, I should never have
chose a filly . . . . Now, boy, you with the lantern, did you
hear what I said? Come here and – Ah!'

One moment he was armed, mounted and dangerous;
the next his horse was trotting off down the road, stirrup
irons flapping, and he himself lay flat on his back, helpless,

as turbanned Sam slowly garrotted him. I ran over with the lantern, seeing by its wildly flickering light that Sam was fully in control, crooning softly and happily to himself as he tightened the noose.

'Let him go, Sam,' I said, as I set down the lantern and picked up the discarded pistols. 'I've got him covered!'

'You haven't with them,' said Tom, coming up behind and taking the pistols from me, which was a great relief. 'One of the blessed things ain't even primed. Strange high-toby man that first drops one and then forgets to prime the other . . . . Let's take a look at him.'

We were none too soon: the victim was still, no longer protesting or threshing about. Sam had either not heard or, more probably, not understood what I had said and now the masked man hung limp from his hands, eyes rolled up and almost starting from his head, mouth frothy and purplish. That was what they said a hanged man looked like if he didn't choke quickly – I put my hands over Sam's and spoke slowly.

'Let go, Sam. Good fellow, good Sam, that's enough . . . .' Gently I prised back his little fingers till he loosened his hold on the piece of silken cloth that bit into his victim's throat and sat back on his heels, smiling.

I smiled back reassuringly. 'Well done, Sam, well done, but that's enough.'

'Should've let him finish it off,' said Annie behind us. 'Nasty piece of work – choking's too good for the likes of him, I'd say. If it hadn't been for our Sam here we'd have been murdered in our beds, most like! I'm all of a dither! Lost pounds, I shouldn't wonder . . . . Be only a shadow of myself in the morning, not fit to put on a show . . . .'

Sam got to his feet and bowed low in her direction, his hand to his mouth, his heart and his head, and gestured grandly at the inert figure on the ground; then he stopped, placed his hands under the man's armpits and hauled him with a swift scooping movement to his feet, propelling him towards Annie like a present.

'Lord ha' mercy! I don't want him! Put him down, for Christ's sake!' and she backed away precipitately.

Upon which Sam dropped him like a discarded toy and spread his hands wide in apology, while I stooped down and examined our prisoner more closely by the light of the lantern. Though his clothes had suffered from the rough handling he had received, he was obviously a man of lace and frills and velvet, for his jacket and breeches were of good cut, his stockings, though darned, of silk, and his cravat, sadly disarranged, of the finest. The elaborate wig that now lay in the road had covered a close-cropped sandy skull and the features were those of a young-old man with a hooked nose and small, red mouth. On his right cheek was a black velvet patch shaped like a star and another was unpeeling from his chin.

'Looks like a real Macaroni to me,' said Tom. 'Jew-boy too, if I'm not mistaken.'

I nodded. 'Could be. But why so incompetent?'

Tom handed me one of the pistols. 'Search me. But these looks more like toys than the real thing: those silver butts must've cost a pretty penny, but they're far too light to manage properly.'

They were prettily engraved with fine scrollwork and the finials ended in exquisitely moulded gargoyle heads, grinning like imps in the lantern light.

'Mmm. Pretty expensive – he's coming round, Tom! What shall we do?'

The colour was coming back into the face beneath us, and our highwayman shuddered and groaned.

'Hit him on the head and be rid,' from Annie.

'We'll tie him up tight afore he comes round proper,' said Tom sensibly. 'Then we'll load him up on the wagon and take him to Jack: he'll know what to do.'

It was a strange procession that finally halted on the square of grass before the inn. First came I with our van, then Sam driving a still-shaking Annie; Tom was at the reins of the wagon, our captive bound and gagged atop, groaning under a tarpaulin. His horse was fastened behind and last of all came the unchaperoned Daisy with Tom's cart. Leaving the others, I lifted the latch and pushed open the inn door. There were no windows, the floor was beaten earth, and the smoke made my eyes smart – indeed, it was a poor place altogether. Jack had his back to me, sitting at one end of the long table, chatting to the slovenly barmaid, stool tipped back and tankard in hand. A trio of farm labourers sitting nearer to me playing dominoes glanced up incuriously as I hesitated on the threshold, then went back to their game. The girl glanced up.

'Ale, young master?'

'Well, Sprat!' said Jack. 'I began to think you had got lost. Another for me – er, Doll, and one for my friend!' I noticed his good humour had returned.

'No thanks, not just now. Jack, can you come outside a moment? I – we've got something to show you.'

'Nothing as interesting as Doll's cleavage, I'll be bound,' and he traced the cleft between her breasts with an idle finger, and to but token protest.

'Jack –'

'Come, lad: say "good evening" to the wench. Prettiest lass this side of Marlborough, eh?'

I glanced at the simpering, greasy barmaid, wondering just how many quarts he had downed.

'Pleased to make your acquaintance, miss,' I said formally. 'Now, Jack –'

'All right, all right, Zo-Zo-Zoroaster! I'm coming.' He downed his ale and tossed the girl a coin. 'I'll be back, sweetheart.'

Outside, he gripped my left ear firmly. 'One thing you'll have to learn: never hurry a man when he's doing some serious drinking – only gives him wind,' and he belched. 'God, that stuff's only half-fermented . . . . Another thing. However fright-awful a female looks, doesn't do any harm to let 'em think you find 'em fetching – 'specially if it's out the window and down the ivy before you've a chance

116

to see what daylight brings! Spread a little flattery when you can, Sprat: like butter, it makes something plain taste better.' He released my ear and swayed a little. 'Now, then; what was it you wanted to show me? Better be good . . . .'

'We've caught a highwayman.'

'Caught a *what*?'

'A highwayman.'

'Rubbish! You lot couldn't catch a three-legged stool.' He glanced beyond me to the vans drawn up on the green. 'You aren't serious, are you?'

'Come and see.'

In a little procession we escorted Jack to the baggage wagon where, with a flourish worthy of a magician, Tom whipped off the tarpaulin, leaving our unbidden guest feebly struggling and moaning. Jack took the lantern from Tom and held it closer, then suddenly he leant forward and pulled off the mask and removed the gag we had thought prudent to insert lest the robber call out for his accomplices. Then he did an even stranger thing: he laughed.

He laughed all the while he was untying our knots, laughed as he dusted him down, laughed as he shook out the wig and clapped it and the hat firmly back on his head. 'Well, Barnaby,' he said. 'I told you you would never make a successful criminal!'

We glanced at each other in consternation and it was Annie who put our question. 'You knows him, then?'

'*Know* him! Of course I do; don't I, you scabby, disgusting felon?'

No answer save a spluttering cough.

'If your mouth's like a bale of wool it's your own fault. What were you doing, anyway, giving my people such a fright?'

'Just thank whatever gods' (he pronounced it 'gads' – indeed he spoke all through in a most affected way: 'town' was 'tarn') 'whatever gods there are that I do not sue you

117

and your malodorous followers for assault and battery . . . .'

'Come, come!' said Jack. 'From what I heard –'

'Lies, demmed lies! There was I, waiting in a friendly manner by the side of the road, willing to guide them to –'

That did it. We all started talking at once and Tom produced the pistols.

'. . . and if it hadn't been for Sam Alley-Come here we'd all've been meat for crows by morning,' finished Annie, who had had most to say.

'And as for that heathen,' protested Barnaby, 'he's no more than a savage! If it hadn't been for your young lad here – pretty-looking youngster, too – that brown devil would have finished me off and then you would have had a corpse to explain –'

'A body armed to the teeth and masked to frighten children –'

'All right, Annie,' Jack said soothingly. 'There were no children, except perhaps for Sprat here – shut up, boy! – and according to Tom the pistols weren't even primed. If, and I say *if*, Barnaby merely intended a practical joke, then it went sadly awry; but if he did intend robbery, then the tables were turned. In either case he was the loser, and –' he turned to our ex-captive '– I'm inclined to think he deserved it.'

'Now, Jack, demme, my dear boy –'

'I'm not anyone's dear boy and neither is Sprat here: don't forget it! All right, everyone; back to the inn. Barnaby is going to buy us all a drink!'

And with some grumbling, that is what he did. It transpired that Jack had met him twice before; the first time was when he had tried to pick Jack's pocket at Shoreditch, the second when he had taken refuge under the van after selling false 'cures' at Nottingham last year. I asked Jack afterwards why he continually forgave him and got a very unsatisfactory answer.

'I don't think you would understand: I'm not sure I do myself. Sometimes I think it is because he can never be truly happy; at other times just because he is so incompetent . . . . Then again, he went to a very distinguished school . . . .'

He wouldn't explain further, and so I was left to make up my own mind about him during the couple of days he travelled with us. At first I felt nothing but contempt, especially when I realized he was what Annie referred to as a 'Jesuit'. I had never met before a man who preferred to love and be loved by his own sex, and couldn't understand why Jack, so much the other way himself, tolerated his attitude, but, against my inclinations, I began to quite like the man. And he posed no danger to me, as he explained one morning before he went on his way, in the candid manner that did much to overcome my initial dislike. I found him fixing another patch to his chin, crescent-shaped this time, having borrowed Jack's make-up glass. His lips were already rouged, and so were his cheeks. I made to turn away but he stayed me with a conciliatory gesture.

'No, boy, don't run away. I shall not harm you, that I swear, and I do not wish to see that contempt in your eyes for ever. Come, talk with me for a while, and perhaps I can explain to you a little . . . .'

I hesitated, remembered Jack's forbearance, and sat down cross-legged on the turf nearby.

'You are wondering,' he said, twisting his mouth this way and that to get the best effect of the patch in his reflection, and thus making his words sound more affected than ever, 'what brings me to this pitch.'

'No, indeed,' I said, untruthfully.

'You are polite as well as pretty, boy. Tell me, have you ever thought – but no, Jack would be displeased.'

'Thought what?'

'Well, you must know you are a more than ordinarily attractive boy . . . .' I flushed and hung my head. 'Nay, I but speak the truth. You have an almost girlish prettiness, and though I am not inclined that way myself there are men, wealthy, titled men, who would pay extremely well for your . . . attentions. Do you understand what I'm talking about?'

I nodded. 'I think so.'

He leaned over and pulled up my chin so I had to look at him. 'Those strange eyes, demme, would be a sensation in London, and with a good barber to tame those curls and a little –'

'I'm not interested,' I said, as gruffly and masculinely as I could, jerking my head away. 'That's a sin I won't commit, not even if I were starving.'

His young-old face looked sad. 'Don't judge from innocence: that's not fair. Wait till you are caught by temptation, whatever it may be, then if you have honestly striven to resist and have conquered – then say, with the saints: "There, but for the grace of God, go I!" Don't think I have not tried. I, too, remember being an innocent child.' He sighed, and set to combing his wig into neat curls. 'But that was long ago. Suffice it to say that some men should have been born women, for though they have all the outward appearance of their own sex, their thoughts, desires and feelings are entirely female. The same is true, so I am told, of some women: this I do not know for a fact, for I have had little to do with the opposite sex, in spite of my proclivities. This is strange, I suppose, for I feel more akin to them every day; I long to dress in long silken dresses, to have the subordinate role to a demanding, forceful male, to wear perfume and lace . . . . You may not know that some men want nothing more than to live together as man and wife, and that that kind of relationship can be every bit as strong as the so-called "normal" ones. Don't pull a face: wait till you have seen a little more of the world . . . . So you see, I pose you no threat: Jack has more to fear from me than you have – but he has been my friend more than once, and we understand each other.'

Later that day I borrowed the glass and scowled furiously at my image – 'attractive boy . . . an almost girlish prettiness . . . .' I put out my tongue at my reflection.

120

'You'll stick like that if the wind changes,' said Jack.

The weather was capricious for the next week or so as we went a little way into Dorset before turning eastward towards London. Some days we sweltered, on others shivered. The custom, too, varied: money was very short in the country areas, less so in the towns. I cannot remember all the places we went through except for Pewsey, Winterbourne Stoke, and Zeals, for there we were hungry, and one remembers hunger. I remember the stones on the plain, too, but for different reasons.

Our road passed nearby, and I slipped down from the van to take a closer look.

'Mind they old grey things, do!' called out Annie. 'Reckon they don't mean anything good, standing there like a mouthful o' rotten teeth . . . .'

This is exactly what they had resembled from the distance of our first view but when I got nearer their sheer size astounded me. Just like the smaller stones at Avebury these lay higgledy-piggledy, in a rough circle, but these were fashioned stones, great oblongs such as a giant's child might play with. Here was an arch, there another; a heap of stones, a single stone leaning drunkenly. As I approached a warm wind blew a scurry of thistledown across the sheep-bit grass and swallows screamed as they swooped scabious-high to arrow through the arches. It was all tremendous, awe-inspiring and rather eerie. I circled the stones, for nothing would make me tread the centre, and at the other side I came upon an artist on a folding stool, his watercolour box at his side, painting a group of four stones forming two arches. I stood and watched for a moment or two, admiring the deft brush strokes that captured form in quick lines and shade, until he looked up with a sigh.

'The light's going . . . . Interested in painting, lad?' He was wearing a brown frock coat and had a kindly face.

'No,' I said honestly. 'At least – I like other people's

pictures. I can't even draw a straight line, myself. I like *your* painting.'

He laughed. 'Just a sketch, just a sketch. Well, if you didn't come with a painter's eye, it must have been to marvel at the trilithon.'

'Tri – what?'

He nodded at the double arch. 'Trilithon. Once, or so it is believed, these stones formed one great circle of arches and here were held some of the most secret rituals of the Druids. Heard of them?'

I nodded. 'They believed in the survival of the spirit, insofar as it went into another person at their death; they also made human sacrifices.'

'Clever lad. One day, I hope, they'll put the stones up again and we'll see what it really looked like. My guess is that this was a temple of sorts with another outer ring of stones, and perhaps where you are standing now they had wooden dwellings and shops – rather like a monastery with its dormitories and refectory outside the church proper. However, we'll probably never know for sure . . . . . Do me a favour?'

'Surely,' I said, wondering if he wanted fresh water for his brushes.

He tossed me a shilling. 'How tall are you?'

I shrugged. 'About five feet and an inch, I suppose.'

'Go stand against the middle stone of the arch while I do a quick sketch. Knowing your height will give me an idea of the true proportions later.'

Obediently I stood for about ten minutes. At first I was warm, then as the sun shifted and I stood in the shade of the big stones I started to shiver, feeling the cold pressing into my back and the long fingers of shadow reaching out in front. All at once I wondered what would happen if the stone leaned just a little, then a little more, and finally fell and crushed me – I found I was sweating, my hands pressed back against the stone as though I were Atlas holding up the world.

122

'All right, now,' called the artist. 'That'll do nicely – why, lad, you're as white as a sheet!'

'I felt the stones – pressing down.'

'If you felt that, then maybe you will never draw like Leonardo, but I'll swear there's a touch of the artist about you somewhere – that or you have the sight.'

At that moment there was a piercing whistle.

'I must go – my friends won't wait.' Already the vans were disappearing down into the valley.

He followed the direction of my gaze. 'I didn't know you were one of the travellers . . . here's another shilling. They are good people, the ones you are with?' ·

'They have been very kind to me . . . .'

'But you are not really one of them?'

I shook my head. 'But I'm trying hard!'

It was as we were going through Blackmore Vale on our way to Sherborne that Jack made his big mistake: he bought a horse. Not such a crime, you might say, for an extra horse always comes in useful; the crime was in buying it without asking Tom's advice beforehand. Jack had been on ahead to spy out the next day's pitch and came back with the prettiest little roan you ever did see, but even to my untrained eye that pony had never been near shafts.

Tom stood with his hands on his hips as Jack approached. 'Stolen,' he said grimly.

'Never!' said Jack airily. 'Got her from a fellow down on his luck. Met him in an inn a little way down the road – said it was his wife's mount, but used also to drawing a small trap and I thought –'

'Stolen,' said Tom again firmly. 'Child's pony. Pet of the family. Ribbon in its mane. Polished hooves. Marks of a child's saddle. You've been had, Master. How much?'

'Ten guineas,' said Jack crossly. 'You're a real Jonah! I'll stake my life the man was honest.'

'Just what you may have to stake if Tom's right,' said

Annie doubtfully. 'Hadn't you better take it back, just in case?'

But of course when we reached the inn the man had gone and the landlord assured us he wasn't a local. We might have got away with it, too, if Jack hadn't been so determined to stick to his itinerary and play at Sherborne.

We came through narrow lanes, deep in grass and daisies, to the town with the winding streets and high-walled houses. That night we camped just outside as there were not enough spaces for all the vans nearer in. Jack decided that we would play Tom and Daisy from one place, with Sam as back-up, and bring Annie's van nearer in, whilst he and I went through our *King Lear* routine to draw an audience to the others. He had wanted us together, but as it was market day and we had no pitch we were of necessity divided. Sam found a space in the road and soon had an audience, then Tom brought in Daisy to go through her counting routine.

Jack waited till they were under way, then decided to go up towards the church with our act; he had worked out that the greatest impact would be made if he rode into town in costume with me leading the horse, dressed in my motley. We should be an unusual enough sight to attract a following and once there were enough we should stop, and Jack would start the act. This had worked well before when there had not been enough space for us to use our stage, for *Lear* was a wandering sort of play, and accordingly, at a few minutes past noon I led Jack, dressed in flowing white robes and a purple cloak, grey beard and long moustaches hiding his face, up the main street, past the market stalls and up towards the church, riding the newly bought roan filly. We had plenty of curious glances, especially when I beat upon the tabor I had slung about my neck, causing the nervous pony to shake her head and tremble.

We paused where the roads divide, one up to the church, the other to the left, and I started my introduction.

'You are to imagine, good people, that this man who

124

sits his horse so dispirited is that mighty King Lear, dispossessed but lately of his throne by his wicked daughters, and I his poor Fool self-condemned into exile with that same monarch . . . .' Et cetera. So far, so good. We went into the lines Jack had extracted from Shakespeare: 'Dost call me fool, boy . . .' normally ending with Lear's mighty rage: 'When we are born we cry that we are come to this great stage of fools!' but we had barely got the first exchanges done, though there was a nice crowd gathering, when out of the blue there came a piercing scream.

'Wosabella! Papa, Papa! That dweadful old man has my Wosabella!'

I think both Jack and I realized simultaneously that the game was up, for we exchanged looks of resigned horror.

'Bloody silly name for a horse,' said Jack in his normal voice. 'Get lost, Sprat: I'll sort this out.'

We were penned in now on all sides: well enough to say 'get lost' but short of flying over the heads of the crowd, now scenting sensation, there was no way, so I took off my fool's cap and crouched down as near the wall as possible, trying to look inconspicuous. Pushing to the front of the crowd came a portwine-faced gentleman in a port-coloured coat and bagwig, preceded by an odious small girl of about twelve – in pink silk, with carrot-coloured hair – who threw her arms about the reluctant roan's neck and sobbed theatrically. She shrieked and wailed about 'Howwid feeves and murderwers' stealing her 'Wosabella' till I could have cheerfully strangled her. Her papa waved his stick at Jack who had obviously decided on his role; cowering, he started to talk through his nose with a lisp to match Rosabella's mistress's and gave forth such a parody of the Shylock we were rehearsing for next week that I temporarily forgot our parlous position and listened open-mouthed.

'I am a Jew: hath not a Jew eyes? Aye, my masters, an eye for a good horse and when a man such as I meeteth on the road a Christian who condescends of his great goodness to offer me this beast, this pound – these pounds of flesh, why, I to usury shall go to purchase such a one. This wandering is my life and 'tis my life you do take when you take the means whereby I live, for many ducats – guineas, did I give for that Rosinante–'

'Wosabella!' yelled the small girl.

'Cease, Dowabella!' said the port-wine gentleman. 'This fellow shall answer to the magistwates for the deed! In the meanwhile he shall weside in jail. A couple of shillings to get the Jew to his cell!'

I started forward in protest, only to be grabbed by the seat of my breeches and a coat flung over my head and shoulders.

'One's enough, young 'un,' came Tom's voice through the folds. 'Horse stealing's a topping offence. I don't know about you being the fool, reckon Master's worse, and as for playing Jew . . . . Now lie still, till all's clear.'

Later that afternoon we held a council of war: Sam, of course, could understand little of what we said, but Annie was in tears and I was little better. Tom had found out that Jack was being held in the jail on the outskirts of town, a one-storey building on a corner with three cells and strong walls. There was one jailor, in residence all day, and the windows were heavily barred. The cell on the corner nearest the town was occupied by a debtor and Jack's cell was on the side next the highroad.

'We've got to rescue him!' said Annie. 'Otherwise they may hang him or transport the poor dear to some slave plantation . . . .'

'Can't he just explain what happened?' I said hopefully.

They regarded me in silence for a moment, then Tom sighed.

'You've not been with us long enough, young 'un, to realize just what folks think about travelling people. To them we're just gipsies, and as you should know, 'tis a punishable offence to consort with them. Gipsies are thieves, horse-stealers too, and maybe that's why Master chose to play Jew. Not that they are liked any better, but they haven't the reputation for getting into as much

126

trouble. He might talk his way out of it, but 'twill take a power of persuasion . . . . In the meanwhile we are stuck, for the jail's too strong to break into and we've not enough to bribe the jailor to look the other way: it would take twenty guineas at least.'

We looked at one another. I had near four guineas saved, Annie must have more, and Tom . . . but that was their winter money, and probably would not be enough, anyway. There must be another way. We argued round the point till sundown, then decided to try and speak to Jack himself.

Leaving Annie to pack up as best she could – for whatever happened, it were best the vans were not near the town the next day – Tom, Sam and I set off for the jail, bread, cheese and a flagon of ale carried between us. We also brought a rope and a file, in case they came in useful.

The part of the jail that was nearest the town was next door to a farrier's, and by the light from his open gateway we crept round the corner. The jail door was open and we could see the jailor sitting at his table, eating supper, a mug of ale at his elbow. He was a big man with greasy dark hair, a soiled red jerkin tucked into his wide leather belt; from that belt hung a bunch of large keys.

Jack's window was at least eight feet from the ground, with a two-foot ditch beneath, and it was small and well barred.

I beckoned to Tom. 'I'll climb up on Sam's shoulders. Keep an eye open, and give us a whistle if anyone comes.'

He nodded, and I beckoned to Sam, explaining what I wanted by pantomime. He bent down and I climbed to his shoulders, feet on either side of his head. As he straightened up I supported myself against the wall, then clutched at the bars as they came level with my nose. I could feel Sam holding my ankles to steady me, so I felt safe enough to peer into the blackness of Jack's cell.

At first I could see nothing, then I made out a very dim light in the farthest corner from a guttering tallow candle;

127

by its feeble illumination I saw Jack stretched out fast asleep on a pallet of straw, for all the world as though he were safe at home.

'Jack . . .' I whispered; then louder: 'Jack!'

There was a rustle of straw from the corner, then suddenly the support went from beneath my feet, my hands slipped from the bars and I landed in a heap in the ditch. The other two were nowhere to be seen but I could hear uneven steps and I lay where I was as a couple of drunken farm workers rolled by, one relieving himself against the wall not far from where I was lying: I was a little worried lest the ale mar his aim. They went on their way eventually, and after Tom had apologized for not giving enough warning, I was hoisted up again, and this time Jack was waiting. I looked down at the wild disguise of Ancient Briton, lit cadaverously from below by the feeble candle.

'Hullo, Sprat,' he said conversationally. 'I thought you'd be along sometime soon.'

'Your moustache is coming ungummed,' I said.

'Yours would in this place: it's damp. Brought some food?'

'Yes, but we must get you out of this place!'

'Well, I think better if I'm munching.'

It took another couple of descents from the window before we got the bread and cheese organized, and then of course the flagon of ale was too large to go through the bars; luckily Jack had a small horn cup of water which he tossed out and we doled out the ale in cupfuls, spilling a good deal in the process, but at last he professed himself satisfied and I passed the flagon down to Tom.

'Jack, we've thought and thought and we still can't see how to get you out. We've got a rope and file: Tom thought we might file through the bars a little and then pull them out, but you're too big – I mean, the window is too small – for you to get through . . . .'

'I've been thinking too, Sprat. As long as this beard

128

and wig hold out I think I can play Jew, and pay my way out.'

'Between us we've only got a few guineas, and Tom says it will take much more than that –'

'I know, I know, and I don't expect you people to find it. Now, listen carefully: in the van, behind the bed, there is a small leather case – I'll pass you up the key. I want you, and only you, to go to that box: inside you will find a pouch containing one hundred guineas.' He sighed. 'You could call it my inheritance, my investment against old age . . . . Never mind. Count out twenty-five guineas and bring them back here. Don't tell the others about the box, or the money. If I can't buy myself out with that, or if anything worse – and I mean very much worse – happens, you'll find papers with instructions in that same box. In that case give the instructions to Tom: he will know what to do. All being well, I hope to join you some time tomorrow; get the vans away tonight, far enough but not too far. There's a good enough stop by the Sturminster Newton tavern at King's Stag, where three roads meet at the top of Peaceful Lane. Give me two days, but if I haven't reached you by the third, one of you had better come and see what has happened. Now, off you go and fetch that money: you can walk past and whistle "Lillibullero", then toss it up through the window. And Sprat –'

'Yes?'

'For God's sake wrap it in something secure!'

At that moment there was a warning whistle and my support collapsed again; we hid as a man bearing a covered dish came by and turned in at the doorway of the jail. Curiosity got the better of me, and I crept as near as I could. The newcomer and the jailor were talking, and I heard the chink of coin.

'Two shilling do?'

'If'n it's all you got . . . . I takes a risk, you know.'

'Oh I 'preciate it, don't think I don't, and the wife and I will be only too glad when he's clear; wife reckons as how once she's chased up a couple more of those that owes, we should have enough. Then, God willing, brother-in-law or not, we'll have him away to the colonies. 'Tis second time, and gets expensive when –'

'I've had him here afore . . . . What's she cooked him tonight?'

'Mutton pasty. Couldn't come herself 'cos the youngest has a touch of the colic. Anyway I'll not keep you: just see him get round this and I can take the dish back.'

'You're not keeping me: here till midnight, can't lock up and go home till then, as well you know. Gets better fed than me, he does: smells right good . . . .'

Poking my head round the door I saw the jailor unlock the cell where Tom had said the debtor was imprisoned, admit the visitor, then relock the door.

I rejoined the others. 'Sam, lift me up again . . . Jack?'

'Thought you'd gone –'

'I've just had an idea about getting you out –'

'Just fetch the money.'

'All right: I'll be back before midnight. But if my idea works –'

'The deaf will hear and lame will walk, blind men see and dumb men talk . . . . Just don't make it any worse, that's all!'

' "Wosabella"'!' I mocked. 'What *could* be worse than that?' I ducked as his fingers came up to tweak my nose. 'And if you would your freedom see, Then 'twill be Sprat to set you free,' I promised as I jumped down.

Walking back to the vans I outlined my plan, but I didn't tell them it was mine. I let them think it was Jack's, by first telling them he had said we must pack up the vans and get out: that was the truth, and for the rest I just didn't mention the source of the inspiration.

'. . . and so,' I concluded, 'Annie and Sam must hitch all the vans together and drive them to King's Stag and Tom and I will try the rescue plan.'

Annie had almost got everything packed and was not too pleased at being asked to unpack the stage-costume hamper from the bottom of the wagon, but when I explained she was the most enthusiastic of us all, suggesting a couple of amendments which we incorporated. Once the clothes were sorted out I slipped away to our van and found Jack's secret box, unlocking it with the key he had given me. At the top were a packet of letters, tied with blue ribbon, but the name and address of the recipient were folded to the inside. Lifting these out I came to a case of Manton duelling pistols, a medal on a ribbon, another bundle of papers that looked like legal documents, a sealed letter addressed to a firm of solicitors in London, and lastly the leather pouch I was seeking. I counted out twenty-five of the gleaming gold coins and wrapped them in one of Jack's handkerchiefs, then started to replace everything, but suddenly felt a sharp prick in my thumb and, dropping the bundle of documents I was holding, heard the tinkle of glass.

On hands and knees I searched, candle in hand, and finally found the offending article: a gold-framed miniature with small slivers of glass still adhering to the inside of the frame. It was clear that it had been broken some time ago, and that it was one of the splinters that had caught my thumb. Sucking the blood off the latter, I sat back on my heels and contemplated the picture. Although the frame was dented and buckled and indeed looked as though someone had ground a heel into it, the face that smiled up at me was untouched. It was that of a beautiful young woman with fair ringlets falling over one bare shoulder, blue eyes staring directly at me and a smile lifting the corners of a small, pouting mouth. The nose was Grecian and the neck swanlike, the whole effect being one of delicate aristocratic beauty.

Jack had never talked about any special woman, but that this one fell into that category was evident, not only because it was with his personal effects but also because of the violence to which the portrait had been subjected.

Beauty and passion: sweetheart, mistress, wife? Was that the one he had been thinking about that day on the Malvern Hills, the one in the house with swans on the river? She had meant something to him once, that was for sure, otherwise the picture would have long gone; the fact that it was still there pointed to the notion that she was still cherished. But the only certainty was that I could never ask him –

'We're nearly ready, young 'un,' called Tom.

'Just got to change,' I answered, hastily thrusting everything back in the box and relocking it. 'Two minutes.'

The only way to keep the blasted wig straight was to tie a bonnet firmly on top, and what with that and finding something convincing with which to pad out the bodice of the dress, it was nearer ten minutes than two; but finally I was nearly ready. Borrowing Jack's carmine make-up stick I outlined my mouth and rubbed some into my cheeks, then stared at my reflection. No amount of disguise could right mismatched eyes, make a retroussé nose aristocratic or a wide mouth into a cupid's bow . . . . I realized I was comparing my image with the miniature and couldn't imagine why: perhaps it was the dress I was wearing. Sod the lady, whoever she was: she would probably be great at organizing a tea party, but it was I that was going to get her precious Jack out of jail.

'It's near ten-thirty . . . .'

'*Coming*, Tom!'

Sticking my thumb at the end of my nose, I waggled my fingers at my reflection. Who cared about a picture of a beautiful woman, anyway? Tucking the handkerchief of money into the pocket in the dress, I flounced down the steps of the van.

'Well, folks, how do you like Rachel, loving grand-daughter of the old Jew?'

'You look a real tart,' said Annie. 'And the right side's bigger than the left . . . . Want to borrow another handkerchief?'

132

7

It was nearly a quarter to midnight when we pushed open the door of the jail and staggered in, carefully negotiating the narrow doorway; the jailor had been dozing, but he jerked awake and scowled as we entered.

'What's all this, then? No one allowed in here without permission –'

'Oh dear sweet sir!' I cried, falling on my knees at his feet. 'Have pity on a poor maid! Here is my dear mother driven near distraction with the news that my poor grandfather is held, all innocent, in jail . . . . She swoons, see, at the thought of it!' I beckoned to Tom, who was doing his best to support a swaying and heavily draped figure on one arm and carry a basket on the other. 'Here, my good fellow, let me take the viands, while you continue to support my dear mother till she feels less faint: in the meantime, here is a guinea for your trouble . . . .'

The jailor's eyes bulged. 'A guinea?'

'Indeed, yes!' I simpered. 'Nothing is too good for my grandfather. This good fellow has helped us on the way, haven't you?' I cooed, nudging Tom.

He rattled off what I had taught him. 'Wending my way home I was, when I came upon this – this pretty maid and her mother by the wayside, heavy with news of the old man's imprisonment. It was the sight of those female tears that made me stop and succour them in their distress, for what be the role of man save to act Good Samaritan to the weaker flower of womanhood . . . .'

It sounded incredibly over-sticky, like Sam Alley-Come's sweetmeats, but the jailor was a simple man; besides, he was trying to look down my front. I stuck out my chest, and hoped the handkerchiefs wouldn't slip.

'See, my good man, we have brought Grandfather two

133

pasties, but I doubt he can manage both . . . .' The juice
was dribbling fragrantly out of the still-steaming crust and
even my mouth was watering. 'And as for this brandy . . . .'
I put the bottle on the table. 'Perhaps you would take a
draught and tell us whether it is worth what we paid, for
indeed we women are not the best judges of what a man
appreciates . . . .'

He choked on the fiery liquid, and wiped his mouth
with the back of his hand. ' 'Tis good stuff, right enough,
but perhaps a little water with it . . . . It might prove a
trifle strong for the old man; I could give him a little, now
and then.'

'What a good idea!' I said approvingly. 'For I should
not wish him to appear before the magistrates in any way
unsure of himself; perhaps you, then, would keep the
bottle, and eat one of the pasties now? In the meantime –'
I glanced over my shoulder '– it seems as though my
mother recovers a little . . . . What time does my grandfather appear before the magistrate?'

'Nine sharp, in the morning.'

'Oh, then there is so little time!' I said, truthfully. 'Open
the door, dear sir, without further delay!'

'The door? Come now,' said the jailor, eyeing us
suspiciously, 'I can't do that without I have permission.
There has to be an arrangement . . . .'

'And so there shall be, so there shall be!' I cried. 'For
from tomorrow, when Grandfather comes back here for
further inquiries to be made as to his innocence, for
innocent he is –'

'They all say that!'

'But I *know* he is! A guinea a night for five minutes'
conversation would be the going rate, I suppose?'

'A – why, yes,' he said slowly, rubbing his hands.

'Well, that is what we shall have to pay from tomorrow –
if she lives that long, of course.'

'What's the matter with her, then?' he said, staring at
the swaying figure Tom was supporting, who was now
moaning as if it wanted to be sick.

'Her heart is not good, but one glimpse of her father would work wonders: otherwise I cannot answer for us returning tomorrow . . . . Dearest mother, bear up under your affliction, I pray! If she succumbs to an attack I shall have to nurse her and will not be able to honour our arrangement, I fear . . . .'

'Well,' he said, considering. 'You can come over to the door and have a peep at the old man, I suppose,' and he led the way over to Jack's cell. 'Here, you: your daughter and granddaughter to see you, old man!'

A groan was the only answer. Peeping through the grille I could see a form writhing on the pallet in the corner.

'Here, what's the matter?' said the jailor, and his hand fumbled at his belt for the key. 'Don't go sick on me, Jew!'

'Ah, ah, I die!' came a keening cry from within that made my blood run cold. 'One embrace is all I ask, to warm these my ancient bones . . . . You see me here, you gods, a poor old man, as full of grief as age . . . . Let not woman's water-drops stain my man's cheeks! This heart shall break into a hundred thousand flaws, or e'er I'll weep! Here I lie, a poor, infirm, weak and despised old man . . . a man more sinned against than sinning. I am bound upon a wheel of fire that mine own tears do scald like molten lead –'

'Quick, jailor,' I cried. 'The old man is in a sorry state! Let but his daughter in to him – see, our friend will go in with her and I shall stay without with you, that you shall see fair play and have me hostage for their good behaviour. Give them but a few moments together and I swear all will be well . . . .' I could hardly speak for choking, for nearly all Jack's moanings had been lifted straight from Lear's mad ramblings.

The jailor hesitated, and I called through the bars: 'Dear Grandfather, take courage! Your moneys are safe: we shall bring some tomorrow to see you better housed. In the meanwhile, your daughter Cordelia is here to give you swift embrace . . . .'

On the word 'money' the jailor inserted the key in the

lock; on the word 'Cordelia' Jack had his cue. Rising to his feet, he tottered to the middle of the cell.

> ' "Pray, do not mock me:
> I am a very foolish fond old man,
> Fourscore and upward, not an hour more nor less;
> And to deal plainly,
> I fear I am not in my perfect mind.
> Methinks I should know you, and know this man;
> Yet I am doubtful: for I am mainly ignorant
> What place this is; and all the skill I have
> Remembers not these garments; nor I know not
> Where I did lodge last night. Do not laugh at me;
> For as I am a man, I think this lady
> To be my child Cordelia." '

I pushed Tom and his companion into the cell, and pulled the door to. Hastily I drooped heavily against the jailor, pulling him away from the grille.

'Alas! I fear I too shall faint . . . . Some brandy . . . .' Nothing loath, he poured us each a stiff measure. I took a quick sip, then pushed across the horn cup. 'Enough, dear sir: I recover. Pray do me a kindness . . . .' I watched him tip the remains into his mug, trying not to look too eager.

From the cell behind came a fine burst of histrionics and the jailor turned his head. Gritting my teeth I pushed him down onto the stool and perched myself on his knees, twining my arm round his greasy neck and laying my head on his shoulder.

'How comforting you are,' I cried. 'How shall I ever show my gratitude?'

I let one hand tighten round my waist but judged it prudent to capture the other as it crept up to my bosom.

'You are so *strong*!' I whimpered. 'A poor maid like me cannot but admire your generosity, your – your *manhood* . . . .'

His fat lips nuzzled my ear: they tickled unpleasantly.

'I could put strength into you, little maid: I could put my manhood where it rightly belongs . . . .'

I had chosen the wrong words, but before his hands moved anywhere else, the rising wind brought the sound of a clock striking.

'By'r Lady! Midnight – Here, I must lock up sharpish! The watch'll be round soon, and all must be off the premises. You'll have to come round tomorrow, my dear, but earlier, and we'll continue our little . . . talk.'

'Then quick,' I urged. 'Drink up the rest of the brandy and finish off the pies: they'll not keep.' I tipped the rest of the liquid into his mug and watched him drain it; he crammed one of the pies into his mouth, taking his keys from his belt as he did so, and stumbled unsteadily towards Jack's cell. I followed him, fingers crossed, but they were ready. As soon as the door was open I pulled at Tom's arm as he led 'Cordelia' out, then swung the door shut; the jailor locked it after a fumble or two, then peered through the grille at his prisoner. I peeped over his shoulder; the shape lay, wrapped in his flowing robes, easy and quiet and snoring a little on the pallet.

'Thank you, dear sir,' piped 'Cordelia'. '*So* kind . . . . I am *much* better now! Dear father will be quiet for *hours* . . . . But I do feel a trifle peckish!' And to my horror I saw a masculine hand shoot out from under her cloak, grab the remaining pie and convey it to the hooded face. 'Come now, Rachel,' continued the falsetto voice: 'We must be over the hills and far away, my love . . . .'

'Thought you were back here tomorrow,' said the jailor, suspiciously.

'Just a figure of speech,' I assured him hastily. 'Very poetical, my mother.' And I pushed them both, Tom and 'Cordelia', out ahead of me, then turned to blow a kiss to the bemused jailor. 'Better hurry up: it's blowing a gale out here.'

We watched, hidden round the corner, as he locked up and, after three attempts, lighted a lanthorn and stumbled up towards the town.

Jack sighed, then laughed, skirts blowing up around his waist. 'Off, off, you lendings: where are the horses?'

*
137

We found the others as arranged where the three lanes met; Annie had a good fire going and the smell of stew blew invitingly down Peaceful Lane as we rode up, Tom up behind Jack on Hannibal, me bumping up and down on Daisy. Annie embraced us all, eyes full of thankful tears and blowing her nose heartily on her apron; Sam was all smiles, repeating his name 'Sa'am Alley-Come' over and over again, with a little bow each time.

Jack tossed the dress, wig and cloak into a heap. 'Thank God for that! How you females manage in all that gear, Annie, I shall never know! On the other hand, Sprat, you make quite a fetching lass: your bosom had me fooled for a moment . . . .'

For answer I reached down the front of the boned bodice and slowly drew out four handkerchiefs, one after the other. 'Now you see it: now you don't,' I said shortly. 'I'm going to change.'

Back in the van I put the twenty-five guineas we had not used in a neat pile on Jack's table, together with the key of his box. Discarding the hated dress and wig, I hastily pulled on a smock over the breeches I had retained. I stared at the money on the table: if things had been different – if I had been different – I could have been away with a hundred guineas in my pocket and Jack would have been – hanged? Transported? But now he was safe, safe to go back to the beautiful lady in the miniature if he wished . . . . I kicked the table so hard that the pile of coins fell into a heap. 'Over the hills and far away': I hoped so.

Jack had managed to knock up the landlord of the King's Head and by two o'clock in the morning we were well fed and decidedly merry, for Annie had insisted on staying up to hear the full story, and we lay round the fire telling one bit after the other, for all the world like a badly disciplined Greek chorus.

'So I found this chap,' said Tom. 'Worse for drink he already was, but after a few more ales and a whisky or two –'

'And all this while I was waiting down the road with the dress, wig, and hooded cloak, so that when Tom found someone –'

'Thought he was coming to his senses at one stage –'

'The bonnet was the worst –'

'And there was I listening to all this going on,' said Jack. 'Hoping against hope they didn't muck it up –'

'*I* thought he was going to spew up –'

'And then you starting spouting all that Shakespeare –'

'It was very appropriate –'

'And I thought you'd never get the switch done in time, and that *jailor* –'

'You nearly raped him –'

'That *stupid* squeaky voice of yours – *and* grabbing that pie!'

I don't know whether Annie followed all this, but she got the general gist, for after we had all done laughing and congratulating ourselves she asked: 'What about the poor fellow you did the switch with? Drunk he may have been but what happens in the morning when they comes to haul the man they thinks is Jack afore the magistrates?'

'That's the best joke of all,' said Tom slowly. 'For he be none other than one of the magistrate's clerks . . . .' He turned to Jack. 'That be one of the best schemes you've ever come up with, Master!'

We all looked at Jack: he grinned.

' "Blow winds and crack your cheeks" and I think they will, fairly shortly. Bedtime, all: up at five-thirty. I want to be away before the town of Sherborne discovers it has been robbed of one of the geniuses of our day . . . . Yes, it was rather a good idea, wasn't it?' and he winked at me.

Next morning as we trundled down Peaceful Lane shortly before six, wheels protesting at the ruts and potholes, Jack pointed to a bonny bright-haired girl who stood at the gate of the white cottage on the right, waving as we went by.

'You deserve something for inventiveness, Sprat: next time we stop for a day or two I'll find you a wench like

139

that,' and he blew her a kiss. Delighted, she blew one back, then, meeting my scowl, her face sharpened and she thrust out her tongue. I stuck out mine in answer and she blushed bright red and disappeared.

Jack cuffed me lightly. 'I see I shall have to teach you how to behave to young ladies . . . . Now, as to reward –'

'I want none. As you said once before, when I suggested that plain bribery would have been better: "costlier . . . but not half so much fun." I owed you last night for Gloucester, so let's call it quits – less four shillings and twopence.'

'Four shillings and twopence?'

'For ale, two meat pies and an inferior bottle of rotgut.'

He fished in his pocket. 'Five shillings: the tenpence is for cheek.'

I pocketed the crown. 'And I don't want any wenches –'

'Well, I do! Roll on, Winchester . . . .'

And towards the cathedral town we went, via Blandford Forum, Wimborne Minster, and Stoney Cross. The weather was alternately kind and cruel, for we were well into the month of thunderstorms, July, and sometimes we baked and sometimes we soaked. Audiences baked with us, but when it rained they stayed at home, and we were no great weather prophets, and often set out our wares when we should have done better to shut up shop before we started. We knew the bits about red and yellow skies and cattle standing up or lying down and Annie had a bunch of seaweed she swore by: the trouble was that it got damp during rain and after, but never before . . . .

Along the ways we went the wheat and corn were ripening, birds were softer-sung, drowsed by summer heat and crops, and already the blackberry fruits were setting into tiny green knobbles. Roses had blown their last petals but late foxgloves were still busy with bees and the honeysuckle was moth-hung at dusk. There were butterflies I had never seen up north, soft blues and those with Argus eyes, and bats swung out of the barns we passed just before the swifts screamed their way to rest. Tom showed me how to tempt fish with my fingers and weave baskets of withy; with good feeding I began to fill out and poor Annie was for ever letting down, letting out, or patching my clothes. Jack had me play Portia to his Shylock but I was not allowed her best speeches: when I questioned this, he retorted: 'Who's the star, you or I?' I reminded him once about my brilliant playing of his so-called granddaughter at Sherborne prison, but his reply was that my performance had owed more to 'padding than play-acting, handkerchiefs than histrionics', so I forbore to argue further.

We fell in with other caravans going to Winchester, and for the last two days of our journey travelled in company. There was a fire-eater and sword-swallower with his family, a juggler (not as good as Sam), and a mender of pots and pans, and with these, who had been on the southeastern circuit, we exchanged news and views. Of course they told us their summer had been the best for years and we said the same about ours but I don't think either side was deceived: it had been a year like any other.

We reached Winchester at dusk, and came down the hill between the narrow streets, the imposing jail on our right. I shivered: try getting Jack out of that one – it looked altogether too efficient and well-guarded. We were lucky to find a fair pitch near the cathedral and as the day after next was market day, Jack reckoned on staying three days. We did well enough, giving three full performances a day and by the last night I had added another five shillings to my rapidly growing money box, which was as much as some labourers earned in a fortnight and with far less enjoyment.

We took the road next day with a couple of acts that were going on to Salisbury; we were to bear east to Chichester, but our way was the same for that first day, and by late afternoon we chanced on a small village with the usual dozen or so cottages, a church and an inn. There,

141

by mutual consent, we decided to pitch camp on a corner of common land. One of the vans held a puppeteer and his daughter; he set up his stall on the green and earned a few shillings. We were content to laze around: I had to learn my part for *Henry V* – and a small enough part that was, for although it was that of the French princess Jack had cut it beyond recognition – and Annie was busy with washing, Sam with his prayers, and Tom with the mending of harness. We decided to eat easy that day, and about six I went across to the inn and came back with cold meats for Jack and Annie, pig's cheek pie and pickles for Tom and myself and a mess of vegetables for Sam (the vegetables were meant to go with our meal, but that way we paid for four and filled five), and I went back to my studying.

About seven o'clock I went to look for Jack, to help me with my French accent, and found him sprawled on the grass, a mug of ale in his hand, watching the ankles of the puppeteer's daughter as she helped her father manipulate the strings in the booth; the curtaining of the booth fell short of the ground, but not as short as her skirts . . . . I had not paid much attention to what the other end of her looked like but apparently Jack had, for he was eyeing her calves in a way I didn't like, stroking his chin in a reflective way, eyes squinting in the slanting sunshine.

'Jack, can you help me with these lines?'

'Go away, Sprat, not now . . . .'

'When then? I want to ask you about –'

'Tomorrow.'

'Tomorrow never comes.'

'It won't if you keep bothering me. Disappear – no, wait: fetch me another mug of ale.'

'Fetch it yourself!' I retorted unwisely and turned to go, measuring my length on the grass a split second later, all the breath knocked out of me. Jack still had hold of my ankles and jerked me towards him; I wrapped my arms round my head to stave off a cuffing and drew my knees to my stomach to save a punch.

142

'You wouldn't have known how to do that six months ago,' said Jack with satisfaction. 'You're learning . . . . Now, go fetch me that ale. And no spitting in it!'

Daylight seemed to linger that night but the air was close and sticky and the yellow light that flared across the sky as the sun went down made us look sickly and pale. I had begged a hunk of cheese off Annie as soon as she was free of washing, but I knew it was a mistake as soon as I gulped it down.

'You'd think eating was going out of fashion,' she grumbled as she rewrapped the cheese and put it away. 'You'll only get stum-mick-ache again, and not sleep tonight; bad dreams, cheese gives you . . . .'

'I think I have . . . .'

'What?'

'Got a pain.'

'Want a purgative?'

'No thanks.' Annie's special infusion was horrid, and very efficacious. 'I think I'll go for a walk –'

'Not till you've filled the water buckets, ready for morning.'

'Oh, *Annie* . . . .'

'Never mind "Oh Annie-ing" me; and fetch Jack another mug of ale.'

'He don't need any more: he's had at least half a dozen.' I glanced over to where he was leaning against the wheel of our van, his arm round the woman from the puppeteer's. ' 'Sides, he's too busy to care . . . .'

She followed my gaze. 'So what? He's got to have it sometimes, and she looks more respectable than most: go on!'

I fetched the brimming mug from the inn with ill grace and walked over to Jack.

'Thanks, boy: meet Lucy – Lucy Lockit, with goodies in her pocket.' He squeezed her waist. 'Going to let Jack pick your pocket, sweetheart?'

She giggled. 'I warn you, I can tell a dip a mile off; how d'you know I ain't got a fierce little rat down there, with

143

sharp teeth to bite your fingers off?' Close to, she was not as young as I had thought: nearer thirty than twenty, with snapping black eyes and a thin mouth. Her teeth were discoloured too, I noticed, but she had a large bosom and dead-white skin, and she smelled of violets . . . .

'I'll warrant there are no sharp teeth where my fingers would like to be,' said Jack softly, and bent to nuzzle her neck.

I turned away, but he called me back. 'Here, take the mug.' He drained the dregs. 'And go take a walk . . . .' Winking at me, his hand went to the woman's backside, stroking and pinching until she slapped his hand.

'Give over, do! You'll have the lad blushing . . . .' Her eyes went boldly to my groin, luckily well covered by the smock. 'Though I bet he's a likely one, under all that cloth – Fancy a bit, lad?'

'Wouldn't know where to start,' said Jack, lazily.

'Time he learned then,' and she leaned forward and made a grab at me, so unexpected that I started back and fell over my own feet.

Their laughter followed me down the lane as I strolled away, very much on my dignity until I was out of eyesight, then venting my ill temper on the cow parsley and angelica till I left a litter of decapitated stalks behind me. I had walked about a half-mile when the first puffs of hot wind and growls of thunder warned me to retrace my steps. Glancing back the way I had come I saw the great banks of black cloud massing on the horizon like smoke from oily rags, and started to run back. The first heavy drops of rain were falling warm and heavy as drops of blood when I reached Annie, struggling to retrieve the washing. I ripped one of Jack's shirts as I pulled it off the bush but she didn't notice, for at that moment came the first soundless blaze of lightning sheeting across the sky, flickering like a gigantic candle, and she fled with her arms full to the safety of her van. I checked quickly to see all else was safe; the horses were hobbled and their feed was hanging under the vans, well clear of the ground. I checked the lashings of the wagon and rescued the crock of salt that lay forgotten, then made sure all the chocks were firm under the wheels; one last look round: Sam Alley-Come had taken refuge under Tom's waggonette, which, typically, was snug on the highest piece of ground, and all the other vans were shuttered and fastened.

Then the rain came down. I fled for our van and, wrenching open the door, collapsed on my pallet and towelled my hair dry. I could see well enough, for Jack had left me a candle burning on the table.

'It's going to be some night,' I said. 'Reckon I won't have to fill the buckets in the morning.'

There was silence from his corner.

'Sorry, Jack: I didn't realize you were asleep.' I flung away the towel and stood up. 'I'll blow out the candle.' Walking softly over to the table, I cupped my hand round the flame and bent to puff it out, but froze as an amused voice came from behind.

'Shall us try a threesome, Jack? Think the lad's ready?'

By the candle's errant flame I saw them, and even as the ready blood rushed to my cheeks I noticed with curiosity how white Jack's skin was where the line of his breeches started, and how her full breasts had flattened and widened under his weight –

Jack's hand shot out and grasped my right wrist, pulling me over to the bed. He had the blurred and shifting eyes of alcohol and his voice was slurred.

'How about it, Sprat? Want to learn to be a mackerel? I'll let you have a go when I've finished. Here, put your hand on –'

With a violent effort I jerked my wrist from his grasp, leaving the skin sore and reddened.

'I wouldn't dream of touching your dirty whores!' I cried shrilly, and ran out into the storm, banging the door hard behind me.

It was a very foolish thing to do and as I huddled under the van I remembered the fool's lines: 'a naughty night to swim in'. And swim I soon did: the vans were all, with

145

the exception of Tom's, on low, boggy ground and I was soon sitting in a puddle. No room in or under Tom's, the puddles under Annie's wagon were as bad, but I was not, *not*, going back to – The lightning flashed, the thunder roared, the rain pelted down, and at last I could stand it no more, and went and tapped on Annie's door. No answer: I rapped louder.

'Who's there?'

'Me, Annie – Sprat. Can I come in?'

There was a considerable delay, but at last the door was unbolted and on a rush of warm, slightly fusty air a curlpapered, nightdressed, shawled Annie surveyed me, candle in hand.

'Whatever in the world are you doing out there, you stupid lad?'

I slipped past her, leaving wet footprints on the wooden floor.

'Can I stay? Please, Annie, please . . . .'

'I suppose . . . . Why aren't you with Jack? You annoyed him or something?'

'It's that woman – you don't know what they – what she –' I stopped.

She stared at me for a moment, then laughed till she shook.

'So he's got her in there and you couldn't . . . . Oh dear, lad, you're such a baby! You should have pulled the blankets round your ears and let them get on with it: can't expect Jack to do his courting out-of-doors on a night like this!' She didn't sound in the least bit shocked.

'But Annie – they wanted me to – to join in. Jack was drunk – and she . . . .'

She composed her face into a semi-serious mask, but I could see she still thought I was making a fuss about nothing and being overly prudish. 'Well, perhaps you're a bit young for that yet, but you've got to learn sometime and I'll warrant Jack'll be a good study for you! Never mind, lad: it'll all come to you one day, and easier than learning all them lines, I promise you! Wait till you've

146

Jack's experience and you'll be good at both!' She was still chuckling, but pulled a blanket from the chest against the wall. 'Here, you'll have to sleep on the floor, but you can wrap yourself in this. Clothes wet?' She felt my sleeve. 'Soaking! Now, get them all off before you catch your death, and hang 'em over the chair: they'll be dry enough in the morning for you to slip on before you go back and get a proper change . . . . Well, what you waiting for? Strip, lad, or you'll get the pewmonia . . . . Bit embarrassed to have old Annie watching, then? I've seen enough lads strip in my time, but maybe you was brought up different; I'll slip back to bed then: blow out the candle when you've finished.'

I waited till she pulled the flowered curtains across her bed, then stripped off as quickly as possible, even my drawers, for all were soaking. Wrapping the coarse blanket tightly round me I disposed of my wet things over the chair she had indicated and blew out the candle. I lay down near the door but it was stifling hot and after tossing and turning for a while I threw back the blanket and opened the top half. It was still raining but the thunder was retreating, prowling round the horizon like some predator stalking a camp fire.

Behind me Annie's snores took the place of the thunder, and I wondered how I should ever sleep; but I couldn't go back – there – and I didn't feel like facing Jack in the morning after seeing him – but perhaps he would be too drunk to remember. The air cooled my flushed cheeks, but even after I lay down on the blanket again, my mind kept going back to what I had seen. I knew that such things happened, that was part of life, but not that it could be so messy and degrading and shameful – I wouldn't, ever, ever! They had been like animals coupling in the open, not caring who saw . . . was it always like that? I had thought lovemaking would be something tender, precious, secret – he could not *love* her and surely one had to love to do – that? But then there was something called lust, too, and I supposed that must have been it . . . .

147

Tossing and turning, hot and sticky, I tried to sleep, but found that a combination of the heat, Annie's snores, returning thunder, my unquiet thoughts and, very probably, the cheese I had gobbled earlier, kept me awake. At last I flung back the blanket completely and lay naked, staring up through the open half of the door at the clouds passing. Gradually I became cooler and found my eyes were closing: I must remember to tuck myself up in the blanket before I fell asleep, but in the meanwhile I could doze off for a while . . . . Just recite a few of my lines, like counting sheep . . . . Katherine and King Henry, Portia and Shylock, Lucy and Jack . . . . No! Othello and Desdemona, Romeo and Juliet, the obscenely coupled dwarves – Never! The girl in the miniature and Jack: had they . . . ? Clouds, black eyes; tears, rain; lightning, white flesh; thunder, snores . . . .

I was in a dream: surrounded by my playmates from the village school days who were dancing round me in a ring and singing one of our old skipping rhymes: 'Nebuchadnezzar, King of the Jews, bought his wife a pair of shoes . . . .' They came closer and closer and now they were laughing and pelting me with flowers, laughing louder and louder as I tried to dodge the petals. Laughing –

I awoke with light, fresh dawnlight, filling the van, and someone was still laughing; I blinked, stupefied by too little sleep, then suddenly saw it was Annie who was roaring. She towered over me, her nightdress shifting and rippling with the flesh underneath as the belly laughs went on and on and the tears squeezed themselves out of her eyes in little spurts till she had to dab at them with her shawl.

Too late, much too late, I remembered: frantically I tried to gather the elusive blanket round my naked body, hot with shame.

'And to think I thought to get up early and fetch your dry breeches myself . . . .' She could only speak in little gasps, between the laughter.

'Annie, please . . . . They'll all hear –'

She shrieked with mirth again.

'I can't help it! Oh dearie, dearie me: just wait till Jack hears! He'll never forgive you!' She mopped at her eyes again. 'Why – why in the name of all goodness didn't you tell us – tell us you were – were – a *girl*!'

BOOK TWO
Zoe

8

'But you mustn't tell Jack,' I urged. 'Promise me. Not yet, anyway.'

Annie had had to have a 'little something', as she phrased it, to calm her shattered nerves, and now we sat on her bed sharing a gin and water and she every now and again breaking off from her sipping to give me a hug or a poke in the ribs or saying 'dear, dear' or 'fancy me not guessing!' I had wrapped the blanket round me very firmly as my clothes were still damp, and she promised to slip across for a smock and a pair of breeches as soon as Jack emerged. From where we sat, with the door open, we had seen the woman Lucy cross back to her own caravan, gown hanging limp and creased, hair all mussed.

'Going to have to tell him sooner or later,' said Annie. 'Them's quite a nice little pair you've got, and they ain't getting any smaller.'

'I bind my chest with a strip of cloth,' I said. 'I can go quite flat.'

'Won't do 'em no good, squashed down like that: 'sides, you've got women's curves, now I come to look at you proper; no lad has hips like that, nor so small a waist. Don't you think you'd better tell him right away?'

'All in good time . . . .' The trouble was, I just didn't know how; I couldn't walk up to him and say: 'Hello: I'm not a boy, I'm a girl' just like that. No, it would have to be done more subtly, and preferably with witnesses, so he didn't flay me alive. 'I'll find a way soon, I swear. In the meantime you must keep my secret; you mustn't look as if there is anything different. It'll be just between you and me for the present. Promise?'

She did, after a second gin. I counted, hopefully, on the fact that she liked me, would feel important at being the sole recipient of my confidence, and would be inhibited to a certain extent by her doubts as to Jack's reaction.

Getting up, she went over to the door. 'He's out, to squeeze the lemon I shouldn't wonder: I'll slip across for your things. Then while we're getting breakfast you can tell me all about it: what made you dress as a lad, an' all.'

That was the problem: what could I tell her, or anyone? I thought back on it all, right from the day my stepfather's sleep had slipped so easily into death and I had been on my own. The days when I had gone on teaching at the little school while the vicar had made inquiries about my distant relatives; how soon the little money left ran out and I positively welcomed the arrival of Aunt Sophia of the soft name and sharp tongue; of her pointed nose sniffing and ferreting among the precious books it had taken my stepfather a lifetime to amass, declaring that 'all this rubbish must be sold'. Aunt Sophia whose nose quivered in anticipation when the vicar produced the sum of money my stepfather had entrusted him with for my inheritance . . . . As I was under age it was decided by the adults that the child should go back with Aunt Sophia and be brought up as 'one of hers', using, of course, my legacy to do this.

I went to the churchyard on the morning of my departure, the spiders' webs in the dawnlight laced with dewdrops in the long grass, and knelt down to put fresh posies on the new-turned grave and the old. I realized then how alone I was, and cried a little, I remember. There was a gentle breath to faintly stir the old yew tree that stood sentinel nearby and I seemed to hear two voices: my mother's, gentle and remote: 'Zoe, my baby, may life treat you well; be braver than I . . . . Remember, you were born of love . . .' and my dear stepfather's dry tones: 'We make our own lives: forget that rubbish about our fates being in our stars. Go and make the world what *you* want it. And remember, the Good Lord or Whoever-it-was gave you a brain: use it!'

I had needed all the love and all the wits I had ever

154

had for the next few months. As soon as Aunt Sophia got me home it was clear that all she thought me fit for was an unpaid maid-of-all-work. Uncle Frederick – not that they were either of them real relations, just distant ones of my stepfather by marriage – Uncle Frederick was a counting-house clerk completely dominated by his wife, whose slaps and pinches were quite as harsh as her words, as I soon found out. They had two pasty daughters in their early twenties but the real passion of their lives was their son and heir, a plump, piggish young man a couple of years older than myself whose face was marred with little black pits where he had picked his pimples. Oliver could not do any wrong and every care was lavished on his spotty person: food, clothes, indulgence to all his whims.

I was given a bed in the attic, shared with discarded furniture and mice, and was up at five every morning to light the fires and sweep through the house. They did keep a slatternly cook but soon dismissed the maid, Aunt Sophia declaring that it was false economy to rest an extra pair of hands: mine. I was only allowed to keep a few of my stepfather's books; *Gulliver* was soon taken by Oliver as his own, once he found there were 'interesting' parts in it, and Uncle Frederick borrowed my *Travels of Odysseus* and forgot to return it and the girls claimed *Clarissa Harlowe*. Milton's poems disappeared but the Shakespeare I managed to keep hidden. Not that there was much time for reading: there were sheets to be hemmed and turned, dresses to be altered and lengthened for the girls, shirts and neckerchiefs to be ironed and starched, buttons to be replaced, velvet to be steamed and cleaned, draperies to be brushed, furniture to be polished, floors to be scrubbed, preserves to be bottled, meat to be salted, pillows to be stuffed, mattresses to be turned, accounts to be kept, herbs to be dried and distilled, ale to be brewed, glass to be washed, candles to be dipped, carpets to be swept – in fact, all the things to be done that I was not very good at. At home, caring for my stepfather, housekeeping had been a rewarding, if somewhat tedious chore, but all I found here were sluttish and untidy girls, a critical aunt, and a cousin Oliver determined to muddy floors as soon as they were clean and tear off buttons deliberately to provoke and cause work: if all else failed there was always the sly pinch or kick when his parents weren't watching.

Many nights I cried myself to sleep, shivering through a cold winter in the icy garret. Only one thing kept me from despair: as soon as I was eighteen I would leave them all and make my own way in the world. My father's will had stipulated that at that age I was to be allowed to live my own life, with whatever money was left from the legacy; it was certain there would be no money, so I would advertise as companion to an elderly, educated lady or gentleman – I sent myself to sleep some nights composing the advertisement. 'Educated young lady, well-read, with some Latin and a little Greek, daughter of recently deceased schoolmaster, desires position in quiet, respectable household as companion or nursemaid; fond of animals, adept at reading aloud. References.' I ticked off the months as they passed: only two years and six months, five months, four . . . .

Why didn't I rebel, refuse to work as a drudge, demand to be returned to my home? The vicar who had traced my relatives retired soon after and there was nowhere else to go; there was an old bookseller friend of my stepfather's in Gloucester, but who would employ a girl of fifteen in a bookshop? Why didn't I complain of the beatings and slaps? Just because I had never been treated unkindly in my life before and I truly did not know how to protest: I even thought that might be the way the rest of the world lived. I soon learned to knuckle under and make myself as inconspicuous as possible; perhaps another two years and four months of that existence would have driven all adventurousness out of me altogether. I shall never know, for it was one more cross to bear that quixotically released me from thrall: the awakening of cousin Oliver's latent sex urge.

I had been aware for some time that his nips and pinches were becoming embarrassing, but thought this was from sheer ignorance until January, five months after my arrival. One morning I had gone to make the beds: the girls' four-poster took a few minutes, then I went along to Oliver's room. As usual his bed looked as though a couple of dogs had held a running fight in the middle of it and after I had emptied the slops into the bucket and drawn back the curtains, picked up and folded discarded clothes and straightened the mats, I turned my attention to the bed. I was just shaking the feather mattress when a pair of arms came round my waist from behind, hands fumbled at my breasts and an inexpert knee pushed up my skirts from behind. I struggled, but he was far stronger than I and it was only when I threatened to scream that he released me.

I ran up to my attic room and stared at my reflection in the cracked mirror: hair wild, cheeks red, and one shoulder bruised where he had held too hard. What was I to do? Complain to Aunt Sophia? Ten to one she would say it was my fault, that I had led him on. Not for the first time I regretted I had not been born a boy: they had a much easier time, and were not at the mercy of lecherous males – I think it was at that moment that the idea first took shape: I was slim and small enough, no one would think to look for a runaway lad . . . .

From that day I concentrated on two things: firstly, never being alone with Oliver and, secondly, gathering together a complete set of clothes for a boy. Breeches that Oliver had grown out of, a couple of shirts of Uncle Frederick's that my aunt had decided were too worn for anything but dusters, smallclothes made of threadbare sheets, my own serviceable shoes, some pocket handkerchiefs and, greatest find of all, a shabby jacket from Farmer Fielden's scarecrow. This I had had my eye on for some time and very early one morning, in the false dawn, I left the house, ran down the lane and slipped through the hedge to the field of spring wheat: apologizing to the straw man with the mangold face I slipped off the jacket. It had no buttons and a great rent up the side but I sewed and scrounged and soon had the jacket wearable. It had only been rained on a couple of times and, though it wouldn't last for ever, at least it might see me through a couple of months or so. All the clothes I kept hidden under my mattress but I do not believe I imagined I should ever have to use them: I had no illusions that the life of a vagabond, boy or no boy, would be easy. But at least I should be free . . . .

Another two months crawled by and I thought Oliver had repented his earlier indiscretion. Easter was early that year and one day I went out to the stables, where Uncle Frederick's old cob was kept, to look for fresh eggs to colour for egg-rolling on Sunday. It was a bright March day, sunlight full of deceptive warmth as I remember, and the haydust hung in the gold, shifting bars of sunlight that lay across the stalls.

I collected half a dozen eggs, for they laid among the straw near the door, but there was one perverse brown hen that delighted in being different: sometimes she laid in the manger, sometimes behind the sacks of feed, and today she was clucking defiantly from the half-loft above my head. This was nearly empty of hay after the long winter but I cursed her as I lifted out the wooden ladder and clambered up. Another time I might have ignored the old biddy but so far we hadn't enough eggs to go round and she was sure to have hidden at least a couple. I found three and transferred them to my basket, shooing her down to join the others, then decided to have a five-minute rest in the sunshine that slanted so invitingly through the crossbricks in the wall.

Lying back on what remained of the sweet-smelling hay I let my thoughts drift back to the times when I had ridden on the haycart at home, for there was no school on haymaking and harvest days. All hands, even the youngest, were needed to gather in and I remembered lying back among the redolent grasses with the children as the big, slow horses drew us to the barns, picking at the desiccated milkweed and poppy and cracking the pods for the joy of scattering the seed, and tickling one another with the long feathery grassheads –

Oliver had no such delicacy. His idea of tickling was to scrabble with short, bitten nails at my bodice, his weight heavy, his mouth seeking mine like a leech. I awoke to find him pinning me down to the boards of the loft, his breath coming in great grunts, his face red and sweaty. At first I tried to pretend it was all a joke, then I became scared as I realized, from the feel of him through my thin dress, that he meant business. One hand was raising my skirt and fumbling at my thighs and with the other he was unbuttoning his long-fall breeches. With a great effort I twisted away and struggled to my feet but he came after me, breeches half-undone and the source of his lust threateningly visible. His hands tore at my bodice again and his right knee thrust between my legs. I was too terrified even to scream and could only whimper as he pressed his mouth to my ear.

'Not going to hurt you, Zoe,' he muttered. 'Just want a little fun, that's all. Not going to deny a fellow a quick one, are you? You'll enjoy it too, I promise. Open up wide, there's a good girl, and it won't take a minute. I'll treat you nice, buy you some pretty ribbons after . . . .'

All at once a memory flashed across my mind; my stepfather had been talking about Greek wrestlers and comparing them with the village wrestling today and I could hear his dry, dispassionate voice weighing up the similarities: '. . . but of course the basic principles are the same. You use your opponent's weight to throw him off balance and create openings. Give way, if he comes forward, hook your foot behind his ankle or swing your hip across his advancing leg and use his impetus to force a fall . . . .' I went limp and stepped back. Oliver followed me towards the edge of the loft and as one knee attempted to raise my skirts again I swung my thigh across his advancing leg, pulled at the corresponding arm with all my strength and watched him stumble, fall, and then slide slowly over the edge of the loft to land with a thud on the floor beneath, sending the old cob neighing and kicking in the stall behind.

Even as I peered over the edge, fearing that he might have broken his neck, he let out a screech and a howl that would have brought answer from far further afield than Aunt Sophia in the kitchen. In a moment he was surrounded by mother and sisters, all tutting and cooing as he sat and nursed a broken arm. I noticed that his breeches were still undone and that after a startled glance Aunt Sophia covered him with her apron.

'Whatever happened to my darling Oliver? How did my dearest boy get into this terrible state?'

For answer, he pointed with his uninjured hand up to my perch. 'Ask her; oh, ask that slut up there, Mamma! Ask her how she 'ticed me up and then wantonly displayed her evil charms! Ask her, Mamma, dearest Mamma, how she totally unmanned me . . . .' He groaned. 'Oh, my arm, my arm! I fear she has done for me . . . .'

Aunt Sophia stared up, then in a voice which shook with emotion she uttered: 'Come down at *once*!' and pointed commandingly at the steps.

I came, complete with basket of eggs.

She helped Oliver to his feet, her apron still hiding his manly parts. 'And how, my beloved son, did you sustain your grievous fall?'

'I was retreating from her vile temptations, Mamma, trying to preserve my chastity – and you can see how she assaulted me, unbuttoned me – but all the time she came on, her hair unfastened (you do recall, Mamma, what the blessed saint Paul has to say about the snare of a woman's hair) –'

'I do, I do –'

'And her bosom – dare I say it – *bared*! Oh, Mamma! How glad I am you saved me –'

I glanced down at my front. True, the most part of my bosom was exposed, thanks to the ruthless application of his nails, and my hair hung down my back like a curtain, curls a-tangle, but that was all his doing, too. I opened my mouth to explain, but got a ringing box on both ears.

'Take that, you immoral hussy! How dare you exploit your position in this household to try and corrupt and seduce my poor boy?'

'But, Aunt, it wasn't me. He –'

'A harlot's trick to try and blame the innocent! What your poor father will say, I have no idea, Oliver . . . . To think I have harboured this snake in the grass, this viper in my bosom! She has had everything, everything you others have had; I have treated her as one of my own only to have her reward me with this ingratitude, this treachery! Get you to your room, miss, till I decide how to deal with you!' And in a different tone: 'Come inside, Oliver dear, and I shall send to the apothecary for that arm. And Oliver: pray attend to your dress – your poor sisters are not used to sights such as those.'

Poor sisters, as I recall, had been far more interested in the undress than the injury.

I was locked in my room for a week on bread and water, with no one to empty the slops till I tipped them down on Aunt's roses; on the second day of my confinement she came in armed with a pair of scissors, and she had to call for assistance before she was done, but a half-hour later my long hair lay in snips and shears about my feet and I was cut close as a boy. Then I did cry, for the first time, tears of rage and hurt pride, for when I looked in the spotty looking glass I saw the reflection of a half-starved lad . . . . Vainly I waited for the day when they would forget to lock the door but after a week Aunt Sophia came herself to let me out, bearing a list of chores a mile long. Obviously managing without my help in the house for a few days had exposed the deficiency of her own children.

'. . . but do not think you are forgiven, my girl: our dear son has been in constant pain since your assault, and you may be thankful that out of his magnanimity he has decided not to lay complaint against you. Of far greater hurt, of course, was the offence to his chastity, and that will take much longer to heal . . . . Enough of that; your uncle and I have decided that, to protect the innocent and remind yourself of your offence, you shall wear this placard around your neck until we give you permission to remove it.'

The card was about a foot square and bore the word 'HARLOT' in capital letters and red ink.

'But when I go out –'

'You will wear it just the same. What with this and your shorn head no one will be in any doubt as to the kind of slut you have become!'

'I can't wear that! Everyone will laugh and point and I didn't do anything. It was Oliver who –'

I was interrupted by a box on the ears. 'Still unrepentant, I see! Do you wish me to add the word "liar" to the indictment, too? No? Then get downstairs and contrive to try and expiate your crimes in hard work, and be thankful I do not cast you out . . . if it were not for the memory of your poor stepfather . . . .'

And the memory of all the money of mine you have pocketed, I added silently.

'You are to speak to no one, understand? I shall do any communicating necessary: I cannot have my innocent girls contaminated as well, nor can I risk dear Oliver being further corrupted.'

And that was the night I donned breeches and jacket, packed my meagre belongings in two parcels, raided the larder, and Zoe became Zoroaster.

Annie came back with smock and breeches.

'We won't tell him today, dear: he's like a bear with a sore head. Perhaps you can think of something 'time we gets to Chichester.'

Jack ignored my behaviour of the night before, or more likely did not recall it, and to my satisfaction Lucy's van and ours parted company that day and I could get a good night's rest again.

It might be supposed that the fact that Annie shared my secret would be a great relief to me, and indeed it was, but I still saw no tactful way of breaking it to Jack, and every day I left the confession made the eventual telling more difficult. I was afraid all the time that Annie might blurt it out, too, for she was for ever chuckling to herself or giving me a sly dig in the ribs or a knowing wink; luckily Jack was busy at this time accustoming Hannibal to being a warhorse in full trappings and he had little time to notice Annie's behaviour. We were to do excerpts from *Henry V* and Jack was to give the speech before Harfleur mounted on Hannibal and, as a contrast, the scene of the wooing of Princess Katherine with me. It was one of the best things he had arranged and the tin armour looked splendid after it had been polished up a little, though it must have been fearfully hot to wear and heavy for the horse to bear.

The fair proper was held in a field on the outskirts of Chichester but there were some pitches available between the market cross and the cathedral and we were lucky enough to secure one of these for Annie and Sam. Jack, Tom and I went up to the field, and though it meant a lot of running between one and the other for me, usually daytime in the town to catch the shop trade and evening up at the field, the money flowed in and there's nothing like success to take the ache from legs and feet.

On the third day Jack gave me an hour off in the late afternoon and I wandered round the other town stalls, pausing for a moment to watch a bear dance to the tune of a fiddle. Unlike a lot of performing animals he looked well cared for and was extremely tame, for he let his owner's daughter garland him with flowers and lead him on a ribbon. I tossed the child a penny and she flashed a quick bright smile, stroking the bear's thick, dusty fur. In contrast to this a moment later I passed a group of people paying money to throw pebbles at a poor tethered cockerel, doing his vain best to dodge the missiles at the end of a very short tie; I hurried past, for I could not bear wanton cruelty. To be fair, the bird was probably destined for the pot, and the spectators did not see anything wrong in the 'sport', but I just didn't like it: Jack would probably have called me soft.

I slipped for respite from the heat of the day into the cathedral; it was cool and pleasant inside and the people wandering in to sightsee or rest were for the most part quiet and respectful; some, even, had come in to pray, I noticed, but for the most part they gossiped or walked about examing the fine tombs and memorial tablets. I wandered up the right-hand aisle to the altar, said my 'Our Father' and came back down the left aisle pausing, like the others, to admire the tombs. Halfway down I stopped, hardly able to believe my eyes: there, among all the stiff, formal representations, was a sudden touch of humanity – of love. There lay a knight and his lady, stiff, cold, long dead, yet the white stone of their memorial was alive. They lay side by side and the sculptor had carved them with a touch to span the centuries: although he was in full armour and she dressed in her best, yet he had laid aside one mailed glove and reached over to take her hand in comfort and affection. There they lay for all to see, a touching affirmation that there was some goodness, fidelity and beauty in human relationships, after all.

'I'll bet she waited till he was dead and then had that carved to please her vanity,' said Jack, who had wandered in behind me. 'Probably as ugly as sin and amoral as a bitch in season but wanted the world to think her marriage was as perfect as – where are you going?'

But I had to get away before I said something that was not fit for God's ears – or Jack's either. Why did he have to make it all so *cheap*?

He was late coming up to the field that night for our performances so I had time for a wander round the rest of the stalls with the now critical eye that travel with my companions had given me. I saw no sleight of hand to rival Sam's, no fat lady – there was a thin man, as wan and lugubrious a fellow as you could hope to see – and no animal to equal Daisy, although there was a pig who counted in grunts (when prodded with a stick), an acrobatic girl who balanced on sword blades and, best of all, a Punch and Joan show. This was still magic to me and although I knew the puppets were nothing without the hands within they still came to life for me with or without movement, partly I think because of the nasal, vibrating little voices that were just unreal enough to make one uneasy about the reality of the wicked Punch and his stupid wife. Real enough was the dog they called Toby, white with black patches, who sat up on his haunches endearingly, barked when the script called for it, and attacked when ordered. I laughed with the rest when he wobbled on the narrow perch and tumbled off though I was not sure he was meant to, for I heard a thud and a yelp as he crawled under the skirting of the booth.

We managed to get our show completed twice that night before it rained and sent everyone home. I took some mending down to Annie later and we had a nice brew of tea on her small stove and I fetched a couple of pies. We discussed once again how to tell Jack of my true identity, but were no nearer a solution when I set off for the field again, sometime near midnight. I passed the other vans and tents, relieved myself behind a hedge, and was about to cross to our van when I heard a whimper. It came again in the late-night stillness and it was such a sad sound that my natural curiosity got the better of me and I followed it to its source behind the Punch and Joan booth. There sat Toby-dog, all alone in the puddles left by the rain, tethered by a frayed rope to an iron stake driven into the ground, crying a song of loneliness and hunger to the dark.

'Shhh . . .' I whispered. 'You'll wake them all. Are you hungry?'

He stopped his keening and whined a little, shifting the weight of his front paws one to the other. He appeared to be winking at me but when I peered closer I saw the lid was split and bleeding and that the eye was actually weeping. My heart turned over and I knelt down, puddles and all, and lifted his head in my hands.

'Whatever have they done to you, you poor old thing?'

For answer the crooked tail stirred briefly and a tired tongue reached for my nose. Feeling in my pouch I drew out the piece of pie I had been saving for breakfast; he was obviously starving hungry, for now I could see the ribs sticking out through his skin, yet he took the food as gently and carefully as a retriever mouthing an egg. From his owners' van across the way there came the sound of quarrelling: his ears flattened and he whimpered softly again.

'Never mind,' I said, and stroked the blunt head. 'They're too busy arguing with each other tonight to bother you again. Try not to fall off the booth tomorrow: I think it annoys them. I'll bring you something when I can.'

He didn't cry again after that, but when I got to bed I lay awake for a while listening for more rain, glad when it didn't come, and wondering what it was like to be at the mercy of such cruel owners as he appeared to have.

Next day I was too busy to check up on the dog till late, but as I passed the Cross that afternoon I remembered to buy a dubious piece of beef and a rind of cheese and carried them back to the van, hanging them under the door out of sight. We were luckier with the weather that night and got in three full performances, so once more it was near midnight before I was free. I waited till I heard Jack snoring before retrieving the food and slipping across to see the dog, dodging ropes, tent pegs and rubbish in the moonless night. When I found him he was lying on his side and though he wagged his tail briefly he made no attempt to rise. As I tried to lift him to his feet he gave a cry of pain and winced away from my touch on the left side, so I laid him down again and offered him the meat. He licked at it hungrily but seemed unable to chew, so I

166

bit off small pieces for him to swallow – overripe raw beef leaves a horrid taste in one's mouth – and he managed most of it and some of the cheese. I ate the rest, to keep him company, then curled up round him and dozed for a while. He was very cold, though it was a warm night, and snuggled up to the curve of my stomach, resting his chin on my hip. As soon as it started to lighten I had to leave him, however, but promised a visit later that day.

Jack announced that we were leaving early the next morning as there were a couple of Sussex villages he wanted to take in before we began the trail up to London for St Bartholomew's, so we brought Annie and Sam up from the town around four o'clock, then put on a couple of shows, finishing just after dusk. For the next hour I helped pack up and after a supper of bread, cheese, and ale Annie retired for her beauty sleep, Sam went off to pray with his mat, Tom sat and repaired harness, and Jack disappeared to the nearest tavern. Taking a couple of pennies from my store I marched off to the Punch and Joan show and sat through the last two performances, at the end almost crying for poor Toby-dog. He didn't fall off this time but he was obviously favouring his left side, one eye was almost closed and once or twice he missed his cue. When the show closed for the night I hung around inconspicuously until the Punch man appeared to tether the dog, grumbling all the while and giving him a cuff when he didn't follow quickly enough.

'You'd better be more lively tomorrow, my lad,' he growled, 'or I'll slit yer throat soon as look at you. Dogs is picked up easy enough and I allus said as how yer was too damned big 'n clumsy.' He tossed him a crust, aimed a kick for luck, then went off to his van. The dog gave one of those deep inward sighs that seem to belong specially to dogs and children, a shuddering intake of breaths in stages, then lay down on his side. He didn't touch the crust. I crept back to the van to wait for Jack who came back very late, singing happily to himself, and tumbled

167

into bed with a perfunctory 'Goo' nigh' ' and was soon snoring.

A little wind was scurrying across the fair site as I left the van, shuffling paper and waste into little heaps; with a bowl of 'saved' milk I walked quietly towards the dog. I could hear him crying softly to himself now and again and suddenly there was the sound of cursing and swearing, the door of their van burst open and there was a yelp of pain. Dodging behind the booth I saw the Punch man, a stick in his hand, beating down at the dog, cursing and swearing horribly all the while.

'Teach you varmint to keep us awake with your whining – give you something to really yell about,' was the gist of what he said. It took me all my self-control not to rush forward and try and snatch the stick from his hand but I had the sense to realize that that was the worst thing I could have done, for not only would he have probably used the stick on me too, but it would have gone far harder for Toby-dog in the long run. So I stayed quiet, though I had to stuff my knuckles in my mouth to keep from calling out.

Suddenly the stick broke in the man's hand and he cursed. His woman peered from the van.

'What you done to 'im? We needs 'im for the act tomorrow, and looks as if you've finished 'im . . . .'

The man stirred the black and white heap with his toe.

'A bucket of water'll stir 'im in the morning. He's not been worth 'is keep for a while . . . get a smaller dog next time, or else do without.'

I waited till they were both back in the van and I saw the woman blow out the candle, then crept forward and gathered Toby-dog in my arms, stroking his head. Dipping my fingers in the milk I trickled it down his throat till he lifted his head sufficiently to lap it up, all that I hadn't spilled. He was very quiet, but his breathing was harsh and distressed. For a while longer I cuddled him, then caught myself out in a tremendous yawn: we would be moving shortly after sun-up, and this was my third late night.

'Sorry, old fellow,' I whispered. 'We're moving on tomorrow, but perhaps I shall see you again some time. Try and do what they want, and don't get into trouble; and don't cry at night – that makes them cross. Goodbye, and good luck.'

I stood up to go and the dog must have sensed the finality in my voice, for he too struggled to his feet.

'No,' I said. 'You must stay, you can't . . . .' I moved away resolutely but he came to the end of his rope and whined softly, shifting from paw to paw of his front feet as I had seen him do before. I stopped, went back and hugged him, trying to explain. But just how could I tell him I was deserting him to a probable lingering death so that he would understand?

Once again I made as if to go and once again he strained at his tether. Then, as he watched me leave him he gave a queer little cry, a desolate wail so full of pain and loneliness that something snapped inside me. It was all the accumulated pains and lonelinesses I had known myself that answered and recognized his call for help and without thought I was on my knees beside him fumbling with the knots of his leash. In the end I tore a fingernail and had to use my knife, the knife Jack had given me for my birthday. Dog and milk bowl were quite a handful but I managed, and ten minutes later, I had cleared a space amongst the boxes in the stores wagon, between the clothes basket and a sack of flour, and padded the space with an old brown doublet too full of moth for costume.

I lifted up Toby-dog. 'There,' I whispered. 'You lie there, very quiet, and I'll come and see you again as soon as I can. We shall be on the move in a few hours, but you must just keep still if you want to stay. I'll square Jack somehow, I promise.' I sounded more confident than I felt, but I bent forward and kissed the top of his head. 'I'll do my best to keep you . . . .'

*

'He goes,' said Jack briefly. 'And that's that: no arguments.'

They hadn't found him till we camped that night, and then only because Annie had gone for more flour. I had managed to sneak him some breakfast soon after we set off and he had been an angel and kept quiet the rest of the long day's journey; I had hoped to keep him hidden for another twenty-four hours and perhaps if I had been at hand when Annie found him I could have persuaded her to keep quiet. As it was I was humping water, but as soon as I heard her screech I dropped the buckets and came running, for I guessed what had set her off. Picking up Toby-dog I clutched him defensively to my chest, his head on my shoulder; he moaned a little as I clasped him too tight. I backed up against the wagon as they ringed me in: Annie voluble, Sam curious, Tom interested, Jack grim. I felt like a trapped animal myself, my heart beating uncomfortably fast, my hands sweating, but I wasn't going to let them take away my dog, not without a fight.

'Where,' said Jack, 'did he come from?'

I explained as best I could, to my dismay feeling the prickling tears at the back of my eyes; this was one time when I had to be cool, logical, dispassionate and I could see I was going to bawl like a baby instead if I wasn't careful.

'So you stole him?' It wasn't really a question, more a statement, delivered in Jack's flattest, most inarguable tones, but I chose to dispute.

'Not exactly stole – more rescued, really. They were so cruel, beating him, starving him: I couldn't let him stay to die. He wouldn't have lasted more than a couple of days. They even spoke of slitting his throat, of getting a smaller dog –'

'You stole him, Zoroaster,' said Jack again, and by the very quietness of tone and use of my full name I knew he was adamant. 'You stole him, and you know the code we live by. It is impossible to live with other people in this environment if you are going to lie or steal. These are our

170

rules and the rules of all the travelling people, and by these rules he is forfeit. We cannot take him back now, it is too far and his people may have moved on; this has compounded your felony, for it proves that it was not just the impulse of a moment, it was the calculation of someone who hoped he would not be found until it was too late to return him. That was what you hoped, wasn't it?'

'Yes!' I admitted, too upset to lie, and then burst into tears. It didn't help when Toby-dog twisted his head round to lick my cheek in sympathy. 'I knew what you would have said if I had come to you and asked if I could buy him from those people; you would still have said no, and they would have made him too expensive and you're just trying to make excuses now, pretending your answer would have been different, pretending you would have bought him for me if I had behaved more honestly! And your answer would have been just the same, you know it would, and I wouldn't have been able to rescue him then, and I think you are mean and cruel and heartless and I won't part with him, ever, ever! So there!'

Annie tut-tutted and Jack scowled but it was Tom who stepped forward. 'Let me have him, young 'un: like to see what shape he's in.'

'You – you'll not hurt him?'

'No need to ask that. He's been hurt, and I want to see how badly.'

Gently I transferred my dog to Tom, who set him down carefully on the turf and knelt to examine him. He whistled under his breath as he felt the dog all over, paying especial attention to his coat, tail and front paws. Toby-dog stood patiently through it all, obviously recognizing the touch of an expert. Finished, Tom stood up and handed the dog back into my arms.

'Put him back on the wagon for a bit: holding him hurts those ribs of his.' He turned to Jack and spoke matter-of-factly in his soft burr. 'Dog's been starved over some long time. Basically he's English bull terrier, but those black patches are a dye: he's white, with a real black patch over the left eye only. That eye has been split recently by a blow, but it'll heal straight. The tail was broken some time back but the base has set: the top two inches are dead and need docking if he's to stay fit, otherwise he may get gangrene. There are two recently broken ribs on the left side, they need strapping. Worst thing to my mind are the front paws. To make the dog sit up and beg without proper training they've tried all the short cuts: his paws have been scalded and singed and now there are two wicked thorns in the soft parts of the pad: must be agony putting paw to ground. Myself, if I'd come across his owners, I'd've been tempted to hand out some of the same to them.' He paused, and bent forward to stroke the dog's head. 'Basically it's a fine animal about a year and half old with, if I judge aright, a sweet enough temper: wouldn't have lasted more'n a few days longer with the treatment he was getting.'

Facile Annie was in tears to match mine, offering warm bread and milk for the 'poor dumb creature', but Jack was unmoved.

'He goes,' he repeated. 'And that's my last word.'

In vain I pleaded, Annie (now on my side) wheedled; Tom said nothing more, and that surprised me; Sam-Sam just looked bewildered, as well he might.

I turned in protest to Jack. 'You're not going – going to kill him?'

'No, we'll just turn him loose. Dog like that can fend for itself.'

Then Tom spoke. 'Not with those thorns in his pads.'

'Well, get them out then!' said Jack irritably, and stalked off.

Tom and I looked at each other. 'Want to help?' he asked. 'Go get some warm water then, and those two pots of ointment in my van on the top shelf. We'll do it now, afore it gets dark. Annie'll not mind getting the supper on her own for once, will you, m'dear? Get that Sam to give you a hand,' and he winked at me, for never once had

Sam touched what was considered 'woman's work' in all the time he had been with us.

It must have been painful for Toby-dog, but he seemed to realize we were only trying to help and stuck it out with scarce a whimper. We bathed his paws in the warm water first, to soften up the pads, then I held him still while Tom pulled out the thorns with Annie's eyebrow pluckers, put ointment on and bound them tight. The ribs he strapped up with some linen soaked in witch hazel, then he turned his attention to the tail. Feeling it very carefully he found the unhealed break at the tip and, putting on a tourniquet, drew out a sharp knife.

'Now hold him still for thirty seconds: he won't be expecting this 'cos it has been bad for some time and he's used to it . . . .'

I pinned him down, Tom splashed some numbing spirit on the tail, then, as I turned my head away, I heard the knife bite through bone and it took all my time to hold the anguished dog still. In a couple more minutes he had folded skin over the exposed bone, inserted a couple of thread stitches and sewn up the shortened tail, but in that time Toby-dog went quiet, then he started panting and shivering uncontrollably and after a quick look Tom went running for a bowl of milk. He slopped in some brandy from a bottle in his chest, thrust the dog's mouth into it, forced it open and held it there till, unwillingly at first but then more eagerly, Toby-dog had drunk it all.

Tom felt his flanks and listened to his breathing. 'Near lost him altogether then: I should've realized the shock might be too much in his condition. He'll be better for the brandy. Now, wrap him up snug in that horse blanket and put him back on the wagon to rest: should be right as rain in a couple of days.'

I flung my arms round Tom's neck and gave him a quick hug.

'No call to get sentimental,' he mumbled. 'Nice dog. Pity we can't keep him.'

*

Supper was a silent meal. My depression affected Annie, and she handed me a bowl of broth for Toby with a muttered 'at least he won't be thrown out starving'. I took my stew and bread to eat with him and we shared the meat. He managed nearly all and looked much better; one ear was jaunty and he had wrinkled his nose up into a smile when I approached. At first I had thought this was a snarl but it was so obviously a welcome, accompanied as it was by a violent wriggle of the bandaged tail, that when I went back I exclaimed to Tom: 'He laughs just like a person!', then realized Jack was scowling into his plate and shut up. After I had helped Annie clear up I asked her for my money box.

'You're not offering that to Jack just to keep the dog? Wait till we get nearer London and ask if you can buy a nice puppy –'

'I don't *want* a "nice puppy"! I want Toby.'

Jack looked at my offering. 'No go, Sprat. I'm not being bribed.'

'There's near five pounds here –'

'And you'll need it all.'

I returned the box to Annie. 'It's no use,' I said miserably. 'He won't let me keep him. Well, if he throws Toby out, I shall just have to go with him . . . .' And I went for a walk, away from them all, the ridiculous tears spilling down my grubby cheeks.

I walked quite a way up on to downland until way below me I could see cottage windows twinkling with candle or steady with lamplight and our camp fire was a red ember. It was quite dark when I descended, deciding to lift Toby down to relieve himself before I went to bed, but as I approached the wagon I heard voices and saw Tom had done the job for me and was just settling Toby back. I thought the voice had been Tom talking to Toby, but then I heard Jack.

'Certainly been kicked around a bit . . . .'

I shrank back into the shadows.

'People like that should be banned from keeping dogs,'

174

said Tom. 'If I had my way there'd be an Act in that Parliament. I'd fine 'em, myself, and give 'em a taste of their own medicine . . . . However, this one's on the mend now, and it'll be a fine dog in a couple of weeks. Wouldn't be surprised if he didn't know a trick or two to put in an act, and is intelligent enough to learn a few more –'

'I can't forgive the way Sprat stole him.'

'Well now, don't know as how I can defend that myself: still, it's a good child and youngsters should be brought up with animals – teach each other a lot about life, I reckon.' He paused. 'Come to think of it now, I remembers a lad myself as did something of the sort; ten or twelve he'd be, no more, and as I recall it he stood up to a bully much bigger than himself and relieved him of the hound pup he was torturing. And, if my memory serves me right,' he went on in that soft, ruminative way of his, 'that lad's parents praised him for his tender heart and let him keep the dog . . . .'

'Fine gun dog,' said Jack. 'Liver and white, old Bullet was.'

'Yes,' said Tom. ' 'Mazing how fond a lad can become of a dog: 'specially when he don't have no family of his own to spend his affection on . . . .'

There was a short silence, then I heard Jack chuckle.

'Curse and damn you to hell, you conniving old rogue, you!' he said, but there was no malice in the words, only a reluctant admiration. 'And you too, you filthy, decrepit hound!'

At that I walked forward, still not sure he meant no harm to the dog, but when I reached them Jack was stroking Toby's head and he responded by wagging his bound tail.

'Hullo there, Sprat,' said Jack equably. 'I've been thinking. Wrong though you were to steal the dog, I think I can appreciate your motives. I think, also, that it would be cruel to abandon the dog in the condition he is in and if he stays till he's better he would follow us if we tried to leave him behind. Besides, we may find he would fit into an act with Daisy or Sam perhaps. So –' he cleared his throat. 'I've reconsidered my decision: he can stay, provided you are responsible for his good behaviour and he makes himself useful –'

I rushed forward to hug Toby.

'– and that until he earns his keep *you* can pay for his food!'

I watched Jack's retreating back thoughtfully, then stretched out my hand to Tom.

'Thanks.'

He returned my shake formally, then grinned. 'Thought he'd come round. Needed the excuse though; so remember, dog's here for tricks, not for company. Don't think myself he'll want to see another act for quite some time, but in a day or two he'll be one of us and Jack'll think of him just like that.'

I tucked up Toby for the night.

'Tom: that lad you talked about – the one who rescued a dog from a bully – that was Jack, wasn't it?'

He didn't say anything about my eavesdropping. 'Could've been,' he said evasively. 'Then again it could've been someone else.'

'You did know Jack before all this, then?'

'Didn't say so, did I?' He glanced over his shoulder. 'Rain tonight, I reckon. Better put the tarpaulin over the dog.'

He wouldn't say more, but his very evasions set me thinking. I remembered how he had turned up with Hannibal at an obviously prearranged place; how Annie said he minded the horse all winter; how they seemed to have that special master–servant relationship that gave Tom such an insight into the way Jack would behave. Their relationship must go back further than either would admit and if Tom knew Jack as a lad he must know all about his background, where he came from, even who the pretty lady in the miniature was –

176

A drop of rain splashed on my nose, and hurriedly I covered up Toby.

'When you are better you can sleep under the van,' I whispered. 'So hurry up and get well.'

He healed beautifully and it was only four nights later that I arranged a sack under the van, settled him down, and tiptoed up to my pallet, where I lay peacefully listening to him rustling about underneath, getting himself comfortable. There was a pause, then a scrabbling noise, a whimper and a scratching noise at the door. I was out like a shot, after a hasty glance at the dim outline of Jack's recumbent form.

'Go *back*, Toby!' I insisted. 'You're cosy enough under here; you can't come inside, *he* wouldn't like it.'

We played this game three times, and each time I became more afraid Jack would waken. After the third time I tethered Toby to the wheel, giving him plenty of slack, and climbed wearily back to bed, only to shoot bolt upright as a dying wail throbbed under my feet.

'Sprat,' said Jack conversationally in the darkness, though I thought I detected a slight edginess. 'If you don't shut that dog up at once I'll throw a bucket of water over you both . . . .'

'He – he wants to sleep in the van with me,' I faltered.

'It doesn't take an idiot to work that one out.' The howl came again. 'Well, boy, don't just sit there: let him in, and we can all get some peace.'

Toby was already snoring gently alongside when Jack fired his parting shot.

'And if I catch a single flea you can *both* howl all night – outside!'

9

I do not think I shall ever forget my first sight of the sea.

For three days now we had been travelling in the lee of the downs, past sleepy hamlets not worth a performance, noting from lazy caravan steps the heavy wheat nodding its goldening head; hearing the treble clap of pigeons' wings as they rose gorged from their feasting; brushed by bumbling bees heavy-legged with blobs of pollen; watching the pattern scimitared by screaming swifts in a sky drained of blue by a bleaching sun. I couldn't help contrasting all this plenty with what I remembered of our Derbyshire village where summer lingered not so long and the sharper-toothed hills bit rain from any cloud foolish enough to pass too close: our harvests were plentiful enough, but nothing near this rich bounty. Not everything was fully ripe though, and I gave myself stomachache from injudiciously gathered crab apples, in spite of Annie's warning.

We rumbled up the side of a down, wheels jibbing at flints and powdered with chalk, and I lingered behind with Toby, now only limping a little, dirty bandage a-wave from mending tail tip, to inspect the developing hazelnuts in the hedge. We saw Annie waving from the top where the vans had halted, and toiled up to join them.

'Come on, you laggards,' said Jack. 'We'll go on a couple of miles and – why, whatever ails the lad?'

For I had taken one look at what lay ahead, and sat down hard on the ground, my mouth hanging open. It wanted about half an hour of sunset and there before me lay the sea. It stretched from the left as far as I could see right round to the right where an arm of the downs flung itself out into the water; it was misty blue, darker than the sky it reared to meet, with bars and shadows of green and purple, and it was beautiful and fearful, for the whole effect was as if I were sitting at the bottom of some enormous bowl whose sides reached up and threatened to tip over. Half a dozen or so little boats, their sails still lit by a sun I could no longer see, crawled like windblown petals on the shimmering surface and farther out a great brigantine, almost becalmed, headed east in a crowd of canvas.

'Is – is that the sea?' I asked idiotically.

Jack laughed. 'I'd forgotten – you wouldn't know. Tremendous, isn't it? Makes you feel . . . oh, all sorts of things!'

'Fish for breakfast,' said Annie practically. 'Bigger boats than at home, but no shrimps.'

'Herring, mackerel – and sprats,' said Jack wickedly. 'No time to go down tonight, but tomorrow Sprat can go down to Brighthelmstone and join his brothers for a paddle.'

Jack was as good as his word; early next morning, while the dew was still heavy on the grass and the others were packing up, he sent me off towards the little town nestling between hills and sea. We were not giving a performance here. Jack said that though it was 'in season' (whatever that meant), the people were not the type to appreciate our sort of entertainment. Indeed, as I wandered down the cobbled streets and through the narrow winding lanes towards the sea, I saw much new housing being built and many fashionably dressed men and women wandering about aimlessly quizzing each other, and when I heard the formal speech and inanities that were offered, I realized what Jack had meant. Fat ladies, performing ponies, and snatches of Shakespeare would not have interested them a bit. I had Toby with me and he eyed the elegance as suspiciously as I did.

We felt more comfortable when we came in sight of the beach and I saw the fishermen drying and mending their nets, the sea creaming like yards and yards of ribbon lace beyond; I could see fish laid out for sale and housewives bargaining and I fingered the coins Jack had given me;

179

enough for half a dozen of those shining mackerel or more of herring, or perhaps some of the white fish . . . . But Toby had the right idea. Bannered tail a-wave he was on his way to the sea's edge, bouncing a trifle uncomfortably over the pebbles. I followed, telling myself it would be for only a moment; within that moment I was regretting that I was, as usual, barefoot, for in spite of my hardened feet the stones found all the soft places and I stumbled like a drunk towards the water.

The tide was going out, and already there were six feet or so of drying pebbles between me and the water, and tiny crabs, shells, and seaweed. I picked up some of the latter and cracked the glistening blebs between finger and thumb, the smell of the sea which had been present all the time becoming intensified in my receptive nostrils. I crushed more, and then more, my feet taking me ever nearer the water till suddenly there was a splash and a shower of sea and Toby, grinning happily, bandages soaked, was shaking himself all over me. I made a half-hearted grab and he backed into the water, barking invitingly. It was no use resisting: in a moment I was ankle deep in the cool, moving ocean and longing to lie full length in the silky, invigorating water. Splashing my face and arms and getting my breeches and smock soaked in the process, I tasted for the first time the salt of the sea and laughed for pure joy: joy in the sun, the water, the light, the taste, the sheer magic of it all, and Toby laughed too, bouncing and barking and splashing all around me.

We lost all count of time and I waded deeper and deeper till I realized that Toby had lost his hold on terra firma and was dog paddling beside me. I heard the wail of seagulls and the ceaseless lap of water and smelled the tides of the world and completely forgot what I was there for until a stone skipped the surface two inches from my right knee and was followed by another and another, skimming across the smooth sea and disappearing in a flurry of droplets. I looked back – and it was a long way now, nearly two hundred yards – and saw a tall, thin figure, arms akimbo, waiting for us at the edge of the water.

'Oh dear, it's Jack,' I said to Toby, who was still paddling happily. 'He's going to be cross.'

Strangely enough, he wasn't. When we came splashing out, he was lying back on the pebbles, arms behind his head and eyes shut, enjoying the sunshine.

Toby, who had never shown the slightest sign of any fear as far as Jack was concerned, rushed up and licked his nose, and Jack sat up.

'Thought you were about to attempt a Channel crossing. . . . Sorry, Sprat, but we'll see the sea again another day: we've got to move on. I want to get within spitting distance of Ditchling Common before nightfall, and Annie needs those fish I sent you for.'

We dined that night off mackerel, baked in a coating of oatmeal and herbs and garnished with cress, and it was one of the most delicious meals I had ever tasted. Sucking the backbone of the second one I watched Toby scrunch up the head in his strong jaws; he was sick shortly afterwards, but that was because he didn't scrunch hard enough and the bones tickled his throat, and after all that he wanted a second go . . . .

'Did you say you lived by the sea, Annie?'

'Not exactly by, my love, more near; 'bout five or six miles from the river but my brother-in-law lives right nearby, less'n a stone's throw. He's a fisherman off Lytham, does a bit of shrimping as well and times there's a salmon or two further upriver, if he waits while Squire's man is looking t'other way.'

'I like fish, fresh-caught like this, but in most towns it looks all green and smells frightful or else is dried up.'

'It's the distance it's got to travel. I learned as a child to eat nowt but what was fresh, else I got fearful stomachache. Wait till you come and stay and you can eat fresh near every day it ain't rough . . . not that there isn't usually a wind of sorts along that coast.'

I glanced over my shoulder: Jack and Tom were discussing a pipe over by the latter's waggonette and Sam was practising his juggling a distance away. I leaned over to Annie and whispered conspiratorially: 'I've got an idea: about telling Jack I'm a girl, that is.'

She looked at me startled, then smiled. 'Mercy me, I'd forgotten: you've been a lad so long . . . .'

'Yes, but it's getting more difficult every day to keep it up, and especially at certain times of the month – you know. And I'm getting bigger up front.'

She grinned. 'Better not let him catch you stripped, then!'

'That's partly my idea – no, don't look shocked, Annie dear, I don't mean let him come across me with no clothes on at all, but more sort of half-clothed. You know we're rehearsing *Othello* for tomorrow night – no, the night after?'

She was frowning, trying to look as though she understood, but it was obvious Shakespeare was not her strong point. I sighed.

'Well, there's this black man, sort of prince he is –'

'Black like Sam?'

'No, not exactly, a bit darker I think. He wears a turban like Sam, but he doesn't juggle and he has lots of money and is very powerful. He comes from a different country than Sam – I think – but he does speak English and has a beautiful wife called Desdemona –'

'Don't think I'd like that.'

'What?'

'Being married to a black. Children could be half-and-half: white faces and frizzy black hair, or black faces and blond curls . . . . 'Sides, they smells queer.'

'The children?'

'No, silly, the fellows; sort of sharp and musty at the same time.'

'Well this one doesn't, least I don't think so, and it doesn't matter anyhow. The point is, this prince is jealous

182

of his wife, unjustly as it turns out, and in the end he smothers her –'

'Poor lamb!' said Annie, the facile tears ready.

'– and in the extract we're doing, I play the wife. The scene takes place in the bedroom and I'm supposed to lie on the bed asleep until Jack comes in and pretends to kiss me; then he accuses me of adultery, which I deny, but he won't believe me and kills me and then –'

'Better not touch you for real –'

'It's only pretend. Now, I have to wear a night robe, that white satin trailing thing in the clothes basket, and a black wig. It looks pretty terrible and makes me appear exactly like a boy dressed up as a woman. Now I thought, as a surprise for Jack, that if I pretended I was going to wear those clothes but instead we make a proper girl's dress out of that length of muslin that's spare and I let my hair loose – it's growing quite long now – and he sees me like that in the right theatrical setting on the stage, he won't be able to do or say anything at the time –' I still had my reservations about this part '– And afterwards he'll appreciate the drama of the situation. What do you think?'

'Tape is in my chest, scissors too. Fetch the muslin and we'll measure you as soon as I've got these pots away. Serve him right if he sees you for the first time as you really are on the stage in front of a paying audience, and can't do a blind thing about it: beats cockfighting, it really do!'

Ditchling was a pretty little village with its duckpond and winding street. We stopped for ale and sausages at the Bull on the corner of the Brighthelmstone and Lewes roads and afterwards I wandered over to the quaint cottage that was reputed, so they said at the inn, to have belonged to Henry VIII's fourth wife – the smelly one who kept her head. The building was a queer, humped jumble, settling comfortably down upon itself, and I sat on the grass outside and gazed across at the church opposite. Some of the villagers were sunning themselves on benches beneath and it was all very peaceful and soporific. I wondered whether Anne of Cleves had looked at this selfsame scene and I found it difficult to realize that she had lived here over two hundred years ago – nearer two hundred and fifty. It seemed the sort of place where time stood still, where yesterday was the same as today and tomorrow was too far away to worry about. I guessed it would look much the same in another two hundred years . . . .

The dress was ready and though I could only see part of myself in Annie's mirror I knew it was becoming: in fact I hardly recognized myself, and in that dress there was no hint of boy. It clung to my shape like a second skin and though I had not as yet unbound my breasts, Annie had allowed for them and I reckoned it would be a near-perfect fit. She had found a green ribbon for my hair, and brushed loose it curled round my ears and down the nape of my neck very like the man's style that had been adapted by fashionable ladies such as those at Brighthelmstone; with a touch of carmine to my mouth and cheeks I reckoned I would look as near feminine as I was ever likely to do. It was perhaps not so great a transformation as I had had to make when I played Portia to Jack's Shylock, for then I had been a girl masquerading as a boy playing a woman pretending to be a man – a situation that outdid even Shakespeare's fertile pen. Indeed it was a situation I think he would have enjoyed, but he would have made glorious comedy out of it, instead of the quiet laugh I had had to share only with myself at the time.

Toby trotted up with a dead rat in his mouth, caught in someone's stable I supposed, and laid his prize happily at my feet, grinning ingratiatingly. I scrambled to my feet and, picking up the horrid thing by its tail, was about to consign it to Queen Anne's front garden when I glanced down at Toby; he was sitting on his haunches, front paws waving up and down like supplicating hands. This was

184

the first sign he had given of any sort of trick since we had got him and I was so pleased that he seemed to have forgotten the association of performance with pain that he had a big hug and the rest of my sausage.

After that it was easy: every time he did something clever I coupled it with a simple word like 'beg' or 'roll' and gave him a reward. In conjunction with Tom I soon had him friends with Daisy and he even balanced on her back far better than I had ever done – but all that took time and happened later, bit by bit. For now I took him back to Jack and explained what he had done, and earned the not unsurprising remark (for Jack) that he 'knew the animal would be an asset, having such a keen eye for the potentialities of performers' which I had the good sense to accept without argument. At the moment I thought it best to agree with him in everything, especially as the moment for my denouement grew nearer and my stomach felt more and more like dough waiting for its first knead.

We took our vans up the hill and a couple of miles further on to the north, and found the heath already busy with other performers come for the fair. This was one of the few times when a fair was held away from a town, but this pitch was in reach of a number of villages and was always well attended, folk walking up to ten miles to attend. Already there were a number of stalls, booths and tents erected, most unfolding like a ribbon along the narrow road that wound its way over the uneven heath, but it was easy enough to find room to camp. Some acts were already rehearsing and the various pie and liquor stalls were open for business, although, as the fair didn't open till tomorrow, their custom was from other fair-folk like ourselves. Now was the time to ensure we had a good pitch, near enough to water and fuel and the road and as far as possible from any similar acts. After we had unpacked I went off to spy out the land, and though Sam had rivals there was no other fat lady or Shakespearean act as far as I could see and of the performing animals there was none to touch Daisy, apart perhaps from a rather cute pair of performing monkeys dressed in the height of fashion, who drank tea and wheeled another monkey in a baby cart.

Our pitch was between a wirewalker and his family and a wrestling booth, the latter graced by a couple of 'Arabian' dancing girls who enticed an audience with their wriggles between bouts. I imagine the nearest the two girls had been to the East was the pages of a book, for though they were comely enough wenches with long dark hair and deep bosoms their voices held the soft burr of the West Country; however, when dressed up in silks and veils they gave a creditable enough performance and Sam-Sam was lost in admiration, jabbering away in his own tongue, of which they understood even less than we did.

Jack and I spent that last evening before the fair in final rehearsal, not in costume, although he wore his turban 'for authenticity' as he put it. The whole thing was rather a shambles as he had taken more liberties than usual with Shakespeare's scenario, coalescing several scenes into one, and had given the revelation of Iago's perfidy to a discovered letter, so that he could get in his own dying speech. He forgot his lines, I forgot my cues and he became quite cross, accusing me, rightly, of not wanting to play Desdemona in the first place, and wrongly, of trying to sabotage the act in consequence. In the end he stamped off to chat up one of the 'Arabians' and I retired to bed with ringing ears and smarting cheeks, all of which made me long for my acceptance as a girl, for they didn't get their punishments quite so often – or at least not so hard, I hoped.

Unfortunately the dancing girl was either not forthcoming or else too well chaperoned, for Jack returned before I was asleep and insisted that we light a candle and run through our lines again, so that by midnight I wished I had never heard of Desdemona, of Shakespeare and, most of all, of Jack.

Next morning dawned misty and full of dew, promising a fine day, and sure enough by midday the sun was blazing

186

down from a cloudless sky and the ground had dried baking hot. Long before noon the villagers and those from further afield had come tramping or riding across the common, some, Jack said, from as far as Lewes; many had brought food with them and dined alfresco, some saved their money for the sideshows and went hungry, others disappeared into the nearest ale tent, but all were ready to enjoy the day and spend. By four in the afternoon Jack was hoarse and I was little better, for he that had the loudest voice and the tallest tale made the most custom. Annie almost melted in the heat, for it was one of the hottest days of the summer, and her pink satin dress bore great patches of perspiration back, front and under the arms. Sam just looked a little greasier than usual, but Daisy was sticky with the heat and my hands slipped on her mane a couple of times; even so, the money kept rolling in.

We slackened off a little towards five-thirty and Jack decided to rest his voice for *Othello* and gave us all a chance to cool off and have something to eat. Fresh crowds were expected for the evening and we were not to present the Shakespeare till eight, for two performances. It was an extract that lent itself to the night, just as *Richard III* had done, whereas *Henry V* and *The Merchant of Venice* were for the daytime. Whilst, at a pinch, Lear's fool could 'go to bed at noon', it was unlikely that Desdemona would don her night robe before candlelight, so we had Annie and Sam for the hour or so before opening and I spent most of the time setting up the stage, fixing the torches and lanterns, and getting the last-minute jitters till my teeth chattered. I think Jack believed I had genuine stage fright for he actually fished out his brandy flask and tried to make me swallow a mouthful.

Eight o'clock drew near, we stationed Sam out front to perform some of his most dazzling tricks, and Jack, hooded, masked, and cloaked to hide his costume and blackened face, stood ready to step forward and give the introduction, including the events that led up to our extract. Now was the time I should have been changing into the muslin dress, combing out my tied-back hair, transforming myself from boy to girl, but at the last minute I panicked and put on the other costume with the stiffened bodice and hideous black wig.

Annie came up the steps just as I was carmining my mouth.

'Thought you was wearing the other, the one as makes you look as you are?'

'Annie, I can't! I'm scared . . . .'

She put a fat, comfortable arm round my shoulders. 'We're in show business, dearie, and however scared you are the performance goes on –'

Just at that moment I heard Jack's hissed cue and, tumbling out of the van, I slipped on to the stage bed to await the drawing-back of the curtains and the Moor's torchlit entrance.

We got through the extract all right, mainly because Jack was in fine voice and mood, covering up my stumbled deficiencies with an excellent rendering. It wasn't that I didn't know the part that made me falter and hesitate, it was just that I was so confused; boy-girl, Desdemona-Sprat-Zoe – I simply didn't have my mind on the perform-ance at all. As Jack pretended to smother me he muttered into my ear: 'Next time better, or I shall be tempted to forget I'm acting . . . .'

There was only a short interval between performances and I sat in the van miserably listening to the crowds outside applauding Sam's juggling and hearing the sing-song in his own language with which he accompanied himself.

'Which be worse?' came Annie's voice from the door: 'Thinking you was dying by the wayside that time we found you; the first time you had to introduce my act and didn't know your arse from your elbow, or now? Think on, and whilst you are, just take a quick sup of this: it'll do you good,' and she handed me a glass.

Blindly I gulped it down, gasping and choking on the

too-late-discovered neat gin. But it did the trick, either that or her words, for without further thought I flung off the heavy dress and wig, unbound my breasts and held out my hand for the muslin dress. It fitted perfectly, and as I brushed out my hair and twined in the green ribbon a flush-cheeked and quite pretty girl stared back at me excitedly from the cracked and chipped mirror. I needed no more carmine on my mouth or cheeks, they were coloured enough by the effect of the gin so, slipping on a cloak, I crossed my fingers and said a short prayer.

'Wish me luck, Annie!'

Jack barely glanced in my direction, but gestured to the curtained stage. 'Put some life into it this time!'

From the security of the bed I heard him launch into the preamble; the barely covered boards of the mock four-poster were uncomfortably hard and the torches spat and spluttered evil-smelling grease: I hoped I wasn't going to be sick. Above the general noises of the fair I heard an owl hoot and Toby's soft whimper of protest at being tied up during performances; the paste-tasting carmine on my lips mingled with the salt from my perspiring skin; the flaring illuminations sent shadows like pools of black velvet into the farthest corner of the stage –

This was it: Tom drew back the curtains, I lay still and then Jack, turbanned and bejewelled Moor of Venice, strode onstage to accuse his innocent wife of adultery.

As was his custom Jack did not look at me during his speechifying, speaking rather to the audience, as was proper on the stage, and my first lines were spoken from the bed behind him: then came the moment I had been dreading. After he had announced: 'For that thou diest!' I was supposed to jump off the bed and run to his side to supplicate for reason; the line came, I slipped down and walked across the stage.

It was only as I set foot on the boards that I realized that with the flare of the torches set before and behind, my dress was practically transparent.

*

189

It may have been the gin, it may have been sheer desperation, and was probably a combination of both, but once I realized that the only things between me and mother-nakedness were a muslin shift and a pair of drawers, I played Desdemona like she'd never been played before. I heard murmurs from the audience as I came forward, a whistle, a clap of hands, and knew the stage was mine as long as I kept going. Treading small, swaying delicately like the fine ladies I had seen at Brighthelmstone, my eyes wide and innocent, the dress clinging like a second skin, I fluttered to Jack's side, put my hand on his arm and spoke my lines: 'Alas, why gnaw you so at your lower lip . . . ?'

Jack turned, and it was just as well he was looking at me rather than at the audience for never, I swear, did such utter amazement fill a man's face. He gobbled like a turkey cock, his eyes almost started from his head, his jaw fell open and he stepped back as though he had been pricked.

As far as the audience were concerned I knew I could do no wrong, so I changed our lines a little to give him time to adjust. Smiling up at him I said innocently: 'Some bloody passion shakes your very frame . . .' and as I heard Annie's throaty chuckle from the side I added: 'Dear my lord, let me calm your dangerous humours with a fair song I heard but yestere'en,' and straightway launched into the pretty 'Willow Song', fitting the words to a tune I had heard Jack whistle once or twice. My audience gave me spontaneous applause, unexpected and warming, and I acknowledged with a curtsey before turning back to Jack, who now looked grim enough even for the murderous Moor.

'I hope those bloody passions,' said I, thinking to extemporize again, 'they do not point at me?'

But I had given him the correct cue and, like the showman he was, he gave himself a mental shake and followed: 'Peace, be still . . . .'

The scene went on from there the way it should, but as

190

he flung me back on the bed, preparatory to smothering me, with a 'Down, strumpet!' I'll swear he meant it. I spoke my last few lines and he leaned forward with a cushion and said, with real feeling, 'It is too late!' then leaned to my ear and hissed, in quite a different tone of voice: 'Just *wait* till I get you off this stage!'

I squirmed in more than Desdemona panic for his fingers were on my throat and my dying 'Farewell!' came out as an idiotic squeak, drowned in the greater than usual audience participation, for some of the less sophisticated took these excerpts to be true – Jack had been pelted with garbage after one too realistic portrayal of Shylock – and I learned afterwards that some fellow had indeed climbed up on the stage to rescue me and had to be forcibly restrained by Tom from his heroic gesture. As it was, the boos and catcalls I heard in the background were very gratifying and Jack, to vindicate his action as the Moor, was forced to give the last five minutes his full attention.

The applause at the end was deafening and, as I joined Jack for our bows, the comments on my face and figure brought a blush to my cheeks. I risked a peep to the side and saw Annie's face all wreathed with smiles, Sam looking as near puzzled as I had ever seen him, and Tom grinning from ear to ear. Then the curtains came to and I ran, past Jack and off the end of the stage, grabbing my cloak and dodging amongst the booths and stalls, near-tripping a couple of times over feet or ropes, cannoning into elbows, backs, or stomachs.

I ran till I was out of breath and the fairground noises were far behind. Here on the far side of the heath it was still, with just the faintest breeze to move the heavy air, and I stooped to a small pool nearby to bathe my burning cheeks. The grass was pleasantly soft and cool between my bare toes, and I sat down to think out my next move, grateful for a few minutes' peace and quiet before I had to face Jack. Which van should I return to? Annie's would be best, she would be sure to leave it unbolted, for she would reckon, as I did, that it were better to let Jack sleep on it.

Far away I heard a chime from some village church, but I could not be sure of the hour. The lights from the fair were being extinguished one by one and I could hear the revellers returning to their homes, a few shouts, the clop of hooves: it was time to return. I stood up, the big red harvest moon swung from behind a cloud and there, clear in the moonlight, was the figure of a man striding purposefully across the heath towards me. For a moment my heart missed a beat as stories of rapists and murderers flashed across my mind, then it missed another two as I realized it was Jack.

He came to a halt a couple of yards away, and his voice, when it came, was low and even.

'Well? What do I call you now? Zoroaster would seem to be somewhat inapt . . . .'

'Zoe,' I squeaked, stepping back a pace.

'Am I to suppose that is your real name?'

'It – it is. Honest.'

'Honesty has had little consanguinity with you so far.'

'I couldn't tell you.'

'Why not?'

'What use is a girl to you? I can't walk on a wire, balance on my head on a pole, sing and dance, wiggle about like the Arabian girls –'

'You weren't doing so badly at that sort of thing tonight. I've never seen such a disgraceful exhibition!'

I wrapped myself closer in my cloak; he was quite right. I felt hot all over when I remembered just how much of myself I must have been displaying.

'And that tune you used to the "Willow Song" – which it was unpardonable licence to introduce at that point anyway – do you know the common words that are used to that air?'

'I don't think so . . . .'

'I should hope not: it's one of the bawdiest ditties this side of London Bridge –'

192

'It just sounded a pretty tune, that's all; besides, the audience liked it.'

'I'm not surprised! Combined with your near nudity it was probably the most debauching thing they had seen in years!' He sighed, and now came a change of mood. Before he had become mightily sarcastic and sharp as I argued and excused but now he quietened down. 'You'd better tell me all about it from the beginning. And this time, please, no omissions, half-truths or evasions.'

Finding a fallen tree trunk he sat himself down, fumbled for tinderbox and pipe, and when the tobacco was drawing satisfactorily, motioned me forward to stand in front of him.

'I haven't yet made up my mind whether to beat you into insensibility or just rape you, so you'd better be sure I have all the facts. Go on, get on with it.'

So, with the moon for lighting, the heath for backdrop, the errant wind bringing curls of aromatic pipe smoke to my nostrils for effects and the dying sounds of the fair for accompaniment, Jack my sole audience and only critic, I told the story of my life to date as briefly and concisely as I could, omitting nothing I thought relevant and giving him a far fuller story than I had Annie. He was an attentive audience, only briefly interrupting for something to be made clearer, but at the end there was no applause; instead he rose, knocked out his pipe, and stood, silent, before me.

'Have you decided?' I asked tremulously, for the thought of possible punishments had been at the back of my mind all the way through my narrative, and I wasn't at all sure that he hadn't meant every word. My heart was thudding uncomfortably in my chest and my knees wobbled a little, but whether this was from relief that my secret was out or dread of what was to come, I didn't know.

'Decided what?'

'Whether to beat me or – or the other?'

'Is there any reason why I shouldn't do either that you can think of?'

'Well . . . .' Was it my imagination or was his voice

more indulgent, nearer to amusement? I wished I could see his face more clearly. 'Well . . . . You've beaten me before and I didn't like that. You've never raped me, and I understand it's a fate to be avoided, but I think I should prefer it, given the choice. At least then I should know what all the fuss is about –' I took a hasty step backwards as he moved towards me '– but on the other hand you could do a little of each, then I shan't be too sore for work tomorrow . . . .'

'You can't have a little rape, you either are or you aren't, silly lad – lass, sorry. Like being pregnant.' He took the cloak from round my shoulders and dropped it to the ground. 'Let's take a look at what I'm being offered. Hmmm . . . hair's still too short, but you're straight and shapely enough, even if too slim for my taste. How on earth did you hide those?' And, accidentally or not, his hand brushed across my breasts, sending the most extraordinary shock and tingle through my entire body. The feeling started in my nipples, his touch hardening them like cold water, and leapt to a point in my lower belly which contracted as if punched; then a warm flush spread over the whole of the rest of me, from my toes to my eyes, making the former curl and the latter widen: my breasts felt itchy and I had a tickle between my legs. I hadn't the slightest idea what was happening to me: it felt a bit like Annie's gin without the unpleasant taste and the muzziness, but it was exciting and I found I was breathing faster.

'I bound them with linen cloths,' I said gruffly, in answer to his question. 'Otherwise they would have got in the way.'

His hands reached out to my shoulders. 'You still talk like Sprat, yet your body is definitely Zoe: which are you, changeling?' His voice now had a caressing, teasing lilt to it and I sensed that there was to be no beating.

His hands were warm on my bare shoulders and the tingly feeling was still there. I thought at the time that I had had a sudden divine inspiration, but I realized later

194

that what happened next was a question that had to be answered for the sudden girl I had become: I moved forward, stood on tiptoe, leaned against the tall figure in front of me, locked my hands behind his neck and pressed my mouth against his.

For a brief instant he stiffened and seemed about to repulse me, then I could feel him relax into a suppressed tremor of amusement and in a moment his arms went around me tight and his lips returned my kiss very firmly: I could taste the flavour of brandy on his breath.

At first it felt strange having someone's mouth on one's own, then he cuddled me closer and moved his head a little so our noses didn't bump and it was much nicer, so much so that the questing tickly-all-over feeling became a melting-all-over sensation instead and I suddenly became aware of all sorts of things I had only guessed at before. That was the moment when I realized what it meant to be a woman, but I had the sense not to say so at the time.

He raised his head from mine, and now I could see his eyes sparkling. 'I've decided,' he said, and pushing me away his hand came down hard on my rump, so hard I squealed. 'There's your beating.'

'No rape?' I said, as well as I could for the wild beating of my heart.

'Too exhausting; besides, I'm not sure you wouldn't enjoy it, and that's not the object of the exercise. Anyway, you reminded me once that I'm no longer a youngster . . . .' The atmosphere had changed, he was teasing, and my emotions were slow to follow.

'Twenty-eight was not too old for Chloe or the puppeteer's daughter . . . .'

'You have a good memory,' he said shortly. 'And now get to bed before I change my mind. You're too young.'

That stung, and all my new-found importance evaporated like a small puddle in the heat of the sun; but I had to have the last word. 'I'm sixteen!'

'Exactly.' But he must have seen my face, for he grinned quizzically. 'Settle for seduction at seventeen, then?'

'If you're sure you won't be too old and decrepit!' I flung at him, tears of rage and hurt pride stinging my eyes, then ran before he could see them to cry a disappointment I didn't understand into Toby's comforting and uncritical coat.

10

But, after all that, it wasn't so very different being a girl; I think I had expected a drastic overnight change, with me as the centre of attention, but in that I was disappointed.

After another day at Ditchling Heath we packed up, to move by easy stages up to London for St Bartholomew's Fair, the greatest event of the showman's calendar. We chose a route where there would be places to entertain on the way – Jack was never one to miss an opportunity – and we spent the actual travelling time on polishing up our words and our wardrobe, for Jack said we must be altogether the smartest and most effective group attending because the Londoners were quick to spot and reject the second-rate. During the journey we performed all the Shakespeare extracts in turn – yes, I played Desdemona again; no, I wasn't allowed to wear the revealing muslin dress – until Jack had decided which two would be most suitable for the city.

He finally decided on *Richard III* for one, and for this I got a new costume for the prince: pale blue breeches and jacket, white stockings and a white tabard, the latter embroidered with a golden Plantagenet sun. I had to do the embroidery myself for Jack decided that though for most things, including outward appearance, I must stay a lad for the time being, this would not preclude me from occupying myself with all the feminine tasks he could find for me to do. We had an argument about this, for I protested that he was getting two people for the price of one, and wanted an increase in wages; upon this unheard-of presumption he raised his hand to box my ears, I spread an imaginary skirt as a reminder and he thought better of his proposed action, merely remarking coldly that unless I were a hermaphrodite I could not possibly be both boy and girl at once, and that therefore I was being paid correctly. Unless of course, he added nastily, I wished to log my work separately and be paid accordingly, remembering of course that women in general were paid less than men and I could expect a reduction for my feminine duties.

So that was that: as far as Jack was concerned the only difference the disclosure of my sex had made was to decrease the buffets but increase the duties, for never by look, word or deed did he refer again to that strange, stolen moment on the heath when he was Jack and I could have been his Jill: it was as though it had never been. He still called me Sprat, made me dress in boy's clothes and sleep in his van as before, and when Annie suggested it were better that I go in with her he had said irritably: 'I hired a boy and as far as I'm concerned that is what I've got; he – she – looks like a boy and folks would think it very odd to see a lad go to bed in a lady's van, so forget it.' He did, however, as a concession, curtain off a tiny corner of our van for me to change in, but as it was so cramped a midget would have had difficulties I thanked him dutifully and continued to wash and dress when he wasn't around.

There was one other allowance to my feminity; the second Shakespearean extract we were to do was *Henry V* and it was agreed I should have a proper lady's dress for the Princess Katharine. I remembered a crusader's wife on a tomb whose gown looked historical enough – for as Jack would be in armour I could not choose the lax modern way of playing in the latest fashion – so I sketched it for Annie and we sewed it together. It was perfect, bosom and all, so for that part of the proceedings I was a true girl and Jack had the grace to say that I almost looked

197

the part, then spoiled it by remarking that it was only when I stayed still for I 'marched about the stage like a ploughboy . . . .'

The others' reaction to my disclosure varied: Sam, I think, believed I had produced some magic more powerful than his own for he avoided me superstitiously for days, and had he been a Christian I'm sure he would have made signs against the evil eye. Tom, on the other hand, had not seemed in the least surprised at my transformation, apart from remarking that it was about time; when I questioned him he said he had known since the beginning.

'Daisy told me,' he said, with a wink and a tap at the side of his nose. 'But I took it as none of my business: reckoned as how you'd sort yourself out when the time came. I never called you boy, nor lad neither, did I now? 'Twas always youngster, or some such. And I was usually there when you was in trouble a girl couldn't handle.' I remembered the death of the dwarves and the time Jack had nearly beaten me up and it seemed he must have been aware of my true state; but I didn't believe Daisy had told him . . . .

Annie, for her part, was frankly relieved that Jack had taken it so well, for his rage, as she confided to me, that night when he strode off the stage after me had to be seen to be believed, especially when he found I had sought refuge in the obscurity of the heath. She had tried to persuade Tom to organize a rescue party when he had stridden off in search of me, but Tom had reassured her that a tramp round would do Jack's temper no great harm and might even calm him down – 'for if he'd had sense he would have taken the dog along to sniff her out' – and that Jack when faced with a frightened girl in a see-through dress would do no more than give her a good telling-off. 'No rape?' Annie had reportedly worried, but Tom had been sure of this too. 'Master's a gentleman and would never touch a lass without she wanted him to . . . .'

'And I knew you wouldn't, so that was all right!' and she beamed at me. Annie always remembered conversations word for word and repeated them the same way, with lots of 'he saids' and 'so she saids' like cues in a play, but ask her for the gist only and she collapsed like a house of cards and declared that the words had 'flocked away like frittened spugs' and if I didn't interrupt so much the world would be an easier place. 'Don't get your drawers in a twist,' was one of her favourite phrases, 'or you'll find yourself bum-bare in the market-place . . . .'

So I wondered about the words Tom had used in relation to Jack, knowing they had been accurately reported. I had long suspected Jack was not just the travelling showman he pretended to be and that the description 'gentleman' was probably right: I also knew it was useless to probe further in that direction with either Tom or Jack himself. As for never touching a lass 'without she wanted him to' – well, I had set the pace there, and for a moment or two I had thought he . . . . But he hadn't, and whilst one moment I told myself I had had a lucky escape, in the next I was regretting the loss of that tingly melting feeling that had been so unlike anything I had ever known before.

Perhaps, after all, it had been something I had eaten: my stepfather had told me of a mushroom that gave one strange and wonderful dreams . . . . I was a fool!

But it was a relief to think as a girl again . . . .

By the beginning of the second week in September we were approaching London. Gradually the rural communities had been left behind; villages became larger, nearer to each other, and there were an increasing number of comfortable gentlemen's residences within sight of the dusty road. From being the only vans travelling north to the city we became part of an ever increasing cavalcade, not only of entertainers but of travelling salesmen, pedlars, beggars, itinerants of all sorts. As a consequence, although there was a growing sense of urgency amongst all the travellers to gain our objective in time, we were of necessity travelling more slowly each day because of the increase in traffic; on the narrow stretches of road the lighter traffic had to pull off the road to let the heavy coaches and wagons through. To argue over the right of way would have been to waste even more time, but all our travelling companions were not so easily persuaded and we spent one complete morning, hemmed in on both sides by ditch and wood, listening to a farmer with a heavy load of cut logs arguing the toss with a coach full of travellers for Brighthelmstone. The farmer and his lad eventually came to blows with the coachman and the postillion and it would have been a rare fight to watch if we hadn't been conscious all the while of the traffic piling up before and behind. In the end the male coach passengers, a real crowd of Macaronis, left their ladies to the smelling salts and vapours and united to heave the farmer's cart out of the way into the ditch and the coach had proceeded on its way, the gallant gentlemen a little dustier and with their pockets a trifle lighter, if the sight of two disreputable characters arguing over the possession of a pocket book and a fine new watch two minutes later was any indication. We helped to right the wagon, of course, but we left the farmer (bloody nose) and his lad (black eye and bruised knuckles) to retrieve the logs.

Now the weather conspired against us also: everywhere was haste to get in the harvest and we paid our share of shillings largesse to the various harvest lords who importuned from the fields, hats gay with bindweed and late scarlet poppies. It was nippy at night and September gales, a week or so early, were whipping the yellowing leaves from the willows before their time, piling the hollows with the dry whisper of leaves and choking streams with a cargo going sluggish to their deaths. Swifts had gone, but late swallows and house martins still flashed past our noses gathering the insects who sought warmth nearer the ground, and the loudest song was that of the robin, clearing his throat for his winter solos. I stuffed myself with blackberries and dewberries, luxuriating in the burst of each tiny bleb on my palate, and also kept my eye on the ripening apples in each orchard as we passed.

At last the houses outnumbered the trees and all roads led in one direction; the way was firmer under our feet, we suddenly came to mean houses and meaner streets and before I realized it, we were crossing London Bridge. The Tower, of which I had heard so much, could only just be glimpsed as a grey blur through the now falling rain, and the romantic Thames (as I had envisaged it) was merely another grey and swollen river, pitted with rain and full of twigs, branches and other debris, roaring beneath us and tugging furiously at the little boats moored against the steps at either side. Further away downriver were the masts of a couple of fair-sized ships proceeding slowly up towards the bridge and over to our left, up towards Blackfriars, strings of barges were being loaded.

Jack led us through another maze of streets, and late in the afternoon of that first Tuesday in September, 1785, we came to the site of the greatest fair in the world. Once there had been a vast open space but that was now filled to bursting with stalls, vans, wagons, booths and tents, and so were the streets on either side. Horses, dogs, chickens and children were everywhere and it was as though everyone had been to the watch-repairer for a new spring because they all seemed to have a brisker tick and louder voices and before long I, too, found myself caught up in this new fever, till I was both moving and talking quicker.

At first I did not see where we could possibly fit in in all this confusion and clamour, but Jack directed us confidently down a side street called New Lane – though it seemed as old as the rest – and about fifty yards from the entrance, after much pushing and shoving, we came to a rather mean-looking inn, the Fair Prospect. Whatever this latter had been once, now there was none save the outlook of multitudinous chimneypots and sloping roofs, and the sad sign that hung from one staple only was no guide, since the paint on the picture had flaked and faded away to a dull blur. Jack looked momentarily disconcerted and scratched his chin, then he shook his head and led the beginning of our cavalcade through the gateway into the inn courtyard. I say the beginning, for directly our van got halfway through the gate there was nowhere for it to go for the yard was already blocked with two vans and a couple of booths. I tried to back up, but of course by this time Annie's van was too close behind and there we were, well and truly stuck.

Jack then lost his temper right royally and called for mine host with many phrases I was not entirely familiar with, demanding to know what was keeping us from our rightful pitch. The man, a small greasy fellow with side whiskers more luxuriant than the few strands that were plastered across his freckled skull like seaweed, stood wiping his hands on an apron greasier than himself, taking the full force of Jack's anger like a schoolboy awaiting the cane. Apparently, from what I could gather, Jack had bespoken exclusive use of the inn yard in advance this time last year and had paid a retainer of five guineas; unfortunately the previous owner had retired through ill-health some five months past, neglecting to inform the new landlord of the arrangement, so that now the space was let to a sword-swallower, an Italian puppet show and a toy and trinket-seller. An interested crowd gathered round to listen to the argument, none being more interested than ourselves and those in possession, and I must admit to thinking Jack's goose was cooked when the landlord, rather unfairly I thought, asked for a copy of the agreement and the receipt for the money.

We had reckoned without Jack's initiative, however, for with a 'Pah! 'Tis easy found!' he leaped up the van steps, pushed past me and inside, pulling the door almost to. Inside I heard a great rummaging and banging, but peering through the crack of the door I saw him setting out pen and ink on the make-up table and searching for a sheet of paper, the while kicking whatever lay near to produce the sounds of searching, so I was ready when he

roared out: 'Boy! Where did you put my receipts?' to play
the village idiot for all to hear, squeaking: 'I disremember,
Master! Could – could they be beneath the bed, now, or
perhaps in the cupboard? Or even they might be in the
trunk . . . 'tis a long time since I put that one away . . . .'
and all the while I was watching in admiration as he chose
a different pen for a spluttery signature and lighted a
candle for the wax thumbprint, roaring all the while a
thousand curses on my careless head. The admiration
dimmed a little when in looking for something to blot the
ink he could find nothing better suited to his purpose than
my clean shirt, hanging up to air: the linen soaked up the
ink beautifully, I could see that. Finally he folded the
paper, rubbed the outside on the dusty floor and tucked
in a couple of handbills he had had drawn up at one of
the towns we had stayed overnight, then strode out of the
van, aiming a cuff in my direction that left me a-sprawl
on the horse's withers.

'Were I not accursed with incompetents at every turn,'
said he, turning to glare in my direction from his vantage
on the steps of the van, 'such a trifle as this paper would
have been more easily found. As it is, it was most cunningly
hidden amongst these handbills – here, fellow, hand these
few out: 'twill give the customers some idea of the delights
in store for you all tomorrow –' and he handed out the
bills to someone who could obviously not read, for they
were handled upside down; from there they were passed
to another three, and it was only the third who turned
them right way up: I could see Jack marking all this even
while he continued, but the reason did not become clear
till a few minutes later. Then he flourished his agreement
and receipt, on which the ink was barely dry, demanding
his rights. The innkeeper made a snatch at the paper but
Jack was too quick, and dandled it just out of reach.

'Think me a fool? No, we shall have someone impartial
to read this and confirm it as a genuine document . . . .
Here, you!' and he pointed to one of the fellows who had
been unable to read the handbills: 'I can trust a worthy

man such as yourself not to tear or mutilate this precious document, and to tell them all is fair writ within.' He handed the paper to the poor man, right way up this time, and said with an air of confidence: 'Now, tell me, my erudite friend, does that not clearly state that I am to have sole use of this inn yard for my troupe during the period of this year's fair? And is it not signed in that abominable scrawl Simon Rouse always had? And is there not a further receipt for the sum of five guineas witnessed by the authentic thumb seal in the corner? Careful, do not scratch it: this weather has made it somewhat soft . . . .'

The man thus addressed obviously did not know what to say, faced with the (to him) undecipherable scribble, but Jack knew his man. Loath to admit he could not read a word, he pointed with relief at the wax print Jack had described.

'Aye, no mistaking that old print of Simon's: clear as a bell, I'd say . . . .'

'There you are,' said Jack, appealing to the crowd. 'Clear as a bell, my friend here describes that document,' and he clapped the bystander on the shoulder and flicked him a silver coin. 'Honesty and erudition together deserve some reward: have a drink or two on Honest Jack!' And thus encouraged a couple more of the man's cronies came forward to attest to the authenticity of the document and receive enough to join their friend in immediate liquid refreshment.

The innkeeper was still disposed to grumble, for he had not received the original five guineas and feared lest he have to return money to the present occupiers of his yard space, but upon Jack's word that things could be sorted out amicably with room for all, and a swift reminder of the powers of the magistrates to the other stallholders, he was left with a free hand and, to my surprise, had everything rearranged and tidy in a very short while. The yard formed three parts of a square, inn on one side, blank wall opposite, and the stables, at present unoccupied save for the landlord's own nag, facing the gateway in which we were temporarily stuck. Not for long: Jack soon had the other stalls lined up along the blank wall, and by dint of taking the large stable doors off their hinges and knocking out a plank or two, soon had our vans neatly lined up inside, leaving only our stage and Annie's booth outside.

There was still plenty to do: with Tom's help I filled the palliasses with fresh straw and bedded down our horses, conscious of the mucking out there would have to be in the morning. We were all to sleep in the spacious loft above, and after heaving up the bedding, fetching water, shaking out the costumes to free them from wrinkles, carrying plates of stew from the inn, and running the hundred and one errands attendant on a new pitch, I thought I should fall asleep as soon as my head was allowed to touch the pillow of herbs Annie had made for me some weeks back.

Not so: it was my first night under a proper roof for many months and the unaccustomed solid walls and heavy beams stifled me and the straw itched. Besides, although the fair proper would not start till the following day there were so many people crammed into the square and the narrow streets looking for space, quarrelling, fighting, drinking, milling around and, by the sound of it, wenching also, that I couldn't sleep, and telling Toby to stay, I slipped down the ladder and out into the yard. Though most of the drinking customers had gone home by now, there was still a knot of the more seasoned topers by the doorway to the inn, so I slipped past them to the gateway where I found Jack, enjoying a pipe before turning in.

He turned to me with an amused smile. 'Too noisy, Sprat? You'll have to get used to the sounds of a big city . . . . Fancy a quick stroll round before bed? I've a package to deliver, and it might as well be now, while I remember it.' Somewhere a clock chimed the half-hour and he knocked out his pipe and pulled out his pocket watch. 'Bart's says ten-thirty: fast again.' He tapped the watch in its silver case. 'Slow down, old friend: you've never been the same since –' He turned abruptly. 'Well, come on then! I daresay that iron stomach of yours can stand a beef sausage or some oysters?'

'Sausage, please! But . . . I thought they weren't open yet?'

'The proclamation will be read tomorrow at noon, but meanwhile folks must eat. Sniff hard: go on . . . .'

And indeed I could smell the most enticing aromas borne on the nightwind that sidled down the street: pease porridge, if I were not mistaken, pies, gingerbread – all the more tempting because they overlaid the stench of the open ditch that ran down the middle of New Lane. We picked our way along the edge, dodging the shadows that moved and blurred and shifted and suddenly were people, begging, stumbling drunk, embracing and importuning. One thin girl in a tattered muslin dress stepped forward and plucked at Jack's sleeve.

'Only a shilling, kind sir, and I'm clean –'

He flung up his arm as though to strike her, then, as she stepped back with a curse that rang in my ears, he felt in his pocket and threw her a coin. I watched her stoop for the silver coin in the gutter – more than she had asked for – and in the light of a passing torch that wavered and dipped in the unsteady hand that held it I saw the tattered and holed stockings, the muddied ankles and then the crooked and discoloured teeth that bit automatically at the coin before she became again just one more shadow. Dreadful as was her profession, I could not help a pang of pity: she could have been no older than I and yet –

'Come *on*!' said Jack roughly, 'or I shall send you back to bed,' and I had to hurry to keep up with him. The lane twisted right, then left, and of a sudden we were in the great square that comprised the fair proper. Late though it was it seemed light as day with all the candles and tallow dips and horn lanterns that spluttered, swung, dipped, and fizzled in the hands that were still busy erecting stalls, unpacking baggage, setting up booths; the air was full of shouting, swearing, hammering, and the running round of folk like imps from hell; the air redolent with the smells of beef sausage, the smoke of fires, and the boiling of black puddings, all of which mingled more or less agreeably with the smells of wax, grease, sweat, dung, and musty, hastily unpacked costumes.

Jack stopped at a nearby stall and a moment later I was juggling with a couple of sizzling sausages which he tossed me from a spitting pan. They were bursting with fat and meat and herbs and as I bit hungrily through the thick skin I burned my tongue and hopped from foot to foot, both hands and mouth greased and smarting. Jack pulled out a none too clean handkerchief from his coat-tail pocket.

'Wipe your mouth,' and if I recognized the cloth he had used to dust his boots earlier, the last few months had taught me not to be too fussy, and I was soon more or less respectable.

Following his tall figure I noted that the stalls with goods on them were mostly arranged in straight lines fronting the tall houses round the square, the booths for amusements and exhibits backing on to them, and the space in the middle, which looked as though it were normally used for cattle or sheep pens, was reserved for the stalls for food, tables and benches for eating, ale barrels and animals. Folk were still moving in; latecomers scrabbling for a foot or two of space, carts and vans optimistically waiting to be jammed into corners patently too small. Avoiding the chaos we walked along the stalls fronting the tightly shuttered houses – shutters, Jack told me, that would remain in place till the fair was over, for safety's sake – and here, well hidden from the constables, one or two of the stalls were open already. One, a gingerbread stall, could, I suppose, have been classed as food, and I eyed with admiration, not unmixed with anticipation, the little men, pigs, and dogs with currant eyes, houses with candied peel doors and windows, moon, sun, and stars; on a stall further down a man was setting out toys: hand puppets, lead soldiers, dolls; wheeled animals made to nod their heads or wag their tails by means of string or lever; wooden horses with bright saddles, some painted, some stitched; hoops, tops, balls, cricket bats, cards, dice, chessmen, backgammon sets, miniature cups and saucers and dishes, tiny doll's cradles and rocking chairs; and trinket boxes.

'Stop yearning, baby!' said Jack's amused voice behind me. 'Time for dolls is past. You're grown now and must put away childish things . . . .'

'It wasn't the dolls: those trinket boxes . . . .'

'And what have you got worth a trinket box?'

'Nothing really, I suppose: the knife you gave me, those shells from Brighthelmstone beach, that blue embroidered ribbon I bought, the old silver coin Toby dug up, the stone with a hole in it I found in Dorset, the –'

'All right, all right!' interrupted Jack. 'I'm convinced. Here, you!' he addressed the stallholder. 'Any chance of a sale?'

The man glanced swiftly up and down the aisle of stalls and nodded.

'Well then: how much for . . . this one?' and he held up a walnut box, heavily inlaid with a lighter pattern of vine leaves.

'I can see you have a keen eye for the best, sir! Finest piece on the stall, that one: inlaid with –'

'Finest means most expensive,' said Jack, interrupting. 'So we'll have another look. Now . . . how much for this one?' and he held up a plain box, long and narrow, unvarnished and with one corner chipped.

'That one? That's too plain for the likes of you, and a little damaged, though the lock is good. Now, if I could suggest –'

'We'll take this one, 'tis good enough for the lad. Just a box to keep his trifles in, nothing too ornate. How much?'

'One shilling and sixpence. That box I bought off a sailor who –'

'One shilling.'

'Now look here –'

208

'Second-hand, and chipped into the bargain. Not really worth more than sixpence –' and he turned away.

'One shilling it is then, but –'

Jack tucked the box under my arm, flicked across a coin and carried on his way, whistling.

'Thank – thank you,' I said, in truth a little disappointed, for the box was the plainest and cheapest-looking on the stall.

'Sprat,' said Jack. 'You will learn one day that I have an unbeatable eye for a bargain. Keep that box tight shut and don't open it till tomorrow when the sun is high and the wood warm.'

'Is there something inside?'

'The perfume of Cathay, that is all, but that in itself is enough to make it worth more than all the other rubbish he has on the stall.'

I looked at the box suspiciously, but decided to take him at his word and tucked it back under my arm. We moved down the second side of the square, and Jack seemed to be looking for something or someone. Suddenly, so quick I almost lost him, he ducked beneath the canvas flap of a booth painted all over with the signs of the zodiac in silver and gold and, hitting my head painfully on the pole that flanked one side of the opening, I followed.

Once inside I blinked, for it seemed dark after the bright lights outside, then as my eyes became accustomed to the gloom I saw we were in a round tent, with another exit at the back. The roof was painted with silver stars on a blue background, adding to the dimness, and round the wall were pinned yellowed and fading posters. I moved closer to one, and in the light from a flickering candle set on a round table at the back I saw that the posters advertised one Katina Petulengro, 'the only true Romany Prophetess' who could 'divine past, present and future, read hands, the crystal or the stars, cut the cards to advantage' and had apparently foretold the future of half the crowned heads of Europe, having learned the art from her ancestors, who had 'partaken of the wisdom of the East' long before history was written down for us lesser mortals. Beneath our feet was straw matting but by the table lay a faded pink and blue carpet, with a key-pattern black border and a yellow bird taking off in the middle. There was a smell of some heavy, sweet, powdery perfume and indeed on the table, beside the candlestick, a couple of twisted paper spills were smouldering quietly in an empty bottle, the scented smoke wreathing up lazily and dissipating into a haze before it had reached more than a foot or so in the air. Also on the table was a well-thumbed jumble of cards, and I recognized a tarot pack.

Jack pulled aside the flap at the back, which seemed to lead into a smaller tent. 'Come on out, Kat; don't keep the customers waiting!'

'Well you know 'tis against the law to deal in aught but food and drink before tomorrow noon,' grumbled a creaky voice. 'And my name is Madame Katina . . .' and a tall woman, near six feet, bony and a little stooped, pushed past into the main tent. She straightened up and I saw the hawk nose, grim chin, thick dark eyebrows and deepset eyes and the white hair that hung plaited on either side of her face as she held up another candle to survey us. Of a sudden her thin mouth broke into a wide smile and, setting the second candle on the table beside its fellow, she reached to tap Jack with her fist, none too lightly, on his cheek. 'If I'd known it was you, graceless rogue, I'd've – Did you bring it?'

'Now would I dare come if I had not?' and reaching into one of his inner pockets he drew forth a small, square package. Her thin brown hand darted out as quick as a cat's paw, but he held the package out of reach, laughing. 'Not so fast: don't I even get a kiss from my old friend?'

'Not so much of the old . . .' but she seemed pleased enough to reach up, though not so far because of her height, and salute him heartily on both cheeks; then she tore greedily at the package like a small child and a

moment later was sneezing fit to burst as she sniffed at
the snuff on the back of her hand.

'Steady, that's the best Dutch –'

' 'Twill do, 'twill do!' she said with satisfaction and
tucked the package away somewhere in the capacious folds
of the red cloak she wore. 'Now sit you down and tell me
what's happened since last I saw you – when was it?'

'Goose Fair?'

'That's it, that's it . . . I told you to sit down, you give
me a crick in the neck a-staring up at you – what's that
you got with you?' She had suddenly noticed me.

'Travelling companion,' said Jack easily. 'Goes by the
name of Sprat.'

The old woman indicated a couple of stools and sat
down herself, producing a bottle of brandy and a couple
of horn cups from somewhere in the magic cloak. She
poured for Jack and herself, then gave me a sharp glance.

'Too strong for you, whatever you are.' She touched
Jack's cup with hers. 'Here's to your lying tongue and
knavish tricks, my lad!'

'And yours,' he said equably, drank, and set down the
empty cup. 'How's Nance?'

Madame Katina spat. 'Don't mention that hussy to me!
If'n that's why you came you've wasted your journey: ran
off, didn't she, with some tinker johnny at Pinner Fair,
and me spending two years trying to teach the little cat
the trade . . . .'

He shrugged. 'Maybe her talents lay elsewhere than in
reading the future. Pity – she was a bonny lass.'

'And as easy to read as a marked deck. She kept her
ace between her legs, not up her sleeve.' She stared into
the gloom beyond Jack's shoulder, filling his glass by
instinct as she did so. 'Aye, but 'twas not the ace of
diamonds as she could have made it; nay, rather to her it
will be the ace of spades, for to dig herself a pretty pit to
lie in . . . .' She poured herself another brandy, then turned
sharply, and her black eyes bored into mine. 'Want your
fortune told, then?'

Taken by surprise I could only splutter and gaze for inspiration at Jack, who was no help at all.

'I – have no – I don't – I've never –'

'No use asking him, he won't say yea or nay. Afraid to commit himself –'

'Rubbish!'

'– and as for silver,' she continued, as if he had not spoken, 'this one's free.'

'Not worth paying for anyway –'

'You're just afraid you'll hear –'

'As I've told you before, I know –'

' "– my past, am living the present and leave the future to heaven, or whatever gods there be," ' she finished. Obviously this conversation had been held before.

Jack scowled, folded his arms across his chest, tilted his stool back dangerously on one leg and stared at the ceiling. 'Go ahead, if you believe in all this superstitious rubbish!'

'I think I have an open mind,' I said carefully. 'After all, the Greeks consulted their oracles, the Romans examined entrails, ancient tribes studied the throw of dry bones, in the East I believe there are sand-readers, and within most of us there is a longing to pull aside the curtain that hides our destiny, whether we admit to it or not. As to whether I believe it can be done . . . . I do not know, but I should like to try, I think.'

There was a silence.

'Travelling companion!' snorted Madame Petulengro. 'If your nose weren't so long and contrary, Jackanapes, you might see clearer what lies beneath . . . . As it is . . . . Draw nearer, you that go by the name of a fish.'

I pulled my stool up to the table and for a moment she stared at me, then laughed. 'Not what you seem, are you?'

I blushed and hung my head, wondering how she had penetrated my disguise.

She read my thoughts. 'Katina has lived long enough to see what lies beneath. Now, give me your hand – no, not the left, that's what you're born with: the right is what you make of it. Not that you've had much time to make anything of your life yet, but you're on the way . . . .' She bent over my palm, cupping it in one hand, smoothing at the lines with her other thumb; her hands were dry and warm. 'Interesting . . . . Now, before I tell you a future you can scoff at if you wish – marriage, children, money, your heart's desire, so that you go away believing I tell them all the same – shall I tell you some of the past, to show you I know a little, at least, of my trade?'

I nodded. The perfumed spills, the flickering candles, the old woman's voice, the smooth rubbing of her thumb over my flesh, the muted dark were all contributing to an acceptance of anything she asked, anything she said.

She jerked her head at Jack. 'What I'll say will have meaning to you, not to him . . . . A troubled womb, a father yet not a father; an aunt not an aunt; a disguise for the world; an awakening even you don't as yet realize . . . . Am I right?'

She knew she was, even though I didn't quite understand the last part.

'Ah, my little one, born under the twins of the sky, with water and earth colours in your eyes and hands that do not know whether to grasp with left or right and a body that wants to be one, yet tries to be the other . . . .'

Behind me I heard Jack's stool right itself and sensed him lean forward, interested in spite of himself.

'She's right, you know, Sprat. You write right-handed and catch left, sew upside down and hold cards back to front.'

I had never thought about it till now and half-embarrassed, tried to pull my hand away.

'Nay, Jack, disbeliever, don't spoil it . . . . Leave your hand where it is, child: this is not meant to hurt but help, and I must confess you have stirred me into speech without thought, and that is good. So, 'tis likely you'll get at least a measure of the truth . . . .' She peered at my hand. 'No wonder! You have the gift too – see, those curves on the Mount of the Moon?'

'The what?'

213

'Mount of the Moon, there on the outside edge of the palm, near the wrist –'

'But how can you tell?'

'All the lines, the mounts, the very shape of the hand tell me!'

'But aren't all hands the same? They've all got lines –'

'Not the same, stupid! Here, Jack o' my heart, give me your right hand, just to show your treasure how I practise my craft . . . .'

'No foretelling . . . .'

'No,' she said impatiently. 'Just to show your little fish I speak truth . . . . There!' She pulled Jack's hand towards her and turned it palm down on the table, then matched my own. 'Now, tell me what you see.'

I glanced at our two hands lying on the table. I had never noticed the shape of Jack's hands before: whereas my hand was small, almond-shaped with smooth knuckles, his –

'Well?'

'His hand is bigger, of course,' I began hesitantly.

'Go on.'

'My knuckle joints are one with my fingers, his are knobbled; his fingers are proportionately longer than mine, and the thumb and little finger lie naturally spaced further away from the others. My hand lies quiet, while his . . . .' I hesitated.

'Jumps like the fish he miscalls you. Good. Now, turn your hand over; yours too, Jack. Look at the lines: 'tis true they are similar, but not the same.' She touched our palms alternately with an index finger. 'There are the life lines, both long but at the beginning yours joins the head line – there – and his always remains independent. Both your head lines are good and straight – if they dipped too much at the outer edge, you would have a potential suicide, and if they're too short there's no brains . . . . That's the money line there: he's more than you. There are more fratchety lines on his hands: means he's more highly strung –'

'Rubbish,' cut in Jack, interested in spite of himself. 'It merely means I clench and unclench my fist more often, fidget –'

'Exactly!' She beamed at him as at a clever child. 'And why do you do this? Just because, being the person you are, you live on your nerves.'

'I see,' I said, becoming interested myself. 'So, a person having a hand with few lines, and those short, would be thick of wits and short-lived?'

'That would be a beginning: you would have to look at the texture of the skin, too, and if the hand were hard and calloused you would surmise a manual labourer –'

'And a woman's hand with soft palm, many small lines and a droop at the end of the head line would mean a nervous, highly strung lady with a death wish and enough money to employ a servant to do the rough work?'

'You're learning, but there is also the shape of the hands, the colour of the nails, the way the hand is held . . . . Open your hands, palm up, both of you, and look again, child.'

'Jack's hand is more open than mine and his thumb is curved back: his little finger is crooked, too –'

'That's what makes him a good talker: gift of the gab and master of the silver, deceiving tongue. Your fingers are closer: you can keep your own counsel. What about the length of the fingers, one to other?'

'His first finger is thicker than the rest and nearly as long as the second.'

'Lord and master, or else! But you've got to look at the mounts, too, the fleshy bits under the fingers and thumb and the outer edge of the palm. See how your hand is padded? Courage, that. You've both got loving hearts: Mount of Venus. Beware the man, or woman, whose hand is flat there: they'll be cold as death. My word! How strange –'

I think we both leaned forward anxiously. I know I did.

'Both of you have the Girdle of Venus; there, running

215

in a loop across the mounts of Apollo and Saturn. Unusual to find two in one day . . . .'

'And what do they mean,' I queried hopefully.

'Can mean good or bad: heightens the sum of the other lines. I've seen that loop on the hands of a brilliant actress and a general: I've also seen the same borne by a prostitute and a murderer.'

This didn't sound too good, so I looked for another line. 'This one, then?'

'Heart line. Line straight, head rules heart: line curved up to first finger, heart rules head.'

Mine curved up: Jack had turned his palm away.

'Depends, too, on the thickness of the line, whether it's double or single; islands, radiating lines . . . . Your line, child, is clear and deep, with two tiny islands: one true love for you, and a couple of *affaires*. As for this rogue –' she pinned his hand '– part of a double line, feathers in all directions . . . 'tis lucky for you, my lad, that it shows a good finish, or else . . . .'

He was looking so forbidding that I tried to change the subject.

'And do you tell your customers exactly what you can see? I mean, would you tell a man he was to commit murder, or someone else that they could die next week?'

'Of course not! We tellers gain the reputation for untruth just because we avoid that very thing. If a young and handsome soldier came to me with his buttons all polished and a pretty wife a-hanging on his arm, do you think I could spoil their bright smiles by telling her she'd be widowed within the year? Besides which, the future is not immutable: we make our own, and what I see in the hand, the cards, or the crystal is merely an indication of how that person will most *likely* behave: it doesn't mean that one cannot change one's fate by changing oneself.' She smiled at me. 'Like me to give you a word or two of advice on your future?'

The outside of me, disturbed enough by what she had already said, wanted to say a prim 'No, thank you'. The

216

next layer said: 'Go on – it can't do any harm, it's only a bit of fun, in spite of what she says.' Beneath that, a little warning voice whispered that it was dangerous to meddle with the unknown, and that it would be better not to know. Overall was indecision and the knowledge of Jack's disapproval, but she took advantage of my hesitation and imprisoned my hand; I noticed she still had her other hand on Jack's wrist.

She closed her eyes, breathed deeply, and her voice, which before had been animated, took on a deeper, more monotonous tone.

'The way ahead is clear for a while, little wanderer, then comes an awakening and a decision; I can only warn you not to flee your love, for 'twill be difficult to find once again, and between lie hunger and cold and a hundred paths to lead you astray. If you regain your love it will keep you in silks and swans and sweetness to the end of your days. A woman will betray you in blood and another will try to sunder you, but fire will cleanse and make a new beginning. Beware a second flight . . . .' Her grip on my hand loosened a little, but she was still speaking, and I knew this was for Jack. 'Knave of hearts, your queen is not where you look for her: you have the wrong suit. By the wayside you gather more than you bargain for and that which is taken is given back a thousandfold. You, too, are always running away, but with you it is no accident. You will find, when you can run no further, that all will be destroyed and yet can be rebuilt. Forgive, and thrice times forgive, before you regret all your life and Jack o' Lantern is indeed rejected by hell and made to wander for ever lighted only by his own –'

She got no further for Jack had snatched away his hand and sprung to his feet, overturning the stool.

'I said I wouldn't listen to your rubbish, and I meant it! Come, Sprat, if you're not abed soon you'll not be up at cockcrow, as I intend,' and he grabbed me by the scruff of the neck and pushed me towards the entrance, adding stiffly over his shoulder to Madame Petulengro: 'Thank you for explaining your tricks to the lad. I'll bring more snuff next year if I remember.'

'Yes, thank you,' I squeaked, half-throttled by the grip on my collar and wondering, if I couldn't make head or tail of my future, why on earth Jack was so angry about his. 'It was very interesting and – and helpful.'

'Remember it then,' came her voice behind me, 'and keep your heads – and your hearts – for the right ones. I spoke truth for both of you for I guided not my tongue, and the strength has gone from me . . . .'

Jack refused to speak a word on the way back to the inn, and for me some of the joy of the fair had dimmed, together with its lights.

11

'The Right Honourable Mayor . . . charge and command . . . all manner of persons . . . keep the peace of our Sovereign Lord the King. No congregation, conventicles or affrays . . . imprisonment and fine . . . . Sellers of wine, ale or beer sell by measures . . . bread . . . good and wholesome . . . true weights and measures . . . .'

It was very difficult to hear the proclamation, perched precariously as I was on the top strut of a swingboat that wobbled dangerously beneath me, half the width of the square from the speaker. The crowd between were anything but quiet, and a wag who had apparently heard it all before was repeating the words, sometimes before, sometimes after, but seldom with the clerk who was reading the Mayor's speech. The whole thing sounded like a long list of dos and don'ts and I caught myself out in a yawn; that would never do, for there was a long day ahead of us, twice as long as had gone before.

Jack had kept his promise to wake us early and I had unstuck gummy lids to St Bartholomew's striking six and a bucket had been thrust in my hand with instructions to fill it as many times as it took to water the horses, fill the cook pot, scrub clean the cobbles round Annie's booth and our stage, fetch Jack's washing water and anyone else's who wanted it, rinse out a couple of shirts and have enough left to wash Annie's pans and her chamber pot: all these in no particular order and I think if I had spent till Michaelmas working out my priorities I should have still ended up as I did this morning, in everyone's way, either too late or too early and anyway spilling more than I fetched to its destination.

I don't remember any breakfast but I suppose we had some, and the next thing I recall was Jack insisting on trying out yet one more idea for his Henry V speech. Unfortunately he had noticed, amongst other things, the large window through which hay had once been off-loaded from the top of wagons in the inn's more prosperous days, and two long ladders lying inside the loft, so that now, God help us, we were going to storm the walls of Harfleur, or whatever the wretched stables had become, as a climax to the 'God for Harry, England and St George' bit. Sam and I, wrapped in cloaks (mine to cover my Princess Katharine costume), had to try and keep the English hordes, consisting of Tom, the puppeteer, and the sword-swallower (whose swords they clenched fearsomely between their teeth) at bay with pitchforks without (a) hurting them, pushing them off the ladders, dropping things on Jack or Hannibal, breaking anything or (b) falling out of the window or injuring ourselves irrevocably and nastily on the real weapons we were using or facing. (Actually we didn't repeat this performance after the first day because the sword-swallower cut his tongue on his sword, but it was interesting whilst it lasted.) I wondered at the time how Jack had persuaded the other stallholders to join in this masquerade, but I soon found out. After the shambles of the rehearsals he had led me to the end of the lane away from the square and handed me some freshly printed handbills.

'In between performances and in your spare time in the mornings I want you to stand at the end of New Lane, here, and distribute these, drawing everyone's attention to the fact that the best entertainment the fair has to offer is in the yard of the Fair Prospect, just a step down the way. Sam will be outside the yard with more leaflets and his juggling, and between you we should get a good proportion of customers before they reach the fair proper. There are only four ways into the square, and of those Cloth Yard and Cow Lane are not as well used as this and Giltspur Street and we can't be in all four places at once. I should have preferred Giltspur but knew of no certain pitch and the square itself is impossible. It's ten-thirty now and the square will be filling up soon, so get rid of these leaflets and be back in an hour or you'll be late for the proclamation.'

It was only when I had distributed some half-dozen of the yellow bills that I decided to take a look at what we were offering. The Great Jack, I learned, widely travelled throughout the Continents of Europe and the Americas, had brought back with him the best of both the Old World and the New, for the delight of all. 'From Europe the flaxen-haired Dutch Beauty reared on nothing but cream till she has become the Fattest Lady in Five Continents . . . .' He must mean Annie: I hope he told her to keep her mouth shut. 'Adults one shilling, children sixpence –' our prices had doubled '– and for those privileged to take a closer examination, ladies two shillings, gentlemen three shillings' which meant, presumably, that Annie would be 'airing the dairy' again. 'From the fabulous Indies the greatest conjuror of all time, a Prince in his own country' captured by pirates and rescued by Jack himself on his 'famed stallion in the wilds of . . . (smudged)!' It should have read Marlborough, but I swear the word looked more like 'Madagascar'. 'Collections taken during performances.' It was lucky for poor Sam he could not understand our language. From the Americas, I learned, we had 'on a once-only visit, the most Intelligent

220

Pony in the World' who would 'count, dance and act in a play three times daily, accompanied by his inseparable companion Sirius, the Wonder Dog!' Poor Toby! 'Collection during performances.' As an afterthought, some privileged youngsters would be allowed to ride a few yards on this peerless creature, at sixpence a time; Daisy was another who could not deny her fabled origins.

And so it went on: our sword-swallower, it seemed, was a white African and the puppeteer an Italian (this last being probably the only truth, so far). But the largest space on the bill was reserved for Jack's own performances: famed actor that he was, he was deigning to lend a touch of the classical to the proceedings and would show 'the Bloody Siege of Harfleur and the subsequent conquest of the French Princess Katharine' twice daily, and, evenings only, 'the Fall and Demise of the Wretched Richard Crooked-Back' all in full costume and with special effects, aided by 'the Famed Shakespearean Boy-Actor from Greece, Master Zoroaster, who spoke English as though it were his mother tongue. Two shillings and sixpence per performance, children one shilling.' And at the bottom: 'Hot pies. Cold ham. Ale. Spirits.'

I couldn't help grinning with reluctant admiration at Jack's colossal nerve and my smile must have been infectious for I found the passers-by were smiling too as they took one of the printed sheets – but perhaps that was because for them it was to be a holiday, unlike poor 'Master Zoroaster'.

Now that selfsame famed boy-actor was clinging to the top of a precarious pole trying to hear the words of a proclamation that would mean more hard work for him than he could remember, for the next three days at any rate. The square had already been full when Jack and I had pushed our way through the crowd at the end of New Lane, but I was an adept wriggler and Jack was an expert bottom-pincher, and taking advantage of the general good humour he had secured a reasonable station for himself and had given me a leg up to my present perch, where at least I could see, if not hear, all. Precisely at twelve noon, as the last chime died away, over in the far corner at Clothyard appeared the great gold coach of the Lord Mayor, who had descended in all his purple finery, wigged and hatted, and taken his stance on a small temporary platform to hear his clerk read the proclamation, ranged about by the Chief Constable and his assistants. These were the men who would collect dues from all exhibiting or trading and would conduct the Pie-Powder Court, where any grievances from the fair-people or their customers – unfair trading, false representation, harassment and suchlike – would be heard.

'Pie-Powder?' I had questioned.

'*Pieds-Poudres*, Sprat: dusty feet. Us. From the French,' explained Jack. I wiggled my hardened toes and remembered the chalk dust of the downs and the clay powder of the vales and realized what a very evocative phrase that was: dusty feet. I wondered, in fact, just how many miles I had walked in the last five months; it must run into hundreds, and they weren't all dusty miles, either. There had been rain and mud and sharp flints and cobbles and setts and grass and even sand . . . . Sand stuck between one's toes was worse than anything.

The speech was coming to its end, for I could see folk eyeing the stall they wished to try first, showmen getting ready to overshout their nearest neighbours, and the rattling of change in eager pockets . . . .

'. . . according to the laws of this land and the customs of this City. God save the King!'

We cheered and clapped dutifully, but even as I craned my head to catch a last glimpse of the Mayor and his entourage as they bowed and turned away, there was a sharp tug at my ankle and I tumbled down from my perch to land with a bump at Jack's feet.

'Come, Sprat: no time to waste. Fair's open now, and seeing there's no prohibition we can get started right away.'

'Prohibition?'

'Against plays or spoken performances. There have been in the past on occasion, and it has caused many a riot. Every now and again some interfering old do-gooder declares the plays immoral and there is not even a puppet show to be seen. Costs a lot of money when you arrive with naught but a play or two and then find you can't perform 'em.'

'But this year – how did you know?'

'I didn't.'

'Then what would you have done if we couldn't have acted Henry and Richard?'

'Doubled up on Daisy and shown a bit more of Annie; I'd've thought of something, never worry.'

I giggled to myself at the thought of there being any more to show of Annie than was displayed already, and it was probably because she was on my mind that I was so quick to see, among the stalls and booths of the tall men, thin men, strong men; monsters, bearded ladies, manikins; stuffed beasts, tumblers and ropewalkers, a very particular poster. There, on a round tent with pennants flying round the roof, was an advertisement for 'The Largest Lady in the World: Lovely Louisa from Lichfield.'

I stopped. 'They've got another Annie!'

Jack's eyes followed my pointing finger: if the poster illustration were anything to go by, she would make two of our fat lady.

'Hmmm . . .' said Jack, stroking his chin. 'This bears looking into. Get back to the inn, Sprat, and tell everyone we start in five minutes. You can get Sam going straight-away at the entrance to the yard.'

'Are you going to have a look at the Lovely Louisa? Won't it mean – if she *is* bigger than Annie – that we are discredited?'

'Not necessarily. I've got an idea . . . . Now, get along, sharp!'

The idea took shape in a brief lull around six-thirty that evening when the fair was less crowded. The day visitors had gone home to their supper and those coming out for the evening were still dining. We were snatching a quick bite in the inn yard where the landlord's wife had been doing a roaring trade all day with pies, ham, cheese and fresh bread; her food was much more inviting than her husband's ale.

Jack speared an onion from our pickle jar. 'I had a word with Lovely Louisa's husband. I've seen her, and he's coming to see Annie some time tonight; I'm sure he'll agree.'

'To what?' said Annie sharply. Nothing in this world would induce her to ask Jack about Lovely Louisa; in all the months we had been together there had been none to rival her, and now that her professional status seemed threatened she was as niggly as a wet hen.

'A contest to see which of you has the right to call yourself the greatest: a grand Weigh-In to be held tomorrow morning in the square. Should bring in quite a lot extra; we shall need some sort of stout weighing machine: I think I know where to borrow one.'

'And what if I say no?'

'You won't, my dear Annie, because if you do you will never know, will you, whether you *are* the greatest?'

'And if I'm not – mind you, I'm not admitting there could be a fatter lady – but, I say, if this – person – should by cheat or fraud prove to be just a tiny bit heavier . . . ?'

'Annie: have I ever let you down? Trust Jack. You won't lose out, I promise you.'

Annie appeared mollified, but I didn't like Jack's smile: that coupled with the admission that Louisa's husband would agree to the contest after a look at Annie could mean only one thing: his wife *was* the largest.

The contest took place the following day, Sunday. Most folk were at church early but, there being no clampdown on trading on the Lord's Day as I understood there had been in the past when the fair was held over a longer period than the three days we were allowed now, we knew we should have a good audience by noon.

Jack had borrowed a massive weighing machine from some warehouse where they dealt in bales of wool or some such, and between him and Louisa's husband they had erected it in the space among some hastily shifted food stalls, and it now stood, a great beam supported by cross-struts on the ground, another beam swinging on a pivot at the top, with a huge brass weighing pan on either side. By dint of threat, bribe or promise the two men had cleared a space around and roped it off and there were crude posters advertising the event flapping from every available empty vantage point and blank space on walls, posts, poles, and tents. Jack had been up all night and I was awoken at five o'clock to pick up leaflets from a nearby printer's and collect sacking from a convenient stables to enclose the weigh-in from all those who did not pay the half-crown (children one shilling) for this 'Once-in-a-Lifetime meeting of Avoirdupois' to decide the 'Championship of the World'.

The meeting was scheduled for noon exactly and Annie spent the morning alternating between depression and optimism. I had helped her dress in her pink and yellow satin with the frills and lace and arranged her hair in a mass of ringlets; at ten minutes to the hour Tom harnessed Daisy to the wagonette and we stuffed Annie inside, enveloped in one of her voluminous cloaks, and made our way down New Lane to the square, clearing a way by dint of having me drubbing on my tabor and shouting at the top of my voice: ' 'Way, 'way! for the largest lady in the world, come to shame her rival in the Great Weighing Contest – Follow me, and see the scales displaced by these mountains of flesh! The greatest entertainment of this or any age . . .' and words to that effect.

Jack was waiting for us in the square and took up my words, adding, of course, others more effective of his own, and we processed through the crowd with some difficulty, reaching our objective at about ten minutes past the hour.

The Lovely Louisa was already waiting, cloaked as Annie was, and seated on a large thronelike chair. She was an imposing, heavy-jowled woman of about five-and-forty, I suppose, and even sitting she looked taller than Annie. The latter we helped, perspiring and cursing, from the cramped wagonette, which gave a thankful creak of springs as she stepped down and earned a quick frown from Tom as he bent to examine the leather straps that suspended the cane and wood contraption. Led ceremoniously by Jack, Annie advanced to meet her rival and at last the latter rose from her chair and they stood side by side. My heart sank: Louisa topped Annie by at least a head.

Jack had obviously been delegated as spokesman, for he stepped forward to introduce the contest.

'Ladies and gentlemen, you are here on a historic occasion – yes, a few more can be squeezed in, I think: make room at the back there, and let the children come to the front – as I said, a historic occasion: never before in the history of Bart's Fair has there been anything to equal this contest of flesh, this measurement of avoirdupois, this magnitude of pulchritude! Ladies, think of the yards of ribbon and lace which go to cover these two contestants; gentlemen, reflect on the armful these two might prove were they yours . . . . Children, how many gingerbread men and meat pies and sausages do you think these two consume?'

Although these questions were purely rhetorical, a fierce discussion broke out among the ladies present and there were guesses of 'fifty', 'hundred, more like' from the children. In a flash Jack was on to it.

'There will, of course, be a Grand Contest later to guess at this sort of thing, where for a few pence a valuable prize will be offered: why, some lucky person may leave here tomorrow with a pocket full of gold! But more of that later . . . .' He flashed me a quick glance and miserably I realized who was going to organize this Grand Lottery, find the paper and ink, take down the names, collect the money . . . .

The introduction went on and on, but eventually the two contestants discarded their cloaks and stepped towards the scales; the Lovely Louisa was undeniably heavier-boned than Annie and must have been six feet tall: I could see who would tip the scales even before, weighing pans held steady, they were assisted to their places. My heart wept for Annie even as Jack clapped his hands for attention and Louisa's husband and his assistant stepped back; for the length of a long-drawn breath the two ladies hung equally suspended, their feet just touching the ground, their hands clutching convulsively at the brass chains which held the pans, then slowly, ever so slowly but nevertheless inexorably, I saw Annie's feet leave the ground.

She ascended up and up and her knees showed beneath wind-flung petticoats as Lovely Louisa's pan touched the ground; there was a roar of appreciation from the crowd and I looked up at her face, expecting tears, but before she would have had time to squeeze even a drop of moisture from her eyes she had disappeared again from view with a squeal and a great clash of brass pans. I ran forward anxiously, pushing my way through the gaping sightseers, to find her sitting in a scatter of skirts and pans, her pride more damaged than her person. The Loathsome Louisa, without thought, had risen from her pan, and consequently there had been nothing to anchor Annie, and in spite of Jack's frantic clutch at the chains, down she had come.

Jack and I pulled and pushed her to her feet, but she was angry, really angry. 'I thought as how you said you'd never let me down!'

'But, Annie, I did! Those chains slipped through my fingers . . . .'

She was too angry to heed his attempt at a jest, however, but he still appeared confident, as if all her plans did not lie in the dust with the weighing pans.

'We're not finished yet,' he said, and grabbed a handful of voluminous skirts as she tried to push her way through

227

the crowds in blind disappointment. 'Have a little faith in the old firm . . . .'

The customers were crowding round Loathsome Louisa and her husband, full of congratulations, but Jack grabbed my tabor and beat a rapid tattoo.

'So now, ladies and gentlemen, we have decided who is the heavier; but that is not all. This contest was to find the largest lady in the world, and it would be only fair to measure the two against each other . . . .'

Good old Jack! I should have realized right at the beginning, when he had accepted the wager, that he had seen more than one side of the question. Of course the contest, right the way through, had been to find the 'largest lady in the world', and on the measuring part Annie should win; calves, hips, waist, bosom and all!

And so she did. Jack produced a long ribbon and proceeded to measure the two, Annie now all smiles and Louisa and her husband with the scowls. The outcome of it all was that the contest was declared a draw: Louisa being the heaviest and Annie the fattest. It only remained to arrange the lottery: one ticket to guess Louisa's weight and one for Annie's waist measurement: tickets twopence each, the winners of this double contest to receive five pounds apiece.

There were plenty of takers, for the prizes were worth over a week's wages for many, a month's for more, and twopence was easily spent. The morning's takings, weigh-in and lottery, amounted to over forty pounds, which Jack and Louisa's husband divided half-and-half, with money still coming in for the lottery, which they decided would be declared at noon tomorrow, the book to be kept open till half an hour before. This book had inevitably fallen to my lot to keep: a list of names, two columns for the guesses and a slip of paper for each contestant with the number of their entry. My fingers were cramped and stiff by the time I had spent an hour or two at this, and Jack left the lists in Louisa's husband's care for the rest of the afternoon, promising to take it over again later in the evening. He escorted Annie back to the inn and tossed me two florins.

'Go and spend some money, Sprat: back in three-quarters of an hour, for I want *Henry* again at half-past three.'

I wandered past the stalls, paying one shilling to see the stuffed tigers and bears, another to marvel at Master Kelham Whitelamb, the smallest man in the world; I savoured a mutton pie, then another, and went at last to see the great fourteen-foot pig and buy a piecrust pig with currant eyes as a memento of the visit. This last I took up to the stables and unearthed the wonderful, sweet-smelling box Jack had given me the day before and placed the pig reverently with my other keepsakes. The box, I had established from Tom, was made of sandalwood, and couched a perfume that was to intoxicate me with its warm, enticing scent for many years to come: what Jack had said about needing warmth to bring out its true aroma was proved right as well.

Later that evening, the last customer having gone, we all sat around for ten minutes before bed, Jack and Tom with their pipes, Annie with her tea, Sam and I with ripe apples.

'What *do* you measure round the waist?' I asked Annie.

'That's a point,' said Jack. 'Thanks for reminding me.' And he reached behind him for the by now distinctly tatty betting lists, pen and ink. 'Tape, Annie?'

She stood up while he adjusted the measure, it taking him all his time to encircle her waist, even with his long arms. ' 'Ave I increased?'

'A little, I believe. Last time it was fifty inches –'

'Fifty-one and a half.'

'Well, now it's fifty-two and three-quarters.' He entered a figure in the lists and paused, the feather of the pen scraping his chin reflectively. 'No one has got within a half inch of that yet: a couple at fifty-two and one at fifty-four. What name, Tom?'

'What am I?'

'Seafaring man – black wig, chew of 'baccy, eye patch . . . .'

'Hmmm . . . Bill Drake?'

' 'Twill do, 'twill do,' and he carefully wrote the name in the lists, with 'Two ton' against the weight and 'Fifty-two and three-quarter' against the waist measurement. Tearing a slip of paper from the list he wrote the name Tom had given him and the figures again, and handed it to Tom. 'And if you do have to say anything, for God's sake try and sound Devon or Cornish!'

'Aye aye, Cap'n!' said Tom, in a passable imitation, grinning and tucking the paper away in his waistcoat pocket.

All this while I had kept silent, but now I could contain myself no longer. 'But that's cheating!'

They looked at one another, then Jack shrugged his shoulders and spread his hands wide. 'So? What else is all we do?'

'But – but –'

'Think, Sprat, think! What else do we show to the public – not just us but all the fair-people, the gipsies, the tinkers, the showmen – but deformity, sleight of hand or downright knavery? What poster or advertisement ever told the truth about a performance? When did you ever see exactly what you had paid to see?'

'I saw the longest pig I have ever seen this very day,' I said triumphantly. 'Fourteen feet long he was, and they had a board at the front all marked out to prove it. And he was real! He grunted, poor thing, and his tummy rumbled and it was so long they had to support him in the middle with a curved stool so his stomach didn't drag on the ground –'

I was interrupted by a howl of laughter from Jack and a derisive snort from Tom.

'What's the matter? I saw him, I tell you . . . .'

'Yes, but just what *did* you see? Think about it again, child. That board in front with the measurements –

230

fourteen feet it showed, you said? – was it nearer to the audience or the pig?'

'Halfway, I suppose: just in front of the man who poked him to make him grunt, poor thing . . . .'

'Perspective! And how do you know it was truly measured: that a foot wasn't ten inches, or even only eight? You were had, Sprat.'

'He was a very long pig,' I said sullenly.

'Supported in his middle by a stool that effectively hid the join between *his* tail and the head of the *other* pig that brought up his rear, all neatly sewn up in a pigskin to make them one? I'm willing to bet he was a saddleback – black 'twixt shoulder and haunch to make it more difficult to see . . . .'

My face showed him all, and he pinched my cheek. 'Never mind: I saw this done with a sheep ten years or so ago and was near took in.'

'But if you know all this, why don't you expose him?'

'And destroy ourselves? We are part of a brotherhood, a guild just as tight as the goldsmiths' or leatherworkers'; we don't give our secrets away to strangers for one who did would soon find his props disappear or his vans destroyed. Rightly too, for we give a service second to none. We give pleasure to hundreds, to thousands, maybe . . . .'

'But *we* don't cheat . . .' and I looked round at the others.

'Don't we? Annie, if she will forgive me saying so, is a deformity of nature, like Louisa or that everlasting midget, Whitelamb . . . .' I don't think she heard: she was nodding happily over her cup of tea, her eyes shut, no doubt reliving her triumphs of earlier. '. . . Sam's gift is that his hands are unusually dexterous, and quicker than most people's eyes; does he really produce eggs from the air? No, they are up his sleeve. And as for Daisy: does she in truth add three and two and take away one? No, she responds to Tom's signals. And my Richard – is he not all padding, someone else's words and a flash of saltpetre?

231

Yet the people pay, Sprat, they all pay, because they want to believe; because they wish, just for a while, to forget their miserable lives in a world of magic and make-believe where giants still walk the earth, all dross can be turned to gold, and pigs are fourteen feet long!' He rumpled my hair. 'You wanted all that yourself this afternoon when you spent that four shillings, and you're only miserable now because I've told you what lay beneath the things you saw.'

'The mutton pies weren't a cheat,' I muttered, defiant to the last, the more so because I knew he was right.

'Maybe not, but they would have been a halfpenny cheaper a street or so further away.'

For what seemed to me no reason, I burst into tears, great sniffing sobs that shook me from head to foot. After a moment Jack hauled me to my feet and led me away from the others, handing me a handkerchief.

'I keep forgetting you're a female: don't be so emotional!' As I made no attempt to use the handkerchief he took it away from me and dabbed at my wet cheeks, then all at once put his arm round me and held me tight to his chest, stroking my hair. My nose was pressed uncomfortably against one of the brass buttons of his coat but his arms were comforting, and after a while I subsided into a couple of choking sounds and was still.

'And now,' said Jack, putting me from him, 'unless you want me to gain the reputation of a lad-lover from those who don't know, you had better pull yourself together and remember you are supposed to be Master Zoroaster!'

It rained hard that night and the lane was still overflowing with rubbish and mud the following morning when I took my accustomed stance at the end, leaflets in hand, a little after one o'clock. The result of the 'Tonnage and Yardage' contest, as Jack put it, had been declared earlier and the disguised Tom had claimed back five pounds for us and we had made a further seven from the tickets, after a split with Louisa's husband. The weight had been correctly guessed by a master butcher, who had caused much merriment by declaring, as he came forward for his prize, eyeing Louisa appraisingly, that he could 'weigh by eye any side or carcase in England – aye, and joint it too, if the lady's husband was of a mind . . . .'

Jack had put all our money in the communal pool, a sum of over fifty pounds, reminding us, however, that the constables would be round before the fair ended for their tolls of three shillings and fourpence for every performance, and indeed they turned into the lane, two of them, after I had been touting for custom some ten minutes or so, and continued in the direction of the Fair Prospect.

Business was slack and I sauntered to the end of the lane and peered out into the busy thoroughfare beyond. Many customers were obviously waiting for the late afternoon, when, as was the custom, prices would be lowered for the last few hours, but there was a smart and discreet coach just pulling up at the corner, and two servants in extremely fine livery jumped down to assist their passengers to alight. The man and woman were heavily cloaked, but within the coach could be glimpsed fine furnishings, a fur rug; my curiosity aroused I ventured forward a few paces, in time to hear one of the footmen address the man as 'Highness' – at least, that is what it sounded like. At once I remembered something Jack had said; the Duke and Duchess of Gloucester had been regular visitors to the fair some years back, but had discontinued their visits after outcry in the press about royalty condoning the merriment and admitted disorder that sometimes prevailed: could it be that they were coming to enjoy it all incognito? Even as the possibility crossed my mind, I was racing back down New Lane and into the yard of the Fair Prospect, skipping heedlessly over the puddles.

There was no sign of Jack, and Tom was walking Daisy up and down giving some child a ride. I ran over to Annie's booth, shook her out of her doze and hissed: 'Get over to the entrance in your cloak, sharpish: quick, don't

233

argue. Just follow my lead when I come back!' Not waiting for an objection I skidded into the stable and pulled on my Young Prince outfit, white breeches and tabard, and grabbed the bunch of flowers King Henry presented to his prospective bride, glad it was a fresh posy. Back in the yard I pulled the surprised child off Daisy's back, leaped into the safety saddle and trotted out through the gate, calling over my shoulder to Tom: 'Back in a minute or two – I'm off to do us all a favour!'

All this had taken less than five minutes and the (query) royal incognitos were only a few yards into the lane, picking their way precariously among the debris and trying to avoid the running gutter, when I came up with Daisy. One of the footmen, trying to look inconspicuous, was escorting them, and my theory was strengthened when the tall and rather unprepossessing lady, lifting her skirts to clear the mud, disclosed highly unsuitable diamond-buckled shoes and silk stockings. The gentleman was rather short and stout and carried a walking cane in his stubby red fingers and I had time to register an involuntary disappointment in royalty even as I slipped off Daisy and stepped forward to execute my best stage bow, addressing myself instinctively to the gaunt woman.

'Ma'am . . . gracious lady . . . may I offer my services? I cannot bear to see so lovely an example of the fair sex muddying her feet in this filthy lane. My little pony here is at your disposal and I would deem it a great favour if you would let us bear you to less noxious ground. That is, dear lady, if your revered husband will allow me . . . ?' All this in my deepest, most husky voice.

The lady glanced at her husband. 'This is my treat, and I am sure he will be grateful for the kind thought, young man . . . .'

The man nodded, and fished in his pocket for a coin: I was not surprised to be the richer by a new guinea. 'As you say, my love. Most grateful. Very.' He put the knob of the silver-topped walking cane back in his mouth and goggled at me, pale blue eyes popping.

The lady turned to me. 'I thank you for your kind offer then, and I accept – But were you not off to visit another – young lady – with your posy of flowers?'

I bowed again, my hand on my heart. 'A mere slip of a girl, pretty enough in her way but not a real woman, if you take my meaning, ma'am . . . . And now that I have had the pleasure of seeing you, though I may only worship from afar –' I bowed to her husband '– I see how empty was my errand. These poor flowers were to be an expression of hope, but now I have seen you – they are a fulfilment! Pray accept them: their very paucity will be enriched immeasurably by your acceptance. Your touch makes a poor posy into a rich bouquet, makes a grey day in London a veritable summer!'

As she took the posy, bridling unbecomingly, I thanked God for Jack: if it were not for listening to his blandishments and cajoleries with the women I wouldn't have thought of all that tomfoolery. It had worked with them because of his roguish smile and twinkling eye and arrant masculinity: I had to play the impressionable young lad, with a diffidence and shyness he had forgot years ago. The important thing was that it had worked so far, so I led Daisy forward and nudged her imperceptibly behind the left fore as Tom had taught me. Instantly she went into her obeisance, left fore tucked under, right extended.

'Why ma'am! She, too, recognizes your magnetism!' I brought Daisy up again and leaned forward, pretending to whisper in her ear, keeping my fingers the while on her neck for the hidden signals. 'Tell me, my little pony, have you ever had the chance of so fair and – regal – a burden?' Daisy shook her head. 'And do you not think it would make our day if we might bear Her Royal – my lady, down to the square?' Daisy nodded vigorously. 'Then show your pleasure that our fair passenger has consented.' Daisy executed the first few steps of a gavotte, then whinnied gently. 'She conveys her thanks at the honour, as I do myself, Your – Royal Highness, I was about to say, but of course we are not allowed the privilege of a royal visit to the fair these days, are we? So, my feeling that you are somewhat special must be a mistake, must it not?'

For a moment I was afraid I had gone too far, then the lady smiled, showing rather yellow teeth. 'You are a very – perspicacious young man, and so I shall ask you to remember that we are just an ordinary couple out to spend an hour's pleasure like any other Londoners . . . .'

I bowed so low I could see my reflection in the puddle in which I was standing. 'Your R– Your Grace – ma'am! You could *never* be ordinary!'

'Tut-tut, young man, you outdo the greatest flatterers at court!' But I could see she was not displeased, allowing herself to be helped into the curved saddle, where she balanced easily side-saddle, one foot in the stirrup, her hand on the child's safety bar in front. Breathing a prayer that Daisy wouldn't find a pothole, we processed sedately down the lane till we came to the gateway of the inn, where, as I had hoped, the cloaked Annie had positioned herself.

I halted Daisy. 'Well, of all the surprises in the world! You could not have come down the lane at a better time, Your Royal – sorry, ma'am! Here, taking the air, is the greatest sight the fair has to offer – and I mean greatest, in every sense of the word! That lady, so demurely cloaked to hide her charms, is not only famous the length and breadth of England, but just yesterday, in a never to be forgotten contest, beat her rival, the disappointingly plain and miscalled Lovely Louisa, into second place for the title of the fattest woman in the world! Come, Annie, show Their Graces – sorry, this lady and gentleman – your famed inches!'

Obediently Annie slipped off the cloak, and holding her skirts free of the mud, attempted a curtsey. I glanced at my captive audience: whereas the Duchess merely looked surprised, I detected another sort of gleam in the eye of her husband, and he even took an involuntary step forward.

236

'Perhaps if you were to jump a little, up and down, Annie,' I suggested. 'Just to show how generously your flesh is distributed . . . and perhaps a turn or two . . . ?'

What she had intended was a graceful dance step, but unfortunately the ground was very slippy, and before she had shaken herself up and down more than a couple of times there was a great flurry of skirts and an almighty splash as she ended sitting in a puddle, with great expanses of garter and much else revealed. The Duchess and I averted our gaze as Tom and Sam rushed forward to try and right her, but the more they heaved and the more her heels scrabbled to find purchase, the more difficult it became, and in the end I was stuffing the back of my hand in my mouth to keep from laughing out loud. To my surprise the Duchess was smiling too, if in a rather superior way, and after a moment her husband handed his stick to the servant and trotted forward eagerly to help, moistening his already wet lips.

Eventually they had her righted, but not before, I regret to say, a lot of Annie had fallen out of her bodice, to be shovelled back by the eager Duke, one at a time and lingeringly. I saw all this but luckily his wife didn't, for she decided her pleasure lay in patting my cheek and pinching my ear, so it was with a sigh of relief that I started us off down the lane again, leaving a muddied Annie thoughtfully clutching a gold coin. The crowd thickened as we approached the square, and I thought I saw Jack, about to come forward no doubt and ask me what the hell I was doing, then thinking better of it and melting back into the crowd. I helped the Duchess down and bowed low, seeking a spare inch of space to kiss between the rings of the ungloved hand she extended.

She tweaked my ear again, familiarly. 'What else should we see whilst we are here, young man?'

'Master Whitelamb, the midget, is well worth a visit; they say Flockton's puppets are better than ever this year, and Mr Hall's stuffed beasts are quite impressive. Don't waste your money on Lovely Louisa or that fourteen-foot pig: they are definitely not up to Your Gra– to your ladyship's high standards.' I thought for a moment 'Then of course if you would like your fortunes told by Madame Petulengro – down the second side of the square – I can thoroughly recommend her. She is quite remarkable: I have visited her myself.'

It seemed the Duchess could not tear herself away. She patted first me and then Daisy, then me again, and suddenly leaned forward and kissed me soundly on the cheek, whispering in my ear: 'Were my husband not here . . . . You understand?' and pressed a coin into my hand.

I was bereft of speech as she sailed away, turning once to wave; as her husband passed he pressed a coin into my other hand and murmured: 'Best show I've seen in years: such *big* ones . . . . If she does visits just let me know . . . . Not a word to the wife . . . . Ah me, what sights, what sights!'

Which made me both fancy boy and pander.

I wanted to pin up a poster straightaway 'Under Royal Patronage', but Jack was in an unexplained bad mood and vetoed it; in spite of this setback I was insufferably puffed up with my feat, enjoying the plaudits of Annie who was over the moon when she finally realized the identity of the portly gentleman who had scooped her back into her dress, and went immediately to trace with a wondering finger the 'crowned heads' bit written on her van.

'As good as,' I heard her mutter, and in an excess of good feeling I gave her one of my gold coins, telling her the uncrowned head had sent it to her so she had 'a piece of gold for each one'. It was a lie, but she was happy; I suppose it in part made up for not passing on the message he had really sent: I think I was afraid she would have been mesmerized into compliance . . . .

Tom was more reserved, and only smiled and shrugged

his shoulders when I pointed out that he could now boast that Daisy had been 'Ridden by Royalty'.

'From what I heard of it, Annie could near make the same boast,' said Jack sourly. 'And not only Annie.'

'Aren't you pleased with the way I handled things?' I demanded, not sure what he meant.

'You pulled a dangerously clever trick, and I should like you better if you hadn't enjoyed it so much.'

'It's no more than you would have done –'

'But I wouldn't have dressed in skirts to do it,' he said cryptically.

I shook my head. 'I don't understand you: here I have brought recognition to our troupe, and all you can do is carp, and criticize my methods!'

'Not the methods: you!'

'Oh, you're impossible to please!'

'Her Grace wasn't . . . .'

'No,' I said triumphantly. 'She couldn't keep her hands off me. Such a pretty boy she thought me: even half-promised an assignation, and gave me a guinea.' I flicked her coin in the air so that it spun golden in the belated sunshine that lit the corner of the yard. 'Heads or tails, Jack?'

'You don't use the one, but seem ready enough to abuse the other,' he said, a scowl on his face. 'I can only hope you are more innocent than you seem.'

I still hadn't the slightest idea what he was so annoyed about, so I took refuge in childishness.

'Sing me a rhyme, tell me a riddle,' I chanted. 'If you can't do either, then go have a piddle!' And, sticking out my tongue, I escaped to the comparative safety of the stable loft and laid my coins lovingly in my treasure box, glad for once that I was a girl, and so might escape the beating I richly deserved for my impudence. I was extremely nice to him for the rest of the day, however, going out of my way to give a good performance, for I suddenly remembered I had a special favour to ask.

*

My ruse worked and the following evening, at six o'clock, Jack and I were seated on benches in the yard of the George Inn; I at least was wriggling in anticipation on my seat though Jack professed boredom, long legs stuck out in front of him, hat tipped over his face and arms folded. It was growing dusk already, and horn lanterns hung from the galleried landings of the inn. The fair proper had been gradually brought to an end during the afternoon, the constables ensuring that showmen packed their gear away and that booths and stalls were dismantled: we had started our last full performance at two o'clock, to an already diminished audience, and I had rushed around like a mad thing helping to pack everything away afterwards. Whether it was my extra efforts – or perhaps because we had taken much more than anticipated during the three days – whatever the reason, my timid and suitably diffident request to 'see the play' had been met by Jack with a condescending consideration and, after a couple of brandies, assent.

So here we were, I in my clean shirt and best jacket, Jack in his fine mulberry coat, waiting for the curtains to be drawn back. I had read the posters over and over again: '*The Beggar's Opera* by John Gay, first produced at Lincoln's Inn Theatre, 29 January 1728. Music arranged by Dr Johann Christoph Pepusch. Performed now by Principals from the Playhouse, including . . . .' and here followed a cast list which meant nothing to me.

'They have very plain names,' I said, thinking aloud.

'So they should: it's been called a Newgate pastorale,' said Jack, from the shadow of his hat, a squashy indeterminate thing that owed nothing to fashion.

'No, not the characters: the cast. Miss Brown, for instance; I thought great actresses would have exotic names –'

'Like Zoroaster Mortimer?' He was laughing at me. 'Don't ever judge people by their names, Sprat, else would you be ever the little fish . . . . That same Miss Brown,' said he, tipping back his hat, 'caused quite a stir ten, no, eleven years ago now. She was the pretty, flighty daughter of a coal merchant who ran away from her father to seek her fortune on the stage. As an actress she was no great shakes, but gained a certain notoriety from the assiduity with which her father sought to carry her back home again. She was staying with an aunt, as I recall, and was on her way to the theatre one night to play this very part when her father waylaid her as she alighted from her coach in Bow Street for the evening's performance. She screamed her head off, and out from the Playhouse streamed the entire cast to the rescue, some already dressed and made up as thieves and whores, and bore her off in triumph. The fright did her good: the chit performed that night better than she ever had before.'

'You were there?'

He glanced at me from the corner of his eye, not bothering to move his head. 'Either that or I read of it the following day in the *Morning Chronicle* . . . .'

Somehow I knew he *had* been there, and an eighteen-year-old Jack would not have been there only for the show: I wondered whether Miss Brown's performances were confined to the stage. While I was wondering someone came out and lighted the candles at the front of the stage; shielded by curved metal, they threw bright, flickering pools of reflection on the gently swaying velvet curtains. A moment later came the customary three knocks and four musicians who had been tuning up on violins, cello and flute, in a space to the left of the stage, were joined at the harpsichord by a fifth, the curtains were looped back, and the play began.

At first I was conscious of my hard seat, the occasional distraction of a latecomer to the audience; the bells of a nearby church, cries from the street outside; Jack's ostentatious indifference; the crude settings, the tawdry costumes, the ranting delivery of some of the older princi-pals, but soon I forgot where I was and the magic of the story and the music had me well and truly held. I could overlook the fact that the famous Miss Brown's Polly was

241

no spring chicken and that Macheath's cloak concealed not a romantic, slim young highwayman but a rather stout, plainfaced man in his forties who was inclined to strike attitudes; so involved did I become that I clapped as spontaneously as the rest at the duet 'Oh Polly, you might have toyed and kissed . . .' and was away in my own impossible romantic dream with 'Were I laid on Greenland's coast . . .'. The fact that many of the tunes were half-familiar added to the ease with which I absorbed it all, and at the end of the first act I turned to Jack with shining eyes.

'It's marvellous, wonderful! Oh, I am so glad I came . . . .'

He yawned and stretched. 'You're easily satisfied: still, it's a change, I suppose. Like an orange or a pie?'

'Pie, please.'

He beckoned to the pie-seller, and we had one apiece.

The second act had me nudging Jack at the very first chorus: 'Fill every glass . . .'. 'That's one of the things you try to play on your flute!'

'What do you mean, *try*?' he growled.

Once again I was *in* the play, with the actors, and more and more on the side of the charming scoundrel, Macheath. When he sang: 'How happy I could be with either, were t'other dear charmer away . . .', I wished I could make a threesome with Polly and Lucy, convinced I could make him forget both, and was filled with dismay when he was borne off to jail at the end of the second act.

I turned to Jack. 'He does escape, doesn't he?'

'Wait and see!' After a moment he started fidgeting and tossed me a coin. 'Go get yourself another pie: I'm for the privy.'

The third act had started before he returned and I was aware of the smell of new-drunk brandy, and a glance at his face in the shifting light showed a smudge of what could be paint or powder on his cheek. But by this time, like the rest of the audience, I was humming the tunes I half-knew: 'The modes of the court so common are grown . . .' and 'I'm like a skiff on the ocean toss't . . .' and soon entirely forgot Jack and everyone else. When the time came for Macheath to be taken and hanged he made an appeal to his audience and though, like the rest, I knew him guilty as hell, I was on my feet, shouting for reprieve. Of course all ended happily, and my eyes were brimfull with thankful tears as the curtains closed. On the calls I was sure Polly winked at Jack and certain it was that he tossed her a coin which she caught prettily and curtsied.

We of the audience crowded into the bar parlour of the George afterwards, and Jack bought me an ale; he was still on brandy, I noticed, and stumbled a couple of times on his way out. At the gateway to the street he hesitated.

'Find your own way back, Sprat? I have – unfinished business.'

I could imagine.

At that moment one of the orange-sellers, her basket near empty, sidled up to us.

'An orange to take home for your suppers, sirs? Only twopence each, fine oranges from the South . . . .'

Suddenly I was Jack, Macheath, Zoroaster, and the Zoe side was forgotten. 'And how much for a kiss, pretty one?' It was what Jack would have said.

She *was* a pretty lass, and she dimpled, eyelashes fluttering.

'For a kiss, young sir, only one penny . . . .'

I fished a coin from my pocket and tossed it on her tray, saying (as Jack would have done): 'Forget the fruit: there is sweetness enough in your smile!' and again as Jack would have done, pushed her tray aside and prepared to kiss her rosy cheek (he never kissed their mouths). I was rather proud of my display as I leaned forward, but to my dismay I found my hand was on her breast, and on flesh, not cloth, and that my lips were not on her cheek but her mouth. Her lips parted under mine and I could feel her tongue dart between my mouth to touch my tongue and her hand squeeze my buttocks.

A moment later and I was pulled roughly away, the grip on my arm so fierce I cried out.

Jack's eyes were slits of rage. 'Leave a man to do man's work, you little cheap-jack!' He turned to the girl. 'Go cry your wares elsewhere, slut; this one's not for you, or the likes of you –'

'Want him for yourself, then, do you? Tell you what, make it a threesome: I'll take the front and you can grease his arse –'

Jack's grip on my arm slackened for a moment and I twisted out of his grasp and ran into the alley, dodging between the remainder of the audience making their way home. In my haste I went the wrong way and it took me about ten minutes to find my way back to the square by an unfamiliar route; all the way resentment was building up inside of me, and I had a bitter taste in my mouth. Why had Jack been so unreasonable and stuffy, not just this evening but yesterday as well? All I had done, as far as I could see, was to play the boy he had taught me so well that I had successfully deceived a duchess and a slut. If we had been on the stage he would have congratulated me on a good performance: in real life it was reprehensible. He couldn't be jealous, surely? He must realize that my disguise would be uncovered were I to risk more than an innocuous kiss and compliment . . . . But it was a pity to waste what was left of the evening in useless recriminations: I thought back on *The Beggar's Opera*, calmed down, and was whistling jauntily as I sauntered back across the almost empty square.

Not quite empty. 'Aye, "Youth's the Season" right enough,' said a voice out of the darkness to my right. 'But how long will it endure?'

Turning, I peered at the old van, horse's head hanging down as though asleep, one hoof tucked up against the pavings. By the light of the one dim lanthorn I recognized Madame Katina Petulengro, hooded and cloaked.

'I've been waiting long enough for you,' she said testily. 'Jump up by me for a moment; 'tis too far to climb down

244

again. No,' she added, as I climbed up with an unspoken question on my lips. ' 'Twas not the "sight". I watched you and Sir Jack on your way earlier and knew you'd be back this way sooner or later. Only later it is, and I must be on my way.' She rummaged in the pile of stuffs behind her and brought out a small package. 'This is for you: it is my book on herbs and palmistry and stars and suchlike: I have a feeling you will use it well: remember, I saw your hand.'

'But you –'

'I shall have no use of it where I am going. I have other roads to travel and they will be far enough from yours.'

'But where will Jack bring the snuff next year?'

'Tell him to save his money.' She glanced at my puzzled face. 'Do I have to spell it out for you, of all people? It serves me right for looking into the crystal for myself. Tell him . . . tell him there will be another gipsy queen by spring: he'll understand.'

I thought I did too, and shivered in spite of the warm night.

She tipped up my chin with her gnarled fingers. 'Naught to fear, my dear, remember that when your turn comes. It is but slipping into a pleasant dream and not troubling to return . . . . Life's but a burden that grows heavier with age: the young can carry it with grace, never knowing it is there, but as one grows older, unless there is someone to share the load, there is a relief in thinking of slipping it at last. Never weep for the dead: they are the lucky ones.'

I leaned over and kissed her cheek. 'Peace be with you . . . .'

'It will, it will . . . . There's another package in there for you: some herb remedies already mixed; you'll find my own recipes writ down at the end of the book. There's one you will need before next year's fair, if I'm not much mistaken,' and she chuckled. 'Now, off you go: I've many miles to go before dawn.'

I slipped down, holding the package. 'Thank you. Shan't I see you again?'

'I'll be there watching over your shoulder if ever you should be unsure of your own skills.' She clicked with her tongue and the horse woke up and threw his weight against the leather collar. 'Three words of advice, child; first, start thinking as well as living: you can't treat others unless you know yourself; second, deal with that graceless lad Jack gently: he has much to forgive and be forgiven, and more burden than most.'

'And the third piece of advice?' I called out after her as the van moved off into the darkness.

' 'Tis high time you became a proper lass again!'

I walked back thoughtfully, package under my arm, stopping only to buy a couple of beef sausages for Toby from a late seller risking prosecution. At the Fair Prospect everyone seemed to have retired early, for the church clock was only striking eleven as I crossed the yard but the place was deserted. I gave the aggrieved-at-his-desertion Toby his supper, then untied him from his post in the stables to give him a short walk. He relieved himself at every projection he could find down the lane, thus convincing me that he had had to hold on for hours, then, point made, trotted back happily at my heels; I retied him and left my package in the van, for it was far too dark and late to examine it now, then made my way to the ladder that led up to the hayloft where Jack, Tom, Sam and I had spent the last four nights.

The hooded lantern that lit the stable at night was turned away from me and, grateful for the half-light, I wearily began to climb the rungs, unbuttoning my shirt as I went. Suddenly, the light shifted to my eyes, a hand gripped one of my ankles and I swung round half-blinded, with a yelp of alarm. By the wildly swaying light I found my eyes on a level with Jack's. He stood at the bottom of the ladder and his breath reeked of brandy; his hair straggled over his forehead and his neckerchief hung loose, but his voice had the hissing precision of a snake.

'Where the hell have you been?'

'Walking –'

246

'With whom? Another of your bitches in heat?' and he struck me across first one cheek and then the other.

'I – I don't know what you mean!' I gasped, through the sting of pain and smart of tears.

'Don't you? *Don't* you? Do I then have to spell it out for you? Have you so forgotten the girl you should be that you do not see what you are in danger of becoming? Do you not realize that when one woman flirts with another, kisses her on the mouth, fondles her, that she is fast becoming one of those unnatural creatures that will so far forget their own sex as to strap on a false prick and service her own kind?'

What a fool I had been! Now at last I realized why he had been so angered with my behaviour over the last two days. First the Duchess and tonight the orange-girl . . . . A shamed blush further coloured my slap-reddened cheeks. I remembered my stepfather discussing those strange creatures who took their name from Sappho's Lesbos in his usual dry, unemotional tones, talking of them as analytically as he would, the next moment, discuss the Greek system of government: they were something that happened every now and again, like eclipses of the sun or swine fever, and of as little concern in his orderly life; that, I now realized for the first time, was his blemish: very little of sentiment had ever crossed his life, except my mother and me. Everything he had experienced had been on the printed page, which made for great knowledge but little understanding. My mother, on the other hand, had been a creature of her emotions and she had not known how to cope when she had lost her love . . . . Neither way was right: they had both failed in their different ways. And I, I was a product of them both: perhaps because of my mother's emotional failings my stepfather had always been as matter-of-fact with me as possible; this had aided the practicalities of my escape from Aunt Sophie but had not helped me understand Jack. Perhaps that was a little of what Kat Petulengro had meant earlier this evening: 'start thinking'. I had done a deal too much accepting. I saw that now: 'deal with Jack gently'; ' 'tis high time you became a lass again'. She saw a great deal more than I had realized, but surely Jack couldn't believe that I . . . .

'I – I'm not like that really, you must know I'm not. I was only doing what you do so much of the time: play-acting, keeping up the pretence of my clothes.'

'How do I know you speak truth?' and he moved closer, a hand going suddenly to my chest, where my half-buttoned shirt hung loose; with a brutal wrench he broke the linen that bound my breasts flat and both hands reached forward and held them cupped. 'Yes, you still have a young girl's breasts: you may bind them cruelly, but the pretty things will not be denied . . . .' His voice had changed: gone was the anger, there was even an air of wonderment in his speech. 'See where those wretched bands have marked the skin: there, where you have bound them too tight, they have raised a weal . . . .'

His thumbs brushed across my nipples, I could feel the pattern of the skin of his hands on my breasts and suddenly, although the night was stifling, my nipples hardened as if touched by a breath of cold air and stood out hard. At the same time my knees felt wobbly, my heart beat loudly and I felt tickly between my legs. Scarcely knowing what I was doing I raised one hand to Jack's bent head and touched his silky hair; he looked up at me and his eyes were burning, burning like hell-coals. He moved closer and now I was aware that his groin was pressed close to my thigh and he was well and truly roused; his head blocked out the light as his mouth came down on mine and his hands slipped to the buckle of my belt. For a moment he raised his head to gaze down at my breasts, then he was kissing me again.

'You need teaching, little Zoe: let me show you what you were made for . . . .'

He moved his hips and now I could feel him, hard and insistent; taste the sweetness of the brandy on his breath; enjoy the touch of his hands as they slipped down over my buttocks to pull me closer, and the dreadful, lovely melting-all-over feeling I had had once before was making me want all this whatever the consequences. Instinctively I opened my mouth for his questing tongue and my hands were reaching to pull him even closer, when all of a sudden everything changed.

Somewhere someone sneezed, one of the horses stamped in their stall, a sleepy hen gave a protesting cluck, there was a smell of hay in my nostrils and I was back in the hayloft at my aunt's six months ago and Oliver was trying to rape me. Suddenly Jack was no longer Jack, he was all the men in the world with only one thing in their minds and I had to stop him before it was too late and I was deflowered and debased. At once I was in a panic, struggling wildly to get free, thrusting him away, striking out at the dark face, feeling my knuckles against his mouth. Abruptly I brought up my knee hard into his groin and turned and scrambled up the ladder, shirt and breeches half-off, to collapse in a heap on my palliasse and bring the blanket over my ears to shut out the sound of the retching groans beneath.

After a while, when all was quiet again, I sat up and looked round in the dim light. Sam was hunched up in a corner, Tom was flat on his back, snoring gently, but of Jack there was no sign. The church clock struck two before I heard him return, stumbling over something below and cursing, then making an erratic ascent of the ladder. I kept very still and presently I heard a rustle as he lay down; soon after his breathing slowed and I knew he was asleep. I hoped he had been treated kindly by Polly: I think I was regretting my panic, even while the sensible part of me whispered that his amorousness was due to drink rather than inclination. Any woman would have done, the state he had been in, but on reflection I was rather sorry it hadn't been me.

Nothing was said the following morning as we breakfasted early and finished the packing. The skies were overcast and already a fine drizzle was falling when Jack turned to me and said abruptly: 'We're ready. Take that dog of yours for a quick run, Sprat, for I want him safe in the van while we cross London. The streets are easy to get lost in, the traffic could be heavy and I don't want you two disappearing down some backstreet when I need you.'

I looked up at him, unshaven and bleary-eyed, an unspoken question on my lips.

'I don't apologize for last night, if that's what you're waiting for,' he snapped, then grimaced and touched his mouth. 'Don't hit quite so hard next time, that's all – girl!'

Suddenly I was glad there might be a next time. 'Well, at least you've a good idea of what you'll be getting,' I said, and ran off before he could answer.

Toby and I went as far as the square. All the tents, booths, and stalls were gone. Some of the rubbish was already piled in heaps, ready for burning, and a bevy of sparrows was turning them over. Already the rain had smeared the ink on the peeling posters and an errant wind blew scraps of torn paper across the empty pens. Some of the houses had taken down the shutters that had been nailed up for the last few days and a rat scurried by with some scrap in its mouth, unnoticed by Toby. From one of the houses a housemaid emerged yawning, milk pail in hand; Bart's clock struck seven. Lights were being extinguished, somewhere a hungry baby woke and squalled, the night-soil cart was making its rounds . . . .

St Bartholomew's Fair was over for another year.

12

It was raining really hard now, and even before we turned out of the lane and headed northish, the water was running off us in rivulets. Jack and I were in the lead, he magnanimously allowing me to take the reins and keeping himself in shelter, remarking that he needed to keep his brains dry to figure out the way; Annie came next, with Sam Alley-Come huddled miserably on the steps beside her (he hated rain even more than he admired her); Signor Grappelli, the Italian puppeteer who had shared the yard with us, came after Annie with his friend the sword-swallower driving our props wagon behind – these two were coming with us part of the way, to catch what was left of the season – last of all came Tom and Daisy, 'to round up the stragglers' as he put it.

I had really been looking forward to seeing the London sights, but there was no chance in all that rain. The weather became worse, a westerly wind drove gustily against the vans, and there was a misty smokiness in the air that made me cough and splutter.

'Cheap pit coal,' said Jack. 'Wood's too expensive to bring in these days, except for the bakers. This rain is keeping the smoke down: we'll be clear in an hour or so, I hope . . . .'

'Which way now?' I asked, some five minutes later.

'Straight on for a while, then right up Ludgate Hill: we can keep going from there to Fleet Market, or on into Fleet Street and up Fetter Lane and into High Holborn, St Giles's and Broad Street. Then it's on to Oxford Road and up Mary Le Bone Lane, or turn off at Tottenham Court Road – no, of course that leads to a turnpike either way unless we go straight across and we want to go northwest anyway – No, keep to the first route.'

'Jack,' I said in despair. 'I've no idea what you are talking about, and the traffic is getting so thick that I shall be piling this van up any minute!'

Indeed, what with trying to sightsee, keep the van straight, avoid pedestrians who darted recklessly in front of our horse's hooves, check that the van behind was following, miss the drays, wagons, coaches, hackneys, horsemen and the odd sedan or two, plus trying to follow Jack's directions, I was in a fair way to bring us all to disaster. Grumbling, Jack took the reins and we progressed a little better; as the rain slackened somewhat he even deigned to point out one or two places of interest, and I nearly fell off the steps of the van craning my head to see the great St Paul's from the top of Ludgate Hill. The traffic now began to thicken in earnest and at its worst Annie called ahead to say that Hannibal, tied to the rear of our van, had cast a shoe. Jack cursed, but he wouldn't risk his horse on the cobbles so we pulled off into Lincoln's Inn Fields, where we lunched at The Ship inn at the northwestern corner on cheese, pickles and weak ale while Jack found a blacksmith. We had finished before he returned so I wandered off in the damp afternoon to admire the impressive gateway to the Inns of Court and wonder at the strange young trees, guarded by wooden palings from inquisitive dogs like Toby, whose branches were heavy with long beanlike fruits.

Once on our way again I tried to take in as much as I could, gazing round at broad High Holborn and at the fine shops, some of which still kept their bright hanging signs, and trying to peep into the small courts and meaner streets that led off our way. Inevitably there were beggars and thin, starved-looking children as well as the more prosperous citizens, narrow tenements as well as glimpses of newer brick-built houses and squares of stone-built mansions. The noise was incredible: horses', donkeys' and oxen's hooves; wheels, both the light carriage ones and the heavier iron-shod giants of the drays; street cries, striking of church bells, beating of carpets, shuffle of shoes, click of heels and pattens; bray of donkeys, neighing of horses, barking of dogs, shrieks of children at play, curses and songs of the drunk, and the ever present twitter of the sparrows.

It was past four before we turned off at last into quieter roads and down Mary Le Bone Lane. I was allowed to take the reins again; the rain had stopped, but a gusty wind still blew from the west and after a while I became aware of a queer, damp, sickly sweet smell that came with the wind. It grew worse and worse and eventually I looked over my shoulder at Jack, dozing with his arms folded just inside the van.

'Jack – can you smell something peculiar?'

He opened his eyes and looked out to our left. 'Not surprising: there's one of the largest burial grounds in London out there. They are a disgrace, the lot of them! A few years ago there was an official inquiry: no one had given thought, it seemed, to the fact that with a million and a half living in the city there was bound to be overcrowding in the few cemeteries. They just buried people one on top of the other till the graveyards over-topped the streets by as much as four or five feet and it only needed heavy rain for the top layers to be washed away into the gutters, so that there were rotting corpses exposed to the public's gaze and putrid humours loading the air for miles around . . . .'

I thought of the quiet graves I had left behind in the churchyard at Leebeck. 'My stepfather used to say there was more sense in burning the dead as the Danes used to; he said it would take up far less room and lessen the chance of disease.'

'Depends on one's religion; some folk expect to ascend in their expensive grave clothes and cannot reconcile themselves to the anonymity of a heap of ashes: afraid St Peter won't recognize them at The Gates, I suppose . . . .'

'I don't think things are *quite* the same Up There,' I said doubtfully. 'But I know my mother was glad to die while she was still young; she used to say my father wouldn't recognize her if she grew too old before she joined him.'

'And how old was she?'

'Twenty-three – I was six.'

'She must have married young the first time.'

'She – she was only married once, to my stepfather . . . .'

'So you –?'

'Was nearly a bastard, yes.' I suppose the bitterness I had felt underneath for so many years crept to the surface in my voice, for he leaned forward and patted my shoulder.

'Sorry: didn't mean to pry. You don't have to talk about it, you know; it doesn't make any difference to me.'

'No, I know – but perhaps talking about it will help. I always felt so ashamed . . . .'

'There's no shame for the child in being born out of wedlock –'

'But I didn't want there to be shame for my parents either!'

'Very often there isn't.'

'I wish you had been there to tell my putative grandfather that when he threw his pregnant daughter out to starve!'

'Your grandfather did *that*?'

'Yes, and he a man of God, too.'

It was a relief to let Jack, somebody, anybody, share what only three people had ever really known: my mother, my stepfather, and myself. I tried to make him see my real father in the only way I had ever seen him, through my mother's loving eyes: gay, handsome Harry Trelawnay with the blue eyes, auburn hair, and ready smile, second son of the local squire, who had fallen in love with the vicar's daughter, the gentle, brown-eyed Mary Harper. I told him how they had become betrothed in secret, for he was promised by his parents to the daughter of a local landowner; how they had kept putting off telling their respective parents and had decided to run away together. My eyes misted as I remembered my mother's husky little voice still breaking as she recalled for me, too young then to understand, of the day they bore Harry home on a hurdle, his neck broken in a reckless hunt two days before their planned elopement, and of how her father had beaten her and thrown her out when he found she was pregnant. 'Your dear stepfather found me wandering in the woods when he was gathering herbs,' she had told me. 'I was crying and I don't know how long I had been wandering, lost and afraid and alone; he asked no questions, just took me home, gave me hot water to wash in, borrowed a clean dress from a neighbour, fed me . . . . Then he showed me upstairs to this room – our room, Zoe – and said: "There's your room, young woman, and there's your bed, and they are yours for as long as you want them, you and the child that is to come." And after a while he said it would suit, if I had no better idea, that we should get married so that you would have a proper father, Zoe. He said also that I could feel I had a father in him too, for he had never aspired to the estate of matrimony, and indeed would esteem it a privilege if I could accept it as being in name only . . . .'

And he had been a good father to me too, though he was near sixty when I was born: I could not have asked for a kinder. When my mother had died of a wasting she had not even tried to combat, he had had her buried as near as he could to the vault where Harry lay; afterwards he had taken me on one side and said: 'Now we will have to teach each other how to live and grow and learn; you will show me how to be a father and I will show you how to be a daughter . . . .' But still through all those years I had borne a bitterness, a resentment; only now, now that I was confessing it, did a little understanding start to lighten the burden; only now did I see how much the resentment had been a purely selfish thing of my own making. *They* had been happy: what right had I to make of it something ugly and sordid?

Jack's voice broke in on my thoughts. 'I think you should be both happy and proud: happy that you were conceived in love, and proud that you had a stepfather who cared for you so well. You were luckier than many, you know . . . . Who decided to call you Zoe?'

'My stepfather suggested it. If I had been a boy I should have been called Harry, after my father, but when I turned out to be a girl my mother wouldn't give me her name: she said it meant 'bitter'. So my stepfather suggested that as I was a new life for them both I should be christened by a name that meant just that, and "Zoe" is Greek for "Life".'

'And your grandfather, the vicar?'

255

'My mother wrote to him when I was born, apparently, but he never answered. He died when I was about four.'

'Well, Sprat-Zoe, suppose we forget the past for a while and live for the present? Run up ahead to that inn at the crossroads and order us something to eat: meat pies, pease pudding or some such . . . .' And he took the reins from me, giving my hair a gentle ruffling, just as he would have run his fingers through Daisy's mane. It was oddly comforting: so, in their way, were the sheep's tails boiled with herbs, the unleavened bread, pickled onions, and watercress that awaited us at the tavern.

It was a golden autumn; after a couple of days at Amersham's famous market, vans tucked away snugly behind the Swan, we took the Aylesbury road and beyond, past great rolling fields of late September quick with rabbit, hare, and pigeon, bright with pheasant's wing and red admiral. The leaves of chestnut were gold and brown, the old man's beard and spider's web laden with morning dew, the hips and haws and honeysuckle berries scarlet, orange and black against the baring of the hedgerows. Sportsmen were out with their dogs and their guns, sheep were being brought down to the lower pastures, and the farmers in Leicester and Northampton were burning off the stubble in great clouds of acrid smoke; greedy wasps in heavy orchards were burrowing deep and sticky before the pigs could scrunch their stomachs full. We rose later and needed a fire at twilight, and Annie made great pies of the late blackberries and dewberries I found and bagged up the nuts Tom gathered in abundance. During the day the weather was still unseasonably warm and there were insects in profusion; the siskins and bramblings arrived early but the swallows left late; with them went Sam Alley-Come.

For some time he had been shivering in the early morning chill: now, by pantomime and (to me) unintelligible gibberish, he made it known, to Jack at least, that his purpose was to follow the birds south to his homeland. He never learned any English except our names and a few odd words like 'rain' and 'food' and 'thank you', but we were all sorry to lose him, for he was always cheerful and hard-working and behaved 'like a gent', as Annie put it; besides, he was a master of his craft. Signor Grappelli, who was to winter at home with his family in Naples, volunteered to accompany him, for they could travel together as far as Marseilles. The Italian was to join us again next year, probably at Warwick, but it was imposs-ible to make any such arrangements with Sam because he just did not understand plans for the future. Jack gave him a list of the towns we were likely to visit early next year, but I don't think he understood what was intended.

So they were both paid off and we clustered round to give them a good send-off, one early October morning with the dew heavy on the ground. Sam had found us all a parting present: for Jack a curiously carved pipe, for Tom a leather purse. Annie's present was really beautiful, a string of ivory beads finely carved with fruit and flowers, and I was more than happy with a length of silk, greeny-blue and very light. Luckily Jack had anticipated this present-giving and gave Sam, from us all, a fine red woollen cloak, originally made for a woman, but he wasn't to know and was all smiles, repeating his name happily: 'Sa'am Alley-Come, Sa'am Alley-Come', his hand fluttering from his heart, his mouth, his forehead, bowing all the time.

We went on up to Leicester's October Fair at Humber-stonegate, then back to Bedford for the Michaelmas Corn and Wheat Fair, where I tasted for the first time the famous Warden pears, sweet and juicy; here Dan, the sword-swallower, left us to stay with relatives, and we were back to our original numbers. There was only one fair of note left, that at Loughborough, the Charter Fair held in November, and we also made what use we could of market days. We had missed the great Nottingham Goose Fair, but it was not on this year's route: 'next year, perhaps', Jack said.

The rest of November was still mild, though damp, as we progressed north, and we played where we could, bypassing the place where my aunt lived, I was glad to see, by using the old salt roads where practicable. We arrived at Preston on 1 December in a river fog. Annie had livened up as soon as we passed 'north of a line', as she put it, and she was positively blooming like a June rose as we clattered over the cobbles towards the livery stables where the vans were to spend their winter. The proprietor obviously remembered Jack, addressing him as 'Mr Landless', which, as I had never thought of Jack as anything but 'Jack', made me blink thoughtfully: 'Landless' was a surname, certainly, but in association with Jack it sounded uncommonly like a pseudonym, a play on words.

During the winter months the vans were to be overhauled, cleaned out, refurbished and repainted and the horses kept fed and exercised, and for all this the central fund which Jack had deducted from our earnings provided enough. Any extra refinements – Annie wanted new curtains for her bed – were paid for by the person concerned, but Jack held the final decision against anything too outlandish. Everything else we didn't need, props, wardrobe, dry goods, was also stored, but these things needed packing up: this took us all the rest of the day. Annie's boxes and my pack were loaded on Tom's wagonette for the last stage of our journey; Jack was to travel back on Hannibal – to where he wouldn't tell us – and Tom was wintering south somewhere with his sister.

It had been arranged, or rather taken for granted, that Toby and I should spend the winter months with Annie, at her brother's house in Kirkham. 'There's not a lot of room, love,' she had said, 'but there's a welcome and warm hearts, and I should be glad of your company.' So there had been no argument and I for one was glad of the offer, for otherwise I should have had to look for lodgings and could not relish the thought of spending near three months on my own, not sure whether to play boy or girl. Annie and I had settled that too: ' 'Tis too late to fit you with dresses, but with the thicker clothes we'll all be wearing for winter, you can still pass as a young lad. If any finds out, we can make up a tale to suit . . . .'

That night was the last we spent in the vans and Annie collected the bedding to take on with us and wash and mend at leisure. We were to pick up the carrier from Penwortham the following day to take us on to Kirkham, and Tom took two trips with the luggage the five miles or so, then came back for Annie. I hopped up behind Jack on Hannibal and we set off together for the Bridge Inn, where we were all to lodge for the night. It was a pleasant enough countrified place with only a couple of guest rooms, and Jack had spoken one for Annie and me and one for himself. Tom was happy enough to bed in the stables with Daisy, Hannibal and Toby.

Jack invited us all to eat with him at six o'clock. 'There's no private dining room, but the food is good, I'm assured, and they have a decent enough cellar. So, on with your best, and we'll have a celebration!'

'Who's paying?' asked Annie, ever suspicious.

'I am – just this once! Think of it as a bonus . . . I think you all deserve it,' he added generously. 'And we've had a good season, all things considered.' As he had also paid for the accommodation, Annie and I felt thoroughly spoiled. Up in our room, almost filled by the enormous four-poster, she fished out her favourite pink satin and hung it up to loosen the creases; she had fresh yellow ribbons to sew down the front. I looked in my pack and spread out the meagre contents: two pairs of worn breeches, three shirts, one waistcoat with a button missing, four pairs of drawers, two smocks, and three neckerchiefs.

'Which, Annie?' I asked. 'Black breeches or brown?'

She looked up from tacking on her bows. 'What's that folded up?'

'My muslin Desdemona dress and the length of green silk Sam gave me . . . .'

We were both struck by the same thought.

'I can't wear the dress on its own, it's transparent – well, nearly . . . .'

'He's not expecting you to dress as a girl . . . . Why not surprise him? Let's look at that length of silk . . . .'

We ended up sewing frantically by early candlelight, but I was pleased with the result. Annie folded the length in half, then cut a generous third out of the middle of one side; this she fashioned into a petticoat underneath the muslin dress. The complete length she fastened at the shoulders to flow down my back like a cloak, and the two panels that were left were sewn down the front of the dress, to swathe my bosom and fall down at either side in floating panels. While she finished the final tacking at the sides, for her needle was much faster than mine, I had a quick scrub and washed my hair in the large tub the housemaid brought up at my request with much grumbling; apparently a lot of water flowed under the Bridge before anyone used any: there was a small cobweb in the tub.

The fire in our room had been lit, so I dried quickly, twisting my unruly hair into smoother curls, and donned my party dress. Privately I thought the neckline was a little low, but Annie assured me it was just the thing, and the spotted mirror we both shared didn't show enough to confirm my doubts. Annie dusted her face vigorously with white powder and touched her lips and cheeks with carmine: I thought perhaps she looked better without, but she so obviously felt better with her large doll's face that I hadn't the heart to dissuade her. I borrowed a little of her clear grease and touched up my eyebrows and eyelashes and decided that would do, with a touch of rose-water also borrowed from her generous make-up box.

I heard the stable clock strike, and glanced across. 'It's six o'clock: you know how he hates to be kept waiting . . . . Do I look all right?'

'Quite, quite different! Don't think he'll recognize you . . . . You wouldn't like a little powder?'

'No, thanks, dear Annie: I should look silly with a white face and sunbrowned arms – I'll leave it to you to do the honours for us both in that direction . . . .'

We went to the head of the stairs. Round the twist that led down to the bar parlour I could see Tom and Jack seated at a table by the bow window, Tom in his best brown jacket and snuff-coloured breeches, with a spotted neckerchief, and Jack – Jack wore his best mulberry coat, a mole-coloured waistcoat and breeches, and had tied back his hair all tidy and smooth with a black ribbon. His frilled shirt and stockings were immaculate, and he had even polished his shoes. I suddenly felt shy, unsure of my dress, but glad that my shabby, black-buckled shoes wouldn't show under the hem. Although the room was only half-full – a round table containing four or five countrymen playing dominoes, two farmers having a drink at another, and what looked like a prosperous tradesman chatting with a couple of friends at the long bar – I was glued to the stairs: I couldn't move.

'Go on, Annie: I've just got to fetch a handkerchief . . .' and I fled back down the corridor to our room. I couldn't go down there, I couldn't! Supposing Jack thought I looked stupid in a dress, supposing the stitches came undone, supposing –

'Sprat! Where the hell are you?'

I went back down the corridor very slowly. He was standing at the top of the stairs, one foot a step down, hand on the balustrade. As I came level with the wall candles I saw his eyes widen and a little smile curve his mouth. Then he bowed low.

'Miss Mortimer? May I have the honour to escort you down to dinner?' And he offered his arm.

'Jack, I –' then I caught his mood. 'Mr Landless: yes, I should be glad of your arm, sir.' Even with this I hesitated for a moment as we started to descend.

He patted the hand on his arm. 'It's a part, Zoe: the

261

young and charming ingénue dining with one of her devoted beaus. She is beautifully dressed in the very height of fashion, intelligent, and fully in command of the situation. All she has to do is enjoy the evening.'

'If it's a part, what about the script?' I hissed, as he drew me down inexorably into the warm, brightly lit room.

'It's one you know, even if you don't realize it. The part was written years ago, when you were born; inside you there was, even then, the young lady you are now. Remember those caterpillar chrysalids we saw earlier in the year, hatching out into butterflies? You were once a little caterpillar child yourself, then you became a decidedly odd brown chrysalis of a Sprat: now's the time for the butterfly!'

'The biggest chrysalis I ever saw turned into a particularly dingy moth,' I said gloomily.

'Well, you look like a butterfly to me – and a very pretty one tonight,' and he squeezed my arm against his side.

'But the dress . . . . Is it fashionable?'

'I wouldn't know a thing about ladies' fashions, and neither, I suspect, would anyone else here. Suffice it to say, it becomes you very well, and that charming décolletage leaves your true sex in no doubt!'

I *knew* it had been too low . . . I felt myself blushing.

'Don't worry,' he added, quite shattering any ego that might have been stirring in my reassured breast, 'they are all looking at Annie, anyway.'

This was quite true. I had become so used to Annie's size that I thought no more of it than if she had been normal, but when we sat down, with me next to Jack in the window seat and opposite Tom, it was in the midst of a flurry to find a large enough chair to accommodate her. Apparently the large stool she had originally taken had given a few ominous creaks, and now they fetched her a great solid Tudor chair in dark oak, the landlord fussing about like a terrier at the heels of a great Shire. He must have been all of five feet tall and thin as a cutout sideways to the wind but his attentions obviously pleased Annie,

262

for she was calling him her 'dearie' already and fluttering her eyelashes at him in a girlish way I found fascinating.

The rest of the customers, too, apparently could not take their eyes off her, and I heard one of the farmers, openly admiring, say to the other: 'By the left! It's a sight fit for Preston Guild – and as uncommon!' and in Jack's face I read the almost overwhelming desire to charge them a shilling a pinch . . . . For the rest of the evening, whenever one of the clientele had to get up for a pint or the privy, they made sure of a detour as near as possible to our blissful fat lady, just to make sure she was really true.

Tom had nodded to me as I sat down. 'Very pretty, lass: suits you,' which, in its way, was better than anything Jack had said. The dinner was delicious: mussels in white wine, pheasant, jugged hare, and apple pie with cream and a great chunk of the local sharp cheese. Annie, for once, tucked in with gusto and drank quantities of gin and water; Tom politely ate everything on his plate, as usual, but stuck to ale.

Jack and I had wine, two bottles of it: I was too excited to eat much, only too conscious of my dress, the unaccustomed luxury of a set dinner, the warmth, the wine . . . . And, most of all, of Jack. He drank his way steadily through one bottle of wine, then started on what I had left of the other, and halfway through the apple pie I found I was eating with my left hand only, my right comfortably clasped in his. For once we two seemed to be apart in a kind of conspiracy, almost as if we were on a different level from our companions and the other customers, smiling down on their innocent enjoyments with a kindly superiority. Besides, holding someone's hand was warm and comforting and to be relished and appreciated and enjoyed like the food, warmth, and wine.

Port followed with the cheese, but my head was swimming already and I leaned back to watch the others. Tom was slowly and methodically masticating the last of his cheese, perhaps a little redder in the face than usual, but otherwise as unruffled and calm as ever; Annie was getting more and more expansive with each gin and water, the little landlord dancing attendance on her, his hands now hovering unashamedly round her plump shoulders, his eyes diving eagerly down the dark cleft between her enormous breasts, tongue between his teeth.

Jack's fingers tightened on mine. 'You all right?'

'Mmmm . . . . A – a little woozy, whiffley, perhaps . . . . Wheeee . . . !'

'What on earth does that mean, you dizzy girl?'

'Bit – 'nebriated, I think. Everything seems to be floating. 'Specially me . . . .'

'What you need is a breath of fresh air: come on, the others won't miss us, and I think we might be inhibiting them a little . . . .' He leaned over and had a quick word with Tom, then pulled me to my feet and unhooked his cloak from the peg near the door. Outside, he slipped his arm through mine and guided my unheeding feet through the mire of the yard to the footpath leading down to the river. It was one of those nights when the air was perfectly calm and still, the stars bright with cold; I stumbled a couple of times on the stony path but after a few minutes' walking we came to the river, chuckling over its rounded stones in a hurry to reach the sea. There we halted, the bridge a darker shadow to our left; above our heads a night bird cried mournfully, answered by a couple of sleepy sheep. Jack released my arm, and I shivered.

'Cold?'

'Don't think so . . . . Don't really know.'

He laughed. 'You're cut, child! Breathe deeply: if you fall flat on your face I'll pick you up –'

I flung away from him in a pet. 'I'm *not* a child . . . !'

'Prove it!'

'Any time, any time, just say the word . . .' but I belied my promise and ran away, laughing, stumbling over the pebbles, dodging behind the twisted trees that clung, bare-rooted and precarious, to the river-bank. There was a slither of stones as Jack followed me, then, suddenly, we both heard it, a tiny piping in the sky. At first it was only a murmur, a voice on the edge of consciousness, then the sound intensified and became a clamour of wild voices and against the dark of sky a deeper wedge of black came winging overhead, the trumpeting call passing down one side and up the other.

'Wild geese,' said Jack at my side. 'They don't usually fly by night; dusk and dawning's their time. Some poacher must have disturbed them.' He slipped an arm and half his cloak round my shoulders. 'I think they are coming down again in that field across the river.'

Sure enough, the wedge was breaking up and veering and a moment later the cold air above our heads was stirred to life as they swooped in overhead, their vibrant honking a warning of the harsh susurration of wing pinions as they beat the night air down on our faces. Instinctively I ducked as their wing feathers almost brushed us as they passed, then stooped and picked up a discarded feather.

'And what are you going to do with that?'

'It's going in my treasure box.'

'Along with the fourteen-foot pastry pig?' he said, teasing me, for well he knew that only a week or two after St Bartholomew's, opening my box to gloat, I had found my souvenir a heap of unhealthy crumbs, tasting of sandalwood. Even Toby wouldn't touch them, although he did nibble thoughtfully at a currant eye before spitting it out.

'I might trim it for a pen to write the story of my travels,' I said airily.

'Small feather for a small history,' he said. 'Wait till you've lived a bit.'

I thought I had, but let it pass. We walked back to the inn, sharing the cloak; I used the privy first, then shivered in the yard, waiting for Jack. I was just about to cross to the stables to say goodnight to Toby when the returning Jack touched my arm and, following his gaze, I saw two figures, closely intertwined, disappear through the double doors and close them quietly behind. One looked like

Tom, the other was a wench. I looked up at Jack. 'I didn't know he was like that . . . .'

'I told you we were cramping their style. You've a lot to learn, Zoe.' He was smiling as he led me back into the inn. Nearly all the customers had gone and I looked for Annie, but the Tudor chair was empty.

'She's gone to bed,' I said, surprised.

'Very probably.' He went across to the bar and brought back a bottle and two glasses. 'Shall we go and see?'

'Expecting a visitor?' I said waspishly, nodding at the second glass.

'One should always be prepared.'

I thought of the maids I had seen at the inn, but could recall none that would tempt even him on a dark night and there were no female visitors except Annie and me: still, one never knew with Jack: he might even have ordered one from outside.

We climbed the stairs together and he took a candlestick from the table at the head. 'Here, you'd better take this.'

I stopped at our door. 'Thank you for the wonderful meal and the walk and – everything.' I reached up and kissed his cheek: it seemed the right thing to to.

'Aren't you going to see if everything's all right?'

'Where?'

'In there,' and he nodded at our door. 'I should, I really should, before you are in too much of a hurry to say goodnight . . . .'

I didn't know what he was talking about, but lifted the latch and peered in. There was a candle left burning on the bedside table and a confusion of dress, petticoat, flounces, frills, stays, drawers, stockings, and breeches – breeches? – littering the floor from the doorway to the bed. And on the bed there was taking place what looked, and sounded, like a battle royal; arms and legs were threshing about, there were grunts and squeals and cries and a snow of feathers. I started forward to Annie's rescue, then suddenly realized what it was all about. Not that I could say I recognized the owner of the little round buttocks valiantly pumping up and down between her mountainous knees, but I knew she would not thank me for any interruptions.

I closed the door carefully.

Jack was leaning back against the panelled wall, laughing. 'Well?'

'How did – Who is it, anyway?'

'The landlord, of course, unless she's changed jockeys in midstream! It didn't take much imagination to see which way that was going earlier this evening. She's quite a girl on the quiet, is our Annie, and this is her last fling before resigning herself to a respectable, dull winter. Now, having answered both your questions, albeit in the wrong order, here's one for you: where are you going to bed down for the night?'

'The stable, I suppose – oh no! Tom is in there with that girl . . .' I glared at him. 'Well, I suppose you have a better idea, grinning away there like a gargoyle?'

Grabbing my free hand he led me down the corridor, lifted the latch of a nearby room with the wrist of the hand that held the bottle and glasses, and pulled me in after him, kicking the door shut. Setting the refreshments down on a nearby table he took my candlestick and lit more candles on the side tables, crossed to the fireplace and poked the logs into a blaze.

I looked about me; it was a larger room than ours, with a four-poster, a large hanging cupboard, two clothes-presses, another table and a large and comfortable-looking leather armchair by the fire. 'But this is your room . . . .'

'So?'

'I can't stay here –'

'Why not?'

'It – it wouldn't be decent!'

'Again, why not? You've successfully shared a caravan with me for the last nine months or so, and you've been perfectly safe.'

'But – but this is different!'

'How different? What is the difference, Zoe?' And he

267

came and took my hand and led me over to the fire. 'Could this be the difference?' and suddenly his arm was round my waist and a hand slipped into the front of my dress, fingers on my breast. 'This different?' and he brought his groin against my stomach. 'Is this what you are afraid of?' His fingers teased my nipples and I could feel him harden against me. I was suddenly afraid, confused, embarrassed: yes, yes! this was a Jack I didn't know, the Jack of the casual encounters. Even his voice was different: husky, provocative, yet harsh, and suddenly I didn't want to be any part of it. I wanted the comfortable, sexless Uncle Jack of the road, who was kind to a starving boy and asked nothing more than a fair degree of intelligence and hard work. Forgotten was the kiss I had forced upon him on the heath at Ditchling, and my unexpected response; gone was the fair Miss Mortimer, in charge of the situation: in her place was a frightened youngster who didn't want to grow up. Jack must have sensed my conflict, though I tried hard not to flinch from his embrace and to pretend I was used to such encounters, for he released me abruptly, walked over to the side table and poured two glasses of wine. 'Here, drink.'

I thought that now I understood the two glasses and hesitated, mind and body in a turmoil.

Flinging himself down in the armchair, he lounged back and regarded me over the rim of his glass. 'What are you afraid of?'

'You,' I said truthfully. 'This drink –'

'For God's sake! It's not drugged, and I've no intention of raping you, seducing you, or even making you take your clothes off, so for heaven's sake drink up!'

'Then why the demonstration?'

'Just to show you that I am as I always have been, a man, with all a man's normal desires. To show you too that I can leave well alone if need be; we have been good companions during our time together – it was only what was in your mind that made it possible for us to change

268

the relationship two minutes ago. And you didn't like it, so I stopped. Simple as that.'

I couldn't explain to him that once his hand had been on my breast we could never go back to the state of forgetfulness; he may have touched so many that one was as acceptable and unremarkable as the next, but in this case it was *mine* he had touched, and they were first-time-tingling still . . . I sipped the wine thoughtfully. It was pleasant and heady, and the fire crackled cheerfully in the grate. I made an effort to return to the normality he obviously thought I should find so easily. 'Who sleeps on the bed?'

'We'll cut for it: high card wins. You first.' He reached for a pack of cards on the mantel.

Obediently I cut: four of hearts. My heart sank; still, the rug would be warm . . . . He held up the two of clubs. 'Your bed.' He blew out the candles on the side table, leaving just one burning on the mantel, and heaped more logs on the fire. 'Go on, before I change my mind!'

Behind the curtains of the bed I slipped out of my pretty dress and drawers and draped them on the edge, wrapping myself snugly in the coverlet. 'Do you want a blanket?'

'No, thanks: the fire's warm enough. Go to sleep!'

I lay back, the bedcurtains undrawn again, watching the reflections from the fire and candlelight on the walls and ceiling, but I couldn't sleep. My heart thudded uncomfortably in my chest; I was too cold, too hot. Raising myself on one elbow, I gazed over to where Jack lay back in the chair. He had discarded the mulberry coat and his necktie, and his shirt lay loose over the half-buttoned breeches; one hand was in those same breeches – All at once I understood a lot of things, and my heart was full of compassion. Silly fool! I slipped out of bed, counterpane draped strategically, and went over to his side. He made no attempt to adjust his dress, just looked up at me.

'Have – have I done that to you?'

'You put the idea there . . . . It's been a long time, you know.'

269

'But you have women all over the place –'

He leaned forward and stood up. 'How would you know what women I have?'

'There was Chloe at Marlborough, one at that place near Malvern when Annie had a cold, and the puppeteer's daughter . . . .' I stopped. There must have been others.

'You see? Of those three, the only ones you can think of, just two were correct. It might surprise you to know, my little spy, that I have only been to bed with a woman three times in the last twelve months, in spite of what you may think.'

'But your . . . .' I hesitated.

'Reputation?' he supplied. 'Ah, yes, that's different. My reputation, my dear Zoe, has nothing whatever to do with my performance. Perhaps you will understand one day.' He moved away to stand by the fire. 'Now, go away, before I break all my good resolutions.'

'You mean – me?'

'Who else? You're the only female within touching distance, I believe.'

I considered this for a moment. Forgotten were any prudish ideas of what was right and what was wrong, all I knew was that Jack needed help, and I owed him whatever I could give. I didn't know anything, except in theory, about going to bed with a man, but I should have to learn some time and I had rather it was Jack than anyone else. If he could bring back to me that lovely tingly melting feeling – I went over to the table and refilled our glasses.

'Drink down, Jack, and I'll give you a toast.'

'Celibacy is good for the soul?' He grimaced, but he drank.

'No, seduction is; but please don't rape me, I don't think I'd like that. Seduction sounds softer and more comfortable.' and I shed the coverlet to lie in a huddle at my feet. 'Is this the best way to begin?'

He stared at me in utter astonishment, then to my complete chagrin burst out laughing. 'Oh, you *idiot*! you dear idiot . . . . Here, drape yourself with that thing again and go back to bed. I'm not seducing you tonight, or any other as far as I can see.'

'Why?' and I'm sure my voice must have been thick with the shame of rejection. 'Aren't I . . . aren't I acceptable enough? I know I'm not particularly pretty . . . .'

He stopped laughing and picked up the coverlet. Very gently he draped it round my shoulders, then bent and kissed the tip of my nose.

'You are *very* pretty at this moment, my dear, and you have a lovely figure – at least, everything's in the right place as far as I can see. But Jack's no man for little sixteen-year-old virgins; what I need tonight is a ripe matron who knows all the tricks.'

'But I could learn . . . .'

'Not from me, and not tonight. You deserve better. One day you will be glad I'm treating you as the child you still are. Thanks for trying to help, just the same,' and he bent to kiss me again, but this time I was determined and he found my mouth instead of a more commonplace area of my face. He tried to draw back but I had my arms around his neck and pressed myself against him. Moving my lips under his I wriggled a little so that the coverlet fell off again and in a moment I felt his hands on my body, pressing my buttocks closer to his hips and there it was, that lovely melting feeling again . . . .

Once more he tried to put me away from him, and his voice was all shaky. 'No, Zoe, no! You're too young and too nice and I'm responsible for you –'

'And I'm responsible – for that,' and I lightly touched his swelling groin. 'I know I'm inexperienced, but isn't there something I could do without – well, you know . . . .'

'If you could have helped, my love, you would have been in bed with me half an hour since.'

'But you won't even let me try . . . .'

'Perhaps I don't want you to grow up too soon: it isn't always fun, you know.'

'Surely there must be some way?'

He smiled, then shrugged and, taking my hand, guided it down. 'See what you can do with that, then . . . .'

The trouble was that I hadn't more than a vague idea, and in any case was afraid of hurting him. Tentatively I unbuttoned the rest of his breeches and stroked him. 'Is that all right?'

'Oh, Zoe!' and suddenly he stooped and picked me up, held me close for a moment, and then we were on the bed together and he was covering my face, my neck, my breasts with rapid kisses. I could feel him shaking with urgency, hear his rapid breathing. 'You know where it wants to be: just give it the next best!'

I did what I could but apparently it wasn't enough, for after a moment or so his hand came down over mine with a violence I hadn't expected and he showed me what he wanted. After that it didn't take long and he groaned and shivered and his head was on my breast, sweat from his forehead on my skin, his now ribbonless hair tickling my neck. After a while he raised his head and drew away, to lie flat on his back, his hand over his eyes.

'Are you all right?' I asked anxiously, wiping my sticky hand on the sheet.

'Of course.' He laughed, a little shakily. 'Now you know what fools we men are, to be ruled by our pricks.'

'Not very often, according to you.' I hesitated. 'Was . . . was it . . . . Did I do it right?'

'Yes, thank you.' He seemed disinclined to go on, but I had to know.

'Is it . . . is it as nice as it seems?'

'Better properly, but you gave me what I needed.' He rolled over and kissed my forehead. 'Now, let's get some sleep.'

All very well for him, but I was wide awake; curious, yes; elated by my discovery of how men worked, yes, but, most of all, unsatisfied, my body still hungering for kisses and the feel of Jack's body. I found I was breathing more quickly and I felt restless and strange all over as I had in Wiltshire, as if my body stretched and moved in the direction of discovery, all the nerve endings taut and touch being the most important sense of the five. At the same time I felt empty – not hungry, but as if somebody had taken out my insides painlessly and the resultant hollow needed filling before I burst inward, like a reverse bladder of air. I wanted to run away from something like the wind, and yet not away but towards . . . .

'Stop fidgeting, child, and go to sleep.'

I tried again, but it was no use.

'Jack . . . .'

'Yes?'

'I feel awful!'

'Sick? It was all that wine –'

'Not sick. I – I just want something terribly and I'm not sure what it is but I think it's you –' The words tumbled out helter-skelter in an unconsidered rush but he seemed to understand, for he laughed, but tenderly, and drew me into his arms again.

'Well, my dear, you've successfully done for me tonight, which is just as well, but perhaps I can give you a taste . . . . Lie still and don't wonder at what I do; if you don't like it I'll stop. Remember, this is what your body was meant for, so let your sensible, prosaic, corseted mind go to sleep for a while.' And he kissed me and touched me and stroked me so expertly that the wanting became desperate and he was both my pursuer and my quarry at the same time. Although I was trembling I was neither frightened nor ashamed, and I could hear myself making little sounds like a hungry kitten or pup.

'Steady, love, steady,' he murmured. 'I didn't realize . . . . Sweetheart, hold me tight: that's it. Now, Zoe, my honey-heart, glove my finger: just so, that's it . . . . Imagine it's Jack that's there . . . .'

Just for a moment it was strange to find part of him in my secret places, then it was all that I had ever wanted. All tickly and tender and like wanting to relieve oneself but in reverse, then suddenly everything tightened up and rushed inwards instead of spreading out and it was like lurching over the bar at the top of the swing and jolting over a humpback bridge and embracing impossible dreams all at once, and Jack's mouth was on mine to stifle the cries.

'Gently,' he said, 'gently. That better?'

I started to cry, but quietly so he couldn't hear, and the tears spilled out of my eyes and trickled down into my ears. The strange thing was that I didn't want to weep at all: I wanted to laugh and run and shout . . . .

'We shan't have any trouble with you when the time comes,' he said, and kissed my wet eyes, first one and then the other. 'Don't cry, girl: you're still mostly virgin. So you've lost nothing but your innocence.' He kissed my nose. 'And that, my sweet, was quite ready to go, and is quite safe with your old Jack.' He flopped back, his right arm still holding me close. 'But don't go experimenting with anyone else for a while; you are still bound to me by your indentures. For everything, and that includes lovemaking.'

'I never signed any indentures –'

'Oh, yes, you did. I've got your signature, or a very fair imitation of the 'Z. Mortimer' inside your copy of Shakespeare: Gloucester taught me a thing or two, so I made sure you were bound to me if the occasion arose. Until your seventeenth birthday that is: then you are free.'

I sat up. 'That's cheating!'

'Prove it: prove that it's not your signature –' He laughed suddenly, then sighed. 'Oh, Zoe, don't let's quarrel! I've never demanded anything of you except a fair day's work – no pun intended – have I?'

I shook my head. 'How am I bound to you, just out of curiosity?'

'Body and obedience; to learn my trade for a tenth of the profits – after wear and tear and clothing, upkeep and so on . . . .'

'And does learning your trade include – what happened tonight?'

I think he smiled in the darkness, because his voice

sounded as though his lips curled round amusement. 'No, my dear, that was my bonus – and yours, for I believe I am qualified to teach the rudiments . . . . Now, go to sleep,' and he yawned, a noisy, jaw-cracking yawn that had me duplicating it a moment later.

He appeared to fall asleep at once: not me. For all the yawn I lay awake till the candle on the mantel guttered, flared grotesquely for a brief renewal, then expired in a gasp of smoke and dawnlight filtered round the edges of the ill-drawn curtains. I was conscious all the while of the man who lay beside me; conscious of the mind-searchings and soul-searchings that went with what had happened this night; conscious most of all that whatever happened in the future, life could never be quite the same for me again.

13

Not that anything appeared different the following morning.

When I awoke, reluctantly, a little after nine, the room was empty except for myself and I crept back to Annie, expecting all sorts of reprisals; I was met by the same chaotic disorder of the night before, except for the breeches, plus a very cross and comatose singular hump in the middle of the rumpled bed. Tiptoeing around, I resumed my boy's clothes and regretfully packed away the Desdemona dress. Wearing it had certainly been an experience.

I went downstairs to find the others. Tom was just struggling with the last of his ham and eggs, and a crumbed plate and empty mug told me Jack had already breakfasted. Tom merely grunted when I wished him good morning, his red-rimmed eyes and unshaven chin telling all. I brought Toby in for his food and he seemed the only bright, alive and bouncing creature in the whole

275

establishment. The serving maid brought my dish of eggs with a slatternly shuffle, wisps of hair escaping from her mobcap, her apron unironed; if she were indeed the one who had gone to the stable with Tom last night, as I suspected, it seemed that here there was to be a conspiracy of silence, for neither even glanced at the other, though I noticed that Tom leaned further over his plate and she kept her eyes fixed on the floor.

I fed Toby under the table with most of my eggs and the rind from Tom's plate, then we went for his constitutional, visiting most of the shrubs and trees down the lane towards the river and starting a hare who lolloped away derisively over the brown grass as I called Toby to heel. This saved his face, for he could always persuade himself he would have caught it, which he wouldn't, and it also spared him the humiliation of returning half an hour later having lost both himself and his quarry amongst the sere and withered clumps of herbage along the river-bank. When we reached the water I leaned on the bridge for a while, leaving Toby to sniff hopefully for water rats; I had half-hoped Jack would find his way down here, but we were alone except for a shepherd and his dogs who crossed the bridge on their way further upstream. The geese had gone from the far pasture, and apart from the cry of a tattered seagull, the bleat of sheep and the chuckle of water over the smooth pebbles, we heard nothing either. There was a thin edging of ice on the banks where the river moved slowly and after a while I shivered in my thin jacket and turned back for the inn, hoping that at least Annie was up by now.

She was, but still not in a sociable mood, her face buried in a mug of mulled ale, her fingers idly crumbling a slice of dry bread: of the little landlord there was no sign. I went upstairs and finished my repacking, then started on Annie's. This took some time and I heard the clock downstairs strike eleven before I was finished. Glancing out of the window I saw Annie emerge from the privy looking distinctly green, passing the little landlord bound on the same errand who scuttled past like a startled cockroach in his dark coat and black breeches. Again without a glance at each other: I began to feel distinctly uneasy. Was this the way one was supposed to behave towards people when one had spent the intimate dark hours in their embrace? Perhaps it was the done thing, a convention to be observed: that was probably why Jack had disappeared, afraid I wouldn't know the correct way to behave. I supposed that I was what one would call a casual encounter; I began to feel ashamed. Calling Toby off the bed, where he had gone into hibernation under the coverlet, I walked slowly down the passage and stairs. All right, I must remember to ignore Jack, and stifle, too, the earlier conviction that what had happened between us was rather special . . . .

I had just walked over to the table where Tom and Annie still sat, the air thick with monosyllables, when the door crashed back on its hinges and Jack strode in, bringing on his clothes and hair the smell of fresh air; his nose was frost-bright, his tangled hair curling up on itself at the ends to keep warm.

'Come on, you lot! Carrier'll be here soon – all packed? Good. Annie, you look thoroughly dissipated: Tom, you look worse. It must be the life you lead,' and he winked outrageously at me. 'Regard Sprat and me, now: a good meal, a glass of wine or two and a peaceful night, after a little exercise, and we are full of the joys of life!'

I doubt if the other two heeded his words, though I felt myself blushing at the innuendos, but when he slapped his riding whip down on the table with a sound like a pistol shot they both jumped and Annie groaned.

'Leave over do, Master Jack: I'm in no mood.'

'And just when I was about to share out our profits!' he tutted, and brought out three paper-wrapped piles of coins. 'That's what's left after all the reckonings have been paid.'

Eagerly I counted my coins: eleven guineas, four florins and two pence. I would need every penny, for I should owe Annie keep for the next three months or so and I needed a warmer jacket. Tom slipped his packet into his pocket without even looking at it but Annie turned her shoulder to us all and counted hers laboriously, at least twice.

The luggage was brought out into the inn yard. Hannibal was saddled and ready but Tom was still harnessing Daisy up to the wagonette.

We all stood around waiting for the carrier, but no one was saying anything. I thought the time had come to break the awkward silence, so I brought out my three packages.

'Tom, these two are to be opened at Christmas: the one with the dark blue ribbon is for you, the other with the pink paper, for Daisy. Jack . . . I'm afraid it might not be as appropriate as I first thought . . .' and I trailed into silence as I handed him the carefully wrapped tube. Inside, only I knew there were prints of Hogarth's 'Rake's Progress' (second-hand from a bookseller in Chichester) that at the time had merely seemed a virtuous warning, but after last night – 'Annie, yours is in my baggage.'

'Well, now,' said Tom. 'That's a kind thought. Seems as though we had a packet for you and one for Toby somewheres . . . here 'tis. And one for Mistress Annie, too.'

Jack said nothing for a moment, just looked at his unopened present, an oddly embarrassed look on his face.

'Well, you little lamb!' exclaimed Annie. 'Bet you've spent all your savings.'

'Not quite –'

'I have something for you too as you're spending Christmas with us, but I didn't think to get anything for the others –'

'And I,' said Jack, 'to my eternal shame, didn't think. At all. Sprat's is my one and only Christmas present, given or received, and I am mightily grateful . . . .'

278

'Well, don't open it till Christmas,' I said gruffly. 'It's nothing special: I only bought it because we always used to exchange presents at home, however little, to mark the season; as I said, I don't think it's particularly appropriate –'

'It's the thought that counts,' said all the others, more or less simultaneously, and we were still laughing the rather overloud release from an awkward moment when the carrier turned into the yard.

His wagon smelt strongly of sheep's wool and fish, his two principal everyday loads as I learned later, but as it was a fine day the tarpaulin was folded back. Annie climbed heavily to the seat beside the driver, addressing him familiarly as 'Chuck', and Tom and I piled the boxes on to the back, where I was to join them. The carrier, who apparently had been as far as Fulwood with his earlier loads, disappeared into the inn for a well-earned pint or two, and Jack drew me aside.

'You all right, Sprat?'

'Of course – why should you think I wasn't?'

'You seemed to be avoiding me.'

'I thought *you* were . . . anyway, isn't that what one's supposed to do?'

He looked utterly confused. 'What for?'

'After last night: like Tom and his girl and Annie and her – her –'

To my surprise he laughed, looked sober again, then laughed once more. 'And *I* thought . . . . No, Sprat-Zoe, one is *not* supposed to ignore one's bedmate – unless the whole thing was so trivial or shame-making or done purely for lust as to make it something to crawl away from the following morning.' He placed his fingers under my chin so I had to look up at him. 'That's better. It was none of those things for me last night, nor, I hope, was it for you. I enjoyed it, and perhaps one day –' He released me abruptly. 'Damn you for still being a child, and damn those mismatched eyes of yours even more! You *are* a witch's brat . . . .' He changed the subject. 'Which reminds me: Kat Petulengro. My spies tell me you saw her again before she went.'

'Yes . . . . Oh hell! I forgot to give you the message.'

'Don't swear. What message?'

So I told him she had foreseen her own death, upon which he frowned, sighed, but did not argue. I did not tell him what she had said to me, but I did mention the book she had given me, which I had only glanced at so far. 'It was all about reading hands and looking at the crystal ball and the tarot pack —'

'Good,' he said, interrupting. 'You'll have plenty of time in the next three months' holiday to get to know the methods thoroughly. I had already earmarked you for a spot of fortune-telling next year: you can't be dressed as a boy for ever, you know . . . .' That was more or less what *she* had said: were the book and recipes then meant to be the way?

In no time at all, or so it seemed, we were ready for off. 'Chuck' flourished his whip, the horses leaned against the shafts, and we swung our way out of the inn yard. The last sight I had of Jack was of him bowing, hand on heart, and declaiming, to me or Annie or both, I wasn't sure which: 'Let not winter's ragged hand deface thee in thy summer prime . . . .'

Annie's brother's house was to the west of Kirkham itself, the middle of three cottages that stood atop the winding street that curved down to the centre of the town. Downstairs was a fair-sized living room with a brick oven to one side of the fire that would burn either wood or peat, a mantel over carrying a broken-handled blue mug, two spotted china dogs (chipped), and a brown box with shells stuck in a pattern on the lid. There was a scrubbed table and four stools, a large rocker, a double bed and a couple of wooden boxes for storage; a lantern hung from the ceiling and there were hooks for coats behind the door, together with a couple of shepherd's crooks. Where horn was missing from the panes in the small window that gave to the street oiled paper filled the gaps.

Through the living room and down a step was the pantry: a cupboard for the crockery and pans, such as they were, a long stone slab and sink with three buckets under. Outside at the back was a minute yard with three scrawny chickens pecking in the dirt and a covered wood and peat store. Beyond were the fields, restless with grubby sheep, and in the far blue distance, rolling hills. The pump was some way down the lane and one of the buckets was used for water; one was for vegetables, mostly potatoes, and the last was for night soil, the pit for which was in the opposite direction from the pump. Up a wooden ladder in the cottage was the other room, ceiling following the pitch of the roof, where the boys usually slept, but now a rough sacking curtain had been drawn across and Annie's brother had taken a pallet up to share eaves-space with his sons, leaving Annie the double bed downstairs and me a straw palliasse to lie by the fire, though on that first night I had to make do with the rug and a blanket, as of course they hadn't been expecting me.

I was made very welcome all the time I was there, though the whole family, in direct contrast to Annie, were quiet and reserved and I found their speech difficult to follow at first, being heavily local and full of dialect names for things which I found rather confusing – ponds were 'pits', sparrows 'spugs', and so on. Mr Sutcliffe was a shepherd, his taciturnity perhaps explained by the fact he spent much of his day alone; his eldest son followed the same profession and the middle boy, who was about ten, was a bird-scarer and helped tend the pigs on the farm where his father worked; the youngest child, a boy of five years old, was tended by the widow next door, who had two younger children. They all obviously adored their Auntie Annie and she soon made the rather sparsely furnished house into more of a home, ranging her boxes against the wall to make extra seats, bringing out a bright cloth for the table, a cushion for the rocker, hanging a patterned material across the darkening window and putting the rose-patterned mug I had given her in pride of place on the mantel, sending the youngest for a spray of berries to place in the blue one, and setting out her tea-things on the table. There wasn't much free space when we were all at home, but being used to the confines of life in a caravan I soon became used to it. That first night we were a merry party round the fire, eating a bought pie and drinking ale the eldest had brought back from the Plough in a jug.

But it was Toby who was the star of the show. The boys were used to working dogs on the farm, but one who entertained for a living was something entirely new. Only one of them had ever seen even a Punch and Joan show, and that had been without a dog, so at first they treated him warily. But Toby liked all children and was so especially at home with small boys (I suspected there was one in the house he must have been stolen from) that his good temper, comical air and desire to please soon had them all won over, especially when he treated them to a run-through of his begging, dancing a jig and dying for his country. That night the youngest had to be picked off the floor at bedtime, him being fast asleep on the rag rug, his arms wrapped round the patient Toby's neck. After that I was quite happy to let the boys exercise him, and they in turn were proud to show off his tricks to their friends.

The next morning I woke in what seemed the middle of the night to a stentorian tapping at the window.

'Five of the clock and a little past, now! Are you awake in there?'

The knocker-up didn't wait for an answer and I heard the same message, slightly diminished, next door, then a heavy tramping away down the lane. Scarcely had the footsteps died away than Toby and I were trodden on by what seemed a whole troop of young Sutcliffes. Hastily donning breeches and jacket over the shirt and drawers I had slept in, I joined the tail of the line for the bowl of cold water we all shared to wash in. Meantimes Annie was up, stirring a huge cauldron of porridge by candlelight, clad in an enormous flowered wrapper and mobcap. Five minutes later there were steaming bowls topped with treacle on the table and I was trying to summon up an appetite for the glutinous mess. Toby seemed to like it, thank goodness, but I was soon gagging. The rest of the family soon had their bowls empty and, I regret to say, in the case of the youngest licked clean; Annie thrust a hunk of bread and cheese into the packs her brother and the eldest, Stephen, had over their shoulders.

'Be off with you now, lessen you be late: supper around six as usual.'

These were the only words that had been spoken so far, and all she got was a grunt in answer as they stomped off. Apparently this was the normal procedure, for no one looked in the least put out. After they had gone she busied herself heating water for the washing up and set out flour, salt, yeast, and mixing bowl while the middle boy, Joe, emptied the night-soil bucket, fetched fuel from the store and refilled the water bucket. The youngest, Anthony, crept upstairs to make the beds, then fed the chickens; I felt like a spare part and slipped out to give Toby a run. It was still dark, though there was a lightening in the sky where I supposed the east to be and frost made the lane slippy. I could hear Toby whiffling and crackling through the underbrush in the hedge and once he disturbed some bird that chirped indignantly and flew away; the quarter-moon was slipping away behind a twisted stunt of trees to my right and a church clock struck six. Some way down the lane was a glimpse of light and the lowing of cattle: presumably the farm where they all worked. It was cold, so I whistled up Toby and ran down the lane again, starting sheep into flight in a field nearby. There was lantern or candlelight in all the cottages now and as I lifted the latch Joe was winding a woollen scarf around his neck.

'Now, do you tell Farmer Moss as how you'll be coming

home for your dinner now your Auntie Annie's home,' she said comfortably. 'Tell him I'll send an order with your dad or our Stephen tomorrow, cash on delivery. And while you're passing, tell the widow as our Tony won't be stopping with her for the next few weeks, but as how I'll pay just the same. Got all that? Good lad.' She turned to me. 'Widow takes in plain sewing and looks after a couple more besides our Anthony, else she'd be in the poorhouse: not fair to stop the lad's money, even if he's with us . . . .'

That morning she did a week's baking, while the youngest and I gave the place a real sweep-out and scrubbed the furniture: while the bread was rising we gave the blankets an airing and Annie put everyone's shirts in the tub to hang by the fire later. Lunchtime we finished off last night's pie and she sent Anthony down the town for neck of lamb from the butcher. 'Tell him it's for Annie Parkinson what's back,' and she went next door, to return with a decent sheepskin jacket that fetched up round my knees. 'Three shillin', and you'll do no better than that, even Pendle way; it were her old man's, and got fair wear, but it's better than a kick in the teeth . . . .' I gave her the three shillings: the coat was very heavy and stank of sheep, but I was to be glad of it during the cold weather.

She decided to shake out the feather beds and, to keep me occupied, sent me, armed with a pair of wood and leather shoes, to: 'Find Matthew Clegg's shop at the bottom of the hill and ask for more clog irons for me. Best ask him to measure you for a pair of clogs yourself: five shilling they'll be, but least better'n those old shoes of yourn.'

Mr Clegg's shop was in a good position facing across to the market cross, tavern on one corner, eating house on the other and the main street winding up away past the Fish-Stones where the market was held. The shop was double-fronted, the windows filled with lozenges of bottle-green glass and the name and trade 'Matthew Clegg. Clogmaker. Boots. Shoes. Slippers', picked out in gold above the door. Inside it smelled of new-cured leather, sweat and woodshavings, in that order; Matthew Clegg himself was tall and thin, with a thatch of fairish hair, protruding ears, and a large leather apron enveloping him from neck to ankles. I explained about Annie's clogs and he lifted them in big, capable hands.

'Won't take more'n a minute or two, lad, seeing as I keep a fair stock . . . . Er, how is she?'

'Very well, thank you, Mr Clegg. She sent you her regards,' I added mendaciously.

'Did she? Did she now . . . . A fine woman, the widow Annie, very fine . . . .' His voice trailed off, and he busied himself fitting irons to the clogs, much as a blacksmith clapped the cooling shoes on a carthorse, for these irons were horseshoe-shaped. He scratched his nose. 'Would she – would she be having any followers, now?'

'Followers?' I echoed, puzzled.

'Aye, lad: interested parties.' He grew weary of my stupidity, and put it plain. 'Is she courting, like?'

I didn't want to sound like an echo again, so I said carefully: 'She's a very popular lady,' hoping I was on the right track. Apparently I was, for he sighed. 'Figured so. Bonny lass like that wouldn't lack for suitors . . . . Any serious, like?'

'Not at the moment,' I said cautiously, trying to remember the look in Annie's eye when she had spoken of Mr Clegg. 'Of course, once you have been solicited by a duke, as she has . . . .' I let my voice trail away.

'A duke, even? Not surprising, not surprising,' and he sighed again, his hammer poised over the nails. ' 'Nough to turn her head, I reckon?'

'Why, no,' I reassured him. 'She's still the same Annie: never forgets her friends. Heart like a lion, she has.' I found I was slipping into his idiom.

'Fancy that, then: never forgets her friends!' And he attacked her clogs with renewed vigour. 'You'll have seen a great deal of her, then?'

I stifled a desire to giggle. 'Yes, a fair amount: we've been travelling companions.'

285

'Did she – did she ever speak of . . . well, of friends at home?'

'Oh, many times,' I reassured him.

'Aye, she would, she would . . . .' He addressed himself to the clog iron again, head bent low, and the next remark was almost lost in the tap-tap of the hammer and a mouthful of nails. 'Any one particular, like?'

Luckily I was saved any further mendacity as young Joe came into the shop looking for me.

'Me auntie says as we needs more candles and can you bring 'em back as I've to do a couple errands for farmer's wife,' and he thrust a shilling in my hand. 'And if you ain't measured yet to leave it till morning, as she needs your help with the rugs,' and he ran off again, clattering over the cobbles.

Mr Clegg handed me the mended clogs. 'Three pence.'

I paid him. 'Annie says I should have a pair: can I come tomorrow?'

'Aye, that you can.' He rubbed his hands on the leather apron. 'Happen – happen you'll pass on a message –'

'Surely.'

'Tell her – tell her,' he glanced round conspiratorially and his voice dropped to a murmur, though there was none but us to hear, 'as how The Encumbrance has gone to stay with my sister Martha – for good!'

I repeated the conversation to Annie later, as I helped her lay up for supper.

'Cheeky sod!' she said good-humouredly, her cheeks red, I supposed from bending over the fire. 'Fancy wanting to know whether I'd thought anything of him while I was away – as if I would! I ask you, is he the sort a woman'd look at twice?' She flapped her apron. 'My, but it's hot in here . . . . Get your clogs off in my clean room, Stephen, or I'll fetch you such a clout round your ear hole! No, happen if he was good-looking, now . . . . You couldn't say as he was good-looking, now, could you?'

'I think . . . he has a very pleasant manner and an honest face . . . .'

'Aye. Can't say fairer than that, I suppose. Did he — did he say as how he'd — well, missed me, like?'

'Not exactly,' I temporized, scenting at last what would have been aniseed to any mediocre newshound, 'but you could tell he was interested.'

She preened. 'No chance, no chance at all . . . . He did say The Encumbrance was away?'

'Yes: for good, he said. Who *is* he, or she, Annie?'

'His mother. It's what we used to call her when we was children together. We used to say "if it weren't for The Encumbrance we could . . ." oh, do all sorts! Encumbrance, you see, after Martha: that were her name, too.'

'Martha?'

'Aye, cloth-head! "Encumbered wi' much serving . . . ." And she served us two wi' a backhander now and again, an' all!' She sighed. 'Still . . . she were right to be stern, I suppose: she brought up Matthew and his sister proper, after his father fell in a ditch at New Year and caught his death.'

'Too much alcohol?' I ventured.

She laughed. 'Nay, they do say as how it were her dumplings as loaded him down! That, or the weight she tied to his johnny!' She nudged me. 'If'n you're going down there tomorrow I don't mind if you happen to remark as I was thinking of taking a stroll down Newton way come Sunday if it's fine . . . .'

Next day I waited to deliver the message till he brought up Annie's name himself. Before he mentioned personal matters, however, he started on my clogs. Measuring my feet by eye, he fetched out two roughly sole-shaped pieces of wood. Then he made me stand in a tray of damp sand in my bare feet, and considered the prints.

'See? Feet like yours needs care. High arch, narrow by nature yet spread by barefoot walking. Small for your age: got used to walking on the edge of heel and ball of foot, so we'll correct that with a bit of extra depth on the outside.' He whittled away rapidly, occasionally consulting my footprints. 'Try them, now.' They fitted comfortably, and he sand-smoothed the wood. 'Now for leather: any pertikler colour?'

'Red,' I said, hopefully.

'Soon gets dirty. Got a nice brown, or black?'

I sighed. 'Black, I suppose.'

I stood on the soles while he measured and cut the double, stiff leather over my foot, then stepped off as he took up the soles and tap-tapped the leather into place with brass-headed nails and bound a metal strip round the outside of the sole. 'Stops the wood splittin'.' He picked up and discarded several clog irons, then fitted some to the underside and prepared to knock them in. 'Hers fit all right?'

I correctly interpreted this. 'Very well, thank you: so well, in fact, that she's thinking of trying them out in a walk down Newton way on Sunday if it's fine . . . .'

'Well, what did he say?' asked Annie, as soon as I returned.

'He's finishing off the clogs tonight: I've to pick them up tomorrow –'

'No, not them! About me . . . . On Sunday . . . .'

'Nothing much. He just said: "Aye: happen it'll rain, though . . . ."'

'Bit of damp hurt no one!'

Which I faithfully reported the next day, and for the first time saw a reluctant grin on his face.

'Allus handy wi' words, our Annie . . . . Like old times it'd be, afore she met and married the other man o' straw. Old Farmer Mortensen's barn down the road . . . .' He sighed mightily. 'Five shillings that'll be, young sir, and as good a pair as ever left the shop. If'n you like I'll take a shilling a week, or even sixpence, while it's paid off – you'll be staying some weeks, I reckon?'

I reassured him on this point, not realizing till later that it was Annie's length of stay he was fishing for, not mine.

'Half-a-crown now, rest tomorrow? That'll do fine, lad. Now, you be careful how you do walk in those things: they won't bend, so you've to stamp or slide, none of your fancy steps. And no standing on the toes as some of the lads do: it'll ruin 'em quicker than owt else.'

It took me some time to get used to the different way of walking, but after a while the clogs became very comfortable, although I never managed to strike sparks from the cobbles as the other youngsters did.

I suppose he and Annie met on their walk, for it was fine the next Sunday; after that she took to slipping out in the evenings and coming back late, her nose cherry red from the frost, a delicate aroma of gin accompanying her through the door, though when I mentioned his name she merely giggled.

It wanted a week of Christmas when it was decided to pay the family's winter visit to Annie's other brother, a fisherman of Lytham. This needed the carrier, for there were gifts to carry, and seven miles each way was a fair way to tramp in winter for someone of her size. The two younger boys and Toby were to be left with the widow next door, but the rest of us were piled into the cart early one morning before it was light, together with the carrier's usual load from Preston. We jogged slowly across the Moss, a flat, bleak, windswept stretch of countryside, heavily ditched and supporting a few stunted trees and bushes, rattling their bare branches and crouching backs to the prevailing westerly wind, though today was relatively calm for this part of the world. The only signs of life were the ubiquitous and restless sheep, an odd hare or two, seagulls and a magpie, though I heard a curlew crying plaintively. Even the farms we passed seemed asleep, huddled behind their fences, a trickle of smoke showing there was life of sorts behind the white walls. At last there was a thickening of trees away to our right.

Annie nodded to the woods. 'Squire Clifton's place behind all them, the New Hall. Grand place. And yon's Old Nan's cottage . . . . Stop here, Chuck: I'll have to take the old body a gift, else if'n she knows I've passed without a greeting she'll likely as not put a curse on us all . . . .'

The cottage hunched behind a thick hedge, and tethered to a post by the gate was a skinny goat that bleated and made a threatening run at us, to be pulled up a foot or two short by its rope, yellow eyes glaring malevolently.

'Now then, Billy,' said Annie nervously. 'Do throw it a turnip or something off the cart, Chuck, otherwise it'll have my cloak . . . .' She put her hand on my arm. 'Now don't you mind what she says, Sprat: they do say she's near ninety and daft with it and some holds as she's a witch –'

'But I don't want –'

' 'Course you do! You wouldn't let poor old Annie, as is your friend through thick and thin, go in there alone, now would you?'

'Your brother could –'

'He'll not cross the threshold, neither'll our Stephen . . . .'

Which was scarcely encouraging: I didn't believe in witches, at least I didn't think I did: it seemed that my beliefs were about to be tested. Perhaps it was uncharitable of me to wonder, at this stage, whether this was why I had been invited to meet the rest of Annie's family . . . .

She rattled the latch. 'Can we come in?' I wouldn't have recognized the little-girl voice.

'Light the candles you'll find by the door, Ann Parkinson, Sutcliffe that was – and soon to be Clegg?' The voice was large, much too large it seemed for the little person who sat on a stool by the fire, black skirts turned back over her knees to scorch the knotted legs into dark circles, grey shawl pulled up over her head. 'Bring in the girl, too: can't abide breeched females, but she'd best be inside, seeing she's a guest at your brother's . . . .'

I never did discover how she knew all she did, but suspected it was a good eye, phenomenal memory – the latter augmented by her obvious power to make passers-by stop with a present and a gossip – and very good guesswork. She made the frightened Annie sit next to her and took her hand, gazing deep into the apprehensive blue eyes with her own black, and soon the pair were deep in conversation: question on Old Nan's part, answer on Annie's.

Left to my own devices, I looked about the cottage. It was cruck-framed, the great timbers at either end meeting in the open rafters where the ribs of roofing spread down from the ridge like fingers. There was a patch of sky showing at the far end where I thought the moth-eaten thatch had given way, only to see a large, rusty bird perched by the hole. That he was no infrequent visitor was obvious by the pile of droppings on the earthen floor beneath: probably the old woman told her more gullible visitors he was her messenger, I thought, startled out of my complacency a moment later by a shuffling at my feet as a large hedgepig uncurled from a pile of rags and scratched vigorously before wrapping itself up in a ball again. After that I looked for the cat and the bats and found them both, the first on a pile of peat by the fire, the others hanging upside down near where the herbs and fish were hung to dry. I glanced across at the others as the inquisition seemed to have ceased, and found the old woman regarding me.

'Aye, and there's lizards under the doorsill and a warty old toad in a crock . . . . Bring that pack over here, and let's see what you've brought.'

Annie had packed some cheese, apples, and a slice of pie in cheesecloth, and these I brought forward for Old Nan's inspection. She sniffed at the cheese, declaring it 'not ripe enough: I like mine with some bite to it!', turned up her nose at the apples 'as wrinkled as my bum', and declared that the pie hadn't enough spice, but I noticed she packed them all away carefully, cheese and pie on a stone slab out of the cat's reach, apples in a basket by her chair. Standing, she could not have been more than four feet tall, though her arms and legs were long; her shortness came from some deformity in her spine which thrust up

291

her right shoulder and curved in her chest, bringing her head forward like a bird's – indeed, with those sharp black eyes, beaked nose, slit of toothless mouth, and sharp chin she did resemble some disreputable old crow, shabby feathers ruffled against the cold.

Food stowed to her satisfaction, she turned again to Annie. -'Where's my fairing, then?'

Annie glanced helplessly at me, then drew out a small package from her pocket, which the old crone snatched almost before it had seen light.

'Thought I'd forgotten, Ann Sly-boots, didn't you now? Them as travels the roads the walking-people do owes a bit of colour to those of us as are tied . . . .' She unwrapped the paper from the three-colour ribbon and drew it through her fingers. 'Ah, pretty, pretty! Fetch my box – under the bedding, girl – and it shall join the others.' I felt under the sacking, stuffed tight with the spring of bracken, and drew out a metal box with rubbed initials on the lid: J. B. H. I opened the box by lifting the hasp and she laid her fairing along with other ribbons, lace, fancy buttons, and a little glass phial which looked as though it must have once held perfume, though now the liquid inside had dried to a brown stain. Taking the box from me she clasped it to her bony chest, then looked up. 'And what have *you* got for me, friend of Ann Parkinson?'

I was looking down at the initials on the box, glinting now in the firelight, and quite suddenly I remembered Katina Petulengro. It was as though she was right beside me, smiling and nodding; almost I could hear her saying: 'She's a clever one, but there's no magic; she hasn't the gift like you and I . . . .' Slowly I stretched out an index finger and traced the initials on the box; I heard my own words, though they had an origin outside of me.

'I have nothing for you, old one, except a message, and it is this: look for him for whom you seek when the hawthorn dons her lace and the chestnut holds candles to the wind . . . .' And for an instant piercing second as I said the words I held a small picture in my mind, sharp

292

and distinct as an image seen at the wrong end of a telescope, of a man, middle-aged, travelling the lane we had just followed, boots scuffing the dust of a late May, long canvas bag carried over blue-jacketed shoulder . . . .

On the road again Annie glanced curiously at me. 'Where did you get that message from, then?'

'Don't know: it – it just came . . . .' I had a slight headache.

'I'll say it did! Fair gave me the creeps, let alone her, and she was knocked sideways. Sounded like your Shakespeare . . . . Who's she waiting for, anyway? And why couldn't you just say "come spring", instead of all that about candles and lace?'

I sighed. 'Annie, I just don't know . . . . It arrived out of the air. There was something about the box, and the initials, and remembering a gipsy lady, and the atmosphere of that place.' And that was true: and that was all.

'Heard tell once as how she had a late-comer son – born of one of those she lived over the brush with – and there was talk of him being lost at sea a few years back; think it was him?'

I was spared an answer by the sight of two young children racing down the lane towards us and leaping up at the cart with cries of welcome for Annie and her brother.

'Well, it's never young Mark and our Alice? My, how you two have grown! I'd scarce have recognized you! Come, sit up at the front with your Auntie Annie, then, and tell her all the news . . . .' She turned to me, her arms and lap full of bright-eyed, ruddy-cheeked children, much of a size, though the girl looked a couple of years older: perhaps ten or eleven to the boy's eight. 'These is the two eldest: then there's Cuthbert, John, Mary and little Ann. Mark's for his dad, Ally for her mam's mother. Cuthbert for the saint who rested hereabouts when he were on his last journey, John for his uncle here, Mary straight for her mam, and little Ann for her grandma and me – that's right, isn't it, my pets?'

'Me mam says there'll be another, come Lent,' said

young Alice. 'If'n it's a boy it's Benjamin 'cos she says as how that's that and final and if it's a girl me feyther fancies calling it after me aunt Bet at Marton Mere but Mam says as how that's too plain and she favours Charlotte after the Queen but me feyther says as how that's too fancy and if Bet was good enough for Aunt then it's good enough for his daughter and –' She prattled on, her accent even thicker than those I had become used to in Kirkham, but accompanied with far more liveliness, and before I realized it we had drawn up in the square and dismounted, heaving down our parcels and packages.

The fisherman's cottage was one of six, in a narrow cobbled street leading down across the common land to the jetty. Neat behind a low wall of pebbles set in mortar, it was a one-storey building, thatched, with whitewashed walls and small windows. Inside there were four rooms: a living-kitchen, small scullery, and two bedrooms, and the place was full of children and the smell of fish, the latter augmented by the nets hanging to dry from the rafters. But we fitted in, and Annie's sister-in-law, a small square woman with sandy hair plaited round her head, had a steaming fish broth and plate of fresh shrimps and bread and butter waiting for us. I had only tasted shrimps in butter before but these were morning-fresh, scooped out hot and 'rough' from a cauldron in the scullery, and once the children had taught me how to shell them in two easy movements I smelt as fishy as the rest, but felt like a gourmet, for they were the most delicious food I had ever tasted.

After we had eaten, the two eldest children volunteered to take me down to the river while their elders caught up on the gossip.

'You can go if'n you take all bar little Ann with you,' decided their mother briskly. 'Mary and John can go in the hand cart, and mind they don't stray. Time you was away from under my feet for a while, any road! And be back afore tide turns because your Auntie Annie and Uncle John must catch the carrier again at five.'

'Do mind the tide,' said Annie anxiously. 'It don't half race in across them sands once the channel's full –'

'Aunty Annie! You *never* remembers! Moon's a slice of cheese these nights and it's near neap as makes no difference,' said her niece Alice. 'Comes in like a slug this time of year and only half-full: our Ann could crawl faster!'

'Never mind tempting providence,' said her mother sharply. 'Just you remember them poor bairns as tried to cross the river this time of year and were all washed up drowned. Whole family gone in one go 'cos they couldn't afford the carrier to Scaresbrick where their relations lived . . . Now, be off with you and don't go getting into mischief with the visitors, if'n there are any.'

'Old Mr Wilkinson gives us a penny sometimes . . . .'

'Yes, well, don't go moithering him just 'cos he's bought the White House for a bit of sea breezes and peace and quiet. There's no call to make him wish he were back in Manchester: 'sides, I've heard as how his sister is visiting, so happen he won't be out for his usual stroll . . . .'

We crossed the green, an open space between the houses and the shore; from the walk, or promenade, that led down to the beach and the long wooden jetty, the sand looked like ash-brown knitting, but once on the reality the ribs of sand were hard and wet, sprinkled with worm casts like pulled threads and scored with the tracks of mussel carts like dropped stitches. The tide wanted half an hour to the turn and scores of dunlin, sanderling, dotterel and oystercatchers were out on the banks of the river in companionable flocks. The few gulls that had overwintered in the estuary were quarrelling over shrimps' heads and mussel shells discarded by the fisherfolk, and a lone heron, long legs trailing, moved to a better vantage spot. On the green behind us nets were being mended by the hardy, for the ever present wind whipped the drying sand into stinging particles that soon reddened my calves and gritted my teeth. Over on the other bank, perhaps three miles away, the weak sunshine picked out whitewashed cottages, windmills, and even grazing cattle.

'Lazy, ain't it?' said Alice.

'Lazy?'

'T'wind; goes straight through 'stead of round, gormless! C'mon, me an' Mark'll show you Squire's place; young 'uns can play in the sand hills while we come back. Our Cuthbert'll mind 'em. Leave them clogs off: sand'll soon fill 'em.'

The sand dunes were full of hollows of soft sand and humps of spiky marram grass, natural places to play bandits, smugglers, highwaymen, and the like, and we left the youngest children there and struck inland a quarter-mile or so, to a high wall of the ubiquitous pink and grey pebbles. Using these as toeholds, we scrambled up and dropped into the thick wood beyond.

'Main gates are away to the right,' whispered Alice. 'Squire's road to St Cuthbert's is to our left, but this is best place to see the Hall.'

We crept cautiously through the wood, narrow at this point, and there was the park, with a small herd of deer snuffing the wind suspiciously, their ears flicking back and forth.

'Careful,' murmured young Mark. 'Wind's right behind us and if'n we scares them . . . . There, that's the Hall: grand, ain't it?'

The modern, square, nicely proportioned red-brick building picked out in white stone lay about a quarter of a mile distant, with a broad sweep of gravel in front and a cloak of trees behind; it was a pleasant-looking residence, and to the children must have seemed both luxurious and desirable. But travelling broadens the mind, as Jack used to say, and I had seen many more imposing edifices during our wanderings. However . . . .

'I've never seen anything so – so grand,' I said, to please.

There were fresh river-caught dabs for our tea, and baked crabs: I declined the latter, after I discovered how the children caught them: 'Piece of string with a bit of fat pork on the end, dangle it in a pool and they come up lovely; hangs on 'cos they ain't going to let go. Catch gulls the same way, only they swallows the string and it ain't always easy to drag it up their gullets again without twisting their necks . . . .' Soon it was time to pack up for the carrier: we were to take a couple of baskets of fish for the market at the Fish-Stones the following day, and also some of the shell-decorated boxes that young Cuthbert produced.

'He's maybe ninepence in the shilling, that lad,' said his mother fondly, 'but he's right clever with his hands, and not a bit of trouble. Came into the world early, he did, and we named him after our saint 'cos he survived after all. Mends the nets a treat, too, and that helpful with the younger ones.'

The boxes were very pretty, especially those where he had used tiny shells as fine as a baby's fingernail, white, pink and pale yellow; Annie assured me that they sold well in both Kirkham and Preston: 'Makes nice Christmas gifts.'

And in a couple of days it *was* Christmas, my second away from the quiet village where I had been brought up – the first had been with Aunt Sophia of horrid memory – and it was the grandest, jolliest, most overindulgent Christmas one could wish for. Everyone had the day off, everyone wore their best and everyone ate and drank too much. We shared our festivities with the widow next door: roast pork, boiled mutton with caper sauce, apple dumplings and cheese. Matthew Clegg brought up sweetmeats for the children and a bottle of port for the adults and stayed on to supper. He was smoking a peaceful pipe by the fire while Annie and I 'redded up' the place, as she put it, when he suddenly clapped his hand to his forehead.

'Well, bless me now! If'n I didn't forget what I came up for in the first place – apart, o' course, from wishing you all the very best.' And he went over to the greatcoat that hung on a nail behind the door and rummaged in the pockets, bringing out at last a couple of small parcels done up in oiled silk. 'Addressed to Master Zor-something Mortimer and Mistress A. Parkinson, Kirkham. Messenger came through from Preston this morning, delivering up as far as Lancaster way: had to make a detour, like, for this place, and asked me to deliver them, seeing as how I knew the area. King's messenger he looked like, but couldn't be that, surely . . . . Had one of they saddlebags with a royal crest, though . . . .'

'Give over moithering, Matthew, do!' expostulated Annie. 'Let's see what we got, then!'

'And who it's from,' I added, examining the outside of my parcel speculatively.

But Annie was tearing the wrapping in her haste and a moment later out spilled a small, rough wooden box like a miniature crate; pasted to the front was a slip of paper and Annie handed it to Matthew. 'Tell me what it says.'

For a moment I felt a small pang of hurt: once, she would have turned to me without question to read anything. Now, it seemed, Matthew was her first choice.

'It says . . .' and he peered down at the spiky black writing. 'It says, "Ay votree grossy belly taily" or some such, and it's signed "Jay-cues" . . . . What's it all mean, now?' and he glared at Annie. 'Sounds lewd to me, all that about tails and bellies!'

Momentarily I was glad the two younger boys were safe in bed and that Stephen and his father were 'visiting' at the Plough, for this had the making of a first-class row. Still, if Matthew were that jealous, maybe it was a good sign . . . . I decided to interpose.

'No, no!' I said, having caught a sight of the handwriting. 'It's not rude at all: it's French. The present is from Jack, Annie: see, that's his name spelt the French way: "Jacques". The box is from Paris: "Deligny et Cie" – that's "Company" – "Confitures. Des Fruits sucrées. Rue de St Jeanne, Paris, France." They are crystallized fruits, I think – lift up the corner and you'll see.'

298

'But what's all that about her belly?' pursued a grim and tenacious Matthew.

'That's French, too.' I hesitated. How on earth to translate 'a votre grosse belle taille' into anything but a hymn to Annie's enormous waistline? Blast the man! 'It means . . . "hope you enjoy these", or something similar: my French isn't very good.' Which it wasn't, but fair enough to make me hide my smile.

'Well, now,' said Matthew, mollified. ' 'Twas a kind thought then. Let's see 'em, lass.'

Each fruit – pear, orange, fig, damson, greengage – was beautifully packed in its own greased paper, a miniature of itself. Annie popped a fig in her mouth, then offered the box to us; I tasted the sweet sharpness of greengage, a taste that took me back immediately to one magic day, years ago, when my stepfather had brought just such a box home from one of his infrequent trips to the south.

'They'll be fattening,' said Matthew.

Annie looked at her second fig doubtfully. 'Won't do no harm, love: I've lost a pound or two while I've been here, and I can't afford to lose too much.'

It was true: I hadn't really noticed before, but now my attention was caught I could see that she was pounds, maybe even stones, lighter. And it suited her, though I knew Jack would be furious.

'No harm, my dear?' said Matthew. 'I remembers you best as merely a plump young lass – not as you are now.'

Annie looked so crestfallen that I tried to console her. 'Just remember your title: "The Fattest Lady in the World", and how the Duke –'

'Depends what she wants, don't it,' interrupted Matthew. 'Plaudits of the common crowd, money off the gentry – or one man's honest regard . . . .'

I took one look at Annie's face, another at Matthew's, and decided it was time to take Toby for a walk; slipping on his new red collar – Tom's present – I mumbled something about 'a bit of fresh air' and escaped.

Outside, the night was sharp with frost and bright with

stars. Glad of the stout leather gloves I wore (Annie's present) I lit the lantern I had taken from behind the door and stomped off down the lane, Toby bounding up and down ahead of me. The moon was a narrow sliver of white and the stars burned red, blue, green; somewhere ahead a barn owl gave a shriek of disappointment as it hunted Farmer Moss's ricks, and the air was still acrid with the sharp smell of wood smoke, for everyone had used their spits and ovens today. Aware of the unopened parcel in my pocket I found a convenient fence post and, setting down the lantern, investigated my present, though not with Annie's impatience.

There was an irregularly shaped lump wrapped in a soft leather pouch, and a letter. I read the letter first.

'I cheated' – No "Dear Sprat" or "My dear Zoe" – 'and opened your present early and you deserve a thick ear for your presumption, child! Still, the engravings are excellent and the subject, viewed objectively of course, does have a certain moral tone.

'I hope you are behaving yourself and doing your homework for our next tour' – Oh, God! I had forgotten the palmistry – 'for I expect to be sending for you both by the middle of March, if not before, and I expect you to be word-perfect in the generalities. You might also browse through *Macbeth, Richard II* and *Hamlet* and explore the possibilities in your spare time.' He *had* to be joking!

'Finally, with wishes for a peaceful Christmas, here is a little curiosity for your treasure box, together with its story:

Ten thousand years ago or so, a prince of faery fell in love with a beauteous maiden. Jealous of their love a perfidious warlock turned the lady into a graceful fern and the prince into a lowly black beetle. For many moons the beetle flew round the fern, bemoaning his lost love, who hung her head and wept green tears of frustration. Then one day came a dilemma: the evil warlock, tired of their continuing devotion, diverted the waters of a nearby stream to flow towards the hapless fern and drown her in its choking waters. The beetle, free to fly away, hesitated

300

but a moment, then flew to his ladylove's breast and clung there with all the strength of his love as the torrent engulfed them both. But the gods above were piteous to their plight and released them from their metamorphoses to live in peace and love. Their former shells were left in a magically hardened bubble of golden light, to remind others of the glory and the price of fidelity.

'That is the story as it was told to me. Romantic rubbish; but the amber *is* beautiful and it *is* ten thousand years old and it *does* contain a black beetle resting on a piece of fern . . . . So, make of it what you will: knowing you, you won't even want to hear the scientific explanation, and perhaps you are right. Magic moments are so rare that to capture the precise instant and encapsulate it for ever is well-nigh impossible. So weave your imagination all you will and pray that one day you, too, will have an amber moment.

'Yours – sometimes anyway – Jack.'

Even in that frost the amber lay warm in my palm, and by the lantern's flickering light the beetle appeared to nestle closer to his green love. I wondered about 'amber moments', as Jack had put it. Surely I – but no, there had not been one single moment that could be for ever remembered as magic. Emotions recollected in tranquillity seemed to be continuous things, as if the etchings of Hogarth finished their gin and the discus-thrower achieved his three hundred yards. Only portraits and still life achieved an arrest that required no sequel. All my memories were of continuous things: a walk with my stepfather when he taught me to listen to the dry ringing of a harebell; the pictures in a January hearth fire with stomach full and *Gulliver* by one's side; hugging a sea-wet and tongue-happy Toby; that night when Jack needed me . . . yes, that night was probably the nearest I had been to an amber moment, but it wouldn't stay still; no one moment was clearer than the rest, gave one an instant of emotion or realization that could be caught forever.

'Happy Christmas, my dear,' I said to the stars.

'Wherever you may be.' I wondered what he had been doing in France.

'Nasty old things, beetles,' said Annie, when I showed her the amber. 'Don't look anything like a faery prince to me: more like the sort of thing you'd find in your shoes or behind the sink!'

Our summons to return, when it came, was unexpected. The same messenger as before left a note with Matthew Clegg, terse and to the point. 'Meet me at the livery stables in Preston, 10 March, noon. Jack.' Considering that we didn't get the message till midday on the 9th, and had to find and engage the carrier specially, it was a miracle that we made it: but we did. Prompt on time we disgorged ourselves outside the stables and there was Jack, watch in hand, approvingly snapping it shut.

'Couple of minutes late – not bad. Hullo, you disreputable hound!' For Toby as usual, didn't stand on ceremony. With Jack, unexpectedly, was Signor Grappelli, whom I hadn't expected to see till later at Warwick: he had brought a shivering monkey with him, wrapped in a little green cloak.

But Jack had seen Annie. 'My God!' he said in consternation. 'What *have* you being doing! You're more like the thinnest lady in the world –'

'I've only lost a pound or two,' said she, defensively. 'And with all this hurry and bother –'

'Sugared almonds,' said Jack promptly. 'And ale.' He turned to me – expectant, a trifle dewy-eyed perhaps, ready to recite my newly learned skills, longing for a hug, a word of welcome. 'As for you! If anything, you're worse. You've put *on* weight. No, you're no longer my Sprat, I'm afraid!'

The world, and the universe around it, dissolved in one brittle, breaking instant: no amber moment here, rather the scattered fragments; a vast emptiness, a black hole that swallowed up all eagerness, all hope, all love . . . .

'No, no longer Sprat,' said Jack. 'Girl's clothes, Annie, and as soon as possible. Those hips and those breasts – whatever happened to the binding? – are all woman . . . and what a delightful surprise! Well done, my Zoe!'

And he came forward and kissed me on the mouth.

14

But after that unexpected Preston kiss it was back to business. Back to the road again, to the rain and the wind and the cold, the half-empty bellies and tired legs, playing the Jack, with Jack and for him. Perhaps I should have been warmer, both in and out, those late March and early April days, if he had made any further gesture of warmth towards me, but there was none. He did make concessions as to my dress, however: during setting up and dismantling, acting with Daisy and Toby, foraging for fodder and water, helping Annie, humping firewood or provisions I was still dressed as a boy, but always wearing a disguising smock. For a couple of hours a day I was allowed to be Zoe in my new dresses, but even then it was merely for training. It had been decided I was to be Gemini, 'Daughter of the Stars, Princess of the Zodiac, Reader of the Heavens and of the Lines of the Hand, Foreteller of the Future,' and to this end Jack had procured a tent from somewhere, a tiny thing, big enough for me, a table, stools, and a couple of small customers. He had us sewing the interior with strips of bright metal and slivers of glass, which were pretty to look at and reflected the candlelight a treat, but were the very devil on hands, hair, and the fabric of the tent itself when it had to be taken down.

I did not know whether to be glad or sorry when Jack converted the front of the provisions wagon into a small space for sleeping for me: it gave me a more comfortable bed and space for a rail for my clothes and a chest for my other bits and pieces, but in the stupid way one has my first reaction was that he was banishing me because he was tired of having me around his van; then I thought he had done it because it would be easier for him to have his lady friends in for the evening; then I had a good cry, although I wasn't quite sure why. I worked it all out of my system by helping to persuade a reluctant Annie to store some of the seldom-used costumes in her van, and by restacking all the other provisions so as to give myself the most space possible, then by scrounging a cracked mirror, a wobbly stool, and a length of mothy velvet curtain: it didn't look very smart, but it made me feel better.

As the weather was still capricious and decidedly cold my debut as soloist was postponed till Chester or Shrewsbury later in April, but in the meantime I was coached unmercifully by Jack, backed by the little I had managed to lift from Madame Petulengro's notebooks. Not only during the day – jolting over the dismal cobbles of some outpost of Yorkshire civilization that appeared to have changed little since Roman times or bogged down in the ruts of a so-called road that wriggled over the winter-retaining moors like a demented earthworm fallen in pitch, burrowing into all the hollows that still held snow – that was bad enough, but at night, too, perhaps drawn in a circle behind some precarious drystone walling waiting for the wolves – wolves in sheep's clothing, that was, for there I would be frantically trying to remember the line of success or shuffle the cards so it was never spades, when there would be a chorus of wild bleats from outside as a pack of shock-fleeced sheep with glaring yellow eyes attempted to overrun the bucket picket and get at our fodder. What's more, they wouldn't be shooed away like southern sheep; they stood their ground, stamped their black hooves threateningly and even rattled their curving horns.

But through all this, Jack kept me at my studies.

'It's not just the lines and shape of the hands that

matter,' he would say: 'You've got to weigh up your customer like Kat did; no amount of learning and long words will make a ha'p'orth of difference to the fact that you must tell the customers what they want to hear. They won't give their sixpences to know they'll never get married, or that their husband will run off with another woman, or the house catch fire, or the rich uncle leave his all to educating the savages in Timbuctu. Even if you did have the gift and could truly foretell all this, you mustn't tell them: they pay for the good news, unless it happens to someone else. You must gain their confidence too, so they *believe* what you tell them; when they first come in you must quickly assess their type, social position, background, in the moment before they sit down. Two men, both reasonably well dressed, with similar accents and around the same age can be as different as tallow dip and altar candle; smell them: assess the stink of indifference to cleanliness against the sweat of emotion and the perfume of fastidiousness; look at their eyes – are they steady and interested, shy, sly, anxious, merry, sad? Is their mouth firm or loose, mobile or stiff, dry or wet? And this is before you come to Kat's bitten nails, polished nails, spatulate nails, or almond-shaped nails, let alone the lines and mounts and joints . . . .'

It was all too much: I was in a muddle. I was sure I could never think so quickly, gauge so rapidly, interpret so exactly, flatter so adeptly – Jack stormed off in a temper, declaring me a feather-pated, woolly-headed, cabbage-brained, feckless flibbertigibbet with as much initiative as a pile of planks. Ten minutes later he was back, a shawl over his shoulders, a wig on his head, a basket over his arm and a falsetto voice.

'Persuade me, Zoe: make this farmer's wife feel happier about life; make me feel there's something more to look forward to than next year's harvest or the grey hen beginning to lay. Make me feel nineteen again, beautiful, wanted, loved . . . . Remember, I'm a simple body and nervous, not sure whether I'm not wasting the egg money

305

coming to a fortune-teller; I'm a devout churchgoer, yet superstitious – see, I've a crucifix round my neck, yet I'll throw that money spider over my left shoulder for good luck. I'm naturally hard-headed and canny, but mystical surroundings, a hint of magic, and I'm as suggestible as the rest. I'll believe anything of you if you turn me child again: convince me!'

A few minutes later he was fussy, dusty lawyer, then by turns languid lady of leisure, local yokel, tremulous old man, lecherous layabout, giggling village girl, shy bachelor, prim elderly spinster and earnest bluestocking.

This I understood, and before long I was reasonably competent at putting customers at their ease and gaining their confidence, which was half the battle. The other half, interpretation of the lines, was left to me and Madame Petulengro's book. I won't say it came all at once, but it was a bit like standing on one's hands or fanning a pack of cards: one day you can't, next day you can – two times out of three, anyway.

I gained a new dress as well, and had to learn all over again how to walk in skirts, with little prim gliding steps instead of my 'ploughboy's stride' as Jack called it. I already had a couple of plain cloth dresses for everyday that I would dress up with a coloured neckerchief, ribbons or a bright belt, but now I was given a special Gemini fortune-telling one: it was red silk with a gold belt and had a dark green cloak to go with it, sewn with golden stars. Jack wanted me to wear a black wig and dye my skin with walnut juice, but after a couple of days getting stain over everything, including him, we compromised: wig, yes; dye, no. 'You'll just have to get sunburned,' said Jack, optimistically, for it was a very wet spring and it wasn't till May that we saw any sun of note. By this time we had met up with Tom and Daisy again, were past Shrewsbury and Ludlow and on our way to Warwick: I remember those first golden days well, for they shone like new-minted coin from a boy's fair hair.

I had just been hearing Jack's lines – this year he had

decided to expand our repertoire with a few of the better-known soliloquys: Hamlet's, Richard II's (both the John of Gaunt and the 'worms and epitaphs'), Mark Antony's confidence trick on the Romans, and the Mercutio Queen Mab speech – when I looked up from the book at the sound of hooves and saw a rider trotting up beside us. The sun suddenly and capriciously broke through the clouds and a golden Apollo reined up and gave me a dazzling smile.

'Am I on the right road for Warwick, young lady?'

I must have gaped like a codfish, for it was Jack who answered, coolly: 'It is to be hoped so, else are we all lost.'

The young god turned his brilliant smile on me again, and I was glad I was wearing fresh blue ribbon on my dress. 'Perhaps we may travel the road with you then, for we are bound for the market . . . .'

'So – so are we,' I stammered, for the golden vision was strangely disturbing. 'You – you are buying or – or selling?'

'Both, I hope: we deal in horses. I shall go back and tell my parents we are on the right road, then perhaps I may return and –'

I *think* he was going to add: '– ride along with you', but at that moment Jack, scowling dreadfully, whipped up our placid horse so sharply that the poor nag must have thought it the end of the world, for he started up with such a jerk I was tossed heels over head into the van. From all this, and the excuses he found for keeping me busy, I gathered he had some grudge or dislike against young Apollo, or John, as I found he was called; I could not imagine why, for I found him a charming person.

We pitched our camp in a water meadow below the castle, together with four or five other showmen, one with the largest collection of freaks and curiosities I had ever seen. There was a shrunken head, perfect in its miniature form, only the large, bared teeth betraying its human origins; there was a poor sheep with five extra legs that had never developed hanging spare from its dirty fleece; a two-headed monkey in a jar and a baby mermaid likewise entombed in pickling juices; a mummified hand with six fingers and two thumbs; a young woman with no arms who poured out wine and cut her meat with dexterous toes; a drooling idiot with but one eye, and that in the middle of his forehead; and a small girl covered all over with hair like an ape. He also had a fabulous horn from a unicorn, all spiralling and gilt, a massive pair of bull's horns from an ogre's castle in Ireland, and a pair of antlers that spread like giant hands.

'Oryx, aurochs and moose,' said Jack succinctly when I came back to report. 'But they fool the masses, I suppose . . . . You took long enough going round; and why are you wearing your best dress?'

How could I tell him that I wore it because John had asked me to go for a walk with him? How could I explain that a warm hand in mine and a fleeting kiss had made me forget the time? Clasped in an embrace in that stifling booth full of monstrosities I had forgotten our macabre surroundings, forgotten Jack, forgotten everything for one blissful moment. His lips had been gentle, hesitant on mine and he smelled of grass and saddle soap. 'You're so pretty, Zoe,' he had said, and in the dim light he had not noticed my odd eyes, I'm sure of it. Never before had I been so aware of my deficiencies: the transient spot on my chin, the freckles that marred my unaristocratic nose, the slightly crooked front teeth, my lack of bosom, work-rough hands, the mole on my left thigh (only he couldn't see that) and my stubby toes. I tried to remember my good points: my hair was thick and curled a little, but the colour, a sort of sun-touched house-mouse, wasn't fashionable; I had a slim waist, but of what virtue was that without the rounded hips and full bosom to complement it? Neither my ears nor my teeth stuck our unduly, but my mouth was too wide. My hands were reasonably well-shaped, but the torn and bitten nails . . . .

I contemplated again Jack's idea of dyeing my hair, stuck an experimental couple of handkerchiefs down my front, added a little horsehair padding to the hip part of my petticoats, decided to wear gloves for the dirty jobs, practised pulling my lips into a becoming rosebud shape . . . .

'You'll have to go on a diet if you're not careful,' said Jack. 'You are getting to be quite a dumpling. And, if you're not sucking a lemon, pray don't make such a face: you look positively vinegarish.'

For the first time I used a touch of carmine on my lips, a little grease on my eyelids, some of Annie's lavender water; I started to worry, not only about my external appearance, but also about what went on inside me: was I shaped right? Did I have all the parts I should? Were they the right measurements, and would they function properly? For no reason that I could see I suddenly remembered a mare belonging to the parish clerk in our village being taken to be covered by a stallion for the first time and how they had to take a knife to her because, as someone put it: 'Key's too big for the lock . . . .'

Jack said nothing further, and I removed the padding, but I couldn't be sure it was just my guilty conscience that made me feel that he noticed everything else and disapproved. We were at Warwick a week, and every day I spent an hour or so in John's company. We walked by the river and he picked me late primroses, we strolled through the town and he made me a present of candy and a lace handkerchief. I listened to his soft voice, tinged with a North Country burr that I thought the most attractive in the world, tell me the sort of things every girl wishes to hear; I looked up into those soft brown, thickly lashed eyes and at that curly hair that was impossibly gold and marvelled that he had chosen someone as ordinary as me to love – for love he said it was. No one had ever wanted to love me before and the very word made my heart go bump as if he had shouted a blasphemy, almost as though I didn't want him to say it again.

After that first kiss in the monstrosities tent he kissed me often when we were alone, and I waited breathlessly for the tingly melting feeling Jack's mouth had given me, but this was different. I really felt nothing at all except an anxiety lest my breath be not sweet, and a thankfulness when he put his hand down the front of my dress that I'd the sense to remove the handkerchiefs. When he fumbled at my skirts it was in the dark so he didn't see my disfiguring mole and I didn't have to look at his rather thick fingers with the grubby nails. I put down my reluctance for the things physical to the fact that Jack was experienced and in my dealings with him I had found a finesse that John perhaps lacked: that, of course, was to be commended, as it proved he had a virgin approach, but it didn't alter the fact that while I had leaped like a spring salmon for Jack's lightest caress, all I really wanted from John was for him to hold my hand, kiss me gently, and tell me how much he loved me, and I told myself that this was how love should be.

On the Saturday night after our performance I met John by the edge of the woods. I was still wearing my red fortune-telling dress and had splashed myself liberally with Annie's perfumes; I saw John's eyes glinting in the starlight as he drew me close.

'Oh, but you're beautiful, my girl! Come for a walk; we'll go –'

'I can't, John!' I interrupted. 'Jack wants us to pack up this evening as we are moving on tomorrow, as you know, so we can be on our way south early in the morning: but I'll see you tomorrow night as we're travelling the same road, you and I.'

He sighed and put me from him. 'I'm sorry, truly sorry, my pet, but there has been a change of plan; my parents have decided we are to go west to pick up some Welsh ponies. I didn't know till today, truly I didn't!'

My heart sank, and though it was a warm night a chill wind touched my heart. I couldn't lose him now, the only man who had ever loved me . . . .

'Don't go, please don't go!' I begged him. 'I shall miss you so much! You can't leave me behind, you can't! If you do I shall – I shall –' I was going to say die, but even

310

at that fraught moment it sounded a little overdramatic, so I stopped and started to cry instead.

He took me in his arms, and I could hear the rustle of some night-prowling creature in the undergrowth, a ready-made excuse for me to snuggle closer. He nibbled at my ear: it tickled.

'Then don't *let* me go; stay with me. Be my love for ever – there is room for you with us; my parents could do with the extra help and I should have you with me every night. Leave that black-avised charlatan you work for and come with us. You won't regret it, I promise!'

It was my very first proposal of marriage and I almost fainted with shock and delight. 'Oh yes, *yes*!' I breathed. 'I must go straight back and tell Jack we are to be married . . . . I'll come back with my things as quickly as I can!'

Was it my imagination, or did he stiffen a little, withdraw his encircling arm? If he did, it must have been explained by his next words.

'No hurry, sweetheart. Now we've – decided, we can afford to play it coolly. Don't tell *him* anything: he'll only try and make trouble, because you are one of his chief assets, and I'm not at all sure he hasn't got his eye on you himself . . . .' My heart gave a jump: but no, it couldn't be true. Not Jack. 'Just pack what is necessary – and keep it quiet – and I'll come and fetch you later tonight. Leave your wagon door open – I know which one it is, for many's the night I have stood and watched till your candle went out – and I'll come to you. We can spend the night together, and talk about our life in the future and steal away together in the dawn before anyone else is awake. It will take some time before we can be married in a church, with us moving around so much, but at least we can show each other tonight what we mean to each other – plight our troth, as it were.' He bent his head and gave me a slow, deliberate kiss. I heard the night creatures stir among the trees as though they protested our decision and I pressed closer to my husband-to-be.

311

'I can't wait to hold you properly in my arms,' he murmured. His cheek was damp against mine; the warm night was making him perspire, and the added intimacy made me shiver. He smoothed my stomach downward with the back of his hand, then his fingers turned and pressed hard into my groin. 'Don't worry: I'll treat you right. I'll bring some wine tonight . . . . Don't forget, no one else must know for the time being, or they will try to stop us.' He stepped back and released me and I was glad, for his fingers were hurting in just the wrong place. He turned me round and gave me a little push. 'Away you go, sweet: I'll keep an eye on your boss and make sure he's abed before I come. I'll tap thrice on your door. Till then . . . .'

I reached my wagon at last after what seemed like time endless. In the end it had been left to Tom, Annie, Signor Grappelli and me to do the packing for Jack had disappeared, presumably to the nearest tavern, and I bet his ears were burning as I donned my working clothes and tied and humped and packed and lashed and knotted; as usual when one was in a hurry, everything took twice as long.

Annie had made stew and dumplings, but I was too nervous to eat. At last something special, very special, was happening to me. I had been chosen, out of all the girls in the world, all the girls John had ever met, to be his bride. To be his wife; to be with him always, cook his food, mend his clothes, wash and iron them, bear his children, share his joys, console in his difficulties. And I was so proud of my handsome husband-to-be: he stood head and shoulders above the rest, except for Jack, and had the most beautiful face and golden curls. I was *so* lucky . . . . The girls in the village at home would have been wild with jealousy.

I wondered how Jack would take the news: I must remember to leave him a note. I was sure he wouldn't deny me my marriage, in spite of what he had said about owning me till I was seventeen; after all, I was only a month away from that now, and if he came after us and made me wait those four weeks or so, we still had tonight, John and I.

Somewhere at the back of my mind I remembered some foolish remark of Jack's made on Ditchling Heath about being seduced by him when I was seventeen, but that had surely been only something to say at the time? My mind sheered away from what had happened between us at Preston, but I still wondered if it would be like that with John and me; somehow I thought not. The tingly melting feelings Jack's persuasions had engendered seemed to belong to him alone, and I suspected they were part of his special magic with women that went along with his talents as an actor. I was sure that lovemaking was not meant to be as violent and passionate and that my life with John would be less exciting but more rewarding; after all, he wouldn't dream of treating me as anything less than an equal. I should be a woman in my own right, not the child Jack sometimes saw in me.

Somewhere a church clock struck midnight, then another, farther away; a trifle guiltily I tied Toby up to the back wheel of the wagon, hoping he wouldn't bark: he wasn't very keen on John, but they would have time to get used to each other later. Lighting a candle, I surveyed myself in the cracked mirror Jack had given me for my dressing chest. Hair tidy for once, cheeks rosy with the carmine from Annie's box; the paste necklace I had borrowed from the props looked well with the red dress; I splashed a little more of the Perfume of Araby I had wheedled out of Annie over my throat and wrists. He wouldn't be long now . . . .

Outside the nightwind rustled the grasses and an owl hooted mournfully; from somewhere came the yap of a hunting fox, and nearer at hand the stamp of a restless horse and a whine from Toby. I stood at the door of the wagon and the breeze cooled my perspiring skin: no need to get so worked up, I told myself. These sort of things

313

happen every day: he is going to be my husband, and I love him. The fact that we are going to anticipate our wedding night will be known to no one but ourselves, and I am looking forward to it. I *am*! He would be gentle and loving and it would be over soon and then I should know once and for all just what all the fuss was about.

Someone was coming across the space between the trees and my wagon, a tall lithe figure: my heart missed a beat. Hurriedly, lest it be thought I was too eager, I stepped back again and draped myself in an attitude of rest on the narrow bed, closing my eyes. The candle shone onto the bed and I felt the wagon sway as footsteps mounted the step and someone stood just inside the open door. Behind my closed lids I saw the flutter of the bent candle-flame steady itself, but there was nothing else: no movement, no voice. All I could hear was my own quickened heartbeat, my breathing; even Toby was quiet. It seemed like an hour that I lay there, pretending to sleep, but it was probably no more than thirty seconds or so: why didn't he move, say something? Perhaps I was so convincing he really thought me asleep and would go away again –

Suddenly there was darkness, a quick breath as the candle was extinguished. I sat bolt upright, immediately forgetting to be asleep.

'John? I've been thinking, my dear: I am of the opinion that we should wait. After all, it won't be for long, and when you come back from Wales I can join you up here for a proper wedding. Jack won't mind, I'm sure . . . .'

This wasn't what I had meant to say at all: the words just seemed to come tumbling out helter-skelter as if I had no control over them at all and part of my mind listened to them bemused even as the other part formed them. 'We are both very young and I think our marriage would have a firmer foundation if we didn't – anticipate. I'm sorry: if you light the candle perhaps we can sit and talk about it.'

What on earth was I thinking about? I had got myself dolled up, perfume, rouge and all, rushed through my jobs, missed my dinner, made up a fresh bed, all in order

314

to lie with my love, and here was I dismissing him with a few words as cool as the midnight breeze that rustled the leaves outside. 'Truth to tell, John, you would find me but a poor companion tonight even were I your wife, for if you must know I at present am suffering from the malady that all women must endure once a month and –'

There was a short, sharp bark of laughter. 'Liar!'

'Jack! What the hell –' But I was hauled off the bed by the scruff of the neck and propelled down the step before I had time to expostulate any further, and once in the open air I was shaken till I let out a yelp very reminiscent of Toby.

'Serves you right, you little – little –' Words apparently failed him and he loosened his hold a fraction. Instantly I turned on him, fists reaching for his shadowed face. For answer I got a slap across the cheek that had me measuring my length on the turf, my head swimming and tears flowing. After a moment I was hauled to my feet and a handkerchief appeared. 'Dry your eyes, slut, and when you've recovered your senses I want an explanation!'

'I owe you none! It's you who owe *me* one: what right have you to burst into my wagon and –'

'By the same right that I wipe that disgusting paint off your face!' and a bucket of water was emptied over my head, the handkerchief was ripped from my outraged hands, and my face was scrubbed unmercifully. 'Now at least you look clean: you still stink of that atrocious perfume I suspect you borrowed from Annie, but that can soon be remedied.' And half-leading, half-carrying me, he made short work of the distance between us and the slow-moving river. 'In you go!'

When at last he hauled me to the bank again, the fight had gone out of me and I was choking and shivering. All at once his mood seemed to change. He made me walk up and down, fetched out his brandy flask and persuaded a mouthful or two of the choking spirit down my throat, then flung his coat over my shoulders and led me back to the camp. Kicking the smouldering embers of the fire into life he added a couple of lengths of dry wood, then sat down on a convenient log. The reviving fire threw flame shadows on his dark face and I could not see his eyes.

I remained standing, still shivering. 'How did you know – about me and John?'

'Wasn't difficult, what with him washing every day – well, nearly – and you tarting yourself up like a Garden whore and the both of you disappearing into the undergrowth every five minutes spare; it would have taken a blind, deaf and dumb idiot not to have seen which way the wind was blowing. I thought at first you were just playing at being grown-up, at fancying yourself as a lovesick country maid, but when I heard what was planned for tonight – well, enough was enough!'

'You spied on us!'

'Yes! and I was justified, wasn't I? If I hadn't followed you earlier and skulked in the bushes like some Peeping Tom you might have made the ultimate error –'

'Which is?'

'To mistake infatuation for love – and stake your virtue on the three-card trick.'

'But I wasn't going to: you heard me –'

'Panicking –'

'Rubbish! I just decided . . . . Never mind. *How* did you know I was lying about – about the time of the month?' It was a silly question, at a silly time, but somehow it was important to know the answer.

Subtly his voice changed again; now it was indulgent, almost loving. 'Before each time, my dear, your eyes look as though you have smudged them with burned wood and you trip over tent pegs that aren't there and swear like a ploughboy . . . don't you think a man notices these things? What the hell do you think I'm here for? For God's sake, Zoe, I *care* what happens to you! I'm not the ogre you seem to think me. I just don't want to see you throw yourself away on a worthless piece of rubbish like that young Adonis. If I had thought him worthy of you, do you think I would have interfered?' He rose and came

316

round to my side of the fire. 'For heaven's sake, child, you're still cold – I'm sorry. Sorry for throwing you in the river that is, not for interfering. Come here: let your old Jack warm you up.' And he put his warm arms around me and held me close.

For a moment I leaned against his chest, then had to spoil it all.

'It's not me you care about, it's your wretched invest-ment! For that's all I am, isn't it? A meal ticket that you invest in your fancy whores! You don't really care for me at all, and you've made that abundantly clear since that night in Preston! Oh yes, you pretended at the time, but you made it obvious that I was useful because there was no one else around, and since then I have been just your chattel, a thing that works to line your pockets, and nothing more. If I wasn't an attraction for the customers you wouldn't keep me on – I'm not beautiful or experienced enough to be your fancy piece, and you only begrudged me happiness with John because I still help you bring in money – Where is he, by the way? You haven't hurt him?'

As I spoke he had gradually released me, and now he stepped back a pace or two, and his voice was harsh. 'Is that what you think? That I keep you here merely for the paltry copper you bring? Oh, sure, you work for your keep, but do you really think I couldn't find others just as good to take your place? Someone, if you believe what you say, who would work for love, not money?' He turned away, and his next words were offered to the trees, the castle, the sky, to anyone but me. 'As for Preston – I told you then why I couldn't make you my mistress. You were too young, and I respected you too much. As for not being beautiful enough – you've just proved to yourself, I think, that that is not true.' He turned back to me. 'Anyway, you're still too young –'

'I'm seventeen in a month –'

'Maturity has nothing to do with age: you are either born a tart, or not. I thought you were not. It seems I was wrong.'

'Getting married has nothing to do with being a tart –'

'Married? Married! You believed him, then . . . . Perhaps I misjudged you: you are more fool than I thought.'

'Believe him? Of course I do!' I hesitated, not liking the past tense of the conversation. 'Where is he?'

'On the way back to Richmond, I hope.'

'Richmond isn't in Wales. He was going to Wales, to get some horses. Unless, of course, you waylaid him or –'

'Or nothing! He went happily enough, with fifty gold pieces in his pocket.'

'Fifty – gold – pieces? I don't understand . . . .'

'That's what it's cost me to keep you: approximately all you've made in profit since I met you. What's that? A gold piece a week, I suppose: nothing to the landed gentry, but more than enough for me. So, for whatever time you condescend to stay with us, you will have to earn double just to stay abreast, even if that means working twice as hard. I can't finance a whole troupe on losses . . . .'

'I don't understand!' I didn't. He just wasn't making sense. Why had he given John money? And, most important of all, why was my intended suddenly going to Yorkshire instead of Wales?

The embers of their fire were cold and the horse droppings no longer fresh. Where the vans and wagon had rested were deep wheelmarks, but of John and his parents there was no sign, except a broken hobble, a discarded brush with no bristles, horsehair from some mane or tail caught in the hedge, a wisp of hay.

'I knew his parents were going to Wales –'

'Yorkshire.'

'Wales!'

'*Yorkshire* –' He broke off. 'This is silly. That boy told you he was going to Wales?'

I nodded. 'To pick some Welsh ponies. We were – we

were to get married when he returns. Tonight – was to be just between ourselves . . . .'

'Oh, Zoe! You – you gullible little idiot! Do you really want to know what was intended?' He didn't wait for an answer. 'They none of them had any intention of going any farther west: this is as far as they go every year. I asked around, you know, and they never vary. They buy up from the Egyptians and Romanies in Yorkshire, break in the best, and travel across to sell at Shrewsbury, Ludlow, Chester and Warwick. Then back again. They've been doing it for years, ever since the lad could ride; and for the past five of those years he's been doing what he nearly did to you tonight: picking some girl up from the towns, or preferably one of the travellers, filling her full of promises, then disappearing when he'd got what he wanted. You've been conned, girl, why not admit it?'

'But – but – he said he – loved me . . . .'

'Don't we all? It's the quickest way to bed I know –' He broke off, for he must have seen the misery in my face, the slow-dawning realization that faery princes exist only in the imagination, that what had seemed solid gold was only a thin plating on base metal –

'Zoe, my stupid little dear, it's happening all the time; why, when he said he loved you, perhaps he even believed it himself for a while . . . .' I knew he was only trying to comfort me, and the silly tears of hurt pride and loss of dream ran down my cheeks so fast his face was only a blur in the firelight. I hiccoughed, and in a moment his arms were holding me close and a handkerchief was busy mopping me up. 'And don't let this – this fiasco make you feel you aren't a very attractive girl . . . . Why, there are times when I could fancy you myself!' and he kissed my wet cheek. 'There, that's better . . . .'

How had he known that John's betrayal might all but destroy my faith in myself, my new-found confidence in my looks, my body, my desirability? Somehow, whenever I had really needed him, Jack had been there with the right words, a comforting hug, a dry handkerchief I

319

had been a fool! Now, with Jack's arms about me I was far more comfortable, relaxed, happy than I had ever been in John's embrace. Even the fact that that same Jack had slapped me around a quarter of an hour earlier and then thrown me into the river didn't change the affection, the very real affection, in which I held him. Every time he had chastised me it had been for my own good, and it had only been with him that I had felt that lovely tingly melting feeling that even now his proximity was stirring in my tummy . . . . And he had paid out fifty guineas to keep me safe: surely, that meant that he did care, even if only a little, for me myself.

'Did you really give him all that money?'

'Money? Oh, that: yes. But what's money, anyway? Just a handful of metal, that's all. Think no more of it.'

'That's not what you said five minutes ago . . . . Why didn't you just tell him to go away, threaten him a little?'

'I wanted to be sure he wouldn't return – he couldn't face you after accepting money to let you alone, I was sure of that. He was an obstinate young man: told me to mind my own business at first. And if I had just knocked him down he might have found a way to get to you . . . . So I made sure.'

'I'm glad you didn't,' I murmured, happy in his comforting arms. And yawned.

'Time for bed. And sleep. Didn't what?'

'Mind your own business . . . . You were right, Jack, and I'm sorry.' I detached myself, reluctantly, from his embrace. 'I'll pay you back somehow, some day. I promise.'

'Don't worry about it: it's over and done with; I'm glad enough just to have my sane, sensible Zoe back again . . . . I'll amend that; my pretty Zoe.' He chuckled. 'And I always am.'

'What?'

'Right!'

320

15

The weeks ahead were filled with work; tramping the drying lanes, performing under the warming sun, sheltering near the burgeoning trees, every day bringing us further into the hottest, dryest summer I could remember. From Warwick we moved east into the Midlands and then south and a little west so we didn't miss Worcester and Tewkesbury. The sun burned our arms, faces, and hands and soon I was gipsy-colour wherever it showed, and somewhere it didn't, dark enough even for Jack's critical eye.

But sunshine wasn't all joys; we grew too hot, sweaty and sticky and irritable, and at last the water began to dry up. First the village ponds, then there was no stream water to wash away the stinks of the towns and there was talk of plague; indeed one day approaching a sleepy hamlet, our mouths full of grit from the dusty road, thinking thankfully of a long cool drink and water to wash away the dust, we were met by flying stones and lumps of turf. It turned out that some tinkers a week or so back were suspected of bringing the vomiting and fever that had laid low half the population, and they weren't going to take any risks with us. This was the first time, but not the last, that we had to pay for our water; Jack also had to compensate Annie for the black eye from one of the flying clods of earth, and that proved expensive; for three days after, she refused to perform, and it was only a gold coin on the fourth that persuaded her.

Water and heat were not the only problems: one dusty evening we were lying in the shade of a few trees, their leaves drooping in the stifling air, when there was an indignant chatter of small birds above us, a couple of loud squawks, and an addition to our troupe dropped literally out of the skies at our feet.

It was a large raggedy black bird with a disproportion-ately large beak. 'If you don't hold your tongue, I'll pull out all your feathers and squawk! squawk!' said the apparition, perfectly clearly. It waddled forward like the big brother of a starling, cocked its eye up at the small birds still twittering in outrage among the branches above, then leaned forward and bit my toe. 'For God's sake put the cover on and let's get some peace!' then in a woman's voice, shrill with exasperation: 'How many times do I have to tell you?' followed by a few whistled bars of 'Lillibullero' and a profanity.

Jack was the first to recover. In an instant he had grabbed Annie's apron and brought it down over the bird. A few moments later, its beak prudently tied with twine, it was being examined by Tom.

'Some foreigner, most like; not used to flying: wings have been clipped. Bit of a strain in the right one . . . . Had a few pecks, too. Spent a couple of days free, but not found much to eat. Fetch us a bowl of warm water, Zoe lass, and some of the dried fruit you puts in puddings – oh, and a handful of oats.'

Before dark we had the stranger in a roughly fashioned box with slats for bars; cleaned up, wing bandaged and crop full, but not before we had been treated to a fine collection of swearwords both from itself and from Jack, after it drew blood from the latter's ear. By morning they had both quietened down, and Tom was of the opinion that the bird was really quite tame. He made a large sleeping box and a high perch for daytime, and after a while Baltasar, as we named him, grew quite used to them and us. All but Toby, that is: they could not stand each other from the start, and if ever one got too near the other all hell was let loose, Toby barking hysterically and the bird yelling: 'Good morning my dear! Oh what a bad-tempered bird! Strike me blind! Will you take a dish of tay?' in a variety of voices and intonations.

It wasn't long before it was picking up phrases from us too, each in the very tone and manner of the speaker. So it was that I jumped out of my skin when Tom's voice said in my ear: 'Come up, then, Daisy,' when he was patently half a field away; and was vastly amused when Baltasar appeared to learn the 'Tomorrow and tomorrow . . .' speech from *Macbeth* quicker than Jack himself, though I must admit that the bird's 'tomorrows' did stretch into infinity . . . . At first he was an unreliable performer, though, for billed as 'The Amazing Talking Bird from the East, with a Vocabulary of Thousands of Words' he would sometimes dry up completely, shuffle along his perch in a miserable heap of untidy feathers and say 'Squawk' and nothing more. It was Tom's everlasting patience that got him to respond in the end, however; for two hours before a performance Tom would shut him in his box in the dark, then when he was brought out reward him with a sultana or raisin every time he spoke.

We never found out where he came from and none claimed him; Tom took him as his own, and he became a big draw and more than repaid his keep. After a while he was even trained to draw cards from a pack to help with my fortune-telling and I grew quite fond of him, though not when Toby was around.

Baltasar came to us in the last week in May, and the sixth of June was my seventeenth birthday. As the great day approached I grew more and more excited: on this day I should be released from my spurious indentures and perhaps – if he remembered, and if he felt like it, and if . . . . And if. So many ifs . . . . But surely, whatever happened, I should have a present from him; I had given him enough hints. During those last few weeks I had made myself look as feminine as possible, ribbons in my dresses and in my hair and, because I knew Jack didn't like Annie's heavy perfumes, I had bought a light cologne water and hung sweet-smelling herbs among my dresses. I treated myself to a beautiful pair of red leather shoes with yellow heels, white stockings with a pattern on the calf and yellow silk garters with roses sewn in a cluster, and scrubbed and scrubbed at my nails every night till they shone clean from even a hint of horse and dog and bird and pots and pans.

When Annie found out why I was prinking and preening, buying and beautifying, she told Tom and Signor Grappelli that my birthday was due. They all asked what gift I would like and though of course I told them I wanted for naught and would be happy with their good wishes, I knew they would take no notice.

Tuesday was the great day and I planned to wash my hair and try it in ringlets. Annie was to prepare a special supper – glazed pork, a pair of fowls, and spiced pudding – but on Monday the worst happened. We were camped near Worcester and could see the Malvern Hills away to our right and Bredon to our left, when Jack suddenly announced that we would have to do without him for a couple of days. Too late I remembered last year when he had ridden off about this time and this place: too suddenly I blurted out: 'But you can't: it's my birthday!'

Coldly he regarded me, and coldly he spoke. 'What's that to me?'

'I'm seventeen tomorrow –'

'Seventeen or seventy, birthdays are naught but an excuse for ill-deserved presents! Well, you'll get none from me until you grow up, and that has nothing to do with the day of the week or the month of the year. Feasts and fallals and gewgaws and junketings are all very well for children!' And at dusk on the Monday he rode away to the west, Hannibal's hooves a low muted clop on the dusty highway, their figures a blur between my tear-tangled eyelashes.

So I had my birthday without him; we worked as usual, but afterwards gathered round an unnecessary fire, had our feast and I was presented with my gifts. From Signor Grappelli a quill pen and blue and white china inkstand, from Tom a covered stool he had made for my wagon and from Annie a pink velvet pincushion, shaped like a heart.

Even Toby had something for me, for I found him trying to extricate himself from the tangle of ribbons – white embroidered with pink roses, green with a darker pattern of leaves, blue with silver shells – that someone had tied in a great bow around his neck. There was a yard of each and I suspected Annie, but no one would say and Toby wasn't admitting anything either. He was just glad to be rid of them, and in fact had managed to swallow two inches of the pink and one of the blue before I rescued him.

They were all very kind, and I laughed and ate, and drank my wine and kissed them all thank you and pretended I was too happy for words: but I had thought my birthday would have been different. The stupid tears that I held till I was alone blurred the moon that swung like a great lantern above the trees, as I blew out my candle and went to bed alone.

Jack returned two days later, his boots and Hannibal's legs white with dust, the great moths flying about their heads in the twilight. This time he was not angry or aggressive, just tired and quiet. Once again no one asked where he had been and he volunteered nothing, just slipped the reins to Tom and went to bed without a word. This time last year I had been in his van, been thrown out and regained it again, but this year I dared not even go near; then I had been a boy to all intents and purposes but even so had felt nearer by far than I was as my true self. Almost I would have welcomed last year's buffetings . . . .

June crawled, hot as ever, into July and rain receded in the mind into one of those things one had heard of but never seen; we heard the growl of thunder now and again but it was always over the horizon and the lightning flickered like an adder's tongue and as dry. Further north, we heard, the rains came, the streams ran sweet and the grass was green, but here in the south an increasing number of the inns we came to had no ale, ponds were all dried up by now and so were the cows. There was little enough water for the horses and none for washing unless we came by a river, and these were running slow and low; there was a brief spell of wetter weather towards the end of July and beginning of August, then the drought settled in again and even the wells ran dry and we met carters hawking great barrels of stinking water they had got from the Lord knows where. Some bought, but we were not tempted: one look at the warm scummy water, alive with larvae, and my stomach revolted. Tom went down with a low fever and Jack decided to find a river town and perhaps stay till the weather broke, or at least follow the water-flow towards London, because we had little enough time before St Bartholomew's.

So we came to Oxford, city of towers and bells and scholars, of books and late-burning candles, and stayed for St Giles's fair in a meadow near St John's College. Pickings were good, Tom got better, we caught up with the washing. Although it was not term-time, there were a number of personable young men hanging about the fortune-telling tent when I finished at night, but they were still callow enough to be discouraged by a Jack in one of his more forceful moods, or by a Toby whose trick of smiling in welcome was generally misinterpreted as a ferocious snarl by those who didn't look as far as the wagging tail. Not that Toby couldn't be fierce when occasion demanded: one young scholar who had the temerity to try and kiss me found he had an irate dog hanging on to his cuff; as I disentangled the young man I reflected that it was strange that Toby had never attempted to interfere in whatever mistreatment Jack handed out to me.

From Oxford Jack struck south through the Vale of the White Horse, and it was there that the rains came.

We had played the night before in a little village for our supper; the latter was meagre enough and I forget the name of the former, but we were away by dawn and winding between lazy lanes, the dust thick in our nostrils. During the day we passed through a couple of sleepy, heat-dazed hamlets, and apart from the shuffle of hooves through dust and dry grasses, the creaking of the axles, the irritating tap-chink! of a badly juxtaposed pot or pan, we were silent. Even Signor Grappelli's monkey was too hot to chatter and run up and down the roof of his master's van: he was the only one to have appreciated the heat, but was still at last; Baltasar I could see perched on Tom's wagonette, a heap of scruffy feathers, his head under his wing . . . .

'What's time, Jack?' I heard Annie call out fretfully.

'A little after four.'

' 'Sgetting awful dark!'

It was. For a while now it had seemed like twilight. The fields on either side were still: no breeze stirred the ripening wheat that usually needed but a dandelion-puff of breeze to send it rippling like silk in a pattern of dark and light. Not that the harvest could be anything but bad this year: the too-early drought had brought it up shorter and thinner than usual and the pigeons had devastated it still further. Ahead there was sudden movement: a flock of small birds flew past, full of urgent chirrupings, and disappeared into a wood a little way ahead, where the ground rose above the bed of a dried-up stream.

'Pull up a minute!' I heard Jack's shout and saw him jump down to walk back and have a word with Tom. Being at the tail of the line I let my horse's reins drop so he could snatch a mouthful under the hedge; as I watched him lip a blade or two a rabbit darted across our path and skidded to a standstill, sitting on its haunches and twitching its whiskers, then dropping to all fours again, thudding a couple of alarm signals with its back legs and making for the higher ground. I glanced back over my shoulder; behind us the sky was the colour of wet iron; no clouds, just a sheet of threatening dark grey-blue.

Jack appeared at my elbow. 'Tom reckons we're in for

327

the father and mother of a storm; we'll pull off the road up ahead and get a bit higher in that field you can see.'

Almost we were too late, for even as Jack's van passed in the lead through the wooden gateposts of the field the first drops of rain, thick and warm as blood, fell on the backs of my hands. Instantly Jack whipped up his horse for the copse at the head of the slope, Signor Grappelli's lighter van passed Annie's, and Tom, Daisy, and Hannibal were ahead of them all.

I was still steering my van between the gateposts as Tom neatly reversed his wagonette next to Jack's in the shelter of the trees and ran down to help Annie, who was floundering. Jack had unharnessed his horse and was leading it through the trees when the first fork of lightning jabbed into the earth a quarter-mile away followed by a crack of thunder that had me fighting my horse, aware of Annie a heap on the grass and Signor Grappelli leading her frightened horse up the hill. Even as I slipped down to lead mine I saw Jack and Tom heave Annie to her feet and propel her up the slope, her skirts ballooning up round her bare behind in the sudden gust of wind that had them all reeling.

The rain increased in volume and it was all I could do to bring my van up alongside Jack's. From somewhere a piece of tarpaulin broke loose and whipped across my arm, stinging like a slap; my horse reared in panic as I unfastened the last straps, my feet became entangled in the greasy harness, there was a sudden blinding flash of light, a sulphurous smell, and a thunderous bang as a dead tree in the middle of the field was struck, and smoke curled up round the burned grass. Temporarily deafened and blinded simultaneously I shut my eyes and clapped my hands to my ears, letting go the horse which reared again, cannoned into me on the descent and left me flat on my back as it careered off down the field with its collar still on, to disappear in a curtain of rain that was practically solid.

I cursed, and bidding Toby 'Stay!' I gathered up my

already sodden skirts and ran out into the deluge. My bare feet slipped and skidded on the wet grass: the earth was so dry it would not soak up the rain and it ran in yellow rivulets between the tussocks of grass. Again the lightning flashed and the thunder roared and I could see my horse gone through the gate and careering down the road. All the breath came out of me in a whumph! as I landed on my nose and rolled the next ten feet or so. By now I could hardly see; rain plastered my hair to my skull, my eyelashes were spiky with it and my dress was a soaking wet rag that clung stickily to my wet body.

Glancing back, the vans against the trees at the top of the hill were a blur through the veil of rain, but I could just distinguish Daisy, who looked like a giant snowdrop, hooves tucked together and head and tail hanging down soaking. Down I went again, but now I was out on the road and could see my horse trotting away in the distance, all fire dampened by the rain, his fetlocks looking ridiculously thin where the feathers were plastered by mud and water, his tail an apology on his steaming rump. I yelled at him but he picked up speed and disappeared round a turn in the lane. I ran, caught my toe on a sharp flint, cursed again and sat down promptly in a puddle. Behind me, above the drumming of the rain, came the harder clop of hooves; looking up, I saw a dripping Jack on an even drippier Hannibal. He handed me down a sodden rope, then held out his hand.

'Up behind: it'll be quicker.'

Even so, it must have taken all of a quarter-hour to corner that horse, and we only accomplished it when I managed to slip past him and drive him back to Jack; in the end he was docile enough and I rode him back to camp and tethered him with the others. It was still raining hard, and as I dodged back between the trees I saw Toby sitting snug in my van grinning happily, and Tom leaning from his wagonette.

'Don't forget chocks under the wheels – only needs earth

to loosen for vans to go rolling down the slope . . . . They're all done save yours and the master's.'

Obediently I wedged my wheels, then turned to look at Jack's van; cursing men, rain, thunder, horses and all, I stomped over and knocked on his door.

'Chocks, Jack?'

The half-door opened and he stood there in his breeches, towelling his hair.

'In the box under the step; thanks; I forgot. Come and get a brandy when you've done; you must be chilled through . . .' and he turned away, whistling cheerfully.

Sticking out my tongue at his back, and feeling thoroughly sorry for myself, being the only one left outside, I busied myself with the wooden wedges. All done, and on my way back to my wagon, I paused. I had no fire, no food, no brandy, and no one to warm me but Toby: why not take advantage of Jack's careless offer, borrow his towel and save mine?

I knocked on his door.

Inside, he had lit the lantern, which swung erratically from a hook in the roof. On the make-up table there was a bottle of wine and another of brandy, some cheese, the heel of a loaf, a knife, two horn mugs and two pewter plates. So he *had* been expecting me . . . .

'Help yourself – God save us, you're soaking! Here, stop dripping all over the floor and dry yourself.' And he flung me the coveted towel.

I rubbed my hair, face, hands and arms. 'That's all I can manage.'

'Rubbish! Get that wet dress off – you can put on that old shirt of mine in the corner – Oh, for Christ's sake, girl, I won't watch!' and he turned his back.

I hesitated, then the shivers got the better of me, for with the rain had come a blessed coolness: after all, I still had a pair of drawers on. Pulling the soaking dress off over my head I hastily rubbed myself down and donned the shirt. Miles too big. Knotting it in front, I rolled up the sleeves.

Jack was lounging on the bed as I turned, a hunk of cheese in one hand, a mug of brandy in the other. He was wearing some sort of long robe of crimson silk tied with a fringed sash, and his feet were bare; I suspected the rest of him was too, especially as his shirt, breeches, and smallclothes were hanging over the chair to dry. I sat down on the stool and got up again.

'Look away,' I said, and pulling off the sodden drawers that clung uncomfortably to my crotch, I draped them under my dress on a clothes hook on the door. Carefully I unknotted the shirt again and buttoned it up all the way: it reached nearly to my knees now and I reckoned it was decent enough. I sat down again and cut some bread and cheese. 'This is cosy, then.'

'Don't talk with your mouth full . . . . Help yourself to wine.'

We munched and drank for a while in companionable silence, and I downed my second mug. Outside the rain seemed to have lessened, at least it was no longer drumming on the roof too loud to let oneself think and the thunder was a dull grumble in the distance. I stood up and brushed the crumbs from my lap into my hand and put them carefully on the plate.

'Thanks very much: that was very welcome.' And after a pause. 'I suppose I'd better go now . . . .'

'Why?'

I considered. Toby would be glad of the company, I could get properly changed, brush up on my lines or the herb lore, darn the hole in my second-best stockings that had been waiting three weeks –

'No reason, really.'

'Then sit down again and talk.'

'You always say I talk too much –'

'Chatter. There's a difference. The first is like a little brook, all fuss and noise and froth and shallows, the second like a slow-moving river, deep and profound.'

I giggled. 'Brooks make streams, and streams, rivers . . . .'

331

'Stop trying to be clever; you know what I mean!' But he wasn't angry: he was grinning at me over his brandy mug. '*Some* little brooks get swallowed up by the earth before they really get going . . . .'

'Potholes. Underground caverns. Stalactites and stalagmites.'

He looked at me in surprise. 'You know about things like that?'

'Better still: I've been in one of those places.' And I recalled for him the cave my stepfather had taken me to see, one hot, sunny day that seemed like a hundred years ago, when I was eight. It had been all of ten miles away and he had had to carry me partway home. The mouth of the cave had only been a small hole in the rock, but once inside and the candles lit, the rocks had stretched out on either side like great fangs, the teeth of the devil himself, gleaming from the floor of the cavern, dripping from the roof, and the water running away like a living tongue to disappear down the throat of Satan, a shaft that fell down too far to see, was too stomach-deep for the pebbles I threw down for sound . . . .

'Have a brandy,' said Jack and I found, after the first stinging gulp, that I was enjoying it, and enjoying talking too, about my life in the village: about the time I taught the children; the times I had helped with the harvest; the long winter evenings studying with my stepfather; skating on the mere; gathering blackberries and wild strawberries for preserves, elderberries and sloes for wine; the long walks over the dales, helping with the sheep; trimming my first bonnet, saying my first Communion; dancing on the green on Midsummer Day.

My glass was full again, and now it was Jack who was talking: about America and the Indies; about battles and soldiers and sudden death; then somehow about a great concert he had attended where music was played on barges on the river and there had been an open-air performance of *A Midsummer Night's Dream* and fireworks –

'– and it looks as if the fireworks are coming back: hear that thunder?'

Indeed, it was much darker again. The lamp, which had been spluttering for a while now, expired with a gasp and left us in twilight. Outside the rain was coming down hard once more.

'Reach me down the lamp, girl, and I'll put in some more oil . . . .'

I stood up, and to my surprise the van seemed to be turning a slow circle. After shaking my head and rubbing my eyes I found to my relief that everything had steadied; after a moment I reached up for the lamp, but it was a good eight inches out of range. I jumped, rather ineffectually, setting the van to swaying, and heard a low chuckle from Jack.

'Don't try to help!' I said sarcastically. 'It wouldn't take a beanpole like you a moment, but I'm not tall enough.' I pulled the stool underneath and after a couple of attempts managed to climb up and unhook the lamp. 'Here you are, then! Well, come on . . . .'

Slowly he uncoiled himself from the bed and came towards me. 'Pity: I was enjoying that.'

'What?'

He reached up and took the lamp, leaving me wobbling precariously on the stool. 'The sight of you stretching up for that light, with my shirt-tails up round your waist like a bare-arsed boy.' He stood back and put down the lamp, considering my furious, blushing face and the hands that were now holding the wretched shirt as low as it would go. 'No, on second thoughts, not a little *boy* . . . .' He was mocking me, and in my fury I aimed a swipe at his head but he ducked and stepped back, laughing. 'Careful, or you'll fall and lose all your dignity, sweetheart, and there's precious little of that as it is!'

I stamped, forgetting where I was, and all but overbalanced. I would have climbed down, but was afraid of the shirt riding up again, and there was no room to jump. 'If you don't want me to forget my – my dignity next time we are on stage together,' I said through clenched teeth, 'you will help me down – instantly!'

'Please?'

'Please!' I shouted. 'And to hell with your niceties!'

'There's no need to yell over a simple request,' he complained, but stepped forward and with surprising strength lifted me off the stool and held me up straight in the air so that I had to rest my hands on his shoulders for support and look down at him.

'Put me down!'

'Now?'

'Now!'

'Sure?'

'Quite!'

Slowly he lowered me between his arms, and it was only when my toes touched the ground again that I realized where the shirt had ended up. Round my waist again . . . . And then his hands were on my bare behind, patting me like a puppy.

'Nice . . . .'

'Let me go! I'm . . . . I'm cold, I must get some more clothes on –'

'Cold? That's easily remedied.' And suddenly his robe was open and I was pressed against his warm body and he was running his fingers up and down my spine and laughing at my furious face. 'That better?'

'Yes – No! Let me *go*!' Suddenly I felt unsure, uneasy, and tried to push him away, my fists clenched. 'Who do you think you are, anyway?'

There was a sudden little silence as he stared down at me in the gathering darkness, his expression inscrutable, then suddenly there was a flash of lightning that lit his face like Richard III on his way to hell and as the thunder rumbled all around us one of his arms tightened round my waist, the other hand twisting my hair and dragging it back so that I had to look up at him.

'Who do I think I am? Why, I'm Jack, and the best

334

Jack you'll ever know. And just now I have a fancy for you to play my Jill –'

I struggled and swung my fists, but it was no use: all I managed was one buffet on his right cheek before his mouth came down, hard, on mine and I was gasping, choking, stifled, by the cruellest kiss I had ever known. I wriggled and twisted, but it seemed minutes before he released his hold and I stumbled back. Not far enough, for as I swayed he caught me to him again and forced up my chin.

'Ever been kissed like that before?'

'No, not like that . . . .'

'And you don't like Jack any more, either?'

'Not particularly . . . .'

'Well, then, connoisseur of me,' he said sarcastically. 'How should I behave to you?'

Had I not stopped then and thought before I answered, my whole life would probably have been very different. Another sense seemed to be working inside me that whispered that the answer would have to be right; the same voice told me, as sure as if he had told me himself, that Jack was chastising some other woman through me, that his punishing hands felt another body: at the same time I knew that he was unconscious of this, and also probably unaware that he was trying to warn me that it was unwise to get involved with him. With this knowledge came a great tenderness, and I realized that to call back the Jack I knew the atmosphere would have to be light, deliberately contrived. I did not try to struggle any more, in fact I moved closer.

'The acting is good,' I said, as if assessing a performance, 'but I think you are reading someone else's lines. Leave Romeo to the callow youths and Caliban to the middle-aged and ugly: how about Antony?'

'Because you're too young to know what Cleopatra knew.'

'And what was that?'

'The answer to the riddle of the Sphinx.' He was

relaxing, holding me less tight, his hands caressing rather than punishing.

'Why it smiles, you mean?'

'If you like.'

'Oh, I know the reason for that!'

'Do you, indeed?'

'Indeed, yes! Bend your head down and I'll whisper . . . .' But as he inclined his head to mine I clasped my arms round his neck and kissed him full on his startled mouth.

Momentarily he drew back, then he chuckled and shrugged. 'Teach me the riddle then, Zoe, my little Cleopatra . . . .'

Good: I was back to being me with him again. But he was still playing a part, albeit now Jack-of-the-road, and to him I was still his hired help, too young to be anything but a plaything to be indulged to the point where he would put me away from him and ask me to feed the horses, wash the pots, hear his lines . . . . But now I was in earnest. This was for real, I wanted to find, with Jack, and only Jack, what – it – was all about, so I closed my eyes and vowed to forget five minutes ago and pretend he was all the princes of Araby, all the knights in shining armour, all the young men I had seen who deserved a second glance, my mind telling me at the same time he was probably more like Macheath than any. But as his tongue parted my lips and his hands caressed and held me close, it was suddenly all true. For a magic moment that I could only pray would last for ever the tingly melting feelings I had had before came back a hundredfold and I responded with all my body, knowing somehow when and where to caress in return, for he too was becoming aroused; I opened my thighs to his insistent pressure and thought he would lift me to embrace his, but then, as I knew it would sooner or later, came the moment of rejection. As if suddenly realizing where his indulgence was leading him, he took a deep breath and pushed me away.

336

'Enough, enough, my dear, or I shall forget you're still virgin!'

Gently I reached forward to touch him, my heart hammering wildly. 'I'm tired of being a virgin, Jack: it's just a word for not knowing what makes all women alike. Please, don't turn me away this time,' and I stroked him more confidently.

He shivered suddenly, as though a goose had walked over his grave, then gave me a wry smile. 'If you don't take your hands away, my pet, I shall spill before you get me to the bed . . . . Come then, let Jack show you how to become a woman!'

Boldly, not giving myself time to think, I walked over to the bed, drew back the covers and lay down on the rough sheet, unbuttoning what was left of the shirt. Outside the thunder played a game of skittles and the rain fell harder; inside there was the spirt of tinder and a flickering candle bloomed behind my closed lids. I opened my eyes and Jack stood over me, candlestick in hand, just looking – My boldness evaporated with the light, and I tried to cover myself with my hands.

Gently he bent and pulled them away. 'Nay, let me see what I'm getting . . . .' Setting the candle down on the table he sat down by my side and his hands pressed me back against the pillows. 'There now, move over a little – just so, and let Jack have a little room . . . .' He eased me out of the shirt and it went to join his robe on the floor and suddenly his warm body was alongside mine, his mouth went to my breasts with a touch like the brush of a moth's wing and his hand parted my thighs and stroked till my mind could think of nothing save a great need that only he could assuage. His lips came down on mine in a long kiss and then he raised his head.

'Zoe, my little dear, are you sure?'

'Not quite –'

He leaned back. 'Then I won't –'

'I want to, but – it's just – just –'

'Yes?'

'Are you sure it's not too big?' I said in a rush, glancing down his long, lean body in some apprehension.

His laugh was full of amused tenderness. 'No, my darling, it's not too big . . . . Leastways I've never found a woman who couldn't accommodate me. You it will hurt, just a little at first, then never again, I promise. Why, you might even grow to like it . . . . Kiss me, kiss me with your whole body and so . . . and so . . . .'

For a moment it did hurt, and quite a lot, but he was so gentle otherwise that the hurt went away and once more I was only aware of his closeness and of my insides drawing him in. He didn't move for a little while, but murmured: 'All right, my sweet?'

'Yes, oh yes!' I hesitated. 'Jack – is it all right? I mean, comfortable, where it is?'

My insides felt him jerk with suppressed laughter, then he drew down one of my hands to lie flat on my lower stomach. 'There: press down. Can you feel it? I assure you it feels *very* comfortable . . . .'

Sure enough I could feel the shape with my fingers. 'I didn't know I had room . . . . Can you feel my finger?'

'Mmm . . . I don't think any woman's done that to me before!'

Suddenly everything was all right and I relaxed. Now he moved his body, slowly at first and then faster and all at once he clutched me tight.

'I can't hold out much longer, my darling – Oh God, God!'

And miraculously as he groaned and shuddered my body, my untaught virgin body, responding as much to his cry of urgency as to the feel of his intimacy, found the way quite on its own and I was suddenly soaring in an ecstasy to match his, a pulsing sweetness that had me stifling my cries in his shoulder and scoring my nails into his back.

It seemed to go on forever, but all too soon I came back to myself and we were lying quiet and sticky with sweat.

'All right?'

I nodded, and two tears squeezed unbidden from my closed eyelids. And they weren't for my lost virginity, for there I had lost nothing of importance. No, for I had given away something of far greater value in that lovemaking, and hadn't been conscious of its importance till I discovered its absence. I had always thought of love as a present to be taken, now I realized it was a gift to be given, and in this case the recipient would have been amazed to know he had received it. *I* knew, and that was enough, that our whole relationship – fear, respect, irritation, comradeship, affection, liking – had all led to this moment of discovery. I also knew that he didn't, couldn't feel the same way, and that he mustn't know . . . . It was enough for the moment that I loved, and should never love another the same. That was why it was all so sad: this might never happen again. Growing up suddenly like this made one aware how precarious was happiness, how ephemeral a relationship that depended on one person's feelings alone – What a fool I'd been, not to realize sooner how much I loved him!

He raised his head and rolled away from me, his back against the van, the candlelight on his face.

'Tears, my love? Don't cry: you have made me very happy,' and his fingers brushed the moisture gently from my face and tucked my damp hair behind my cheeks. 'You know something? I hadn't realized until this moment just how beautiful you are . . . .'

And I hadn't realized, I thought, gazing up at him, how his eyes were the bright blue of speedwell; had never noticed the single frown-line between his thick, dark brows; the laugh-lines at the corner of his eyes, the hollows beneath his cheekbones, the smallpox scar on his right cheek, the creases at the corner of his mouth when he smiled; had not noted the one crooked incisor in his otherwise even teeth, the small cleft in his chin, the little white nick slightly left of centre in his lower lip, the couple of silver hairs in his widow's peak, the high bridge to his definitely crooked nose, the pulse that beat so clearly in his left temple – Had he said 'beautiful'?

Then something suddenly happened to him. It was as if he mentally held his breath, and for a heart-stopping moment for me the rain stopped beating on the roof, the leaves no longer rustled, the thunder died, the candle-flame burned true, for as I looked up into those incredibly blue eyes I saw a strange expression, the first flicker in a newly caught fire and as quickly gone. It was as though he had suddenly caught sight of something unexpected, something over which he had no control; but it was gone too quickly for me to identify it, and just as suddenly he changed.

Slipping over me, he donned his robe, then pulled me to my feet and kissed the tip of my nose.

'Rain's almost stopped: run along and see if there is any dry wood in the back of your wagon, and we'll see if Annie can think up some food. I'm hungry!' He pushed me towards the door, draping his shirt over my shoulders, and handing me my damp clothes. 'Oh, by the way, have a look in that herb book of Katina's: there must be an infusion of sorts to counter what – what we have done. Just to be on the safe side: I don't want you out of action for any reason now that St Bartholomew's is so near . . . .'

It might never have happened: all that loving tenderness and heavenly passion wiped out by a man's mundane stomach and mercenary mind. I went back to my wagon and howled into Toby's warm, sympathetic, uncompre-hending coat, only too glad of his uncomplicated, uncritical tongue to mop up the stupid tears.

16

The next day, and the next, I waited for some sign, some indication of the momentous act that had taken place between us and perhaps an invitation to share his bed again: there was none. Rather did it seem Jack was avoiding me, for if at any time it looked as though I might have the opportunity to speak to him alone, he conveniently disappeared. At first I was too happy to care, then I was hurt, then I despaired.

It is not easy when you are seventeen and have given yourself for the first time with a whole heart to have the recipient behave as though you were a one-night romp with no redeeming features worthy of recall; for a while I almost thought I might have done it all wrong, had some deformity of body he had not dared to mention. The humiliation was something that still hurts even in recollection, and the bitterness stayed with me for a long time.

At first, too, I thought he was afraid he had landed me in trouble, but a couple of days later I knew he need not have worried; besides, Kat's book had a handy astrological table which showed me there was no chance of conception and there were a couple of herbal remedies that doubtless would have done the trick. Looking at these I recalled her words at St Bartholomew's Fair last year: 'There's one there you will need before next fair if I'm not mistaken . . . .' How had she known? Or was it just a clever guess? By now I knew how much there was of trickery in fortune-telling, and yet there had been something beyond the usual chicanery in the way she had talked . . . .

For the next two days it rained nonstop, more than making up for the drought of the weeks before, and we were a bedraggled enough troupe that reached Maidenhead later that week. A couple of minor roads were impassable where the volatile Thames had burst its banks and flooded and we were trapped a couple of nights at Bray, our way out being blocked by water rushing across the road in a torrent, sticks, branches, drowned sheep and hens making an impossible hazard. Reaching our objective at last we found dryish ground in the meadows above the town, but we had run out of dry kindling and it was a miserable enough first evening. The ever present threat of more rain kept most customers away and Jack disappeared after only one performance; the nights were drawing in too, and it was with thankfulness that I closed up for the day, dowsed the lantern and made my way back to my wagon, the paltry coppers too few to count. Discarding the wooden pattens I had worn for the mud I climbed the steps wearily and lit the candle left just inside the door. Pulling off the Egyptian wig I wore for my fortune-telling I hung it carelessly on the stand and sank down on the stool, propping my chin on my hands and gazing at my reflection in the cracked and spotty mirror. I stroked Toby, who had come nuzzling at my knee; because of the crack in the glass my mouth and chin looked as if they had slipped, and I sighed, addressing my dog, who was the most appreciative – and often the only – audience I had.

'A sight, that's what I am, my lad, and no mistake. It's been a terrible day and Jack will hit the roof when he sees how bad the takings are: if he bothers to ask, that is . . . . He's away down to the tavern again, I shouldn't wonder, avoiding us once more. If only I could tell him to forget what happened and pretend I had, then we could go back to the old ways: sometimes I wish it hadn't . . . . Dear dog; you're really the only one who cares –'

'No, he isn't,' said Jack quietly, from the shadowed corner of the bed. He rose, and as he did so he swayed. God! he's drunk again, I thought, and with that came the unbeckoned thought that if he were, perhaps he would want me again – No! I swore to myself that I wouldn't be

342

his whore again just for a tipsy moment. But knew I would. If he asked . . . .

'You gave me a fright! How long have you been there?'

He disregarded the question. 'I had to see you.'

'Well, you'd better have the stool: you look a little the worse for wear.'

'I'm all right,' he said impatiently. 'Just a trifle dizzy, that's all. I think I have a touch of fever.' And he swayed again.

A touch of the brandy, too, I thought, but didn't say so.

'This is – is a little difficult to say,' he began, then stopped.

'Don't bother, then,' I said quickly, and brightly too, I hoped, thinking I knew what he was about to say. 'What happened the other night: you can forget it – I have. It was very enjoyable and I appreciate the care you took to – to break me in, and I'm very grateful. But you mustn't feel you have any obligation to do more about it than you have, and you may rest assured that I shall never take advantage of what happened. So – so let's try and get back to the old footing, where you're the boss and I'm – I'm Sprat . . . .' It was hard, but I had rehearsed it often enough during the last few days.

Was it just the light, or did he looked relieved? Or puzzled?

'Is that – really all it meant?'

'Of course,' I said lightly, wanting all the while to cry out instead: 'No, no! you great idiot, you beautiful, wonderful simpleton: I want you and it over and over again for ever and ever, amen!'

'You are making it easier for me,' he said, but now he was frowning. 'I'm glad you didn't take it too seriously, then.' I had an idea he had not meant to say that at all, though what instead I had no idea. He took a deep breath. 'God! I feel terrible . . . . What I came here to say was that you mustn't think I didn't enjoy – the other night, but that it mustn't happen again, for all sorts of reasons.

343

If I told you half of them now I don't think you'd believe me . . . . But it seems from what you've said that it's not necessary to explain. Anyway, whatever you felt about it, I should just like to say that it was one of the most delightful evenings I have ever spent: and it reminded me, amongst other things, that I hadn't given you a seventeenth birthday present.'

'Presents . . . "you'll get none from me until you grow up",' I quoted.

He gave a ghost of a smile – he really did look ill – acknowledging the dig. 'Exactly.' He handed me a flat parcel. 'I hope one day this will reflect the beauty of a bride on her wedding day, and I hope too that when you find the right man you will be happy to come and tell me, and perhaps invite me to the wedding.'

He stumbled rather noisily down the steps, and my eyes were too blurred with tears to see my reflection properly in the hand mirror I found in my parcel. 'Damn him! oh, damn him!' I whispered, unable to appreciate yet the fine smooth grey harewood of the reverse, the silver love knot set into the handle and the tiny seed pearls round the rim of the mirror itself. There was a roll of parchment on the floor: taking it up I smoothed out the indentures of one Z. Mortimer. Written across from side to side in Jack's spiky, angular handwriting were the words: 'Discharged in full' and the date was the date of our lovemaking.

I was woken before dawn by a thumping on my door and Annie's voice raised in great lamentation.

'Oh Lordy me. Zoe my dear, do come! Summat terrible's going on in that van of his, I'm sure!'

Throwing a shawl round my shoulders I stumbled out onto the dewy grass in my shift.

'What's happened?'

'It's Jack! He's swearing and hollering and says he's afire, though I don't see no smoke –'

Now I could hear it also: the crash of a body throwing

itself from side to side of the van, the tinkle of broken crockery, a deep groaning. My heart in my mouth I tried to think sensibly. Signor Grappelli was dancing up and down and chattering like his monkey, Toby was barking, and the bird Baltasar was shrieking, appropriately enough as far as I was concerned: 'Show us yer boobs, then!' over and over again. Slapping a cover on his cage, bidding Toby 'Quiet!' and shouting '*Pace*, damn you, *pace*!' at the Italian, I only had to deal with Annie's threatened hysterics.

'Where's Tom?'

'Taken the horses off somewheres, I reckon: down to water them at the river I shouldn't wonder –'

'Well, go fetch him back here as quickly as possible,' and I did not wait to see whether she had obeyed but mounted the steps of Jack's van and knocked as loudly as I dared. 'Jack – Jack? Are you all right?' There was no answer save an awful moaning that tore at my heart and frightened me half to death at the same time; here outside the dawn was breaking and a pearly pink flush touched the fluffy clouds overhead: red sky at morning . . . . Nothing to fear on a September morning save that he was ill or hurt – 'Jack! *Jack!*'

Still no answer, so I lifted the latch and peered in. Inside was darkness and a rotten-sweet stench of vomit. Throwing the door wide I made out Jack lying on the floor, still in shirt and breeches, in a shatter of broken furniture, plate and china. He was twisting and groaning and muttering and, tossing my shawl out of the door, I crossed the floor to his side; as I bent over him he retched again, but nothing came up save a clear froth; his eyes were open but he was obviously not aware of me. Running back outside I unhooked a couple of buckets from the side of the van, thrust them at the dithering Signor Grappelli with a brief '*Aqua, presto!*' and returned to my patient.

Luckily the bed was not soiled, so when the Italian returned I stripped Jack off, washed him as best I could in cold water, then we half-led, half-carried him to lie down. Prudently shoving a bowl into Signor Grappelli's hand, I stationed him at Jack's head, then grimly set to work clearing up the mess. By the time Annie returned with Tom it looked much better, so I left her to get a fire going and heat some water and went back to my patient. He would not lie still and was burning with fever, tossing and turning, muttering and raving.

Tom shook his head. 'Nasty old fever he got there: don't like the look of him. Best get a doctor.'

I agreed, and Tom set off for the town at speed, returning some half-hour later accompanied by a small fussy man with a rumbling stomach and glasses, who tutted and stifled a yawn or two as he poked and prodded at Jack. He prescribed bleeding.

'You will not!' I said sharply. 'He's weak enough.'

The doctor took a pinch of snuff. ' 'Tis a low fever that has irritated the blood and till the ill humours are drawn off he will burn.'

Annie looked impressed, but I glanced at Tom, who shook his head. 'Mebbe 'tis in the blood now, but it started in the stomach. Still there: he's got the gripes something terrible!'

I looked at the doctor.

He shrugged. 'I can make you a purge of feverfew and –'

'He doesn't *need* purging!' I said furiously. 'He's thrown everything up already! He needs something to reduce the fever and calm him down –' I had suddenly remembered a village remedy and could not wait to get at Kat's herb book to confirm it. 'Have you laudanum?' I asked the doctor.

It cost three guineas and I had to use my savings as we had no idea where the expenses money was kept, but it was worth it to get rid of the quack. Once he had gone I asked both Tom and Annie whether they had seen any motherwort growing thereabouts but they both looked blank, so I got dressed and went to look for myself. I was lucky enough to find some growing in a cottage garden down a nearby lane and when I knocked up the old dame she had some made up already and was glad enough of sixpence for the infusion, promising me more if I needed it.

At first he couldn't keep it down, but I fed him drop by patient drop, and then a little laudanum, and at last he fell into a restless sleep. Tom and I took it in turns to watch over him all that day and the next while Annie and Signor Grappelli did their best to earn our meagre suppers; luckily the weather had improved and we kept going somehow, although I was exhausted by the second night. I had relieved Tom at midnight, promising to call him at six, and sponged down my hoarse-voiced, semi-conscious patient, then fed him some more of the infusion by spoon; before I had had to dip a rag in the mixture and put it on his tongue, but for the last few hours he had swallowed obediently and was sleeping for longer periods.

I found myself nodding off but was wakened with a start at two for Jack had tossed off the bedclothes and was trying to get up; it took all my strength to hold him down, but after a while he quietened. I sponged him down again and gave him a few drops of laudanum, and it being stifling hot I went to throw open the door for a few minutes (my stepfather having taught me that fresh air was healthier than stale), when the mutterings from the bed behind me seemed to turn to more coherent speech. His previous mumblings had been an uncoordinated gabble like a child talking in its sleep, but now the words were coming slower and more recognizable. I crossed back to the bed again and gazed down at the unprepossessing, stubble-chinned face of the man I loved, then smoothed the damp hair back from his forehead and put my lips to his drawn cheek, knowing he could not protest.

'It's all right, my dear, you'll feel better in a little while. I'll not leave you . . . .'

' 'Thea . . . ! 'Thea?' he repeated, then groaned and muttered again. He appeared to doze, then suddenly sat bolt upright and pointed at the wall behind me, his eyes staring wide. 'Murdering harlot!' he said quite distinctly,

347

and there was such venom in his voice that I shrank back. 'Harlot!' he repeated, and tried to spit, but his poor mouth was too dry. 'I loved you, God knows! but you couldn't wait, could you? You're like them all ... never forgive you ... treat them all the same ....' He sank back on the pillows again, his eyes closed. I tiptoed forward and sponged his face once more, and suddenly his eyes were open again. 'Forgive me, *Maman*, but I can't – no man could. Haven't I paid enough?' I soothed him, but he grabbed my wrist. 'Let *him* have her! And may they rot together in hell!' I tried to release myself but he held on the tighter. 'There's no more money, I tell you .... Haven't you had enough? And now there is this girl .... She has the most beautiful ....' He sank back and released his hold. 'I forget. I forget ....'

I rubbed my aching wrist, remembering that I hadn't the 'most beautiful' anything. But he had said something like that to me the night we .... But that way was foolishness: all men said things like that: 'the quickest way to bed I know'.

He started to talk again. 'Let's get this show on the road! Stupid boy ... two left feet and a heart like butter ....' That must be me. 'Scrawny scrap .... "To be or not to be ..."' I endured the next few lines, then took advantage of a pause to feed him another spoonful of the infusion. 'Thanks, sweetheart,' he said unexpectedly, then for a moment his eyes opened and he looked up at me like the old Jack, fully comprehending. 'You'd make a lovely whore,' he said clearly. 'Make a man feel it's all worthwhile: once with you is like a dozen with the others ....' He shut his eyes again, and I couldn't believe he had really been talking to me. 'Could I make you love me? And would it be fair?' He frowned. 'No, because Jack loves no one but himself .... Give your heart and have it gnawed away. No, love 'em and leave 'em, that's Jack's motto. Pity: I could have loved ....' His voiced trailed away and he fell straightaway asleep.

And all I could think was: who was 'Thea? She was the

348

one who had started his ramblings, the one he had felt so strongly about. Was she someone he had met on the road? Was she, perhaps, the mysterious lady of the miniature? And why had he used the French 'Maman' instead of 'Mother' or 'Mamma'? And who was the girl with the 'most beautiful' whatever-they-were? And *had* he been seeing me when he had said 'once with you is like a dozen with the others'? No, it couldn't be, otherwise he would have sought me out again. Questions with no answers chased themselves through my mind for what seemed like ages before I dozed off on the floor by the side of the bed, but then it was just a moment before daylight streamed into the van and Tom was shaking me awake.

'Your potion's worked, praise be! Look now: he's sleeping natural and that old fever has burned itself out. See, his cheek is cool and damp . . . . Give us a hand and we'll change the sheets and make him comfortable like.'

Breakfast tasted good that morning, although it was only bread and cheese and very weak tea. Jack still slept, breathing easily and slow, and it did indeed seem as though the fever had abated. Tom thought he would need feeding up, but gently at first, and we decided on trying a bone broth, with whatever vegetables I could find in the town. I was to buy a bottle of port wine, too, 'to give the soup body' as Annie put it: I imagined it would be a very well-tasted brew . . . . Privately I thought some nice hot bread and milk with sugar would go down just as well, but the others pooh-poohed the idea of any 'pap' as Tom put it, so I took some more of my dwindling pile of money and set off for the market, just like any other housewife, except that I also carried some bills advertising our stay, for I was fairly sure we should be back in business before very long.

I had Annie's big basket over my arm and dreamed a little, I must confess, of what I should be feeling like if I were really just going shopping for myself and my imaginary family: carrying back the viands to our little cottage by the river, with the lavender and pinks under the front window, Toby dozing on the front doorstep in the sun and the swans gliding by on the river at the bottom of the garden, and Jack – no, I just couldn't see Jack sitting in a chair by the door waiting for my return, a pipe in his mouth and whittling away at a doll for one of our children . . .! I must have looked a real idiot, grinning away at my dreams in the marketplace then giving myself a mental shake at my presumption like the rag rug I used to air on the steps of the wagon to rid it of dust.

I found and bargained for a nice piece of shin on the bone, fresh eggs, onions and greens, butter, bread and a twist of tea and left some of the advertising bills at the grocers'; the basket was heavy by the time I had gathered all my purchases, so on the way back I rested it for a moment on the bridge. The morning was hot and heavy, so I leaned back against the stones, brushed the flies away from my sticky, sweaty face, and watched the crowds go by. After a moment or two I became aware I was being watched too, or rather stared at, by a young man outside the inn across the way. Thinking he was merely an impudent passer-by I ignored him, but was aware the scrutiny continued and a moment later saw, out of the corner of my eye, that he was crossing the road towards me. Oh dear, I thought to myself, here we go again! wishing I wore a ring and could pretend to be an outraged wife. If he had been prepossessing it could have been different, a smile and a pleasant conversation might have enlivened the day, but even without looking at him directly I could see his linen was not of the freshest and that he wore a spotty complexion on top a stout body. As he neared me I picked up my basket, ready now to walk on.

'Pardon me – Zounds! I was not mistaken! Cousin Mortimer, by all that's holy . . . .' And a hand shot out to grasp my free arm.

Horrified, I found I was gazing at my loathsome Cousin Oliver.

Not stopping to think, the sweat of sheer panic pervading

my whole body, I attempted to break free, but his grip was too tight.

'Oh, no, you don't, Miss! Mamma will be *very* interested to know you are –'

Desperate, I twisted my head and sank my teeth into his detaining wrist, wrenched free as he howled in anguish, picked up my skirts and ran, instinctively taking a circuitous route back to camp, the basket swinging and bumping against my thigh, my heart beating a tattoo loud and thick enough to choke me. Behind I heard a yell and hullabaloo, but fear lent me wings and by the time I reached the vans all I could hear was the roaring of blood in my ears and my own harsh breathing. Instinctively I made for Jack's van and ran up the steps, only to find Tom barring the way, his finger to his lips.

'Steady, lass: he's sleeping. Anyway, what's the hurry?'

I stared up at him. How could I answer? He, I supposed, knew nothing of my domestic history, Jack was out of action, Signor Grappelli would not understand, and Annie would panic. Hastily I glanced back: there was no sign of pursuit.

I took a deep breath. 'Nothing that won't keep,' I said. 'How is he?'

All the rest of that day I kept glancing up the road towards the town and jumped at any unusual sound, till even Annie exclaimed at my irritability but, thank the Lord! there was no sign of Oliver, so that by the evening I began to think I might have been mistaken, especially when we were joined by the comfortable company of half a dozen other vans stopping off, as we were, on their way to St Bartholomew's. There was a strong man, performing dogs, a pair of conjurors, a bearded lady, and a fire-eater, and for a while the noise and bustle, familiar show cant and exchange of news and views kept me from tension, but when we all bedded down after a quick evening's show,

351

the lanterns were dowsed and I took the night watch with Jack, I had time enough to think.

Part of my mind still cherished the idea that I had been mistaken, that Oliver was safe in Cheshire, that the man I had seen had borne him a fleeting resemblance and that the rest had been supplied by an overactive imagination. But could my fancies have supplied the 'Cousin Mortimer!' I had so plainly heard? No, by some dreadful mischance Cousin Oliver was in Maidenhead, he had definitely recognized me, and now he would discover my where-abouts, perhaps through those damned advertising bills I had left in the town, and come and drag me back to Aunt Sophia, for I was sure I was still legally her ward and the law was on their side. It would be goodbye to freedom, to the road, to Annie and Tom, Toby and Jack – and surely they could have Jack punished for harbouring a runaway? I tiptoed over to the bed and looked down at him: he had taken his medicine two hours ago and was sleeping peacefully, but he was still very weak. Whatever happened, he mustn't become involved; I loved him too much to risk his freedom or a fine. Besides, he was still ill, and nothing must hinder his recovery, even if it meant I had to keep to my wagon till we moved on.

The following morning he was much better and even tried to sit up, so that when I brought him a nice bowl of gruel for his breakfast I found him perched on the edge of the bed, nightshirt crumpled round his thighs, calling for hot water for a shave.

'And take that muck away, girl,' he ordered. 'I'll have some cheese and ale.' And promptly he collapsed back on the bed again.

Still, he was obviously on the mend, and it was comfor-ting to hear him roaring away again, albeit at cub-strength only, as Tom attempted to keep him still enough to shave. That day I persuaded one of the women from the other vans to do our shopping for us, and when plenty of folk came up from the town for the afternoon's and evening's performances I felt brave enough to do my fortune-telling

352

again, though I pulled the wig down almost over my nose and wore a gauze veil, so that with luck Oliver wouldn't recognize me, if he came.

Next day I had even begun to hope that he had only been passing through, and when I went to see Jack and found him demanding tobacco I felt hardly apprehensive at all about hurrying to the nearest tobacconist's, although I took care to wear a shawl and take a stick, practising my crippled-old-lady walk. The day was cloudy again, promising rain later, and I hurried as well as I could across the bridge. It took some time to get Jack's special mixture blended and I grew increasingly impatient, for now that I was actually in the town my fear returned and every time someone entered the shop I was afraid it might be Oliver; at last all was ready, I paid, stepped out of the shop blinking in the sudden midday sun, peered anxiously to left and right, then scuttled for the encampment as fast as I could, glancing back over my shoulder now and again. I walked the last few yards to the lane that led home backwards, so on tenterhooks was I, and so backed into the strongman, slip-bang! and bounced off his stomach with a grunt.

'Looking for someone?' he inquired, in the rather high, squeaky voice that assorted so ill with his hefty frame.

'No,' I said. 'Not particularly.'

'Missed a bit o' fun quarter-hour or so back,' he said, falling into step beside me as I walked down the lane. 'Constables was 'ere.'

'Constables?'

'Aye. Lookin' for some heiress that's been spirited away from 'er guardian and is lyin' bound and gagged somewheres hereabouts –'

'*What* did you say?' I was all attention now, and suddenly the bright sun had lost its warmth.

'Just as I said. Came trampin' around the tents and booths they did, demandin' a beautiful lady as was locked up. 'Course there was none, but then they started looking in the vans and had only got halfway round when they came to Madame Zelda's van with the little dogs and opened that up, without she was there. Out hopped the little buggers and, they thinking it was a performance, started tumblin' and screechin' and barkin' fit to bust, dancin' round they men o' the law like they was payin' customers. The Madame 'erself comes runnin' up and shakes her fist in they faces and says – wait for it, you'll laugh as never so – she says: "I'll have the law on you!" she says, and we fair to split our sides . . . .' He hesitated and glanced down, probably thinking me incredibly thick. 'That was the joke, see? They *was* the law!'

'Yes, yes,' I said impatiently. 'Was there – was there a young man with them: plumpish, with spots?'

He rubbed his chin. 'Not that I did see: but I was laughing so much . . . . Still they'll be back, I daresay, 'cos they looked awful mad!'

I waited for no more: gathering my skirts up in one hand, basket swaying precariously in the other, I made for Jack's van once more, to be met this time by Annie with the inevitable finger to her lips.

'Hush now, Zoe: we just got him to sleep. Had a restless morning he has, and Tom's gone off for more of that lordy-mum. Says he's not to be disturbed, like, 'cos he tried to get up when them constables came round and made a spectacle of himself with his nightshirt a-flapping round his shanks like a scarecrow in a sheet, and where he got that sword –! *Now* where you off to?'

For I had thrust the basket into her hands and fled. No Tom, Jack out of action, Signor Grappelli a waste of time, Annie apt to get too flustered: I would have to do my all my own thinking and planning, and that quickly. Ten to one Oliver and his lawmen would be back, and I must not be found anywhere near for fear of compromising us all. Safest thing to do was hide, but where? I could run to the fields for the night, but I should have to rejoin the others sooner or later, and would they not wait, and therefore make our departure more noticeable? They might even ask the constables to search for me . . . . No, it would have to be farther away, much farther. Struck by a sudden brilliant idea I dashed to my wagon and wrapped my second-best shawl into a parcel round my boy's clothes, herb book, and smallclothes. Tipping what was left of my savings into my purse, I searched for an advertising bill and considered for a moment, quill in mouth, then wrote quickly, ink spluttering.

'Can't risk constables: explain later; see you at THE Fair. Look after Toby.' I hesitated: to sign my real name might be too compromising. 'Love, Sprat.'

Now no stranger would connect us. I whistled for Toby, who was fruitlessly snapping at a pair of dancing white butterflies, and tucked the note in his collar. Kissing his nose, I led him over to Tom's wagonette and fastened him to a wheel with a length of twine: I still couldn't trust his 'Stay!' if I went any distance.

There was a commotion over in the lane: I guessed the constables were back with reinforcements, but could not stay for confirmation. No time for goodbyes either: when Tom returned he would find the note and they would understand I would see them in London. After all, it was only for a week, ten days at the most . . . . Hugging Toby again, in a passion of love for them all, I dodged behind some elm trees, jumped a ditch into a field of mustard, and doubled along the hedge till I reached the roadway into town. Glancing back I could see nothing except the smoke of our fires, but there was plenty of noise and commotion, so I kept going. I knew there would be coaches going from the George, and determined to take the first that offered even if it meant doubling back, but I was lucky. The coachman was already up, the horses clattering impatient hooves on the cobbles as a couple of inebriated young men were being hauled up to the roof.

'Any room inside?' I asked.

'Going Lunnon way?'

I nodded. His sharp eyes took in my breathless condition, the fact that I had not asked the destination, and assessed my need accordingly.

'Room for a small 'un: hop aboard. Should be in around ten if all goes well and the 'Eath's clear.' He was hauling back on the heavy reins as he spoke. 'Lay still, damn you! Slough first stop: guinea right through . . . . Give over, yer brutes! Hurry up then, missy, take it or leave it. Ain't another goin' through till evening.'

I gasped at the extortionate rate, but we both knew I would pay it. I parted with my one gold coin, only then realizing how much I had paid out while Jack had been sick, and squeezed myself in between a fat and heavily perspiring old gentleman and a thin cleric, the latter edging away from me as if I were Lucifer himself and the former moving correspondingly closer. As soon as the coach was on the highway he tried to pinch my thigh, but I was too miserable to care, for now every mile we travelled took me further from those I loved.

We passed through sleepy villages and busy towns, horn blaring; we kicked up mud from the byways and stones from the highway; chickens scattered from under our wheels, dogs barked, children ran alongside to jeer or cheer. We stopped three times as I recall: twice to change horses, once for the passengers to relieve themselves as the coach rumbled slowly up the steep last hill before the valley in which lay London. I saw the sun decline slowly and then shoot down the sky in a fury of sunset; saw starlings flock home to roost in the card-cutout trees; heard the rattle of harness and jingle of bits as a troop of horsemen rode by, their uniforms dimmed by wear and twilight; held in my nostrils the acrid tang of burning stubble that for a while overrode the musty smell of the coach itself and its passengers.

My eyes were dry, but inside I felt as if each mile were taking a little of my stomach with it, leaving me starving of homesickness for the vans, the road, the company: Annie, Tom and Daisy, Baltasar, my darling Toby, and Jack.

And Jack. And Jack . . . .

BOOK THREE
Gemini

17

For the second time in eighteen months I was cold, penniless and starving, but this time there was no robin, no crumbs, only the sleepy, protesting chatter of disturbed sparrows in the eaves above the doorway where I crouched, shivering and alone. Once more my situation was entirely of my own making through lack of planning; rather, perhaps, my reckless impulsiveness had landed me again in destitution, with the very real threat of extinction only a day or two away . . . .

Of course, looking back, it had been foolish to run away from the threat of Oliver; at best I could have left a proper explanation with Jack and gone forward to the village of Slough until they caught up with me; at worst I could have faced it out, relying on Jack's ingenuity; I could have hidden in one of the vans that had already been searched . . . . Looking back, the possibilities were endless, but it is easy to be wise after the event. I think I had realized even as I climbed into the coach that I was being foolish, and I believe on that long journey I should even have welcomed a high-toby man on windy Hampstead Heath, because I should have been given pause enough to think: to stop, to consider the position and perhaps even then turn back. As it was, sleepy and confused, I had alighted at the King's Arms on the outskirts of London, where the coach had let off most of its passengers, instead of sticking to my seat and going through to the final destination nearer my goal of St Bartholomew's. This had meant a bed for the night and a further depletion of my resources: I had had a moment of real horror when I opened my purse and found how little I had to exist upon. During the time Jack had been ill I had been using my own money for food and medicines, and I remembered too late that Annie still had the major part of my savings in the greater safety of her van, as usual. Now I was down to a bare subsistence level, and to save money I should have to sleep and eat very cheap and walk the rest of the way.

It had been a long walk. I had descended initially at quite a large hamlet called Hammersmith and by dint of asking, found I had two ways to my destination down south by the river: to follow its bends southeast and northeast, or to keep to the road east and find the river later. I chose the latter course as I was assured it was quicker: probably it was if one knew the way in the first place, but I soon became hopelessly lost as I came to the maze of streets that was London proper. I followed the Oxford Street and thought I was heading in the right direction until I came to fields again; I had turned left when I should have kept straight on. That night I spent in a convenient stable near a Foundling Hospital, breakfasted off a penny loaf and a gill of milk, and resumed my journey. Again I strayed, for the second afternoon found me part of a throng of gaping sightseers outside the ill-famed Bedlam, notorious madhouse. Fine ladies and gentlemen were paying well just to visit the inmates, to quiz and gloat, while the poorer townsfolk outside were either throwing refuse at the supplicating hands stretched through the bars or thrusting scraps of food into gaping mouths. It was both a pitiful and a sickening sight: pitiful for the afflicted inmates and those whose compassion and help was merely one herring in a day's catch: sickening in the unhealthy curiosity and stupidity that shone from the silver and the avid eyes of the majority who came to view only, and go home congratulating themselves on their sanity.

Back again I went through narrow streets till I found Cheapside, and expensive lodgings. That night I counted the pence remaining to me and, going to bed a young woman, left by the back door next morning once more a lad. I reckoned that my dress with its pretty ribbons, my shawl, petticoat and shoes should fetch enough to see me through the next couple of days, and I was lucky. The old Jew in the second-hand clothes shop chaffered and grumbled but in the end offered a reasonable price, and I ran off down the road richer by two shillings and twopence and poorer in my old tight-fitting jacket, torn breeches and bare feet. Even then I had not learned my lesson: I spent the morning gawping and dawdling like any country boy at the fine shops, some still defying the ban against hanging signs: glover, provision merchant, milliner, tobacconist, saddler, chemist, topographer, tea merchant, coffee shop, tailor, draper, hatter, baker, chandler, coach-fitter, stationer, outfitter, dressmaker, bootmaker, pastry cook . . . . Inevitably it was the last that appealed most and I left the shop some pennies lighter with a pie scant of filling and a pastry with shavings of apple and sour cream.

Night seemed to come more quickly in those streets of tall houses, and lodgings were more expensive, for it was not safe to sleep in the streets. On the fourth day I tried to pull myself together, and marched on without eating till I became lost again, this time in a narrow tangle of streets near St Martin's full of refuse, rats, hungry ragged children and their raucous parents. Someone threw a stone and I ran, bruising sore feet still further, and suddenly cannoned straight into a burly figure at the end of the lane.

'Curse you for a clumsy gallows-cheater! Can't you see I'm blind? Why do I tap-tap away so with this stick if I –' and then in a completely different tone: 'Now where's a pretty lad like you a-going?' I peered up at him in the gloom. Tricorne hat, bushy beard, eyes hidden behind dark wire-rimmed spectacles that sat snug on a snubbed nose like an overripe Worcester, and a scabbed mouth empty of teeth save the canines. Bit-nailed hands rested on a knotted stick, but even as I noted these things those same fingers were to his lips in a piercing whistle I knew for a signal. I backed away hurriedly as his stick groped towards me, dodged round his detaining arm and ran, pursued now by a sudden horde of ragged children, some not more than six or seven years old. They overtook me with ease and pushed and buffeted past, sending me tripping and stumbling into the gutter, grazing my knee and filling my mouth and nostrils with unmentionable sludge. I picked myself up, only too glad I had not been their quarry, and limped into the comparative brightness of the place I learned later was Covent Garden. The herb book and bits and pieces I had slung round my neck under my shirt for safety had winded me a little as I fell, and I was glad enough to crawl into the shelter of a water butt at the side of an inn and take time to recover from my fright.

Here was fresh air, a broad thoroughfare, fine buildings, a church, a theatre, and comfortably-off citizens taking the air. This was one of the anomalies of London: step but a couple of yards and it was a different world: the difference of light and darkness, of goodness and evil, dream and nightmare. On one side were the fine streets, well lighted and well paved and well dressed, and less than a stone's throw away were the stinking hovels, the rookeries, dens and stews of a different world where men, women and children had the pallid complexions, swollen stomachs, poxed skin and twisted bones of generations of privation, disease and neglect. These creatures of the underworld lived – nay, survived – on a diet of poverty, vice, and crime, and I had been lucky, so far, to have survived as an onlooker, but the blind man had given me a nasty fright. Before I had been neither too well nor too poorly dressed to attract attention in either environment and had achieved the anonymity of a shadow: for that blind man I had had substance. If he were indeed blind, how was it he had called me 'a pretty lad'? I shivered, though the patch of sunshine in which I lay was still blessedly warm for the time of year.

I must have dozed a little, I think, for a grumbling, empty stomach woke me to the fact that I was hungry.

Thirsty, too; I dipped into the water butt at my side, taking off the cracked wooden cover, only to find to my disgust that the water was scummy and alive with larvae. Still there was no other nearby and I could not afford ale, nor a dipper of milk from the girl who crossed the square with buckets swinging from a yoke, so I held my nose with one hand and scooped water with the other till I had slaked my thirst. Thankful that I still had a few pence to spend – surely I should reach the site for the fair tomorrow, and by my reckoning Jack and company should be there by the day after – I resisted the temptation to sally forth in search of food for the moment and contented myself by feeding on the sight of the world passing by my refuge.

By my side, so near I could touch them, gregarious sparrows quarrelled over the straw and chaff that blew from the stables further down; starlings and pigeons pecked and waddled in the gutters; a peacock butterfly, far from its nettle-patch inception, gorged on a fresh pile of dung. A cur cracked a dubious bone in the shadows behind me and a plump black and white tom jumped to the wall above, licking the taste of mouse from his whiskers, to settle, paws under, and enjoy the last of the sun. Carriages, carts, wagons, the odd sedan rattled and creaked past me, the clatter of hooves magnified by the high, enclosing buildings. An ancient lady, her hair still dressed high and powdered in the fashion of years back, tottered past in pattens, her outmoded panniers swaying, escorted by a grim-faced maid, a footman carrying parcels, and a diminutive blackamoor, his turban gleaming with what looked like a real ruby. Offer me her money, I reflected, and I'd wear powdered hair and panniers . . . . A gentleman in a mulberry coat and dove-coloured breeches strolled by, his nose in a book; a sanctity of nuns scuttled past, eyes lowered to their beads. Here came a handsome youth in shirt and breeches, his quick eyes taking in everything, even me, the sun catching a glint from his gleaming brown hair and the outlandish gold earring in his left ear. Small children screamed like swifts as they chased each other and the fallen leaves through the melee of traffic: a crippled girl limped past, a basket of posies round her neck, to settle on the steps of the theatre and wait for custom. Round the colonnades of that same theatre her night sisters yawned awake, their cheeks too rosy by far for the early evening light, but soon to be softened by the gentler touch of torch and lantern light. Now, their cheap finery showed tawdriness; then, they would be transformed into the fairies and princesses of a different stage. One or two were rehearsing their parts already, mincing steps and swaying hips complimented by heavy bosoms and rolling eyes; I noticed the youth with the earring come by again and stop for a word with a couple of them. Perhaps he – but no, no one as young and handsome as that, even allowing for his casual dress and unfashionably curly hair, would lack for less expensive fare. He walked with the swagger of a dancer, I noticed, and seemed to know plenty of the regulars, for he called a boy by name even as he cuffed him lightly for tearing at one of the posters advertising the play, then stopped for a word with a respectable groom exercising a gleaming chestnut stallion.

I dozed again, and when I awoke a man and woman occupied the bench some yards away from where I lay. She was large and somewhat pitted with pox scars, dressed respectably enough in black with a lace shawl of the same colour over her carefully arranged hair: he seemed a parsonical sort of fellow, some years her junior, with a pasty moon-face and thin legs. From where I reclined it was not difficult to hear their conversation, though they were unaware of me.

'What time, Noggs?' From her.

'Near enough six-thirty.' He coughed, and spat.

'Shouldn't be long, then.'

' 'Tis often late . . . .'

'Then we'll just have to be patient. Once a week for a nice little plump chicken ain't too bad, is it?'

'We had trouble enough with the last one!'

'Because you would insist on . . . never mind. Leave it

to me, leave it to me: I know a good accommodating little bird when I see one.'

My attention wandered; the sun was disappearing behind the tallest chimneys, sending down a last strike of fire to burn gold the windows of the inn; a smell of pork reminded me I was hungry. Still, I could wait for ten minutes, half an hour longer . . . . Ten minutes. I felt thirsty again and drank of the water butt, aware that if my stomach were full of liquid, I should need less food. Perhaps a quartern loaf, some cheese or a twopenny pie, a slice or two of the roast pork whose aroma was tickling my nostrils – A stage-wagon creaked and clattered to a halt at the side of the inn and the man and woman on the bench eyed each other and straightened up. The driver, in battered tricorne, dusty cloth coat and leathern leggings, climbed wearily down and unfastened the ties at the back of the wagon. Down clambered a couple of young men in caps carrying satchels and an elderly man and his wife and their parcels: that took care of one of the benches along the inside. Perhaps the fowls the two were expecting were on the other side but instead of the crate I expected there descended a young woman with two young children, who hurried off across the square, and lastly two country lassies, from their dress. The elder had a thin face and sly expression; the younger kept her eyes to the ground, and even to my inexperienced eyes she was well gone in pregnancy. The couple on the bench eyed each other: the man shook his head doubtfully but the woman shot him such a glance of venom from her black eyes that her rather ordinary face became an instantaneous mask of Medusa and even I, unheeded in my corner, instinctively recoiled. A moment later I thought I must have been mistaken, for the face now merely held an expression of pious disappointment and I'll swear there were tears in her eyes as she tottered to her feet and approached the coach driver, a hesitant hand on his sleeve.

'My – my niece? My dear Nancy . . . . You have not brought her?'

The driver looked as though this were a well-rehearsed answer. 'No, my good woman, there was no Nancy on this trip. It was from *Witham*' (he emphasized the name) 'way as you were expecting her? Now, these two young ladies come from thereabouts, so if you was to ask them . . . .'

'Oh, my dear niece, what can have become of her?' She bent forwards to the country girls, who clung together, their eyes wide both with being in London and with being singled out for attention. 'My dear young ladies – you have travelled from Essex: from Witham?'

The sly one nodded. 'Nearabouts.'

'And you did not see a young lady waiting for the coach? About your own age, but not perhaps quite as – pretty?'

The girl blushed. 'Not as I remember . . . .'

'Then it will be the next coach she will be taking; Cousin Susan must be still poorly . . . . What a disappointment! And here's me with a great double bed a-waiting and hot bricks for her feet; and in the oven one of her favourite beefsteak pies and the kettle on the hob singing away like a canary bird all ready to welcome her . . . . When I think of that pie, gravy dripping on the plate and the oysters a-squeezing themselves out of the crust! And there's the bottle of port I opened: it'll not keep, once uncorked . . . .'

The sly one licked her lips and nudged her companion. 'Your Nancy may be on the next coach, but that's not till Thursday, and I reckon as how that pie won't keep till then . . . .'

'Nor it will, nor it will! And the bed so comfortable . . . .' She paused, as if struck by a sudden idea, turning to the man she had called Noggs earlier. 'What say you, brother dear, would it not be a kindness? My dear brother is in holy orders,' she confided to the girls. 'A celibate, and much respected; I heed his opinion, left as I am a poor widow woman with none to guide me . . . .'

She nudged her 'brother' sharply. 'Well, Mr Noggs?'

He shook his head doubtfully, but she had her own interpretation. 'Just as I thought: he is of the opinion that the pie won't keep, neither. I hesitate to offer you two young ladies my humble hospitality, as I can see you've been used to better things, but if it should be that you've no one meeting you and have not yet bespoke lodgings for the night, I should be glad with some help with that pie and a little of the port . . . . And if you're thinking that I'm the sort to charge for a night's lodgings, well you're mistaken, for I wouldn't take a penny piece, not if you were to press me ever so! Why, it would be you as was doing me the favour, for you could tell me such things of the countryside around Witham that I could almost believe I was there with my dear Nancy . . . .' And all the while she was drawing them away, her arm linked with the elder girl, who still held in turn to her companion. Mr Noggs lingered behind to speak to the coachman; I heard the chink of coin.

The coachman spat. 'I were promised two guineas each!'

'For whole goods: the younger's well gone and we had trouble enough with the last one like her; had to change our lodgings after her young man came looking. No, you'll be paid for the other and be thankful!'

The coachman hawked and spat again. 'As you say, Reverend . . . .' He watched the man's retreating back and made an obscene gesture. '*That* for your poncing, you old turd!'

Even if I had realized earlier what their game was I could have done nothing. No one would have believed a shabby and starving boy and I should have probably have ended up beaten or worse; as it was I watched those two led off into probable prostitution and was only too glad it was not me.

The coachman threw down an armful of hay for his horses and made off into the inn, spinning a coin. I decided to follow his example though, strangely, my appetite seemed to have lessened; a penny loaf and a couple of slices of meat should see me through. I felt in my purse for the pitifully few coins I had left then, disbelieving, felt again. Feverishly I pulled it from its fastening on my belt and opened it, pushing my fingers up as far as they would go till they waggled through the torn stitching. Not torn, cut. Cut very neatly with a sharp knife along the seam. Frantically I cast my mind back: those boys in the narrow street brushing past me, knocking me over – that must have been when it was done. But it didn't really matter when; what did matter was that now there was nothing, no money, naught left to pawn. There was my herb book, but who would give me a shilling for that? It was probably valuable only to me, and I thought it were better to starve than part with it, anyway. It was my last link with the others . . . . My heart began to thump uncomfortably, my head ached, and I felt hot and sticky. There was another twenty-four or forty-eight hours till the fair opened – I had lost count of days – and I was still nowhere near enough to the site. I began to doubt whether my strength would last the extra miles, and was afraid now to chance asking the way, lest I be taken up as a vagrant. I had been hot before, but now I was so cold.

Dusk had fallen and a dry and unsympathetic wind blew chaff and grit in my eyes; I shivered, and decided to look for a more comfortable hiding place: by morning I must surely feel better. The torches and lanterns were lit up by the theatre and I could see well-dressed men and women going up the wide steps from their carriages and chairs. The crippled girl with her bunches of flowers was rid of half her basket already; I could see her lips move, crying her wares, but her thin voice was lost in the clatter of hooves and scrunch of wheels. Nearby a chestnut seller was roasting his wares and I crept nearer his brazier for a warm, only to be kicked aside with a hoarse: 'Piss off, you varmint! You'll keep the customers away with your Bedlam looks . . . .' and I had crept away to find the doorstep where I was now crouched, hearing the church bells strike the slow hours while the streets quietened and even the prostitutes sought their beds. Wrapping my arms round my shaking body I dozed off, only to wake with a start as some drunken reveller stumbled past, swearing to the sky and cursing his mistress. Somewhere someone moaned on and on, a baby woke and squalled, a dog barked, rats scuffled in the heaps of refuse, cats yowled, and as the false dawn smeared the sky and a sleepy cockerel crowed on a cracked note, I rose wearily to my feet and set off towards the dawn. If only I could keep going, that was the way to St Bartholomew's, and surely Jack must be there today . . . .

The beginning was easy, for the streets were only just coming alive and I could stumble a little way unhampered and then rest awhile without hindrance. I was definitely weaker; my head ached, I was deathly cold and my empty stomach kept twisting itself into knots. I helped myself to another drink from a rain tub and found a mouldy piece of cheese rind on a pile of refuse, but though my teeth chewed mechanically my throat refused to swallow, and I had to spit it out. Once I thought I caught a glimpse of the comforting square tower of St Bartholomew's itself, but I had to slip aside into a side street for the traffic was getting heavier as the day lengthened, and twice I had narrowly missed going under the wheels of a wagon. Passers-by jostled me aside, and one young swell deliberately thrust his cane between my legs and laughed to see me tumble. After that I crept into a niche behind some steps leading to a stable loft and dozed uneasily: now I seemed to see Annie's warm smile and perspiring red cheeks swimming in front of my eyes, and her North Country voice saying: 'Ay-oop, lass! You want a nice drop of Annie's soup and then bed wi' a brick at your feet . . . .' Toby's bark and warm smile . . . . Jack's erratic piping . . . . The soft nuzzling of Daisy, and Tom's voice: 'Lie easy, girl, and get some rest . . . .'

I woke with a start as something stung my cheek and gazing round wildly, temporarily disoriented, saw a mischief of small boys, one stooping to pick up another stone.

'S'not a deader . . . 'tis live.' I heard one say, and there was disappointment in his tone, even as another stone hit the wall behind my head.

In a panic I scrambled to my feet and ran, knowing only that I must escape and that in the direction of the now reddening sun, for like one possessed I still had it in my mind that St Bartholomew's lay in the direction of the rising sun and I had forgotten in my fever that it was now evening. I could hear, or fancied I heard, footsteps behind me as I ran, and fear lent me some reserve of strength for I seemed to run for ever, faster and faster, across thoroughfares, down streets, through alleyways, under washing that spanned narrow byways, over piles of rotting refuse; shouted at by pedestrians, cursed at by drivers, snapped and barked at by dogs, clattered by the wings of pigeons, half-drowned by a pail of slops flung by some servant; struck by obstacles I did not see; deafened by the clamour of bells that struck jangled hundreds; bruised by cobbles; and driven all the while by an inexorable whip of fear that beat about my shoulders, curled about my thin ribs, stung my ears, and gave to me the numbness of unreason.

Suddenly I could go no further: a blank, high wall smashed into my shoulder and scraped my outthrust hands. I think I tried to run up it like a trapped rat, for I found myself on my back in the cul-de-sac, my head ringing, my knees scraped. There was a thundering in my ears, and still I could hear the beat of following feet. Frantically dragging myself upright I hobbled to the nearest door and beat upon it with bruised hands: no answer. The gloom was deepening, but I saw a double door that surely would lead to stables or a yard, and twisted at the iron rings that held them fast, but they would not yield. Beside hung a bell on a rope and I pulled on it with all my strength and kicked on the lower panels of the gates with my bare feet, unaware of pain. Surely someone must hear, would give me sanctuary from the nameless thing that ran at my back? I heard with awful distinctness the sound of footsteps right behind me and a voice: 'Here, boy!' and then suddenly the doors were open and I fell to my hands and knees on the cobbles of a yard.

Around me I felt, rather than saw, shadowy small figures; suddenly I remembered the terrible dwarves but even as I shrank back rough little hands hauled me to my feet and I was thrust forward to where a burly figure stood holding a lantern.

'Well, what 'ave we 'ere then? Aha! 'tis the uncouth boy what almost knocked me flying t'other day . . . . Remember, my brave boys? Gave 'im a chase for old Bob, didn't you? His voice was a whine. 'Cruel 'ard and thoughtless, runnin' into a blind man, that was . . . .' His voice changed again: now it was sharp, peremptory: 'Come 'ere, lad, let's see what you got a-tucked up that there shirt of yourn!'

Shrinking back from the half-menacing, half-wheedling voice, I recognized the man I had collided with the day my purse had been slit and turned to fly, not stopping to wonder how a blind man could see I had a package strapped to my chest, but a hundred clawing hands reached out, and I saw I was surrounded by boys: ragged, dirty, with avaricious eyes. The lantern was thrust in my face and the 'blind' man ripped my shirt down, then reached again to tear aside the bindings across my chest. There was a sudden silence and I was released, to stand swaying with fatigue and fever, the chill air hardening my exposed nipples.

The pause was only momentary for my captor moved forward again and I saw the yellow tongue flicker like a snake in the black beard.

'What 'ave we 'ere, then?'

'Not one of yours, you old devil: one of mine, I think!' The voice was light, gay, amused.

I turned, and the young man I had seen yesterday stood in the gateway, arms akimbo, his earring glinting in the lantern light. I tried to say something but instead was horribly sick. The world spun round like a whirlpool, but before I was sucked down into the vortex a pair of strong arms closed about me and I was lifted till my eyes were level with the golden earring.

371

'Well met, lass! You're safe now. Better young Nick than old Beelzebub, eh?' were the last words I heard before I spun into unconsciousness.

18

'Not a virgin . . . clean . . . reacts quickly . . . .' I was conscious in my dreams of odd words, phrases, of inquisitive handling, but soon persuaded myself that these were indeed only fevered imagination. 'Keep her under . . . easier later.' Another puzzling thought, but again, quickly forgotten. Not as easily dismissed the sickness, the purging, the ache in my limbs, the headaches; one half-conscious part of me knew I was very ill, the other half that I was dosed, warm, bathed and changed and, most of all, safe. This did not stop the nightmares – back came the drowned dwarves, the blind man with his stick, and even the childhood terrors of window-tapping trees and shrouded furniture – but increasingly I was aware of a calming constant, a face that swam in and out of my fever but became steady and still as my illness diminished. It was a face I seemed to remember from a carving in some cathedral church, an angel then complete with halo and half-folded wings, and it was easy to associate the name 'Angel' that somehow accompanied it. The face was such as one would find in a medieval painting, the ones before they got the perspective right; oval, pale, and pure, with downcast eyes, straight nose, high forehead, and a small, bloodless mouth. No passion there, only selflessness and compassion: sexless, but compelling. And yet, even as the image registered itself my inner mind knew that this was not all: the face held not the calm of innocence but rather the containment of experience; the eyes were downcast, not from humility, but rather from a need to hide their fierce longing. When I recovered I believed that this impression had been merely another manifestation of dream: for once I should have trusted that first intuition.

I remember beginning to feel well again. I had been dreaming, quietly this time, of sunlight and children playing in a field of flowers. Opening my eyes, I felt warm and refreshed and the light no longer hurt. I was puzzled, for the room that revealed itself to my wondering eyes was totally unfamiliar. During my sickness I had been aware only of darkness and light, heat and cold, and that calm face, but now I was conscious I realized I had been ill, knew I was feeling immensely better, and was curious as to where I had spent my time. Without moving my head I could see a bar of sunlight that fell across the foot of my white-counterpaned four-poster; the windows, directly opposite, were draped with half-drawn muslin; beyond I could see chimneypots, a jumble of roofs and the smallest patch of blue sky. The blue was echoed by the sprigs of forget-me-not that patterned the wallpaper; there was a washstand and a tall press to my right; to my left a chest, a fireplace and a heavy oaken door. I turned my head: a red-faced woman in a huge mobcap and white apron dozed in a high-backed chair, her lap full of coarse mending. As I watched her head nodded forwards, startling her awake.

'Hello,' I said. 'Could you tell me where I am, please?'

With a queer snorting noise she threw cotton, linens and scissors into the air and bolted out of the room; her demeanour somewhat alarmed me, but a moment or two later the lady with the angel face glided into the room and laid a cool hand on my forehead.

'Don't worry about Nancy, my dear: she is dumb, but a good enough creature. Are you feeling better?' From anyone else a 'my dear' would have been an expression of warmth, but not from this one. Her eyes were a clear, pale grey, outlined with a deeper colour that matched her dark grey dress with its white collar and cuffs. She was all puritan, and her voice as cool as her eyes and her hand. She repeated her question. 'Feeling better?'

'Thank you, ma'am. May I ask –'

She interrupted me. 'Not ma'am: pray call me by my Christian name, for I feel sure we are to be friends. I was named Angelina, but you may call me Angel, for that is how most of my acquaintances address me.'

'I thought – that is, I dreamed – but perhaps it was no dream? Did you not bend over me while I was ill, and did I not address you as Angel in my dreams?'

'I do not recall: you did say much that was wild and disjointed in your delirium, but I do not think you told us your name?' She waited.

Who was 'us', I wondered: her and the dumb Nancy? But there had been other voices, I was certain of it, and surely there had been a bonny lad with a gold earring? Memory of my rescue came flooding back, and I eluded her question, wanting to be surer of my ground before I committed myself. I asked a question of my own, feigning lack of memory.

'Who brought me here?'

She frowned. 'You were – found – in an alley. Some young thieves were trying to rob you, remember?' Long lashes swept down to cover her eyes. 'Shall you try and sit up for a while? Here, Nancy,' and she gestured to the dumb maid, who came forward and propped me up with work-reddened, capable hands.

I tried again. 'Is the man with the golden earring a friend of yours?'

She did not answer, but instead rose with a gesture of irritation and crossed to the window to close the muslin curtains. 'The sun is too strong: you are not well enough yet.' She turned, and came back to the bed. 'And now, seeing that we have cared for you as best we could, perhaps you could tell us a little about yourself: your name, where you came from to be dressed in so out-of-the way a fashion?'

It was a more than reasonable request, under the circumstances, and she had every right to make it: yet she had not answered even one of my questions. Some vague feeling of disquiet told me that it would be wiser, till I found out a little more of my hostess, to tell her as much as would satisfy her curiosity and no more. To gain time to think I feigned a sudden faintness and in a moment had them fetching burned feathers and a bowl of broth. The latter was most welcome, for my stomach was concave and I could feel all my ribs, and while they waved the former under my nose I decided on my story.

I took the first delicious mouthful of broth. 'My name is Gemini, after my birthsign . . . .'

So I was a fortune-teller (that explained away the herbs and Katina's book which I was thankful to see on the chest) who had joined a troupe of fair-folk after the death of my parents. The troupe had been led by a Mr Landless (I was sure that was not Jack's real name) and I had been nicknamed Sprat because I was small and skinny. The rest of the troupe had been laid low with sickness and I had travelled ahead, dressed as a boy for safety, to reserve them a good pitch for St Bartholomew's but had been robbed and then fallen ill.

'. . . and I was on my way to the fairground,' I concluded, 'when your – friend – with the earring found me.' She had not mentioned the blind man, so neither did I. 'And now, if you don't mind, I must get dressed and make my way to the fair as soon as possible or they will worry about me. There are certain performances for which I am needed, and I should not like to let them down.' I smiled, in what I hoped was a confident manner. 'Mr Landless will want to reimburse you for your care and attention during my illness.' And he still owed me for the food and medicines I had bought while he was ill, I remembered.

'St Bartholomew's Fair?' questioned Angel, glancing at Nancy, who shrugged her shoulders. 'Why, my dear, that was over and done with a week past! More than a week . . . . How long do you think you've been lying there? Near eleven days.'

The world cracked into fragments about my ears, but still I tried to catch hold of the pieces. 'It can't be! You must be wrong: it can't have been that long! They will wait for me . . . .'

'Well, they haven't. I was that way yesterday, matching some silks, and the place was deserted except for the usual rubbish and some torn posters. They've gone, I tell you, and,' she pushed me back against the pillows, 'you are certainly not well enough to get up and go looking for them.' She frowned, for tears of weakness and disappointment were coursing down my cheeks. 'Don't be stupid: you will ruin your eyes . . . . If you wish, I can send – someone – to ask specifically after these people of yours: what did you say your manager was called?'

When they had both left me to 'sleep and preserve your strength' as Angel put it, I crawled out of bed and over to the window, but it took me all of my time to stand upright and gaze out over the rooftops, hanging on to the sill for support. She was quite right: I was still far too weak to think of going out there to look for Jack. But what must he think of me? I had promised to meet them at the fair, in the note I had left tucked in Toby's collar, and I had let them down. Perhaps they even thought me dead, lying in some ditch with my throat cut . . . . Tears of self-pity welled up, and the rooftops blurred and shimmered. Where had they gone? How could I ever find them again? They could be anywhere in the country where there was a market or fair or holiday, and I had no money to go searching, even if I were well. And no clothes either, as I found when I managed to look in the clothes-press: just another nightgown, a wrapper, and a pair of rather down-at-heel slippers. 'They' had probably burned my boy's clothes. Miserably I climbed back into bed and cried myself to sleep.

More dreams. Now I was running up a hill, flying a kite, and Toby was bounding up and down just ahead, turning now and again with a breathy bark and happy lolling tongue, encouraging me to run faster . . . . The dream changed, and Jack was exhorting me to try harder with my lines on one of those days when the words were like a ravelled skein of wool that would not knit straight. 'You're giving up too soon: use your brain! You have got one, I suspect, though it seems asleep at the moment. *Think* what your character is trying to say: come on, now. Quitters don't get to play the lead!'

I started awake. Someone was coming up the stairs with a blithe tread, gaily whistling a snatch of 'Lillibullero'. For one idiotic, heart-stopping moment I thought it was Jack, that they had found him, then the door was unlatched and the lad with the gold earring poked his head round.

'Can I come in?' Not waiting for an answer he stepped across to the bed, and one finger touched my cheek. 'You're better, but you've been crying . . . . We thought at one stage we'd lost you, you know.'

'We?'

'Angel and I.'

'Is . . . is she your sister?'

'Not exactly, but I suppose you could call her an honorary one. We are spiritual twins maybe, but not blood kin. She brought me up from the time I was just a snotty-nosed little kid, and she scarce older.' He grinned, an infectious, healthy grin. 'She was old enough to tan me though, if I got out of line! I think she still would if . . . . But I was forgetting. She sent me out to see if I could find any trace of that troupe of yours.'

I sat up expectantly. 'And?'

'Well, I asked at the inns, for all the travellers had gone, and from one surly fellow I learnt that a Mr Landless's troupe had used his yard for the fair. Fat lady, puppeteer, white pony, with a bit of reciting and magic thrown in. Stayed a day later than the others, they did, and were asking after a boy or girl called Sprat. Even advertised for you.' He pulled a tattered bill from his pocket. 'Had a couple of those stuck up on the wall.'

My eyes blurred with tears as I recognized the spiky handwriting.

Five guineas reward for information leading to the safe return

377

of one female aged seventeen years. Low stature, slim build, mouse-colour hair, odd-eyed. May be dressed as a boy. Apply to Mr Landless, care of Fair Prospect Inn.

'Did anyone come forward?'

'I doubt it, otherwise they would have stayed longer and searched farther.' He paused. 'Still, you can write to them, tell them where you are?'

'They could be anywhere, anywhere at all! I wouldn't know where to direct my letter. Christmastime they will be in winter quarters, and then I could write to Annie – the fat lady – for I know where she will be.'

Was it my imagination, or did his eyes hold a sudden satisfaction?

'There it is, then: you will have to rest, get well, and by Christmas –'

'I shall go up north to Annie.'

'You must be fully recovered first.'

'I feel nearly well again already, thanks to your – to Angel's care.' I paused, not sure whether to continue, but he seemed so friendly and relaxed, and the propriety of his visiting my bedchamber unchaperoned never entered my head, so I threw my earlier caution to the winds and asked just those same questions Angel had seemed so reluctant to answer. 'Where am I, sir? What sort of establishment is this? Why have you been so kind to me? And how can I ever repay you?'

He laughed, and leant to raise my chin in his fingers. 'Questions, questions, pretty girl! Answers: London; private; common charity; and no need.' And before I could protest that these were answers yet no answers, he went on: 'Gemini, isn't it? Truly named, for your eyes, mismatched though they be, are like twin gems: a peridot and an amber . . . .' His voice was husky, with an undertone, not unpleasant, of what I had come to recognize as a London street accent: a tendency to pronounce 'th' as 'f', and sometimes the loss of a final consonant, especially 'g': 'I shall call you Gem, and you may call me Nick. My full name –' and he bowed exaggeratedly '– is Nicholas Ivanovitch Kelly: the first two are for my father, who my mother, God rest her! swore was a titled Rooshian nobleman; ordinary seaman, more like, who went back to Moskie or St Petersburg with a sigh of relief, leaving a Slav bun in Irish Kelly's oven . . . . I was declared an orphan at three years old when Ma succumbed to pewmonia through being on the streets . . . .'

'Your mother was a –'

'Whore, darlin', a whore, and a poor one at that, else she'd never have had me nor needed to walk the streets, neither.'

I wasn't quite sure how to take this young man, this remarkably good-looking young man with his white teeth and curly brown hair with the golden gleam to match his earring. His eyes were as grey as house-mouse fur: not clear and still like Angel's but more the surface of a pond, glinting with sun and ruffled by wind.

'Didn't – didn't you *mind*?' I blurted out.

'Mind? Why should I? I was off the streets and in the warm, with Angel to knock some sense into me and Madame Bonneville to sponsor me.'

'Madame Bonneville?'

'Yes; next door. Runs a gaming house, and for the young and uninitiated a –'

'School,' supplied the cool voice of Angel from the doorway. 'Come, Nick: you mustn't tire Gemini, and talk of this kind can wait.' She glided over to the bed and placed her cold hand on my brow. 'Just as I thought: the poor child is well on the way to getting another fever. Drink this.' She held a glass to my lips. 'And get a good night's sleep. Nancy or I shall be around if you need us.'

So I slipped easily into another drugged sleep, without my questions answered.

One day merged into another; the shadows outside grew longer and soon we needed candles lit inside through most of the day. I was allowed up, still in my wrapper, to sit in the tiny parlour one floor down by a fire of sea coal and help Angel with mending and sewing during the day, or read one of the surprisingly light novels that filled her bookshelves, while she puzzled efficiently over columns of figures at her desk in the corner. My room was under the eaves at the front and I understood that Nick's room was behind mine; down the narrow stairs was this parlour and Angel's room, and on the ground floor was the kitchen where Nancy prepared our meals, a hall and a locked front door. Beside it was another door, locked also, that seemed to lead next door; I wondered about this, for sometimes at night when I could not sleep I fancied I could hear music and laughter and feminine shrieks – but perhaps the latter were only cats on the roof.

I wondered, too, where all Angel's mending came from, for none was delivered as far as I could see, but there was always plenty to occupy us both; good-quality stuff it was too, perhaps a little garish and overtrimmed for my taste, but expensive. Her clients must have been very careless, for their garments suffered more from tears than wear, and often looked and smelled as though a whole bottle of perfume had been used in one go: still, my sewing was good enough for hems, seams, and rips and I was reasonably content, especially as every day brought nearer the time when I could write to Annie and escape back to the life I knew. Angel gave me a couple of lengths of serviceable cloth to make dresses for myself, and with a little help they turned out quite creditably, although petticoats and drawers were easier, mistakes being hid. I saw little of Nick during this time, for he seemed to spend much of his time out, both rising and returning late, the latter sometimes through the door in the wall. I asked Angel about this: she primmed up her mouth, then explained that it led directly to Madame Bonneville's establishment next door, and that as she and Nick were both employed by Madame, it was a convenience. Emboldened by the fact that, for once, I had had a direct answer, I asked if perhaps the good lady could find me something to occupy myself for the next few weeks.

'For I do not want to be a burden to you for longer than I can help, and that way perhaps I can earn a little towards my keep. You mentioned a school, I think: my father kept the village school, and I have a smattering of most subjects. Perhaps the younger children . . . .'

Nick happened to be with us the night I asked this and I was answered by his peal of laughter. 'There's nothing in that line, darlin' –'

'That they have not got good tutors for already,' interrupted Angel swiftly, frowning. She tapped Nick's bent head with her thimble as he leant over the back of her chair. ' 'Tis a pity *you* did not profit more from your schooling. Still,' and she pondered for a moment, her industrious needle for once still, 'there *might* be a way you could help, Gemini: these children speak roughly, for they are mostly – charity children, rescued from the streets –'

'And perhaps I could help with their elocution?' I supplied eagerly. 'Indeed I should welcome the chance to try, for I myself improved immeasurably when Ja – when Mr Landless taught me to speak from a stage. Indeed, I believe that is one of the best ways to teach people to speak properly. Perhaps I could write them a little play, based on a faery tale or a classical myth . . . .'

For once Angel looked animated. 'I believe you have the germ of an idea there,' she said slowly. 'I shall speak to Madame.'

She was as good as her word. Two days later the door in the wall was unlocked and I was received by Madame Bonneville in her dark and stuffy boudoir on the first floor. Although it was daylight outside the curtains were drawn tight; a small fire spat and cracked in the grate and there was a queer powdery smell in the air. A silent parrot shifted nervously on its perch and small tables set with ornaments were a trap for the unwary in the dim light afforded by the single branch of candles. From a high-backed chair behind a desk a shapeless bundle of black silks rose to greet Angel and myself and extended a mittened hand for me to take.

'See to that dratted fire, Angel, while Miss Gemini and I have a chat . . . .'

For one awful moment as I inclined over her hand I thought she was afflicted with some dread disease for the flesh seemed marked with great black spots, then I realized her mittens, like the stockings I caught a glimpse of above her leather pumps, were patterned with haphazard patches of black velvet from weevil to cockroach size. It was a pity her skin was so white and doughy, like a puffball in a gloomy dell, for the spots stood out twice as alarming.

'Sit you down, my dear, and we'll talk of your offer to help teach the little ones. Angel has told some of what you propose – wonderful girl, that: don't know what I'd do without her. Does all the accounts as regular as clockwork, and *such* a help in other ways –' But there was no liking in the look she cast in Angel's direction, and the latter did not look up from mending the fire, though I fancied I saw a faint smile on her lips.

Madame questioned me closely, sometimes not seeming to wait for the answers. I supposed Angel and Nick had told her already the little they knew of their guest, and she was merely confirming that my story tallied. I was careful to add nothing, and assure her I was eager to help in any way I could with the children's speech. After a while she appeared satisfied and rang a silver bell on the desk to summon a surly-looking maid with sherry wine and sugared cakes.

'It is agreed then, miss, that you will teach my young 'uns to speak proper: I'd do it meself, but for this dratted shortness of breath – Angel, light one of them pastilles – and perhaps you could put on a playlet, something to show off their talents to the best advantage?'

'May I see them?' I said hastily, for the particular cloying sweetness of the pastille Angel had ignited on its dish was making me feel sick. 'The sooner we become acquainted the sooner we may go to work.'

382

'Of course, my dear: Angel, show her up. The children are in a deportment class; a little dancing and how to hold their knife and spoon and not wipe their noses on their sleeves . . . . And for Gawd's sake, Angel,' she added irritably, 'get the girl summat brighter to wear: looks like a funeral in that drab. I distinctly remembers a bolt of yellow silk and some lovely red velvet in the store. Get her used to the idea . . . . Well, get along, do!' and she poked the indignant parrot, who squawked in outrage but still did not speak.

She doesn't give the bird a chance, I thought; Madame, from her speech, had never been what was known as a lady. Still, she surely did not need the trappings of fair speech and good birth if she were both rich and kind enough to run a sort of orphanage for the unfortunates of the streets and also keep Angel and Nick. I dismissed my first instinctive dislike as mere prejudice and the smell of the pastilles, and determined to try and like Madame better, as I trailed Angel up to the next floor.

It was a large room, lit brilliantly by many candles, and with the unwashed smell of stuffy classrooms I remembered so well. Some twenty or so children were trying out steps, bowing, curtseying, walking with books on their heads, or trying to sit or stand gracefully, under the irritated instruction of a pale young man in yellow waistcoat and purple breeches who was vainly trying to keep an eye on everyone at once. While the children were occupied I glanced round the room, noting to my satisfaction that there was a platform at one end which could be used for a stage, with the addition of a few screens. The children could be taught to give recitations, sing and dance for Madame and her friends . . . . There were twenty-two of them I counted, between the ages of five and fourteen at a guess, more girls than boys; they were dressed for the most part in what seemed cut-downs from adult dress, for the girls' bodices were scandalously low. They were all good-looking, and some of the girls decidedly pretty; one or two were thin and pale, but at least two of the girls were decidedly plump and I was pleased to think Madame had fattened up the little starvelings so conscientiously. And if the orphans of the London streets were all so pretty and appealing, it was time more people looked under the dirt and grime and brought these little angels in from their wilderness.

Angels they may have looked, but once they opened their mouths all the filth of the kennels, slums and rookeries poured forth. I heard words, phrases, even whole sentences, that meant nothing to me, even used as I was to the cant of the fair-folk, the obscenities of drunks, the familiar swearwords that some of the uneducated used as constant adjectives and that meant as little as 'Goodness!' in a governess.

I decided at once that to appear shocked was the worst thing I could do, so after the first half-hour with my charges when every attempt to make them repeat polite phrases after me was met with the sly innocence, the deliberate ineptitude, and the daring with which all schoolchildren will try their new teacher, I decided to outdo them all. I had kept my temper, though sorely tried, and now I remembered something my stepfather had once said when he had been struggling uphill against the wind to instil in me the rudiments of Greek: 'If a pupil cannot – or will not – learn, then it is the teacher who should be punished . . . .' Stepping down from the platform where I had been standing, crossing my fingers behind my back, tasting mentally the proverbial soap with which Jack would surely have washed out my mouth had he heard, and blessing both my good memory and my ear for accents, I launched into a five-minute résumé of all the gutter filth I could remember, delivered in as good a London street whine as I could muster. When I finished there was silence for a moment, then they gave me a spontaneous cheer. I waited for silence, then walked up onto the platform again and turned to face them.

'I've just proved to you that I can lower myself to your level – can you raise yourself to mine?' I asked in my normal voice. 'It's easy enough to talk like you: I've just proved that. But I'll bet a silver sixpence that none of you can say: 'Good morning: what a beautiful day. I hope the rain keeps off till tomorrow,' as a lady or gentleman would –'

'Sixpence, Miss?' came a hopeful voice from the back.

'Sixpence,' I repeated firmly, 'and a seat on the platform with me.'

After that, with only a few regressions, and a small bribe or two, they were mine. By mid-November I was pleased enough with their progress to submit a short play in rhymed couplets to Madame Bonneville for her approval and assure her that her protégés would be ready to perform it at Christmas.

By the end of November I, too, had progressed: by the end of November I had become Nick's mistress.

19

I'll swear I had no idea it would happen that way.

I know all women, even with the little experience I had had, on first meeting a man have him mentally measured for a wedding suit or the grave within minutes of the encounter, and in many cases have assessed his probable physical performance to a nicety as well. This was not true of my attitude to Nick. At first I had been too ill and distressed to heed him, and when I was better he had always treated me with the friendliness of a brother and an easy courtesy. I saw him perhaps once or twice a day, usually fairly late in the evening, and never but in the company of Angel as well. True, I was aware of his good looks, his youth and vitality, his undoubted charm, but there had been no impetus to deepen our relationship for I was too busy with the children's lessons and, besides, all I looked for was to return to Jack and the others in the

385

spring. There was probably another, subconscious reason: although Nick often carelessly referred to Angel in her hearing as 'little mother' or 'big sister' I fancied she did not care for these titles, although she never said anything. I noticed, however, that whenever he came into the room her usually pale cheeks gained colour and her manner became more animated; I pitied her a little, for after seeing the easy familiarity with which he had chatted with the whores on the steps of the Covent Garden theatre, that day when, despite my destitution, I had noted the lad with the golden earring, I knew it would take more than her stone-angel prettiness to stir him to anything other than the careless affection he gave her.

My better acquaintance with him was the result of an accident: if this had not happened I doubt whether our relationship would have developed as it did, in spite of what I learned later of Madame Bonneville's intentions . . . .

It was now the last week in November and my mind, never far from my travelling companions, registered the fact that by now they would be nearing the end of their peregrinations and heading for winter quarters. Annie, I knew, was bound to be back in Kirkham for Christmas and I was determined to write to her at once, care of Matthew Clegg, so that she would know I was safe and hoping she would invite me to stay till we rejoined Jack. Accordingly I sought out Angel early one evening to ask her advice about my letter. As I approached the parlour I heard her voice raised in an anger that made it almost unrecognizable.

'You'll have to! It's your job: you know the rules. That's what she hires you for! "Find them and bind them," she says, and this one's no different.'

'She was brought in for that mebbe, but she's doing the other now —'

'For how long? Till she finds out, and then it'll be that more difficult. And if Madame gets wind of your reluctance she'll end like the other, and —'

She broke off as I knocked on the door.

386

'Come in, Gemini. We – we were just have a disagreement over a – a friend. Don't pay any heed.' She must
have known I would have heard some of the argument,
though I was only curious from the point of view that it
had been something over which the normally self-contained
Angel had obviously felt very strongly. 'Nick! Don't
go . . . .' But too late: he brushed past my advancing form
without his usual courtesy and disappeared down the
stairs at a run. Angel was flushed and her delicate nostrils
still flared with repressed anger: her hands, I noticed, were
trembling, but she took a deep breath, shrugged her
shoulders and said lightly, 'He always was so
impulsive . . . . Now, what can I do for you!'

I explained, and her brows drew together in a frown. 'I
thought you said you had no way of contacting these
people?'

'Not while they are on the road, but I know where one
of them will be – the fat lady, Annie – during the time
they are in winter quarters.'

'And you wish me to write a letter for you?'

'Oh, no: that I can do for myself. I wondered if you
could let me have paper and ink, if it's not too much
trouble.'

'Of course: no trouble at all,' and she smiled suddenly,
her secret, sly smile. 'At the desk you'll find paper, ink
and wax. My quills are sharpened and there is a blank
seal.'

Once with ink on the nib, however, I hesitated. I did
not like to ask for more than one sheet and Annie and
Matthew were plain folk and to try and explain all would
only confuse them. Best to keep it short and simple
anyway: the important thing was to let them know I was
safe and well. Dipping my pen in the ink again I scratched
the first few sentences, tongue between my teeth. 'My
dearest Annie: please get Matthew to read this to you. A
short note to let you know that I am all right. I became
ill on my way to the fair and could not meet you as
arranged.' I paused. 'Angel, where is this place? I need

387

some direction for them to reply to. Jack will write –' Too late: his name had slipped out.

She was quick enough. 'Jack? He will be this Mr Landless you spoke of?'

'Yes. Annie will have this read to her, and even if I don't go up to her she will show him the letter in the spring and he will arrange a rendezvous.'

She appeared to consider. 'Does he . . . know London well?'

'I imagine so: he knows his way around it, and at one time lived the life of a gentleman, I'm sure.' I remembered the lawyer at the inn in Shrewsbury and the talk of money and a Lady Something-or-other.

'A youngish man?'

'He would certainly consider himself so, I believe . . . .' And how angry he had been when I had guessed older! I smiled involuntarily.

'Does he – Is he what you would call a man of the world?'

I nodded. 'Oh yes, definitely.' I wondered what on earth all this had to do with a return address.

She moved to stand behind my chair. 'Tell your friends that you may be found at Madame Bonneville's establishment off St Martin's Lane, then.'

I glanced up at her. 'That is sufficient address?'

'I assure you your employer will have no trouble finding you at that address. To any man who knows London Madame's premises are well known. She has spread her – philanthropy – far and wide, and many ladies and gentlemen have good reason to be grateful for her – understanding, shall we say – of the problems which face our society at this time.'

I thought of her charitable work with the children and nodded. 'I haven't really room to tell them of my situation and your kindness . . . .'

'I should just say that you have a position that suits your talents, you have some pretty new clothes, and want for nothing,' she suggested, her breath warm on the back of my neck.

There was just enough room for this and remembrances to them all. I signed it 'Sprat', and squeezed in a postscript. 'Please show this to Jack, and ask him to let me know where you will be.' And then, written round the edges in capitals: 'A kiss and a hug and a bone for Toby, if you can spare it.'

I sanded the letter, folded it, and blobbed it fast with sealing wax, pressing the seal Angel handed to me. As I lifted it I saw that it was not plain at all: round the circumference were letters that spelt out 'Pleasure'. I glanced at Angel, but she had turned away, so I addressed the plain side to Annie, care of Matthew Clegg's shop.

'Where do I send it from? How much will it cost?'

She turned. 'Nothing, my dear: you will recall that it is paid for the other end by mileage – what is it: about two hundred miles or so? – but I am sure it will be worth it for the reassurance that you are safe. I myself will ensure it is put on one of the mail coaches. We have nothing to worry about now, do we?' and she smiled, showing her small, perfect teeth; her eyes, however, were shaded as usual by those downcast lids.

Something uneasy touched me for a second, as fleeting as the shadow cast by the flight of a bird between one's eyes and the sun, but leaving the same impression of a black streak that only faded slowly. The unease had no name, for I was sure she would see the letter on its way; somehow I felt I had been cheated, had been persuaded into folly, but I could not see how and mentally shrugged off the doubt. Annie would be so pleased to hear from me: I could imagine Matthew spelling out the words to her, and she saying 'Fancy!' and dabbing at her eyes a little with her apron . . . . Jack would be relieved as well, I hoped, though no doubt he would curse my ineptitude before penning a note for me to meet them – somewhere. I reckoned it would at least be two to three weeks before I could expect Annie to answer, and by then it would be too late to go up there for Christmas. Still, that gave me longer to perfect my charges in their playlet.

Angel and I spent a very pleasant evening playing piquet and she let me beat her so obviously that once again the unease touched me: it almost seemed that she had beaten me so soundly at another, more important, game that mere cards were trifles to be tossed away as carelessly as stale crumbs to the birds.

Nick did not come back that night, nor the next: the quarrel with Angel must have been more serious than I thought for him to forgo his bed. In his absence Angel was so very kind to me, unbent so graciously, chatted so amiably that I almost began to like her very much. I even decided that her normally cold and reserved exterior was a disguise for shyness, and soon found I was chattering away to her with little heed to my tongue, telling her of my travelling companions, our lives on the road, Toby and Daisy, and I even once or twice mentioned Jack – quite impersonally and objectively, of course. She paid me the compliment of appearing interested in all I had to say, and although she would never be the sort of cosy girl to put her stockinged feet on the fender and fold back her skirts to the fire the better to enjoy the butter-dribble of muffins on her chin, she unbent far enough to give me advice on the cut of my gowns, augmented by Madame Bonneville's instructions, and dressed my hair in the latest becoming fashion.

'We shall soon have you quite the young lady of fashion,' she said approvingly. 'You have a slight but graceful figure and you stand well. Pull your shoulders back a little – you're a woman, not a flat-chested boy – and take smaller steps when you walk. That's better . . . .'

The third night of Nick's absence she sent me up to bed with a journal containing the latest fashions. Some were wildly grotesque, others looked merely uncomfortable, but I saw that I could if I wished adapt some less extravagant ideas. Hats were out, as far as I was concerned; of the dozen or so pictured two looked like coal scuttles with feathers, one resembled nothing so much as a roof ridge hung with ribbon, another was a cake dish with lace curtaining, and the others were either feathertops or pie dishes with herb gardens for decoration: there were a couple of mobcaps that looked rather pretty, however. Shoes were nicer, in satin or kid, and with the discreet Italian flared heel and bows and ruching they looked both comfortable and attractive.

I was momentarily diverted by an advertisement for rouge, patches, and false eyebrows of mouse skin, and another for false bosoms. Breathing in deeply and thrusting out my front I considered the 'Spring Bodice' and 'Bosom Friends' of a Mrs McCorkquindale of Regent Street and the cork 'Rump Improvers' and 'Cheek Plumpers' which were obtainable 'by post only' from a lady in Tonbridge. There was a shop advertising from near us, in Covent Garden, that sold only accessories: feathers of ostrich, pheasant, cock, duck, guinea fowl, swan, and eagle; artificial fruits that included strawberries, cherries, grapes, plums, and apricots; there were velvet and stuff flowers: lily of the valley, sunflowers, roses, tulips, peonies, forget-me-nots, and stocks; artificial ringlets and hairpieces in black, brown, auburn, flaxen, and grizzly; everything for dressing the hair: combs, bandeaux, pins, hairnets, cushions and rolls. Further on in the journal there were the usual offers of hair powder in small or large quantities, and a warning article on the fading fashion of white lead on the skin. In the jewellery line apparently pearls were in and jet out; diamonds and garnets were to be had at a price, and marcasite and paste much cheaper.

I turned back to the clothes and tried to imagine myself having a dressmaker to hand and unlimited material: a red velvet fur-trimmed pelisse and muff, with under it perhaps a green striped poplin with a matching necker-chief, or a brown polonaise over a yellow petticoat, or even a closed dress in white satin with pink roses . . . . I put aside the *Ladies' Journal* with a sigh: life in a small Derbyshire village, followed by Aunt Sophia and then by my life on the road had not given me much opportunity to indulge in fashion. Now, of course, I had a couple of serviceable dresses, one in yellow satin for best, and a blue woollen hooded cloak, but so far I had not even passed through the front door: I should have liked a stroll through the busy streets, even if only for a change of scenery, but Angel insisted I was still too delicate to risk the cold.

The fire beside which I had huddled gave a dying spirt and I hunted for the last coal knobs in the bucket, hoping to keep the room warm for a little longer after I got into bed. The pitcher Nancy had brought up earlier for washing was cold but, teeth chattering, I gave myself a cat-lick and dived into my night robe, a much frilled castoff from the ladies we did all the mending for and still bearing ridgey mends from all the rips I had hastily cobbled together. Crouching down by the fire again I blew the dying embers into a last blaze and hung on stupidly instead of snuffing my candle and leaping into bed while there was still some warmth left. I was half-dozing, one side cold to the room, the other still warm against the hearth, when I heard the stumble of feet on the stairs. The church clocks had struck the quarter after eleven not long since, and Angel had been long abed. Nancy slept in the kitchen – lucky woman – on the hearth by the fire that never went out, and the only other person with a key was Nick, who had been missing for three days. But if it was Nick, why the stumbling hesitation? If he ever came in after we had gone to bed he would tiptoe up the stairs in his stockinged feet, with exaggerated caution: I had heard the stealthy creak on more than one occasion when I had had a restless night. Whoever was out there rebounding clumsily off the wall on the narrow stairwell was either drunk or . . . Or a burglar. Armed with the courage of stupidity and the poker, and carrying my candlestick in the other hand, I lifted the latch on my door and peered out.

'Who goes there?' I hissed dramatically. Remembering our bogus highwayman by the Savernake forest eighteen months ago, I almost added: 'Stand and deliver: your money or your life!'

'Gem . . . Gem, dear, is that you?' whispered back the ghost of Nick's voice.

I almost dropped the candle in my relief as he came round the bend in the stair. 'Nick, you idiot, you gave me the fright of my – What's happened?' for as he came into full view I saw both his haggard, strained expression and that one arm hung useless at his side, a dark stain spreading from near his shoulder to the cuff of his jacket. Reaching out, encumbered as I was with the superfluous poker, I steadied him as he swayed with weakness. 'For God's sake, come inside before anyone sees you like that!' By 'anyone' I suppose I meant Angel, but didn't stop to analyse. Once inside my room I latched the door, drew him to the stool by the fire and recklessly threw on next morning's kindling to make a blaze. In minutes the fire was roaring away happily, and once I had thrown a blanket round Nick's shoulders his violent shaking lessened to an intermittent shiver.

'Any brandy on you?' I asked.

'Bottle – half-full – in my room. Not locked.'.

Taking the candle I crept to the room down the passage, registered that it was sparsely furnished but tidy, and found the bottle on the chest under the window. Tiptoeing back I found he had tossed away the blanket and was trying to pull off his jacket with the uninjured hand.

'A drink,' I said firmly, 'and leave that to me.'

Luckily there was some water left in the pitcher, and I brought the bowl over to the fire to take the chill off. There were some linen squares in my chest that I had been going to hem for handkerchiefs or make into pads for my monthly times, but this was an emergency. When I had removed his jacket I slit up the seam of his shirtsleeves with my sewing scissors. The wound was deep but the blood was starting to clot, flowing slow, dark red.

'Knife?'

He nodded. 'Fellow in an alley. His doxy detained me,

393

then he came out of the shadows. Must have thought I had more on me than I did. They ran off . . . .'

'Keep still: I must clean it,' and I dipped a piece of linen in the water, wiped the dried blood from his arm and gently dabbed at the wound itself. He winced, but allowed me to finish. The puncture started to bleed again with my messings, but slowly, and it looked clean enough. 'Right: this will hurt.' Taking the bottle he was holding I poured a generous measure over the wound, anticipating the sudden jerk and gasp. 'There, now, that should keep it from infection – don't touch it!' The reek of spirit filled the room as I mopped away the liquid that had overspilled onto his breeches and the rug.

'Waste of good liquor . . . .'

'Nonsense! Best place for it. Clench your fist; good: the muscles aren't affected. Now, this is going to need a stitch: do you want me to do it or see a doctor in the morning?'

'No quacks . . . . Are you sure you can?'

'Of course,' I said, with a confidence I was far from feeling. 'Have another drink, and don't watch!' As I threaded linen onto my needle I tried to recall how Tom had dealt with Toby's tail, and another time when he had stitched a gash in one of our horse's legs; pull the edges of the wound closed to encourage them knitting together, one stitch at a time and tie off securely. Not too shallow, and not too deep . . . . I dipped the thread in brandy and tried to equate Nick's torn skin with other sewable material. It took two stitches and he was gasping and white-faced by the time I had finished, but it looked far better than it had before. 'There: we'll leave those in for a week. Nearly done.' I poured a little more spirit onto the wound, then made a pad: there was a large spider's web over the window and I reached up and transferred it to the bandage.

'What on earth . . .?'

'Don't worry: it's one of my special recipes.' Half-closing my eyes, I intoned: 'A gipsy woman, and she the queen of her tribe, sold me the spell for a silver shilling . . . .'

He laughed as I had intended, and it was a welcome

sound. 'Spiel, Gem, pure showman's spiel!' but he let me bind the linen pad tightly round his upper arm without demur. Then he picked up the bottle for another swallow.

'My turn.'

'You weren't stabbed.'

'Nervous shock.' I took a generous swig, then another, gasping at the fiery liquid. But it was warming . . . . 'That's better! Now bed, my lad!' Hooking my shoulder under his uninjured arm, I hauled him to his feet.

'Hang on . . . .'

'No. Bed. Now! Or you'll never get there,' I added, as he swayed. 'Come on, we'll take it in easy stages.'

But something went wrong with my calculations; I had intended of course that he go to his own room, but a couple of minutes later he was lying back against my pillows, grinning up at me in a way that suddenly made my cheeks feel hot.

'Nick! I meant you to . . . .' But my voice trailed away as with his good arm he pulled down my head.

'Do this?' he whispered, and his warm, brandy-flavoured mouth presumed mine.

'Don't be silly!' I jerked my head away. 'You're injured and should lie quiet. Besides, the brandy has gone to your head. You *must* go to your own room.' But even as I spoke I saw the tangled dark lashes shutter his eyes and lie quiet on his cheeks. A moment or so later his breathing slowed, his head dropped to one side and he snuggled down like a weary child.

I told myself as I huddled by the near-extinct fire that the sleep would do him good, I would wake him in a couple of hours, that he hadn't meant to kiss me the way he did, that – But my hands were at my flushed cheeks, and I could not quiet the wild thumping of my heart. The trouble was that he was so attractive, and it was a long time since I had been kissed . . . .

After a while reaction set in and I began to shiver: it was ridiculous to stay huddled over the hearth in this absurd fashion all night. Outside I heard the first clock chime two o'clock and I determined to seek Nick's room and lie down for a couple of hours. Then, as I paused by the door for a last look at my patient, I wondered whether anyone called him in the mornings. Nancy usually just tapped at my door when she left the pitcher of hot water and removed the empty one and slops pail I left outside the door, but once or twice she had peered round the door to make her strange clucking 'good morning' noises, and if she found Nick in my place she would probably have dumb hysterics, which clatter would be bound to bring a disapproving Angel at the scene. Then again, if it were Nancy's job to call Nick and his bed had not been slept in that would be no surprise, because of his many absences, but if I were there in his place . . . .

There was only one thing to do.

As carefully and quietly as I could I slid under the blankets next to Nick. There wasn't much room, but luckily I was on his uninjured side and he was as warm and quiet as Toby would have been, so I snuggled up and closed my eyes. Just a short nap, and then I could be awake when I heard Nancy coming up the stairs . . . . I *was* awake, briefly, to hear the first cock crow over by St Giles's, then I closed my eyes again. Another half hour before I needed to get up . . . .

It was a pity that Nancy had had the toothache and had taken some laudanum drops to ensure oversleeping: it was a pity I slept more soundly than I had for weeks. It was an even greater pity that it was Angel who climbed the stairs with the hot water, and that when she woke us I had found it necessary to sleep with my head on Nick's chest and that his good arm was holding me tight. But, strangely though, there was no condemnation; in fact she almost seemed pleased, gazing at us thoughtfully, then suggesting we sleep a little longer. It was not until after she had closed the door quietly behind her that I realized she had not noticed Nick's injured arm under the bedclothes, had not listened to my protests, had just accepted the fact that he and I were lovers.

'And we're not!' I said furiously, sitting up and glaring at him lying at his ease, an impudent grin on his face. 'It's – it's not fair to be suspected of something like – like that, when it isn't true!'

'No,' he agreed comfortably. 'I think we should do something about it as soon as possible . . . .'

'Such as what? She'll never believe that we're not – you know – now.'

'Probably not. In which case . . . .'

'Yes?'

'In which case, I believe the time has come for action.' He sat up beside me, the bandage on his arm in sharp contrast to his warm brown skin. 'If you can't convince people in this world of the truth, you might as well make what they believe of you as enjoyable a fact as possible.'

'Meaning?'

'Meaning it's a good job I'm right-handed. Meaning, she did say have a lie-in, didn't she? Meaning . . . . Well, what do you think I mean, silly girl?' and once more his mouth sought mine.

And this time I did not draw away.

I could have said no, but being honest with myself, I didn't want to. Not that I had forgotten Jack, far from it: this just seemed different. We were two normal, healthy young people who needed each other's bodies like some crave alcohol or a pipe: an excitement, a comfort, an experience. Then again, while my lovemaking with Jack had roused in me no question of morals – or the lack of them – I was conscious of sin with Nick; conscious too of the need to take preventive measures. The former I quieted with extra prayers and the knowledge we weren't hurting anyone else: the latter I ensured with diligent application to Kat's book and herbs. I suppose the difference really lay in the fact that I had been in love with Jack. And

Nick? I wasn't sure. We were happy together, good companions, we made love often and rewardingly, but –

He was a most inventive lover: even I, with my limited experience, realized this, and it was not long before I responded eagerly to all he taught me. Initially, of course, I was somewhat shy and diffident, but he had such delightful ways of overcoming my inhibitions that soon I became bolder. Quite apart from the fact that he was young, virile, and charming, we shared the same sense of humour; he also had a beautiful body, firm and well-muscled, very like the Greek statues in my stepfather's books, and his skin felt like velvet rubbed the right way. He made making love fun, something to be treated with irreverence and enjoyment; he would never let me become serious, and though he had special endearments for me and my body, he made it clear from the start that our association was not a permanent one.

'You're here and I'm here, Gem darlin', and you want me and I want you and the devil take tomorrow – let's enjoy today, shall we?'

And we did. For the time being at least I was happy. I had the children to coach during the day and at night I luxuriated in the release of all my other physical needs in Nick's arms. Angel, too, was surprisingly kind, and appeared to accept the situation with equanimity. She insisted that my gowns were cut too high in the bosom, and when I altered them to suit her she found me pieces of lace to trim them, and ribbons for the bodices. I must admit I was surprised at her good humour, for besides the puritan streak I thought I had detected, I imagined she nursed a certain intensity of feeling for Nick herself. But now she was all smiles and pleasantry, though I could never quite catch the expression in her eyes, for she still kept those white lids downcast. Madame Bonneville was all affability when at last she came to see the children rehearse, and had complimented me, hinting that she had another little job for me after Christmas which she thought I might find interesting.

When I reported this to Nick, blithely surmising, he had looked at first startled, then he frowned.

'After Christmas? That's too near –'

'Why? Do you have any idea what she has in mind, then?'

'It doesn't matter whether I do or not; I want you to myself a bit longer.'

'But I shan't be going away from you! Whatever it is will only mean helping out next door, and we shall still have the evenings!' For he no longer came in late: whatever he did – and I never asked him – he was only away during the daylight hours.

But he didn't answer me, at least not in words. Instead he took me in his arms, laid his cheek against my hair and held me tight. 'There's helping out and helping out . . .' he muttered. Then: 'Are you happy with me, Gem?'

'Of course! How can you ask?'

'I don't think you understand –'

'Yes, I do!' I interrupted, reaching up and placing my hands to frame his face. 'What you're really asking is do I mind us living together like this when there can be no permanence in it? Well, of course I don't; I'm glad you found me, you have been good both to me and for me, and I shall never forget your kindness, wherever I go!'

He caught at my hands and pushed me a little away from him. 'You know, then, what is in store for you? And you don't mind?'

I considered. 'No, not really. For a while I have been warm, well fed and with no need to wonder what the next day will bring, and you have been the nicest thing that ever happened to me – well, nearly – but all in all I shan't be sorry to be on the road again in the spring. I know there will be times when I shall be cold and wet and hungry again, but I love the excitement of a good performance, the new sights and sounds that each day's travel brings, even the hard work – and I do miss the others, you know! As soon as I hear from Annie I shall make plans to travel north to join up with them again in time for the new season. I have enough money for the coach fare now, thanks to Madame, and in a week or so I shall have enough extra to stay for a while in lodgings if necessary.'

He loosened his grasp on my hands and smiled, rather bitterly, I thought. 'So you are still determined to go back to your friends? I thought –'

I realized just how churlish I must have sounded. Perhaps he was really becoming fond of me, as indeed I was of him, but I had known all along where my future lay and, dear though he was and much though it would be sadness to say goodbye, yet I knew there was only one man for me, whether I was welcome there or not. Strangely enough, when Nick had first made love to me I had not considered him as a rival for Jack, nor had I ever thought I was betraying my first love. It had been as different as wine and ale, both answering a need, but one a cherished speciality, the other a daily custom. Also I had felt, rightly or wrongly, that whilst Jack would have understood my need for Nick, the latter would never have comprehended what I felt for the former. Gold and silver, lace and homespun, love and liking . . . .

'But, Nick! You never expected me to stay with you, did you? Indeed, my dear love, if it had not been for my friends I should have been content to stay with you till . . . till we tired of one another!'

'I don't think I should – not now.'

'That's the nicest thing anyone has ever said to me!' And I meant that sincerely. 'But you know how life changes people; one day you will see a prettier face, or –' and I grinned '– a larger bosom. You know how you say you admire women with large fronts!'

He gathered me to him, his voice husky with, I thought, laughter. 'Just don't suppose you females have the edge on constancy, that's all! And, puffballs or balloons, I'm happy with yours, Gem darlin' . . . .' He kissed me very satisfactorily, and I forgot to ask him what he thought my new job with Madame was to be.

400

There was a setback with the children in the next few days, as a couple of them went down with croup, so we had to put off our playlet till after Christmas, and I found time lay heavy on my hands. However Nick, with Angel's permission, took me for a stroll or two in the streets, and I really enjoyed these, having once more the smell of (comparatively) fresh air in my nostrils, people to see, shops to visit, sights to admire. It was after one of these outings, when we had ended by buying a bag of chestnuts from the surly vendor in Covent Garden, now all smiles and servility for paying customers, and had strolled back burning our fingers and our mouths and throwing the shells over our shoulders, that Nick introduced a new element into our relationship.

'Like to learn a game or two?'

'A game?'

'Like you used to do when you were learning your fortune-telling spiel, I suppose: weren't you taught to adapt yourself to each new customer afresh? What if we pretend I'm not me, but someone else? Older, younger, more experienced, less so: come on, Gem, we can make it fun!'

It was remarkable how like Jack's tuition it was. He had been preparing me for my different customers in fortune-telling,. Nick seemed to be doing the same for customers in bed. Just as Jack had pretended to be many different people, so Nick was by turn young blade, shy first-timer, seen-it-all roué and forgotten-it-all old man. He appeared too easily aroused, then not arousable; under-eager and over-eager; to each impression he encouraged me to make what he considered the right response, and after an initial doubt I found it a novel way to start what always ended up with us in a glorious tangle of arms and legs on the bed, both happy and satisfied. I ended by understanding a lot about a man's anatomy, and more about mine: once I asked him why he wanted me to learn all this.

He smiled, then turned his head away.

'Once you leave me, Gem, who knows what men you may encounter? Maybe you will be glad of my teaching some day.'

'I shall never marry an old man, nor yet a roué or a pervert. I hope.'

'I hope so too, Gem my sweet, but life plays funny tricks sometimes.' He turned to me and kissed me, hard. 'Whatever happens, I meant it for the best, remember that!'

I kissed him back. 'At this rate I shall know how to deal with any man the dear Lord sends to my bed – but I'd rather have you!'

'If you really mean that . . . .'

'I do.'

'Then perhaps all I've taught you may yet be but a diversion. I hope so, oh, I hope so!'

Christmas came and went, and in January my charges, now fully recovered from their coughs and croup, were to perform their little entertainment. They had all worked hard and I was fairly satisfied with the result. The individual items – reciting verse, singing songs and even a solo on a penny flute – were passable, but it was the classical playlet on which I had spent the most time. This was based on the choice of Paris between the three goddesses Hera, Athene, and Aphrodite and gave all the children besides the principals a chance to take part either as chorus or walkers-on. I had been dubious of the choice of subject at first, much preferring the children to act something they might be familiar with, but Madame had persuaded me with little difficulty; the choice between agreeing and escaping as against staying for any length of time in her stuffy, overcrowded room with the overwhelming, cloying smell of those burning pastilles had been no choice at all. So I had written some simple couplets for them to learn by ear, as none could read, and provided a linking commentary which I was to deliver from behind the curtain. I would have liked some accompanying music, but did not wish to ask Madame for more money; she had already bought the muslin Angel and I made up into simple tunics and dresses for the players and some curtains which were hung from a frame round the stage. There had had to be a few props also: a gold paper crown for Hera, silver paper helmet for Athene, wreath of paper flowers for Aphrodite, and a shepherd's crook and wooden flute for Paris; all very rustic, but we were not professionals.

All went well until two days before the performance, which was to be on Twelfth Night, and then I went down with an unaccountably severe attack of the gripes. Angel promptly dosed me and sent me to bed, promising to take the final rehearsals. I fretted and fidgeted, but was really too ill to do much except worry, sleep and try to keep down the medicine, which, strangely enough, seemed to make me feel worse. On the morning of the concert I decided I had had enough and threw away the dose once Angel had left me. Struggling out of the bed I opened my herb bag; as I thought, the powders were still there. I took a tongueful of Katina's bitter concoction and swallowed hard, mentally noting that the other powder that I had had to use during the last few weeks with Nick had nearly gone. After a while I felt decidedly better, but thought I had better remain in bed till the afternoon in case I was sick again. Angel brought me some gruel, but I wasn't hungry, and instead took another secret dose of the powder.

I woke from a doze to find it was getting dark already, and a nearby clock set off all the others by chiming four. Hastily I lit my candle, put more coals to the fire, washed in cold water, and changed into my best dress. I had half-expected Nancy with a hot drink before this, but there was no time to waste. The concert was due to start at six and I must see the children into their costumes and ready before *Madames* guests arrived. Impatiently I tugged on stockings, pulled a comb through my tangled curls, and wrapped myself in my woollen cloak, for the corridors were cold. My stomach still felt queasy, but I took another dose of Katina's powder and felt, if not fully recovered, at least well enough to think of going next door. Picking up my candle, I rolled back the rug in front of the fire in case of sparks and, going to the door, lifted the latch.

But the wretched thing had stuck. The wood must have warped with the damp weather we had been having over the last few days. I pulled again, but nothing happened, so I set down my candle to try with both hands. Still the door would not budge; a dreadful thought struck me: perhaps with all my rattling and shaking I had shifted the bolt that lay on the other side. I glanced around the room. There on the chest lay the paper and ink I had penned the playlet with, the quills and, thank goodness! the knife I had used to sharpen them with. Sliding it between the edge of the door and the lintel, I carefully worked it up and down, for the gap was scarce wide enough for anything but the thinnest blade. For a moment I thought I must be wrong, then I heard a faint chink! as the knife struck metal. Desperately I tried to work the knife against the bolt, hoping it was only just across, but the working gap was too narrow. Deliberately or not, I was made prisoner.

I must have shouted and called for twenty minutes or so before I realized it was no use. Banging on the door only hurt my fists and the heel of my shoe and there was no sign of any response. Of course Angel must be already over at Madame's getting the children ready. Nick was either out or with her and Nancy was half-deaf and too far away in the kitchen to hear me. I tried the window, but that was too small for anything but my head, and all I was faced with was a blank wall across and an empty alley way below. I heard the clocks strike five, then six, and then half past. Sick at heart I crouched by the dying fire. Sooner or later Nick would come back and find the mistakenly bolted door, but by then it would be too late.

I think I must have dozed again, for when I was next conscious of sound it was to hear the clump, clump of Nancy's feet on the stair. I ran to the door and banged and kicked: she must hear me, she must! I heard her

pause, heard a mumble, then the blessed sound of the bolt
being slid back. In a moment I had the door open, had
brushed past her astonished figure without a backward
glance and was speeding down the stairs. The door through
to Madame's was unlocked and I ran up the two flights
to the concert room. Already I could hear children's voices
declaiming and the murmur of applause, and I slowed
down to catch my breath. They would be performing the
playlet now, and all I could hope for would be to let myself
in quietly, stand at the back and watch what remained.
It would be better than nothing, so I turned the handle of
the heavy door and slipped inside. The room was illumi-
nated by the candles from the stage at the other end and
yes, they were into the Paris' choice scene from the playlet.
I saw someone from the audience rise and come towards
me: it was Nick, and his face was full of alarm. I glanced
back at the stage, and saw what I should have seen
straight-away: a horror I would not have believed had I
not seen it with my own eyes . . . .

20

The three little girls playing Hera, Athene, and Aphrodite
were waiting for Paris' choice, but any resemblance
between innocent children playing at mythology and these
little monsters was purely coincidental; they were the same
children, but there the similarity stopped. They wore the
Greek costumes I had sewn, but even as I watched each
in turn slipped the dress from their shoulders. The youngest
girl was only eight, as I remember, and the eldest twelve,
but even the smallest one's nipples were rouged so that
they resembled tiny unformed cherries; their skirts, too,
had been ripped up the side seams, and every time they
swayed and undulated to an unseen flute playing strange,
erotic music, the cloth slipped aside from naked thigh and

buttock. And who had taught them those obscene gestures? My cheeks grew hot and the blood thundered in my ears as I saw Paris, his powdered buttocks uncovered, offer himself to the audience. The audience? I shook off Nick's detaining hand and stepped forward: not that any of those perverts watching the children would have noticed had I taken off all my clothes and screamed.

There were perhaps two dozen of them, mostly elderly men with powder, patches, and wigs, and a couple of them were masked; one was so immensely fat that he occupied two of the gilded chairs Madame had provided. She sat, in the inevitable respectable widow's weeds, near to the stage, her restless black-mittened hands twisting in her lap, her eyes watching less the performers than her guests. There were women, too: a couple of well-dressed ones with keen, hard faces and a plump one in her late fifties in drag of powdered wig and blue breeches. Nearest the stage a young fop dressed all in shades of grey watched avidly, a thin, red tongue running continuously over his thin, red lips; at the back an elderly stick of a person in wrinkled clothes to match his pocked face and liver-spotted hands had slipped his hand openly into his breeches, trying to stimulate the old flesh with audible gasps and sighs. Somewhere in my consciousness I heard words of utter filth intoned in the halting pure tones I had taught those children – I felt I was in a nightmare and clapped my hands to my ears and shut my eyes, trying to deny both senses the truth before me. Perhaps I felt that I should suddenly wake to find I had been in some hideous fevered dream, and Angel would be bending over me, her cool hand on my brow: but no, as I opened my eyes on this waking nightmare she was there too, dressed demurely as a nun, and her quiet, deliberate tones had just prompted one of the children into another ribald speech. And not only Madame and Angel, but Nick, too, was part of this horrible scene!

I turned to him, ready to scream, to shout, to cry with

bitterness and rage and incomprehension, but the only sound I could utter was a whisper.

'Nick – oh, Nick! I don't understand.' But even as I said the words, my mind understood, and only too clearly.

His strained, oddly embarrassed grin was ready. 'Just watch, Gem darlin', and you'll savvy right enough. But keep quiet for Gawd's sake! Open your mouth just once, and you're a goner!' His words were all the more impressive for the low, frightened whisper in which they were made: fear for me? 'And if there's anything you still find difficult to *comprenez* after, I'll let out the rest of the cats. Now remember, keep your trap *shut*, and watch. They're coming to the auction now . . . .'

The auction. Those helpless babes, as I still thought of them, were placed one after another on a raised box and made to shuffle and prink, wriggle and pose, while Madame Bonneville auctioned them off one by one to the highest bidder. I saw the old dodderer who had been playing with himself outbid twice for a couple of young boys; three girls went to one of the women, and the prettiest of the remainder to the woman in drag. So it went on; the prices were fantastic; two rosy-cheeked, plump girls from the country went to the grossly fat man for a thousand guineas and a particularly young girl – she was seven – was worth seven hundred and fifty to the man in grey with the red lips. By now the helpless tears were running down my cheeks and a couple of those in the audience had turned to stare; I saw Angel lean forward and whisper to Madame, then they both glanced in my direction. But Nick had had enough; pulling at my arm he opened the heavy doors and pushed me out ahead of him down the dark corridor and into a small deserted salon, full, it seemed in the flickering candlelight, of heavily ornamented mirrors. He thrust me down in a chair and stood over me, arms akimbo, a flush on his cheeks.

'Do you still not understand?'

I began to sob hysterically and heard his swift slap on both my ears almost before I felt the blows.

'And there's more where that came from if you don't pull yourself together and grow up!' Then in a different tone: 'Oh Gem, my love, I'm sorry! Of all things I wouldn't have wanted you to find out like this . . . .'

'Is that why you bolted me in my room?' I was guessing.

'I wasn't sure whether the medicine would keep you indisposed long enough. Angel said it would, but –'

'I threw it away –'

'I only wanted to spare you . . . this.'

'I should have found out sooner or later!'

'Later was better. I – I wanted to explain to you myself before anyone else told you. Or you discovered for yourself.'

I was dry-eyed now. Giving myself a little shake, mentally as well as physically, I tried to pull myself together, think calmly and constructively. I must be objective: if Nick knew how frightened and desperate I felt, anything might happen. I could be locked in my room again, my food drugged, I might even be – but my mind shied away from anything so terrible. I must find out what else went on in this ghastly place, appear to accept all I saw without any more fuss, and so lull them into a sense of false security that it would be easier for me to get the hell out of it and back to the security of my life on the road. I had enough money saved to go up to Annie's tied up in a handkerchief in the chest, and I would not wait any longer for a reply to my letter. I could trust no one but myself now, not even Nick, who I had believed had had some affection for me; but perhaps it was still there. Locking me in had been his way of protecting me, I supposed. But from what? Even now I was sure there was worse to come, more horrors to face, but I must appear unshockable, even curious about what else went on, just so that he didn't suspect the almost overwhelming desire I had to run: run now, run anywhere . . . . It was too late to do anything for those poor children, but once away from this place I was sure that if the authorities knew just what was going on, something could be done about this horrific traffic in little bodies. And to think I had had a hand in it! The fact that they could now speak in the passable tones of gentility I had taught them must have put up their price, as Madame and Angel had intended.

'I . . . I'm sorry. I'm not used to being caged. I must admit it would have been less of a shock if I had had some idea of what was going on . . . .'

The smile he gave me was relieved, grateful that I had understood.

'It's not so bad for them when you come to think about it. Those kids were taken from the gutter, half-starving most of them, others cold and homeless. What sort of life would they have been able to look forward to, else? Half of them would have been dead before they grew much further, the others thieves, pickpockets, molls and doxies. Why, some of the parents actually bring their prettier kids straight to Madame: she gives them ten shillings for the pick. And don't forget she has to keep them, dress them, feed them, tutor them till they're ready. Some of those kids today are going to a life of luxury: remember those two plump little ones that went to the Burgomaster, the fat bloke? He comes over from the Continent every two or three years and always takes a couple back. Regular customer, he is; got an invalid wife and no children, so he takes ours back with him and brings them up as his own. 'Course, they have to perform a few – services – in return, but he likes them young, and when they get older he trains them up as servants for his wife. Then when they're of marriageable age he gives them a dowry and they wed back into their own class. And then he's back for more: there's no worry about them.'

No worry about two little girls who should have been still playing with dolls having to exchange that for a stifling four-poster and a fat pederast!

'And the others?'

'Most of them's all right: Madame hand-picks her customers. Only one I don't like.' He frowned. 'That fellow dressed all in grey: children don't seem to last, and he takes them younger and younger. One day there'll be a scandal.'

I shivered, remembering the thin red tongue over the thin red lips.

'You mean . . .?'

'They die! Fever, accidents – so he says.'

'What happens if . . . if they don't suit?'

'Madame has them back again, for another customer. Original buyer doesn't get back all the purchase price, of course; after all, a virgin ten-year-old who knows how to suit can't be repeated as such the same next time, can she? Still, a few weeks discomfort in luxury is better than crawling round the gutter with an empty belly, isn't it? You should know.'

I shivered, remembering those days in London, lost and starving. I didn't know, couldn't know, because I had not experienced the alternative these children had to face. But I was not convinced. However, I mustn't argue . . . .

'Hunger is a great incentive, I agree . . . .' For no reason my mind went back to the starveling boy who had staggered out of a ditch in Derbyshire to halt Jack's van all that time ago; no perverted luxury for that child, just food, warmth, hard work and, eventually, love of a sort. God! the sooner I shook the dust of this corruption from my feet the better! In the meantime . . . .

'Does . . . does Madame have any – er, sidelines?'

'Sidelines? The kids *are* her sideline!'

'Then what –'

'Is the rest of the charade? Gawd, Gem darlin', where are your wits? Come here, girl, let me show you. I'd have thought with all that mending you'd have some idea.' He grabbed my hand and hauled me to my feet. 'We can have a look, but there won't be too much going on at this time of night.'

He pulled me over to one of the ornate mirrors and pressed a knob, unsatisfactorily concealed as a protruberant nipple on one of the undressed nymphs that held up the gilded contraption. A portion of the gilding slid away and I looked down through a peephole into a candlelit room filled almost to entirety by a large four-poster containing two very capable females and a naked man trying to deal with both at once. Nick released the knob and the peephole slid shut. Two other small rooms were empty, another held two women, and in the last a young lad who looked no older than fourteen was getting into bed with a woman old enough to be his grandmother. Luckily my mind seemed numb, as unresponsive as my expression, which I had schooled into unshockable lines, though I knew that when I could think again those scenes would come back to haunt and disgust my waking thoughts.

'There!' said Nick. 'This room is for our special guests, those that want a bit of extra. The customers don't know the peepholes are there but our lot do, and they play up special if they know there's to be an audience. Madame pays them extra for a good performance, and we can always call on a big negro and a dwarf for the real kinks. Mostly, though, it's normal traffic, which takes care of the other rooms, and the gambling is downstairs.'

I tried to look reasonably intelligent and not too shocked, though my whole being repudiated what he was saying. I must get away . . . .

'This, then, is a brothel?' I said, realizing how stupid I sounded.

'What else? Brothel, bordello, whorehouse, palace of fun; call it what you will, it's all the same thing.'

'And you? What is your role, Nick?'

'Me? He hesitated, then he glanced away. 'A bit of this and a bit of that. Sometimes I find the customers, sometimes the goods. Depends.'

'And the blind man? The one who isn't blind: what was it you called him? Old Bob? Beelzebub? Is he one of Madame's – procurers – too?'

He winced. 'He looks after the lads we don't use. They become his spies, touts; run errands and maybe . . . .'

411

'Slit a purse or two?' I supplied, as he seemed disinclined to go on.

'Sometimes, if they're bored. That's why they chased you. They thought after that perhaps you'd make a likely lad for Madame's, and I had noticed you too: put them up to a little harrying. Of course when I got there they'd just discovered you were the wrong sex, and that's where I took over.'

'And this is why you rescued me? To put me in here with the rest of those – those – those –' and I gestured for want of words to the now closed peepholes. 'Was I just to become another of Madame's whores?'

He flung out his hands in a gesture of repudiation. 'No, not one of them! Perhaps at first that's what you were intended for, but not after I got to know you better. Don't you realize after all we did together, all the fun we had, that I couldn't just turn you over to her?'

I noticed he was using the past tense, and my heart sank. He was my only chance of getting out of here: did his tone now mean that I was, after all, to become nothing but a permanently caged bird of pleasure?

He clutched my arm. 'Don't look like that, darlin'! We mean something to each other, you and I, and she's not getting her maulers on you just yet, I promise you!' He pulled me to him, and so had he trained me to his use that I automatically responded to his touch. 'At the beginning, see, you were just another female, pretty enough to attract a customer or two, and that's what you were brought in for. But after a while I sort of got used to you, and didn't want to train you up like the other doxies. That's when I had a real argument with Madame, and Angel too.'

I remembered that night he and Angel had quarrelled: had it been over me?

'So you see, I had to make it up to them both. I found another girl those nights I was away, and luckily she didn't take much persuading: took to it like a pig to swill. Madame was pleased, Angel laid off me 'cos she thought

I'd soon get over my scruples with you, so Nick was favourite again. Then I had that – accident – and there I was, in bed with you after all! They think I'll get over it pretty soon, but I'm not so sure: you've sort of got under my skin. Funny little thing, you are too: not the sort to . . . . Never mind.' He rumpled my hair, then scowled. 'Of course we had to think how you'd take this thing with the children's concert lark: Angel gave you a couple of doses of a purge, but I thought you'd be better locked away. Who let you out anyway: Nancy?'

I nodded: I felt as if cold water was running through my veins instead of blood. 'Do you always – break them in?'

'Well, we don't get many volunteers, if that's what you mean! Then, neither do we press-gang them. The art of gentle persuasion, that's what I'm best at.'

I remembered now those curious remarks I had thought I heard when I was so ill at first: 'Not a virgin . . . clean . . . keep her under . . . .' Angel's voice or Madame's, after a crude examination while I lay helpless. I could not help it: my empty stomach revolted, and I retched.

He was all concern. 'It's that last dose she gave you: I told her she'd made it too strong. Come on down the corridor; there's a friend of mine off duty for a couple of days, and she's always got a dish of tea and a bit of cake going . . . .'

Lil was plump, generously so, fair and talkative. Nick went off on some errand, to do with those wretched children, I supposed, and left us alone. I was glad of the tea with cream and the seedcake with which she generously plied me; glad, also, of the soft cushions in her fireside chair; glad most of all of the unceasing chatter which flowed around me like a comforting shawl.

'. . . glad to welcome a friend of Nick's . . . best house-girl breaker I ever knew . . . always had a soft spot for the lad . . . 'course I remembers him as a youngster . . . I've been here meself near ten years, but still only twenty-six . . . sometimes I look at meself and I says: where would you be now, my girl, if it weren't for Madame?'

She looked nearer forty than twenty-six, but her comfortable curves, generous manner, and increasing flow of chatter reminded me of Annie.

'. . . lots of different faces – and the rest, know what I mean? Still, makes a break to be off with the usual: working twenty-three days of the twenty-eight makes a girl relish a rest . . . . They are all the same really, when it comes down to the fundamentals, you might say. Still, whiles they're with us they're not taking it out on their wives or raping an innocent girl, that's what *I* say . . . . Mind you, there's some of 'em wants it funny, lots of surprises you get in my job . . . . You don't look the sort to be in this place, if you don't mind me saying so: not enough fat on you, for a start. 'Course, there's some as prefers bones instead of meat, but not many. Still . . . . How did you come to meet lover boy, then?'

But she did not wait for an answer.

' 'Course, I always thought as Miss Angel-Face had more than a passing interest in the lad, always hanging round him as she does. Sort of girl who'd scratch out your eyes one minute, and go to confession the next. Meek as pie . . . . Must say her mending's always nice and neat, though: a girl doesn't get much chance for any fancy undoing of buttons and unfastening of laces in my job. You all right?'

I realized now what Nick had meant with his reference to 'all that mending'. All that finery Angel and I had sewn was the direct result of the life of these whores: the stained satin of seduction, the slit silk of sex, the lace of lust. I felt sick, and probably looked it.

'It's . . . it's nothing.' I thought of an excuse for my revulsion. 'Those children – I didn't realize . . . .'

'Auction day, is it?' she said comfortably, turning her skirts up over her knees to the fire. The flesh of her calves was mottled like a leopard with reddish-brown scorch marks, and she wasn't wearing drawers. 'Well, it has to come to us all sooner or later. Bit of a shock to you, was it?' She leant over and patted my knee. 'Don't worry, dear: I know how you feel. Makes you feel sentimental, don't it, to think of kids of that age going through what we has to?' She dabbed automatically at her eyes with the hem of her skirt. 'Still, it isn't as though they weren't the dregs: no fancy little ladies and gentlemen there. They all knows what's coming to them, and if they aren't suitable Aggie upstairs sorts 'em out before they're trained, poor little sods.'

'Trained?'

'Oh, yes, just like we were when Madame's breakers – like what Nick is now – had finished with us. They gave us a taste, and we were easy for the rest after. Children's the same; most of 'em knows what their parts are for, but Aggie gives 'em exercises and things that gets 'em tuned up to play a merry jig-a-jog or two. Any that's too delicate is weeded out. Mind you, some of them are due for a surprise or two: why, there was a gent last week who wanted, would you believe . . . .'

I let her ramble on; after all, the variation she was describing was one Nick had shown me during our lessons, for that is what they had been, I realized now. Lil's words about the children were a small comfort, anyway; not that I believed all her self-deception. You can teach most people something in theory: that does not stop them losing their wits and panicking when it comes to the reality. I remembered again the man in grey with the thin red tongue . . . . And then my mind went back to Nick and the expert way I had been conned. What I had taken for a game, albeit a loving one, had merely been a prelude to the sort of existence Lil endured, counting the days of the month until she could relax in front of a fire, scorching her legs to the accompaniment of seedcake and tea. Was that all Nick had intended? Somehow, among all the lies and deception, I still felt there was something more, for both of us. Or was that what I was supposed to think?

415

'How long – how long does Nick usually take? To train us, I mean?'

'Up to a week, usually. Depends, I've heard, on how much he fancies the girl. Had a little faery-looking thing a while back, as died of a fever before Madame got her over here; always wonder if Angel-Face didn't wish that on her . . . . She lasted near a month before she died. Before that there was another who Prissy-Mouth had moved over in a twinkling when he wasn't watching; she settled after a while, but cried her eyes out at first. Reckon he'd promised more than Angel'd stand for: that one reminds me of someone who'll bake a juicy pie and then just a-sit looking at it go bad, 'cos she's no appetite. She don't indulge much herself, to my way of thinking: mebbe that's how she keeps him a-hanging round her skirts. Makes him feel inferior 'cos she don't need his little weaknesses . . . .'

'I've been with Nick for over a month now.'

'And I'll bet,' she said shrewdly, 'as what started with Miss all smiles is now like her arse, crack-tight!'

I laughed. I couldn't help liking Lil, tart though she was; she had a warm heart, a fund of common sense, a tidy philosophy of life and an accommodating nature: and, after all, what else was a whore? She must have been a good one. Thinking of what she had said, I wondered how long it would be before Angel decided that Nick was getting too fond of me and had me forcibly removed to this side of the door in the wall; but of course I wasn't going to wait for that. I was going to be away as soon as I had bundled up my belongings, wrapped myself in my warm cloak, and collected my hoard of money from the chest. I was just wondering if I could leave Lil and find my own way back to my room in the other part of the building, when Nick came back.

He was flushed, talkative, gay, and he kissed Lil soundly before hauling me to my feet and repeating the process with me. 'Come on, darlin', we're going to a party!'

'No – no, I don't feel like –'

416

'Rubbish, sweetheart! It's a celebration. Thanks to your help, Madame's made half as much again on the kids, and we're to join her in a drink.'

I twisted myself violently from his grasp.

'Not me! You know perfectly well I had no idea what was going on: I'm taking no credit for the deception!' I might have added that I would have had no part in it if I had known, but prudence stilled my tongue. Even Nick must not realize how much my whole being revolted to think what I had done.

'Now, come on, darlin'; you're not going to let me down, are you? I'd've thought you'd have got over your squeamishness by now.' And he really believed what he said, I could see that.

'Who'll be there?'

'Why, you and me and Angel, Aggie from upstairs, and a couple of Madame's cronies: her accountant, and her mascot and bodyguard, Jimmy Spade. Black as the cards he's named after, that one! Got muscles like an all-in wrestler; does the heavy work and a bit in here on the side. He produces a nice act with a couple of the girls; in one he dresses up as a savage and pretends to rape the two of them, and in the other he plays a slave who is teased by his mistress till he breaks loose and turns the tables. Very effective. Customers'll pay a lot extra for that kind of thing.'

I was thinking hard: what a perfect time this would be to get me tight and inveigle me into staying in this part of the house. Nick had already had a drink or two, to judge by his manner and flushed face, and they would only have to give him a couple more for him not to notice till it was too late if the black man carried me off and locked me in one of the cell-like rooms and worked me into submission. Perhaps my subjugation would be one of those visual treats Madame allowed her more privileged customers . . . . No, tonight – and every other moment till I crept down and unlocked that front door – must be spent in my own room. If possible I must get a relatively sober Nick to come back with me, persuaded that I was the most desirable female in Christendom, for his active presence was my only safeguard at the moment. Two stages then: one, no party; and two, Nick back to my room and in my bed.

It was not so difficult, after all. After I had bid an affectionate farewell to Lil, I followed Nick down the corridor until I suddenly came all over faint. It was a trick I had learned with Jack; once, when we had been relatively flush, he had decided for fun to teach me one of the beggars' tricks. He had dressed in rags and made me do the same, as his crippled daughter. Flints in my stockings had ensured a hobble, but the interesting pallor was provided not by powder but natural methods: first my shoes were stuffed with newsprint, to draw the blood from my head to my feet, then, as encouragement to the process, Jack made me whirl around in a circle as fast as I could whilst keeping my eyes fixed on a book in my hand. The result was instant sickness and a face as white as bleached linen: the method so horrible that the mere memory was enough to induce instant queasiness, and induce a similar attack at a moment's notice. I held my hand to my head, willed my blood down to my lower extremities; rolled my eyes, staggered, took deep gulps of air and moaned, and in shorter time almost than it takes to tell, I was back in my own room lying on the bed with Nick bending anxiously over me, rubbing my hands.

'Water!' I breathed helplessly. 'And some brandy, if you have any . . . .'

My one fear had been that he would go for Angel, or perhaps call on Lil's assistance, but I had leaned on him so heavily on the way back that he had scant choice but to keep me clasped in his arms. Now, as I heard him pour water from the pitcher and fumble for his brandy flask, I willed myself into the role of the temptress. Once, Jack had attempted to write Shakespeare, arguing that if Will had lived he would have been bound, sooner or later, to write a play based on the Biblical tale of Samson and Delilah, and he had started the play with great enthusiasm

418

in the middle. It had not survived more than a week's
pen-nibbling, but I remembered the seduction scene where
Delilah persuaded the reluctant Samson to spend the night
in poppy-induced slumber in her arms; I remembered it
because we had actually got round to rehearsing it as 'part
of Will Shakespeare's forgotten play, miraculously drawn
from obscurity by a famed scholar and here performed for
the first time on any stage by . . .' etc. I believe Jack gave
it up eventually because he could not stage the collapse of
the Temple with our limited resources. I recalled part of
the scene:

Samson: My lady, you are ill?
Delilah: Not ill, my lord, save in that quiet spirit,
    Which dwells within the hidden fastness of my heart,
    Lighting its narrow room like the consolation candle
    That stills the stricken whimpers of a child
    When, assaulted by the shadows of the night,
    It fancies the unicorn of faery doth do
    Battle with the roaring lion; creatures all
    Wove by infant substance from the insubstantial
    Hangings of his bed. Not ill, my lord, save in that
    Trust the sighing lover breathes into his
    Lover's mouth, that all their secrets are as one.
    Bellowsed into a fire of mutual love
    Until it doth flame like a beacon from the top
    Of Cleeve, a signal to all alike that their
    Love is an invasion of the heart, a bloodless
    Conquest wherein the conqueror is himself
    Bound prisoner of his mistress' heart. Not ill,
    My lord . . . .

And so on. I had never been able to learn it to Jack's
satisfaction and he had eventually abandoned the idea of
being Shakespeare's successor.

The point of all this remembering was that Delilah had
successfully waylaid her lover with words, endless rhetoric
of Jack's that I suspect would have sent the real Samson
running to the nearest tavern; on the other hand, he might
have been bored to death. In reality Delilah had dosed

him with poppy juice, and I recalled part of her soliloquy as she sat with his sleeping head in her lap, waiting for the shearers:

Rest now, my strength, in the weakness of a
Woman's arms. Rest, and let the golden
Harvest of your hair await in sleep the
Stealth of untimely reaper's hook. You
Tonight have drunk the cloudy poison of
Demeter's bane, that will you give dreams
Too deep for waking. See, I kiss your brow, and
Like a child you frown a little and then smile,
Escaping for a span the realities of Life,
Running free in dream as a galley doth take
The south wind in her arms and tread the waters
Into a path to Africa, to see the winter sun
Strike sapphire from the back of screaming
Swallow . . . .

But I had no poppy juice.

'Here,' said Nick's voice, bringing me back to reality. 'Drink this.'

Obediently I sipped at the brandy and water, peering up at him over the rim of the mug.

'Thank you, my dear love: I think I shall be all right now. Silly of me to get so upset over what she said . . . . Of course she couldn't really know . . . .'

'Know what?' he asked, sitting down on the edge of the bed.

'Nothing. Nothing really, I suppose. And yet . . . I near enough believed her . . . .'

He was almost shaking me now. 'Believed *what*?'

I turned away and buried my face in the pillows, trying a sob or two.

'I believed that you – that we – that we were something special!'

'But we are, of course we are!' He grabbed my shoulders and turned me to face him. 'Who's been saying anything different? I'll kill them . . . .'

'No, no, my darling Nick; I believe you, of course I do. I knew she must have been wrong . . . .'

'Wrong about *what*, for Gawd's sake?'

'Just hold me in your arms, my love, and the doubts will disappear . . . .'

Of course there had to be only one end to that, and afterwards he fell asleep before he remembered to ask what I had been worried about.

Which was just as well. Because I couldn't have given substance to my insubstantial fears – except for the fact that Angel and Madame wanted me for a whore, and I was equally determined not to be one. And I did not believe at that stage that Nick would have understood my fears; to him, notwithstanding what had happened before to his other mistresses – the one who had been whisked away when his back was turned, and his 'faery' who had died in a fever – he would still believe whatever Angel told him when she turned her guileless face to his gaze. I realized that he had started to train me for the profession with his 'games', but I also knew that, at the moment, he felt I was too dear to him to relinquish willingly. Time would blunt his desire, I knew that also, but my craft must be to hang on as long as I needed, long enough to effect my escape. The strange thing was that, although I only felt fear and disgust for Madame and Angel and their machinations, I felt a true affection for Nick, and still enjoyed his lovemaking. The tarnish of the disreputable business he was engaged in had produced in me only an emotional desire to excuse and forgive as far as he was concerned. But perhaps that was my excuse to my conscience, because I should have to go on using him . . . .

I slept late the next morning, and when I woke Nick was gone. I flew out of bed and tried the door: Heaven be praised! It was not bolted. I was free to go. Perhaps today would be the only chance, for if Angel got any inkling of how desperate I was the front door, normally unlocked in

421

the mornings when Nancy did the marketing, would stay fast all the time and I should be trapped. It would not matter not having breakfasted; I would dress in my warmest things, make a bundle of necessaries, take my money from the chest and run as far as I could before finding a bite to eat and the first available coach north. If my money ran out I should have to walk or rely on lifts, but I thought that now I was far abler to cope with whatever fate had in store for me than I was four or five months ago: life had a way of teaching one things, will-she, nill-she. As honestly as I could (for all my clothes had been provided by Angel one way and another and my boy's clothes had been consigned to the fire long since) I donned the plainest and cheapest garments I could find and made up my herb book and other necessaries into a parcel with my head-shawl. Now I was ready: just my cloak to put on and the money to tie in an inside pocket of my dress. A quick note to Nick, thanking him for all he had done; he was the only person I should leave with regret.

Pen and ink were on the desk; hurriedly I sharpened the pen, drew out a piece of paper, and hesitated. 'Dearest Nick'? 'Darling Nick'? No. 'Dear Nick'? No, again. Better just to start with his name. Hastily I scribbled 'Nick', followed by a dash. Just what was I going to say? Ah, yes –

'Another letter to your friend in the North?' asked Angel from the doorway. How long she had been there I could not tell, but as I whirled around, paper screwed up guiltily in my hand, my cheeks were flushed enough for her to have guessed something was amiss, even if she had been too blind to see my parcel and cloak lying ready on the bed. But she was not blind, that I knew, though she gave no indication of having noticed anything as she came further into the room, holding something in her hand.

'You can stop wondering; here is a letter for you. It came a couple of days ago, but with you being ill I quite forgot.'

I took the folded paper, noticing without surprise that the seal was broken. I hesitated to unfold it, for I knew now that if the news it contained were in my favour it would never have reached me, and my heart was heavy.

'You have read this?'

She made no attempt to prevaricate. 'Of course. If I engage to play a hand I do not revoke. And it would be stupid not to know the colour of my opponent's ace, would it not?'

I looked at her: pale queen of diamonds, a declared trump to my highest heart. She had no need to play a higher card.

I read the letter quickly, wanting to know the worst, but it made no sense the first time around so I read it again.

Written by Matt. Clegg at the dictashun of Annie Sutcliff.

My dear Zoey, whatever have you dun? I was so glad to know you was Safe and Well and not come to a Dreadful End and I told Jack straitways for Matt bort the letter to Preston to meet us as it came to him before we did and Jack was Ever So Upset. He curse and swor something Terrible and tear the letter into little pieces and I had to pick up all the Bits to find out Where to Write. How cood you be so Norty an Wiked? Mind you, I don't suppose as how you ment it and are hartily sorry for being Bad. I woodnt have knowed but for Jack saying as how Madame Bonnevilles place is the Most Note Orious House of Ill Fame in London Town what caters for every Vice and you to say as you were well suted to Your Posishun and were Well pade was The Last Straw. Howsomever my dear I am sure you did not mene it and were Forced and I am sure you are still Welcum Here. You were never That Sort, leastways I dont think so and so Rite Soon and let us no you are not so Bad as Jack Makes Out. Matt joins me in Affechunate Remembrences. Toby is with Tom and Well Looked After.

Yore Loving Annie.

It was difficult enough to decipher the thick, black writing even without the blur of tears in my eyes, but there was no doubt what it meant, even with the variant spelling.

Jack and Annie and probably Tom, too, believed that I was living it up as a well-paid and willing whore. And the message had been given to them clearly by a few apparently careless words that Angel had put in my mouth; that was why she had asked me whether Jack was a man of the world and knew London well: the address for the return of the letter had been enough, and my innocent words, suggested by the demure, nunlike figure at my side, had merely confirmed what suspicions had been planted in Jack's mind.

'Why?' I said, and she did not pretend to misunderstand.

'I work for Madame: that is all. You came here, like all the rest, but you were ill: that was the only difference. You stayed with Nick and me longer because of this, but as soon as you were better you were destined to follow the others before you. That's why we wanted no relatives or friends to start asking awkward questions. So, the letter, to put them off.'

So, the letter. No welcome any more from Jack, who now obviously believed me damned. Still, there was Annie; she would receive me for my own sake, and I could try and explain to Jack in the spring. A sudden cold shiver ran down my spine; now Angel had seen my preparations she would lock me in again until someone came to carry me forcibly across to that part of the house on the other side of the door in the wall . . . . But surely Nick wouldn't let her? Then I remembered how he had lost the other girls.

'So?' I said, trying to brave it out.

'So,' she answered equably, 'for Nick's sake, because I care for – his good opinion, you will stay here. Till he tires of you, that is.'

'Suppose he doesn't?' I asked defensively, knowing I was being stupid.

She just smiled.

'Aren't you going to bolt me in? Aren't you afraid I'll try to run away?'

'Where to? Your friends don't sound too keen to have you back and you have no means of keeping yourself.'

I remembered the bag of money – surely not!

She followed my glance to the chest behind me and nodded.

'You owe me for your food and keep, so I took what was due: there was just enough to cover it.' She turned to go, leaving me defeated. 'But, of course, if you decide to try and escape and chance your way, there are still Old Bob's boys; the blind man, remember? They have specific orders to stop you and bring you back. Not my orders: Nick's. For the moment he still wants to keep you here. For your own sake, you'd better pray he doesn't change his mind.' She smiled. 'So you see, my dear, there is no need to bolt the door.'

21

It was a fine June morning when we set off for Tyburn.

'We' were all the girls from Madame's establishment, deaf Nancy, Nick, Angel and I. Madame declined to accompany us, pleading a megrim, but as all London would be having the day off (for it was rumoured that this would be the last public hanging, many of those with an ear to listen in Parliament insisting that it was a degrading spectacle: in my innocence, never having attended a hanging, I thought that so much spoilsporting, like those who would close down St Bartholomew's Fair) she had allowed us a free day. Nominally we were in the charge of the black man, Jimmy Spade, but he disappeared on his own devices soon after we reached our destination. The hangings were not to take place till noon, but it was nine months since such a day's entertainment, there having been only twenty death sentences passed during the past six months, and the fact that five were to be topped at one go, plus the uncertainty of any such future entertainment, made it certain that only an early start would ensure a decent viewing. We had risen at three, some of the girls not having slept at all, and were ready for the wagon at four: our breakfast and luncheon had been packed by Nancy to take with us. Looking round at my companions as we set off, most still half-asleep, it seemed like an outing for any innocent and pretty young girls. Scrubbed of their rouge, free of gewgaws and dressed in their plainest, the girls had the freshness of the morning: some, indeed were scarce more than children, Lucy and Audrey being but sixteen and the oldest among them not yet thirty. It was only a certain coarseness of manner, a wariness in the eyes, a hardness round the mouth that would have distinguished my fellow travellers from any other cart of young women that travelled the same road as we that morning. The day promised heat, being heavy and sultry even at this early hour, so we all wore our thinnest cotton or muslin and Nick was in shirtsleeves, lolling at my knee.

'Wake me when we get there,' he said sleepily, and yawned. I ruffled his curly hair affectionately. Since that day five months ago when Angel had spelled out the terms of my imprisonment my relationship with Nick had not changed. In spite of his double-dealing he was genuinely fond of me and I of him, though in different ways; he still thought of me primarily as a bedmate, I am sure, while I found him a delightful companion as well. At first, after I had found out about the children and the real function of Madame's, I had doubted whether I should be able to respond to him as once I had done, but this fear proved unfounded, luckily for me, for I could not have pretended for long even to save myself from the purgatory of the other side of the door in the wall. I should have tried, no doubt, but the body can be a traitor too and I should have been sure to lose concentration or eventually display repugnance. But luckily, as I said, he still had the power to turn me on with so little as the flick of a finger, and underneath the brashness and assumed charm I found a

426

vulnerable and lonely young man with as much need of genuine affection as Toby had had. We shared the same bed and the same sense of humour and so far – touch wood! – there had been no signs of his tiring of my company, in spite of Angel's hopes. I glanced across at her now and saw, as always, her eyelids shutter those betraying eyes. I knew that she still resented my presence, resented the attention Nick showed to me, and was surprised that I had lasted so long, but she had never shown by word or deed since that dreadful day that our relationship was anything other than perfectly normal; the second letter from Annie she had even handed to me with the seal unbroken, or so I had thought until I saw the point where the hot knife had slipped under the wax.

The letter was short and spelled out a final farewell to any thoughts I might have had to joining my former companions this year; it was dictated to some letter-writer she had found near Preston:

My dear, just a Hurried Note to let you know that we are Off On our Travels again, but I do not know where as Jack would not let us know, in fact when I spoke of you he told me to Shut my Mouth, so I daresn't say I was writing. If'n I get to know I'll Write Again but I'm not Hopeful. Tom sends his Regards and to let you know as he'll care for Toby like it was Daisy. Love, Annie. Postscript: Matthew would've sent his regards if he knew I was writing. A.

Once I had resigned myself to staying prisoner at Madame's, at least until there was a chance of moneyed escape, I had reconciled myself all too swiftly to my life in the shadows. I had even persuaded Nick to take a note across to Lil, asking her to pay a visit next time she was free, and she had duly come, though it was strictly against the rules to escape from that side of the house, and we had to be careful Angel was out of the way. We had a cosy chat – or rather I sat and listened to her – while we drank tea, fortified with a little spirit. Lil drank her tea in the same refined way Annie did, her little finger extended, but there the refinement ended. I learned quite a lot about her life, for a 'prime crack', as she assured me she was, became the receptacle for that side of some men's lives that neither their wives, colleagues, employers, friends, servants, children nor enemies ever suspected. In fact, as she said, there was probably more of the frustrated mother in every whore than the world imagined for, as she put it: 'Most of our customers might just have tumbled straight from the womb, for like infants they are piss-proud, demand attention at once, squall if they don't get it, and are all greedy, fumbling, sucking, grabbing creatures with no thought but for themselves; full of body feelings and no mind; fall asleep as soon as they are satisfied, and indulge their private parts as if we had nothing better to do than mop up and powder them after . . . .'

In time Nick gave me a spare key and when the coast was clear – Angel out and Madame either asleep or with the megrims – I would slip across to Lil, and sooner or later I met all the other girls: Meg, the dark-haired beauty from Salcombe; Sal of the red hair; short-sighted Nan of the dimpled cheeks; Emma, who had been a contortionist and found her training useful; Lucy, the youngest and prettiest; Sukey and Liz, twins who specialized in working together; Aggie, who was tallest and oldest; Audrey, smallest and cheekiest; Sabra, half-negress and Louise from France. None of them had more than a smattering of education or refinement, and of necessity their conversation was mainly limited to discussions of their clients, clothes, and food, but they were in the main a cheerful and friendly lot and made me very welcome, especially when they found out how useful I could be.

I had asked Lil one day if she were not afraid of becoming pregnant.

'That, and the clap,' she replied gloomily. 'For the second, there's no cure for women that I know, and as for the first . . . . You must either be lucky, or try a charm or two and a prayer or three, and if Madame likes you it's an abortion and if that doesn't work, three months off to have the little bastard. I've had two,' she added, 'abortions, that is, and painful they was too. And one born dead, poor little sod.'

'What medicines do you use?' I asked curiously.

She named two loathsome concoctions, three spells, and some other mumbo jumbo, and I remembered the preventative in Kat Petulengro's book and her chart of days to avoid: forget the latter, these poor girls would have no chance to refuse their clients on a critical day, but the herbal mixture might work. Tentatively I offered my help.

'No harm in trying: tell you what, let Louise try it first. She's dropped three in the last four years: all born dead, but that's going it, even for one of us.'

'Is she pregnant now?'

'Probably. I'll ask her.'

She was: about two months, she reckoned. I made up some of the mixture, and she aborted cleanly and easily some twelve hours later. After that I was in demand, and had to send Nick out for more herbs and spices to mix a reasonable quantity. He was pleased, for he not only appreciated that there would be less time taken with the girls out of action, but he also believed I was helping them out of the goodness of my heart, reconciled to the life they lived. This was not true: in the first place, they paid me: only pennies, all they could afford, but these were mounting up, and I had found a loose floorboard under the bed where my hoard was relatively safe. Nor was I reconciled to the way of life they led; I helped them get rid of their unwanted pregnancies only because I could not bear to think of the life any survivors would have: more children for Madame's auctions, if they were allowed to live that long, which I doubted. Any live children were probably smothered at birth; what I was doing was wrong enough, but that was worse.

So, I quietened my conscience, and the pile of pennies grew. There was not nearly enough yet to even think of chancing an escape, but if my luck held I might have enough by Christmastime to go and join Annie, for I was still determined to explain to Jack what had happened; somehow, somewhere, sometime . . . . To this end I had even started to steal; a coin or two from the sleeping Nick's pockets, not enough or too often for him to miss; once a sixpence from Angel's purse when she had left it in the parlour. Never again from her, for she had made such a fuss over the money she supposed she had dropped that she even had poor Nancy take up the carpet. In the end I dropped it into the ashes of the parlour fire and then pointed it out to her, gleeful when she burned her fingers, uttered a most unladylike oath and dropped it to the floor where, without the covering of carpet, it rolled down a crack in the floorboards and was lost. I had already examined my conscience against the count of procuring abortions, and now arraigned it on a charge of thievery: it vanished like a snowflake on the tongue. Less than six months ago the only things I had ever stolen were food from Aunt Sophia's larder, the coat from a scarecrow, and, I suppose, Toby – though that latter I still preferred to think of as rescue – but now my conscience appeared to be blunted, and that even though if my total of pence taken from Nick's pocket amounted to more than twenty-five shillings I was liable to transportation or the death penalty. My mind justified the thefts and sheered away from the consequences by remembering the deceptions that had been practised upon me, but wondered how much close proximity with a dozen prostitutes and a procurer, to say nothing of Madame's and Angel's lack of scruples, had to do with it. Perhaps, like that curious reptile the chameleon my stepfather had told me of, people could and did change their colours with their surroundings: and if their colour, why not their morals in reflection of their companions? Perhaps even the garish colours of a whore would seem like my true skin one day – Never! I clenched my fist in denial.

'Stop pulling my hair!' complained Nick. 'You're hurting.'

Back in the wagon on our way to a day's forgetfulness

I bent my head and kissed his cheek. 'Just practising a little torture,' I said lightly. 'Thought you might like a change.'

'If there's any of that to do, I'll do it myself,' and he pinched me under my skirt, so sharply and intimately that I jumped, and dared not look at Angel for embarrassment.

It was some three miles to Tyburn, and it was as well we had started out early for the traffic thickened step by step. There were people on foot, on horseback: in carts, carriages, wagons and drays, and even the odd old-fashioned sedan. Our sedate trot turned to a walk, then to a succession of halts and starts. Luckily we had chosen the wider streets and were keeping away from Newgate itself and the procession from the prison, otherwise I doubt we would have reached the hanging place at all: as it was we had difficulty enough in forcing our way through the crowds to a good vantage point not far from the gallows – perhaps a hundred yards away. I was kept too busy either hanging on for dear life as we rumbled and clattered over cobbles and potholes, or repelling the hordes of small boys who were trying to hitch a free ride on the side of the wagon, to have much time to look around me, until our driver announced 'That's it!', stuck his whip in its stand and went forward to attend to the horses.

It was the noise that struck me first of all. All of humanity seemed to be shouting, swearing, yelling, screeching, cursing, calling, crying, laughing, sobbing, muttering, murmuring, laughing, complaining and singing all at once; add to that the animal sounds of neighing, barking, chattering, screaming and buzzing and it was a veritable Tower of Babel. Already it was almost unbearably hot, although we were drawn up in the temporary shade of a grandstand which was filling up with the wealthier citizens able to afford a seat, but even so I was aware of the sweat trickling between my shoulder blades and the dampness underarm. We were jostled and shoved by those

431

who attempted to pass on either side of the wagon and those who had time to spare eyed us up and down and, the men especially, were only too quick to guess where the girls were from, aided to some extent by their ready repartee. I shrank back in my seat as a couple of respectably dressed women shook their fists at the cart, and the colour flooded to my face as I heard what they thought of us; it was clear from what both men and women said that they considered a whore's place was in bed and not on the streets.

Nick woke up sufficiently to chase off some young lads that fancied their chances with the girls and unpacked our breakfast, which consisted of cold pasties, thick boiled bacon between slices of bread, cheese, and ale well shaken, warmed and frothed with its journey. There were purveyors of food and drink all around us but I suspected their prices would be exorbitant, though I did wheedle Nick into buying me a couple of oranges. As I sucked out the sharp, refreshing juice I heard a nearby church clock strike nine: three hours to go. And still the big open space was filling up, though it did not seem possible even now to fit anyone else in; and what about their need to relieve themselves? And suppose they all felt faint? As for the former, we ourselves were provided with a couple of receptacles under an awning, as I supposed those in carriages were, and the rest of the populace were already emulating dogs and relieving themselves carelessly and unselfconsciously wherever there was space. As for the latter – if they fainted, they would have to do it standing up. Nick informed me that at this moment they were unshackling the prisoners from the floors of their cells in Newgate, forming up the escort of military in the prison yard and bringing the priest from his breakfast, for it would take all of two hours and more to pass along the crowded route from Newgate to the gallows.

The sun rose higher in the sky, the place grew more crowded, if that were possible; the heat increased. Now the greatest consciousness was that of smell. All of a sudden I inhaled the stink of unwashed bodies, excrement, stale ale, overripe fruit and rancid milk, bad meat, cheap perfumes, sweaty dogs and horses, dust, raw spirit, lavender, pomade, wet straw, cloves, fresh paint from a new-decorated trap nearby, musty cloth, damp leather and cinnamon cakes, and felt sick. Beneath our wagon a young woman gave the breast to her children, a baby and a child of two or three, while her man vomited carelessly against the wheel. A stray draught of air and suddenly, over all, the smell of new-planed wood from the gallows itself: immediately I was terrified. Turning all ways I could see nothing but a sea of faces and shoulders as far as the limits of the buildings and still more were pressing in from the streets around. The high wall across from the packed grandstand was festooned with onlookers hanging precariously from the bricks or perched on the top; our cart creaked and groaned under the pressure of passers-by. The noise was louder, the smells viler, and I could not escape from this throng of bodies, could not breathe, could not move without touching someone, could not shut my eyes and ears to people, people, more people, crowding in and crushing me till I stifled –

'Hold your nose, darlin', take a couple of deep breaths and put your head between your knees,' advised Nick's husky voice. 'Like a drop of brandy?'

I shook my head and leaned against him. 'Just a little faintness: it'll pass. It was just – all these people . . . .'

'Crowd sickness,' he said, nodding. 'Takes some people that way, like height or open-space sickness. I thought for a moment . . . .' He hesitated. 'You aren't – aren't in the family way?'

I shook my head, wondering for a startled moment what his reaction would have been if I were.

He heaved a sigh of relief. 'That's all right then: just thought I'd ask . . . . Perhaps it's something you ate. You had strawberries yesterday, remember?'

'I think it's your crowd sickness – Listen: what's that?' For above all the usual noise there crept a new sound.

433

'It's the drums and pipes – they're coming!'

There was a huzza of sound, a sudden uncontrolled surging forward of the crowd nearby that rocked the cart, but above it all I could hear the faint, mournful beat of drums and a shrill and discordant piping and the wild cheering of a crowd away to our left. Instantly all sickness was forgotten as Nick lifted me to the coping of the cart, his hands round my waist to steady me.

'Can you see 'em yet?'

I strained my eyes. 'Yes – I think – yes, here they come! There are some soldiers – they're having a job clearing a way through the crowds, though! Then there's a cart – no, two. There's one man in the first and a parson reading from a book, and there are four men in the second. They've all got their hands tied. Why is there only one in the first cart?'

'That'll be Robin Rich; they'd put him on his own 'cos he's been a high-toby man for five or more years, Hounslow Heath way. Near caught a dozen times, but always got away. Heard tell it was one of his doxies got jealous and shopped him this time. The others are just petty thieves . . . .'

I thought at once of Macheath and Polly and Lucy and all became suddenly transformed into a play – romantic and exciting. Like everyone else I was smitten with a fever, a desire to be in the front row for this special entertainment, and ignoring Nick's restraining hands I tore away, slid down the side of the cart and began to battle my way towards the scaffold. Wriggling and twisting, I clawed my way through the press of people, glad I was small and reasonably wiry, for I could squirm my way where others were jammed solid. At last I could move no further forward but, glancing to the side, I saw a carriage, abandoned by coachman and footman, with a couple peering hazardously from the curtained windows; the whole thing was shaking and creaking with the weight of those were were using the roof as a gratis grandstand. Wriggling to my left and hearing the pop of buttons as I slid across the chest of a portly tradesman and treading on the toes of another I reached up to tug at the sleeve of a fresh-faced young man who had found himself a precarious perch on the step of the coach.

'Room for a little un, mister?'

He reached down and hauled me up; I heard my sleeve rip, but found a foothold and hung on. He slipped an arm round my waist to hold me steady, and inevitably his hand moved up to my breast, but it was with an abstracted air and I could see he was more interested in the spectacle than in me, and I decided it was worth it for the view.

The cart carrying the first condemned man had reached the gallows, and the soldiers, behind the flimsy wooden barrier that protected them from the spectators, were glad enough to rest their muskets, though they still kept a wary eye on the crowd; men had been spirited away from the gallows before now. The second cart, with its escort, waited some way off. The crowd swayed this way and that as the prisoner was helped roughly out of the cart and on to the scaffold; he stumbled a little because his hands were tied, and the fine mulberry coat that had been slung over his shoulders fell away to the ground, where it was snatched up by an enterprising bystander who filched it from under the noses of the military. The highwayman was only young – not more than two-and-twenty, I guessed – and handsome in a florid sort of way; he was wearing canary-coloured breeches and waistcoat and his fine linen shirt still showed traces of starch, even in this stifling heat, though the front and back were wet with sweat. The crowd had quietened to a murmur now, and I distinctly heard him ask in a low voice for 'something to lay this confounded dust'. Someone handed up a flask, and he spluttered and gulped, turning to wipe his mouth on the shoulder of his shirt. Now a steward stepped forward with a recital of his crimes: two murders, five woundings, and numerous robberies.

I stared at the condemned man but he seemed indifferent to his indictment, tossing his arrogant head and glancing

435

at the crowd as though we were here for his amusement, monkeys behind bars in some fairground instead of the other way about. His sentence was read out with a certain relish: 'To be hanged by the neck until you are dead' and I expected then that he would show some trace of fear, but he only jerked his head and asked for ale. This was brought, with some delay, from a tavern nearby, but so thick was the press of people round the scaffold that it had to be handed over the heads of the crowd for the last distance, spilling much on the way, so that he could finish the remains in one gulp. Some woman in the crowd began to sing 'My Bonnie Sweet Robin' and soon the refrain was taken up on all sides. It was more like the play than ever, for when we had finished the song he stepped forward and began his farewell speech, prefaced with the warning: 'Now, you balladmongers, scriveners and chaunter-culls, get it right: I don't propose to waste prose prepared for posterity in the mincer of mangled mouse-talk!'

A propitious beginning, and in the main the long speech that followed would have been worth a penny or two of anyone's money, though I doubt that even the most experienced court clerk, let alone a plain scrivener, could have taken down above half. There was no remorse, no begging forgiveness for his sins; quite the reverse, in fact, for he described in detail a couple of his more successful escapades and positively boasted of the time he had stopped a coach on the Heath, robbed the elderly passenger and then seduced his young (and willing) wife. 'Friends, her name was Rose: Rosie by name and rosy by nature, for never did I come upon a bud that was in full bloom, so to speak, at one and the same time. What a woman! Even now, if I close my eyes I can see those pink – cheeks!' And much more in the same vein, loudly appreciated by the crowd, and in the end I was laughing and applauding with the rest for he would have been entertaining enough to stop and listen to at a fairground, let alone with his now captive audience.

I quite forgot what we were all gathered here for, and

so I suspect did many others, for it came as a shock when one of those on the platform interrupted his flow of reminiscence, tapping him on the shoulder and nodding back at the noose that hung like a halo behind his head, motionless in the heavy air. Robin Rich stopped in mid sentence, his recollection of what a certain dowager had said when he attempted to remove her jewelled garters to be for ever in his memory alone. For a moment he seemed at a loss; then his back straightened, he frowned and then smiled wryly, and his voice was now quiet and subdued.

'I have been reminded there is a debt to pay, and that I have kept you waiting an unconscionable time, my friends. Forgive me: I am but the prologue, there are other actors to fill this little stage, but we shall all end with a dying fall, methinks . . . .' I congratulated him silently, both on his knowledge of the Bard and on the pun, though I do not think many of the others caught the allusion. 'I have few regrets, no remorse, and no last-minute repentance to titillate your palates. My regrets include all the mouths I have not kissed, all the skirts I have not lifted, all the – But enough of that; my prick will still be standing after all the rest is but a limp rag doll, a stringless puppet!' He laughed, but I thought I detected, at last, a hint of hysteria. 'Watch closely, my friends: at the last it will be Sweet Robin who decides when he is to die, and not our doleful friend here; I always swore I'd cheat the hangman, and so I will!'

A man dressed in black, with a black mask that hid all but his eyes, stepped forward and slipped the noose over Rich's head, drawing it tight. Someone in the crowd moaned, then all was deathly quiet, so that his last soft words were clearly heard by those of us within fifty feet or so: 'No prayers, parson; where I am going it will all be singing of bawdy songs and warmth and merriment; I have no desire for your cold temples and towers. The devil himself will stir to greet rogue Robin.' Then, so low I had to strain my ears to hear: 'Loose your arms around my

437

neck, sweeting: you have me now, and I shall not run away –'

There was movement around him, the rope tightened and creaked on its pulley and of a sudden – so sharp and quick it took all by surprise – the bound man took a great spring up in the air away from the platform, bringing his knees up high to his chest like a man with the gripes; for a long moment he seemed to hang in the air, the rope loose like a loop on his shoulder, then he fell, legs straight and back arched to a bow.

There was a terrible soggy snap like the breaking of a rotten branch and he swung at the end of the rope, legs quivering, head on one side, eyes open and tongue lolling, while down the front of those bright canary breeches crept a darker stain as he voided himself in death. There was a moment of utter silence, of mute horror, then a woman screamed hysterically and all was hubbub.

'Jesus Christ!' said the man at my side, whose presence I had truly forgotten in the trauma of the last few minutes, when what had been a compelling play had turned into a ghastly nightmare. 'He's cheated the gallows!' There seemed real disappointment mixed with the awe. 'No five-minute dance . . . . Still, there's always the death-dew.'

'Death-dew?' I questioned, still numb with shock.

'Death-dew,' he repeated impatiently. 'Where's your cloth?'

I must have sounded like an idiot. 'Cloth?'

Quick for his place in the front and impatient for my stupidity, he explained. 'As he dies, the hanged one sweats and chokes, and any such liquors from his body, mouth or, best of all, his prick, is proof against all devilment and a charm against infertility – see, the others are there before me! Wait there!' And he was gone, amid the whirl of arms and legs of those who were pressing forwards to avail themselves of the special charms of a hanged man.

I remained where I was, not because he had expected me to be there when he returned, but because I was still in mental turmoil. There was in me the surface

438

disappointment of the rest of the crowd who had been robbed of the expected dance of death, but deeper down there was a cold, sick feeling that I could not as yet explain. It had been my first experience of a hanging, and it had not been at all what I had expected. Two minutes ago, on that tiny platform, there had stood a virile, intelligent, and handsome young man in the prime of his life, and now all there was was an ugly, lifeless puppet dangling on the end of a rope, and the two bore no resemblance to each other. I knew of life and death, or had thought I did, for was not the dancing March hare tomorrow's dinner, and the crop-heavy pigeon, flying to the sun, just another day's pie? They had been as real in their lives as this man, and had died as quickly and violently, so where was the difference? Because he had been a man? But I had seen dead people before: the old ones, at peace now, in their grave clothes; the infants too young to look more than dolls; the odorous scraps of rag and bone that hung at the crossroads . . . . Never before, though, had a man been alive, vital, breathing one moment and the second later become this obscene remnant that hung ready to be mauled in posthumous affection by a sensation-seeking crowd. And as for punishment: punishment for a zest for life, a way of living that did not conform to that usually accepted by society? True, he had killed, but the poor wretches that were to follow were mere petty thieves – and who could guess at their temptations? I, too, was now a thief; I was finding it easier and easier to accept the life that Lil and her kind lived, see it as a necessity, but society said that that, too, was wrong. Society said it was wrong that Jack and I had been lovers and that Nick and I were sharing a bed. God said that too, but I do not believe He would have hung Robin Rich; after all, His son saved a place in paradise for one thief . . . .

My companion returned, fighting his way through the seething mob to my side, and thrust a sweat-soaked rag against my nostrils.

'There! You're lucky; his shirt was already torn, and by

the time those old whore-mongers have finished, I doubt whether even his drawers will be safe . . . .'

My senses sick with smell and sensation I glanced back at the scaffold: a disorderly mob, mainly women, were fighting and weeping over a half-clad form that was only now being freed from the noose and lowered from the platform. The soldiers, ostensibly there to prevent riot, were making half-hearted gestures with the butts of their muskets, but there seemed no official policy to prevent the pillage of the body. The shirt had disappeared, scissors and a knife were busy about the disordered, damp hair, and women were embracing and fondling his most intimate parts. An infant, crying bewilderedly, was lifted up and pressed against the corpse's stomach, and all the while someone was shouting and screaming. Glancing to my left I saw the cart where the next ones for execution were fast; they were writhing against their bonds, sobbing and hysterical. All at once nausea rose like a tide in my throat and nostrils and, jumping down from the step of the carriage, I started to fight my way through the mob and away from the scaffold, careless of tactics and careless also of the bruises and buffets I received in consequences.

It seemed like an hour but it could not have been more than five minutes later that I found myself in comparative seclusion in a street away from the crowd, leaning gasping against a convenient projecting chimney breast. My hair hung in rat's-tails in my eyes, my dress was torn in two places and I was dripping with perspiration. People were still pressing foward eagerly towards the hangings, their faces alive with expectation, but they were too busy to notice me and I shrank back into shadow, only afraid that they would hear my gasping breaths above the growl of the crowd, the creak of the cart as the next consignment was brought forward, and the sobbing of the hapless victims. I was cold and I was hot, I breathed deep and I breathed shallow, and my fingers were still clenched around the scrap of linen from Robin Rich's shirt; I was about to fling it from me in revulsion, when suddenly I stopped. Why throw it away? Because I felt sick? Because I found it difficult to condone hanging? Because the mob had disgraced themselves and degraded Rich's brave attempt to give the manner of his dying a dignity the living of it had lacked? Because of the blind superstition attached to the sweat of a dying man? In facing death the condemned man had shown a courage denied to many, a courage that not only had kept him upright and laughing till the last moment, but also gave him the impetus to play his last trick with the hangman and cross the boundary between being and unbeing in his own way . . . . My breathing quietened and slowly I folded the scrap of linen and tucked it in my bosom. It would serve to remind me in the future, perhaps, that given a little courage we can still shape our own ends.

'Last words of merry Robin . . . his message to the ladies . . . exploits of the famous highwayman . . . words of repentance from the gallows . . . .' The voice had been in the background for some minutes, but it was only now that the words began to make sense. A balladmonger in crimson coat, blue embroidered waistcoat, snuff breeches and shoes with red heels and blue bows was hawking his wares. A mincing walk, languid air; pale face with delicately hooked nose and a patch on the left cheek; a young-old face –

'Barnaby!' I shrieked, and ran out and hugged him, much to his dismay and the danger of the sheaf of papers he was carrying. Instinctively he tried to avoid my embrace, pushing me away with futile little gestures, backing up till he was against the wall I had just left. 'You must remember!' I almost shouted, wild with delight to have found someone from my other life. 'The big forest – you played highwayman and then stayed with us for a while – Jack and Tom and Annie and Sam –'

'Jack? Jack! Yes, of course I remember Jack. But – that was two years ago. And I don't remember you.' Delicately he dusted me from him, affront in every movement. 'And how is the dear man?'

441

Despair reduced me to momentary silence. I had hoped – oh, so much! – that he would have had more recent knowledge of Jack, would have come across him somewhere, would have exchanged news with someone who had seen him . . . . Now I felt as though my recently inflated world of two minutes since had collapsed like a soap bubble.

'I hoped you would know – would have seen – You do remember me? I was the boy, the one you said was too pretty. Sprat.'

He gazed at me in stupefaction. 'Demme, yes! The lad with mismatched eyes and an inviting arse! Did you change your mind, then?'

'I just changed my clothes,' I said impatiently. 'Not my mind, nor my sex. I was a girl all the time, only nobody knew then.'

From somewhere he produced a quizzing glass and eyed me from top to toe.

'You are, too. A girl, I mean. Always said you were too – Never mind. What are you doing in London town?'

The question caught me unprepared, so I told him.

'Living in a high-class brothel? Not your style, I shouldn't have thought. Can't see what the dear man was about to let you do it: thought he had an eye to you himself that time, though if he didn't know you were skirt . . . .'

'Oh, he soon found out.' I was desperate to explain before the others – before Nick – came seeking me. 'But he doesn't know I'm here. We became separated when I came on ahead to find lodgings –' Out of the corner of my eye I could see a familiar figure pushing its way through the press of sightseers at the fringes of the mob, even as a loud roar signalled that another of the poor wretches was swinging. 'Quick, Barnaby: where can I contact you?'

Like me, he was surprised into truth. 'George Inn at Southwark, across the river. Scrivener and chaunter-cull, at your service. But –'

I gave him a little push, grabbing one of his papers as I

did so. 'Now go, and for Christ's sake don't look as though you know me!'

After one startled look at the oncoming figure of Nick, obviously and vengefully bound in my direction, he tripped away hastily as I collapsed to the cobbles crying, the ballad paper clenched in my fist.

Nick jerked me to my feet, none too gently.

'What the hell do you think you're doing? One minute you can't abide crowds and are pleading sickness, the next you're into the thick of it and cheering with the rest! Hanging on to some bumpkin on a carriage and tearing your dress – or did he do that? Then you do the disappearing act, and now you're sitting in the dirt bawling your eyes out!' He shook me again, and I could understand his anger and bewilderment. For a while, one way and another, he must have thought he had lost me, and that he could not bear to do; not because of love or any such unmanly emotion, but because I was his uneasily won possession, and until he decided to sell me, swop me, or simply throw me away I was his, to behave as impeccably as Caesar's wife. Then again I was behaving like all the temperamental females men hated to admit they couldn't understand: he had probably convinced himself I shouldn't behave that way just because anything he chose must be above such things. 'And who was that you were gossiping to when I came up?' he asked, between shakes.

'Oh, just some Jew-boy catamite that was selling a rubbish report on Robin Rich's death,' I said apologetically. 'And I wasn't gossiping: I was giving him an earful because of the lies he had printed, even before the poor man swung.' I pulled away and straightened my dress. 'I even threatened him with the magistrates, and you saw him scuttle away like a naked crab looking for its shell –'

I had thought he would smile, but he was scowling, and his handsome face momentarily lost its boyish charm, becoming sharp and cunning.

'Just don't you ever go near those magistrates, my dear, not ever! Because if you do . . .' and he drew his hand in an expressive gesture across his throat. 'Madame don't like magistrates, and neither do I.'

It took me quite five minutes to bring a smile to his face, and another ten to get his arm around me again, but I had learned my lesson and watched very carefully what I said and did from then on. So, we were friends again, and lovers, and for a while I pushed the providential meeting with Barnaby to the back of my mind. But sometimes, when Angel eyed me thoughtfully, or Nick was late in at night, or the sounds of screams and cries from next door could not be ignored; sometimes when I counted over the pitifully few coins I had managed to collect; sometimes when I heard the sound of a pipe or heard a dog bark; then I remembered that Barnaby could be a person to run to and hide.

I could not know how soon I was to need that haven . . . .

22

It was about three weeks later that Angel tossed a letter into my lap after dinner with the remark: 'It seems your friends fully deserve their name of travellers; I suppose they will be doing the Grand Tour next . . . .'

Of course it had been opened and read; I only hoped the postage she had had to pay was worth it. It was postmarked 'Bristol' and dated 20 June.

'My Dear – I am getting this Writ in Haste by a clerk near the docks. I know I could not hear from you as you did not know where we were but I hope this finds you as it leaves me in Tolerable Health and Spirits though I daresn't think how I may feel on the Crossing! For you see Jack has taken it into his head to –' I turned the page '– go for the towns of Ireland! I am sure they be full of little better than Savages for my sister up North do say as they comes across to Trade but dress poorly and spend it all on Ale. But Jack says he has his Reasons so we shall not be in London for the Fair but I hopes to see you in Kirkham for Christmas if you can come. Love, Annie.' The next bit was written round the edges of the letter. 'Post-scriptum: must not forget as Tom sends his regards and Matthew would too I'm sure. Post-post-scriptum: Toby and Daisy well as ever so is that Wretched Bird worse luck.'

Tears stung my eyes: she would have said if Jack had forgiven me. She had remembered to reassure me about my darling Toby, with his grin and his crooked, wagging tail . . . . I blinked hard, but a persistent drop trickled down my nose and blotched the ink; the word 'Ireland' was drowned in a salty sea.

'Thank you, Angel,' I said as calmly as I could. 'Would you like to read it again?' Glancing across I saw that those normally hooded eyes were full of a hideous gloating enjoyment, and I realized at last how much she must hate me. A moment later she had shaken her head and her eyes dropped once again to her stitching, but I was left with a cold shiver running down my spine. I had been aware that she disliked me as a person and was determined to get me across to Madame's where she obviously thought I belonged, but I had not realized the extent of her loathing. I supposed it mostly had to do with my monopolization of Nick, and I determined to stay out of her way as far as I could until I could make good my escape. And now there would be no quick running to Barnaby for a few weeks while waiting for St Bartholomew's, as I had planned, for I could not be sure of seeing any of them till Christmas came round again; that was five months ahead, and I had barely enough saved to last three weeks.

Taking up my mending I savagely cursed both Ireland and the Irish to myself so effectually and with such venom that I pricked myself badly twice.

July was a hot month but August was worse, and

445

September was hotter still. The air was breathless, everything stank, there was no way of cooling oneself. All the
windows, even those that were normally nailed fast, were
opened as far as they would go in the hope of catching a
late-night breeze, and the freshest food smelled putrid by
the time it came to table. No one had ventured to eat fish
for some time, even on Fridays, because it was not worth
bringing from the ports, and pies were crawling as soon
as they were cut open. I do not know how the very rich
fared, but there was no ice locally for chilling the white
wine and we all took to drinking tea, for at least it brought
one out in a refreshing sweat that cooled down the blood.
Nick and I slept naked with the sheet and cover thrown
back and it was too hot to make love. We all became
increasingly irritable and the business across the way
fell off considerably. This was seasonal, of course, at
Madame's, for the gentry went to their country estates at
this time of the year, so Lil told me, but this year was
worse than usual. I had taken to going across to her rooms
in the early evenings, for it was cooler than in my stuffy
little attic, and she had few enough customers for it not to
matter. We drank tea and gossiped and scandalized whilst
the air cooled by a degree or so and the moths flew through
the open windows and flirted with the candles until I felt
I could not breathe with their fluttering. Bats had a fruitful
time amongst the eaves, as did the rats on the lower levels:
so much food was left at the markets or thrown away as
we grew more disinclined to eat through the heat that the
rats were soon as fat as the tabby cat across the way that
was fed a diet of seedcake and cream, and they soon grew
casual and bold in their manner, strolling in the daytime
with the confidence of those who knew that there are none
with enough energy to hinder them to any purpose. In
mid-September came a rumour of a cholera outbreak near
the docks and Madame decided to send the majority of
the girls for an enforced holiday in the countryside till the
danger passed.

'It's not that I can't get the gels,' I heard her explaining to someone as I crept back from Lil's room one night (she had left me her key to feed her canary bird and water her orange tree). 'It's not the supply, it's the training. My gels is quality, and it takes time to make 'em that way . . . .'

In fact Lil came back home only a few days later: she had been badly bitten by some insect, and had insisted on being returned to the dangers she knew.

'Not that the countryside don't look nice, dearie, but it's so boring! All those cows and sheep and horses and fields and trees! Not a decent house for miles – no theatres, no gaming houses! And the hours they keep . . . . Crack of dawn and the day not even aired, and there's all those wretched birds a-scrawkin' and a-hollerin' with no one to put the cover over 'em: there's people as should know better driving cattle down the lanes all a-bellerin' to be milked; there's pigs squealin' and dogs barkin' and cocks a-crowin' . . . . And then there's the food! Bread 'n' cheese 'n' ham's all they live off! No tea, no coffee: milk, all the time, would you believe it? They eats at six in the morning, and it's ale for the men, if you please, and but a drop of cider with your dinner if you're lucky. Give me civilization every time, collery or no collery! Got anything for these bites, dearie? Ain't half giving me the screams and fidgets!'

They were nasty indeed, and embarrassing too; up her thighs, at the backs of her knees, on her buttocks and round her waist, and she had made them worse by scratching.

'Thought at one time I'd had a nasty old wassup up me drawers, I did! Lots of them little striped horrors about too, and worse; couldn't reach for a spoonful of preserves without they came buzzin' out and went for you. They was gollopin' away at the fruit in the orchards too, and that's why at first I thought it was one of them, you see, 'cos one day I lay on the grass under the pear trees at the back and snoozed off a bit – it was all that gettin' up early and I'd had a glass or two of that cider; stronger than what it looks that stuff, and doesn't half give you the rumbles, and the other – What was I sayin'? Oh, yes; I falls asleep, and keeps feelin' little nips like it was a feller in my dream when he wants to jolly you up a little; you know, a nibble or two to make you screech a bit; there's a lot that likes you to show you're 'preciating it; gets 'em excited and often brings 'em off without the actual . . . . Tell you the truth I was beginnin' to come all over sweaty and restless meself when this rotten fruit from the tree drops on me left boob and I wakes up all of a jump and there's all these little red marks all over and I has a good scratch, makin' sure there's no one watching first, of course, then I gets up and goes in but these bites gets worse all the time till they all swells up and I can't sleep and for the love of Jesus find summat to sooth 'em!'

I poured out some of her rose-water. 'This'll do for the time being, but you mustn't scratch them! I remember my stepfather saying that insect bites affect people differently: we had one woman in our village that was stung really badly when a hive overturned, and she couldn't breathe and choked and went into convulsions . . . but the beekeeper wasn't affected,' I added hastily, seeing the alarm on her face, 'and you weren't stung by a bee anyway; I think it was ants in your case, and stepfather said they had an acid in their bodies that made their sting swell up.'

'Recall watching some of the little devils earlier, come to think of it,' said Lil. 'Just near where I was sitting there was a little mossy mound and I pokes at it with a stick and they all comes a-runnin' out like a market-full tryin' to get out of the rain, so I laughs and tickles 'em up a bit more and then they was like a fox among chickens . . . . Never have thought the little sods would have had it in them!'

I found a recipe for soothing poultice in Kat Petulengro's herb book and smeared Lil's bites, threatening to tie up her hands like a naughty child that bites its nails or sucks its thumb, if she dared to scratch. I left her sipping hot gin thoughtfully, no doubt regretting the soporific qualities of cider.

That night was hotter than ever; there were abortive rumbles of thunder in the distance and the attic room seemed airless so that we slept hardly at all. In the morning Nick and I had a silly quarrel, over what I cannot now remember, and he flung off at midday to a cockfight, leaving me to tiptoe over to Lil's room, dress her bites and listen to her moans till she dozed off and I could creep back to a desultory supper with Angel, more taciturn than usual. After supper we sat in silence in the parlour, she busy altering a dress, me stifling my yawns over an excessively tedious book of sermons, which was the only book in her collection I had not read at least twice. Outside a church clock struck ten and she stood up briskly, picking threads from her dress.

'There is no call to waste more candles: time to retire. I think.' Turning away to fold her dress she inquired, honey-sweet and bee-sting sharp: 'Expecting Nicholas home tonight?'

Only too aware that Nick had been staying out much later recently I was about to tell her to mind her own business, my usual guard of politeness breached by the heat and her sly attack, when there was the pound of running feet in the normally quiet alley outside, followed by the door below being crashed back on its hinges, then just as violently slammed and bolted, and the noise of someone stumbling erratically up the unlighted stairs. For once we looked at each other as equals, united in alarmed surmise, then the parlour door burst open and Nick staggered into the room, jacket missing, shirt-tails hanging, face pale and strained, sweat dripping from his forehead. For a moment he made as though to come to me, then suddenly turned to Angel, to kneel clumsily at her feet.

'Help me . . . .'

I shall never forget the look of triumph she flashed at me from those iron-hard eyes before stooping to Nick in a rustle of skirts, her face soft and attentive.

'Gently, my dear; tell me all about it, and take your time. You are safe with me, so relax. Sit down, and take a

449

glass of madeira. Gemini!' She pointed to the decanter on the sideboard. Hastily I poured a glass, my hand trembling so that I spilled some of the golden liquid on the wood, to lie there unheeded, blooming the polished oak. Strange: I worried long after whether someone ever bothered to wipe off the wine before it stained irreparably . . . .

He drained the glass and held it out to be refilled.

'Christ! Angel, I never thought I'd make it back here! The other one said he recognized me . . . .'

As I poured the second glass I glanced at them in the mirror above the sideboard. They were like a picture, sufficiently distorted suddenly by being back to front for me to see them for a moment with startled objectivity. He was still kneeling, his face raised in entreaty: a knight suppliant at his lady's feet. And she? A soft, graceful, protective Angel in whom there was no pretence. The slim hand that stroked his disordered curls was full of the tenderness of true affection, the mouth was compassionate, the shining eyes held only solicitude. Fixed in stone she would have had the loving curve of wings to embrace and soften his sharp entreaty; as it was they held their own private moment of time and emotion and I was outside: outside as though I was merely the reflection of my shocked mouth and questioning eyes and they were the true and only reality.

I turned away from the mirror to thrust the refilled glass in Nick's hand, and my voice shattered their still moment.

'Perhaps you will tell me what the hell all this is about?'

Rising to his feet he drained the glass. His face was still dripping with perspiration, his hair wilder than ever; there was a dark stain on his shirt and street-ordure on his breeches. I could smell, too, the acrid sweat of fear, so like that of excited love, yet so different.

'He was an old fellow,' he said hoarsely. 'Christ! I'd've thought his head would've been thicker than that – it was only a little tap, honest it was, a goddamn tickle with a stone wrapped in my jacket – And all for a mangy couple

450

of ha'pence and a broken watch! He looked well-sprung, but . . . Jesus! Who'd've thought he'd bleed so!'

Macbeth . . . . 'He's dead, then?' I said, hearing with surprise the lack of emotion in my voice.

'You must be jokin'! Of course he's bleedin' well dead!' he snapped at me, not noticing the grisly pun.

Ridiculously I wanted to giggle: it was all so dreadful, so shocking, that I needed a relief from tension. I felt that Shakespeare had known what he was doing when he used Macbeth's porter . . . .

'What are you going to do?'

But it was Angel who answered.

'Get away, of course, and as soon as possible!'

'I don't – I can't –'

' "I" nothing! We go together.'

'We – we're runnin' then?'

'And fast: I'm not having you topped for an accident,' and she took his arm.

An accident? That a man had died, perhaps, but he would still be alive if Nick had not committed a felonious assault. So that made him a murderer.

'Nick, up to your room: Gemini, fetch hot water from the kitchen. When you are thoroughly cleansed of that dirt, Nick, bring all that you are now wearing and burn it down here.' She put a light to the fire. 'Both of you pack what you will need for, say, two weeks.' She was rapping out her words with a sharp authority I would not have believed possible, and her face was full of animation; gone was the self-effacing Angel with the meek mouth and downcast eyes: here was a woman with purpose who would almost seem to have rehearsed her part a dozen times, move- and word-perfect.

I suddenly realized the full implication of what she had said. 'I am to leave as well?' I asked, hopeful I had heard aright.

'You have been trying to escape for months: don't tell me now you would rather stay? Besides, I shall need your

451

help. Hurry now, both of you!' and she clapped her hands as though we were children.

'What will you be doing?' asked Nick, and for the first time his face showed some of its old animation.

'There are a number of – arrangements to be made. We need transport, a clear start and no pursuit. Trust me,' and she turned him to face her. 'Have I ever let you down?'

He shook his head. 'No. And you do know I never meant to –'

'Enough of that!' she said briskly. 'I told you it was an accident, but the law is the law. Now, hurry: I want to be away in three-quarters of an hour or so, and the time is against us.'

For the next half-hour or so I had no time to think, for I had to organize both Nick and myself. He seemed in a daze still and I had to push and pull him like a doll into washing, shaving, and changing; when I had helped him pack a valise there were still my own belongings to parcel up: a complete change, toiletries, my herb book and sewing things. As I tied my shawl with twine I smelled smoke and guessed that Nick had tipped all his clothes straight onto the fire with no attempt to feed them on bit by bit. Setting the house on fire or choking to death was all we needed and it took another ten minutes to draw the flames up, dispel the smoke and set Nick to work cutting and tearing the cloth into reasonable portions. It was hot work, and I noticed that he helped himself a couple of times from the madeira decanter, without benefit of glass. Sitting back on my heels by the fire, I had time for a couple of minutes of thought.

I remembered guiltily how easily I had slipped into the condonement of what Lil and her companions did; how the memory of the children's fate had slipped into an uncomfortable blur; how I had stolen to provide myself with enough to escape: and now, the worst crime of all – murder. If I went through with this I should be an accessory after the fact and condemned as such, although

I had been nowhere near at the time and had not made the decision to run. Suppose I stayed, though, and let them escape? At worst I should find myself over at Madame's within an hour of discovery, at best I should still have to face a charge of concealing a crime: no chance of pleading ignorance with the house in the state it was. What alternatives were there? I could run out into the street and cry havoc, let them be caught and have Nick face the gallows, but the idea was unthinkable. I could have let Angel face the music with little heart-searching but Nick was another matter. We had been lovers and I knew that whatever he did I should always hold him in fondness, if no more; the idea of seeing him mount the scaffold to dangle in a slow, terrified, agonized suffocation was too horrific to contemplate, however evil the deed he had committed. Angel had been half right: he had not, and never would, I thought, intend to kill in cold blood – all the same I could not dismiss it with her blithe assumption of accident, as if that excused everything. So what to do? There was no question after all: I should compound all my previous felonies, help them as far as lay in my power to get away, then disappear to the safety of Barnaby for a while till I could return north to Annie; perhaps for a time it would be safer to become a boy again, once we were clear.

I glanced across at Nick: strange how quickly his adherence had altered when a crisis threatened. Once, he would have turned naturally to me, but now it was all Angel, Angel, Angel; granted, she had showed a determination and leadership I would not have thought possible, and she had been the one who had had the task of raising Nick from a child, so she was a sort of surrogate mother, but the irrational, feminine part of me still felt a twinge of unreasoning jealousy. A stupid time to find out that I had been fonder of Nick than I thought, and I gave myself a mental shake, smothered the emotion and went down to the kitchen to see if I could find some easily portable food for our journey, for God only knew when we should feel free enough of pursuit to sit at a table again. Nancy was snoring on her truckle bed and I quietly helped myself to cold chicken, half a loaf, and a bottle of red wine. Wrapping these in a clean cloth I tiptoed out again, glancing fearfully at the bolted front door as I did so. Every sound from the alley outside had my heart thumping, afraid the watch would be turned to any minute and batter down the door to find their murderer: in spite of the closeness of the air I found I was shivering. But the street outside was quiet, and the only noises came from next door, where the depleted staff were just starting their long night.

I turned to go up the narrow stair and was halted by the sound of the door into Madame's opening and then closing, and the squeak of a stealthy key. Turning, I saw Angel by the light of my candle, her back pressed against the door, her arms full of a great bundle of what looked like clothes. For a moment we stared at one another and I noted the quick rise and fall of her breast, the greenish pallor of her face, the uncharacteristic shine of sweat on her skin: her eyes were almost closed, but not in their usual demure masking of expression. They looked as though the lids were swollen with crying, or the aftermath of sex . . . .

After a moment she moved, pushing herself away from the door as though it was an effort and coming to the foot of the stairs. She smiled, still with that sleepy look in her eyes.

'All ready, Gem?'

I nodded. 'I've just packed up some food – in case –'

'Good thinking: we shall be hungry before the night is out. Up you go, then; we haven't much time.'

Some ten minutes or so later she joined us in the parlour. She was as immaculate as ever: hair smoothed behind her ears, dressed in sober grey with a white neckerchief and a straw bonnet. She brought a small valise, a large bundle

454

and a dark cloak; in spite of the relative sizes, the valise looked the heaviest.

She surveyed us both with disapproval.

'If we are to travel together I intend we shall draw as little notice as possible: at the moment you would do nothing but attract attention. Nick, a tricorne to hide that unruly hair of yours, and a proper cravat, not a silk scarf.' She turned to me. 'That dress looks as though you cleaned the grate with it: upstairs on my bed you will find another. It's not new, but better than the one you are wearing. And tie your hair back with this ribbon.' She took the candle from my hand. 'You won't need that: I don't want lights on all over the house.'

The curtains were not drawn in her room, and I found the dress without difficulty; she was slimmer than I, and taller, but it fitted tolerably well and I was pleased, and a little surprised, to find that it was a dress I had thought one of her favourites: in fact I was almost certain she had been wearing it this evening. It was pale blue, with a round neck and a row of yellow velvet bows down the front of the bodice, and as I struggled with the fastenings in the bar of moonlight which touched the bed I realized that my fingers must have been clumsy in their hurry, for when all was done I found that the top bow was missing. There was no time to search for it, for I heard Angel's urgent voice on the stair. When I joined them by the front door I noticed she was still carrying the valise and the wrapped bundle: I made to take the bundle from her to lighten the load, as Nick was carrying my parcel and his own parcel, but she shrugged away my hand.

'Thank you: it is not heavy. Now, down the street, one at a time, and I'll meet you at Nixon's stables about a hundred yards down the first turning to the right and then right again. Nick: you first, and *don't* hurry. Remember, you're a respectable citizen, out a little late, it's true, but you have been staying with a friend and are carrying your belongings back to your lodgings, so *think* that way as you walk. Gemini, the same applies to you: think innocent,

455

but don't dawdle. If you're stopped, Nick, drop the bags and make it to the yard: I've got a couple of the boys on watch. If you are stopped, Gemini, they will create a diversion, but you must make for the stables just the same: I'll find you.' She opened the front door a trifle and peered out. 'All clear: off you go, Nick!'

She watched him to the corner, then gave me a little push and I stumbled after him. At the corner, before I turned into the brighter road ahead, I glanced back. There was no sign of Angel at all. For a moment I wondered in panic whether she had decided to ditch us and run on her own, then realized that for the moment it made no difference to me: I was out on the street on my own with only the few pence I had saved between me and penury. My first task was to keep up with Nick, for if she had reneged we would at least have each other and two heads were better than one. Accordingly I followed instructions and thankfully found him some five minutes later, crouching in the shadow of the stables.

Rising, he held me close and I could feel him shaking. 'All right, girl?'

I nodded. 'And you?'

'Sure. Just wish I could get the sight of all that blood out of my mind . . . . Where's Angel?'

'She'll be along in a minute.' And I hoped that I was right.

But it was longer than that; I heard the quarters from a nearby church twice and listened to the stamp and shuffle of restless hooves from the stable till they sounded like pursuing feet, before a figure detached itself from the shadows and a small urchin pulled at Nick's sleeve.

'She says to go on to the next street and turn left. Carriage with black and white nag,' and he was gone, back to the darkness. I wondered if he were one of the 'blind' man's boys, even as I followed Nick and we shrank back into a doorway as a couple of late-night roisterers wavered down the middle of the road.

The carriage, an old rickety one with torn leather seats

456

and floor covering of evil-smelling straw, was already occupied.

'Hurry!' said Angel.

The contraption swayed and jolted over the cobbles and the horse's hooves made an uneven sound, so that I wondered if it had cast a shoe: I tried to unfasten the leathern window flaps but Angel pulled back my hand.

'Be still . . . . Do you want to advertise our presence?'

After what seemed an age, and no further word spoken, the carriage drew to a halt and the driver tapped on the roof with his whip. It was misty, and I could smell the river. We watched the carriage disappear down a side street, then Angel hitched her skirts higher, picked up the bundle and valise and nodded towards a narrow alley.

'Right: we walk from here.'

'But I thought . . . . The river . . . .'

'Exactly! Easier, quicker; that's why we are going the other way. *They* will all think –' and I could hear the scorn in her voice '– that we have gone by water; especially as I sent one of Beelzebub's boys ahead to bid me a boat: it will be waiting by the steps now.'

I could not but admire her foresight even as, stumbling and cursing, Nick and I followed her down the mean, narrow, deserted streets. In time we came to broader and better-lit thoroughfares where some clubs and dining houses were still open for business, but we must have been walking for nearly an hour before she stopped at last before the yard of a large inn called the Lamb and Fleece. A late coach had just swung through the gateway, and ostlers were uncoupling the horses even as the half-dozen or so passengers alighted.

'Ideal,' said Angel's voice in my ear. 'Better than I had hoped for. Here, take Nick's valise with your bundle and you can be just another passenger. Get in quick and take a room – any room – for the night. As soon as you can, come down to the bar parlour and order some food to be sent up. We'll be somewhere around and you can let us

457

know – discreetly, mind – where they've put you. We'll follow you up. Go on, hurry!'

It worked because I did not have time to think of failure. They gave me a room on the second floor overlooking the courtyard. Small, but clean; bed, washstand, table, two chairs, and hanging cupboard. Whatever the impropriety of a young lady travelling alone, they accepted my explanation that, being so late, my father would think I had decided to travel another day, and dealt with me without trouble. I passed the location of my room to Angel, and shortly after hot water, a pie, bread, cheese, and a bottle of wine had been brought up to me there was a soft double scratch on the door panels and the other two joined me, bolting the door behind them.

'I told them I would leave the plates and glass outside the door for them to collect,' I said, as Angel swiftly crossed to the window, closed the shutters and pulled the curtains across.

'No point in drawing undue attention to ourselves,' she muttered. 'Well done, Gemini. Now, food. Then we shall have to rest, taking it in turns on the bed. The coach we want doesn't leave till ten in the morning: we can slip down when the maid goes to order your breakfast. We'll divide out the food we have as best we can. Nick, you sit on the bed with one of the plates, and Gemini and I will manage with the other on the table. Now, with the other bottle of wine and the fowl you packed, my dear, we should dine tolerably well . . . .'

It was after one by the time we had eaten. As the hour struck Nick yawned and Angel shivered.

'The dark hour . . .' she said. 'Someone walked over my grave. Now, we must arrange some sleep. I shall lie down for an hour and you can call me at a quarter past two.' And she lay down, her cheek pillowed on her hand, and appeared to go to sleep at once. I envied her her relaxation – I had never felt further from slumber.

458

Nick went over to the window and, forgetting her earlier injunction, opened the shutters and pulled aside the curtain to peer out into the night.

'Still misty,' he said.

I joined him, looking out over the dim, sleeping, crooked roofs of London town. He slipped an arm about my waist and pulled me awkwardly against him.

'Wonder when I shall see them again – if ever . . . .'

'What?'

'London chimneypots, London fog . . . .'

'Where are you two going, then?'

We had been speaking in whispers, and he nodded back at the sleeping Angel. 'She knows: I shall find out when I get there, I suppose. Always told me from a kid as she'd make our fortunes. Abroad, she used to say: used to tell me tales of how we would eat off gold plate and have hundreds of black servants a-waiting on every whim. Never get up till noon, eat meat every day and lie out on silks and satins under a sun that shone all day.' He smiled reminiscently. 'Believed every word she said, I did.'

And you still do, I added silently. I hesitated; I wanted to know the answer to my next question, but dreaded the answer.

'And me: what has she planned for me?'

'You? Oh, she has some money put by for you; enough to see you through till you can join those travelling friends of yours. She told me that; good friend to you is Angel – can depend on her all right.'

I should have felt reassured, but . . . .

'She's always looked after you, hasn't she?'

'Always; got me out of a scrape or two before this. Nothing serious, mind, just embarrassing. Taught me a lot about life in general, too: made me learn my letters, and beat me when I wouldn't concentrate. She was my first – A man couldn't ask for a better woman: she'll make someone a fine wife someday.'

I was unreasonably hurt, unreasonably jealous too, although I knew he could never mean the same to me

459

again after the events of the night: not only the murder, but the way he had gone to pieces, shrunk down to a helpless child again, no longer strong and dependable. For no reason at all I suddenly thought of Jack: he would not have panicked.·

'You said the same sort of thing about me, once . . . .'

'Oh, you; you know how I feel about you! Quite, quite different . . . .' and for a moment he was the old Nick and his lips were on mine; for an instant I felt a return of the strong urges he had so often awoken in me. Then I pushed him away.

'It's too late, Nick: that's all finished, it has to be. Our roads lie in different directions now.'

'But we're still friends? I shouldn't like to leave without it being all right between us . . . . A kiss for goodbye, little Gem?'

I gave it to him, and willingly, for I had almost loved him once.

'God! You're enough to turn a parson . . . . We could have been a good team, you and I, couldn't we, girl? Never fancied another like I did you – and remember I saved you from . . . the other, didn't I? Know what I mean?' Suddenly he chuckled. 'Christ! I'd give a lot to be a flea on her tits when she wakes and finds all her birds are flown: the girls'll get all hell for a couple of days!'

I thought of Madame Bonneville, that fat black spider with her spotted mittens and unctuous attempts at gentility and was glad, glad! that she had lost these two.

He yawned. 'What I wouldn't give for a proper kip!'

'Sit down at the table and rest your head on your arms,' I suggested. 'I'll wake Angel when it's time.'

I remained at the window, listening to his restless shiftings and the creak of the chair; outside, the maze of rooftops were dim in mist. I could see as far as a clock tower some two hundred yards away, but farther there were not even the shuttered eyes of windows. Somewhere cats were courting, a dog barked, someone quarrelled, a restless horse whinnied down in the stables, someone was

460

snoring heavily in a room down the corridor, there were slow footsteps on a stair, and, far off, the cry of the watchman: 'Two of the clock, a fine night, and all's well . . . .'

But all was not well; Nick had killed a man, however accidentally, and we were all fugitives from the law. I had no idea how long it would be before I could find Jack and the others, nor how I would live till then. I supposed I could make my way north to Annie in December but that was nearly three months away, and I had no inkling of how much Angel would give me. My only hope was the doubtful hospitality of Barnaby at Southwark, but he could not be expected to keep me. I should have to ask him to find me work, however menial, and hope I could save enough for the journey north. So, first stop the George Inn at Southwark. Once back with Annie and I had explained and been reunited with Jack, everything would be all right again: it must be. He might take time to forgive me but in the end he would, he surely would. He must . . . Toby would; if he had not forgotten me. And surely Tom –

There was a hand on my arm. 'It's near half-past two. You forgot to call me.' Angel stood there as neat and tidy as she always was. 'Never mind; you get an hour or so and I'll keep watch.'

I was sure I should not be able to sleep but as soon as I closed my eyes, it seemed, I was dreaming. Dreaming myself back in the sunshine with a Jack dressed in a robe hung with glass that glinted and flashed in the light, riding that wretched Wosabella and juggling with six turbans he had borrowed from Sam Alley-Come. Toby, dressed in small breeches and coat and smoking a pipe, was walking on his hind legs, and John – I had forgotten John! – was dancing a reel with Annie in the altogether. Nick, in a large flowered apron, was washing out Annie's smalls and I, back in my boy's clothes, was flying up and down in the trees crying: 'Look at me! Look at me!', until Jack rode up and, binding me like a webbed fly, hung me from the bottom branches of an oak tree while a whole crowd

461

of dwarves with wooden spears ran at me with mouths wide open on evil grins –

I think I must have called out, for I woke in a panic sweat with Angel's hand over my mouth. I was all tangled with the bedclothes, and she tutted as she pulled me loose.

'You were dreaming. It's four of the clock: Nick's turn.'

He needed no persuading and was snoring gently in a moment of his head touching the pillow. Angel flung a shawl over his legs.

'There: he can sleep until six.'

Going over to the washstand I splashed my face and arms with the now cold water and hastily combed my tangled hair. Seeing Angel's continued neatness made me doubly aware of how sticky and untidy I felt, and no doubt looked. But the cold water went a long way towards waking me up, for I was still half asleep and could not stop yawning in a cavernous, unladylike way.

Angel watched me for a moment, then motioned me to the chair opposite her at the table. 'Have you decided what you will do?'

'I – I think I shall try and find the troupe – Mr Landless.'

'I thought your friend Jack was in Ireland?'

I remembered she had read my letters from Annie. 'Yes. Well, it depends. I think I know of somewhere I might get work till they return. A friend . . . .'

'South or North?'

'South, actually: Southwark.' I was annoyed with myself the moment I had told her: I was still unconvinced that she wished me well.

'How convenient: we ourselves are taking the coach to Plymouth in the morning. We can travel partway together – unless you fancy the longer trip?'

'Longer?'

'Hush! I do not want to wake Nick.' She glanced over her shoulder, but he was so obviously oblivious that she turned back reassured. 'Yes; I said longer – and further. We go to the Americas.'

'America?' It was half the world away.

'A land of opportunity, I am told. A new beginning for us both.'

'But what shall you do? How will you live?'

'My dear Gemini, do you not think I have planned and schemed and saved for this very day? I have known, ever since I was about nine years old, that there were two things I must accomplish in my life: one that was mine alone, and the other that would be accomplished only with the company of Nick: us two, together. Together, Gemini!' And now she looked straight across at me, her eyes no longer veiled by those heavy lids. 'For I have known that ever since they brought him to me as a child that he belonged to me. To me, Gemini, and once we leave these shores we shall be bound by an even stronger tie than that which holds us now, for he will be mine in name as well as fact. When we are on board ship I intend that the captain shall marry us, and Nick will not refuse. He will agree with gratitude, for he will remember only that I have saved him from the gallows – or so he will believe,' and she smiled. 'It was well planned, was it not?'

'But – but you couldn't have known he would kill that man?' Even as I spoke a dreadful suspicion of the truth robbed my words of surprise.

'Kill? He killed no one. He thinks he did, and that is enough. I should have left it longer, found some other way, but you, dear Gemini, you were proving a trouble; he was becoming foolish over you and forgetting his true loyalties. None of the others had lasted so long and I had to precipitate matters a little. So, you see, it was all your fault that I had to deceive him.'

The girl was mad: how could she sit there so quiet and contained, speak of murder as though it were something that could be conjured out of the air and disappear as easily and then blame the whole terrible business on me?

The candlelight shone like twin yellow flames in those strange grey eyes and she continued as if I had asked a question out loud.

'How did I do it? An out-of-work actor, a handful of silver, a bladder of pig's blood under a soft-crowned hat, and the blind man's boys to arrange transport as far as the river; they know there was a boat waiting, but not that we did not take it. Our trail is cold.' She anticipated me again. 'And if you attempt to tell Nick what I have just told you, I shall deny every word; I shall have no hesitation in telling him that you have concocted a wild tale – a fortune-teller's trick – to hasten him to the gallows for your own selfish ends. I shall tell him you have concocted the story of murder-no-murder in order to escape us both and go back to your travelling friends, having taken Madame's jewels, ready to blame us for that too.'

She was not mad after all: just diabolically cunning. 'If you wanted to be rid of me so much, why didn't you let me leave long ago?'

'At first you were meant for Madame's, so I had to be sure you would not escape. Afterwards, after he – had become fond of you, it was he who made sure you would not leave. That was when I knew I should have to – dispose, of the threat you posed to our happiness.'

'You did not seem to mind our relationship at first . . . .'

'He broke them all in that way, told me it meant nothing, and when I found you both in bed that morning I only thought it was the quickest way to get you across with the others. A week at most, they usually lasted. But you – you had to be different. I hated you for it. I still do.' Her voice was quiet and unemotional as ever, only her eyes were now those of a bird of prey, fierce and wild in the shifting candle flame.

In spite of the closeness of the room I shivered. 'I never wished to hurt you; all I wanted was to rejoin my friends. As to Nick – he has been very kind to me and I shall always be fond of him but I am not, and never was, in love with him. We both knew right from the beginning, I think, that our relationship was only a temporary thing; and tonight we said goodbye.'

'I know: I heard you.'

'I thought you were –'

'Asleep? You miss a lot that way. I manage with very little. As for now – time enough for sleep when we are safely aboard.' And she looked down at her left hand as if she could already see the gleam of a gold ring.

'What shall you both do once you arrive?' I asked, for this strange girl – no, not girl: woman – was sure to have made even more comprehensive plans for her future with Nick; I had reached the stage when I would have believed anything was possible with her. I must have looked much like a terrified rabbit watching the deadly dance of a stoat: I could not have ceased to listen in horrid fascination had the building caught fire.

'Do? Why, what we best know, of course. I shall open a small – at first, anyway – and discreet brothel, catering exclusively for those with more money than sense. There will be music, soft lights, gaming, a little dancing perhaps; entertainment to titillate the most jaded palate, and my girls will be the most beautiful and accommodating in the country. Everything will be run on genteel lines, a model for others . . . .'

She sounded just like a handbill, but her voice held the conviction of truth.

'That will take much money, surely?'

'No problem: I have been thrifty over the years. I have also taken what was rightly mine. See?' From beneath the table she brought out the leather valise she had insisted on carrying earlier; it was fashioned like an overlarge purse. She placed it on the table between us. 'In there are coins and jewellery worth over eighteen hundred guineas.' My brain was numb: it could not absorb amounts like that, but automatically I reached out to take momentarily the weight of the case. 'Heavy, isn't it? In there are a hundred guineas, or mostly the equivalent in gems, for every year of my life since – I became aware of certain facts. The facts of life, you could say. Two guineas for every week, seventy-two pennies for every day, three

465

pennies an hour for all those years of slaving, pain, misery and fear . . . . Oh, yes; I was cheap at the price!'

'But you couldn't have saved all that, surely?'

'Some of it.'

'And – and the rest?'

'You don't listen to what I say! It was owed to me, and as I said, I took what was mine.'

'You *stole*?'

Her eyes flashed sudden fire, then once again the white lids hooded them. 'It was not stealing; you do not understand. Nick would.'

I said nothing, for I was shivering; even if I were to believe her tale of the masquerade of murder she had contrived for Nick we were still runaways and now thieves, to a sum that meant the nearest gallows for all – Dear God! Let me but escape from this and I would go to church every day for a year –

'You would not understand, Gemini, because you could have no comprehension of that kind of existence. Let me tell you a little of my life, then perhaps . . . .' She went on talking, still in her usual soft, emotionless voice, but as I listened I felt the hairs prickle at the nape of my neck, for somehow the dreadful story I heard became all the more macabre, all the more horrifying, just because it was related with all the animation of a cookery receipt.

'I was the illegitimate daughter of a dancer and a young and impoverished artist: he died, so I believe, of the consumption before I was born, and my mother went on dancing to support us both. When I was a baby she carried me into the dressing room in a hamper, and as I grew I was tethered to a convenient piece of furniture when she went on stage. I believe I·can remember the smell of the sweat, the greasepaint, the tallow; the bright lights, the prettily dressed ladies, the sound of applause like rain on a metal roof – but perhaps that is just wishful thinking. I do remember, however, what she herself looked like. She was tall and slim and fair, and invariably dressed in pale greys or violet; in season she always wore a bunch of those flowers pinned at her breast for that was also her name, at any rate the name she was known by: Violette D'Asprey. She never spoke much of my father, but I heard her pray for him every day: "God keep you, Francis; God give you rest . . ."

'One day when I was five or six years old she dressed me in new clothes and took me to visit her friend, one Georgina Bone, a widow who let out rooms in Cauthery Street. This lady had been, so I understood, my father's landlady and had become acquainted with my mother when she visited him in his illness.' She broke off to snuff one of the candles. 'It will soon be dawn. To cut a long story short, my mother left me with this lady, promising to send money for my upkeep. I remember her kneeling before me to say goodbye, her fingers straightening my hair ribbons and the tears running down her cheeks: "Be a good girl, my Angel, for Mamma is sick: she will soon be with your father, God be praised! Mrs Bone will be your new mother and you must heed what she says and be a brave girl: then you will grow to be a good and gracious lady and be a credit to us both." I was bewildered, but I remember the kisses she gave me and the great hug, and the coughing fit that followed: I believe she had the same disease my father had suffered from. She gave Mrs Bone a purseful of money, for I heard the coins chink, and then turned to me: "God helps those who help themselves, Angelina, remember that; remember too, and never forget, that love is the greatest gift in the world; worth all the dancings and paintings man ever made . . . ."

'I never saw her again.

'After a while I was not unhappy. I had a fixed abode, and my surrogate mother made a great fuss of me, treated me like a little doll, dressing me prettily and making sure all her friends and visitors brought me sweetmeats. I was a comely enough child, I suppose, and she was content to refer to me as her adopted daughter. I believe my real mother forwarded money when she could, for every now and again Mrs Bone would say she had heard from her and that she sent her love and I was to have a new dress or a doll. She must have died some eighteen months later, for Mrs Bone no longer gave me messages from her, and new dresses were few and far between. We moved to a larger establishment and my stepmother had little or no time for me in her new business: I started to outgrow those clothes I had, and I can remember vividly constantly trying to pull down my cuffs to cover my wrists, and walking small to hide my exposed ankles.'

Nick mumbled something uneasy in his sleep, and she rose and drew the covers over him; I watched her tender hand on his disordered hair.

She sat down again. 'Where was I? Oh, yes: the new establishment. Well, Madame Bonneville as she now called herself –' she glanced across at my involuntary start, then lowered her eyes again '– somehow forgot the many promises she had made on my behalf, especially those on treating me as her own daughter; for a time I was truly neglected, and it was only Madame's "ladies" who fed and petted me: without them I think I would have succumbed. The summer of my eighth year was as hot as this one has been, I recall, and I was dressed in a somewhat threadbare shift and nothing else when a gentleman came to call on Madame over some matter of a gambling debt. I was privy to the visit as I was in the little closet off her parlour, cleaning her jewellery with soap and water – I had been given many menial tasks to do at that stage, Madame insisting that a great, fat, lazy young thing like me must earn my keep. The gentleman who called could not take his eyes off me where I worked, and came over and stroked my cheek and ran his hands – cold even in August, I remember, so that their touch sent chill-pimples up on my skin – over my bare arms and calves. Madame called him away and I was sent off on some excuse, but the next time he called I was present too, and wearing a new dress. Madame was ever so loving towards me once more, sitting me on her lap and feeding me comfits and sugar cakes. The gentleman was not allowed to touch me

468

this time, but Madame kept hugging and kissing and tickling me on her knee so that my skirt rode right up to my thighs. He came again the next day and the next, and for each day I had a new dress and my hair in ribbons; and after a week of this . . .' Angel's voice became lower and even less emotional, if that were possible, and I had to lean forward to hear what she said. 'After a week, Madame informed me that he was my new uncle, and that I was to stay with him for a while; I found out later, much later, when I was searching through her papers, that he had paid a couple of hundred guineas for me. When we reached his house I was shown into a large, cold bedroom, given a box of sweetmeats and told to get ready for bed. I must have fallen asleep, for the next thing I remember was the feel of a body next to mine and the smell of violets. I must have been half-awake only, for the smell of the flowers made me think of my mamma, and I reached out to the person next to me for an embrace.

'My shift was torn from my body and cold fingers plucked at my unformed nipples; a mouth slobbered on mine, and after a moment I felt my legs forced apart, and he tried . . . .' Her voice died away and I made an involuntary gesture of repudiation, but after a moment she continued, as calmly as though we had been discussing the weather. 'The next day he insisted I sit with him in the library and listen to him read; he read me fairy stories and recited poems and fed me from his own mouth as though I were his little lap dog, and for a moment or two I believed the night before had been a wild and hideous nightmare, but I was soon disillusioned; that night he rubbed me all over with some nauseating oil and then tried again. His fingers were always so cold . . . . On the fourth night he tied me down between the legs of a table, then draped the top with a big cloth so that it made a tent and crawled in beside me in the dark. He said I had been a naughty little girl and must be whipped for my own good. He beat me for a while with a knotted cord, and then said it was time for the big stick. He kissed me all over, starting with my feet, then tickled me, and said I would like my punishment, because his big stick knew just how to make little girls scream and squirm.

'Then he raped me, not once but three times.

'I was eight years old, I was slim and small, and I stayed conscious through it all. He left me tied and bleeding onto the carpet, but the next morning he came back, unfastened me, bathed, kissed and cuddled me. The next night it was the same, and the next. I haemorrhaged on the fourth night and he panicked and threw me unconscious into the gutter. One of the footmen saw me and told the coachman, and whether it was disapproval of his master's ways or guilty conscience I do not know, but he wrapped me in a dirty horse blanket and had me conveyed back to Madame's. She was away, probably seeking fresh custom for the business, so I was lucky insofar as it was the girls who took me in, or my story might have ended very differently. They did not know of her treachery, so called in the doctor who gave them abortions and treated their minor ailments, and it was he who sewed me up there and then on the gaming table. I was very ill for many days, but the girls – God bless them – looked after me with all the affection and care they would have shown a younger sister, or perhaps even the child they were not likely to have.

'When Madame returned I was recovering – superficially, that was, for the good doctor was no surgeon and I healed as crooked as his stitches – and she put a good face on it, pretending she new nothing but good of my "uncle" and that it was all a terrible mistake; but I never trusted her again, nor did I ever allow her to kiss or fondle me as before.' She looked across at me. 'That experience of mine is one of the reasons, Gemini, why the children you were so distressed about are trained for what is coming to them; even their bodies are prepared for intercourse, and mentally they are deflowered long before they come to us. That is the main difference between them and the innocent child I was: you think me callous and unfeeling towards

470

them, but I can remember what I suffered and that is why I insist on supervising their training.' She stretched like a cat. 'Time to wake Nick.' Snuffing the remaining candle, she went to the window and, pulling aside the curtain, threw open the shutters. 'Another day: the day we begin the rest of our lives . . . .'

'I'm sorry,' I said, and meant it. 'I didn't realize.' And how could I? Even now her tale was so full of horror, of the terror and pain of a betrayed child, that if I had read of it somewhere I would have treated it as fiction. But, from her, I believed every word. And if that had happened to her body, how much it must have affected her mind, her awakening emotions; it explained much of her coldness, her obsessive neatness and self-control. Poor, poor Angel! 'I didn't realize,' I said again.

'Why should you? But perhaps you can now understand a little of why Nick means so much to me.' She glanced over at his sleeping form. 'He was brought to Madame when he was three years old, soon after my – experience. His mother had died of the clap, and he knew no father. She had been one of Madame's first girls, but had been thrown out when she became pregnant. Madame did not want the burden of a child to look after and would have had him put in the poorhouse, but that I asked if I might care for him; perhaps she was surprised into consent, maybe she was still uneasy at her betrayal, I do not know the true reason, but she agreed, providing that I "kept the snivelling brat out of the way and taught him something useful when he grew older". Those were her conditions, and I agreed. When he was seven or eight I saved him from the auctions she had just initiated and sold myself once a week to an elderly schoolmaster so I could learn to read, write and figure well enough to teach him in my turn. He was all I had to love, all I have ever had since my mamma went away. He was by turn my baby, the baby I can never have (for thanks to that rape and the doctor's bungling I am sterile), and then the brother my mother never gave me, and when he was old enough I

471

was his first taste of sex. He hurt me, for I shall never be able to enjoy lovemaking: the doctor sewed me up so that it will always be pain. I never let Nick know, for I loved him more than the hurt. When I could stand it no longer I passed him over to the girls as a willing pupil, and they taught him all that a woman needs. In the meantime I gradually made myself indispensable to Madame: my figuring was good enough to take over the household accounts, my sewing adequate for the girls. I trained the children and encouraged Nick to become her procurer: my reasons for the latter were not unselfish, for by taking one girl after the other and passing them on, he would never grow too fond of any one. I soon knew everything that was going on, where the money was kept, how it was made, the names of our customers, their foibles and idiosyncrasies, Madame's own weaknesses . . . . My first moneys came from blackmailing a young husband with an ugly, but wealthy and jealous wife, who did not know where he spent his evenings. Then I falsified some of the household accounts; not for much, but little and often. Soon, what with one thing and another, I had saved near three hundred guineas.

'Then you came. I had not saved nearly enough, but knew I had to get Nick away before you made a groom of him –' She waved away my demur. 'I do not care what you believed to be true: I know Nick, and I had never seen him so besotted. Besides, you have a brain.

'I had promised us both a life away from all this, a new start in the world with enough money to see us comfortable, and I was only a third of the way there when you arrived. So, something had to be done, and quickly. There was also another debt to repay, and I had not seen my way clear to that either; when you took him from me things became much sharper in my mind and I saw what I must do, for us both. It had been the only way all the time, but the veil of comfortable time had hidden it: you tore that veil aside, and I was no longer blind. And I needed you also, whether you realized it or not; not only for clearing

472

my sight but also for the execution of my plan. Now my debt has been repaid, we have the money we need, and today we start a new life.'

She felt in her pocket and drew out a curiously fashioned silver tube on a chain. Through a glass window I could see it was full of half-guineas, some two dozen or so; at the bottom was a little spring that released one coin at a time. She demonstrated, then slid the coin she had released back onto the top.

'Here is the money I promised you; it should keep you going till you find your friends again. A distinctive little contrivance, is it not?'

I took it and thanked her, wondering at the strange repoussé work: it made the tube into an upside-down old woman who took the coins up her skirt and spat them from her grinning mouth. Not very pretty, in fact rather repulsive, but the money would see me through the next couple of months easily.

'I hope you and Nick will be very happy together,' I said formally, still trying to quell a faint feeling of unease that skulked in a corner of my mind. I should have been relieved and glad for them both and, although she was a thief, I should be safe enough if I hid away for a while until the inevitable hue and cry died down, being innocent even of intent. I hoped, after all she had told me, that they would get clear away. And she had been kind and considerate to me after all, taking me with them, and even giving me one of her better dresses.

I had forgotten to thank her for that, but remedied the omission straightaway.

For the first time since I could remember she laughed, a creaking laugh rusty from disuse and sufficiently unusual to wake Nick, who sat up and yawned.

'Think nothing of it,' she said, amusement still evident in her voice. 'It suits you better than me. But don't get too fond of it: remember, a sparrow is always a sparrow, even if he borrows the peacock's plumes. And sometimes

473

it is better to stay a sparrow.' She laughed again. 'You'll see!'

It was agreed not to risk ordering breakfast in the room, so we went our separate ways down to the bar parlour where I greeted them as acquaintances and we ate together in the obscurity of a corner table.

Angel finished her second cup of hot chocolate and sighed. 'Seems a pity we have to part so soon: are you sure your mind is made up, Gemini?'

I nodded my head. 'Sorry, yes.' But I was not really; much as I should miss Nick, I had no real desire to stay with them any longer than necessary, not only because I was afraid we might be caught if we stayed together, but also because I could never feel Angel was my friend in spite of all she had done for me recently. She deserved her heart's desire, however, and now I knew Nick was innocent I felt he would be content enough in the New World with her to look after him.

He looked happier this morning and had washed, shaved, and brushed his tangle of curls into some semblance of order. Grinning across the table at my serious expression, he stretched out and took both my hands in his warm clasp.

'I shall miss you, Gem!'

'Me too!' I said truthfully.

Angel rose to her feet abruptly. 'Well, we have two hours to fill till the Plymouth coach: I shall go up and do the packing and stitch that – Oh, drat!'

'What is it?' I asked.

'In all that hurry to leave yesterday I forgot my sewing things.'

'I have some upstairs –'

'Yes, but probably not the colours I need. Besides, I may not have time to purchase any before we board ship, not knowing the times of the sailings. I had rather be sure. Gemini, would you be so kind as to slip across to

474

Marksman's while I get everything else ready? I cannot ask Nick, he would not know how to begin.'

Put like that I could not refuse and Angel gave me hurried directions.

'First left, then the second – no, the third – turning on the right and right again at the crossroads; it's a little way down on the left-hand side. I shall need – let me see . . . . A packet of darning needles, another of sewing; a small pair of scissors, a thimble and a darning mushroom; skeins of black and grey darning wool and black, white and grey silk. Oh, and a measure. Here's five shillings; that should be more than enough, and I would not have you break into your own money. We shall settle for the room and breakfast. Do not hurry: there is plenty of time. Did you get the directions?'

I both repeated and followed them precisely, but found myself in a maze of mean streets with no shops except a second-hand clothes and a gin parlour. I heard a nearby clock strike the quarter, retraced my steps and took the second turning on the right with no better result. In the end, mindful of the time, for nearly three-quarters of an hour had passed since I left them, I turned into the first haberdasher's I could find. Again I was at a loss, for I had not thought to ask Angel about the correct shades of grey she required, but in the end I settled for a pale and medium silk and medium and dark wool, trying hard to remember the shade of her dresses and stockings and Nick's hose. As I left the shop I heard the three-quarters strike and congratulated myself, glancing up at the clock, that in spite of all the delays I had still over an hour before the coach at ten o'clock.

I looked again.

The clock must be wrong. When I left Angel had distinctly said there were two hours before the coach at ten o'clock, and the timepiece on the church of St Stephen said fifteen minutes before ten. Not nine. I ran.

When I reached the inn the stable clock said eight minutes to the hour and breathing a mental sigh of relief, for physically I was completely breathless, I noted that the coach had not yet arrived and climbed the steep stairs to my room. Angel and Nick must still be up there packing, or waiting for me; she must have mistaken the time. Thankfully I flung open the door, ready to hurry us all down to the stable yard.

But they were not there.

23

They were not anywhere to be seen. On the bed lay my bundle of belongings and the larger package Angel had been carrying, but of my companions there was no sign. I rushed down to the bar parlour, but they were not there either. I searched in the other public rooms, gaining a few surprised glances for my dishevelled appearance; more worried than I would admit I went back to my room, looking for a letter, a note, something to explain their disappearance, but there was nothing. Apart from Angel's bundle there was nothing to show they had ever been there. I picked it up, hoping for perhaps a note pinned to the underside, but nothing, except for a passing surprise on my part at the weight of the whole thing. I peered out of the window: no coach as yet, but the stable clock said three minutes to the hour.

I hurried down to the yard, where there seemed no hurry to put horses to and no prospective passengers. I approached an ostler who was rubbing down a patient grey.

'Excuse me . . . . The Plymouth coach: does it not leave in a few minutes?' Perhaps it came from further up the road and only called here to pick up. The ostler straightened up and scratched his head, eyeing me up and down familiarly, the ancient straw in his mouth rotating unpleasantly between the gaps in his teeth.

'Well now, little lady,' he said slowly. 'I reckon that somewhere, somehow, there's a coach leaving for Plymouth right this minute; stands to reason as how there must be, some place. But not here. Don't reckon as how I've ever known a coach for Plymouth leave from hereabouts,' and he spat, accurately, by my left shoe. 'Ever heard of a coach going Plymouth-way from hereabouts, Ned?' he inquired of an ancient who was polishing bridle leather in the doorway of the stable.

The old man also spat, but on the buckle of the bridle, then rubbed in a leisurely fashion at the bubbly smear he had left. 'Never known one,' he said. 'Bristol, yes; Oxford yes; York, yes; Plymouth, no. Wouldn't be any sense in it, now would there? Wouldn't cross the Atlantic Ocean if one wanted Paree nor yet the Channel to reach Ameriky . . . . Same here; we sends coaches north and east and west from here 'cos we're north of the river; coaches for the south and southwest goes from south of the river. Common sense.'

'But my friends said they were catching a coach for Plymouth from here at ten o'clock,' I said desperately.

'Well, your friends must've been wrong, 'cos ten's just struck and there ain't no coach. Ain't no more till eight tonight, and that's the Bristol overnight. York went at a quarter after seven, Oxford at nine and a half: tomorrow's the same. Every day, 'cept Sunday, of course . . . .'

I scarcely heard his mumblings, for I was struck by a fresh thought. 'Then perhaps they got on the wrong one. How many passengers were there for the Oxford coach? Did you see a young lady and gentleman – she is fair and pale, and he is handsome, with curly hair and a golden earring?'

They looked at one another, then the ostler winked. 'Lost your young man, then? Gone off with your friend, has he?'

'No – yes – no!' I said angrily. 'He isn't my . . . . We were travelling together, that's all. Were . . . were there none like those two?'

477

'An old gentleman with a lot of luggage . . . .'

'Couple of young fellows outside . . . .'

'Man and woman with two little boys . . . .'

'Fat lady with her maid: all shawled-up she was, with the toothache . . . .'

But not Angel and Nick.

I left them staring after me as I turned and went slowly back to the inn. Surely they would not have left their bundle behind? Perhaps they had discovered their mistake about the coach and had gone seeking alternative travel. In that case they would be back very soon; in fact –

As I opened the door of my room there was a fair-haired figure leaning over the bundles on the bed.

'Angel!' I cried, never having thought I would be so glad to see anyone I did not really care for. 'I thought you and Nick –'

The chambermaid turned guiltily, the bundle Angel had carried free of its ties.

'Ever so sorry, miss: just thought as how I'd tidy up a little, make the bed . . . . I've brought up the soap and water you ordered. It's a bit late but we've been busy this morning. You going to wash the dress up here, then? It won't dry in this weather, you know, even if you hang it from the window. Wouldn't you like me to take it down-stairs for you now, and have it dry by the fire in the kitchen?' She was talking rapidly and fast, more to distract me from the fact that she had been rifling through the bundle on the bed than to do me any service, I guessed.

'Wash? Dress?' I asked sharply, only too eager to get her out of the room. This must be another excuse, just to give the maid a chance to go through the guest rooms.

'Yes. That Jenny, she who does this room regular, had to go and see to her sister what's took bad with the one she's expecting. Afore she go she gave me the message about your dress. She told me that you'd had an argument with your intended and needed strong soap and hot water to wash the bloodstains from your skirt . . . .'

'Blood?' I said stupidly.

478

She pointed to my dress. 'On the side, there.'

I glanced down, then pulled the side of the skirt forwards; there was a rusty stain on the hem and a fainter mark nearer the waist, as if someone had dirtied her hand and wiped it hastily, surreptitiously, behind her back.

'I asked for no soap, but now you've brought it –'

'She said definite as it was the single lady in number nine – and that's you. Told me most particular not to make a song and dance about it, as the lady had given her sixpence to keep it quiet that she'd had this quarrel with her man and caught him with the scissors: looks like dried blood to me . . . . Be wanting this room another night? They said downstairs as I was to ask. It'll be two shillings, service and food extra.' And she held out her hand.

What to do? I had understood Angel to say she would settle for the food and the room, but if she had not it must mean they intended to return. For that, and the bundle on the bed. I did not want to break into my store of money as yet and took out the change from my expedition to buy Angel's sewing things. If I gave this girl a shilling or two and bought something to eat upstairs I could put off settling for the room until they came back.

I handed her the money. 'Fetch me some bread and cheese and a cup of chocolate,' I said as imperiously as I could. 'You may keep the change. I shall certainly be staying another night, and I shall settle with the landlord before I go. You can make the bed later.'

Once she had left me I realized I had been a fool to give her so much, for even with the food she would easily have a shilling for herself and that kind of tip merely drew attention to oneself, the last thing I wanted to do at this juncture. The afternoon drew on in hazy sunshine, but I dared not leave the-room and paced restlessly the few steps between the bed and the window, starting with every sound and drawn irresistibly to the casement with each sound of activity in the stable yard below. I washed the stains in the skirt, not too successfully, and hung it up to dry, thinking as I did how unlike Angel it had been to give me a dress that was dirty: she was usually so scrupulous about everything she wore. I must have brushed against something in our hasty flight of the evening before, that was the only explanation. But it did resemble dried blood and it was difficult to wash . . . . I wondered, too, about the hot water and soap: surely Angel had not noticed the stain and sent for them? But, then again, there was that preposterous story about a stabbing with scissors – no, it must have been some other guest who even now might be wondering where their order had gone. And all the while my brain was racing like a terrier in a barn of rats, wondering what had happened to the others. At one stage I even wondered whether the law had caught up with them while they had been away from the room for a few minutes, but surely then someone in the inn would have heard of it and it would have been gossip enough on the chambermaid's lips when she had brought up the hot water; the law would have surely searched for me too, for if one were discovered missing, all three would be too. After an hour or so of unconstructive thought I lay down on the bed, suddenly aware that I had slept only a couple of hours the night before; if I just closed my eyes for ten minutes or so . . . .

When I awoke it was quite dark, and a chill breeze blew through the open window, bringing with it the smell of burning fat from the kitchens below. The skirt of my dress was still damp and I shivered at the clamminess as I put it on. There was still no sign of Nick and Angel, but perhaps they had not been able to slip up the stairs again and were waiting in the bar parlour. I still had the small store of money I had been able to save, and donning my cloak I went downstairs for something to eat for by now my stomach was clamouring for food.

The bar was full, but they were not there. I thought it best to stay as inconspicuous as possible so bought a lukewarm pie and took it outside to eat. The yard appeared quiet, so I chewed my way through the unappetizing mess

480

seated on a mounting block. I was not unobserved, though: the ostler appeared at my elbow, still with a straw in his objectionable mouth, murmuring: 'Short of company, little lady? He won't turn up now you know, and me and you we could –'

Jumping up I flung the remains of the pie in his face – they deserved each other – and fled back to the obscurity of my room, to spend a miserable night tossing and turning, my broken sleep disturbed by evil dreams.

Morning saw me risen by six, determined to wait no longer for Angel and Nick. I decided to leave the large bundle to be collected if they ever returned, for it was heavy and cumbersome and I did not wish to be overburdened, so I emptied it out on the bed in order to pack it more tightly. To my surprise it contained a very strange collection of apparently unrelated objects. The whole had been tied loosely in a large and ornate black silk dress with jet trimmings and a torn bodice, stained with some rusty mark. There were a couple of tortoiseshell hair combs set with brilliants; a pair of large silver-plated candlesticks; a silver letter-opener and inkstand; several fine lawn handkerchiefs; a mother-of-pearl and gilt box about six inches square and empty; a rather beautiful set of ivory gambling dice with garnet spots; a well-fingered pack of playing cards, and one lady's black slipper.

The dress and slipper were obviously too large to have belonged to Angel and none of the other articles seemed to be associated with her, neither were they of any obvious value, except perhaps the dice. I picked up the cards and idly arranged them to tell my fortune, but remembered in time that it was unlucky to cast one's own, and packed everything away again in the dress; my own bundle was still tied, but one corner was loose so I tightened the string. Making a quick toilet in the water left from the day before, I left the bundles on the bed and went down for a hasty

481

breakfast, for I wanted to be on my way to Southwark as soon as possible, now that my mind was made up.

It was too early for full breakfast, not yet seven, but I was provided with a bowl of gruel and a couple of warmed-up sausages and ate at my leisure, for the room was almost empty. As soon as I had finished I would pay my reckoning, pick up my bundle and find a carriage to take me to the river, for I fancied for once cocking a snook at London from the luxury of a seat, rather than on a pair of dusty feet like last time. An early traveller was already on his way and I watched idly as his horse was led from the stable, breath steaming, for there was already a nip to the early mornings and the sun did not reach the yard till late afternoon. The traveller, a middle-aged man with the fussy manner of a lawyer, picked up his saddlebags, chose some coins from his purse and placed them neatly on the table then departed, leaving, however, a morning newspaper lying folded on his chair. I was about to call his attention to it, for he looked the sort of man who could find an excellent use for even a twice-read paper, when my eye was caught by the headline nearest me: 'Murder off St Martin's Lane!' then in smaller type: 'Woman with throat cut: killer escapes with jewellery and hundreds of guineas.'

For a breathless moment everything stood still; I was freezing cold and yet could feel the perspiration break out on my forehead and the sweat dampen my armpits. The words blurred and ran into each other to make no sense as a dreadful formless suspicion took the very breath from my body. My teeth ached from clenching them as though I had a mouthful of snow and I felt as if everyone was watching me and could read my mind as though it were a poster unrolled on the wall for all to figure. I knew I must have gone white as goose down and felt as insubstantial; hardly realizing what I was doing I picked up the newspaper and tucked it under my arm, leaving the rest of my money on the table; I have no memory of climbing the stairs, except that I reached my room as breathless as if I had run up Silbury Hill at midsummer. Shooting the bolt across I sank down on the bed and unfolded the paper again. The first reading might have been in Welsh for all the sense it made, but then I steadied myself, took a couple of deep breaths and started again.

The *Morning Chronicle* had done itself proud. Without all the hyperbole and italics and capitals and sermonizing and sensationalism it boiled down to this: yesterday morning, at about ten-thirty, for the household rose late, the maids had gone upstairs to Madame Bonneville's rooms — yes, it was of her they were writing — to start the cleaning and the lighting of fires. One of the girls, expecting Madame to be still abed, had gone into her parlour and found the body. She had run screaming into the street, alerting the watch and a passing horse patrol, who had accompanied her back into the house. The body was examined by a surgeon who was of the opinion that she had been hit repeatedly on the back of the head with a blunt instrument and that when she was unconscious her throat had been cut; the instrument must have been extremely sharp, as her head had almost been severed from her body. Her fingers had been stripped of rings with considerable force, one finger having been hacked off to detach the ornament, and her earrings had been ripped from the lobes. The body had been stripped of dress and petticoat, and one shoe was missing. A further search revealed that a large sum of money was missing from a safety box, as also was her jewellery; the total sum of these two was estimated at twelve hundred guineas. Also unaccounted for were a pair of candlesticks, writing materials, and a gilt games-box from her desk. In addition, her faithful companion, one Angela D'Asprey, was believed murdered also: her room had been ransacked and there were bloodstains on the walls and bedding. The only firm clue to the assassin was a yellow velvet bow found clenched in the murdered woman's hand; the Runners were seeking an itinerant fortune-teller called Gemini — no other name given — who, they believed, could help them with their inquiries.

There followed a description of the wanted girl: of low stature and slight build with light brown hair and glib tongue; she was described as being of persuasive manner and immature years. It was assumed that she would be carrying a large parcel or bundle and would be dressed in a gown with a yellow bow missing from the bodice or sleeve.

There was no mention of Nick.

It was hoped there would 'be a Speedy Arrest of the Murderess'.

For a long while I could not take it in, let alone believe it; I might have been reading fiction, something that had happened on another world. Mars, perhaps, the bloody planet who always shone with a baleful red glare, the red of blood . . . . Blood. Blood – oh, my God! I shrugged up small in the dress Angel had given me, the dress with the stains that would not wash out and the missing yellow bow on the bodice . . . . Now I understood.

It was the angelic Angel who had murdered her employer; the unemotional Angel who had struck her down from behind and then cut her throat to make sure; the self-righteous Angel who had systematically and cruelly stripped the body, who had stolen what she believed was due to her by right; the uncomplicated Angel who had embroiled Nick in another murder that had never happened to suit her urgency for escape; the fair-faced Angel who had known all along where to find a knife so sharp it 'almost severed the head from the body'.

Had Madame realized, I wondered, in those last few moments what devil she had had so close to her all those years? I thought not: the passionless face would have deceived till the head was turned away and the weapon, perhaps a candlestick, was wielded from behind – Candlesticks! With the hair crawling at the back of my neck I reached into the bundle I had so carefully wrapped, hesitated, withdrew my hand again, then cursed myself for a coward as I plunged in recklessly and drew forth one of the pair. There was a sticky stain and a couple of black hairs clinging to the base –

The candlestick fell to the floor with a shattering crash as I realized what else Angela D'Asprey, Angel-Face, had done: in that bundle were the missing articles from Madame's desk left deliberately as an encumbrance for me to carry round with innocence. On my body I wore the dress she had given an unsuspecting fool as a surprise gift; the dress with the bloodstains, Madame's blood, and the missing yellow bow that had lain in a dead woman's hand. It had all been a deliberate move to incriminate me, even to the description she had probably paid one of the blind man's bum-boys to give to the Runners. And they could have been paid twice to forget Nick . . . . No wonder she had smiled at me when she had admitted she had needed me: of course she had! She needed someone for the hue and cry, someone to run one way while she and Nick escaped the other, and I was convenient. And that was not all; she would have used anyone who came to hand, but she had a special reason for making me the cuckoo in the wren's nest, the albino fawn: I had captured Nick's affection, however temporarily, and I must be punished. I had not really believed her when she had said the night before last, 'I hated you for it. I still do,' and she must have known I could not imagine how far that hatred would carry her, and despised me for my incomprehension.

How confident she had been! I realized now that she must never have thought of failure, and that even when I had surprised her coming through the door in the wall only moments after the crime had been committed, she could still talk to me as calmly as if she had just been to afternoon tea. I remembered again the sleepy, satisfied look I surprised in her eyes as if she had just come from a lover's bed: I had not realized that the satiety of blood-letting could be a substitute for sex.

I remembered, too, how I had inadvertently drawn attention to myself all the way through; a young girl on her own hiring herself a room; a distraught seeker rushing around looking for nonexistent travellers; a persistent questioner of coach timetables: a guest who had carelessly left incriminating evidence on her bed for the chambermaid to rifle through; a visitor who insisted at inconvenient times for hot water and soap to wash through a blood-stained dress – no, wait! That must have been another of Angel's refinements. I had not asked for water, but she must have found a maid who was going off duty, a maid who would not connect us, and got her to pass on the message: my denials had merely ensured that the girl would remember. Was there no end to Angel's invention?

I tried to reason out what had happened to them in the light of what I now knew. I had been sent, I realized now, on a deliberately fruitless errand to give her time to disappear. That had given her forty minutes or so to get away, with a presumably willing Nick; she probably told him some cock-and-bull story of having got the coach times wrong, and had promised to leave me a note: he would not have disbelieved her. Maybe she had played on his fears of the discovery of his 'crime' to persuade him to board the Oxford coach while I was hunting the sewing silks: I tried to recall the description of the passengers that revolting pair in the stable yard had given me, although I was sure none had sounded the least like those I sought. They could have just moved to another inn, or taken a coach for hire, but somehow I thought she would not risk the streets again till she was far from London. What were those passengers again? An old man, a young family, a couple of youths, a lady all swathed up with the toothache, and her maid . . . . Of course! She had dressed Nick in another of Madame's dresses and a disguising shawl – it was as plain as the way to the parish church. She would not risk his disguise too far, but they would alight at a convenient posting station and continue the journey as themselves, or even in fresh roles. And if they changed transport often enough no one would be able to follow their tracks. I guessed they would make for one of the northern ports, Liverpool perhaps, and take the first ship out. Even if it took the long way round, calling elsewhere on the way, and the voyage was of three months instead of three weeks, there was no one to pursue, and even if I was caught and betrayed them they would be anonymous in that new continent, lost among thousands more seeking their fortunes. And they had a head start: they had Madame's money.

It may be strange that I believed Angel, after all the lies she had acted and told, but believe her I did about three things: her love for Nick, her terrible childhood, and the fact that they were going to America. Even now I could almost find it in my heart to find excuses for what she had done to Madame, for her obsession with Nick and the ill-treatment as a child must have gone a long way to unhinging her mind and warping her judgement. The beginning of understanding I had for her; forgiveness would take more time.

I suddenly realized that while I was sentimentalizing over her escape, and hoping, for Nick's sake at least, that the law did not catch up with them, I was forgetting the most important thing as far as I was concerned: the law was not after them at all.

It was after me.

As far as the authorities were concerned I was a murderess, all bar the confession, and I must run like a hunted hare till I could find a safe form or a high enough hill to run up: hounds ran better downhill or on the flat. I put away my toilet things in a hurry and tightened up the bundles, for there was no question now but that Angel's incriminating evidence could not be left behind: I must find the first opportunity to ditch or destroy it –

There was a sharp scratching on the door, and I froze. I could hear whispering: it sounded like a man and a girl. The chambermaid and the ostler? After a moment I forced my stiff limbs over to the door; lifting the latch and drawing back the bolt I opened it a crack and peered out. All I could see was the maid, fresh sheets over her arm,

487

but I could sense there was someone else beside her in the shadows.

'Are you staying another night, miss?' Attuned as I had learned to be in the trade of fortune-teller, I could tell from the slightly aggressive tone of voice that she was 'talking from her own territory' and that she therefore was sure she had got me at a disadvantage. Which meant that she, and whoever was with her, knew, or suspected they knew, that I was the person wanted for questioning for the murder of Madame Bonneville. She moved forward a little and now I could see her eyes, alight with the first lively curiosity she had shown. 'If'n you're staying, I've to make the bed . . . .'

I had to think fast; something to lull their suspicions, make them leave me in peace for a while to escape –

'Yes,' I said, in what I hoped was a sufficiently calm and matter-of-fact tone of voice. 'I shall be staying until my friends come back; in the meantime I have a headache and will lie down for a while. You may come back in, say, an hour. Bring me a bowl of broth and the day's newspaper: the *Chronicle* or *Morning Post* will do. Please see I am not disturbed till then,' and I shut the door firmly in her face and made loud walking-over-to-the-bed-and-lying-down-with-a-megrim noises.

There was more agitated whispering outside the door, then I heard their footsteps move away down the corridor; infinitely cautious I opened the door an inch and watched their retreating backs: it *was* the ostler. My summary treatment of his advances the day before must have given him the incentive to dig and delve till he had come up with the murder; by hearsay, I would imagine, for he looked one for the pictures rather than the print. They went slowly down the stairs to the kitchen, still obviously in disagreement; now, by all the clocks winding down the seconds, minutes and hours of time passing, I must be quicker, more agile and defter than I had ever been . . . .

*

I reckon it took me about five minutes to get clear and away. That included a complete change into the only other clothes I possessed, a swift trim of my hair down to the scalp almost, and a repacking of the large bundle so it contained also my hair trimmings and the dress Angel had given me. Then it was a quick look down the corridor, a rush for the front stairs, a casual negotiation of the blessedly empty yard, a dive down the nearest alley I could find, and a losing of myself in the anonymity of the London streets. Damp with the perspiration of relief, I made my way as near south as I could judge, towards the river. This was nearer than I had thought; obviously Angel had not led us due north the other night, as I had imagined at the time, but more northeast, and it was not long before I came out on the riverbank.

I had wanted to fling my burden into the water and forget it but unfortunately the tide was out, and I was faced with acres of evil, slithery mud, slimy with the smell of rotting fish, drains and decay. I walked upriver for a while, but found I was coming to an area where the houses overlooked the water, so I retraced my way till I found a flight of rickety steps leading down to the mud, with a small wooden pier nearby. I could see tide marks quite high on the retaining wall, and the channel came relatively near and deep at this point, so I settled down on the steps beneath the level of the wall to wait, the incriminating bundle by my side. I judged the progress of a froth of yellow bubbles and a half-submerged crate: they were moving slowly upriver, so obviously the tide had turned, and it was only a matter of time. The sun was shining directly on the water in front of me and warming my hiding place; I watched the light dancing on the smooth grey water; as the flow of the tide increased the water became brown with sand, and every now and again there was a swirl and sudden cloop! as a fish rose after gnats. It was warm, it was peaceful, and I had had a traumatic thirty-six hours: I slept.

I dreamed a long, slow dream of nothing I could recall

that merged into a dream of escape; again I was a runaway, but this time I was an accused witch. Above me, as I ran and stumbled over cobbled streets, great birds like Baltasar screamed overhead: 'Burn the witch! Bind the witch! Drown the witch!' like the raucous cries of street vendors and guttersnipes. Now I was fast, surrounded by a mocking crowd, and there was the green and scummy pond below, the ducking-stool hard beneath me, the bonds cutting into my flesh, a gloating silence as I dipped nearer and nearer to the stinking pond; I whimpered, but no sound came from my throat and I could feel the water, the icy water, creeping over my feet, soaking my ankles, dragging at my skirts, and all the while I screamed a silent scream and the great birds overhead sounded my terror in their mocking echoes –

I woke in a sudden cold sweat, and the gulls were screeching overhead: the water was soaking my feet, my ankles, the hem of my skirt. While I slept the tide had risen and was now lapping the steps on which I rested. It was late afternoon, for the sun was behind the buildings to my right and my refuge was chill with shadow. Now I could be rid of my incriminating burden. Thankfully I put my own package on the top of the steps and, glancing round swiftly to ensure I was unobserved, picked up Angel's bundle and swung it back and forward by a fold of the material to give it momentum and then let it go, to watch it arc into the water now surging past upriver near the full. Shaking out my damp skirt I picked up my bundle and set off in the same direction as the tide, only to be halted a moment or so later by a sudden shout and loud splashes behind me. Turning in dismay I saw two small forms, naked by the looks of them, swimming like otters towards the still floating bundle. A moment later a small skiff shot out from behind the wooden pier, a hunched figure plying oars vigorously, heading also for the same target. I had heard of the scavengers of the river – mudlarks, the children were called – but had not realized how quick they could be, nor how unwilling the bundle

490

would be to sink. A moment later the first swimmer had grabbed it to be joined a few seconds later by his companion, and I could see fists flying as they tore at it between them. The boat was coming up fast too, and I saw a glittering oar-blade swing high to smash down on the swimmers, even as I panicked and fled back into the maze of streets and passageways behind the river.

After a few minutes I slowed down again, fairly sure the flotsam retrievers would have been far too busy with their own quarrels to remember what I had looked like, even if they had noticed me at all. The smell coming from a nearby pie shop was also conducive to recalling other things, like hunger. I had not eaten since this morning, and I reckoned I looked harmless enough, if a little damp, and could risk breaking my fast. Accordingly I went in and sat down, ordering two small pies and a glass of ale, and considered my next move. I should go to Barnaby first, as planned, and then, with the unexpected amount Angel had give me in that curious little dispenser, I should probably have enough to go up north and wait for Annie to return from Ireland; why, brilliant thought! I could find lodgings near the livery stables where they wintered the horses in Preston, and be ready and waiting for them when they returned. And Jack would be there . . . .

'More ale, miss?'

Looking down at the crumbs on my plate and the empty glass, I shook my head: I had successfully daydreamed my way through my meal. Taking the coin dispenser from my dress pocket I pressed the little spring and dropped a half-guinea into his outstretched palm.

He stood staring down at it, then gave me an uneasy grin. 'A joke, miss?'

It was my turn to look uneasy. 'I don't understand: surely that is more than enough?'

'Two small meat and 'tater pies and a mug of ale: ninepence, please!' and he slapped the coin back on the table. He was overcharging, I was sure of it, but I had no choice but to pay: I did not want to draw undue attention to myself. I pushed the coin back at him.

'Surely you have the change?'

'For what?'

Really he must be half-witted, and surly into the bargain. 'For a half-guinea – here!'

'Oh aye, we've change for any amount of half-guineas, or whole guineas come to that, but the only change you'll get for that gaming token is a spell in Newgate, my girl! Now then, pay up and get out, or I'll have the law on you!'

Unbelieving, sick in my stomach, I picked up the coin – no, token, as he had correctly described it. It was weighted like the real thing, and on one side was the head of the king, but the gilding was too bright and the image crudely cast. The obverse held the representation of a naked lady, blindfolded, and the inscription 'Lady Luck': I recognized the piece as one used at Madame's. Luck was on the side of the wrong Angels, I thought bitterly, for once again she had contrived a bitter joke to play on me: anyone who knew of the murder might guess where the token came from. In growing suspicion I emptied the dispenser and the useless tokens glittered and spun on the table top, all tinkling a hollow laugh at my incredibly trusting nature. Every single piece was counterfeit except the last, the one she had shown me before slipping it back on top. By now the proprietor of the pie shop and his wife were watching my sorry performance. A wave of hopelessness overwhelming me, I proffered the one genuine coin.

'A – a joke.' I said feebly. 'My – fiancé, a gambling man . . . .'

The waiter took the coin and tried it dubiously on his teeth, but the proprietor was still suspicious.

'Just a minute, then,' he said. 'Better take a closer look at what else you've got there –' And he made a grab for my small bundle of possessions, his other hand hard on my shoulder.

Desperately I hung on to my bundle and, twisting out of his grasp, kicked over the table to impede their pursuit, running out once more into the warren of streets. Behind I could hear a hubbub and cries of 'Stop!' but reckoned that they would eventually be satisfied enough with the genuine coin I had left behind, and perhaps would not connect the tokens with the horrible murder I was being hunted for. Now there was no question of a ride in a carriage, no chance of an early journey up north to Annie's, no sign, even, of the next meal for, thanks to Angel's duplicity, I was now penniless as well as wanted for murder: now, indeed, there was only Barnaby at Southwark, and I would bring nothing but myself: how long, I wondered, would he be willing to hide and succour me, if at all? But there was nowhere else to go.

It was dusk now, and I took care to keep out of the main thoroughfares, so it was dark by the time I had crossed Blackfriars Bridge, and a cold, windy night. I kept walking till it was too dark to see, then bedded down miserably, and hungrily, in an outhouse behind a low tavern. I made a bed for myself, of sorts, from some noisome old rags I found by touch in a corner; I discovered later that these belonged to a large and smelly dog. Luckily he decided I was harmless, and settled down on his larger-than-fair-share of the bedding, breathing old-bones breath into my ear noisily all night.

It was well into the following afternoon before I reached Southwark, and by this time I was dizzy with hunger and tiredness. I staggered up to the side of the George Inn aware of my tattered and dirty state, but too weary to care. There was no sign of Barnaby, but there was an empty scrivener's stall on the left-hand side of the entrance: a battered card announced 'Back very shortly'. Crouching beside the stall, I waited, but I had dozed off before I felt a rough hand on my arm and heard a voice I knew apostrophizing me to: 'Go away, there's a good girl, and stop cluttering up the pavement –'

493

'Oh, Barnaby!' I said feebly. 'Don't turn me away! I didn't do it, honest I didn't . . . .'

And fainted clean away at his feet.

24

It was a very hard winter: the hardest, folk said, since 1739–40.

After his initial displeasure at finding me flung, unwanted, on his mercy, Barnaby had mentally shrugged his shoulders and made the most of it. All in all, he treated me very kindly, though I am sure he would have preferred me to be the boy he remembered. I shared a room with him and his 'friend', a slaughterer's assistant called Luke Taylor; I had a curtained-off pallet in a corner of the room under the window, but my presence must have been inhibiting for them as they were affectionate lovers. Often I had to count stars desperately or recite Shakespeare under my breath, pretending all the while to snore, while the murmurs, creaks, gasps and squeals of joy from the bed they shared made me feel embarrassed and, at the same time, almost envious.

It was decided it would be easier for all concerned if I dressed in boy's clothing again, and Barnaby found me appropriate wear, exchanging what little pieces I had left and paying for the rest. There was no work at the George itself, nor any nearby, but he took me on as his assistant scrivener, giving him more time, as he said, to concentrate on balladmongering or chaunter-culling. It was a good pitch we had, for the mail coaches left from the inn and the postal receiving office was just across the way, and we charged for reading letters to our customers as well as writing the replies. The landlord took a nominal sum for our space but the business was profitable enough through October and November; adequate to keep us clothed and fed, that is, but not lavish enough for any noticeable saving. Then the real cold set in; it snowed in the first week of December, and an iron-hard frost took a grip it did not relax, with a few days' remission here and there, until early in March. The sun only found its way to our pitch for an hour or so every day, and then mittened hands would slowly thaw and I would start to remember I had toes, but by afternoon the shadows created their own chills and a northeasterly whined down the alleyways to chafe my joints into chilblains and make my nose run. The ink froze and the parchment and paper became unmanageable, the former stiff as a board, the latter brittle as ice. There were few events of note Barney could turn his rhyming talents upon, for gossip was in short supply; the king had had another relapse, but who was anything other than sorry for the poor old man? The Prince, Gorgeous Georgie, with his Gentleman Jack that rose to every occasion, was always worth a verse or two but, once composed, who was there to buy? Even tarts and whores could not keep themselves warm enough to walk the streets, and their customers were shrivelled by the cold.

Commissions grew scarcer, and I was increasingly glad of the chestnut-vendor's stall down the road a piece, for I could always shuffle down and warm myself fleetingly. There could be no thought of going to Annie's, for there was not a penny to spare; I wrote to her at Christmas, not telling her much except that I had changed my job and was working under my old name of Sprat, and that she could answer care of the receiving office. How was Jack? Love to Toby, as usual . . . . In time I received an answer that took all the few pence I had saved, for they charged me full for two hundred and thirty miles between Southwark and Preston, where it was posted. Annie had married her Matthew two days before Christmas, and had brought the youngest nephew down the hill to live with them. She told me that Ireland had been cold and wet, the people were 'mad as March hares' and very poor. They had seen but little of Jack, he being about his own business more than usual, and he had disbanded the troupe permanently once they had arrived back to England. He had announced that he had 'other fish to fry' and had disappeared south with Tom, Daisy, Hannibal, Toby and the bird Baltasar after selling up the caravans, excepting his own, and giving Annie a generous wedding present. She concluded by inviting me to stay with her and Matthew whenever I liked.

Part of me froze inside when I read that letter. It had been nearly eighteen months since I had seen any of them, and although I knew I would be welcome at the shoe shop at the bottom of the hill whenever I wanted – if ever I could afford the coach fare – Jack and Toby had gone forever, and I could not bear to think I would never see them again. All through my hardships and adventures there had always been the thought that before very long – next month, next year, perhaps – I should see that tall scarecrow figure, hear that alternately rasping and caressing voice, feel either a slap on my rump or be enveloped in a bear hug: either would have been equally welcome. And once I had explained all that had happened to me it would have been all right; it was always all right with Jack. The small, hopeful bit inside me had always known that. Somehow I had come to believe while I was with him, although I had not realized it at the time, that he could always run my life for me in the way best for me; I was willing to be organized, told – ordered, even – what to do; have the messes cleared up after me, be chastised when necessary and encouraged and educated where needed. And I knew he liked me a little; perhaps rather more than a little, otherwise he would not have bothered so much.

While I had been so close to him day after day, there had been many things I had not understood about his attitude towards me, especially his seeming rejection after I had slept with him that time, but I had been too near, too subjective, and my time in London at Madame's had taught me, if nothing else, to stand back a little and evaluate rather than judge, understand rather than censure. I could see now that he had gone out of his way on many occasions to shield me, care for me, excuse and tolerate me even when he thought me a boy, but even more so since that night when I had upstaged him in *Othello*. I knew now, too, without being quite sure how I knew, that what he had said about not being a womanizer was true also, and that he had tried hard not to seduce me for my own sake and that afterwards he had been sorry, not for the act, but for the effect it might have had on me. I guessed, looking back on his actions, his mysterious comings and goings, his apparently meaningless outbursts of temper and his obviously educated background, that he had hidden responsibilities and worries, even some secret that chafed at his temper; some task, perhaps, that sat uneasily on his temperament and desires. If I had met him again our relationship would have been very different, for I had grown up a great deal in the last year or so.

There would have been no need, either, to try and explain my part in Madame's death; even before I reached Barnaby – and he had not understood what I was ranting about – I was in the clear. When I had recovered sufficiently to explain he had shown me the issue of the day after the one I had read, which painted a very different picture. My friend Lil – God bless her prying eyes – had heard a disturbance, opened her door an inquisitive trifle, and had seen Angel leave Madame's rooms carrying a large bundle and looking agitated. Something – a bloodstained knife, she thought – had dropped from the bundle, and Angel had stopped guiltily to retrieve it.

So now the hunt had switched: but they did not catch her.

The knife, the last of her attempts to shift the blame, I found in my pack: Barnaby disposed of it for me. It was a good, sharp kitchen knife, and I suspected it went to Luke for use at the slaughterhouse, but I knew better than to ask; life was cheap, and good tools hard to come by and

497

expensive. I found this fact borne out only too horribly early in January.

We were always cold, but were spared the worst of hunger by the fact that Luke regularly stole offal from his place of work: others were not so lucky. Our room was on the third floor of a four-storey building and one morning I heard the snapping and snarling of dogs from the attic above; curiosity got the better of me, and I went up to investigate. Two dogs were quarrelling on the landing, growling and baring their teeth over a large bone in the open doorway. The bone was human, and the rest of the dead bookbinder who had lived above us was lying on the floor, whence he had been dragged from the bed by the dogs.

I retched, clinging to the doorjamb for support, and luckily Barnaby came up to see what was the matter. His face grew paler, but he merely drove away the dogs and took the one tattered blanket from the bed to wrap the body. He and Luke carried it to the steps of the nearest church later that night and left it with a note that the man had died a pauper, name unknown. That last was true, for there were no papers in his room to reveal his identity, and the landlord never asked for names, but we did find a handsome set of engraving tools. Barney fingered the worn leather case. 'Should have sold these, poor bastard: he'd have lived a week or two on the proceeds. Probably the last of his possessions . . . . Pity to let the landlord, God rot him, get all.' So we ate well for a week instead. Once I should have cavilled at the death, the inhumanity, the fact that no one had bothered to be neighbourly enough to notice the man was dying, the sin of stealing his last goods, but life in this cold and desolate winter was merely a matter of existing from day to day, no time or space for conscience or suchlike niceties. Looking back, I wonder now how I managed to live with such a philosophy, but then to live another day was an achievement in itself; in a way we lived like those starving dogs: food was food wherever it came from, and that, plus warmth, was the be-all and end-all of our precarious existence.

I would have been colder, and hungrier too, if it had not been for my little old lady down the street. She wrote – via me or Barnaby – home to her family in Yorkshire regularly, and came to us to have her answers read. It must have cost a fortune, for besides our charges all letters were paid for, of course, at the receiving end by mileage, and her son-in-law's farm was even farther away than the two-hundred-odd miles Annie's letter cost me. She was a plump little person, but I daily saw her grow thinner as the winter progressed, for I suspect she spent much of her food money on keeping in touch.

'It was my idea,' she explained to me, 'me coming down here when my dear Mary got wed. No good ever came of two women sharing a kitchen. I found a good post down here with a retired gentleman, but he's been gone now this year or more, and though I takes in washing and some mending to keep me in vittles, I find I miss the family ever so . . . . Do you know, I haven't ever seen the grandchildren? And it's not the same, down here; folks aren't as friendly, somehow. Oh, they'll pass the time of day civil-like, but they're not really interested.'

She more or less adopted me as family, I think, for she came every now and again, even when there were no letters to write or read, with a pasty or a sweet shrivelled apple – and, more welcome still, a pair of knitted mittens, socks, and once, oh joy! a knitted waistcoat. This was especially welcome, for as I grew thinner (and I definitely looked more like a half-starved boy than a girl, now) I found I became correspondingly colder: 'thrawn', she called it. The letters she received were cosy, warm family letters; two children already, with another on the way, and there was always a plea for her to go up, if only for a visit. Even while her eyes grew misty with longing for them all, she would tell me firmly to write and say how well she was, how London suited her, how her old gentleman could not manage without her, how she might

take a week or so later in the year to pay them a visit . . . .
When I ventured to urge that she was pining away and
would be much better off up North she cuffed me – not
hard – and gave me the edge of her tongue, telling me to
mind my own business. I did for a while, but when I saw
the tears run down her cheeks at the news of the safe
arrival of the third grandchild, I took matters into my own
hands, not without some trepidation, and enclosed a note
of my own with her next letter, without her knowledge of
course. I explained what I was, said I was worried for her
health, and asked them, if they really wanted her, to find
some excuse for insisting on her return up North. The
answer came, not by letter, but in person. Some two weeks
later, on a particularly unpleasant February day with
snow and sleet, she came tripping across to me with a
basket full of goodies.

'The last of the food, my dear, and a warm scarf –'

'Are you going somewhere, then?'

'Going? I've been fetched, that's what! My son-in-law
came down by wagon some two days past, found my
lodgings, and will stand no refusal! He's packing my things
now – all of 'em – and says I were a fool, and daft into
the bargain, not to let him fetch me before. Says as Mary
needs my help with the littlest, and that with the boys
growing fast it's getting too much to cope, what with the
hens and ducks and the spinning . . . . Told me as how a
friend down here wrote as how I wasn't doing too well.
Don't know who that could be, I'm sure, 'cos I don't
speak to a soul save my customers . . . . Still, there it is;
I'm off in an hour or so, and going by coach, too: no
mucky, slow wagons for me, he says! And to think they
really needed me all the time! Beats cockfighting . . . .'

And off she went, to live happily and usefully ever after,
I hoped: as I watched her bustling retreat I wound the
scarf around my neck, took a gingerbread biscuit, and
part of the cold, dumb misery I had surrounded myself with
over the past few months thawed a little; I remembered the
bookbinder who had died so alone: that had nearly

happened to my little old lady, and could happen to me as well if I did not pull myself together. I should have to try and forget all that had happened before and make the decision to plan the rest of my life in a sane and positive way. Now was the time to stand on my own feet, put my shoulder to the wheel, plough my own furrow, make my own bed and see it soft to lie on – and mix all the metaphors in my vocabulary, so long as I got the message.

Having pen, paper, ink and time, I decided to set out my advantages and disadvantages, pros and cons, and see how they would fit me for a new lifestyle.

It was a little discouraging to find, after a great deal of pen-nibbling and head-scratching, that there were only two courses open to me, two occupations which would suit my talents; to become a whore, or take to the road again.

The in-betweens that I had hoped for were impossible, if I was to be entirely honest with myself: I had had too little experience of domestic economy to become a competent servant, too little proficiency in sewing to become a milliner or dressmaker, too little aptitude in drawing, playing and French to be a governess, and was without the essential knowledge of etiquette and the decent clothes to be a lady's companion. References for all of these would not have posed too much of a problem, because Barnaby was adept at copying or inventing handwriting – I hesitate to call it forgery, for he never used the gift, as far as I knew, for monetary gain – but the supply of all these respectable positions far exceeded the demand in London these days. More and more people were coming in from the provinces and the countryside, convinced that the streets of the metropolis were paved with gold, and there were just not enough positions to go round. I had taken to looking at the advertisements whenever I could get hold of a fairly recent paper, but it was obvious that no one wanted a small, scrawny female of eighteen whose only positive accomplishments appeared to be an ability to light a fire with two twigs and a twist of birch bark; tell a fortune in the cards, the tea leaves, the palm, the crystal, the sand, the bones, the stars or (mostly) out of her head; make a passable boy; read aloud and play a part tolerably well; and who knew the tricks of her body and those of a man well enough to ply her trade in any bawdyhouse north or south of the river. As I said: fortune-teller or whore?

The latter I rejected out of hand. If I had fancied lying with anyone who could pay – and I did not, in spite of Nick's teaching – there was still the question of suitable clothes, and the ever present fear of infection and pregnancy, however careful I was and however efficacious Kat Petulengro's herb remedies continued to be. So, that left fortune-telling. I remembered that Jack had told me there was a great fair held in Southwark itself each year, but I did not know when. Barnaby would know, and once I had explained the few tools of the trade I needed, he might be able to stake me and I could pay him back. I knew there was no money to spare at the moment, but if I could hold on till the warmer weather came I should only need one pretty dress, a table, two stools, an awning, some cards, and a crystal . . . . Then I should probably find there was a showman, like Jack had been, who would let me join his troupe for a pooling of the take and a share of the profits. Or I could even set up a troupe of my own: find a couple of like-minded folk who would rather travel in company, or a foreigner or two like Sam Alley-Come . . . . My mind spun on, as clear and shining as a sand-scoured pan, and I was as excited as a small potato with two pints of bubbling water to itself, but I gradually came off the boil as I realized that a very impatient young man clutching the bridle of a lathered horse was practically shouting in my ear.

'The Plymouth coach! Is it in yet? Wake up, boy! The Plymouth coach?'

Pulling my scattered wits together, I peered through into the inn yard. I knew the times of most of the coaches by now, for we often had commission from newly alighted passengers telling of their safe arrival.

'It wants a few minutes of eleven, sir: the coach is due within the next half-hour. It is sometimes delayed, I fear, through bad weather and the poorly made roads, and I believe they have had more snow down there in the past few days –'

'As long as I am in time,' he muttered, and began walking his horse up and down, first, I was glad to see, loosening the girths and flinging a blanket over its heaving sides. He had interrupted my daydreams of becoming an impresario and I had no customers to claim my attention, so I amused myself by watching his pacings to and fro, imagining his background and trying to weigh up his character, much as I used to do with my customers at the fairs. He was a personable young man, quietly dressed, and his hair was tied back neatly by a black bow; a nice fellow, I guessed, judging by the consideration he had paid to his horse, but it was a pity he was wearing such a scowl; he was probably a clerk to a shipping agent or a lawyer, for he was well spoken but not dressed as one of independent means. I wondered why he was so impatient for the coach's arrival; perhaps a relative or friend was due to arrive, or an interesting package, or maybe some long-awaited news . . . but in all these cases one would have thought he would have been clearer as to the arrival times of the conveyances; no, this was something unexpected, judging by the haste and the frown. I attempted some pleasantry about the weather, which was its usual foul self, but he was too full of his own thoughts to notice I had spoken. At last I heard the coach rattling up the road, and almost before it had turned, mud-splattered and creaking, into the yard, he had thrust the reins of his horse into my hands and was dodging to one side and the other as the passengers alighted. Curious as to his purpose in spite of myself I eased forward to peer round the edge of the gateway, his unwilling horse in tow, just in time to see a pretty, wan young woman dressed soberly in brown alight from the coach only to be snatched up in his arms. She gave a little scream, dropped her parcels on the cobbles, from whence I darted forward to retrieve them, and flung her arms around the young man's neck.

'Richard! Oh, Dick, my dear! How did – what – when – Thank the dear Lord you are here! I thought you would not get my letter – it took me ages . . . .'

'It only arrived some two hours ago, and I was so afraid I should miss you!' And he covered her face with enthusiastic and, as far as I could judge, welcome kisses. His tricorne fell off, disregarded, into the mud and I retrieved that as well, mentally counting the pence that might come my way from so happy a couple. It took some time for them to become disentangled, but at last he drew her towards the parlour of the inn, remembering me, the horse, and the packages with a tossed shilling that I caught in his hat, having no hands free.

'Mind the horse, boy: we shall be with you in a little while.'

The little while was nearer an hour, but I kept myself warm by deciding that the shilling would be the foundation of my savings for a new career: I did not owe it to Barnaby as it had had nothing to do with being a scrivener, so it was all mine. To justify myself I rubbed the horse down with a wisp of hay from the yard and pinched a handful of grain for it from the bin. But he like as not would not notice; all he would see would be his ladylove's great brown eyes, all he would hear would be her soft West Country burr, all he would feel was her hand in his . . . .

'I've given him a good rubdown,' I said, when they returned.

'Eh? Oh, yes, good lad: here's a shilling.' He continued to gaze at his love, but now I did not care; he could gaze all he liked and all day at a shilling an hour.

He spoke, still looking at her as if he could not gaze his fill. 'Did I see you at a scrivener's stall? Are you a writer of letters, boy?'

504

'Why, yes, sir: I have a good, clear hand and write on first-quality paper and –'

'Yes, yes!' he interrupted. 'Well, go take up your pen and Esther – Miss Tregorran, that is – will dictate to you. 'Twill save you time, my dearest,' he said, turning back to her. 'And I know how little you care for the writing of formal letters.' He laughed, as though the word 'formal' had a special meaning for them both.

I wrote as she dictated, my eyebrows mentally raised. A young lady, bound for some seminary in Buckinghamshire, was instead to elope with her sweetheart. The letter was to inform the proprietress of the school that her prospective pupil was not to be expected as 'thanks to dear Mr Bright I shall be married within the week and require no further imposed schooling'.

'Will that do, my love?' she asked him prettily.

'Admirably, my sweet. Should you not also let Lady Margaret know our intentions? After all, she is your guardian . . . .'

She pouted. 'She would have me a spinster: you know that. Besides, she only wishes to get rid of me by sending me away to that horrid place, and I don't think she deserves to know; not at least till we have been well and truly wed. I could only get that note sent to you because she was so busy packing for their trip to Europe . . . .'

'I do not think even she could object now I have been promoted to chief clerk and have such excellent prospects with my uncle . . . .' He gathered the reins of his horse and took her arm. 'Mother will be waiting; I can get a sedan for you round the corner and I shall ride alongside . . . .' They walked off down the street.

'Sir – Miss!' I called out after them. 'Your hat – the parcels – the direction for the letter . . . .'

They looked at each other, and laughed, and came running back like two children let out early from school. Retrieving his hat he refused the parcels.

'In that larger parcel there are some dowdy aprons and suchlike that I would not let any pretty wife of mine wear:

give them to your sister, if you have one. In the smaller parcel is correspondence with the Seminary that you may tear into small pieces when you have extracted the direction –'

She opened her purse. 'I wish to have nothing left to remind me; in here you will find the two guineas my aunt gave me for travelling expenses: I have not touched it, and you look in more need than I, poor boy . . . .'

And they walked off into their particular happy ending, the horse trailing behind, leaving me with my hands full and the beginnings of a wild surmise nibbling at the suggestible margins of my vulnerable imagination . . . .

BOOK FOUR
Esther

25

I could not have managed it without Barnaby, and Luke Taylor, too, if it came to that.

Barnaby at first said that I was mad, and said it very colourfully, too, but I had had the foresight to load the table upstairs with a beef pie, sausage, bread and cheese, and two bottles of red wine – which took care of the tips I had taken this morning plus the cost of writing the letter and sixpence I had besides – and by the time we had dined on these and Barney had sent out for apple pie and another bottle of wine, he was far more amenable. I spun the two guineas so they caught the candlelight, we unpacked the bundles, and Barnaby examined the correspondence we found in the smaller package minutely, especially a letter from Esther Tregorran's sponsor, Lady Margaret.

'Can do,' he pronounced at last. 'What's in the other bundle?'

Two large plain white aprons, two mobcaps, a grey woollen dress; two shifts, two pairs of drawers, two pairs of black woollen stockings, two night-shifts, one pair of felt slippers; one hairbrush, one comb, one horn mug, one horn spoon, needles, thread; a Bible (new), a prayerbook (old), a box of pins and a pair of scissors, a jar of handcream (half-empty), six cotton handkerchiefs and a number of lavender sachets. These were itemized in a list from the smaller bundle, pinned to a brochure for the establishment, which read:

Thoroughgood Seminary for Domestic Economy, Chesham Bois

Proprietors: Miss Hester Thoroughgood; Septimus Thoroughgood, MA. A thorough grounding in all Domestic Affairs is taught against a background of Christian Virtue and Humility. Girls are encouraged in the Arts of Thrift, Cleanliness, Economy, Modesty and Gentleness. Those suitable will be taught their letters and simple Figuring. The Advanced Course includes Reading Aloud, Haute Couture, Conversation, Hairdressing and Flower-Arranging. Positions Guaranteed. Pupils who are accepted must be sponsored and provide the clothing etc. shown on the attached list. Fees: 5 guineas for the Basic Course: 10 guineas for the Advanced Course, payable in advance. Absolute Secrecy guaranteed. All Transactions Confidential. Anonymity Assured. Complete Responsibility Undertaken. Highest Patronage.

I was not sure about 'Christian Virtue' and 'Complete Responsibility Undertaken' but the 'Positions Guaranteed' were what I was after, so I read Lady Margaret's letter again over Barnaby's shoulder, complete with too many capital letters and underlinings.

I send Esther Tregorran with this letter. Thank you for your acknowledgement of ten guinea fee; tho' I consider this Excessive it will no doubt ensure that my Dear *Niece* (for this is what she imagines herself, as I explained in my earlier letter) will have the *Best Care* you can devise. Altho' she is in general *a Good Enough Girl*, she has that *Waywardness* I discussed in my earlier Missive that tends to put My Dearest Georgina *At A Disadvantage*. She has, of course, the Family Good Looks, tho' a More Aristocratic Demeanour is described in my Dear Children, but *Unfortunately* she appears to appeal to the *Baser Instincts* of the Local Gentry. If I had not Promised my Late Lamented Husband on his Death Bed to care for the Chit, I should have Disposed (crossed out) found a Genteel Position more suited to her *Lowly Birth* some time ago. Unfortunately she has latterly Attracted The Attention of a *Quite Unsuitable Young Man*, a *Mere Clerk* in some London Office, who has Local Connections. I wish her away from the Neighbourhood as soon as Possible and would be Obliged if the Position she takes eventually may be as far North or Ruralized as you can devise. My Dearest Georgina and I go abroad shortly to Winter with Lady Ormerod in Rome, so you may dispense with the usual Reports on Esther's Progress for some time. Your Acknowledgement of her Safe Arrival will set My Mind at Rest.

You ask me for a List of her Accomplishments: she is moderately well-versed in the Arts of Cookery, Dressmaking, Plain Sewing and Embroidery, and Draws and Sketches with some Facility. In herself she keeps Neat and Tidy, tho' I do find a *Needless Frivolity* in her preference for Lace and Ribbon: I beg you see her Dress Plain. She has been taught to Read and Write, but for these shows *Little Aptitude*: she can barely form a simple Letter of Thanks, tho' she can follow the Services in her Prayer-Book. I have been told she has a Pleasing Singing Voice, tho' I have no ear for such Myself.

She made it sound a virtue.

There had obviously been an interruption here, or a lengthy pause for thought, for when the letter resumed it was in thicker, more emphatic downstrokes.

As I mentioned in my First Communication, I should Appreciate the *Utmost Discipline* exercised in this case: you have My Permission to use whatever *Confinements* or *Chastisements* you deem necessary to bring her to a Meek and Pliable Disposition, fitted to what must be her *Lowly* and *Humble Station* in Life . . . .

'What an old dragon!' I exclaimed. 'Miss Tregorran was a sweet and gentle creature, from what I saw of her, and she was so pretty –'

'Exactly,' said Barnaby. 'You're not using your brains, girl. That letter would never have been written, nor the lass herself sent away from home, if she were plain and ungifted: as it was, the lady's own daughter must have had her nose put out of joint. Miss Esther was probably her husband's by-blow . . . .'

'Then I'm glad she found her sweetheart!' I said stoutly. 'But Barnaby, that letter just won't fit me at all. I can't embroider or sing or draw, and my cooking isn't that good. But I can read and write –'

'Whole letter will have to be redone; at first I thought I could maybe alter it a little, for the emphasis on the sewing skills could just be any prospecting sponsor's ploy to get the girl accepted, and would be recognized as such by any employer, but her lack of reading and writing skills . . . .'

He shook his head. 'Those are the ones that would catch you out, strange as it may seem – Are you sure you want to go on with this?'

'Of course: I don't foresee a better chance to be trained to a position, and one where the tuition is already paid for, do you? And there isn't much chance of discovery for a while: you can see from the letter that Lady Muck is going abroad for a while and only wants confirmation of Esther's arrival – and one Esther's very like another. Besides, Esther herself was against telling Lady Margaret she was going to marry her Richard until after it was a fact: and by then she will be abroad anyway . . . . Why did you say that the skills I have would be more likely to trip me up than those I haven't? Surely I can pretend not to be able to read and write well?'

'Anybody can lay claim to those skills they have not, provided they are reasonably quick-witted and are willing to learn, but can you, for a day even, pretend enough to convince others that you cannot, say, see or hear, or walk and run? Could you pretend you were a cripple, or could not move your fingers? Best of all, could you remain dumb in company for an hour, let alone twenty-four?'

I had to laugh: he was right, of course. So, we composed another letter; ink was easy enough to match, but he had to go to two or three stationers before he found a match for the fine cream-lined paper, then had to spend some time trimming pens to get the right, thick, angry strokes to the paper. We kept the general tenor of the letter, reckoning that if the Seminary had some of her earlier letters they were probably written in the same self-congratulatory, waspish style. I was allowed to be reasonably proficient in those things I could do but passably well, but halfway through Barney declared it sounded more like a paean of praise than an excuse to send me studying and proceeded to denigrate my lack of sewing skills till I sounded as though I had never touched a needle in my life. When I protested, he fixed me with his sharp gaze.

'Remember offering to repair that tear in my shirt? Remember wearing those breeches with a great tear in the arse for three days because you couldn't cobble together a patch? And who was it who finished off both jobs when you made a dog's bed of them? Me!'

Writing the letter took most of the night: we snatched a couple of hours' sleep, then Barnaby sent me round to the old-clothes shop two streets away with one of the guineas and a cryptic message to the Jew who ran the place, which resulted in no questions being asked, twenty-five per cent off the price with no haggling, and my pick of the shop: I wondered if he and Barney were related. Luke arrived back with news of his own; a carrier friend was going Buckinghamshire way next afternoon and would be glad of my company and cover.

'Cover?' I said sharply. 'What's he carrying then?'

'Didn't ask,' said Luke, who was a man of few words. 'Odds and ends, s'pose.'

'I can imagine,' I said tartly. 'Oh, Barnaby, this dress looks terrible! I took one that measured the same, I thought, but I must have lost two stone –'

'Well then, take it in.'

'But – Oh, please, Barnaby: you're much better than I am; you said so!'

'I can't write this demmed letter, make all the arrangements, keep an eye on the business downstairs, and be a dressmaker all at once – Luke, my dear, go fetch us some brandy and a couple of pasties; that is, if her ladyship has a little change from her expedition to the gown-maker?' and he glared malevolently at me. But my clothes had been cheap enough, in spite of his sarcasm: a minimum of cleanish undergarments, a brown and green striped dress, black bonnet and shoes, brown gloves and a rather nice dove-coloured half-cloak, fully lined, and I still had nine shillings and my other guinea left. So by evening we were all tight and I was trying to stand straight in my new dress while Barnaby pinned up the hem and I endeavoured to darn one of the gloves while it was on my hand . . . .

In spite of all this I was up at six, feeling sick in my stomach and with aching head; I knew the carrier did not leave till ten but I could not lie abed and was glad enough to be finally rid of the uncomfortable little pallet anyway so I went down to the inn and begged a pail of hot water, then toiled upstairs again and washed my hair and myself all over as best I could, drying myself on the rough curtain before donning my girl's clothes: the rest were only fit for the ragman, but I kept the scarf my little old lady had knitted and wound it round my waist, to hold in the dress that was still too loose.

There was a groan from the big bed where the other two lay.

'Demme, my *head*! Confounded cheap cognac . . .' and: 'Christ! Mouth like a snake's armpit!' from Luke.

There was enough bread and cheese for breakfast and a small packet for me to take on the journey. Of the money there were two shillings and a couple of pennies left and these I pocketed before tossing the remaining guinea to Barnaby.

'With my love . . . .'

'Can't pretend that this room won't be less crowded without you,' said Barnaby, 'but you've been surprising little trouble – for a girl.' He blew his nose. 'Near enough ten: better get going. Luke'll show you.' He turned away and busied himself tying his cravat.

I knew he would only be embarrassed if I embraced him, so I blew him a kiss.

'Bless you: I'll send you a line or two if I come out of this smelling of roses . . . .'

The first part of the journey – up to the river, across, and through the more crowded thoroughfares – took till late afternoon. That night we accepted a bed in the stable of a farm on the outskirts of Pinner, and while I snuggled down warm enough in the straw my companion slipped away, as I thought to the nearest tavern, but next morning the

514

cart was noticeably heavier, and the packages, carefully concealed under an old oiled cloth, more abundant: having lived with Barnaby and Luke I knew better than to ask why. The carrier was a merry enough man, small and spare, with a wink for all the women, a London accent you could cut with a blunt butter knife, and a habit of slapping his thigh to emphasize a point. On the first day I had ridden on the wide seat alongside him, but after Pinner he asked me to ride on top of the cart, ostensibly to keep an eye on a crate of hens we had acquired somewhere.

'Lends verisimilitude,' he said. 'Makes it more convincing.'

We stopped off at a place called Parsonage Farm, near Rickmansworth, where some packages left the cart and others were added, and the farmer's wife gave us milk and oatcakes, which we ate under the bare branches of a young beech tree near the piggery, so it was early afternoon when the cart drew up at the foot of a steep hill at the southern end of Amersham.

'Place you wants is up there, m'dear,' said the carrier, pointing with his whip up the hill. 'Up the Jack-and-Jill, turn left at the top, and the Half-Fairy is about a mile further on the right-hand side. I won't take the pony up, if you don't mind. He's got quite a load on as it is, and 'tis not fastened well enough to take such a slope – and we can't have that lot tumbling off the back now, can we?' He winked knowingly.

I asked, at last, what we had been carrying.

He considered. 'A bit of this and a bit of that, you might say. I exchange things. Things people don't really want I exchange for things they do; only few miles more and I can unload this lot and take fresh back . . . .'

I could see I was not going to get a straight answer, but I could not forbear one more question.

'Do the people who own the things they don't want know they haven't got them any more now?' I was rather pleased with my delicacy.

515

He winked at me. 'Sometimes; sometimes not. Good luck, m'dear!' and he clicked tongue against teeth and urged the tired pony to nod its way along the winding road of the village.

I watched them go, an odd ache in my heart as the last link with all that I knew disappeared, then I turned and began the steep ascent. I passed a church on my right with shivery coffin-shaped tombstones in neat rows above the ground and a large house to my left, then passed into thick beech wood. Already, in the milder February weather, tiny three-sided beech pods were bending on thin stalks, waiting to unfurl their green parasols, and squirrels raced the silver branches above. It was nearing dusk, but a blackbird chinked his alarm as he hopped the road ahead, and a hedgehog uncurled leaf-pockled spines and shuffled off into the bushes. A pair of immaculately dressed magpies made cat-and-crow noises, flicking their tails, and everything smelled wonderful and open and heady, like wine on an empty stomach; I breathed in deeply, the smells and staleness of London lost in the heavy intoxication of the country: all at once I remembered the caravans, and to leave behind the sadness those thoughts engendered I ran up the last of the lane.

Miss Thoroughgood's Seminary was set back from the road, the trees surrounding it confirming the discreet distance; a double iron gate was set in a thick beech hedge still untidy with last year's browned leaves. I studied the neat brass plaque.

'Thoroughgood Seminary, Chesham Bois,'
I read. 'Tradesmen's entrance down lane to right. No tinkers. No gipsies. Trespassers will be prosecuted. No one admitted after dusk. Please ring for attention.'

Two hours later I wished I hadn't. I wished myself, instead, back in Southwark, starving and cold; I even wished myself back at Madame's, warm but threatened; most of all I wished myself back with Jack and the others, in the worst weather, with an empty stomach and the cold rain trickling down my shorn head. Because it was, shorn I mean, but now there was no Annie-stew to look forward to, no warm, crackling, pungent camp fire, no hot-water-bottle Toby to cuddle.

I banged and thumped on the door of my prison, but no one came. I had snuffed the candle inadvertently with a careless whisk of my shift, and the bread and milk I had flung against the wall, from whence it had probably trickled dismally down the stone, but that I could not see for there was only a faint seep of moonlight through the barred window, and this in a dim ribbon that only reached half across the floor. I yelled, but was too far from the house for anyone to hear. Miserably I squatted down by feel on the pallet in the corner and let the tears trickle down unheeded, my arms wrapped round my shivering body in an unborn-animal position, every now and again allowing a hand to pass unbelievingly over the scrubby, sticky stubble that had been my head of hair: not even Aunt Sophia had cut so close. The smell of the ointment was sickening and I retched between the bouts of shivers; somewhere there was a coarse blanket, but I could not see it and was afraid it was now inextricably intermixed with the discarded bread and milk, for in my temper they had both gone in the same direction.

I had been met at the gate by the lodge keeper, a shuffling old dame who had taken my new name and bade me 'wait quiet on't step and don't wander' while she disappeared in the direction of the house. I shared the step with a suspicious tabby cat for what seemed an age till the old woman returned.

'Along the path to the left to't bughouse: they thought you wasn't coming.' And with that she turned and tottered back to the lodge, preceded by the cat.

I made my way along the path indicated, noting with approval the neat half-hedges of box and rosemary and wondering whether it was her lack of teeth that had made me think she had said 'bug' house; certainly this was not the way to the main building, and I was more puzzled when I came upon a small stone cabin enclosed by tall laurels: a guesthouse? There was a lanthorn set just inside the open door, but I hesitated.

'Go and bathe,' said a voice from somewhere the other side of the laurels. 'I had almost given you up: you were expected earlier in the week, you know.'

I faltered something about bad roads, then heard footsteps receding. It seemed a strange greeting, to have a bath before being allowed to enter, but the lure of the water overcame my doubts and I stepped inside, to find a large tub of warm water, soap and towel on the floor, and two hooks on the near wall. Latching the door – there was no bolt on the inside – I stripped quickly, hanging my clothes on one hook and my parcels on the other, and was soon luxuriating in the first all-over I had had since leaving Madame's. The water was not overly hot and the soap evil-smelling, but at least I felt clean. Some quarter-hour later, as I was towelling down and rubbing my hair dry, the door was opened and a big, strong-looking girl with red hair entered, carrying a clean shift, a stool, a jar of ointment, and a pair of barber's shears.

'Welcome, Miss Esther: I am sorry the water was not hotter, but –'

'What are those scissors for?' I interrupted suspiciously.

'Your hair, of course. I do hope you are not going to be one of those lassies we have trouble with: it'll only take a minute or two. Now, just sit still and we'll –'

'No, we won't!' I backed away. 'My hair doesn't need cutting.'

'Rule of the seminary, dear. Just let me –'

But I would not 'just let' her and in the end it took four of them to hold me down while I was cropped close and ointment from the jar was rubbed into my almost naked scalp. Indignity was not complete, however: the same noisome stuff was smeared between my legs and under my arms. In between my struggles I heard the big girl say calmly: 'It's for your own good, you know: Miss T won't allow any in that's not free from the fleas and lice –'

'I'm clean!' I can remember yelling furiously. 'I've not had lice for years!'

'Just making sure . . . .'

In the end there were too many of them for me, and this is why I was now shivering, hungry and afraid, for temper after they had left me locked in for the night 'to let the ointment work' had resulted in loss of candle, food and warmth, and now that I was alone I was afraid. Afraid not only of the immense dark of the countryside after the snug noises of London: on the road the rustles, squeaks, hoots and scurries would have been a natural part of our shared life in the vans, but now I was without my companions. But that was not the only fear: I was afraid of the future, afraid even of the next day and what this strange place would bring, for thanks to my noncooperation and refusal to accept rules and regulations I was now a prisoner until they decided to let me out: and what could I do but accept their ways, with no money, nowhere else to go, and an unsightly cropped head into the bargain? The knowledge that I had behaved unreasonably did not help either: it would be a long night.

Dawn came eventually, however, with an early missel thrush and a lightening under the bolted door I had tried so often during the night, and it was a chastened, cold, starved and grateful Miss Esther Tregorran who welcomed the big red-haired girl as she unlocked the door, a little after six by my reckoning.

'Slept all right?' She looked at my woebegone figure, then round the cabin. 'God help us! You haven't half made a mess . . . . Wait there.'

Two minutes later she was back with a bowl of gruel, a bucket of water and a scrubbing brush.

'Eat that quick, now, and then we'll clear up this mess: I should really make you do it all, but I reckon you've been punished enough for your sins.'

I scooped up the gruel ravenously, not even bothering

to look for the spoon in my bundle which, forgotten, had hung on the hook all night, and then licked my fingers.

'Thank you, Miss . . . ? I – I'm sorry for being such a nuisance.'

'The name's Jessie, but while we're with anyone else it's Mrs Lachie. As for being sorry, poor lassie, you can work that off with a hand to this spilt bread and milk: it sticks fine to the wall . . . .'

Ten minutes later she was satisfied and I was warmer.

'Still hungry?' she asked. I nodded and she pulled a chunk of bread from her pocket. 'That was for my birds: half each, and then I'll get the girls to bring hot water to wash away the ointment and you can get dressed.' Chewing on the crust I watched the thrush, a robin and some sparrows come almost to her feet for the crumbs she scattered; I noticed some tits picking at a lump of pork rind that hung from a branch of laurel, and I suddenly liked her very much and felt much more hopeful.

Once washed clear of the horrid ointment – and indeed there were a couple of unsuspected fleas in the dirty water – I dressed in the sober clothes I had inherited from the real Esther, hiding my shorn head under a comforting mobcap.

'There, now,' said Jessie. 'That's better. Now I'll take you to see Miss Thoroughgood: remember to call her "ma'am": she and her brother and I and any other staff will call you by your surname; between yourselves, while on duty, you will address each other as "Miss" and your surnames, just as you would if in service: off-duty you may be as informal as you wish. Now, you've a long day ahead of you . . . .'

Lying back on my none too comfortable truckle bed, gazing up at the plaster and lath ceiling dim in the small light of my candle, conscious of the sleepy murmurs and sighs of the couple of dozen girls around me, I thought back over the day's happenings. It had been a long, confusing time. After breakfast of porridge and boiled ham I had been taken to the kitchens to learn my first lesson: how to light a fire. To be strictly accurate, I suppose, I had taught *them* how to light one. Having had many times in the past little more than a couple of dryish twigs, a curl or two of birch bark and wet flint and tinder to coax flames to life in competition with a howling gale, thick fog or torrential rain, I was something of an expert; so a snug kitchen, lucifer matches, a warm hearth, a good updraft and dry kindling were no problem. Nor did I have any difficulty in starting the spring-jack spit or the movable Dutch oven, nor in lighting the wood-burning bread oven and the smaller hob grate: but that instant success was the only one of the day – still, I had passed my first test.

I was to spend a great deal of my first few weeks in that kitchen: it was a large, light, airy room; apart from the three fireplaces, designed to give every girl experience of all conditions for cooking, there were two tall windows with stone sinks under and the house door beside; the outside door was at the other end, next the fuel store; the wall opposite the fires was covered with cupboards full of crockery, pots and pans, and a long, scrubbed table occupied the middle of the floor. Behind the fuel store and the sinks were other rooms: pantry, scullery, laundry, dairy, still room, buttery and brewhouse, and most of the time they were a scurry of busy girls. The kitchen was divided from the rest of the house not only by its door and a short passage with storerooms off, but also by another door; beyond lay the hall, dining room (used on Sundays, otherwise we ate in the kitchen), the morning room, the linen room, Miss Thoroughgood's parlour and her brother's study. On the first floor were the drawing room, the music, weaving and embroidery classrooms, the housekeeper's parlour and bedroom, occupied by Jessie, the bedrooms of Miss Thoroughgood and her brother, and two seldom used guest bedrooms. These latter were used for the practice of french-polishing, mending and repair of furniture, drapes and china, apart from the more mundane tasks of bed-making, which was the first 'upstairs' job to be learned. The top floor, under the eaves, had been turned into two vast dormitories where we girls slept; there were fifty of us, and any spare space was taken up by baskets of apples, pears and nuts, trays of dried and drying herbs, wool waiting to be carded and spun and by broken pieces of almost anything that could, or might be, mended. I was in the dormitory whose nailed half-windows faced east: this was probably to facilitate our early rising, for I was in Group A, those beginners who had paid the initial five-guinea fee but had not progressed beyond the kitchen as yet: after we finished that part of our training satisfactorily there was still more work to learn in Group B for our five guineas but this work was outside. I had asked Jessie how long it took to complete a set of tasks to the satisfaction of Miss Thoroughgood, and she had smiled.

'Depends on each one of you, hinny, but of course we like to get you through as quick as possible, because that money doesn't go far. We do all our own work, both inside and out, and grow a deal of our own food, but to keep the place going we need a quick turnover; on the other hand Miss T won't let girls go till they are a credit to the place, so it's a bit of a battle. She gets a fee of two guineas from the new employer for every girl placed, and that helps but there's occasionally those that don't suit, one way and the other, and that money has to be returned: I should say we aim for nine months for the first five guineas and longer for the full course, unless the girl can already read and write, in which case it is shorter. The quickest I ever knew was a girl who went through like a dose of salts in six months altogether, but she had been well trained before we got her: an orphan. On the other side, we've had some of those in Group A for over a year . . . . So you see, it's largely up to you.'

For the fiftieth time I drew the list Jessie had given me from the pocket of my apron, where it hung on a hook at the head of the bed, and studied my duties. Until I passed my first tests I should wear a yellow ribbon on the right shoulder of my dress; I should rise at four-thirty, light fires, fetch kindling and coals, scrub floors, dust, bake, brew, wash dishes, launder, starch, iron, sweep, spin, plain-sew, black-lead, whitewash, peel, slice, cut, bake, broil, roast, simmer, steep and clean as the occasion demanded. There was not much incentive to progress to the next course either, for that list seemed longer, if that were possible. I should rise later, at five-thirty, but then I should be liable for gardening, mowing, scything, clipping, sowing, harvesting, manuring, weeding, pruning and trimming; for gathering wood and splitting it; for feeding hens, horses, pigs, goats, cows and sheep, and for milking the last three; would gather nuts, windfalls, potatoes, berries, fruit, mushrooms, honey, and go to market with the excess. I smiled to myself: no one could possibly master all that in less than a lifetime. Yawning, I blew out my candle, the last to do so, and heard the tall clock in the hall downstairs strike a silver ten. My bed was becoming more comfortable and I had a stomach reasonably full of stew and lentils: I said a quiet prayer for all those without bed and victuals, then fell to remembering, as I often did, of Jack, Annie, Tom and Daisy, and my beloved Toby: I could almost imagine myself back at the reins of one of the vans, creaking sleepily down a sun-dusty lane: I could almost hear the clinking of those wretched loose-packed pans under the van . . . .

'Up, Miss Tregorran!' came a voice in my ear. ' 'Tis four-thirty! Last one down scrubs out the slops buckets . . . .' And she went on ringing that horrid bell in the darkness and cold of the frowsty attic room till I was glad enough to get up just to escape . . . .

That was the beginning of one of the hardest-working periods of my whole life. For weeks I rose tired and went to bed even tireder: in between my whirling brain, sore fingers and aching bones were a bewildering tally of polishes, dough, and irons, plackets, hops, sides of ham, crystallized cowslip petals, icehouses, charcoal, dripping, twice-dried tea leaves, mousetraps, beer-warmers, rush-lights, syllabubs, hem-stitching, tallow, root sauce, oil and ash soap, feathers and down, Bible readings, saffron cakes, goffering, saltire and daily prayers. Eventually it all made some sort of sense, and within three months – even in spite of my abominable plain-sewing – I had passed all my tests in Group A, and was promoted to the outdoor shift, with a green ribbon replacing the yellow, and all the good weather of summer to come. This I enjoyed much better and grew quite unfashionably brown in the sunshine; I was pecked by the chickens, trodden on by cows, leaned against by horses and splashed by pigmuck; I was stung by bees, scratched by brambles, spiked by garden forks, sliced by pruners and soaked many times, but I was well fed, healthy and, surprisingly, happy.

By the end of July I had passed my second set of tests. I sewed a blue ribbon to the new grey cotton dress I had made – both symbols of my increased status – and reported as requested to Miss Thoroughgood's parlour.

'Good morning, Tregorran.'

I curtsied.

'Sit down, child, there by the window where I can see you.'

The soft summer sun, interrupted by fluffy baby clouds and diffused by the thinnest of muslin drapes, glinted on silver candlesticks, glowed on brass bowls, was kind to the threadbare rose-patterned curtains and warmed the faded pink wallpaper. By its light Miss Thoroughgood's face was a thousand tiny scratches of wrinkles, with pale lips and rain-washed eyes. From a corner came a breathy sigh, and I glanced in that direction: Mabs. She was of indeterminate age, spent nearly all of her time in the kitchen, and taught us all by example how to peel, scrub, quarter, scrape, clean, stone, husk, core and prepare all the vegetables and fruit. I suppose she was what one would call a 'natural', for there was no sense or thought behind those tiny currant eyes and slack mouth, but everyone was kind to her. She was of small stature, crooked-backed, and her skin was soft and doughy like under-baked bread, but she smiled so sweetly and her fingers were so deft that none questioned her right to remain at the bottom of every class except the one of her speciality.

Miss T followed my glance, then rose and beckoned me to follow. Mabs squatted in a tangle of skirts and drawers over a large brass tray on which were a myriad of coloured beads, mostly the small glass ones used for embroidery, all the colours of the rainbow and the softer ones between, and she was transferring the beads to a smaller wooden tray lined with soft leather in a pattern that grew before our eyes so swiftly it seemed like magic. Mabs looked up and grinned happily, then mouthed some words of which I understood none, but apparently Miss T did, for she stroked the creature's cheek affectionately.

'Good girl, Mabelle: that will be lovely when it is done. Tell me when you have finished.' She motioned me to be seated again, then looked across at Mabs. 'My one failure: she has always been as she is now, with the brain of a child of four or five, and it seems it is only her fingers that have attained maturity. I made the mistake of placing her once as vegetable cook in a house nearby, but she disgraced me by running back here as soon as the back door was opened . . . .'

'Surely not a failure, ma'am? She is an artist in her own way, and she has the sunniest nature –'

'Perhaps, perhaps: who is the judge?' She sighed, seemed to slump into herself, then drew herself up into her usual tight person again. 'But it is you we are to discuss today. You have satisfactorily completed the First Course, so Mrs Lachie assures me. I have seen some of your work and applaud your energy and enthusiasm, but do not altogether share your guardian, Lady Margaret's, optimism about your plain-sewing,' and she placed her hand on a sorry little heap on the table beside her, which I recognized as

525

my latest attempt to hem half a dozen handkerchiefs. 'These will have to be unpicked and done again . . . . However, I do not consider I can hold you back for the only fault we have found, so I shall expect you to spend extra time improving this deficiency.'

Coming from her it was a command rather than a hope, and I nodded meekly. 'Yes, ma'am . . . .'

'Good. Now, you are ready to progress to the Advanced Course: so far you are a competent below-stairs maid who would make some yeoman a good wife, but the extra tuition is to fit you for the position of at least an upstairs maid, and hopefully under-housekeeper, lady's maid or even companion.' She consulted a notebook by my discarded handkerchiefs. 'Luckily you seem to be halfway along the course of instruction already, for Mrs Lachie notes that you can read and write competently which is borne out by your letter of introduction, and that you have done simple figuring. She also says that you have had experience of preparing herb remedies, and have a book with some new ones which you have found efficacious.'

Again I nodded: Kat's herb book was my most precious possession, and had survived even Angel and Barnaby.

'Then you will only have to concentrate on the finer refinements of attendance on a lady, with dressing, pressing and refurbishing clothes, hairdressing, accounts, keeping a linen cupboard, french-polishing, embroidery, conversation, light massage, make-up, washing jewellery, polishing silver and other metals, arranging flowers, ordering meals, quick repairs to tears and rips, mending crockery, cutlery and light furniture and furnishings, and the day-to-day running of an average household . . . .'

She left me no time to be even more daunted by the list than by the earlier ones I had faced, for she produced pen and paper and proceeded to confirm to her satisfaction that I could indeed manage simple accounting, write a fair hand, and read aloud. And in this last I nearly betrayed my unconventional background, for after a dull account of a visiting preacher's sermonizing she asked me to read a little Shakespeare, giving me the Portia speech on mercy. The words swam into my mind with the ease of familiarity: white swans on a golden river Avon. There we had rehearsed *The Merchant of Venice*, Jack and I, he in his false nose and wisped beard of horsehair, I in my boy's garb and lawyer's cloak, and he had taught me how to say the words with sweet reason in my voice . . . . There was a little silence when I had finished, and in that silence there was not only surprise, but also censure. Mabs broke the uneasy quiet by clapping her hands and Miss T bid her sharply to silence again.

Realizing my mistake I made a hurried excuse. 'I – I saw the play, once . . . .'

'There is no need to read the piece with such histrionics, whether you saw it on the stage or no,' was the sharp answer. 'You are not, thank the dear Lord, one of those terrible play-actors . . . .' There were little spots of colour on her faded cheeks, and I could feel my blood rising to an unwise retort, but bit my tongue: Esther would not have argued. Esther would not have read it like that, either . . . .

'No, ma'am . . . .' and I studied the pattern on the carpet with fierce concentration.

'Very well: from now on you may read the chosen lesson at prayers on Tuesdays of every week, and we shall take it that that part of your education is complete. There is the matter of your plain-sewing: I wish you to make the time to show me a piece every day until I am satisfied. You will find you have more leisure on this course, rising later, so the task should not prove too onerous. Now, have you anything else to say?'

'Nothing, ma'am, except to thank you –'

'Good girl!' But she was not addressing me. Breathing heavily with concentration, Mabs was carrying her small tray over to the table by Miss T's side. Setting it down carefully, she clapped her hands.

'Mabs good girl . . . .'

I looked with Miss Thoroughgood: a green cockerel trod

527

his drab hen in rising high-combed splendour, while a winter sun cartwheeled its red face above the fence behind, seeming to smirk approval. It was very good: bold, primitive, indelicate, but real. No snows would have shrunk that cock: for a moment I was reminded of Nick . . . .

Miss Thoroughgood gave me a sharp glance, then patted Mabs's arm. 'Very well observed, my dear: now, back to your work. Come and see me again on Wednesday, the day we do the wash, remember? That's a good girl . . . . Don't spoil it all by crying: we can't always do just what we want, can we? Next time you can do me a nice picture of flowers: roses and forget-me-nots and daisies, perhaps. Off you go: they will be needing you in the kitchen to show them how to peel the carrots wafer-thin and make flowers out of the radishes, won't they?' And she pushed Mabs gently from the room. When the door shut behind her Miss T crossed hurriedly to the tray and poured the beads back with a clatter onto the brass tray: her face was flushed, and she did not look at me.

I rose to go, but hesitated. 'Miss Thoroughgood . . . .'

'Yes, Tregorran?'

'Why didn't you let her stay and make another picture? She wanted to . . . .'

'Just because she is — what she is, there is no need to overindulge. Besides, her pictures are sometimes — overdramatic, too realistic.' She sighed. 'However limited the intellect, the emotions are still strong: a pity, a pity. No, if I had let her make another picture it would have ceased to be a treat. One sips at wine, my dear, one does not gulp it down like water, otherwise one becomes dulled in time to both the flavour and the intoxication . . . .'

True: my own sips of the intoxication of real happiness had been few, mostly unexpected, and all very heady, perhaps more so for the combination. I supposed I was happy enough now, however, but it was the custom of a lesser brew. The time with Nick had been more exotic, like madeira, while my life on the road could be likened to strong ale. And Jack? Ah, he was the best brandy, the kind one smuggled into the cellar in casks that were both hard to open and evaporated easily when broached. But they left their flavour on the tongue; that kind of spirit could have made of me an alcoholic . . . .

I moved into the other dormitory, the one that faced west, where there were only nineteen girls, instead of the twenty-nine that lay as close as bottled gooseberries in the other. We luxuriated in a rising hour of six-thirty and had no fires to light, no heavy chores, no continually dirty hands, but in my case there was always the wretched plain-sewing from which I had no respite until the day I left. A lot of the course I enjoyed: practising hairdressing on the horsehair wigs on stands and on the other girls (my own hair was growing nicely now, and I no longer wore the disguising mobcap but had graduated to a dainty lace saucer-cap); arranging flowers; concocting lavender water and colognes; mixing face powders and rouges (though never allowed to wear them); marketing, and even teaching in the local Sunday school. Miss T's brother not only took us for religious instruction and conducted morning and evening prayers, he also taught the village children their catechism, and once when he had been ill with his stomach, as he often was, I deputized as an emergency measure, but apparently did well enough to take over the babies on Sundays. Septimus Thoroughgood was a thin, paler echo of his sister. Although he was the younger, he had been forced to give up his living some years since through ill health and was now retired. He taught the girls their letters gently and patiently, heard their reading with fortitude, corrected spelling accurately and fell asleep every night directly after supper. We all liked him, and he did not inspire the fear his stricter sister sometimes did. But neither he nor Miss T were getting any younger, and even while I was there I noticed how Jessie Lachie was gradually taking over more and more of the running of the school, sparing the other two as much as she could. So it was Jessie who came to me with Lady Margaret's letter one autumn morning when the ripening chestnuts were stretching and splitting their knobbly suits like brown-skinned ragamuffins and the robin's song held a dying fall.

I had always known that one day Lady Margaret would write, either to inquire as a politeness after her 'niece', or to demand my instant dismissal as an imposter, but after the first three months, when I had daily expected a call to Miss T's parlour and my forcible removal, I had imperceptibly relaxed, the tension had grown less and I think I had almost persuaded myself that she would stay abroad indefinitely with Georgina; to tell the truth, I had not thought of her for weeks. Now, lulled as I had been by a false sense of security, I could only stare in horror at Jessie as she stood there with the letter in her hand. I must have looked like a classic statue of guilt discovered, my mouth gawping like a fish and my hands clapped to my cheeks.

'A – a letter – from my – my aunt, Lady . . . .' I couldn't go on.

But dear Jessie misunderstood my dismay, and hastened to reassure me that my 'aunt' was well. 'She writes how pleased she is to hear from us that you have satisfactorily completed the first stage of your time with us: we always inform the sponsors, as you know. I must say I am surprised that she has not written to you before, nor you to her, but I suppose that was because she was abroad, and I know the Continental service is notoriously unreliable. However that may be, she is home now, and reports that they have had a most enjoyable time. Your cousin Georgina had a number of admirers, as I understand, but – Why, Esther, my dear, whatever is the matter?'

For I had burst into tears, I who had prided myself on my ability to act the part of another without cracking up or betraying myself. Jack would have blamed my lapse on the time of the month . . . . Oh, Jack! I need you, I need you, with your common sense, your large handkerchiefs and your comforting hug! I cried harder.

In no time at all Jessie had waved her vinaigrette under my nose and escorted me into the privacy of her room, where she seated me firmly in a comfortable chair, poured a glass of madeira, and wiped away my tears with her own dainty handkerchief.

'And now,' she said firmly. 'I think you had better tell me all about it.'

So I told her that I wasn't Esther, but Zoe; I skipped over my life on the road, merely telling her I had run away in disguise from my Aunt Sophia and had been earning a precarious existence as a scrivener in London when Lady Margaret's letter had been given to me, together with the rest of Esther's belongings. I kept the telling as simple as I could, for if I judged Jessie aright she was an uncomplicated, loving person and would understand things plainly enough if I kept to the essentials. I was right: she wiped her own eyes and gave me a swift embrace.

'Poor wee mite! How could you have – but never mind. Your secret is safe with me; I could never condemn your actions after all Miss Thoroughgood has done for me!' And I learned for the first time how she and her Dougal had been in a company driving cattle down from Scotland when he had caught a low fever in Yorkshire and the others had had to leave them behind; how Miss T, journeying to fetch her brother to live with her, had come across Jessie nursing her dying husband by the road near the village of Bingley . . . 'and she stopped the coach right there and then and took us both up and conveyed us to the nearest inn. My Dougal died that very night, God rest his soul, but she was not satisfied until he had had the neatest of Christian burials, and her bearing all the cost. I was fair worn with watching and grief, but she would have no pining and had me down here in the twinkling of an eye and no time to mourn.'

And Jessie had been Miss T's prop and stay ever since.

Being a good, tidy Scots girl she was diligent, careful, and frugal, and now was repaying her benefactress by taking as much of the burden as she could from the older woman's frail shoulders.

' 'Tis no more than I owe her, and she will not forget. She had a will drawn up two, three years ago, for she knows her days are numbered, and I shall get the care for her brother and Mabs; there will be enough to buy a wee cottage for the three of us and provide an annuity. This place will have to go, but none shall be turned out till they have places to go to –'

'Mabs?' I queried. 'Is she special to Miss T?'

'Aye. Miss Hester was a maiden lady with a bit put by in the savings line – I tell you this to keep as close as I keep your secret – and she approaching middle years. She was cozened by a wicked play-actor who stole both heart and money, and left her with nothing but a poor bairn with half the wits she should have and no marriage lines. That she started this place with nothing but her wits and hard work is to her credit, and she has paid off near all she owes. To save disgrace she sent out that the babe was adopted, and the girl herself knows no different, nor would care, I suppose: that sort loves just the heart that is kind and the hand that feeds; she will be my loving care, as will Mr Thoroughgood, and with my sister's eldest to help, we shall be cosy enough, I imagine.' She paused, and seemed to draw herself together. 'But as to you, my dear Esther, as I shall still call you: it is clear that we shall have to get you placed as soon as possible, before your "aunt" finds out you are here under false pretences. In the meanwhile you had better read the letter and know how the land lies.'

'Should I? It's not really meant for me –'

'Look, girl, if you decide to do something, do it properly: no point in having false conscience now. The real Esther would have been given this to read and you're still her to all intents and purposes, so – read!'

To save paper my 'aunt' had written on both sides of

one sheet and on the inside of the enclosing fold as well. Her letter, like the one Barnaby and I had studied, was full of exclamations, underlinings and capitals, to the exclusion of style or content. It appeared that Venice had not lived up to expectations: '. . . and Georgina has had only One Serious Offer, and that from a So-Called Prince, who dressed little better than a Tradesman, and had no fortune to Commend him . . .' and: '. . . the smell of the Drains was Abominable – dead dogs in the Canals and *Worse* . . . . Mould on the Walls and Ceilings of even the most Pretentious Palaces . . .' and: '. . . Society very Tight-knit and Standoffish; prouder still are the Paupers . . . .' I skimmed through, wondering once again how she could think Miss T would be interested in hearing all about her gossip: perhaps, however, it was the only time anyone took note of her endless chatter. The part that concerned me was near the end of the letter: 'We are Home for a few days then go to the Polreaths', where My Dear Georgina has High Hopes of the eldest: in the meantime I hope you will keep Esther hard at her Studies: we shall be at the Town House for the Season of course, and she may write her duty Letters to me there: I look forward to a fuller report on her Progress then. As we have travel Acquaintances in Chesham Bois, we may well pay a Visit . . . .'

Jessie had missed that piece. 'All right, lassie, don't get your drawers in a pucker, or you may find yourself bum to the wind! How long have you been with us now?'

'Since . . . March, I think; And I passed my first tests by the end of June.'

'And it's now the beginning of October; apart from a wee bit of polishing up you are as ready as you'll ever be. Do you mind what position you take?'

I shook my head. 'Anything, as long as I am gone before *she* arrives . . . .'

'Leave it to me, then. Nothing too lowly or Miss Thoroughgood will suspect. The next suitable post I'll speak up for you special, though there's others with more seniority.'

I hugged her. 'You're an angel!'

'Not me! Now, away with you: down on your knees tonight and pray for a place . . . . And in the meantime, a bit of plain-sewing wouldn't come amiss . . . .'

26

The little two-wheeled cart I had hired from the inn trundled off down the lane and I was left, carpetbag in hand, peering through the wrought-iron gates into a swirl of falling leaves.

The October wind was chilly, and I drew my new cloak thankfully round me and fastened it at the throat. The length of dark green serge had been a present from Jessie, and she had helped me line it with some scarlet silk we found in one of the attics. The frogging I had managed myself – strangely I was far better at complicated stitches than plain – but the neat hemming and finishing was entirely Jessie's, as were the delicate lawn collars she had appliquéd for decorating the two new dresses I had made, plain and sober as befitted my new position. And all I had given her was a Daily Book, price one shilling and threepence, with an uplifting verse for each day, and space for cut-out pictures or recipes. But I had copied out some of the more useful (to Jessie) herbal remedies from Kat's book into the back, and her face had lighted up when she saw them, for the cough remedy and the balm had sold well at Amersham market each week, and were the main reason I still had one shilling and elevenpence in my pocket. At Miss T's we had been given a percentage of anything that went to market: most girls made preserves, or hemmed handkerchiefs and made lavender sachets, but I had concentrated on my one proven skill, dispensing, and had been lucky in my sales, for horehound candy, cherry linctus and witch-hazel lotion had all proved popular, nicely packed in straw baskets and tied with scraps of gaily coloured ribbon. I had had to buy some material for my dresses and underwear, and though the coach fare from the Kings Arms in Amersham to High Wycombe, mail from there to Oxford and an overnight stop, mail again to Cheltenham and packet to Evesham had been forwarded by my prospective employer, there had also been apologies that there was no coach to collect me from Hink. I had hired the cart for sixpence, the drink of milk and bread and butter I had consumed while waiting had been another twopence . . . . Still, I had nearly two shillings more than I had had when I arrived at Miss T's eight months before, I was warmly and neatly dressed with a change of underwear and dress, and came with a recommendation that I was proficient in all the arts to make me an ideal companion-help to Lady Jestyn.

Lady Jestyn . . . Jestyn. That was the name that, less than a week ago, had sent a shock through me as if I had been caught catnapping and had suddenly been jerked awake: something had pricked my consciousness so sharply that I even had had the temerity to interrupt Miss T . . . .

And I still had no idea why; I had repeated the name over and over again to myself till repetition had taken away sense, and it was only a two-syllabled sound. I had searched my memory as far back as childhood, worried over the less likely connotations, delved into remembrance until it became less productive than ever, and still I was baffled. All I knew was that the name meant something important to me, good or bad.

Miss Thoroughgood had called a conference, as she called it, of the more senior girls, as two offers of employment had been received in the post. It was the usual custom, a pretence that everyone had a fair chance to choose their position, although in fact the lucky ones had usually been picked by Miss T beforehand, and the others were usually included merely to show them how unfitted they were as yet. As Miss T was paid a fee of two guineas by the prospective employer, it was obviously in her interest to choose the most suitable applicant, the girl who would be most credit to her, as much of her custom was engendered by word of mouth. She had even been known to leave a post unfilled rather than send someone she considered unsuitable, and she only advertised in extreme cases. She always investigated a place thoroughly before sending out her girls, and with this combination, together with our thorough training, there had been few failures.

This particular evening there were five of us seated in the dining-room at dusk, a couple of candlesticks at either end of the table throwing pools of wavering light on the highly polished surface. We dined at five in the autumn months, and as this was a Sunday the senior girls had dined with Miss T and her brother in here instead of in the kitchen with the others as usual on weekdays, and had been waited on by the junior girls as part of their training. We five clustered at one end for warmth, for the day had been chill but no fires were lighted in the public rooms till November, to save fuel: that was why the kitchen was always crowded in winter, and with the few candles we were allowed we must have looked sometimes in the gloom like a bundle of bats in a belfry wriggling into the warmest spots.

Miss T and Jessie bustled in and took their places at the other end of the table. Almost immediately she noticed something wrong.

'Mrs Lachie: there is a spot of pork grease on the table here; those girls must be more particular. Please see to it.'

'Of course, ma'am,' said Jessie in her soft voice. 'Some of our newer girls have come from such dismal homes that all this polishing and tidying must seem very strange to them. But they will learn.'

A mollified Miss T placed two letters on the table. 'Thank you. And now to business. I have to tell you girls of two excellent offers I have received. I have considered carefully the positions open and discussed your various capabilities with Mrs Lachie and the result of our considerations is that you shall all have an opportunity to decide whether your talents would fit the posts offered.'

I glanced round at the others. It was my first time at one of these meetings and I imagined that Jessie must have pressed my case hard for me to be included, for the others all had seniority. On my left was Rosemary, twelve months a student, round, cosy, good-natured; competent at most things, with happy, coaxing ways and a talent with the village children. At the bottom of the table sat Jane, an excellent seamstress and always ready for a tease, and next to her was Betty, who had been here longer than anyone else, and with a history to match of cracked pots, dropped stitches and burned meats: no one, however, was more willing, and generous with her belongings. Across from me sat Prudence, a student two months longer than I: a grave, somewhat austere girl who was, however, better at everything than most, though I considered her reading aloud to be colourless and stilted.

Miss T studied the first letter. 'This is from Mrs Wellborough: you may recall that Nancy Roberts went to her from here some two years ago, on the birth of the fourth child . . . .' Betty was the only one who had been here long enough to remember, and she nodded. 'Nancy has given great satisfaction, but now the family has been increased by twin boys and there are six children under ten years of age: Mrs Wellborough requires an under-nursemaid to assist Roberts. This will be an exacting post, with patience, good humour, cheerfulness and excellent plain-sewing obvious requirements: the girl who takes this post must be responsible, fond of children, and prepared to work hard. The wages are ten shillings a month, and every second Sunday is a free day. The house is on a moderate estate some ten miles from here, the nearest town being Kings Langley. The premises are relatively modern, and the establishment is run on Christian lines, Mr Wellborough being a prosperous tradesman with an interest in local welfare and a seat on the board of the local school. The food is adequate, the servants' quarters a little cramped but the staff appear content, and the children are well behaved. I believe Roberts has found a steady prospect in one of the under-footmen.' She glanced up. 'Now, what do you all see as your fittedness for this post?'

Clever, I thought: the qualifications sounded ordinary enough, but even as she stated them she was automatically debarring one or other of us. 'Excellent plain-sewing' obviously excluded me and left the four others: 'exacting post' would not suit poor, careless Betty, while 'good humour' and 'cheerfulness' did not apply to Prudence. That left Jane and Rosemary: both responsible, both good seamstresses, with Jane getting the edge on the last, but she would be the last to call herself patient, and had two months' less seniority. It went as I expected, with Rosemary all aglow at the thought of having a clutch of children to care for – and, who knows, a little intrigued at the thought of perhaps another free under-footman.

Miss T was reading the second letter, and I suddenly realized I must have been brought in for some consideration on this one, so listened carefully.

'I am afraid I know little of the lady inquiring; she writes that she heard of my establishment through a mutual acquaintance, but omits to mention the name. She writes, however, as a matter of urgency: it appears the lady has recently lost the services of her French companion-maid, who has gone abroad to nurse a sick relative. She writes that she is "desperate",' and Miss T raised a disapproving eyebrow at the use of such an extravagant word, 'but as I believe she is of French extraction herself, she may be a trifle short on patience: I believe most foreigners are in a hurry. She writes that she is a partial invalid, having suffered a stroke some time ago, and needs someone to keep her company, help dress her, do her hair, attend to light mending, do some polishing of silver, arrange flowers, accompany her on local visiting, write letters and read aloud. There may also be some nursing duties; I understand the post may well be temporary, but, dependent on the return of the French maid, the lady promises to see that whoever takes the post gets good references and is helped to find another post, dependent of course on the satisfactory performance of her duties.

'The house is a large one, near the village of Crum Potting at Hink: I understand this is some ninety miles away. She is the stepmother of the present heir and occupies part of the house, Riverwood, as a separate establishment.' She paused. 'I know the sparse information I have to offer, and my lack of knowledge of the lady, coupled with the rather unsatisfactory question of it being a temporary post, is discouraging, but I might mention that the lady herself is conscious of this and as an added inducement is offering a wage in excess of the usual: twenty guineas a year. She adds that there will be at least two hours of free time during the day as well. I suggest you consider the offer carefully.'

I looked at Prudence and Jane; at a pinch we could all three fit the bill: Betty was obviously thrown in as a makeweight, and she happily dismissed herself from the running with the remark: 'My silver gets tarnished in no time at all, and my flowers wilt: I don't think I'd do at all, ma'am.'

There was a little silence as we three avoided looking at one another, then I heard Jessie's voice. 'I think you said to me ma'am, that the lady was a Catholic? And that she would be pleased to teach the girl some French conversation? Now, I think that is a very kind idea, but I was wondering about the question of religion: some of our young ladies may have strong feelings about popery . . . .' She let the suggestion hang in the air like a worm on a line, and Jane was quick to rise to the bait.

'My family have always been good Protestants, ma'am,' she said. 'I should not wish to offend them by working for a Catholic establishment.'

Which left Prudence and me. The post seemed tailor-made for her, for it sounded like a quiet, gloomy household: I did not fancy the idea of being forced to learn French, nor of waiting on a fussy invalid all day, in the intervals of polishing silver and mending clothes, and yet there was the awful thought of Lady Margaret lingering in the background, time was wasting, and obviously Jessie had tried hard to recommend me –

'I have no real objection to the post,' said Prudence slowly. 'Provided the lady is not too much of an invalid: we are not trained nurses.'

Miss T consulted the letter. 'She had a seizure a year ago, and this has left her a trifle unsteady and with a definite weakness in the left arm. Her eyesight is also affected, which is why she wants someone who is prepared to write letters and read aloud –'

'Tregorran reads aloud most delightfully,' came Jessie's voice again: she really must want me to have the post.

'A little histrionic for my taste,' said Miss T: she had never forgiven my 'The quality of mercy . . .' but after Jessie had told me of her betrayal by an actor, I could appreciate this.

'If you are losing your sight, however,' persisted Jessie, 'perhaps this is just what you would need: someone to create word-pictures for you, so real you can see them in your mind . . . .' She was doing her best, but really she must see that I did not want –

'Lady Jestyn also wished for other qualities,' said Miss T repressively, but that was when I woke up and knew I had to have the post. Forgetting my manners I addressed her directly.

'Whom did you say?'

She frowned, but let my lack of courtesy pass. 'Lady Jestyn, Lady Marie Jestyn, a widow and –'

'Then I must have the post!' I burst out, heedless of Jessie's warning frown. 'I know of her – know the name –'

It was true: somewhere in my past I had heard the name, Jestyn, but I could not for the life of me remember where. It was an unusual name, and I should surely be able to recall: but all I knew was that somehow it was important. I saw Miss T frown, saw her turn to Prudence, and all at once someone whispered in my ear and nudged my brain into action, any action, as long as I did not miss this chance; for a moment it was as if I felt Kat Petulengro's warm breath on the back of my neck, then I opened my mouth and told a string of lies.

'Miss Thoroughgood, ma'am: I am sorry I sounded so discourteous, but you startled me. I am acquainted with the lady in question, although by hearsay only. My dear aunt, Lady Margaret, engaged a tutor for Cousin Georgina and myself who came of good family, fallen on hard times. He had occasion to speak often of those people of quality with whom he had acquaintance. He had travelled extensively on the Continent, and it was there he had met Lady Jestyn.' (Where were the words coming from?) 'He spoke to us at length of her gentle manners and affable condescension, and of course of her many titled connections, both here and abroad.' I drew a deep breath: in for a farthing, in for a florin. 'In fact I remember Lady Margaret deploring at the time that we girls did not have the opportunity to meet many such in the restrictions of our life in the country . . . .'

Which left me with a position I had not wanted, a name that nagged like a sore tooth, and four days' frantic sewing, pressing and ironing before I caught the coach.

The gates were plain, no bearings graced the rusting iron, and the drive twisted away between tall trees so that I could see no further than the first hundred yards. Everything bore the signs of neglect, like a long-forgotten grave; I shivered suddenly as a magpie croaked from one of the evergreens, flicking his tail irritably. There was a small wicket gate in the wall and over the high bricks I caught a glimpse of a curl of chimney smoke; there was a large bell by the gate but the wicket was open, so I stepped inside to a squeak of hinges and over to the lodge. Among the brittle leaves of dead hollyhocks a large ginger cat stretched and yawned, then padded up to the front door at exactly the same time that a spare, middle-aged woman opened it.

'No hawkers, no 'tinerants,' she began automatically, and the ginger cat slipped past her knees into the house. 'Dratted animal! If'n he brings in just one more – Beg pardon, miss; didn't see as how you were respectable. What can I do for you?'

I explained, and my eyes strayed past her to the frayed curtains at the windows, the unscrubbed step, the dingy window glass. I would dearly have liked to ask for a glass of water, but the appearance of the lodge deterred me: I could only hope that my new home would not be as shabby and derelict. When there had been no carriage to meet me I had accepted the written explanation in the letter to Miss T that the coachman was ill and his son away, but now it would almost seem that the excuse could well have been poverty.

The woman shrugged as I explained. 'Someone came down from the house two, three days ago sayin' you was expected, but I didn't take much notice, tell you the truth; usually when folks come 'tis more of those roistering friends of Sir George's; had the gate near off its hinges, last time, and up till all hours . . . .'

Looking down the drive I could see that the thin gravel was well scattered and deep with wheel ruts, though these, and the ditches on either side, were thick with fallen leaves. I hoped my twenty guineas a year were safe.

'You say it's Lady Jestyn as you've come to serve? You'll want the old part of the house then. Quickest way's down the path you'll find to your right just round the corner; if'n you take the drive it's all of a mile, to take in the views, like, but the path'll save you half and bring you out by the back of the old part; you can't miss it.'

I found the path with no difficulty, and at first it was easy going for the path was well trodden, and in spite of the gales and rain of the past week it was dry enough, for flat stones had been placed some time ago over the places that might have proved muddy. There were recent traces that a horse had passed by, and my spirits rose: my goal was nearly reached, the late afternoon sun struck warm through the thinning branches, and life was surely all a big adventure. Every now and again I caught tantalizing glimpses of roofs or chimneypots, so it was with distinct annoyance that I rounded a turn in the path and found my way effectively blocked by a large fallen tree that had obviously come down in the gales. To my left was an impenetrable thicket of briars and bramble, to my right a thick hedge of laurel that yielded but a few inches to pressure then sprang back as thick as before. Sprat would have been able to climb over that tangle of branches and trunk that was the fallen tree, but Esther in her new dress and cloak dared not even try. I had no wish to retrace my steps all the way to the drive and walk the long way round, so looked for an alternative route and found it two minutes later. My mind had noted a faint track leading off to the right some fifty yards back, and I could now see that there was a secondary path, and that this was the way the horse had taken. As I hesitated I heard the faint thunk-tug! of someone chopping wood, and a woman's high laughter. Reassured I took the new path, hoping for an alternative way to my destination, or at the least help from the woodcutter to move the obstruction.

I had been expecting a humble cottage, but when I stepped round the screen of bushes that marked the end of the path I could not have been more surprised. In front of me was a half-gate some three feet high, and beyond that a small grass lawn edged with flowerbeds, still full of yellow, white and purple flowers in profusion. The garden rose to a small terrace, where stood a house that could have come from the pages of a child's picture book. It was half-timbered with a thatch roof, like many others I had seen, but this was so clean and sparkling with whitewash, shining windows, and clean brown wood that it did not look quite real. It was bigger than a cottage, for I counted four windows on the ground floor and as many above, yet it seemed like a toy house, so perfect was it in its setting of velvet grass and late-blooming flowers. The autumn afternoon sun threw long tree-shadows across the grass, but the terrace was still bathed in a golden glow, and by its light I saw a girl, a woman perhaps, with golden hair, dressed in white and sitting in a low chair, rocking a cradle with her foot. As I hesitated she began to sing, a high, wordless song, and stooping picked a bundle from the cradle and held it to her breast, swaying back and forth. Lifting the latch of the gate I began to walk up the path towards her, but even as I did so an older woman came out of the house with a shawl in her hand.

' 'Tis getting late, my dear, and we don't want you to catch cold: you might give it to baby, and we don't want that, do we? Supper will be –'

They both caught sight of me at the same time, and my appearance could not have produced greater consternation and aversion had I had two heads and been ten feet tall. The fair girl screamed, her pale doll's face blank, the baby clutched close to her breast; the older woman appeared to try and protect her, flinging the shawl over her head and thrusting her behind her own greater bulk. She shouted at me: loudly, angrily.

'Go away! You have no right to be here! Husband: a trespasser!' And she moved threateningly down the steps towards me. 'Get out this instant, or I'll set the dog on you . . . .'

As if on cue I heard a menacing growl and heavy footsteps right behind me and turning, saw a burly, tall man with a woodman's axe on his shoulder and a large, rough-coated dog at his heels.

Taking a deep breath I started to explain. 'I'm sorry if I'm trespassing and frightened your – your wife, but I was taking the way through the woods to Lady Jestyn's – I am come to be her new companion – and there was a large tree blocking the path, so I looked for another way and – well, here I am!' I ended up out of breath, and to hide my confusion bent down to stroke the dog. 'Good

544

boy . . . .' The dog's reaction was to bare a perfectly fearsome set of teeth and inch forward.

'Down, Rusty! Don't 'tempt to touch him, miss, he's been trained as a guard dog and will respond only to the wife or me. Wait there,' and he strode up to the other two, still watching from the verandah, and obviously explained the position to them. Without thinking I stooped to pick up my carpetbag, only to jump back in shock as a perfect fusillade of barking reverberated round my ankles and teeth flashed within an inch of my fingers. As I leaped back there was a scream of laughter from the terrace and the fair girl pointed a finger of ridicule at my discomfiture. Her lovely doll-face still held no expression, and the only indication of emotion was in that high, tittering laugh. The woman at her side said a few words to her husband, nodding back in my direction, then led the girl into the house; as the door closed behind the girl I distinctly heard her say, in very ladylike tones: 'She did not come to steal my baby? You would not let her take my baby, Nannie?' and it was all of a piece with this that suddenly the sun had gone and a dry, cold wind rustled the dead leaves at my feet.

The man came back, this time without his axe, I was thankful to see, for by this time I was not only tired, cold and hungry, but a little frightened, too.

'Stay, Rusty: stay and guard!' and the dog slunk off to the terrace, still eyeing me suspiciously. 'Come, miss: there's another path leads from the Dower House here to the old part of Riverwood. I'll get that tree seen to tomorrow, and then you mustn't come this way again; trouble is, there's just too much for one man to do, and I can't be everywhere at once,' and grumbling he led me at a rapid pace down the side of the house and struck off down a paved pathway, somewhat overgrown, leaving me breathlessly half-running behind. In no time at all, it seemed, we emerged at the side of the great house, and he pointed me to a door.

'That's Her Ladyship's part of the house; the path you

should've come by is over there,' and he pointed to an opening about fifty yards to our left. 'As I said, I'll have that cleared right through by tomorrow, and you're to use that if you want a way to the village. The way we've come is trespassing, and the dog will have you if there's none to stop him; besides, Lady Jestyn herself wouldn't like it that you came this way and saw – what you did; if she wishes she may tell you herself what's out there, but till then it's best you don't say what you've seen, nor that you came by that path. Off you go!' and he gave me a shove between my shoulder blades that set me stumbling over the thin gravel towards the house.

Lady Jestyn was not at all how I had imagined her; she seemed in her sixties, was tall and slim, almost gaunt, with a sallow complexion, plainly dressed grey hair and dark purplish marks under her brown eyes. She was dressed in simple muted colours, with an exquisitely worked lace widow's cap her only concession to extravagance. Her voice held hardly any trace of her French ancestry and, apart from a slight hesitancy in her step and the stiffness of her left hand, she showed little sign of her affliction, either. She made me instantly welcome and I was drawn into warmth and comfort, my cloak and carpetbag were taken by the maid, Kate, and moments later I was seated on a low stool by the fire in the sitting room with a bowl of vegetable broth and a glass of wine.

'Now, my dear,' she said: 'No questions from me and no answers from you until that is inside you, though I should dearly like to know of your journey. When you have supped and warmed yourself I will have Kate show you your room, and after you have unpacked and washed, perhaps you will join me for a talk before bedtime?'

The room I was allotted was under the eaves, and from it I could see all the way across the front of the newer part of the house to the southern wing, and to my left was the wood through which I had come; the part of the main house that I could see was built of honey stone, picked out in white, with a parapet along the roof, a gravelled courtyard, and a columned entrance. The part I was in was obviously earlier, Tudor perhaps, although the wood and stone work were not in as good a state of repair as the little Dower House I had just left. I thrust open my ill-fitting window to its fullest extent and leaned out past the leaded panes to breathe in the last of the autumn twilight; the sky was greening already, making of the bulk of the house to my right a deep silhouette, although the woods to the left still held that sudden livid brightness that is so ephemeral, a memory of the sun, light before the dark. Beyond the woods lay a little hump of a hill that at home in Derbyshire would be no more than an obstruction on the horizon but that here, on a plain, was definitely a hill: I learned later it was called Bredon. Below me on the gravel an aimless heap of leaves twirled suddenly on a twist of air, shuffling and spinning anticlockwise, their voice a surprised dry whisper. A late-summer moth blundered against my hand, and for a moment its ruby eyes and dingy wings hesitated on my palm, tiny feet clinging to my skin: then it hurled itself into the dark. A little like me, I thought.

I turned back to my room; some nine paces by six, it held a small truckle bed with a patchwork coverlet, a washstand, a cupboard for my clothes, and a shelf by the bed for my candle and perhaps a book; the uneven floor was brightened by a rag rug. Quickly unpacking, I had scarcely put away my things when Kate, the housemaid, appeared with a jug of hot water.

'Am I glad you've finally arrived! Not that Her Ladyship isn't a dear and not unduly fussy, but she's been like a wasp in an empty jar without someone to read to her since that Hortense went back to France – you do read, don't you?' Having been reassured she bubbled on happily, not offering to leave as I got washed; I knew it was not the done thing to listen to servants' gossip, but in the position I was in I was neither one thing nor the other: besides I

547

was curious about the household I had come into, with French maids, hints of roistering by the present baronet, and secret houses hidden in the woods I was not allowed to refer to. 'I've got the room next to yours down the corridor,' chattered Kate, perched on the bed like an animated sparrow, her hands fluttering like wings, her toes waggling with enthusiasm at someone to talk to: 'Cook and Charles are just across the way – Charles is the butler-cum-everything-else, been with the family for years – and just below us is Her Ladyship's room and next to that the one Hortense had. Jeremy sleeps across from them.' She blushed as I glanced up at her suddenly softened voice. 'Jeremy is the footman . . . . He's, well – you'll see him tomorrow.' I noticed with amusement that her restless toes hung momentarily still, dejected. 'He's awful strong; carries Lady Jestyn like a baby up the stairs if she's tired. Used to work in the stables when she first lost her husband and Mr James was only a lad, but has come up in the world. Got a good position and could have any girl he fancied, I reckon . . . .' The toes were still dejected.

'Is that all the staff?' I asked, as she had come to a temporary halt.

'No: there's the scullery maid, Sukey, that sleeps in the kitchen, and Sal what comes in daily to do the rough; then there's the coachman, Old Bob, and his son, Young Bob, what helps with the horses. If we has company there's two maids who'll come in from the House, but mostly we don't have visitors since Mr James left. Her Ladyship has been ill the last few months and has quite got out of the habit of visiting and she only receives the doctor and his wife, the priest, and sometimes Miss Tabby Pritchard and her sister Dorcas from the village: for others we're to say she's indisposed. Except, of course, for Mr James.' A sudden sparkle came into her eyes, the toes pointed heavenwards for a moment, and then she jumped up and investigated the clothes I had put away. 'Nice piece of cloth that, and I like the collars . . . . When *he* comes everything's upside down for days! Trouble is, he's always giving but two days' notice, or less, and gone within the same. Still, he always brings a present: last year I got some scarlet ribbon and he kissed my cheek right soundly and said he dreamed of such as I . . . . Called me Thisby or some such and swore he wished himself Pyramids and hoped we could have a perpetual Midsummer Night: Jeremy didn't know what to make of it when I told him!'

' 'S Dream,' I supplied. 'He sounds fun!' and I could not repress a smile, for I suspected the erudite James had been having a tease at the expense of the decidedly buxom Kate.

'He's very lively, I know that! A gentleman, of course, but somehow he's the knack of getting on with all. 'Course he comes secret, as Sir George is sort of set against him and won't let him near. Comes on Her Ladyship's birthday, Christmas; times like that.'

'He is Sir George's half-brother, then?'

'And so unalike as cob and hunter! Sir George takes after his mother, so I've heard tell: fair and pink and white and plump; Mr James is tall and thin and dark, like *his*. He's a temper all his own though, and a way of looking down his nose when things aren't quite right – like the mistress if the fish is too high or Old Bob has a swear . . . .'

It did not take me long to settle into the new routine, and I learned quite a lot of the family's background and present set-up from my new employer. Our establishment was completely separate from Sir George's, and as I had surmised our wing was the oldest part of the estate, dating from Elizabethan times. It was thought that it had been originally part of the extensive stables as it faced south, and any house in those days was built facing north because the sun was considered unhealthy. Our part was actually connected to the newer part by a ground-floor gallery, but this was permanently closed off by a heavy oaken door.

The land had been granted to the Jestyns in the 1660s

by a grateful King Charles II – no one seemed to know what had happened to the original owners – and as a mark of respect all the male children since had borne a Stuart name. Thus the present incumbent – hedging his bets – was named George Charles and his half-brother James. There had also been two daughters of the first marriage, Anne and Caroline, who had died in infancy, but the only child of the second was the dashing James. Lady Jestyn was obviously very proud of this self-exiled son – for permanent absence was his own choice – and before long she showed me the miniature she always wore about her neck: a plump, dark-haired child clutching a toy soldier and scowling at the painter. There were other paintings, too: a child of four standing in the grounds with a dog near as big as he by his side; a curiously stiff boy of seven leaning against his seated mother's lap. She had changed but little, except that her then black hair was dressed in ringlets; a multicoloured kitten played with the ribbons of her dress. That kitten was now an incredibly old, stiff-jointed cat called Gipsy, who lived her life in the hearth, her ancient hip bones sticking up like knobs through her fur. She was carried out ceremoniously once a day to a patch of earth by Charles, the butler, who waited for her to perform; she had beef tea for breakfast, cream for tea, and fish and rice for supper, because of her teeth. I felt sorry for her at first, but I soon saw that age had come to her so gently and gradually that she had forgotten how to be spry and supple: and who knew how young she was in her twitching dreams? I learned she was the monumental age of twenty-three or -four – Lady Jestyn said that made her one hundred and sixty-odd years old in human terms.

I said it did not take me long to learn the new routine: what it did take some time to become accustomed to was the fact of being confined to one person for exchanges of ideas, social contact, affection; I do not think I ever let my employer see that sometimes I felt like a finch in a cage, caught in adulthood, with all the dangerous and

550

heady freedom of outside to contrast with stuffy gilded bars and imprisonment. If I had not had the liberal upbringing of my stepfather, the excitements of the road, the uncertainty of Madame's, the sheer physical effort and companionship of Miss T's – and if I had not fallen in love with Jack so irrevocably – it would have been easier. The memory of the times I had had with Nick did not help either, for we were a celibate household. I had not realized how much one can become accustomed to turning for the sheer physical relief of one's body to another till I had it no longer: I had felt restless in the hot summer nights at Miss T's but, wisely I think in retrospect, she had kept us generally too busy to think of our physical needs: not, I suppose, that many of those girls had spent the best part of a year with a virile lad like Nick as their bedfellow.

Our routine was simple: we rose early, breakfasted, and I read the papers aloud as directed. While Lady Jestyn answered what letters she could, in a large, unsteady hand, leaning away from the paper (for she had become very long-sighted), I polished the brass and silver in the sitting room, hall and her bedroom – candlesticks, boxes, trinkets, bowls, vases and jugs – and then we looked together at the mending. This, of which I had been so apprehensive, proved no difficulty at all: a little mending of tears, an occasional dropped seam, resewing on of cleaned collars and cuffs or ribbons: any mending or patching of household linen was done by Kate. At eleven precisely each morning, unless it was wet, Lady Jestyn and I strolled in the grounds as far as the Italian garden that lay beneath the southern wing of the main house. The walks and arbours and hedges were sadly in need of clipping and the gravelled paths choked with weeds; the great basin where the fountain had been was empty and silent, but the tall cypresses still retained an air of grandeur as they marched away into the distance, though some were taller than others, due to the neglect of their smaller brethren. Over to our right could be caught the occasional glimpse of sparkling waters where the Severn provided our western boundary, although it was only a babe at these levels – and farther still the misty hump that was the Malvern hills.

Luncheon, usually a frugal affair of soup, pâté and toast, was at twelve. During the afternoon Lady Jestyn rested on the day bed in the sitting room and it was then that I escaped, always outside. Into the October gales, November mists, December frosts, January snows, I ran; joying in the open air, the tossing bare branches that scribbled frantic messages on the blue, grey, white sky; the wind that brought with it the smell of rain – or was it the sea? – the crisp snow crossed and recrossed by the tracks of robin, rabbit and the slot of deer; the haunting gabble of wild geese flying still farther south to the marches; the cry of a dog fox, the scream of a vixen; the spectral call of owls, the winter song of the chaffinch, a pretty dying fall. . . . But I had to be back by three-thirty, when we took tea. Afterwards I read to my employer: a poem by Cowper, part of Mr Pepys' diaries (a lovely discovery), articles from the *Spectator* or the *Tatler*. We dined at six and afterwards Lady Jestyn would try to practise a little on the out-of-tune harpsichord, her crippled hand making a sad sound out of the Bach and Scarlatti she loved so much, but she would soon tire and come back to the fire, to teach me some more French.

At first mere politeness had kept me from fidgeting, but her enthusiasm, patience and, probably most of all, her commendation of my quick learning and excellent accent made the lessons more of a pleasure than a chore, and in the end I even began to look forward to them. I kept a small notebook in which I noted new words, genders and conjugations, and before long was able to hold a simple conversation in her language, so long as we kept to generalities like the weather and, to a certain extent, the daily news. I say daily, but in reality the papers came up from London about twice a week in a bundle, together with a couple of magazines and journals. Eagerly we would catch up with the news I had once neglected or despised, being too busy merely living; now I began to appreciate how it mattered to all of us how firm Mr Pitt was in his foreign policy, how many troops we had, how well or ill His Majesty became, how much the price of tobacco had risen, because all these were indirectly connected to us through James, for he worked secretly for the government, in part of the new Foreign Office, and had to spend much of his time on mysterious trips abroad in dangerous circumstances. And the tobacco? James loved his pipe of tobacco, and proudly his mother pointed out his jars and pipe rack on a shelf in the corner. I was allowed to open one of the jars and sniff: certainly there was no smell quite like it, and how much better it smelled than it tasted. . . . I remembered, of a sudden, picking up Jack's pipe once when he had been hurriedly called away and taking a surreptitious draw; remembered, too, the awful coughing, sneezing and retching that had followed, and the clip round the ear and 'Serve you right!' I had got from him – I was still Sprat, then – and the honey Annie had found for my reddened throat.

But the day James came home I was not there.

It was February; the willow in the sheltered dell behind the house a haze of yellow, not quite trusting its first thin slivers of green, the woods shining in odd corners with celandine, shock-headed coltsfoot growing by the drain in the stables, and an optimistic frog testing the shallows of the pond – but I was on my way to Cheltenham. We received the Cheltenham paper erratically and in the last issue, tucked away amongst the local births, marriages and deaths, the out-of-date London news, homilies on manners and dress, amateur verse, writing up of subscription concerts, and many advertisements, we read of their subscription book club. Apparently they had over five thousand volumes in stock, and always welcomed new subscribers. I had by now read all the few books in the house and yearned for new reading: Lady Jestyn did not take much persuading to write to the club and arrange for me to pay them a visit, choose half a dozen volumes and leave a list for the next time we needed something fresh. I was given money, a lift in the trap to Evesham from whence I caught the regular coach, and the address of one of Riverwood's former housekeepers, who had retired to live with her widowed brother in a cottage just outside Cheltenham. They had intimated they would be glad to put me up for two nights, meeting the coach, escorting me round the town the following day, and taking me to the coach for the return trip.

Cheltenham was very pleasant, and it was a real treat to be amongst crowds again, to admire the shops, to quiz the passers-by, to take time to eat in a pastry shop; I managed a nice selection at Prewett's, the book club, and made a list of a couple of dozen others we should try at a later date; I bought the silk stockings my employer had asked me to find, and the sheer exuberance of the day persuaded me not only into the purchase of a length of fine lavender-sprigged muslin to make into summer dresses for myself from a pattern in the *Lady's Magazine* but also a length of daffodil watered silk, a reckless extravagance I regretted as soon as the yardage had been cut and wrapped. Luckily there had been no problem with my wages: these had been paid every month without fail, and not only had Lady Jestyn not deducted the fee she had paid Miss T, she had also professed a diffidence with figures and the original twenty guineas a year, when divided by monthly portions, came nearer twenty-four. Consequently I was better off than I had been since the travelling days, especially as the clothes I had brought with me were adequate, if not exciting. But I still had misgivings over the lovely yellow silk, and on the way home in the coach the following day my mind was scurrying round like an ant on the first day of spring, devising ways of using it so that I got the maximum usage and could persuade myself it was an advantage rather than a luxury.

To my surprise the trap with Young Bob aboard met me at Evesham, instead of the usual stop at the inn at Hink, but after I heard his news I could not wait to get back as soon as possible. Apparently, so he told me as we rattled back along the highway and turned into the twisty lanes to Crum Potting, James Jestyn had arrived the previous morning at dawn, on a lathered horse and unannounced. He had spent but twenty-four hours at home, most of the time closeted with his mother, though he had had a quick round of the estate, in the continued absence of his half-brother. He and his mother had talked far into the night, and when he had finally dropped asleep on the day bed she had stayed up through the small hours to watch over him; he had left at dawn for foreign parts, and Lady Jestyn had waited till he was on his way before collapsing. The doctor had been called and ordered her to bed, speaking severely of undue strain and exhaustion and calling in a body from the village to help with the nursing.

Parcels and books forgotten I went flying up to her room as soon as I arrived and, forgetting all propriety, embraced her and told her she must not send me away on errands if she were going to take no care of herself in my absence. Afterwards my temerity amazed me, but it all seemed so natural at the time to be worried about her; I suppose I had not noticed how fond I had become of her in the short time I had been with her, and it needed a shock at her illness to realize how I would miss her: besides, I had not had much experience at being dependent on another woman for the affection I clearly felt for my employer. My mother was a cuddle in a child's memory; Annie, bless her heart, was too large to embrace; Angel neither gave affection nor expected to receive it, and Miss T had been above such softnesses. However my employer was not: she returned my embrace affectionately and without embarrassment, and from that moment on treated me more as a near relation than as a servant.

'I'm glad to have you back, my dear,' was all she said, but her eyes were loving and kind. 'So silly to feel unwell after the happy day I had; see, what my darling brought me!' And she indicated the two tortoiseshell combs with silver inlay that lay on her bedside table, together with a large box of French glacé fruits, just like the ones Annie had had all those Christmases ago. 'Take one, *chérie*: my letters had not reached him, the ones that told him how good a girl you were, otherwise I am sure he would have brought you a little gift as well . . . .'

To please her I took a greengage, spitting the stone through my forefinger and thumb into the palm of my hand, as I had been taught at Miss T's.

'He is not well, my dear son,' she continued. 'He looks overworked and tired, and he had not shaved for some days . . . . I worry for him, all the time. And he has gone back to such danger, although he tells me it is quite safe. But my country is changing all the time, and it is, I am afraid, only for the worse.'

'But he writes to you –'

'When he can, when he can – and then it is always through a third person and sometimes takes weeks to arrive; everything also goes through our solicitors in London, lest he be traced. And it all takes such time; I can never know where he is . . . .'

'You must not worry,' I told her, angry at this careless son who came and went without apparent thought to his mother's well-being. 'From what you have told me he is both brave and resourceful. He will come back safe, never fear.'

But his visit had exhausted her; she kept to her bed for nearly a week, and was deathly pale when at last she was allowed up again. The priest had been a constant visitor, and she seemed to gain great comfort from his presence. I scoured the grounds and the woods for flowers, finding the last snowdrops under some ivy leaves close to the house, windflowers from the woods, violets from the ditches, and grey mousetails of sallow near the river. I read to her from the new books, showed her the latest fashions from the *Lady's Magazine*, shone the silver till it reflected light like moonglow, encouraged her to take the air – in fact quite forgot myself in my anxiety to see her better. At last she seemed to respond, and by the end of the month seemed almost her old self again; once more we started the French lessons and I was so determined to please that I became reasonably fluent in day-to-day conversation, and could even read and understand some of the poetry and plays she kept in the bookshelf in her room.

It was too good to last; one day in April I was brought right down back to earth with a bump. We were in the sitting room when Kate brought me a letter from Jessie at the Seminary. We had corresponded irregularly since I left, and I had not heard from her for some time, so unfastened the letter eagerly. As I read my heart sank; she wrote that she had been up to Scotland to visit her parents, but on her return had found Miss T too ill to carry on. Taking over, she had sorted the correspondence, and amongst the letters in the bureau had found one from Lady Margaret, denouncing me as an impostor. Whether it had been attended to she had no idea and was unable to discuss it with Miss T as long as she was ill. She sent her love.

Dropping the letter to my lap, I gazed out at the spring sunshine; I had known it would come eventually, but why now, with the new life springing up all around, Lady Jestyn so much better, my life seeming at last settled and happy? I made up my mind: better to know the worst as soon as possible.

I went over to Lady Jestyn's side and knelt at her chair. 'Dear ma'am: I have a confession to make . . . .'

Perhaps I was only doing it because I was frightened: better to admit a wrong before one can also be blamed as much for the deceit of concealment as for the crime itself; but the real reason, I think was that the time had come when I truly wished to be honest with this woman, this fine and gracious lady who had been so kind and gentle with me. If the worst came to the worst, I reflected, I still had three guineas and the clothes to my back . . . .

'You have broken an ornament, perhaps? Such a little thing to be down on your knees for . . . .'

'Worse than that, I'm afraid.'

'You have overspent on that pretty material and wish for a little loan?'

'No, ma'am!' I wailed. 'Far, far, worse! You see – I am not really Esther Tregorran at all: I am here on completely false pretences!'

I waited for the thunderbolt, the tirade, the dismissal.

For a moment she was silent, then she shrugged her shoulders in her exaggerated fashion, sighed, and patted my hand.

'I wondered when you would get around to telling me: you see, I have known this for at least six weeks . . . .'

I stared at her in utter amazement. She *knew* . . . . But I should have realized that if Jessie had found Lady Margaret's letter filed in the bureau it must have been attended to long since: the reputation of the Seminary depended on straight dealing.

Lady Jestyn went on to tell me that the letter had arrived soon after Christmas; 'Aunt Margaret' had explained, via Miss T, that her ward was married and had never been near the Seminary, but had given the introductory letter and the money to a scrivener on the understanding he would write and explain her defection. Apparently the young man that the real Esther had married had won Lady Margaret over – some relative was in line to become the next lord mayor of London – and all was now forgiven in that quarter, but Miss T was most apologetic about the impostor who had taken Esther's place, promised to send a replacement, and had advised Lady Jestyn to send me to a House of Correction, or at the least turn me out penniless and without reference.

'But you didn't?'

'No, *chérie*. I was hurt a little, perhaps, that you had not trusted me enough to tell me, but was intrigued with the thought of learning the whole story one day. Besides, anyone can see that you are a good girl, and I do not

558

believe there is an ounce of badness in you, not real badness. There is nothing that you have done or been or said since you were here that could not have been the real Miss Tregorran, so I came to the conclusion that there must have been a good reason for the deception. I wrote back to Miss Thoroughgood and said I was more than satisfied with your behaviour, I did not need anyone else, and I would deal with the situation as I thought fit; I also sent back the ten guineas Lady Margaret had expended on the wrong girl, in case she thought to pursue the matter further . . . .' She held up her hand to forestall my thanks. 'I have perhaps also a selfish reason.' She paused, and I saw her smile reminiscently in the firelight. 'My boy lives at times by the charity of others, and sometimes he sleeps under the stars and goes hungry: so, in accepting you, perhaps I am bribing *le bon Dieu* for James's next time of need. . . .' She leaned back against the cushions. 'I want to ask you so many questions, but I also love a story; so perhaps you will tell me what led you to this place, tell me about yourself. But not all at once; a little at a time, like the Arabian princess who kept her life by telling the sultan a different story every night, finishing at the place that was most exciting . . . .'

'Scheherazade?'

'That was it; it is a pretty enough name, but I am sure your real name is prettier: tell me.'

So I told her, and she then made me start right at the beginning, in Leebeck with my mother and stepfather, and stopped me that night at the point where Aunt Sophia came on the scene.

'Tomorrow is time enough for that: I shall sleep well enough tonight with a picture of you in my mind, and before we have finished, I shall know you as if you were one of my own! I think you should still be Esther, though, for the servants might become confused if you were suddenly someone else . . . .'

'And – and you are not going to send me away?'

559

'Just when I have successfully taught you to conjugate the verb *demeurer*?'

She must have seen hope struggling with suspicion on my face, for she leant forward and stroked my cheek. 'I jest, *chérie*: of course I shall not send you away, unless you wish to go. I really do wish to know how and when and why and who, but if there is anything you would rather not tell I shall understand. We trust each other, you and I, do we not?'

Over the next few days therefore I told her my story, introducing her to my companions of the road, and as I told her so many forgotten incidents came to mind, making me sigh or smile with the remembrance, that I determined there and then to fill whatever was empty with my days in writing down what I recalled as accurately as I could. In that journal I could remind myself what really happened between me and Jack, and not the watered-down version I gave to my employer. I could also write down what happened at Madame's, the story of Angel and Nick, for this was another part of my life I preferred to gloss over with her: besides, I truly do not think she would have understood. For her I made my life on the road as interesting and amusing as I could: she especially liked Annie's adventures with the weighing contest, my rescue of Toby, and Jack's ingenuity in disentangling me at Gloucester. At the end of my recital she was kind enough to say that she quite understood why I had done as I did, and that for her part she was doubly lucky to have such a well-travelled companion.

'A great pity you lost touch with your friends, though,' she said. 'I should have enjoyed meeting them all; especially the resourceful Jack: he sounds a little – unconventional, shall we say, but so kind.'

I stifled a giggle: it was hard to imagine careless Jack in Lady Jestyn's quiet and ordered drawing room.

April started windy and cold, but Easter Sunday was fair

and warm and Lady Jestyn announced her intention of attending Mass at the little Catholic chapel midway between Lesser Beedle and Hink. This was the first expedition of any distance she had made since I arrived and I was apprehensive for her comfort, but Old Bob assured me she quite often used the carriage to go to church or pay social calls during the better weather. He drove carefully, he said: 'Not that the old hosses is up to much more'n a gentle trot, and there's always that idle great lunk Jeremy up front to help her down and lift her in and out.' Kate's Jeremy was a nice, youngish man, not overly bright but kind and strong, and I thought she had chosen well, although she had not yet managed to get him to agree to marriage: 'He don't half need a great shove, miss!'

I asked Lady Jestyn whether she wished me to accompany her and wait in the carriage, only too conscious of the fact that I had only found my way to the village church myself some half a dozen times since my arrival, but she shook her head and assured me she was perfectly content to travel alone, and as I was not a Catholic it would be a pity for me to waste the time waiting for her.

'So you may have a free morning, *chérie*: do just as you like.'

Whenever people say that it is always a false freedom: there would have been nothing I would have liked more than to run free in the lanes nearby, pick primroses and look for the first lambs and the mad March hare, but duty dictated that I write to Jessie and bring her up to date with my acceptance. After that there was the material I had bought to make a determined effort to turn into the creations that had so taken my fancy in the *Lady's Magazine*; the cutting out and tacking had all been done, using a brown paper pattern I had adapted, but unless I sewed a detested seam or two they would never be ready . . . .

It must have been nearly two hours later that I first became conscious of the noise and commotion outside my window: below, someone was hammering on the front door with their fists and carrying on as though the skies had fallen.

'For Gawd's sake, Milady, you must come, otherwise she'll murder us all!'

27

Pushing open my window, I saw below me on the gravelled sweep in front of the house the middle-aged woman from the cottage in the wood.

I had not been near the place since my escape last time; when next I went through the woods, the fallen tree had been cleared from the path and I had hurried past the other turning. The cottage and its occupants had never been mentioned by anyone in the household and, contrary to my usual inquisitive nature, I had asked no questions either, although when the wind was in the right direction I had heard the sound of axe on wood, and knew all our fuel came from that part of the estate. Sometimes I almost persuaded myself I had imagined that pretty doll-like creature with her baby, but now –

'Milady! I can't deal with her –'

'Stop it!' I called down crossly. 'Lady Jestyn is away from home. What is it you want?' But she only cried and wailed the louder, so that I was forced to go down to the front door that Kate should have answered – but of course she was over in the main part of the house, visiting one of her friends among the staff there; I had forgotten. Charles the butler was conspicuous by his absence – possibly had walked over with Kate – Cook was dozing in the kitchen, and Young Bob was probably rabbiting, ferreting, or ratting, depending on the opportunities.

I opened the door. 'Now, calm yourself: there's no one here but me. Her Ladyship is gone to church, and –'

'She'll kill us all, miss! With that great knife an' all . . . .'

562

'*Who?*' I leaned forward and shook her violently. 'Who is going to kill whom?' Could it be that some vagrant had attacked the young woman and her baby? 'Where is your husband? And the dog?'

'Dog's there, but Jem's doing a bit of – he's out. A walk with the coachman's son, along by the river . . . .'

Just so: poaching. Did they have salmon this early, I wondered; or trout?

'So, you're alone with – with the young lady?'

'Yes, and it's she what's gone off her head. Clean gone, and sly with it. When she gets those moods there's only Her Ladyship as can calm her down, shame her into quiet – and you say she's away from home?' She broke into fresh sobs. 'She don't come so often to see her now, so as she don't get upset remembering, but I can't manage her when she's like this! It's too much, to have to keep my eyes open all day and half the night . . . .' She hiccoughed, and I could smell spirits on her breath. 'Went for me, she did, then locked herself up in the attic with that great knife from the kitchen: no telling what she'll get up to!'

'I'll come,' I promised. 'Wait there.' Rushing upstairs I grabbed a pretty blue head-shawl Lady Jestyn had given me and a rolled strip of linen, and downstairs picked up a pack of cards from the bureau: fortune-telling often distracted the most unamenable . . . . I remembered the small flask of brandy Lady Jestyn kept for medicinal purposes: the younger Miss Pritchard – all of sixty – sometimes came over faint when she and her sister paid us a visit from the village. Medicine, bandage, a present, and a distraction.

We ran down the path to the Dower House, the path I had never dared travel again since my arrival.

The track was coming alive with the early innocence of ground elder, soft primroses, the folded hoods of lords-and-ladies, bright celandine, and new tentacles of ground ivy, and I had much ado to keep up with my frightened companion. At the side gate the dog, Rusty, growled at me but let us pass at a word from the woman, and we hurried round to the front of the house. The sun, pale and heatless, shone full on a calm scene. The small house looked again like a picture from a child's book: smoke curled lazily from the chimneys, a chaffinch sang loud and clear, and by my feet an early pasqueflower unrolled its furry stems. A ubiquitous robin straddled a large worm in the middle of the lawn and everything seemed peaceful enough.

'Where is she?' I whispered, though none would have heard.

'Up there.' She pointed to a window set like an eye under the thatched brows of the eaves. 'See: there where the window's open . . . .'

'She doesn't seem to be doing any harm to anyone,' I ventured.

'Locked herself in, hasn't she? No telling what mischief she'll be up to.'

'Leave this to me,' I said firmly, though at this stage I had no idea what I was to do. However, there was no point in just standing around, so I marched down the path and came to a halt under the window indicated. 'Hello, there!' No answer. I turned to the woman at my side. 'Are you sure she's there?'

'I'm sure; she's done this before. Last time Jem had to break the door down.'

I called up again, and this time a face appeared momentarily at the window, the pretty pale doll-face I had seen before.

'Go away . . . .'

'Wait!' I called. 'Don't go: I have a present for you –'

'A present? What present?'

Holding the blue shawl behind my back, I walked forward a couple of paces. 'A surprise – for the baby.'

'They want to take him away . . . .'

'Nonsense,' I said disarmingly, though if the girl were really mentally disturbed, it would seem the safest thing to do for the child. I had heard that some women became temporarily deranged after the birth of a baby, and perhaps

564

this was the case with her. I turned to the woman at my side. 'You wouldn't try to take away the baby, would you?'

She shook her head. 'Been told never to touch it.'

'You hear that?' I called up. I whispered to my companion: 'Go upstairs and see if she has unlocked the door again; I'll stay here and keep her talking.'

She was reluctant but moved away, the dog at her heels.

I addressed the window again. 'It's not very polite to shut out your guests.'

'You're not a guest!' came the imperious voice from above. 'You are an intruder!'

'No, indeed! I live at Riverwood with Lady Jestyn –'

'Her!'

'– and I've come to visit, with a gift for the baby, and to tell your fortune with the cards.'

There was a pause. 'Can you really tell fortunes?'

'Of course: I was taught by the great Gipsy Queen herself. Shall I cast your baby's horoscope as well, while I'm about it?'

'And mine . . . .'

'And yours. Just come down and –'

'I threw away the key . . . .'

'Where?'

A white-gloved hand gestured towards the shrubbery. 'Down there. Somewhere. I don't know . . . .'

The woman had returned and stood by my side. 'Can you get in?'

She shook her head. 'Locked tight.'

'She says she threw the key down in the shrubbery,' I said quietly. 'You have a look around and see if you can see it, and in the meantime . . . .' I raised my voice again and called up to the window. 'If you can't come down, I shall have to come up. I am afraid it would not be convenient to call back later,' I added, to forestall any resistance to the idea, 'as I have to read the Duchess's tea leaves at four.' I had not the faintest idea what I was

565

talking about, but it seemed to work, for the figure in the window nodded her head.

'You'll have to climb up . . . .'

The woman and I found a ladder in the shed: it was heavy but we managed, propping it up under the window and grounding it as best we could on the terrace. Unfortunately it was short, reaching only just beyond the first-floor windows, but it would have to do. I mounted the first few rungs.

'I'm coming up,' I called. 'Leave the window open as wide as you can –'

But apparently she had changed her mind, for as I climbed higher I felt the ladder being shaken from above quite alarmingly, and a voice hissed: 'You're not to: I don't trust you!'

As I was by now halfway there, and further encumbered with shawl, brandy, cards and bandage, I felt disinclined to do other than continue upwards.

'If you don't let me come up I can't explain the cards to you –'

'Cards?'

'Here in my hand. The ace of hearts for an affaire, the nine a letter from over the sea,' I tempted. 'The queen of diamonds a false friend . . . ?'

She appeared to consider, but I could no longer see her face above me because of the acute angle.

'Very well, but you can only come as far as the window, not inside. Don't be too noisy, you'll wake baby . . .' and the voice assumed a high, childish whisper.

'As far as the window ledge,' I promised, and started to climb again. At last I was high enough to peer into the room; inside all appeared to be in deep shadow, the more so because of the bar of sunlight reflected blindingly off the gilt mirror on the wall opposite the window. Propping my elbows on the ledge I tried to see further into the room, looking for Doll-Face. Over by the fireplace was a bundle that could be the baby, and in the hearth itself a heap of smouldering paper; as I looked the paper shifted in the draught from the open window, and quite a large piece rolled across the tiles and, unencumbered by any fender, burned energetically on the polished floor. Instinctively I half hauled myself up through the window but was brought up short, the ledge cutting painfully across my stomach, by the sight of a large and sharp carving knife waved in front of my nose: the girl had been hidden in the shadows to my right. Instinctively I recoiled, remembering almost too late that my feet had left the top rung of the ladder –

'No further, or I'll slit your throat!'

Precariously balanced on my stomach muscles, unable to turn my head, I tried to recall how I had behaved when faced with other deranged people; we had had one such poor woman in Leebeck village, but she had been born daft: we always treated her gently and kindly as one would a child, and any miseries she had were soon chased away by a song, or a tune on the flute – I had no flute, no free hand to play one if I had, and no breath to sing a song. Then there was Sly Sanders, the old hermit in the woods. He was harmless enough if you didn't leave your drawers out on the line, for his penchant was for ladies' underwear . . . . There was the epileptic girl at school who had to be restrained for her own good, but was normal enough most of the time; the various touched people who turned up at fairs, sometimes used as exhibits at sideshows; the crazy preacher who wandered the roads dressed as John the Baptist, eating honey and sometimes grasshoppers because he thought they were locusts –

I tried to think what Jack would do in the same circumstances and remembered his teachings about how everyone appeared to want something different in life, but that in the end it all boiled down to the same: inspiration, anticipation, reassurance, the allaying of secret fears, and that we, the fair-people, could make all these things larger than life itself for a little while. He had also said there was no such thing as a balanced norm in people, we were all tipped a little one way or the other, and that the secret of

567

a show person's success was to balance that tilt to the greatest effect.

I should fall off the ledge any moment if I didn't think of something fast. Already the flames from the burning paper were charring the floor: we did not want a conflagration as well as a madwoman with a knife.

I nodded at the bundle by the hearth. 'Don't you think the baby might choke?'

'Choke?'

'Yes: the fire. There is too much smoke, and it is really quite warm for the time of year.' I spoke calmly and conversationally.

She glanced over at the flames and giggled. 'He's cold, poor lamb. Needs the fire. Likes the pretty flames . . . .'

'He won't be cold any more if you let me come in and give him the nice present I have brought; he will be lovely and warm. Let me come in and I'll show it to you.' I deliberately did not look at her, as one does not stare an animal out if one wishes to gain its confidence.

'How do I know you won't try to hurt him?'

'You have the knife,' I said reasonably. 'I have only the present – and the cards for fortune-telling . . . .'

'Just inside, then, no further.'

Thankfully I kicked out to give myself leverage, felt my left foot catch on an obstruction, then heard the slither and crash as the ladder slid sideways down the wall to land on the terrace beneath. Simultaneously I landed in a heap on the attic floor, knowing my escape route was gone. I peered at the girl from my lowly position, nursing a bruised elbow. Her face was in shadow, only the hand with the knife was still sharp in the band of sunlight. I unfolded the blue head-shawl and held it between my outstretched hands, getting to my knees as I did so.

'See, isn't it pretty? That pattern is a shell design, and there are little silver threads crocheted between . . . .' The sun glittered on the shining threads as I knew it would, and she crept forward slowly with her hand outstretched, as I had hoped.

568

'Give it to me!'

'Certainly,' I said, at last rising to my feet. 'But you can't wrap the baby up with only one hand, can you? Why don't you put the knife down on the table over there, and I will stay here by the window out of the way.' I glanced over to the fireplace: luckily the fire had burned itself out, but there was a nasty charred patch of floorboard. 'Go on, now: you don't want him to catch cold. I won't move from here, not till you tell me to.' I still avoided looking at her, and hummed 'Lillibullero' under my breath to show I was completely at ease. I must have convinced her, for with a complete change of mood she snatched the shawl from my hand and danced away from me, laid the knife on the table without a backward glance, and bent to pick up the bundle by the fireside that had lain quiet all this while. Tenderly she wrapped it in the blue shawl, her gloved hands deft and capable . . . . Gloved hands? It wasn't that cold, surely? I gazed at the plump, rounded figure bent so protectively over her child: what a pity she had had this disturbance, she was such a pretty –

She turned to me, rocking her child at her breast, her eyes wide and guileless. 'Thank you: he likes being warm, and he hasn't had a new shawl for ages . . . . What's the matter?'

Although my face was in shadow now, she must have seen my dismay. In spite of her animated conversation the doll's face turned to me stayed blank and fixed in its vacant prettiness. My God! She had no face! It was a mask; convincing at a distance and very expertly fashioned, but nevertheless a mask –

Rapidly I improvised. 'Nothing . . . it was just a spider over your left shoulder – Keep still!' Moving quickly I clapped my hands over the imaginary insect. 'There! All gone.' Now I was between her and the knife, and had composed my features to look back at her with an expression as blank as her own.

'What a beautiful dress,' I said. It was too, a pale blue

silk, with rather too many frills and furbelows for my taste, but seeming just right for her.

She glanced down, apparently pleased at the compliment. 'Just an afternoon gown, but I am assured it is in the latest fashion. I have all my clothes made by a dressmaker in London, of course; she has my measurements, and when I feel the need for a new wardrobe she sends the patterns and I choose whatever I like. So much less tiring than going up to town, don't you think? Still, they are rather a waste I suppose, with my being immured in this backwater and scarcely anyone of note to entertain . . . .' Her voice trailed away. 'I am afraid I cannot offer you any refreshment, but perhaps a –' She gestured towards the table, and her glance fell on the knife. 'How stupid of the servants to leave that nasty kitchen knife there! I have told them time and again to leave all sharp things locked away – my baby might get hurt . . . .' She glanced at the empty mantel as though she saw a clock there, and her voice changed, became indulgent. 'It is time for his feed – would you excuse me?' Without waiting for an answer she pulled at the strings of her bodice and bared her breasts, caressing one with her free hand. The flesh was smooth and white and fair with faint blue veins, the nipples pink and pointed. 'James says I have lovely breasts . . . . Have you met him yet?'

'Not yet.' Another shock – but perhaps not such a shock after all. What other reason to hide this poor woman away, look after her so carefully, dress her so prettily, guard her so rigidly, than that she was the flawed mistress of the so-near-perfect James?

With good manners I turned away to look discreetly out of the window as she fed the child; besides, I wanted to find out what was happening below with the missing key. The middle-aged woman was trying ineffectually to lift the fallen ladder back; as she glanced up I made a key-twisting gesture with the hand furthest from my hostess, but she shook her head. I pointed to the shrubbery, and after a moment's hesitation she went back to the search.

Turning back to the room I saw the young woman had refastened her bodice.

'That didn't take long,' I said politely.

'No; he's such a greedy boy! Like James, he never tires of . . . .' She looked around her with a vague air, then back at me. 'Who are you?'

'Your visitor; remember? You asked me to call . . . .'

'So I did. Did I? I don't remember . . . . Well then, now you're here – Why *are* we here? This is the attic: I don't entertain in the attic . . . .'

'We lost the key,' I reminded her.

'So we did!' She clapped her gloved hand guiltily to her mouth. 'How naughty! Nan *will* be cross! Never mind, now we are here we will play a game of cribbage; I seem to remember there is a board up here somewhere . . . . Would you hold baby for a moment while I have a look in that cupboard?'

'Certainly.' I held out my arms. 'Is he always so good?'

'Oh yes! He has to keep quiet, otherwise they will take him away. That doctor was here again this morning to spy on us so we ran away and hid, didn't we, baby?' She handed me the blue-shawled bundle. 'Now where is that board?'

I do not think I was really surprised this time, but nevertheless the flesh crawled at the nape of my neck as I looked down at what I held. Gazing up through the tangle of shawls was an unwinking stare from the sewn-on eyes of a rag doll!

It was a tattered and filthy object, with the remains of what had been black wool hair clinging to its linen scalp like little tussocks of burned grass.

'What's his name?' I asked, in what I hoped was a normal tone.

'We haven't decided yet. If he had been a girl I fancied Elizabeth Anne, but as you know, being a boy, he must bear a king's name; somehow I don't think he is a Charles, do you? I can't find that game – it must be downstairs.'

'What about calling him George?' I suggested.

At once she rounded on me like a maniac; snatching the bundle out of my arms she backed away, the gauze mask somehow twisted in fury. 'Keep away from me, you slut! You're just like all the others!' I was disturbed to see she had picked up the knife again in her free hand. 'You're all the same, insinuating things about . . . about. . . .'

'You could call him William,' I said desperately. 'William was the first king of England. Or Edward, or Henry. Or –'

'You know perfectly well he has to have a Stuart name, either as first or second –'

'I like the name Charles, then,' I said quickly. 'There never was a bonnier prince than Charles Edward, remember?'

She relaxed a little, and I seized my advantage. 'You could call him your own favourite name first, and Charles second . . . .' I recalled the Catholic connections of the family. 'How about a saint's name? John, perhaps? John Charles has a fine ring to it, do you not think?'

She nodded. 'Perhaps: but there is no hurry; it can wait till James returns home . . . .' Her mood changed abruptly. 'Now, I'm bored with you: please go home.' She paced up and down, hugging her 'baby'. 'I want my tea . . . . Why don't you go?'

I looked out of the window again. The woman's husband had joined in the search now, and it seemed more systematic; I turned back. No point in upsetting her once more with the added frustrations of the lost key: a caged animal is dangerous. My hand found and picked up the cards I had left on the windowsill with the brandy and the bandage.

'It would be a pity for me to leave without telling you your fortune, now I am here,' I cajoled. 'Why don't we sit round this table and I'll shuffle the cards? I need you to help with this; you will have to choose the cards.' She looked doubtfully at her gloved hands, but I reassured her. 'No need to discard those, you will manage fine as they are.' With all the shocks of the afternoon still fresh in my mind, I did not wish to invite further horrors by encouraging her to disclose anything that was obviously usually hidden away, so I hurried on. 'Perhaps if you were to put baby on the other chair and the knife on the mantelpiece . . .? That's right!'

Outside the sun had gone and the attic room was gloomy, but I put on my professional chitchat as I made good play with the gambler's tricks (learned so arduously from Jack eighteen months ago) of fanning and showering cards, until I had her full attention. 'Now, what kind of fortune would you like?'

'What kinds are there?' she asked excitedly, wriggling in her chair like a child.

'Well, if I had all my gear with me there's past, present and that to come; there are trends and portents, lives and loves; pictures in the crystal, casting of horoscopes, throwing of bones, tracings in sand, reading the tea leaves, consulting the lines of the hand –'

She gazed down at her gloves. 'I'm not supposed –'

'– but with the cards,' I continued briskly, 'there are answers to immediate questions.' I plonked down the superficially well-shuffled pack, knowing the positions of the favourable ones to a card. 'Now, you can divide the pack for me with your gloves on, can't you? It needs the personal touch for them to respond as they should . . . . I want three piles: past, present, and future, with at least five cards in each.'

Carefully, clumsily, she divided the cards, then scratched at the palm of her hand through the thin fabric which covered it. 'It itches. . . . What do I do next?'

'Show me which pile you wish to represent the past, which the present, and which the future; carefully now, you must give this some thought. Concentrate hard, for it may influence the reading if your mind is not fully on the matter in hand. Shut your eyes, let your mind go empty, then think of the past; open your eyes, and point to which cards represent that which is gone , . . .' It was very quiet in the room now, and I was so used to the bustle, cries and clatter of a fair as my background that I found myself humming a tune again to lighten the silence.

'That's his tune,' she cried, opening her eyes. ' "Over the hills and far away . . . ." Far away: that's where he is – far away . . . .' And I saw the tears begin to spill from her eyes, soaking into the gauze mask beneath.

'That's just what we are here for,' I said quickly, fearing another sudden change of mood. 'To find out just when he's coming home again! Now, show me which pile you wish to be the past . . . .'

Like all my clients all she wanted was the future, but in order to make the customers swallow the lies we told them with credulity, it was necessary to build up their confidence by telling them the truth of past and present first. 'Truth' in this instance was not difficult: like any other art it needed experience. People like me, trained in the hard school of the fairground, learned quickly and learned well. It was easier to be accurate with a background of the lines of the hand to work on (for whatever people said, they *were* an indication of the types we worked with) but otherwise it was necessary to suggest, and watch the eyes: the slightest widening of the pupils or flicker of an eyelash was enough to tell you if you were on the right track.

I talked swiftly and fluently of gentle parents, a moneyed background, a fine house, of many suitors: this was easy enough to guess at from her voice, her taste in clothes, her acceptance of servants and deference, and the fact that, in spite of the disguising mask, she must have been pretty. The present was not difficult either: a waiting for one's love, loneliness, impatience – the cards she had chosen were in sequence, as I had hoped, so it was not difficult to deal out hearts and diamonds and suit them to my interpretation. She was at her ease now and, again as I had hoped, she began to talk about the missing James herself.

'We fell in love at first sight: he was *so* handsome in his uniform! Mama and Papa had no objection, of course, even with him being the younger son, and we courted for only four months before we were married —'

'Married?'

'Of course. He had to go abroad, you see . . . . It was a beautiful wedding: I wore the prettiest dress, all pink silk with lace and pearls and the artist painted me in it afterwards. The portrait still waits for James's likeness –'

Yet another shock: this was not James's mistress, as I had supposed, but his wife . . . .

'– with him still being away. And of course Baby was born then too, and they tried to take him away when I wasn't looking. The doctor said he had been born dead, but I knew better than that.' Her voice was rising, and I put out a reassuring hand.

'Don't get yourself upset, the baby is safe with you now.'

She jerked away from my touch. 'Yes, he is safe now, but only because I heard him crying in the night and went looking for him! They said I was too ill to leave my bed, but I could hear him somewhere, calling for me, and I had to go and find him . . . . I cannot bear to hear a child cry and not go comfort it, can you? And do you know where they had hidden him? In the old nursery, there among all James's discarded toys! I ask you, is that any place to put a baby? He might easily have smothered among all that other rubbish! And they had no right to remove him, to try and deceive me, did they? He's mine, I tell you, all mine, and no one shall take him away –'

'Of course they won't,' I soothed: I wondered how long ago the poor real baby had died: a year, two?

'Whatever I did, they had no right to take him away,' she repeated, the cards forgotten, her grievances the only thing that mattered. 'If *he* will only come back and forgive me, then everything will be all right, I know it will! The baby will be all right, I shall – be better, and can take off these – *things*,' and she gestured to the mask and her gloved hands. 'It is only a rash and must be better soon, and then he will love me again as he used to at the beginning. *He* is mine too, he belongs to me only, and no one else shall have him, no one shall come between us as long as I live . . . but he *must* forgive me, must he not? It would not be right for him to go on hating me, would it? You will ask him to come and see me as soon as he arrives, will you not? *You* will tell him he must forgive me?' She paused. 'I am here all the time, I shall not be going away till later in the season . . . . At least I do not think so: if only my head did not ache so much sometimes I should remember. I did not *mean* to do it, you know,' she added, then to my distress she fell to her knees by my side and clutched at my skirt. 'You *will* tell him, will you not, that it was not all my fault? I was lonely, you see, and he gave me presents and told me I was beautiful . . . . How was I to know what would happen? You must help me to get him to forgive, for I have much to be forgiven . . . .'

Amidst all this garble of words of which I could make little sense and less meaning, my wandering mind caught a phrase, a sentence, and slid back immediately: once again I was saying farewell to Katina Petulengro at St Bartholomew's Fair, and she had said almost the same words about Jack: '. . . he has much to forgive and be forgiven . . .'

I stopped and pulled the girl to her feet. 'Of course I will do what I can; shall we have a look at the cards again now?'

But her mood had changed once more and she preferred to ignore me. Picking up her 'baby' she sat down at the table again, rocking back and forth on her chair and singing in a high, sweet voice, 'Over the hills and far away', her gaze on the window. A moment later I heard footsteps on the stairs, a key in the lock, and a voice I recognized saying anxiously, 'Are you all right, child?'

It was Lady Jestyn, breathing far too fast, her hand at her heart, and behind her Old Bob and his son and the woodcutter and his wife. Thankfully I stretched out my hands to my employer, only realizing now how tired and frightened I was, when there was a wild scream behind me and a figure rushed to the open window.

'They'll take him away, they'll take him away!' and in a flash I had turned and was struggling with the frantic girl as she attempted to throw herself out of the window. She seemed all at once to have tremendous strength and flung me away, to crack my head against the wall, even as the others secured her and soothed and comforted.

I stayed where I had fallen, my head ringing, and was suddenly violently sick.

Back at Riverwood Lady Jestyn insisted I went straight to bed and stayed there for the rest of the day.

'No questions today, my dear: I shall explain all tomorrow. Kate will bring you something to eat, and a draught to help you sleep.'

And the next morning she forbade all questioning till we had broken our fast, then she led me without further words down the long passage that connected with the main part of the house.

I had never been this way before, and watched with interest as she took a large key from her reticule and inserted it in the lock. Once through the heavy oaken door I found myself in a large panelled hall, light and airy. To the left were closed doors to what could have been a sitting room, across the hall open double doors to a room that led to a terrace, and ahead of us a graceful flight of stairs leading off to the left past a tall window. All was clean, but the floor had not been polished for some time, and there was not the usual furniture one would expect; it seemed almost as if the owners had just moved out, or the house was waiting for new tenants.

Lady Jestyn led the way up the stairs, and I hurried to draw level and take her arm, fearful for the strain on her heart, but she put my hand aside.

'No, child: I must learn to manage. Besides, what I am to tell you will take far greater toll than a flight of stairs . . . .'

We paced a long corridor with doors on either side,

then came to the head of the stairs proper: ahead stretched another corridor similar to the one we had traversed, while below was an enormous hall with marble patterned floor and doors leading off at either side of the double front doors; behind us was a tall window that stretched the height of the house, or so it seemed.

'What a wonderful view!'

She smiled. 'James's favourite. He used to walk up and down on the terrace below, smoking his pipe an hour at a time, then we would go into the music room, near where we first came in, and I would play a little Scarlatti . . . . He loved to watch the sun go down behind the hills; he used to say it had a long way to go after it had left us, all the way over the green Welsh hills till it met the sea.'

The terrace below us was grey with lichen and banked with lavender bushes which straggled untidily down to the sloping lawns that tipped towards leaning willows and the glint of running water. And on the water the high-banked wings and looping necks of a pair of swans –

But even as something stirred at the edge of my memory, fretful and teasing, Lady Jestyn took my arm.

'Come: I must show you the Gallery, for that is where it all begins.'

The long Gallery stretched the whole way across the front of the house, lit by tall windows that faced towards the east and Bredon Hill. The morning sun slanted in across a dusty carpet runner, and touched the gilded frames that hung in neat rows the whole length. The portraits started in the 1660s with a picture of the first Jestyn kneeling to kiss the hand of his benefactor, Charles II: in the background was a representation of Riverwood as it must have been then, mostly the Tudor wing where we now lived. Little could be seen of the ancestor as he was in profile, and the whole thing was obviously painted by an amateur; the thing that lifted it from the rut was the portrait of the Merry Monarch himself. The face showed a lively, ugly attractiveness that totally eclipsed the mediocrity of the rest.

'The King even gave the first Sir James a wealthy wife to go with the estate,' said Lady Jestyn. 'It was said she was one of his discarded mistresses. Their first son she insisted on calling after the King, and ever since then it has been tradition that the eldest son at least should have either the name Charles or James. Now, here is a portrait of his wife, then their eldest son and his family, and . . . .'

Dutifully I followed her down the length of the gallery, past paintings good and bad, past nondescript husbands with beautiful wives and striking men with plain spouses, obviously married for their dowries; staid children, large dogs, fine horses, and devoted servants, until we came finally to the last three portraits.

'Here is my husband,' said Lady Jestyn. 'Painted when young, of course.'

A bland face, perhaps a little weak in the mouth but with lines of merriment near the eyes, and two dogs, a horse and the 'new' Riverwood as background. Next to this there was a family group: the first wife and their children. She was a fair florid woman with high-piled hair who sat on a sofa with her youngest, a baby, on her lap; a small girl leaned at her knee, and a boy of about fifteen posed uncomfortably with his elbow on a marble stand. While still masked by the undeveloped lines of adolescence he had his mamma's rather prominent blue eyes and high complexion and his father's indecisive mouth, and was dressed in the height of fashion.

'The little girls died of a low fever some two years later, within a week of each other, and their mother a year later of a stroke. She always favoured George, though, and I am afraid he was a little spoiled even then.'

'George?'

'My stepson, the present baronet. Here is a more recent portrait: he must have been in his early thirties then.'

This portrait was by a more competent artist than most and I saw an arrogant, petulantly handsome man, aged about thirty-five, splendidly attired in court dress against a background of draped red velvet curtains and attended by an obsequious negro slave bearing a bowl of exotic fruits. The present bearer of the title was inclined to corpulence and I did not care either for the indication of a self-indulgent mouth or the protruberant eyes, though these were suggested rather than emphasized by the artist. There were no dogs, no horses, no clue that this was the portrait of a country squire rather than that of a man about town, and in this lay the main difference from the other paintings.

'He has aged a great deal since then,' said my employer. 'And he has an unhealthily high colour, like his poor mamma. He – he does not care for the country life, and spends the majority of his time in town.'

'He does not bear a Stuart name?'

'His mother had German connections, I believe, and wished him called after our present king, but his second name is Charles . . . . And now, my dear, perhaps if we descend to the terrace – slowly, if you please – I can tell you a little more of my unfortunate daughter-in-law . . . .'

We sat out on the unpainted iron chairs; a soft breeze ruffled my hair and nesting sparrows flew past, busy with beakfuls of straw and twiglets; an advance guard of ants was investigating a likely mound of moss. Lady Jestyn spoke low, so softly I had to lean forward in my chair to hear properly.

'After George's mother died,' she began, 'his father took him abroad for a year to do the grand tour. While they were in France I met his father again for the first time in some twenty years, for the last time I had seen him was when I was a child and my father had had him as a paying guest to improve his languages. On that second meeting we fell in love almost instantly, and although I was near thirty years of age and had never been tempted to leave my parents, I accepted his offer of marriage gladly.' She smiled reminiscently. 'He was still a handsome, upright man with great charm, and such a sense of humour! I think it was that that appealed to me most for I was, I am afraid – and perhaps still am – a rather serious-natured

580

woman. Be that as it may,' she continued, smiling again, 'we returned together to try and make a home for young George here in England. Unfortunately he had no use for his new *maman*, making it very clear from the start that he resented my presence. Perhaps, too, he was afraid that his father would turn his affection to any children I bore, in preference to him. As it transpired *le bon Dieu* blessed us with just the one, James, but he was a delight to us both. My husband and I were very happy together, for he said to me once: "It is not many men who can marry tolerably well the first time for a dowry —" Lady Arabella was wealthy in her own right "— and have the good fortune to marry for love the second time around!" My poor Charlot . . . we had only the ten years together . . . .' She sighed. 'After his father died George went through the money his mother had left him in trust, and without his father's restraining hand it was soon wasted in riotous living, gambling, mistresses . . . . And he hated James! They were so unalike, those two: the one so obsessed with good food, wine, excesses, fashion, and my boy content to run about the countryside in old clothes with his dogs, Pistol, Trigger and old Bullet. Out in all weathers he was, and barefoot and bareheaded much of the time. . . . Not that he did not study: before he went away to school I had taught him French, some German, and a little Italian, and his local tutor pronounced him excellent at both history and literature . . . .' She sighed again, and I laid a hand comfortingly on her knee. 'Good child,' she murmured; 'What should I do without you? To continue: before he died my husband could see the way George was going, so although the estate was entailed, of course, he managed to tie a good deal of the money that was left into a joint trust to be managed by both George and James, when the latter reached his majority. He had hoped this would bring the two closer together, but in fact it produced the opposite result. Charlot had hoped his sons would be reconciled, but the bounds that were imposed merely made George spend more wildly than ever, and James has had to spend what little would have been his to help with the bare upkeep of the estate.' She waved her hands. 'Look at the state of everything! We keep but one step ahead of the debtors all the time, and everything is falling to pieces, is crumbling through neglect! Look at the gardens! Look at the rooms, so bare of all but the most essential furniture! Look at the cracks, leaks, the peeling paint, the broken glass! 'Tis all we can do to keep the place from falling down, and to pay the few wages we can –'

'Why didn't George marry a wealthy bride?' I interposed. 'Surely as a titled landowner he could have had his pick of well-dowered ladies?'

'George contracted a – disease – when he was living his rakehell life in London, and although he is pronounced cured, the story went around society and no father would lend his consent to an alliance so doubtful; in latter years he has been heard to declare that the advantages of freedom far outweigh the bonds of matrimony, and has made no attempt to form an alliance; the money is still enough for him to lead the kind of life he likes, and he has no apparent wish to continue the line, especially since James can no longer –' She broke off, and I guessed that now we were coming to the part that concerned the poor mad girl in the house in the wood.

'She was a delightful, sweet girl, the one that James chose for his wife,' she continued, 'although perhaps a trifle flirtatious. He was head over heels in love with her from the first moment he saw her, and nothing would do for them both but marriage as soon as possible, so I gave my blessing and took her to live with me while he went abroad on military service in the Americas. They had only two weeks together before he had to rejoin his regiment on its posting . . . . Before long Dorothea confided in me that she was enceinte, and James wrote home full of plans for the future. Some nine and a half or ten months after they were married she was brought to bed of a boy.' Her voice had deadened, become lifeless. 'The child was born dead, *pauvre enfant*,' and she crossed herself, 'and it was as

582

well. It weighed but two or three pounds and was deformed and diseased; the doctor who attended her would not tell me what I believe the poor girl did not at that stage know herself – instead he waited until my son came home and accused him of infecting his wife! It was not true, of course: my boy was clean, clean! Then the doctor told him of the circumstances of the baby's birth and that his wife was –was –'

She buried her face in her hands and her voice was muffled so that I had to strain to hear. 'After that he would have nothing to do with her: her mind was already unhinged with the combination of the disease and the loss of her baby, but this finally set the seal on their relationship, for she would not reveal with whom she strayed from that day to this. She has had the best treatment, the best doctors, but there can be no reversal, and James has never forgiven her for destroying his son and their marriage for the sake of what could only have been a passing fancy, some chance-met stranger who infected her unborn child. My poor James! My poor girl! For ten years he has refused to see her . . . .'

Ten years! Dear God . . . . And she thought it was yesterday, and that her husband would be home any day; and yet she knew there was something she had to be forgiven. What a tragedy: it was a mercy her mind had made of time a mockery. But she had a pleasant enough retreat, pretty clothes, her rag-doll baby substitute, and those masks –

'And the masks she wears?' I asked.

'Those gauze masks, so expensive, so carefully made, are to conceal the fact that under their protection the flesh beneath is eaten away: yes, my child, one side of her face, her nose, her chin, her hands and arms are infected . . . .

'My daughter-in-law, the once so pretty Dorothea, is in the last stages of an incurable syphilitic disease . . . .'

583

28

The gauze masks that had given me the horrors when I
had first seen them were made for Dorothea in London,
at three guineas a time. They were exquisitely fashioned,
to resemble as near as possible the real thing, and in fact
they had deceived me at a distance when I had first seen
her. Because of the weeping of the skin underneath she
could only wear one for two or three days at a time, and
as washing them destroyed the stiffening of the fabric, they
had then to be thrown away. She was under the care of
two excellent practitioners, Doctors Francis and John
Willis, and at various times they had treated her at
their own establishment in Leicestershire whilst they had
studied the best way for ameliorating her disease. The
syphilis they could do nothing for directly, except to
recommend soothing tinctures and the masks, but the
softening of the brain they countered with gentle, understanding care, the removal of mirrors, and accepting her
'baby' as though it were indeed real. This was why the
house in the woods, the old Dower House, had been
adapted for her use, and the woodcutter and his wife, a
former nurse, employed to give her as stable and easy a
life as possible. She was told that she had a nervous rash
that would disappear with time, the mirrors were removed
– except for that forgotten one in the attic – and she was
provided with gewgaws, games, and pretty clothes to
distract her. All papers with dates were kept away from
her, and gradually, as she lost all sense of time, she truly
believed that it was only a few months since she had seen
James, and that it was his military duty overseas that kept
him from her side. The rag doll she so cossetted, had he
been real, would now be a boy of nearly ten years old.

I wondered for some time about Lady Jestyn's account

of the birth of the baby: obviously she, probably influenced by the masculine outlook of her son, and to a lesser extent by the biased prognostications of the local doctor – who I learned had died of old age some years back – was convinced that the baby Dorothea had conceived had been James's, and that she had thoughtlessly let herself be infected with the disease she now bore by some stranger no one seemed to remember while she was pregnant. This did not seem to me to be at all likely. Given the times and intervals quoted by my employer, it was highly improbable that the child was indeed that of her husband. To be born some ten months after his departure, weighing but two or three pounds, was well-nigh impossible: my life since I had left home had given me opportunity to hear of all the tricks that women had to employ in an embarrassing plight, and it was far more likely, given the birthweight, that the child had not been conceived till three or four months after her husband had left, and that she had taken one of the many concoctions available to make it arrive before time, in order to make it seem his. This was a deliberate risk, for even discounting the many side dangers of these drugs the child was patently premature, and might not have survived had it been entirely healthy and unharmed by the potion. However, she and her husband were both young, and the death of a first-born would not have mattered overmuch: it was the disease which had upset all her plans. I wondered long and often, not only what sort of man could have tempted her so soon after her marriage, but also what villain could deliberately infect so pretty a girl, so that she could have no more children. I remembered Lady Jestyn's remark that she had been 'a trifle flirtatious' and wondered whether she had felt as I did after having been made love to for the first time: it was such a marvellous feeling that it must be repeated, much as I had repeated it with Nick, scarce four or five months after that first time with Jack.

I called on her once a week, after that unfortunate encounter in the attic; sometimes she was not rational enough to receive me, but often we would take tea on the terrace and tell our fortunes in the leaves, and afterwards stroll in the garden, gossiping of fashions or the 'baby's' health. All the time I could see the accelerating deterioration and pitied her the more; it was like visiting a petulant child, who never questioned where her pleasures came from but accepted them as her due – just as she accepted me as Miss Tregorran without the slightest interest in where I came from or why I was there, except to provide a diversion once a week.

These visits started without the knowledge or approval of Lady Jestyn, but after a couple of them I asked her permission: she did not withhold it, but neither did she thoroughly approve; I could see that she was still more influenced by the harm Dorothea's actions had done to her son than by the sufferings her daughter-in-law was now undergoing, and I could understand this. Blessed as I had been with a logical and reasoning stepfather this same example had cursed me, or so it seemed, with an increasing ability to see both sides of a question – looking back I could now begin to appreciate how I must have irritated Aunt Sophia, with my education and manners so vastly superior to those of her less gifted children. At the time I had put all the blame on them for being deficient; now I realized that I had been the lucky one – an attitude of humility that had completely escaped me at the time. This was only one example, but I supposed it was possible to be objective about the problems of others – my own, only at a comfortable distance. If my stepfather had been other than an agnostic, he would, I am sure, have had me embroider my sampler with 'There, but for the Grace of God, go I', instead of: 'The Cultivation of an Enquiring Mind within the Ordered Confines of Logical Thought assures a Bounteous Harvest of Wisdom', which latter thought, though doubtless excellent, left very little room for the cross-stitch Tree of Knowledge and its attendant birds and beasts, which were the main pleasure of a sampler . . . .

Now I could see, all too clearly, how easily people fell into what we regarded as sin: through laziness, carelessness, good intentions even. And once down it was easy to stay; I had loved Jack and always would, whether I ever saw him again or not, yet had yielded easily enough to the temptations of Nick – and had enjoyed them, too. Once, and that not too long ago a time either, I could not have envisaged compassion for a girl who had wilfully abandoned her marriage lines after a few weeks to enjoy a clandestine affaire, and then had tried to deceive her husband into fathering another man's bastard, but after Annie, Barnaby, Angel, Lil, Miss Thoroughgood, and even Jack himself, all creatures with a past of doubt and a present of compromise, I could the more easily comprehend and excuse a fall from grace.

The month of May brought a spell of fine, warm weather, which encouraged the farmers – 'a pinch of dust in May, is worth a load of hay' – and enabled me to persuade Lady Jestyn to be driven about, very sedately, in the park and down the lanes nearby. Young Bob looked out and refurbished a small open trap, and with the quietest horse in the stables we even ventured into Crum Potting to visit Her Ladyship's most faithful visitors, the elderly Misses Pritchard, and one day went as far as Lesser Beedles, to consult her priest. Driven by Old Bob in the ancient carriage we visited a couple of Lady Jestyn's friends for a musical evening, supper party and cards, and once, to my joy, took a box at the Little Playhouse in Hink; a travelling company gave a most moral tale, *Miss Muffin's Downfall, or: The Erring Daughter*. As a troupe they were not very good: the acting was less able than Jack's, and of the accompanying acts the acrobats were less nimble than the dwarves had been and the juggler was not a patch on our Sam-Sam. But it had been so long since I had seen entertainment of any kind that I clapped and cheered as loud as any at the lights, the colour, the music, and was wrapped in the warmth of the dusty drapes and the mixed smells of the audience: perfume, sweat, fur, grease; pomade and powder, unwashed hair, oranges and stale meat pies.

I believe my employer had as much pleasure in watching my enjoyment as in anything else, because she told me afterwards how happy she was to see me laugh. 'You grow too serious with me, child,' she chided, and though I protested she was wrong, at the same time I could see that much of my natural ebullience, which had stood firm in much harsher circumstances, was being gradually eroded by the gentler tyranny of our quiet and subdued life together. True, I still rebelled, when everything inside of me wanted to run free in the wind and the rain, to take my shoes off and feel the velvet surprise of grass between my toes and the tickle of running water push against my ankles, but these times were becoming less and easier controlled, and I doubted now whether my softened soles would stand up to a day walking barefoot in the lanes.

Even my memories of my time on the road with my companions were blurring into a comfortable landscape where the sun always shone, like the remembered summers of childhood; the traumas of London and Madame's seemed a thousand miles away and Miss T's a pleasant interlude, but luckily for me Lady Jestyn found an unused journal among her possessions, a fine volume bound with red leather, and suggested I use wet days for recalling in my own words the story of my adventures. Although she assured me she intended it to be as private as I wished, I often found myself reading out to her some of the more amusing parts. At first I had not known where to begin my story of myself, but finally decided that my rescue from that April ditch four years ago would be as good a place to begin as any. At first I found I was writing in a stilted and pompous way, but as I recalled more and more it became easier and more fluent. I found I had a good enough memory to be able to quote whole conversations and keep what happened in chronological order; Lady Jestyn heard some of my recollections with eyes round with amazement or crinkled at the corners with responsive amusement: I do not think she really believed it all (and in the reading I left out the more compromising bits), but she was kind enough to declare that it was 'Much more interesting than that dull book we had from the circulating library this month', and 'not to stop!' Much of it she knew already, from the résumé I gave her when I confessed my deception, but she seemed not to mind hearing it again.

Apart from my other duties, I had taken over my employer's task of distributing the various comforts and food we could spare to the poorer people of the village: Kate had taken as much as she could while her mistress was confined to bed, but she had enough to do with her other duties, and I was a willing volunteer. Alas! for good intentions. At the beginning of June, with a joy of roses in the hedgerows and the sneeze of new-mown hay drying in the meadows, I caught an infection from one of the cottagers' children. The humiliation of measles made me miss James Jestyn's visit on the occasion of his annual return on or around the anniversary of Lady Jestyn's wedding day: this, like her birthday and Christmas, were the times when he could be relied upon to return home, even if for only a day or two, so she told me later.

I, too, had had a special reason for hoping to enjoy those first days of the month, for the sixth brought my birthday, though I had told no one. I had missed my birthday last year at Miss T's, not knowing whether the real Esther owned to a known date, and it was with a real sense of amazement that I realized I should be twenty this year. My sixteenth birthday had been enjoyed with Jack on that day out in the Malvern Hills, my seventeenth was the day he had ridden off saying birthdays were for children, my eighteenth was spent in Nick's arms, my nineteenth at the Seminary . . . .

On the third of June I felt shivery and out of sorts; on the fourth my head ached and so did my throat, and on the fifth I went to bed early and tossed and turned all night in a rising fever, remembering the spotty, heavy-eyed children in the hovel by the stream, and hoping that what I had caught was no worse than their infection. On the morning of the sixth I could not have cared had it been Christmas twice over; I staggered to my feet and washed and dressed, then collapsed in a heap halfway down the stairs. Lady Jestyn heard my fall and I was rescued by the strong arms of Kate's Jeremy, who put me, under my employer's instructions, in the room next to hers, the one normally occupied by her absent maid Hortense. She sent for a woman from the village to alternate with Kate in caring for me, and I remember the latter struggling to undress me and the doctor forcing some horrible concoction down my throat, then it was blackness and fevered dreams in alternation. The night-mares brought back the crooked cross of the drowned dwarves, Angel with a smile and a bloody knife stooping to cut their dead throats; Madame Bonneville smothering me in her black velvet dress and the brothel children laughing and applauding as she did; the hangings at Tyburn with rats the size of hounds gnawing at the swinging ropes; Lovely Louisa of St Bartholomew's Fair sitting on my chest till I thought it would crack; Jack with his arms full of Arabian dancing girls with spots; Death from the tarot pack stepping larger than life from his cardboard backcloth with a rattle of bones; a blind man with his stick pursuing me endlessly down darkened alleys full of shuttered windows and bolted doors . . . . I do not remember the next twenty-four hours except as a hot burning inside and out, night and day the same; the light, any light, hurt my eyes; a candle looked like the sun.

Then, suddenly, I felt a little better. I was still hot, but sticky too, and that meant the fever was breaking: I touched my burning cheeks and could feel the little bumps of the spots coming up. 'Water,' I whispered and somebody heard, came across with a rustle of petticoats, lifted my head, and I drank the cool liquid gratefully, and asked for more. The same person bathed my face and hands and gave me fresh pillows, then retired to the corner again, and I was drifting back to sleep when I recognized Lady Jestyn's voice.

'How is she?' I did not hear the reply, but I heard her again, this time speaking in French, and was aware of the flicker of an approaching candle-flame behind my closed lids. '*Pauvre petite. . . . Vois-tu.*'

The candle hurt my eyes and I screwed up my face. Instantly it was shaded, and I opened my eyes to a tall shadow and some gleaming coat buttons.

'I am a little better, I think,' I murmured, and the candle dipped and wavered wildly for a moment before steadying. I felt a sudden sharp burning on my left forearm, and as I reached my other hand to rub the stinging pain, I heard a man's voice, speaking also in French.

'*Merde!*' it exclaimed, and with a hint of incredulity: '*Gringalet . . .?*'

Then the candle and the shadow with the coat buttons walked away and I heard Lady Jestyn say: '*Elle est belle n'est-ce-pas, Jacquot?*' and I fell asleep at once, wondering why a Froggie should be so surprised at a few spots.

All was explained when they were fading to a more respectable sprinkle. Lady Jestyn told me her son had been home for her birthday, and had peeped in on me at her urging.

'He was very impressed with all I had to tell him of your devoted service; once he had seen you for himself he was most insistent that I was not to think of parting with you, even when Hortense returns to take over your duties –'

'She will be back soon, then?'

'James told me he had seen her in France; her father is dead, God rest his soul, but she stays for a while until his affairs are in order: so, until you are quite well again, you will stay in her room where I can keep an eye on you.'

I smiled and thanked her. 'You called him Jacquot,' I added, thinking of the coat buttons.

'But yes: when he is here we often converse in French and "Jacquot" is a pet name for James. It is good practice for him, I can use my own tongue again with pleasure, and if there is anything he wants to say to me that he wishes kept secret – well, none of the servants understand.'

I frowned. 'He said something when he burnt my arm – look!' And I held it out for her inspection. 'He dripped candle grease . . . .' The red mark was fading with my other spots. 'Now what was it? Ah, yes: "*Merde!*" He sounded quite startled.'

Now it was her turn to frown. 'You will oblige me by forgetting it instantly and not using it again: it is a most indelicate word, and one that should not pass the lips of a lady. I am sure you must be mistaken in his using it,' and she looked so forbidding that I dared not ask what the other word had been, lest it was worse. A pity; if I had, then things might have been very different.

I recovered quickly, and within a couple of weeks was as good as new. The latter half of June was cold and wet with uncertain starts of showers more like April than summer, but once I was on my feet again I went back to my task of exchanging our subscription library books with the Misses Pritchard in the village, and one afternoon, after nearly a week of heavy showers and blustery winds, I judged it fine enough to make my errand while Lady Jestyn was taking her usual rest. I was to exchange *Pamela* for *Rasselas*, and I took care to wrap the latter volume well in a piece of oiled cloth on my return, for black clouds were racing up from the Malverns. The sisters had begged me to stay till the threat was past, but after a weak cup of chocolate and a biscuit in their dismal front parlour which always smelled of uncleaned birdcages and faced north, all I wanted was fresh air, laced with rain or no. I walked round the village green, its duckpond overflowing with the recent rains and ducklings, past the inn, the blacksmith, the stocks, the row of cottages, the Church of St Michael and All Angels and the vicarage. As I passed the latter the wind gusted, died and rose again, and the first few drops of rain splashed the puddles by the track I was taking. I could have sought shelter under the huge chestnut trees by the churchyard, I could have run up to the vicarage through the neat, laurel-edged path, even retreated to the church porch, but instead I decided to chance it and make a dash for the lane and home. Even as I picked up my skirts to run, the heavens opened and poured forth a positive sheet of water that had me soaked in twenty yards. As if that were not enough I tripped, slipped on the muddy path, my feet shot from under me, and I ended rump down in a large puddle.

'Damn!' I yelled to the sky, then clapped my hand to my mouth, glancing furtively round in case any had heard, though it was highly unlikely anyone else would be out in this rain, which was now cold as charity and soaking up second-hand into my drawers. There *was* someone, though: a slight man was leading a tall horse away from the smithy, both heads down, both protected to a certain extent by layers of sacking, but they had not looked in my direction. I struggled to my feet, shook out my draggled skirts, and started off again only to slip and trip once more, this time face down into a rut that had become a stream. Now I opened my mouth and let rip, remembering with aston-ishing ease most of Jack's choicer profanities, not caring that the man with the horse was staring at me openly from the other side of the green; I thought I detected a shake of the head, as though he deplored my lapse.

Infuriated, I yelled across as loud as I could. 'Go *away*!' Somewhat mollified, I saw him turn and lead the horse in the opposite direction, even as I rose to my feet for the second time and prepared to set off again. At the same time I chanced to glance back again, and became aware of a curious phenomenon.

A whitish blur seemed to be crossing the green diagonally towards me, accompanied by strange yipping noises, like a trapped rat; there seemed to be about twenty-four legs working like pistons beneath the apparition as it took the shortest course, straight through the middle of the duck pond, scattering shrieking birds and sending up sheets of spray to mingle with the rain. The yelping continued as

593

the blur rapidly gained in size: mouse-size, rat-size, cat-size, dog-size –

A third time I went down, this time flat on my back, as a weight like a sack of potatoes hit my midriff: a weight with a tongue as warm as the rain was cold, and a moist, steamy, wriggling body that had my dress covered with paw marks in two seconds flat. Struggling to my feet I fended off the recalcitrant animal, thinking it had gone mad.

'Down!' I yelled. 'Behave yourself, you wretched dog – Oh dear!'

For it begged, offered a paw, walked on its hind legs, died for its country, turned a somersault, and finally just sat and looked up at me; wet, muddy, eyes shining, lifting one paw after the other from the ground as if they still remembered the burns and the thorns . . . .

'Oh, *Toby*!' I cried, and dropped to my knees uncaring, my eyes as wet and shining as his. 'Oh, Toby! Toby *darling*! My dearest, dearest dog: where *have* you come from . . . ?'

I carried him secretly up the back stairs and we both had a good wash and I changed before we crept down to face my employer. I had no idea how she would receive the news that I had found – or been found by – my dear companion, but I was so happy to have him back that I would willingly sleep in the stables to be near him, if she did not want him in the house. I need not have worried. Once I had explained in my muddled way who he was, and he had gravely offered his paw, then retreated discreetly to sit at my side, she was won over.

'My dear James always kept a dog, and I have quite missed them around the house. He had three at one time, I recollect: a gun dog called Trigger, a hound named Bullet, and a little terrier – now, what was it called? Ah, yes: Pistol. And your dog: he is not noisy or destructive, is he?'

'Why, no,' I said truthfully. 'He has been well trained –' but I stopped there, for I had seen Gipsy, her cat, stalking stiffly into the room, tail high. Reaching the middle of the room she became aware of the intruder and her tail bushed. But Toby had better sense than I thought: on seeing her he had dropped nose on paws submissively.

Gipsy growled. '*Tais-toi, p'tite!*' said Lady Jestyn, comfortingly, but after a moment's thought the cat stalked forward in Toby's direction.

'*No*, Toby!' I said warningly, but I think he had already accepted the position for he stayed still, quivering a little in a suppressed way as the cat approached. She lifted one paw and rapped him sharply once, twice, thrice on his skull, making hollow box sounds and raising three scarlet pinpricks of blood on his scalp. He winced but stayed still, eyes shut protectively, and after a moment she licked the middle claw of the damaging paw reflectively, flicked her tail irritably, and walked to her customary place in the hearth. Toby opened one eye cautiously, then the other, and glanced up at me, his tail wagging briefly.

'So now you know who's boss,' I said. 'Just don't forget it, my lad, or it's the stables . . . .'

Lady Jestyn stooped to stroke her old cat. 'I am so glad he has found you, my dear: have you no idea where he has come from? Or how he happened to see you in the village this afternoon? It seems very strange to me . . . .'

It seemed strange to me, too: I had thought about it all the way home with him, intermittently during the afternoon, and long into the night, with Toby stretched out beside me, his loving head on my shoulder. There was not really room for us both on my narrow bed, but just this once . . . . An attitude that I knew was conducive to creating a precedent, but then he had always snuggled up next to me in the van, and I loved him so much.

There were all sorts of possibilities to conjecture with; it was June, and he might have been travelling with Tom and Jack and wandered away; he could have been bought or stolen by someone and run away; he could have been living nearby and found me by accident; he could have been deliberately planted. I had examined him all over from head to mended tail: coat, eyes, ears, teeth, paws and claws, and as he had obviously been well cared for and defleaed that would seem to rule out a thief or a bad owner. There had been no fairs or shows nearabout, and Annie had said Jack had sold up, so my happiest thought could be discounted. It seemed unlikely he had been living nearby in the village and had caught sight of me accidentally: I remembered the man with the tall horse, but it had not been Jack or anyone else recognizable under those coverings of sacking. And yet, that same man had hurried away as soon as he saw Toby run to me: so, the inference was that he was known to me, and that Toby had been 'allowed' to rejoin me. But whom had he been with, who had decided, and why?

I fell asleep with the resolution to seek an answer to these questions as soon as possible by spending all my spare time in discreet enquiry, but fate decided to play a hand, and her first card was George.

The elder son and heir came back to his ancestral home at the end of June, accompanied by a weird assortment of 'guests' in two large coaches. The housekeeper at the main house had sent over two days previously – no separate note of courtesy to Lady Jestyn had arrived – saying that Sir George had ordered the best bedrooms to be prepared and the principal rooms aired, and that he would need the services of our butler, Charles, and Jeremy and Young Bob. In spite of the deliberate slight, her increasing fragility, and the drain on our resources, my employer insisted on going over to supervise the staff in the cleaning and preparation, and of course I went with her. It was heartbreaking to see how years of neglect had depleted the fine furnishings and linens: in the end we had to provide most of the latter from our own thin stocks. The small resident staff did what they could in their master's absence, but it needed all our efforts, plus two cleaning women from the village, to wash the glass and windows, bring out and air the hangings, wash the paintwork, polish the floors, dust the few bits of decent furniture left under the dustsheets, light the long-disused fires, and bring enough provisions in from Hink to keep the place going at least for a few days; I suspected the latter were paid for by Lady Jestyn herself, as were the wages for the extra help.

At the end of forty-eight hours of frantic work the whole of the southern wing was more or less habitable. The faded velvets, silks too delicate to be mended again, bare patches on the wall where pawned pictures had hung, empty spaces where the larger pieces of silver had stood, peeling paintwork, rotten sills, and damp marks on the walls could not be hidden but were as well disguised as they could be by the judicious placing of those pieces available and the robbing of other parts of the house. The stables were always kept in good shape by Old Bob and his son but the one decent carriage was now brought out and given an airing, and two extra carriage horses were borrowed from the doctor. The gardens we could do little about except to have the longest of the grass scythed to a moderate length below the south terrace: luckily the boxes and yews were soon clipped and the flower beds, with a little weeding, did not look too bad with the roses at their best. It was too late to think of clearing the moss from the terraces or the ivy that clustered round the windows, but perhaps they hid much that was better so: all in all the place looked better than I had ever seen it, after two days of really hard work.

We heard the party arrive late in the evening of the second day. The main gates had been oiled and opened and we heard the cavalcade long before we saw them. I happened to be up in my room changing for bed when there was a whooping and hallooing off to my left, the sound of hooves and wheels, and out into the open space in front of the house careered two carriages, closely followed by three horsemen. With much shrieking and laughing the conveyances disgorged five females and a quantity of luggage, and five more 'gentlemen'. They were of various shapes and sizes, and seemingly dressed in the height of fashion. The last to alight was a portly man of middle years with a face very red in the light from the carriage lanterns, who appeared incapable of keeping his feet and showed a distressing tendency to sit on the newly raked gravel.

'Drunk again, Gorgeous?' said one of the 'ladies', quite distinctly. 'Oh Lor'! Do help me get the bleeder to his feet, one of you, there's a dear! Come on, ducks: you *are* the host, you know . . . . Lead the way, or we'll never get any supper!'

He was assisted to his feet and greeted by an expressionless Charles at the main door, while a round-eyed Young Bob and a disgusted Jeremy helped with the luggage. The guests stayed up late that night, the house a blaze of candles and echoing with shouts, laughter, and feminine shrieks, and the pattern was repeated for the next few weeks, with much comings and goings and change of company. Lady Jestyn said very little and kept her window fast shut at night, in spite of the oppressive July heat, but many nights I lay awake unable to sleep, my ears assaulted by the sounds of revelry, the ribaldry, the smash of breaking glass, and my mind blenching from the imagined excesses.

George did not pay his courtesy call on his stepmother till nearly a week had passed, but I had encountered him two days before.

Toby and I had been visiting the poorer villagers on my usual round with soup, bread and comforts; this I did regularly for my employer, not purely from charity because that would presuppose that we were wealthy, and this Riverwood definitely was not: we did it to try and alleviate as much as we could the miserable conditions some of them lived under, owing to Sir George's extravagance and improvidence. In his father's day there had been more than enough work on the estate and nearby farms to provide for many more than were now living in the village, and all the cottages had been trim and well cared for.

Now most were tumble-down, with threadbare thatch mended with green reeds from the river, rotting doors and windows, damp walls, and empty cupboards. James Jestyn had apparently won a concession from his brother in that the villagers were to be allowed to collect fallen wood from the estate, a certain amount of grain from the home farm was to be set aside for the needy, and a number of cattle salted down for their winter use, and from what I had seen a blind eye was usually turned to the odd poached rabbit or hare. Nevertheless these people, those who had not moved away to chance their luck in Evesham or Worcester, and those who were not lucky to have a steady job on one of the farms or helping at one of the bigger houses, suffered real despair and poverty, and it was these we tried to help: I say we, but now it was nearly always I, since my employer's illness. Many of the families had a great deal of children, and it was on these we concentrated, and on the old people who could no longer work nor care for themselves adequately. They did not all accept what was offered graciously, for some were proud and all wished to be independent, but the children soon became friends with me and often would bring a gift in return: a daisy chain for my neck, a posy of bluebells wilting in hot, grubby hands, a bird's egg blue as the sky and speckled with sun freckles.

This particular day I had brought linen to Mrs Cosgrove for shifts for her three little girls, milk for the Tanner children, soup for old Mrs Scrope, and cough linctus of my own distilling for the youngest Sayle, suffering from croup. On the way I had met Bet Chiney who, with two illegitimate children under the age of five, was desperate against conceiving any more, and I had promised her a mixture, though where I was to find horehound around here I did not know, and Kat's recipe was insistent on that being an ingredient. Perhaps down by the river on the drier, sunny slopes . . . . I was busy thinking of Bet, the village whore and no worse for that, and Toby was running ahead in the field next to the road, druffling down all the molehills, when I became aware of three horsemen trotting down the lane towards me. They were in single file because of the narrowness of the lane, and I stepped into the hedge to let them pass. The first moved past with no more than a curious glance, and I recognized him as one of the guests at the house, but with a 'Whoa, y' brute!' the second man pulled up and sat gazing down at me. The man behind was forced to rein in pretty sharply, but it was not he that held my gaze.

Pressing back against the hedge till I could feel every twig through my clothes, making myself as flat-chested and hunched as possible, all I wanted was for them – him – all of them to go away. I tried to squeeze past, but the horse at the rear looked like a kicker, and the first horse's quarters were almost up against me.

'Just look what I've found,' said Sir George softly. 'Not bad for around here, b'Gad!'

'Dem' pretty villagers you got, what?' said the third man vaguely.

The first man said nothing, but his gaze raked me from head to heel with a professional air, and he winked.

I was hemmed in on all sides by sweating, restless, blowing horses, and they had never appealed to me in general; not like the particular, darling Daisy and big, gentle Hannibal – Quite irrelevantly something ticked in my mind: the tall, dark, dripping horse in the village the day I found Toby: but the teasing thought flashed away as soon as it had come, like the streak of a swift across the sky, and I was no wiser.

Now was more important. 'Let me pass!'

'Not so hasty, girl!' said Sir George. 'Here, Egerton, hold my brute,' and dismounting he moved towards me. He was a tall man with wide shoulders, a deep chest, big head and thick neck. His eyes were small and restless, set between puffy lids; his nose was a small beak, his mouth loose and wet, his complexion scaly and high-coloured. Now I really became panicky: suddenly he was all the people I had feared since Oliver: he had Madame's hypnotic complacency, the blind man's hidden power, the ugliness of the fellow with the clap. I could feel the sweat trickling from my armpits, my knees trembling, yet I was as transfixed as a rabbit I had once seen charmed by a stoat. I had been contemptuous then of the rabbit's suggestibility even as I had clapped my hands to break the spell, but now I understood its fascinated terror only too well. I wanted to scream for help, to claw at the marred face so close to mine, to turn from the foetid breath smelling of stale wine and rancid meat; I wanted to run, to push past the crowding horses – but all I could do was to stand and tremble like any scared animal.

The pudgy-fingered hands came nearer, rested on my shrinking shoulders. 'How about a kiss, sweetheart? Come on, now: don't be afraid.'

But I could only press closer to the hedge. 'Please . . . . Please don't . . . .'

'Polite, too. Now then,' he said more briskly: 'Let's just see what's hidden under all those skirts –' and he reached down to grab the material.

Suddenly Kat Petulengro's voice was whispering in my ear, and I repeated what I heard without thought.

'Touch me but once with your pocked hands, George Jestyn, and I shall tell what I know, and all that is hidden shall be open to the world . . . .'

It did not even sound like my own voice, and I had no idea what relevance the words had, but the reaction was gratifyingly immediate. He drew back, his face more blotched than ever, and raised his hand to strike me, but in that moment there was a yipping, growling hurricane behind me and Toby burst through the badger-run at the bottom of the hedge, the horses reared and bucked, and my gallant dog launched himself straight at Sir George. Toby's leap was about two feet ten inches off the ground and impelled by all the force of his strong back legs: consequently the point of impact was that part that can incapacitate a man most, but I did not wait for the full effect. Calling Toby off urgently before he decided to try teeth, I pushed past the startled horses and we were off down the lane as fast as we could go. Across the ditch, over the bank and into the wood the quickest way, I spared one backward glance: George Jestyn was doubled up on the ground, groaning, while all around the trio of neighing, prancing horses kicked dust into everyone's eyes.

I did not tell Lady Jestyn of the meeting but Kate guessed after seeing me arrive back all dishevelled and without my basket; when Sir George came to pay his courtesy call on his stepmother she warned me in advance: 'Do you keep away from that one: he's poison!' so I took care to be out. I was afraid of what I might do or say if I met him again; most of all I think I was afraid of the fear itself.

Towards the end of July the maid Hortense came back to her mistress. She was a small, spare woman in her late fifties, and even I, who had not known her before, could see her exhaustion and fear: her skin was drawn and sallow, her dark eyes circled by black shadows, and although she made light of her travels to Lady Jestyn, only saying that Monsieur Jacquot had arranged a most comfortable journey for her, she was more expansive to me when we were alone. I was busy vacating her room, where I had continued to sleep after the measles were long past, when she came in, dumped her travelling bag and, sitting on the edge of the half-made bed, began to cry. I hurried to her side, but for some moments could make nothing of it, for she was muttering and moaning in a French patois I could not follow; then she tried to pull herself together, wiped her eyes, blew her nose, straightened herself up and turned to me, speaking in heavily accented English, but every now and again lapsing into her native tongue.

'You are ver' kind to try to comfort, but there is nothing you can do: I am a foolish, easy upset old woman, that is all to it. But my lady must not know: she has enough to worry without my weakness: you will not tell?'

'Of course not,' I assured her. 'You are tired after your long journey –'

'Not only that: *ma foi!* Do you think I would cry only for a journey and a death? *Non, c'est plus que – Mon père est mort, mon pays est mort* . . . .'

'I don't understand . . . .'

'Ah, how could you? You, the little one who has looked after my lady so well, the one of whom Monsieur Jacquot spoke so highly, you who must help to keep the worst from her –'

'Monsieur Jacquot – James, spoke well of me?'

'But most highly: you have cared so well for his *maman*. At first, you understand, I was – how you put it – *un peu jaloux, peut-être, mais . . . Je regrette*, it is some time since I spoke the English: even Monsieur Jacquot . . . He told me that you were a good girl who was to help me and read the books to her; that you loved her as well as I did, so that I was not to mind. But we must keep the truth of what is happening from her, over there in France.'

'We have heard nothing.'

'It will be in all the papers soon: they let them all out of the Bastille, you see, and for a while everyone went mad and the streets ran with blood. And they shut up the poor King and his Queen . . . .'

'When did all this happen?' said I, having but the sketchiest idea of who 'they' were, those who had opened the biggest prison in Europe.

'Five days ago: *le quatorze juillet*. I only come here safe because of him; he arrange everything, even the disguise I have to wear across Paris, through the mobs. *Il est très gentil, très brave –*'

'And he is still there?'

'But yes, and this is the big reason why we must not tell my lady how bad it all is: she must not know he is in danger! So, do not read all the bad bits from the newspapers, my lady's heart is not strong, and the shock –'

603

'But why does he not come back?'

'He is – how you call it? – spy, for his country. He tells them what is going on – the truth – so that we shall not fight each other. I do not approve of spies, but he assures me that it is to prevent *la guerre*, and I believe him.'

I had not her naiveté, but she was obviously convinced.

'Does he speak French well?' I ventured.

'Enough to pass as a native; a French mother to teach him when he was young. . . .' She spread her hands. 'What more could one want? He even learn a little German and Italian; in France he can pass as native, and with the disguise – the wig, the patch, the old clothes – you would not know it was him: even his sainted mother would not recognize!'

We could not keep all the bad news from Lady Jestyn; the Misses Pritchard were full of it on their next visit and the priest called round to offer up prayers for her countrymen. She bore it well, but became paler and thinner; one day she had a bad fall coming down the stairs and Hortense seized upon it as a heaven-sent opportunity to get her to rest in bed for a few days, using as an excuse the time-honoured housewife's one of the place needing a good clear-out, and that the dust and upset would do her no good.

'Not that there is much to do,' she confided to me once Lady Jestyn was safe upstairs, 'but she must rest, and we shall bang about a little just to show how hard we are working.'

Of course we did not 'bang about' at all, we were quiet and careful, but it was surprising to find how much the rooms in general, and the cupboards in particular, needed a good clear-out. We spent a week turning, tidying, renovating, cleaning and refurbishing, and although the wallpaper remained dingy and faded and the curtains and carpets threadbare, they all at least looked brighter and fresher once we had done. Then we turned our attention to sorting the contents of the brimming cupboards and drawers, some of which had obviously not been touched for years. All this, of course, was undertaken in between the intervals of tending to Lady Jestyn's wants and keeping her company, for we each in turn spent some good part of the day with her lest she find her enforced idleness irksome, and it was early one August afternoon, when it had rained hard enough to dampen the ground and darken the harvest, that I came down to the small drawing room to find Hortense on her hands and knees by the small chest in the corner.

'She's having her rest: how far have you got?'

Hortense sat back on her heels. 'The bureau and the corner cupboard, they are done, and Her Ladyship's desk we will not touch: it is for her private. But this chest: I have no idea of the rubbish it hold! See, piles of old newspapers and magazines . . . .'

'Perhaps they have news she wishes to keep?'

'*Mais non*: they are ten, fifteen years old, and the fashions antique! But perhaps then, the news we shall put back: the magazines they will help to light the fires.

'And there is this!' She held up a battered sketchbook. 'I have wonder where this go. The young artist came some five, six years ago; he beg for his supper in exchange for drawings of the people in this house: see, he did me!' It was a quick drawing, more an impression, but the artist, though no genius, had caught very nicely Hortense's bright eye and the suggestion of bustling movement in her momentarily stilled body. 'He came from Paris, of all things, and he said he travel the country to broaden his mind and practise his art: the illustration of new articles for a paper of quality was his aim. The fact that he was one of my mistress's countrymen ensured him not only that free supper but also *le petit déjeuner* and five guineas in his pocket.' She held up another drawing. 'A nice young man: see how he draw Kate.' Kate had a flirtatious smile on her face: she had obviously found the artist attractive, too. 'He do two, three of Her Ladyship too: see how he has made her look proud and *très elegante*.' There were two pages of sketches of her: profile, full face; studies of her hands, her eyes; a full-length figure. I would not have recognized the still-youthful person I saw portrayed, but this had been before her stroke, of course. 'That was one of the times that Jacquot was here to stay . . . .'

'Did he have his likeness taken too?' It was a natural enough question, yet I had no idea as I asked it how important it was going to prove for me.

'Oh yes! He would not pose, shrug the young artist aside, but his *maman* ask privately that he should catch the likeness; he was to pretend to sketch her, but was instead to draw her son. There were two sketches, I believe . . . .' She flicked over the pages. 'Ah, yes, here they are.'

The first showed a seated man, face shielded by his hand, book on his lap, long legs stretched out to the fire: it could have been any moderately well-dressed, tall, thin, dark, youngish man with untidy elflocks falling forward to hide that part of his face not concealed by his hand, but my heart should have known . . . .

'And here: here he is full-face. The artist talked about Paris politics while he pretend to draw my lady, so Jacquot was attending. Perhaps I could find a small frame and put it by my lady's bedside to remind her: it is good likeness.'

It was indeed.

Dark, disorderly hair framed the long thin face with the strong crooked nose, the frowning eyebrows, the alert eyes, the mobile mouth. The hands were clenched on the arms of the chair, those long fingers with the knobbled joints . . . . I felt nothing, like a foot that has gone to sleep all over. Memory of a word came back, but I marvelled at the stranger with the calm voice who asked for the confirmation already guessed.

'Hortense: what does the word *gringalet* mean in English?'

She must have been surprised at the switch in subject matter but she humoured me. '*Gringalet*? Is a word for a little fish, good to eat but full of bones. Fry it quick in oil,

606

first coated with seasoned flour . . .' She snapped her fingers searching for the word. 'Ah, yes: sprat.'

I had known before I asked, and now I must not explode into a thousand pieces of happiness in front of this woman, I must not, I must not – 'Perhaps it would be just as well not to show the sketches to Lady Jestyn just now; it might remind her of happier times, to her present detriment. Keep them till she is better. And now – and now, Hortense, I feel in need of fresh air. Can you cope if I take a walk as far as the river?'

'Of course – but the grass, it is wet: you will drench yourself!'

But I could not heed her warning. Calling Toby I ran all the way down the river path, my hem brushing the reddening pods of jack-in-the-pulpit that lined the way, my skirts wet with the rain that bent the tall grasses, my hands brushing aside the ripening sprays of blackberries, my face cooled by the drops of moisture shaken from the twisted fluff of traveller's joy. I did not stop running till I came to the stone pier where they filled the buckets for the horses, to save the well-water. Then I walked out as far as I could and sat down, my hem trailing unheeded in the water, and looked across at the familiar sleeping dragon of the Malvern Hills. There, four years ago, Jack had said, staring through his spyglass towards the place where I now sat: 'Just this side of Bredon there is a house whose western windows look to these hills; the green lawn slopes to the river . . . there are . . . banks of lavender on the terrace . . . .' In that same Jack's private box there was a miniature of a beautiful fair-haired girl with golden ringlets, and the glass of Dorothea's portrait was splintered as if by an angry heel . . . . When he had been delirious had he not spoken of ''Thea', short for Dorothea? Had he not also imagined he was speaking to his *maman*? And I remembered now, too late, where I had heard the name Jestyn before: the inn at Shrewsbury where I had lost my way and overheard Jack talking to the lawyer. 'Tell Lady

Jestyn that . . . I send her my fond remembrances . . . as for George . . . tell him nothing . . . .'

All of a sudden I had the shakes and had to get up and pace, forwards and back, to and fro, round and round, while my teeth chattered and my heart thumped like a drum: 'Jack! Jack! Jack!' So at last I knew it all; he was a government agent of many disguises who tried to keep together a crumbling mansion by the Severn whilst his dissolute half-brother endeavoured to dissipate the whole. Jack, my Jack of the road, was in reality a gentleman called James Jestyn, ex-military captain with an invalid mother and no land to call his own. No land, Mr Landless, but you have a wife, a girl as mad as Ophelia who bore you a stillborn son . . . . There had been so many clues I had missed! The gun dog, Bullet, that Tom Fallon had talked of when Jack agreed to keep Toby, and the dogs Bullet, Trigger and Pistol Lady Jestyn had mentioned; Jack riding off to an unknown destination whenever we had been in this area, and arriving back dispirited after his visits to his mother, his clothes smelling of the lavender from the terrace that she hung in all the closets: even now my cheeks flared with sudden burning embarrassment when I remembered how the boy Sprat had tried to warn him of the dangers of the clap; after having left his diseased wife behind him so shortly ago, had it been any wonder that he had struck out so violently?

At first I was wildly excited, hugging to myself the fact that after all this time, after all my travels and hardships, all my longings, all my hopes, I was, by the most extraordinary of coincidences, here where Jack could find me whenever he wished. And, after all, he had recognized me already, when I had been drowsily recovering from the measles. I had been allowed to have Toby back again, and that was why he had told his mother to have a care for me . . . . As soon as he came again I could explain all the mistakes that had kept us apart and he would understand and forgive –

Forgive! The word brought me to my senses with the

suddenness of an April shower: he had a wife to come home to.

Mad she might be, diseased she certainly was, but in law she was his wife, the woman to whom he owed his devotion and his love. No wonder he had said to me so shortly after our own brief lovemaking: 'It mustn't happen again, for all sorts of reasons: if I told you half of them I don't think you would believe me.' It was no wonder, either, that he had regretted that wild impulse, and I blushed now when I remembered how naively I had cajoled him: a married man, a gentleman, with responsibilities I could not have dreamed of – how could I have ever had the temerity to suppose he would lose his head, even momentarily, over a penniless waif of the road! Flinging myself down on the damp grass I sobbed and sobbed till Toby came and whiffled in my ears in sympathy; his cold nose did much to restore my equilibrium: it wasn't in the least bit romantic, and besides, it tickled.

Pulling myself together I sat up and held him by the ears and we stared at each other eye to eye. I had a good idea by now where he had been in the months before he was deliberately released to come to me, remembering that figure leading the tall horse by the blacksmith's, and from him alone I could get the most up-to-date news of Jack – James Jestyn. He might never again be mine, but I still loved him and always would, and I was desperate to know when I might expect to see him again.

'Right, my lad!' I said to my dog. 'You've been kept in hiding somewhere not a thousand miles from here while Master Jack was off on his travels, and I want to know where; so, tomorrow we are going on an expedition to find our mutual friend, and I want your fullest cooperation! No use looking vacant: I know you are perfectlyhappy here, but it's time we paid a visit to you-know-who, and no arguments!'

Easy to decide, but where to start looking? I tried taking him to the front gates and saying 'Seek!', but he didn't want to, so finally I went to Young Bob and asked about the roads that led from the village, pretending I wanted some interesting walks. There were three ways altogether: the widest and best kept led more or less straight to Hink; then there was another longer way round to the same destination that took in the three largest farms on the way before linking up with the main road; the third way went south, splitting into two forks, the first of which joined the Cheltenham–Evesham road some two miles further on, the second a mere track that led back towards the river; 'Only fields down there, miss, and not recommended for pretty walks: best keep nearer home.'

That first afternoon I strode out along the Hink road, Toby trotting happily at my heels but evincing no interest whatsoever in the houses, cottages, huts, or farms we passed. We came back by the loop road, arriving late for supper as dusk drew in, no nearer finding Toby's hideout. The next day we walked down the southerly road and took the left fork, and still there was no reaction from my dog; I began to think that perhaps he had been kept a further distance away, too far for me to walk. There was only one more road to try, so we tried the right fork the day after. Young Bob had been right: it was no way for a pretty walk, though there was plenty of evidence that shod horses had passed recently down the narrow, twisting lane. It did not help that a small stream meandered down the middle of the way, and I had to keep dodging from side to side to escape wetting my thin shoes. I was so occupied with this that I did not miss Toby at first, then of a sudden I heard his excited yip! ahead of me, and was sure at last that I was on the right road.

The end of the track opened out onto gently rolling pasture on which grazed several fine-looking horses. The whole area was carefully fenced, and at the end of a short driveway stood a small two-storey brick house with a thread of blue smoke streaming from one of the chimneys. It was backed by a stand of trees and surrounded by extensive stabling; I could hear the clucking of hens and the sound of someone chopping wood. Toby was already on his way down the driveway: he looked back at me, tongue lolling happily, as though to say: 'Come *on*! What are you waiting for?' and I followed, gazing round me at the sheltered vale. All at once my heart gave a ridiculous-lurch as I caught sight of two horses peacefully grazing high on the slopes: a tall iron-grey horse and a small, white pony. Half unconsciously I put my fingers in my mouth and emitted a most unladylike two-toned whistle, and I saw the pony raise her head; there was not time for any more, for suddenly two towheaded boys of twelve or thirteen appeared on the path in front of me, then one dashed away, yelling: 'Mam, Mam! There's a strange lady . . . .'

A tall, slim woman with a pleasant, weatherbeaten face walked round from the side of the house, a basket of eggs on her arm: of Toby there was no sign.

'Can I help you, missy? Lost your way, mebbe? Or did you want to hire a horse for the day?'

'Yes,' I said. 'You can help, and no, I haven't lost my way, nor do I need a horse. I've come to see Tom Fallon.'

29

'Tom? Who's that asking for Tom, then?'

Running forward I precipitated myself into his arms and we ended up on the front doorstep in a tangle of arms and legs and sticks, for he was hobbling around after badly spraining his ankle a couple of days since. He insisted that I greet a plump and rounded Daisy again before we went indoors: she was in foal to a white Arab cross, and he had high hopes of the result, due in a few weeks. She remembered me, I think, and nuzzled my palm, lipped my sleeve and whickered, much as she had used to do when we were on the road. I had also paid my respects to the grave and gentle Hannibal, the horse so dark with

611

rain that I had not recognized him that wet day near the blacksmith's when Toby had been returned to me; now he was his usual iron-dapple. In the end Tom's sister had to send one of her boys out to fetch us to the parlour, insisting that cheese scones and tea were waiting. Tom had told me once that he had a widowed sister with two children, but I had forgotten; she was as quiet and pleasant-spoken as he was, and the boys were well-behaved, without being angels.

After an excellent tea they left Tom and me to catch up on our adventures, the boys taking Toby for a run down to the river, for he was well used to them, having spent most of the last year at this house. The bird, Baltasar, was in a large cage by the window, and for a moment I was startled to hear Annie's voice again: 'Supper's ready!', but I quickly gave Tom my latest news of her for I had kept in touch, albeit intermittently, then started to ask my own eager questions.

'Whoa up, there! You females have no patience, no method! If'n I answered your queries in the order you ask them, you'd be none the wiser! Let's take all this quiet and comfortable-like . . . .'

Once he had realized I was aware of Jack's true identity he answered most of my questions readily enough; no, they weren't going on the road any more; yes, Jack had recognized me when he had seen me at his mother's, spotty though I was; yes, it was he who had decided I should have Toby back again; no, Tom did not know exactly when he would be back; yes, he was somewhere in France on secret business; yes, he did know how to get hold of Jack in an emergency, and no, he wasn't going to tell me how.

'An emergency would be something like Lady Jestyn getting worse, wouldn't it? That must mean you're in touch with someone up at Riverwood . . . .' I remembered how I had been verbally steered away from this last way I had taken. 'Young Bob?'

'Likely enough lad, but a bit suspect under fire, as the

Master 'ud say . . . . No, 'tis no use you trying to ferret more out of me than you have, for all that you've brain enough in your little finger to scoop out the truth quicker'n a pig empties its trough – *You* can tell *me* a few things, now: how is it you've managed to turn so easy into the young lady I feared you'd never be?'

'Young lady?'

'When I first knew you you were a scrap that behaved like a boy and could have become anything . . . . Reminded me of an orphaned lamb we had once: brought it up with a bitch and her pups, and that lamb grew into thinking itself a dog like all the others. Did everything but bark.' He shifted in his chair to ease his ankle. I remembered how he had known all along that I was a girl, how he had shielded and protected me as best he could. 'Thought you got soured when the Master couldn't promise himself no further to you; thought for a while that was why you disappeared that day near Maidenhead – that is, till we found that chewed scrap o' paper you left and that fat old Cousin Oliver came looking for you. Right flea in his crutch he got from the Master, too . . . . Mind if I has a pipe? Eases the nag from this old ankle: Master left me some of his 'baccy last time he was here, and I must say it comforts a man . . . .' I lit it for him with a spill from the fire and he puffed away contentedly, while that evocative smoke that reminded me of so much that was past stole round the room, settling in a haze four or five feet from the floor . . . .

Tom's voice broke into my nostalgia. 'Master was right upset that day the first letter came from you: he reckoned you'd landed yourself in the biggest bawdyhouse this side of Sodom. Said as that Madame's place was known from one end of London to the other; thought you must have got it wrong, somehow . . . .'

There was a questioning lift to his voice, although I knew he would not ask me outright what I had been doing in a brothel, so I told him, as briefly as I could, exactly what had happened. I even told him about my true relationship with Nick, for I was somehow sure he would be dispassionate enough to understand and accept, and indeed, his next words showed a certain degree of approval.

'Sounds just what you needed: turned a raw lass into a woman, anyway. But those words you've just spoke to me in confidence is better kept as such, unless you be very sure of who hears them; for such, it would be best for them to think you grew up natural-like.'

I understood what he meant: when I came to tell Jack of my adventures my relationship with Nick would have to wear different clothes.

'Now, tell me where you went next?' and he settled back to enjoy the rest.

It was almost suppertime when Toby and I scurried back to Riverwood. Luckily Lady Jestyn had slept most of the afternoon and Hortense had made the tea and taken it up; our employer was now closeted with two doctors.

'Oh, she's not worse?' I asked anxiously.

'*Pas du tout, petite*: the doctors are those who attend Jacquot's wife, the poor Dorothea. They come this morning to see how she progress, and now they tell my lady what they have found. It is not good news, I think,' and she shook her head so vigorously that her lace cap nearly came adrift. Later Lady Jestyn confided in us both what the doctors had said: I think she needed to share her troubles in the absence of her son. It appeared that Dorothea's disease was taking its inevitable course more quickly than they had anticipated; they dared not use any more mercury in the ointment and the sores and infection were spreading rapidly over her whole body. There was evidence of softening of the brain too; latterly she had become more unstable, with brief intervals of remission and a more rational behaviour pattern, but these sane moments would become fewer, and the doctors feared she might undergo periods when she became violent: they recommended that she be returned permanently to their nursing home in

Leicestershire, but to this Lady Jestyn would not agree without her son's approval. She did arrange, however, that a trained woman came from Lesser Beedles to help with nursing and supervision at nights. The fact that it was only August and in the normal run of events she could not expect to see her dear James again till Christmas did not deter her resolve to keep Dorothea at hand: 'I know they are kindness itself in that home, but she still waits for him to come home and forgive her . . . .' She sighed. 'If only he would; but he finds it so difficult . . . .'

Forgive! There was that word again. Dorothea wanted Jack's forgiveness, his mother also wished him to forgive his wife, and Kat Petulengro had said he needed both to forgive and be forgiven. Something within me rebelled fiercely: I did not *want* him to forgive Dorothea, I did not *want* him to go back to a woman who had betrayed him so flagrantly. I wanted him to go *on* being unforgiving, disliking her even, I wanted him to turn to *me* . . . .

Now it was in the open. I had said just that thing to myself in a quiet, unheard voice for so long that it had become as easy to ignore and accept as daylight through half-closed curtains when one is willing oneself to sleep that little while longer. I knew I should be ashamed of my reaction and part of me was – but not the loudest part. That still said that soon I should see him again, and perhaps he might turn to me once more if he realized how much I cared. I knew I was wrong to think in this way, knew it was hopeless to set myself up against the traditions and habits of the landed gentry in this way, knew that to Jack his family name was worth far more than all the chance-met flibbertigibbets of the highway, but still I dreamed: irrationally, sinfully – and hopefully.

In all that had happened it had been easy to ignore the continued presence of Sir George and his cronies so near at hand in the main house, but at the beginning of September the news was relayed to us by Jeremy (via

615

Kate), that there had been an almighty row and the ladies had all departed back to London, together with one of the gentlemen, leaving only Sir George himself and three of his cronies to rise at noon, ride in the afternoons and dice and drink away the nights till daylight threatened through the closed blinds. Since that afternoon in the lane I had not seen any of them and, lulled into a false sense of security, I set off one sunny afternoon to gather a pound or two of the juiciest blackberries for preserves. The village children had stripped the lanes nearabouts but I knew of some promising bushes down by the river and well within our boundaries. I left Toby behind, for the last time near the water he had disgraced himself and emerged dripping with stinking mud. I clad myself in the oldest gown I could find, tied a sacking apron round my waist and hitched my skirt up through the waistband, tucking my hair up in a kerchief and donning thick gloves to protect me from the bramble's thorns. For an hour or so I picked happily, two for the basket and one for my mouth, moving upstream, the sun hot on my bare arms and ankles, the rich fruit blebs bursting into sweet-sour juices between my tongue and the roof of my mouth. When I reckoned I had picked enough I lay down for a moment on the bank, closing my eyes on the slanting autumn sun dappling the flowing water of the river and blinding back from the gleaming feathers of gliding swans: they floated past with their grey, ruffled cygnet brood, the parents with high, proud-folded wings and necks as still and curved as shepherds' crooks . . . .

Lying there asleep I must have looked like any village girl, my skirt rucked up round my knees and my mouth and chin stained with purple juice, so perhaps I cannot blame anyone for what happened next. Suddenly there was a suffocating weight on my body and, wildly opening my eyes, a shadowy head blotting out the sun.

'Lie still, my pretty wench: I'll not harm you!'

Violently I heaved and twisted, for I recognized the high, affected tones, but my wrists were imprisoned in one large, dry hand whilst the other slid up my right knee to grasp the thigh, the fingers groping even higher.

'Let me *go*!' I gasped. 'Sir George . . . I'm not one of your village girls, I'm companion to Lady Jestyn!'

The seeking hand hesitated for only a moment before continuing its ascent. 'So, the old lady'll never know. Just a little feel, m'dear, just a stroke. There's a good girl . . . I'll give you a good time and no harm done.'

I could not move and screaming would have been useless, we were too far from the house. There was nothing, nothing I could do. I tried to bite the hand that held my wrists, though my mind revolted from the thought of that dry, scaly skin touching my mouth, but he easily foiled the intent by raising my hands above my head and pinioning them to the grass. I could not move my legs for he had scissor-gripped them between his own, but I writhed and twisted as though I had been a snake. All to no avail: he was a heavy man, all of sixteen or seventeen stone, I was a bare eight. I tried pleading, I tried threatening: he merely sniggered and started to talk filth above my protests, until my mind squirmed as much as my body. He told me just what he was going to do to me in abhorrent detail, and all the while I could hear his breathing quicken and harshen, and feel him harden against my right thigh. I knew I should be sick, really sick, in a moment, and tried one last trick. Pretending to swoon I lay limp, closing my mind and shutting off my physical responses from what should happen next. For a moment he went on with his hideous fumbling, then I heard him chuckle; he released my wrists and leaned back, fumbling with his breeches. That was enough for me. With a violent wrench that tore my skirt I rolled away from under him and tumbled headfirst into the river. Once there I paddled away from the bank and came upright with the largest stone I could find clenched in my fist. My teeth were chattering with the shock of the gasp-cold water, but anger – and fear – kept me defiant.

'If you come near me again, I'll kill you!'

617

He was angry, and came right to the water's edge, face ugly and red with rage and wasted effort, a walking stick I had not noticed clenched in his right hand. 'Come here, my girl, or I'll have you whipped!'

'Leave me *alone*!'

'You can't stay there for ever: I can wait!'

However, he did not set foot in the water, and I suspected he could not swim. Unfortunately, neither could I; if I attempted to wade for any distance – and I could not judge the probable depth of water – he could follow with much greater ease along the bank. If I kept to the shallows the stones would hurt my feet through my thin-soled shoes, and besides he might wade in and grab me. I suddenly remembered falling into the duckpond at home when I was about seven years old and my stepfather hauling me out, hushing my screams, and then deliberately sending me back into the water to see if I could learn to float. I could hear his voice now: 'You're wet already, and I have a theory . . . . Now, lie back, spread your arms wide, lift your legs off the bottom and breathe naturally . . . .' Of course I had ended with my mouth full of duckweed, but after fifteen minutes or so of trial and error came that magic moment when I lay like a grubby water beetle, suspended between earth and sky on a cushion of water that sang in my ears its own rushing lullaby . . . . I supposed I could try an Ophelia now and float away out of harm, but she had been buoyed up with her robes, and mine were sodden and waterlogged already.

He must have sensed my hesitation, for all at once he stepped into the water towards me, his stick raised threateningly as though to strike, and I screamed helplessly, for all there was none to hear.

But as the scream died away, and above the gurgling of the water, the cry of birds, the rustling of bushes on the bank, I heard a sweet, high voice singing a descending tune of three notes, over and over again. Someone was in the lane I had come down, for I caught a glimpse of a pale shape through the hedge. Sir George stumbled and

turned, and we both heard the words that accompanied
the tune:

> 'Ding dong bell,
> A secret to tell,
> A secret to sell:
> Ding dong dell,
> Of how he fell,
> Fell down to hell . . .
> Ding dong, well.

Without a word, without a backward glance, Sir George
climbed out upon the bank and strode off down the river
path, ignoring both me and the singer. Scrambling out on
to dry land, tipping the water from my shoes, wringing
the water as best I could from my skirt and apron and
retrieving the miraculously preserved basket of blackberries all took a few minutes and by the time I reached
the lane the singer had disappeared, though I thought I
caught a glimpse of a fleeing figure heading into the woods
at the back of the stables. I almost called out, for I thought
I recognized Dorothea, though what she was doing out by
herself I could not imagine. But guilt stopped me. Not
only the guilt of the visits that had ceased since I discovered
she was the wife of my Jack, rather than the acceptable
James, but rather the reason for their cessation: I had told
myself at the beginning that it was anger at the way she
had treated him all those years ago, but I now knew it
was more than that. Right deep down inside I realized I
was guilty of a most sordid and useless emotion: I was
jealous of her position as his wife.

I said nothing to anyone of what had happened that
day, brushing aside inquiries as to my soaked appearance
with some tale of having fallen in the river. This was
mainly for Lady Jestyn's sake, for she had so far recovered
as to be allowed downstairs, and I did not want to disturb
the delicate equilibrium of her recovery by making a song
and dance about her obnoxious stepson. After a week she
was well enough to be taken round the grounds in the old

pony cart whilst the weather was still fine, but my heart bled for her as she gazed around the familiar scenes as though she was both discovering them for the first time and saying goodbye to them for the last. She looked at her domain with a kind of desperate hunger as though it were food and she starving; sometimes I could catch half-heard phrases like: 'There is where Charles and I used to walk when we were first married . . .', or: 'That is the pond where I used to take James to see the fish . . .', or: 'I planted that rose to climb up to our bedroom window: the sun shone through the petals like gold . . . .'

Jeremy reported that all the guests at the main house were to return to London next week for the autumn season, and Riverwood was to be effectually shut up till the spring. I was glad: no more chance of encountering Sir George.

That Sunday Lady Jestyn went to Mass for the first time for weeks, and I risked a visit to Tom and his sister. His ankle was on the mend, though he could only just hobble about on it even now and had not been able to exercise the horses as much as he would have liked. During the visit I managed to coax out of him the secret of his long-distance communication with Riverwood. It appeared that both Jeremy and Young Bob were in the secret; 'You see,' he said, 'depends on which of 'em's there. Whoever 'tis, they'd fly a yellow flag from the corner of the stables if there'd be anything urgent to know – see, you can just see the flagpole from here – or if it's night they'd haul up a lanthorn. I always look, just to make sure, two – three times a day, and always bedtime and on rising. So far there's been no need . . . .'

How often it is in life when people say things like that do they tempt fate! It is almost as if she is perpetually waiting for someone to assume she does not exist, just in order to confound them. 'Tempting' fate, they say, but I reckon she needs, unlike poor Eve, very little persuasion. Be that as it may, that very night, while we all slept, our complacency was shattered: the impossible, the unlooked for – the inevitable – happened.

I was woken by a tremendous hammering on the door downstairs. It was still dark, although beyond the din I could hear the sleepy, protesting chatter of waking birds and somewhere a sheep called, lonely across the river. Toby scratched at my door to get out and barked, a sharp imperious sound; suddenly I knew something terrible had happened, and that it would need all my strength and determination to cope with the hours ahead. My first thought was that Jack was in trouble, and I flung on my wrapper and ran barefoot down two flights of stairs to find a sleepy-eyed Kate, similarly attired, struggling with suddenly stiff bolts and a door that moisture-laden air had swollen till it stuck.

Together we managed to open it and outside in the grey light stood one of the guests from the hall and the butler, both half-dressed and unshaven. As they pushed past us into the hall Jeremy stumbled downstairs, half-awake, and everyone spoke at once.

'What has happened? Why all this commotion?'

Glancing up we saw Lady Jestyn descending, her face yellow in the light of the candles she bore. Pausing at the half landing, she repeated her question, and in our sudden silence the words hung heavy and threatening.

It was the guest who answered, in a rush as though he feared to lose his tale. 'Sir George – the maid found him but ten minutes ago when she went to lay the fire. He's dead, ma'am, dead. Dead, and a face on him like a man that has seen the devil himself!' He crossed himself, and in the silence his words engendered someone sobbed: I think it was Kate.

The candles in Lady Jestyn's hand dipped and flared, but her voice was steady. 'How – how did it happen?'

'No one is sure, ma'am. We were playing cards in the small sitting room last night – it would be near enough eleven, I suppose – when a footman came in with a note he had found lying in the hall. Georgie — Sir George perused it, then screwed it up and tossed it into the fire. He – he said: "Sorry gentlemen, we shall have to cut it short –" the game, you know, ma'am "– I have an assignation for tonight. Never thought the little doxy –" pardon me, ma'am but I merely report what he said "– never thought she'd come round." He gave us to understand he'd had his eye on some local girl, but that she had been playing hard to get. Said she'd written that she'd like to keep an anniversary with him or some such, and that it had to be this night. So we all went up, leaving him down by the fire, with the glass doors open to the night. Tell you the truth, ma'am, I was on a devilishly bad losing streak, and was glad enough to retire . . . . I heard nothing more from downstairs till I was woken by the maid who came screaming up the stairs. I was first down, ma'am, as, to tell the truth, I had taken a bottle up with me and had fallen asleep before I could wholly undress. Met the butler at the door of the small drawing room and we went in together; curtains were drawn, but the glass doors to the terrace were still open and leaves had drifted in onto the carpet. Butler lighted some candles – maid had dropped hers in the fright – and we found him lying on his back, with those demmed leaves rustling around the body like mice . . . . Thought they were at first, tried to kick them away . . . . Obviously dead, he was, and on his face such a look of horror, of shock . . . . There was froth at his mouth, and his face was purple and his eyes – Never wish to see the like again, preserve us!'

Halfway through his narrative my heart had given a sudden jolt when he mentioned a 'local girl', but had resumed beating when I realized nobody knew of our two meetings, except me and perhaps – Dorothea? Even as her name came to mind, I dismissed it: there were many girls in the village, and he must have been meeting one of those. I glanced at Lady Jestyn as the tale finished: she was still, still as a statue.

'And there was nothing to indicate what brought on this – this attack?'

'No, Your Ladyship,' It was the butler who took up the question. 'There were no marks on the body, no signs of violence. There was just one thing that seemed – well, a little out of place.'

'Yes?'

The man licked his lips nervously. 'Over a nearby chair there was – if you'll pardon the expression, Your Ladyship – a lady's under garment, a slip; it looked for all the world as though some–one–had shed their garments and then had run away too fast to clothe themselves again properly. In the grate there was something that looked like a crumpled face, but when I stirred it with my foot it broke up into ash, so I reckon I was mistook. I took the liberty, Your Ladyship, of removing the – the garment to a place of safety, and counselling this gentleman to disremember he had seen it. I hope I did right?'

'Quite right, Charles,' she said automatically, and though she did not glance in my direction, she must have known I was remembering those words of the butler's: 'a crumpled face'.

We were all looking at Lady Jestyn now: she held the centre of that little stage by a dread stillness that seemed to emanate from her. Yet when she spoke, the question seemed an irrelevance.

'What is the date today?'

It was the butler who answered, and even as he spoke I marvelled at the habits and training of a lifetime that reasserted themselves in his demeanour, that conquered briefly these moments of distress and conjecture. He bowed, and answered as though the question were the most natural in the world. 'It is the twenty-second day of September, I believe, Your Ladyship.'

'The twenty-second . . .' said Lady Jestyn. 'The twenty-second. How right: how very just. Ten years . . . . Now I know. God forgive –' and on those words she suddenly gasped, shuddered, and fell like a stone down the last half-flight of stairs, to lie in a crumpled heap on the floor of the hall.

Even as they all rushed to help, and I could see in the dawnlight filtering through the side window that she still

623

breathed, I turned and grasped Jeremy by the sleeve, drawing him away from the others.

'Quick, the flag! Tom always looks across first thing in the morning –'

'The – the flag?' he questioned, his eyes on the scarcely breathing figure of his mistress.

'Yes, you fool, the flag! I need Tom Fallon's help: don't pretend you don't know what I'm talking about. If there was ever a time we needed him to fetch Jack – James Jestyn, back home quickly, it is now!'

No, not James Jestyn. Not Jack. Sir James, now.

During the time I awaited Tom we got Lady Jestyn upstairs to her bed, and Young Bob raced off for the doctor. Dr Richardson took a quick look at her, then went across to the main house to examine the body of George Jestyn. When he returned I had Kate make him a dish of eggs and some coffee before he went upstairs again to tend his patient. This time he was with her over an hour, and came downstairs to the sitting room looking grave.

I offered him a glass of madeira.

'Thank you, m'dear, but I'll take a brandy, if you don't mind: it's been quite a morning, one way and another.' He sat down with a sigh, and accepted the glass. 'Now: you'll be in charge for the time being, I suppose?'

I hadn't thought about it. 'Well . . . . As her companion, I suppose so, yes. Her maid, Hortense, has been with her for a long time, and she will wish to be with her as much as possible, so I expect I can cope until Ja– Sir James returns and makes other arrangements.'

'Mmmm . . . . It'll not be easy for you: there's all this unpleasant business up at the main house to clear up, and Her Ladyship is far from well. I would not be surprised if she were not to follow her stepson before very long –'

'Oh, no!' I cried, for I had convinced myself she had merely swooned away from shock, and would be well

624

enough to get up in a few days, with careful nursing. 'I thought – I thought . . . .'

'She's much worse than I've ever seen her, m'dear. Suffered another stroke, I think; don't forget she's had a couple before, and they all leave her progressively weaker. At the moment she has scarce strength left to breathe, and there is a definite weakening of the muscle tone in the left side; you'll find she has difficulty with her speech as well. I'll prescribe what I can, of course, and you must keep her warm and quiet, encourage her to eat something, even if it is only sops, and keep her propped up in bed, to aid the breathing: she finds it easier that way. No more disturbances or worries, or I won't answer for the consequences.' He drained his brandy, but shook his head when I offered another glass. 'No thanks: a doctor can't afford to indulge, not when he has no idea what's coming up next.' He sighed. 'Pity that son of hers is away: best tonic she could have, to see him come striding through the door . . . .'

I thought furiously: this was far worse than I had feared. Now it was doubly important that Jack return as soon as possible; it would have been necessary to bring him the news of his stepbrother's death, and to know that he would return sooner or later – but now it must be sooner, for his mother's sake. I could not risk something fatal happening to her without giving him every opportunity to return.

The doctor must have been following at least part of my train of thought.

'The new lord of the manor is abroad, I understand?'

I replied guardedly, for I did not know how far he was in the family's confidence. 'He is out of the country at the moment, yes. Something connected with the government, I understand. A courier service, perhaps . . . .' and I let my voice trail away, playing the dumb female to whom masculine pursuits were a mystery.

'But can he be brought back home fairly shortly?'

'I believe so. I – I have never met him, but there is a servant who has some idea of his whereabouts, so I'm told. He was never keen on Sir George knowing of his plans, I understand, so he thought the less people knew the better.'

'And I am relieved that he was so far away last night. He and his stepbrother were known to be at odds, to put it mildly, and if he had been in the district there would have been those who would have somehow connected last night's death with their feud – all the more so because no one could be happy about the way he died.'

'I understood it was some kind of fit, apoplexy?'

He sighed, and frowned. 'That's mebbe the explanation for the stopping of the heart, but I'd like fine to know what brought on the seizure; no man dies with that expression on his face without the devil's been at him. It's as though he saw something so terrible his brain burst. Not to say that his brother was the devil, mind you, though I recall when Master James was but a lad of twelve or so, his putting on one of those hideous festival masks and one of his mother's petticoats and dressing up as a ghost, to frighten Sir George. It worked, but he got the beating of his life! Meant no harm, I'm sure: always was a lad with plenty of imagination.' He rose. 'Still, no point in complicating the issue: we don't want inquests and investigations, do we? No, I shall certify that he died of a surfeit of good living, aggravated by the very deterioration those dissipations entailed. No need to mention village girls and assignations, for there was no mark on him that nature did not put there herself. Natural causes, hey?' And he gave me a broad smile.

So he had heard the rumours.

'Perhaps it was all just a fancy to impress his guests: perhaps he had been losing heavily at cards, or just didn't feel too well and wanted an excuse for an early night,' I ventured, though I knew perfectly well after Lady Jestyn's reaction that there was more to it than that.

'Possibly. The less said the better, I reckon, and so I have counselled those I have seen. Now, down to details. I'll prepare a death certificate, and send you down a copy by the boy as soon as I can. You'll need to contact the family solicitors as soon as possible; I suggest you send the large young man – what's his name, Jethro? No, Jeremy – with the certificate and a short note of explanation. They'll send someone down when convenient, for there's much to sort out. I would suggest to them that the funeral be held back for say, ten days: that'll give 'em time to make their arrangements and for the new lord of the manor to take his place. Solicitors are Messrs Slane and Boddihead of Lincoln's Inn . . . .'

Thankfully I took down the direction. 'The undertaker?'

'I'll call on him on the way to see old Mrs Tooley. I'll suggest his best lead-lined coffin – if we're to hold on for a few days in this weather . . . . Best send up a woman too from the village to help with Lady Jestyn: you will have enough to do. Perhaps you would send a note to the vicar to call and arrange a time and date for the funeral service?'

I nodded. The priest must also be told of Lady Jestyn's relapse: I would send Young Bob to both clergymen. 'The newspapers?'

'Leave that to the lawyers. Now, I think that's all. Oh, the mourning . . . .'

I had forgotten the mourning. 'Could you send up a seamstress from the village?' And I should have to order silk and bombazine from Hink . . . . I hoped there was enough in the housekeeping to cover it all.

There seemed too much to accomplish in so short a time, but it was only a couple of hours after Dr Richardson left that I took a package for the solicitors out to the yard where Jeremy stood waiting, a horse saddled and ready.

I handed him the package. 'Can you read the direction?'

He nodded. 'If'n I gets lost, I'll ask the way. I can get a fresh horse partway. Don't fret, miss: I'll get there.'

'I know you will. Take it steadily, now: we'll expect you back some time the day after tomorrow. Oh, I almost forgot!' and I leaned forward and gave him a quick peck on the cheek. 'That was from Kate: she's gone up to the house to help clear up. Said you were to remember not to look at the London lassies too hard!' And I watched him blush a slow deep crimson, though whether it was the message or the kiss, I could not be sure.

Back in the house I counted off on my fingers: doctor, funeral, undertaker, vicar, priest, seamstress, solicitors, nurse; what next? As I considered I heard a faint, rusty mew and something brushed against my skirts. It was Gipsy, looking for her mistress, and obviously bewildered by the grate still full of last night's ashes. I hesitated, then bent and picked her up firmly, sad to feel the stiff, uncared-for fur and the lightness of her body. Daring – for she had always ignored me where possible – I cuddled her briefly as her mistress would have done, and kissed the top of her head.

She was too unhappy to protest. 'Quite right, old lady,' I said. 'Your disapproval is plain, however. The next thing to do is to get the household organized, fires lighted, and breakfast done. Your mistress is very ill, I'm afraid, but there is a fire upstairs and I'm sure you'll both be happier together.'

I took her up and put her on the bottom of the bed. Lady Jestyn's colour was better but her breathing was still ragged and uneven, and she seemed in deep sleep or coma. I told Hortense that there would be a trained woman to share the nursing, and nodded down at the cat, who had curled up at Lady Jestyn's side. 'She will be all right here?'

Hortense nodded. 'I have no great liking for cats, but Her Ladyship loves this one and when she wakes will be glad to have it here. When the woman comes to help I will go down to make something to tempt my lady, and will bring some warm milk for the cat also. Do not worry about us: we shall manage.'

Reassured by her competence I descended to the kitchen and had just got Cook started on ham and eggs for everyone when the person I had been waiting for tapped at the back door.

'Saw the flag early on, but had to send one of the lads

to borrow Farmer Bent's cart; I saw that Jeremy on the way going hell for leather, and he told me the news. Not sure I've got everything straight though, for he was full of ghosts and devils; suppose I sit down at this here table and you tells me it all again so that I – why, whatever's the matter?'

For I was staring in despair at Tom's stick and still heavily bandaged ankle. Obviously Jeremy had not told him of Lady Jestyn's serious condition and the need for Jack to return at once – and how could he ride with the speed necessary when he could not even walk properly yet?

Lady Jestyn was awake and smiled a queer lopsided smile as I bent over her. 'M'dear . . . .'

'Just you rest easy, now. Do you feel a little better?'

'Mmmm . . . .' Her eyes took in my cloaked figure and widened and grew anxious. 'Not go . . . away. Not away . . . .'

'Just for a little while. Can you understand what I say?'

She nodded almost imperceptibly, but her eyes filled with tears that trickled helplessly down her cheeks.

'Don't cry, dear Lady Jestyn, don't cry! I know you find it difficult to talk, but you will soon be better.' I leaned over and kissed her forehead. 'I shall only be gone for a few days, and I go for a good reason. Kate and Hortense will take good care of things for I am going to fetch Jack – Sir James,' I amended hastily, mentally cursing the slip. 'I know where he is to be found and there is no one else to send. I'll bring him back as soon as I can: in the meantime you mustn't worry – promise?'

I was leaving Kate in charge, with more or less full confidence. She had Jeremy's strong right arm to back her up, and these few days of increased responsibility could well turn an efficient upstairs maid into a competent housekeeper. She would not only have to keep Lady Jestyn's household running smoothly, but also supervise

the preparation of Riverwood itself to receive an unspecified number of guests for the funeral. One of Sir George's
cronies had returned to London but the other two were
staying on: Kate was ruthless in that they had the
minimum of attention until the place was put in order for
the expected mourners.

'There'll be the solicitor and his clerk, Miss Esther, and
probably Mr – sorry, Sir – James himself. There's the two
that are there and bound to be others come, even if only
out of curiosity. Cook will have to get busy with funeral
meats, and there's wines for the butler to bring up from
the cellars – if'n there's any left. Don't you fret: everything
will be in good order when you gets back. If'n I needs
any extra help or advice, I'll call in that Dr Richardson:
he's a man with a good head on his shoulders. Now, off
you go!'

I had told her that Tom Fallon, whom she knew by
sight only, had knowledge of Jack's – Sir James's –
whereabouts, but that he had a damaged ankle, so that I
was going in his stead. If she wondered at the propriety
of a young lady travelling unescorted to find a gentleman
she had never seen, she did not voice it – at least till I
was out of sight.

Tom had not been idle while I briefed Kate and said
goodbye to Lady Jestyn, as I noticed when I joined him
in the cart. 'Is that what I need?' I asked, nodding at the
bundle in the back.

'More or less,' he growled. 'But I still think you're off
your head –'

'That doesn't matter if it brings back Jack in time,' I
interrupted. 'Lord! It is a relief to call him that without
having to think of curbing my tongue. And I just can't
think of him as "Sir"; not yet, anyway.'

'Reckon as how you'll have to, soon enough.'

'Easy for you! You knew all the time, back there on the
road!'

'I had the same trouble as you now, not to call him
Master James . . . . And when he went off those times to

630

visit Her Ladyship, and you all a-speculating where he'd gone: 'tweren't easy. Remember that time you let slip that remark about not catching the clap? Took me all my time to remind him he were supposed to be playing the part of a traveller of the road.'

'You knew him long before – all that?'

'Second groom to his father, God rest him! Taught the Master to ride, and a good pupil he was, too: took to it like a pig to truffles. When Sir Charles died Her Ladyship got me off serving Sir George, and I became her son's personal servant and groom. I was there when he met and married Miss Dorothea, poor young lass . . . .'

I wondered whether he mentioned her to remind me that now he was Sir James, Jack had other obligations and responsibilities. As for me, I must admit I had completely forgotten her in all the drama of the last few hours: Sir George's death would not affect her directly for the moment, and she would likely not miss me or Lady Jestyn. Of course, now she was the new Lady Jestyn, and Jack would have to decide how far he would have to change his attitude: you cannot ignore your husbandly responsibilities if you are a baronet.

'Pretty little thing she were, too,' mused Tom. 'Real taking ways she had; could wrap the Master round her fingers like knitting wool. Sad thing about it was, though, she were like a bitch in season once she knew what it was about – not that she would have any animals about her: reckoned they took the attention off her, for she was always one wrapped up in her own feelings, a parcel of self-love, that one. Only person she ever cared for, save herself, was the Master, I reckon.'

'You saw all of this happening, then?'

'Not all, for I were in the Amerikys with the Master, but when I came back I used my eyes and ears. But he wouldn't listen to me; wouldn't see how the explanation was not only self-indulgence on her part; couldn't see as how it took two to ruin their lives together.'

He would not say more, and I could not draw him

further in the time before we drew up in front of his sister's house. I had brought Toby with me, for I knew he would be well looked after by Tom's nephews, but it almost broke my heart to have to be stern and tell him to 'Stay!' so soon after we had found each other again, and I spoiled the effect by dropping to my knees and hugging him, kissing his broad forehead and whispering: 'Back soon . . . .'

Young Bob's second-best breeches and jacket fitted me tolerably well, though I had to turn back cuffs and pull the waist in pretty tight on the breeches. After Tom and I had argued the toss earlier about the quickest way to fetch Jack and he had finally agreed I would be faster, it had taken further persuasion to convince him I would be better travelling in male attire. I had left him to find suitable clothes, and now, with the addition to Young Bob's things of my own buckled shoes and cloak, a shirt and woollen stockings from one of his nephews, and a ribbon to tie back my hair, I looked reasonably convincing. A money belt with twenty guineas, a rolled map, precise verbal instructions and a horse completed the preparations, though as to the last I had, at first disbelieved my eyes.

'That's a *horse*?' I queried, as Tom led him round to the front, for a sorrier-looking animal I had scarcely ever seen. He was thick-coated, with a deep chest and massive quarters, long ears, a Roman nose, heavy fetlocks thick with feathers, a short neck and shorter legs.

'Best horse for distance I ever knew,' affirmed Tom as he helped me to the saddle. 'Welsh cob cross. Looks like something a child drew, I know, but got a heart like a lion and will take you the whole way; no other horse I know could do it, but you're a light weight and provided you don't drive him too hard at first he'll have you in Dover day after tomorrow. Take him as far as you can today, but don't 'tempt to ride at night. That map's good, but it needs daylight. You know what to do once you reach Dover, and I'll follow with the cart and Hannibal, leaving him at the Golden Goose tell Master if I miss him, so he can have the last part back at a gallop.'

His sister handed up a packet of food, the boys opened the gate and patted the horse goodbye.

'What's his name?' I asked.

'Mumps,' said Tom. 'Got him when the lads were both bladderfaced with it.'

'Mumps!' It was as bad as 'Wosabella' all that long time ago at Sherbourne.

'Don't you mock till you've ridden him a few miles! 'Sides, he and you've got something in common . . . .'

'What's that?' I called back as we jolted off down the lane.

'Both got odd eyes!' Tom yelled back, and I saw him grin for the first time that day.

Jack's map was a great help, especially with the short cuts. It was one of those that unrolled like a scroll, easy to follow one-handed. We climbed up out of the valley on to the Cheltenham road, then went southeast on tracks over the Cotswolds and down into Stow-in-the-Wold. That night we slept out, for the weather was with us, and I snuggled up in the lee of a rick, too tired to bother about the squeaks and rustlings, comforted with the sounds of Mumps's steady munching nearby. We were through Oxford and on to the London road by noon next day, and I rested him during the afternoon, to follow the London coach in at dusk. Safety in numbers, especially after all the highwayman scares we had read of in the London papers. That night we lay up at the Fleece in Thames Road as near as we could for the crossing by London Bridge.

Mumps was noticeably tireder the following morning, but I urged him on and, courageous and likable beast that he was, we were through Greenwich and on to the Canterbury Road before we had to have an enforced rest, for he cast a shoe. It took time to find a free blacksmith, and it was dusk before we toiled up the hill beneath Dover Castle, to find the inn called the Two Pigeons. For the last part of that road I dismounted, for the poor pony was really exhausted and I was little better, being saddle-sore and stiff. He had not been an easy ride, having an action and gait peculiar to himself, but Tom had been right: he had the heart of a lion and was unbeatable over distance. I saw him stabled, rubbed down and fed before seeking my own refreshment, then I ate ravenously of fish pie, cheese and bread before slipping out in the starlight to find my contact, the 'Third Pigeon', a misnomer for two brothers who ran a fishing smack – and other things – out of the harbour below. Here was the first disappointment of my journey: both brothers were out, and were not expected back before the first tide in the morning. I gave one of their wives a guinea to fetch me at the inn as soon as they arrived back, then trudged back up the hill again, more asleep than awake, to topple into bed and fall asleep to the sound of the sea far below and the cry of gulls.

I awoke to a grey day, a freshening wind from the southwest, and a sense of urgency. No message arrived for me, however, until past midday, by which time I had regressed to an old childhood habit, nail-biting. I was sent for to meet the two brothers, and after I had explained what I wanted and they understood I came from 'Mr Landless', I parted with five guineas and was hurried down to the harbour, a net flung over my shoulder, a stocking cap jammed down on my head. Once there I was bundled into a small, rocking, smelly, creaky boat. The sail was hoisted, and before I knew where I was the boat was lifting bluff bows to meet the chop of waves at war with the current out in the Channel proper.

'Not the day as I should've chose for a crossing,' said one of the brothers. (I never did find out their names: they just went by their code words: Third Pigeon.) 'Have to beat up and down a space, and it may get a mite uncomfortable later. Been fishing afore, youngster? Thought not. Should kip down snug by those barrels if I were you, and hang over the side if her gets too uneasy . . . .'

I prefer to forget that trip across the Channel, even

now. Suffice it to say that it did get 'a mite uncomfortable' and it was 'too uneasy' – though those were not the words I would have chosen – and I sicked up everything I had eaten for a week, or so it seemed. At one stage it seemed so bad I almost begged them to turn round and go back, but even then it would have probably taken longer to return. At least I felt too ill to be frightened.

We made landfall on the French coast at dusk, and a wild, flat, unwelcoming place it looked. We had come too far west on the last tack, but the brothers knew what they were doing and reached cautiously along the coastline, now with the lessening wind at their stern, and finally brought down the sail and rowed quietly up a hidden creek to beach the boat under an overhang of willow.

'Now then, youngster,' said one of them in a whisper. ' 'Tis near enough nine o'clock, Cally's up there two miles or so. Take that track up through the wood and t'other side you'll see the road below and the lights of the town plain enough. Tide's on the slack: we can give you three hours, no more, or we'll be stuck fast here on the ebb, and can't wait another tide: too risky to be caught in the daylight. So, if you're not back here by midnight you must swim . . . . Wind's backing southerly: should be a fair run home. Don't lose your way,' and, with a very poor imitation of the French, he added: 'Bonny voyage!' and chuckled.

Scrambling up the hill and through the wood took some time in the dark and a church clock on the outskirts of Calais struck ten as I shadowed my way down the ill-lit streets, stopping for a moment by a lighted doorway to peer at the roughly drawn map I had been given. Stopping just there was a mistake. Within five seconds I was addressed familiarly by two females, one on the pavement behind me and the other from within the house. I could not understand the rapid patois word for word, but I sensed the invitation without any difficulty and fled, luckily in the right direction, for a minute or two later, slowing down to a walk, I found I was in the Rue des Petites Soeurs, with the convent at one end and the harbour at the other. For all I knew there might have been a curfew in force for the streets were deserted, and I resumed my trick of dodging from one pool of darkness to the other, glad there was no moon, but having difficulty deciphering the brown numbers painted on the peeling doors. Most were shut, but I was lucky with *numero dix-sept*, for one of the half-doors was open. I slipped inside, blinking and straining my eyes to get my bearings, for everything was in darkness, only a faint illumination from the window in the stairwell indicating where they ascended. I knew the apartment I wanted was on the top floor, and had my hand on the greasy banister rail when a door in the hall opposite me opened and a woman emerged, smelling of garlic and perspiration and carrying a candle. She let loose a gabble of French, but I pointed up the stairs. 'Monsieur Sansterre?' I said, and those were the first words I had uttered since I had landed in France.

'*En haut*,' and she pointed up the stairs and shrugged; if I had hoped she would lend me her candle I was disappointed, for she shuffled back to her room without a backward glance. Climbing the stairs with caution, for the pools and pits of darkness hid worn steps, half-steps and no steps without discrimination, I suddenly realized that I was within moments of seeing Jack again face to face for the first time in three years, and for a moment I felt nervous. Then I remembered why I was here, why I had had this horrendous journey, why I was in danger every moment I stayed on French soil; all that mattered was the message, not the messenger. He must know as soon as possible that his brother was dead and his mother dying, and with this thought I took the stairs of the last half landing at a run. There was a light showing under the ill-fitting door at the top of the flight and I paused only for a peremptory knock before trying the knob. It turned easily and I burst into the room: over by the window stood a tall figure with his back to me.

'Jack!' I exclaimed thankfully, in English. 'Thank God I've found you!'

The figure turned and I saw to my horror, by the light of the candles flickering on the table in the draught from the door, that it wasn't, couldn't be Jack! A greasy fellow with fat jaws, reddish straggly hair and huge yellow teeth that stretched his mouth into a permanent grimace as he rapped out some command in French – Instantly I found myself seized from behind, a knife glittered, my scream was stifled by a hard hand across my mouth.

'An English! A spy!' I heard dazedly through my terror, the French words at last making sense.

The tall man strode towards me and said, in execrable English: 'You have no business here, *cochon*! How is it you find this place? You look for the trouble, is it not?'

My captor took his hand from my mouth and: '*Non, non, pas du tout!*' I found myself gabbling. '*Je – je cherche –*' I was thinking desperately, then remembered the alley where the women had accosted me. '*Mon ami Jacques – la rue des Prostituées, si'il vous plaît . . . .*'

'*Fiche-moi le camp!*' roared the tall man, and grabbed me from my captors. Shaking me by the scruff of the neck he propelled me towards the door, muttering over his shoulder something to the other two about getting rid of me '*très rapidement!*' We clattered precipitately down the stairs; I tried once or twice to explain I was looking for the wrong person in the wrong road and the wrong town, only too aware that if I got away from here with a whole skin I had not the slightest idea where to start looking for Jack, but the tall man would not listen; he pushed me roughly down the stairs ahead of him, muttering something in French which I took to be swearing, and we did not stop till he had propelled me out into the empty street and stood, arms akimbo, glaring down at me. Then he repeated what he had said on the stairs, and this time it, and he, made sense.

'*Tais-toi, Gringalet!*' said Jack.

30

He repeated it in English.

'Quiet, Sprat!'

I gazed up at the tall figure incredulously. The height and the voice were Jack's albeit the latter somewhat muffled – but the red hair, the fat face, the grotesque sticking-out teeth?

In spite of everything he must have seen from my face that some explanation was due, otherwise I should be too busy puzzling to pay heed.

'It's a wig; the cheeks are padding and the teeth are extras that I am having great difficulty in keeping in my mouth: satisfied?

'Now, before you interrupt me with an irrelevant question, in order to allay the suspicions of those acquaintances of mine in the top window and anyone else who may be interested in us, we are going to stand in the middle of the street here and I am going to wave my arms about – like this – and make some very rude gesticulations and you are going to follow my lead, just as if it were a dumb show. In the meanwhile we shall talk in English, but we shall keep our voices down – understand?'

I nodded. 'But Ja—'

'Quiet, till I've finished. When I finally dismiss you you will go left, back the way you came, which is the right direction for the dubious street you had the temerity to mention; I shall tell those people upstairs that the friend you are looking for is an American; that will explain those stupid words you let slip in English.

'Right. Why are you here, what's the trouble, and why not Tom?'

'Sprained ankle. Your brother is dead of an apoplexy.

638

Your mother had another stroke and – and the doctor does not hold out much hope. I'm – I'm sorry.'

I was sorry, too, about the brusque way I had to break it to him, but we could not stand here in the street forever, or those watching would be more suspicious than they probably were already.

For a moment he was silent, though he continued to point first one way then the other as though questioning my route, and I pantomimed with him.

He sighed, then seemed to come to a decision. 'When is the funeral?'

'Six – no, five days away. Everything is arranged.' I remembered just in time to continue the pantomime, and pointed in an entirely new direction. 'Tom is leaving Hannibal at the Golden Goose and should be at the Two Pigeons by midday tomorrow. Oh Jack, I'm so glad to see you! There's so much to tell –'

'Enough for now! We'll catch up later. Get back by the same way you came. If I miss Tom, tell him I'll see him back home. And thank him.'

'You could come back in the boat I came in. I'm sure they –'

'I have my own transport,' he interrupted. 'Now, go! I'm going to kick you, so watch it! It will lend verisimilitude to a meeting that has gone on far too long for comfort or the convincing of the suspicious.' His voice softened. '*Bon voyage, petite.* we'll catch up later. Thanks.' He raised his voice '*Dépêchez-vous, stupide!*' and he kicked me, none too gently, into the gutter. 'Christ! these bloody teeth are biting back!' and that was the last thing I heard as I fled back the way I had come.

I turned once, at the end of the road, but he had disappeared.

I slept most of the voyage back; the wind had dropped to a steady breeze, and the motion of the boat was more of a lullaby and less of a tumult. I had expected we would be back in harbour by noon, but when I woke I found we were some miles to the west of Dover, placidly fishing: it seemed the two brothers needed their own verisimilitude to account for our absence. Luckily they found a shoal of herring fairly quickly and I learned quickly, too, how to become an honest fisher-boy. If I had thought the boat smelled of fish before, I had not been anywhere near the truth of it.

The one advantage this enforced lull had was to give me time to remember all that had happened in that meeting with Jack, and to crystallize my reactions. At first, when I awoke, I had been full of the mere fact that I had met him again; my head carolled 'Jack, Jack! Jack!!' like an ascending lark, and I felt giddy and drunk with the mere thought of having seen him. I treasured every word, made a caress of his ungentle handling, a promise of his curt arrangements . . . . But then I began to think. What had I really seen? A man in a disgusting smelly disguise, who only sounded like the man I had built all my childish dreams upon. Yes, childish; that was the key word, for since those (to me) halcyon days on the road there stretched a great gulf of time, of experience, of life – for us both.

I was no longer the callow lass who had seen him first as an uncertain and volatile showman, then, as we got to know each other better, as the magician who made magic of the commonplace, and finally, when he indulged my body, as the fairy prince, seven feet tall, and Don Juan to boot, who was the most wonderful thing since Dr Johnson's Dictionary. Since then I had grown up a little – a lot, I suppose, for Madame's and the heady intoxication of Nick, followed by fear of murder and the gallows and the rigid discipline of the Seminary, had shown me life at its extremes. I would be a fool to deny that I was changed from the gullible girl who took my first experience of sex as a fairy-tale ending, and Jack himself had grown without me, he must have. Besides, I had now caught a glimpse of him from the other side, from those people who could be said to know a part – perhaps the greater part – of Jack as he really was. I had seen him on the road only, but there was a lifetime of devoted son as his mother saw him, a kind and promising master as Tom had known him, a devoted and loving husband as Dorothea – but no, I would not think of that aspect. And because of that denied thought I realized that I still loved him as I could never have loved Nick or the John of long ago. But now, perhaps, I loved him as a woman should love a man, not with the uncritical and adoring eyes of a child, but with the more mature understanding and affection of a grown woman. He was a man, not a prince: he was human and fallible and frail, as all men are. And in my heart I was glad, for the Zoe I was now could never have been satisfied with a story-book hero who was perfect. But what would – did he think of me?

I gave the taciturn brothers another agreed five guineas when we reached the safety of harbour, and when I returned to the Two Pigeons Tom had arrived but Jack had gone, some three hours since.

'He'll be well on his way, now,' said Tom. 'Beyond Canterbury, I reckon. Well, he told me for us to take it easy on the way back . . . . I brought the trap, and Mumps is rested, so we'll start off in the morning, as it's near dark now. Fancy roast chicken and apple pie?'

'Anything,' I said. 'Just as long as it isn't fish . . . .'

We returned to Crum Potting on the evening of the day before the funeral, and the boys rushed out to welcome Mumps. 'Best horse in the county, ain't he?'

'In the country, I reckon,' I said. 'Like to swop him?'

'Only thing we'd swop him for is your dog, and bet you'd not consider that!'

No, I wouldn't. Mumps was a character (his odd eyes were only two shades of brown, not my mismatched colours) and had been just what I needed at the time, but Toby was a love, useless, and for keeps. I believe he thought I had abandoned him again, for his incredulous greeting was almost more effusive than our initial reconciliation by the village pond.

I changed back into my own clothes and, tired though he was, Tom himself drove me back in the trap to Riverwood. After I had given him a quick hug of thanks he went off to return Young Bob's second-bests and seek out Jack; in that last he was luckier than I, for Jack was closeted over at the main house with the lawyers, so I was told, and there was enough for Miss Esther to do to prevent Zoe from going in search of him.

I could see that Lady Jestyn was much recovered, mostly because she had her beloved son back again, I think: she was sitting in a chair in her room, insisting she was well enough to attend the funeral on the morrow. I could see she was still affected by paralysis on one side but there was no dissuading her.

'No arguments, my dear; I have already had this out with dear James.' She paused, visibly gathering the strength to continue as though she were not afflicted, and I could not but admire her courage. 'You are – good, sweet child to – to fetch James. I know what is – best to do now. You must help me – help me to dress – in the morning. Hair, clothes . . . .' The look she turned upon me was fraught with determination, pain, anticipation, love. 'Must. For James. Please!'

What could I say?

The only glimpse I had of Jack the following morning was when he arrived to help his mother into the carriage they were to share; Jeremy and one of the footmen from the hall were to ride with them to provide a hand carrying-chair so that she would not have to walk to her pew. Jack looked deathly pale, drawn and haggard, his pallor accentuated by the dark clothing convention demanded. He glanced at me once and inclined his head, but all his attention now was for his ailing mother.

After the funeral there was a gathering for the mourners at the main house. We had our own description of the happenings from Jeremy, who had been relieved of his duties temporarily after ensuring that Hortense went over to attend on her mistress, who had insisted on carrying on. We staff all sat round the kitchen table; it was like listening to the pedlars in the village at home, when they used to bring us news of the births, marriages, and deaths from the great houses hundreds of miles away.

'Lots of mourners there were,' said Jeremy, gulping down the tankard of ale Cook had thoughtfully provided. 'More'n what was expected, I reckon. Most of 'em come to pay their respects to Lady Jestyn, I shouldn't wonder, and to welcome Sir James, rather than to regret Sir George; then there's always those as comes out of curiosity . . . . Still, a bigger gathering than we've had for years. There was Lord Mulberry from the other side of Bredon, Sir Edward Jessop and his lady, Squire Mostyn, Mr Peabody from Evesham way with his family, those two of Sir George's guests as stayed, plus some more from London I never seen before, and of course the lawyers. Thank 'ee, Cook, a kind thought,' as another pint and a slice of pie appeared before him. 'Thirsty work, it's been . . . . Well, as I were saying, there was a fair old crowd at the funeral itself. Village people stood at the back, but there weren't many of them: he never was a popular master – not to speak ill of the dead, mind. Could tell they was all thinking less of the old than the new, hoping things would be better in the future.' He drank deep and munched at the pie. 'As good fare as they'll be getting up there, I reckon. Anyway, when 'twas all over the new master, Sir James, he went and thanked all the tenants and villagers for attending and said as how he had arranged that the landlord at the inn were to serve free bread, cheese and ale 'twixt noon and three for all that had attended.'

There was a general sigh of approbation round the table.

'Go on, Jeremy,' I urged. 'How was Lady Jestyn?'

'Not bad, not bad at all! We carried her up the church path, but once at the door nothing would do for it but

that we place her on her feet, and she walked to her place
as steady as you please on the arm of the new master. Sat
in the family pew with him during the service, then came
back down the aisle with her head as high as the church
steeple. We carried her the next bit down to the family
vault on Sir James's instructions, for on her own I think
as how she might have 'tempted it, but he could see she'd
had enough. But her stood for the committal.'

'What's the family vault like?' inquired Cook, passing
him another generous slice of game pie. 'We've heard
tales . . . .'

'Strange place, that,' and he wiped his mouth with the
back of his hand. 'I must say as how you brew a good
pint, Cookie . . . .' The hint was taken. 'Thanks. Now I
thought as the place would be all dark and gruesome, like
what they say tombs is, but that h'edifice on top, like a
little church in itself, why it's all pierced with holes at the
sides what lets in the light and fresh air. Once we'd walked
down the steps we saw as there was a stone table in the
middle set with candles, enough for us to see that three
sides was like a giant honeycomb all carved out of stone,
with little wooden doors with their names on that sealed
'em up like cells in a hive. They had to put his coffin on
one of the bottom rows, it was that heavy with all the
lead. What with the light coming slanting in from the
churchyard and the candles a-winking back from they
nameplates – gold for the men and silver for the ladies,
someone said – place seemed almost bright as day.'

I thought of that gross, angry, pathetic man, now only
another dead cell in a dead hive, and I shivered. Still, that
was what we all came to, and one day Jack would have a
place there, too. No! I thought: some bodies stayed
clamped where they were, heavy as the clay that cushioned
them, but others, the bright, light, impulsive souls, escaped
their entombment and whirled up and up into the clouds
to join the sky. Bodies should not be buried so deep they
were no comfort to the earth; they should lie near the
surface where they could become part of the land from

whence they came, nourishing even in death so that they might bring better crops from their bones –

'Miss Esther,' said Cook. 'You're looking quite morbid.'

I laughed, then shivered, then laughed again. 'Goose walking over my grave . . . .'

'Don't go talking about no more graves, there's a dear; though they do say as how these things go in threes . . .' and she looked at me almost hopefully.

'No one else is going to die,' said Kate sharply. 'And I'll thank you not to go putting ideas in people's heads!' But I knew she was thinking of Lady Jestyn.

There was a pause.

'Don't know about more deaths,' said Jeremy ruminatively. 'But I saw a ghost the night Sir George snuffed it.'

'Go on!' said Cook and 'Rubbish!' said Kate at the same moment.

' 'Tweren't rubbish,' objected Jeremy. 'I were coming back along the drive – remember, it was my night off, and I'd been over to Ted Smith's to see his new ferrets – and it were past midnight when I slipped into the woods for the last part, being quicker. I was just at the edge, treading quiet, 'cos I come to the gravel at the front of the house, when I saw something flitting across the front, coming from the South Wing –'

'You must have been drunk!' interrupted Kate. 'Ferrets, indeed! More like a skinful down at the King's Head.'

'Tell you I weren't!' said Jeremy. 'May have had a jar or two with Ted earlier but I was stone cold when I saw that there white thing tripping along. I was that scared I dropped to my knees there and then on the stones, and they was so sharp they cut my knees, but I wouldn't stir till it had gone. You remarked on the knees of my breeches having a tear in 'em following day,' he added, turning to Kate. 'Asked me if'n I'd been saying my prayers: remember?'

'Never said nothing about seeing no ghosts, though!'

'Well . . . thought as how you might laugh. Thought I

might have been – mistook. But I wasn't, come to think now, I'll swear I wasn't!'

'What was this ghost like?' I interjected, more to keep the peace than because I believed one word of it.

'A woman, it was, all dressed in white. And I'll tell you what: she was laughing to herself all the while. Not loud, you understand, but soft and low: it was that that scared me most of all . . . .'

I remembered, then, what those who had discovered the body had said: he looked like a man who had seen the devil himself. Or herself . . . .

Lady Jestyn spent the next day in her room, although she insisted on receiving those who came to pay their respects and offer condolences, sitting by the fire swathed in a large black wrapper. The Misses Pritchard from the village were the first to call; staring about them with bright inquisitive eyes – for they had never ascended the stairs before – twittering in their soft, singsong Welsh voices, they still managed to bring with them the odour of their dusty, frowsty cottage. The doctor soon shooed them away and tried to get Lady Jestyn back to bed but she refused, her voice strong, though her hands trembled. I persuaded her to one of my herbal brews and she quietened, comforted too by the arrival of the priest, who brought his own form of medicine. I left them and Hortense, who came to join in the prayers, and went to my room with Toby, who had been waiting for me outside the sickroom door, patient head on paws.

'A walk for us both, my lad,' I said. 'Let me fetch my cloak.'

On the bed, lying there as carelessly as though someone had just put it down, was a box, an ordinary brown box with a dent in it. '. . . . You'll learn one day, Sprat, that I have an eye for a bargain . . . .' It was *my* box, the sandalwood box Jack had bought me at St Bartholomew's and – yes, they were all here: the new guinea, the amber memento, the harewood and silver mirror, my cancelled indentures and, right at the bottom, an alien thing, a tiny black leather box. Carefully, my hands trembling as much as the invalid's in the room beneath, I lifted it out and opened up the lid. Inside, nestling on black velvet, was a huge pink pearl, the colour of a rose. No note, no indication of the sender. My heart beat so fast I felt I was suffocating. Carefully I rolled it in my palm; I did not need to touch it to my tongue, I knew it was real. As real as Jack.

Toby and I took our walk up by the main house, but though there were carriages at the door and people leaving, there was no sign of Jack, and it was dusk before he came.

We had put Lady Jestyn to bed and Hortense had carried broth up for her supper when there was the sound of hooves on the gravel outside and a moment later I caught a glimpse of Jack on his way up to his mother's room. Outside Hannibal, his coat gleaming, was loosely tethered to the ring by the front door; slipping out, I pulled the reins free.

'Off again, old boy? Where to this time, I wonder? Never mind, let's walk you up and down a little till he comes . . . .' He whickered, and bent his great head to nuzzle my hair. Toby disappeared into the undergrowth on some urgent, rustling errand of his own, but the horse and I had completed the full circuit of the front of the house before Jack appeared. I missed his arrival at the front door but he whistled, Toby came running, and Hannibal pricked his ears and dragged me in the right direction. I might have been a bag of feathers for all the effect I was having on him so I released the bridle and regained my dignity. I saw Jack stoop for a quick rub of Toby's ears, then he swung himself up into the saddle as I came hurrying to his stirrup.

'Jack –'

'Good evening, Miss Tregorran . . . . Or is it Sprat? Or Zoe?'

I could not see his face in the gloom, but his voice was remote, impersonal. Hannibal was tossing his head and lifting his hooves much as Toby had once done with his injured paws, eager to be off.

'Thank – thank you for the present. And for my box back. You – you are going away again?'

'The present was for what you've done for my mother, Miss Tregorran – or may I call you Esther?'

'*Don't –*'

'Don't what? Call you by the name everyone but me recognizes as the one you have always held?'

'Your mother knows –'

'A little.'

'I can explain – I must tell you –'

'No time for that now. I'm off to London: we'll talk about it when I return. Take care of everything.' He swung Hannibal's head, but I caught desperately at the bridle.

'Jack! Wait – oh, blast! Sir James . . . what *do* I call you? Damn you! Can't you try to understand?'

'That's more like it! You were never prissy-mouthed. All right, Zoe. I'm off to London to report and ask for a month's leave. It's more than due, but with the situation in France I'll be lucky to get a couple of weeks. However, with my mother's condition . . . .' He paused, and there was only the scrunch of Hannibal's hooves and a whine from Toby. 'I'll be back. Soon. And then we'll catch up with each other. Promise.'

'I didn't – do – anything. Anything really bad, I mean. I . . . Oh, God! Why can't I . . . ?' I had no idea what I was trying to say, except that I had always loved him and now I needed him so much, and please would he stop being so remote and un-Jacklike, but the words, luckily enough, wouldn't come. Instead, I burst into tears, cursing myself mentally for my weakness even as I did so.

The tall figure on the tall horse was silent for a moment, then the voice coming from the face I could not see was infinitely kind. 'There's really no need for explanations, you know. You're here, and that is all that matters just now. And . . . .'

'And –?'

'And you are still my Zoe, I think. Your eyes have the innocence they always had, mismatched or no. What happened in between does not really matter, unless you yourself let it. Look up!'

I lifted my face, all runny with tears, and Jack, Mr Landless, Sir James, Monsieur Sansterre – my darling – bent from the saddle, scooped me up in his arms, and kissed me with a mouth both fierce and tender.

'I'll be back, my little runaway, I'll be back!'

There was a scream, a tiny scream as of an animal in pain, from the woods behind us, then he was gone and I heard nothing but the beat of hooves down the long drive.

I remembered a candle, fashioned in the image of a naked lady, that I had seen at Madame Bonneville's. As it was lighted and the flame flared and grew, the wax of the figure gradually melted, and the wick that ran down through the inside glowed red as blood. That was how I felt now: melting and yet glowing. The nightwind brushed cold against my flushed cheeks, but I was warm right to my heart. I had thought I loved him before, but that was a pale, numb love compared with the colour and ache of this new emotion. I loved every inch of him, head to toe, nails, skin, muscle, voice, brain and flesh, and all my feelings were concentrated into a Lilliputian me that he could have carried in his pocket with ease, yet at the same time they had expanded so much they could have been a huge cloak to envelope him completely. I knew now that I belonged to him for ever, whether he wanted me or no –

'Whatever are you doing out there, Miss Esther?' said Kate, standing in the front doorway. 'You'll catch your death! I've been looking for you a while: Her Ladyship would like you to read a little to her.'

'Coming,' I said. Above me the moon shone clear for a moment, lighting the sky and catching a gleam of silver from some bush or tree in the wood. 'Coming, Kate!'

Jack was away nearly a week and during that short time

649

his mother slipped back visibly. The doctor came, shook his head, and diagnosed the added complication of an infection in the chest. 'Going to that wretched funeral, I don't doubt,' he said. She spent all her time in bed now, propped up against the piled pillows, her head tossing from side to side, her breathing short, her cheeks hectic with fever. No longer was she interested in my reading aloud, except from the newspapers, and then all she wanted was intelligence from France. Often she would be wide awake at night, or would doze and mumble to herself in French, but words so fast I could not follow. Hortense shook her head and sighed, and explained that she was going back in her mind to her childhood days.

'Is not a good sign, *petite*: I wish Sir James would hurry back.'

He returned on a night of late October storm, the last leaves clinging desperately to the branches of the trees in the wood, the wind roaring down the chimneys to puff soot and smoke in our faces. We none of us heard his arrival for the noise outside, and the first we knew he was taking the stairs to his mother's room at a run, stopping on the threshold abruptly as his eyes took in her desperate state.

'My God,' he said, but so softly only I heard. '*Pauvre Maman* . . . .' But the next moment he was striding forward, coat-tails flying, boots ringing on the polished floorboards, the wake of his passing making the candles flicker, the still life of the sickroom suddenly an action painting.

'How's my favourite woman, then?'

I saw her smile, saw her stretch out her thin arms for his embrace, and slipped away to prepare the empty room across the way from mine, for I guessed he would wish to be near at hand rather than up at the main house. Kate brought him a tray of paté and veal cutlets up to his mother's room so that they could be together, and it was quite late when I descended to the small drawing room to mend the fire, and found him standing in the hearth drawing impatiently on a reluctant pipe.

'Your mother is always so particular about keeping the tobacco fresh against your return,' I said without thinking, embarrassed at finding myself alone with him after all this time; then realized what I had said, realized that she would probably never come down the stairs again to check that the jars were tight-sealed and the pipes arranged as he liked them, and sat down abruptly, my face hidden by my hands. 'I'm sorry: the doctor says . . . .' I trailed off miserably.

'Says there's no hope. I know. She's dying, and there is nothing anyone can do.'

I looked up at him. 'All she wanted was for you to come home . . . .'

But that was not true: that was not all she wished for. There was something else she wanted, something I had suddenly remembered, but how could I explain? If I told him she had been muttering in her sleep about him and Dorothea during the last couple of days, and that several times I had heard her say: 'Forgive! must forgive her . . .', and if I reminded him of Kat Petulengro's words on the subject and then related how Dorothea herself had begged me to ask him to come and see her and forgive, where did that leave me? I loved him jealously, I realized that now, and if I sent him back to her I could not hope for any further involvement with him, at least not on the level I would wish. So I kept quiet, and cursed myself for my cowardice even as I did so.

He went over to the sideboard. 'Brandy?'

I shook my head. That way would remind me of the day of that other storm, the time of my initiation. I could remember the effect brandy had had on me that day, the melting, dizzy feeling its consumption had engendered. That way madness lay, the fever of unquiet emotion –

He turned, inquiringly.

'No,' I said. 'No, thanks.'

One eyebrow rose quizzically. 'Afraid of the effect?'

I could feel myself flushing and bent my head, furious that somehow he still had this uncanny instinct for understanding my thought processes. But perhaps I was just so sensitive to what had happened that I was crediting him with an intuition he did not possess. 'I shall be sitting with your mother for part of the night until the nurse takes over, and I don't want to feel sleepy.'

'Just a little will do you good: too much sitting up late has taken the roses from your cheeks – or I thought it had till a moment ago. Why *are* you blushing, anyway? It can't be the heat, not with that damned draught under the door!'

'Nothing – no reason, really. It's just that . . . . Well, we haven't seen each other for three years, and so much seems to have happened between. One just can't pick up a relationship in five minutes and expect it to be – I know I have changed, and . . . . I don't know.'

'Stop burbling, child,' he said comfortably. 'And come and tell your Uncle Jack just what did happen to change everything so drastically. Which I doubt.' And he settled back in the wing chair by the fire, and patted the low stool at his side invitingly.

But I took the chair opposite: I was not ready to tell all and was afraid his proximity might weaken my resolve.

He heard me through in silence, his eyes on the fire, just occasionally glancing in my direction, usually in those moments when I found myself faltering, glossing over, covering up, dissembling just a little . . . .

'You were lucky,' he said, when I had finished. 'Everyone who is anyone, at least at the levels of society it might concern, knew, or had heard of, Madame Bonneville's. I read somewhere of her murder and wondered again what had happened to you. You know, when Annie produced that first letter, I went out and got very drunk; I believed, as that girl Angel intended, of course, that you had of your own free will become a whore; and what was worse, that you were actually enjoying it. No man likes to think of a girl he has been to bed with preferring to be paid for it by the dozen.' He paused. 'It was fortunate for you that that young man had a fondness for you and kept you from such a fate.' His voice had the faintest, the very faintest, interrogative lift on the last words, and if I had not been guilty of gross misrepresentation I would not have heard it.

'Yes,' I said, remembering only too well what that fondness had led to and just how enthusiastically I had responded to it. How sensible that I was going to listen to my head instead of my heart: let him believe it was all innocent; gloss over the *affaire* instead of confessing all and flinging myself on his mercy as my foolish heart told me to. After all, I was an adult now, not some tell-all chit that needed a confessor! Hadn't he just said that no man likes to think of a girl he has slept with going to the arms of another, with the inevitable comparisons? Doesn't he want to pretend, however foolishly, that he has been the only one? And Jack had more cause than most to despise unfaithful women, for had not Dorothea betrayed him, with disastrous results for them both?

Even as I told myself all these things, even as I congratulated myself on my diplomatic reticence, I knew it would not do: whatever the consequences there would have to be truth between us two, on my part at least, or my love for him would not be the splendid thing it should be. Even if he turned from me in disgust, even if he thought me the whore I was not . . . .

There was a curious lump in my throat. 'Nick didn't have just a fondness for me, Jack: he was my lover, and a jealous one at that. But I don't regret what happened between us; basically he was a decent lad, and he treated me well.' I could not look at him, yet I had to. 'Do – do you mind?'

Oh God, why didn't he say something at once, quickly? Why the hesitation?

'Mind? Of course I mind. But he did save you from a living hell, and if he were here now I should thank him for that – before showing him the door for preferring that conniving Angel and for being too weak to keep you.' Leaning forward, he knocked the ashes from his pipe. 'I don't know why you were so afraid to tell me; after all, we are not married, or engaged, or even sleeping together. During the last three years I slept with one English girl, one Irish and two French: you would not call that betrayal to you, would you? Transgression is much a matter of intent, you know: you seem to think you have sinned by being unfaithful to me, but we are both free agents and I distinctly remember giving you carte blanche to marry whom you chose – and "marry" meant the other, as well. In any case, I could not name your sins so very great without calling myself hypocrite. And if you are afraid my pride is hurt – well, that is more than outweighed by my relief at finding you safe and well.'

I burst into tears.

What I had wanted, needed, hoped for, I suppose, was a furious jealousy, an anger, a reaction that would tell me that he cared what happened to me, just a little: I mean *really* cared, not the polite interest he had expressed so far. Instead of passion was this measured, logical appraisal, almost, I thought, as if I were a material possession that had been mislaid and then found again, to mild rejoicing. There were perhaps a couple of dents in it, but better to have it back damaged than not at all –

'*Now* what have I said?' He rose from his chair, almost with an air of irritability. 'Once you would have snapped back quick as light "What was wrong with the girls of Wales and Scotland?" but now you're behaving as if I were an ogre! Oh, come here, child, and let your Uncle Jack cuddle away the niggles!' And he opened his arms to me.

God knows what would have happened if I had yielded to what, at any other time, would have been an irresistible invitation, but now I was angry, with the anger of the rejected.

'No!' I spat back at him. 'I'm too old now for "Uncle Jack". Uncle me no uncles . . . . I'm not a baby any more to be bribed by sweetmeats and a hug! I'm a woman grown now, and it's time you realized it – and time you grew up too!'

He halted in his step towards me, his arms still ridiculously open to enfold me, then slowly they dropped to his sides. 'Grow up?' he queried, and his voice was as stiff as his back, although there was that still in his voice to humour a wayward child if I had chosen. Even then I could have backtracked, could have submitted like a chastened pup; instead I deliberately chose to be a cornered dog, and like one snapped and snarled, bared my teeth and growled.

'Yes, grow up! You have responsibilities over and above those you call your work, your filial duty, your inheritance!'

'You are talking about Dorothea,' he said, and now there was no pretence of an avuncular relationship; now he was cold, hard, distant. 'And what business is that of yours, may I ask? She was my wife, true, but –'

'Was? Is! *Is* your wife! As for what business it is of mine . . . . I met her for the first time quite by accident, but after that I felt sorry for her, went to visit her regularly. This was before I knew you were James Jestyn, and at first I thought she was merely a cast-off mistress. I was being entirely objective; I knew she had done wrong, grave wrong, but I then believed and believe now that her lover, her husband the so-perfect James Jestyn, should find it in his heart to forgive!'

His brow was as black and menacing as the unseasonal growl of thunder outside and his voice harsh as the October gale. 'So you think after a couple of do-good visits and a chat about the weather, that you know the ins and outs of a relationship between a husband and wife better than the participants themselves? You know just what words have been said, what things done between them? You can turn all that into ounces, pounds, stones and weigh the scales with such a nicety that I, the innocent party, am guilty?'

'I did not say that –'

'As good as! But it was not I who ran to someone else's arms as soon as my spouse's back was turned; it was not

655

I who became diseased from dallying; it was not I who killed our son!'

'No, but it was you who went off gaily to the fight and left a beautiful and susceptible girl to the mercies of some man determined to win her; it was you who awakened in her the meaning of bodily loving and then turned your back on her; it was you who misjudged her character to such an extent that you expected her to be faithful for ever; it was you who came back and condemned a weak and foolish girl before she could try to explain, try to apologize; it was your blind pride that assumed she had conceived your child and then run the risk of infection in another man's arms; and it was you who took one look and said: "She is mad and a whore", and probably, too, said these things to her face –'

'What do you mean: "assumed" she carried my child?'

'Just what I say. As I understand it, the child was born some ten months after you went abroad –'

'Pregnancies have been known –'

'And the child only weighed some three or four pounds at birth?'

'Yes, but –'

'It was *not* your child, could not have been! Carried to full term it must have weighed at least two or three pounds more. My guess is that it was a six-month child and that she took some brew to bring it on, knowing that she could not leave it longer than ten months after you left. Imagine the desperation that could engender such an action in a young and comparatively inexperienced girl! God knows where she went for such a potion!

'Some bastard seduced her, probably initially with a tale that he had your permission to "console" her for your absence with a friendly caress or two, and she probably let it get out of hand – she was, and is, an innocent you know . . . .'

I was speaking now as though with the words of another, the words of someone objective like Kat Petulengro; indeed, I could almost feel her hand on my shoulder, see her nod of approval out of the corner of my eye. And yet I had not meant to say any of this: I wanted Jack to hate Dorothea and loathe what she had done so that he would turn to me – but the words still tumbled from my mouth like apples from a split barrel.

'It may have been just the once – once is enough, you know! Perhaps she had too much wine, or maybe he persuaded her to a drug, who knows? Then when she found she was pregnant she may not immediately have realized it was not your child. And she would not necessarily have known she was diseased, especially if she did not let the doctor examine her too closely.'

'The fact remains that she betrayed me –'

'Yes, she did. As I said, it may have only been the once, and she may have been stricken with terrible remorse – you just don't know. But when she realized what had happened, to whom did she turn? Not, as far as we know, to her seducer. No, she turned back to you, her first, her real love, hoping against hope that you would understand – and forgive.' I remembered the child-woman with the rag-doll baby talking of what would happen when her husband returned, remembering her kneeling at my feet begging me to promise to ask him to forgive her . . . . 'She still loves you, you know, and thinks you will come back to her any day; she believes you will forgive her, and has forgotten all that went between. She nurses a doll, a doll always newborn, that she imagines is her baby – your baby – and her madness is increased by not understanding why you do not come. Time has stood still for her all these years, and I believe that now she does not know why she needs forgiveness, only that the need itself is there.'

'Forgiveness? Does she not realize what she did? I loved her, God help me, I loved her! She was the first woman I lost my heart to –'

'Yes, I know. And you placed her on a pedestal, an impossible pedestal from which she could not help tumbling. Love is not fairy stories, gods and goddesses, Jack, it is loving someone who is an ordinary person like you or me, and loving them not because of some imagined perfection but because they are as imperfect as we are. True love is *because*, not *in spite of* . . . .

'Another thing: we all know that men may have mistresses and lie with any doxy they please, provided they are discreet; they excuse this by saying that men are by nature polygamous, having stronger desires; is that altogether fair? A woman may have as strong desires as a man, but for her to stray is unforgivable – if she is found out. Your peccadilloes are even envied by your peers, whereas your partner must be chaste and above suspicion. In truth, if Dorothea had not become pregnant and diseased, the latter through no fault of hers, would you ever have had to know? And might she not have been a better wife, having made her mistakes?'

'I'm not listening to –'

'You *have* listened, and if you were honest with yourself you would admit it was only your pride –'

But he had gone, slamming the door so hard behind him that the ashes from the fire gusted out with a puff of smoke and sparks glowed on the rug for a falling-star moment before charring, and I blamed the stinging fumes for the helpless tears that ran down my cheeks.

I thought maybe he had run out into the gale and rain to shout his anger to the wind, but when I went up to his mother's room some twenty minutes later to relieve Hortense for an hour or so before the nurse came up from the village, I found her asleep in a chair by the fire and Jack sitting on the bed holding his mother's hand. She looked as though she were dozing, but there were the traces of a frown between her closed eyes, as though she drifted through some unpleasant half-dream. I bent over Hortense to wake her and when I looked up Jack had gone. Taking over the vigil I roused my patient briefly to take her medicine, then sponged her hands and face and rearranged the pillows more comfortably. Down at her feet Gipsy, the cat, hardly breathed at all and I forbore to disturb her for all I knew she had not eaten all day. After

658

a while Lady Jestyn started to mutter and her breathing harshened, but she was talking so rapidly and indistinctly in French that I could make nothing of what she said, so I contented myself with soothing words and the smoothing of her wasted cheek till she quietened. Towards midnight I mixed her laudanum drops with water, and heard the outside door slam downstairs: the nurse must have had a rough walk from the village.

But it was not the nurse. Jack stood in the bedroom doorway, his hair wild about his face, a dried leaf caught in his collar, his boots muddy. His face was pale, his eyes ringed with weariness, and there was a strange, haunted look to him.

'Is she awake? I have something to tell her.'

'I am just going to rouse her to take these drops –'

'Give them to me. Tell the nurse when she arrives to wait in the kitchen till I fetch her – I'll sit with my mother for a while.' He had been looking down at her from the opposite side of the bed, but he now glanced across at me, holding out his hand for the glass. 'Get you to bed: you look half-asleep already,' and, taking no further notice of me, he bent to rouse his mother.

I crept away downstairs, only too conscious that my swollen eyes were due more to crying than to tiredness, but after giving Toby five minutes' run in the noisy dark I was only too glad to snuggle down in bed and fall immediately into an exhausted sleep.

It must have been two or three hours later that some noise brought me awake; I had forgotten to draw the curtains across and a wild moon, three-quarters full, swung like a windy lantern between tattered curtains of cloud. The gale still prowled among the chimneys but its roar was muted, and between buffets I heard a strange groaning, as of some animal in pain. Toby's silhouette was clear at the foot of the bed and his ears were pricked in the direction of the bedroom door, though he appeared more interested than alarmed. Relying on moonlight I slipped out of bed, my toes curling in protest of the cold floorboards. Donning wrap and slippers and bidding Toby 'Stay!' I went out on to the landing and down the flight of stairs towards Lady Jestyn's room, fearing she was worse, but her door was closed and the noise came again from the floor I had just left. Remounting the stairs I paused; the moan came again, nearer at hand, and with it a restless muttering. The noise was coming from the room opposite mine, the room where Jack was sleeping.

For a long moment I hesitated, then lifted the latch of the door. The curtains were half drawn back but the moon was on the other side of the house and it had nothing to illuminate but the dark tossing trees at the back of the house. On the bedside table, however, a thick, guttering candle cast an uncertain light over a scene of disorder, and as I stepped to the side of the bed I made out a restless tossing form and an empty bottle rolled from under my feet across the uneven floor to fetch up noisily against a chest in the corner. The sleeper sat up, only half-awake: his voice was thick and his speech slurred, and I could smell the stale wine on his breath and the sleep-sweat on his body.

'Wha – wha's that? Who – who –'

'It's all right, Jack, it's only me: Zoe. I heard you call out. A nightmare?'

'Some – something like that. Kept seeing face. Face at the window . . . .'

'Well, there's nothing there now and the moon is away on the other side dodging the clouds, so she hasn't stared into your face and taken your wits.' I spoke gently, as one would to a child. As I mended the candle as best I could I saw by its steadying glow that Jack was still in shirt and breeches, jacket and waistcoat having been flung haphazardly over the foot of the bed, stockings and shoes in a muddle on the rug. Moving discreetly I folded the clothes and hung them from the back of a chair and tidied away his shoes, all the while not looking at him, but giving him the chance to pull himself together. Out of the corner of my eye I saw him swing his feet to the floor and sit head in hands. Crossing to the washstand I poured a little water into the bowl and dampened a cloth; there was water in the carafe so I filled the glass and carried cloth and glass over to the bed.

'Drink this: wine always makes one thirsty . . . that's it. Now, wipe your face and neck with the cloth; you'll feel better in a while.'

He did as he was told, then, rising rather unsteadily to his feet, went over to the window and pulling back the curtains opened the casement so that a freezing draught blew my thin wrapper against my body and threatened the candle. Hurriedly I straightened the bed and pulled back the covers. 'There! You'll sleep better now: back to bed, Sir James!'

'I went to see her,' he said, his voice quite steady now. 'This evening. My mother asked – asked me to see her.' He did not turn from the window.

I took a breath to interrupt, to say I did not need to hear what he had to say, but he went on talking in the same quiet, remote way, and after a moment I sat down on the bed and pulled my wrapper around me more tightly, realizing that he needed an audience.

'She was still up, playing patience with those dreadful gloved hands of hers. She did not seem surprised to see me, she just accepted my visit as though I had announced my coming in advance. "You look older, James," she said, "and much thinner. Was the war so bad then?" I could not answer, for the most terrible part of it was that at first I did not recognize her. There was this plumpish creature wearing a parody of the face I thought I recalled, a face made of gauze and paint, looking nothing like the slim, beautiful girl I left behind, the girl I remembered from my initial return. Then she came over to embrace me, and God help me! I stepped away and she just stood there, only her eyes flickering behind that doll's mask. "What's the matter?" she said. "Don't you want to kiss me?" And then she laughed, but as a child would giggle, and putting her finger to her lips, showed me where that obscene rag doll lay cradled. "You must be quiet," she said, "for he is a light sleeper . . . ." '

Turning away from the window he took to pacing between it and the door, and his voice was hurried now, his forehead damp with sweat though the room was quite cold.

'I said – what I had come to say, and she just stared at me. "Forgive you? For what? For being away so long, dear James? But surely you could not help that, you were away at the wars . . . ." I hated to do it, but I had to tell her, to remind her of what had really happened, of the years between. When I had finished I thought for a moment she had not understood one word I had said: she just stood there. Then, slowly, almost imperceptibly, I saw her manner change – it was difficult, you see, for there was no expression on that doll's mask of hers – but I could see at last that she understood, was her normal self, even if only for a moment or two. "Then we shall live again as we used to, only this time we shall be at Riverwood, for George is dead and you are now the master. We shall forgive and forget, and entertain again, and go for rides together and live as man and wife?" And I, dear Lord! said we would come to some arrangement. What else could I do? She sounded so normal . . . . But all the loving, the caring, even the affection – it had all gone! The jealousy and hatred I nursed so assiduously through all those bitter years had vanished – she was a stranger, a disfigured stranger who had nothing to do with the woman I once loved. And now I have promised to live with a – thing – that can be nothing but a creeping reproach, a diseased reminder of the arid years between . . . . And I am tied to her now for ever, for ever . . . . Ah, God! Did I deserve so much, so little?'

There was nothing I could say. I had encouraged him to this, for Dorothea's sake, for his mother's sake, for his own: and yet it was a bitter denouement, a hard punishment. Not only for him, for me also. I had no doubt that he would honour his word, make some pretence of living a normal life with her, enlist the aid of doctors and nurses to give her, however briefly, all but the intimate side of married life once more – but where did that leave me? However little or long she lived, Dorothea was his wife, mistress of Riverwood, and I could have no part in his life under those circumstances. I should have to go away, find somewhere I –

'Don't leave me, Zoe! I need you . . . .' But it was not a command it was an entreaty, spoken so low I scarce heard it, but his hands were stretched out to me and slowly I rose and went into his arms, laying my head just above his thudding heart, my cheek against the dampness of his sweat-stained shirt. He held me so tightly it hurt and the candle behind us flared up and threw our shadows against the window, out into the wild night. The sentimental, selfish, romantic, loving Zoe wanted to be held like this for ever, imprisoned both in his arms and in a delusion of the rightness of a stolen, illicit love. The girl I had been three years ago would have accepted, would have become his mistress and damned the consequences, but I had grown up a little since then. An *affaire* on the side was an immediate solution, but in the end it well might go sour on both of us, for it would mean that Jack could exchange a penance for an irksome chore – taking tea with his wife in the drawing room while his mistress lay waiting in the attic. No, he and Dorothea must have a chance, alone together. And me? Ah, that was another matter: time alone would tell whether my sacrifice proved its own reward, or whether I should curse myself for a righteous fool.

In the meantime, I had precipitated this state he was in and I knew that, for this next hour, what he needed was not softness, sympathy and tears but a way to forget it all, take out his anger, frustration and sheer tiredness in the easiest, the most masculine way. So Gemini took over, the cynical Gemini who had been taught so well, so thoroughly by Nick. I realized how well I had assimilated my teaching by the degree of detachment with which I began my seduction of Jack: this was to be an exercise in play-acting, and I must not become involved, however bitter the part. Accordingly, I accidentally, very innocently, moved my body so that I knew it would arouse him. I had to be careful, for he was experienced as far as women were concerned, but I was satisfied when I heard his sharp intake of breath.

Then I stepped back from his embrace, subtly allowing my wrapper to outline more firmly breast and hip, and pretended to answer the question, the entreaty that had engendered all this.

'Leave you? Why not? What else have you to offer?' I asked lightly, lifting my arms and stretching, allowing the wrap to open still further. I settled back with one knee bent, hand on the other hip, my breasts pushed forward. 'A job as dairymaid? Kitchen maid? Lady's maid?' With my free hand I absent-mindedly rubbed my middle finger along the line of my groin. 'Or am I to don breeches again as your stable-boy?'

'Don't –'

'Yes, I think stable-boy would be best, for I am sure you would enjoy – Sir James would enjoy, I beg your pardon – seeing a female rump in tight breeches leaning over –'

'Shut up, Zoe, or I'll –'

'Forget that Jack is now a gentleman? What will you do to make me? Put me over your knee and spank me? Or perhaps that is too common a thing for Sir James to do . . . Jack would smack, but Sir James would order a whipping, I am sure, and then stand by and watch. It is a great pity that becoming a gentleman so emasculates a man: I remember –'

But it was enough. He was now both aroused and angry, as I intended he should be. Gone was the tenderness, the despair, the weakness, all he wanted now was to belt me or lay me, and luckily the latter won, for I took care to back away from his threatening gesture and fall back on the bed, my wrapper wide open and my nightrobe up round my thighs. After that it was easy, and as I felt his hard body across mine, sensed his urgent need rising to overcome my only partially simulated struggles, heard the angry, frustrated epithets, and willed my eager body to lie quiescent despite an almost overwhelming desire to respond to his caresses, I knew I had done right. Within a few moments his amorous temper had found its release, and he slumped against me; I felt his muscles slacken, his breathing slow down, the tension unwind. I think he meant to say something, to apologize perhaps, but he was too exhausted. A minute or two later he was asleep, but it was a full hour before I dared – or wished – to slide from beneath an imprisoning arm and leg, and seek my own room and the comfort of Toby's warm, welcoming tongue on my cheek.

Lady Jestyn died just over forty-eight hours later, as dawn was lightening the sky over Bredon Hill. The priest had given her the last rites at midnight and she just slipped into a sleep from which she did not awaken. The doctor, the priest, Hortense, Jack, Kate and I all kept the vigil, but none of us recognized the precise moment when her life ended. One moment she was asleep, the next she had escaped her bondage. The doctor had roused himself for the dozenth time to check her breathing and pulse, but this time he was more thorough; after a long moment he laid his hand on Jack's shoulder, where he had been kneeling by the bed.

'It's all over, Sir James: I am sorry. She is at peace now, and she would not wish you to grieve . . . .'

The priest was praying in Latin and Hortense, between sobs, joined him; Kate was crying too, but I could not mourn as readily. Lady Jestyn had been in pain, tired and unhappy, but her beloved son had returned, her daughter-in-law was forgiven, and she had now escaped into whatever world her spirit would take her. I remembered the ritual and opened the window so that her soul, after making its farewells, was free to rise into the ether as it pleased. I would weep later, but my tears would be for those left behind; going on any journey, it was always worse for those remaining.

I bethought myself of someone who had no idea of such philosophies and bent to the foot of the bed to remove Gipsy so that the women could lay out the body, but I was too late: she too had escaped. I gathered the cold little body, already stiffening, into my arms, and found that I was crying too. Why was it so much easier to weep for animals than for people? Was it because they knew nothing of death, had no anticipation and little retrospection, lived only in love and trust? Kissing the top of the bony head, I made her a silent promise: there would be a place for her besides her beloved mistress, however anyone else might disapprove. In the event it was easy: once Lady Jestyn was laid in her satin-lined coffin, the flowing lines of the shroud-dress she wore hid the little curled-up bundle I laid at her feet. I remembered the tomb in – was it Chichester? – where the knight and his lady lay, clasping their stone hands in eternal courtliness and love, pet dogs at their feet sharing their sleep . . . . I wondered if their love had been as peaceful and calm as their memorial, or whether it had been as stormy, passionate, hating-loving-liking as mine was for Jack? At least their affection had been mutual and marital, whereas –

I knew I could make Jack desire me, that he liked to tease me and kiss me, and that he could be tender and loving upon occasion, but there was no consistency, for he could be angry, impatient, intolerant and cold as well. Since his brutal lovemaking of two nights ago I had managed to avoid him and now, in the stress and sorrow of his mother's passing, it would be easy enough to keep out of the way, but after? Much as it would hurt, I must go, leave him and Dorothea to sort out some kind of life together without any distractions. Perhaps they would find a peace and tolerance they could share – or would he find another mistress if I were gone? For a moment I rebelled fiercely against my decision. I wanted to be with Jack in whatever capacity he chose, even as stable-boy . . . . But I knew that I could not go through with it. My persistence in encouraging him to go back and forgive his wife had its roots way back, beginning with Kat's wise words and culminating in my own pity for Dorothea and respect for Lady Jestyn's dying wishes. I could indulge our desires now, but could I live with myself after? And could he?

So, I wrote to Jessie at Miss Thoroughgood's, asking if I could come back for a while until I got things sorted out. I did not give her the chance to refuse, but packed my bag ready and told her I would be with her as soon as I could. I had saved most of my wages, after the indulgence of the yellow silk dress I had never worn – and which hung, a pale reproach, in my otherwise empty cupboard: but I did not feel like pretty dresses now – and for a while I could support myself. It should not be too difficult to find a new position with Miss Thoroughgood's Seminary as sponsor.

The day of Lady Jestyn's funeral was clear and sharp, the first frosts riming the edges of the fallen leaves that shuffled down the paths on the errant wind. She was buried in the family's honeycomb vault; the Anglican vicar took the service but the Catholic priest attended to say his own prayers for her rest. There were many mourners and most of the villagers attended, for she was well loved and in her quiet way had done much to ameliorate her stepson's neglect of his tenants and the carelessness of his neighbours. I kept well in the background, watching a pale, grieving Sir James lead the procession to the interment. I heard the last prayers and then slipped quietly away to say my own to the sky, sorrowing now with the heaviness of rainclouds. I had left Toby at home, but decided to chance getting wet and walk the long way round through the woods, hoping perhaps in the quiet of my own company to get my thoughts into some kind of order, to reconcile my rebellious nature with the path I knew I must take. I would go in the morning, early; I had only stayed this long in order to pay my last respects to my dear employer.

The wind had dropped, but the morning's frost had encouraged the fall of leaves, and every so often a yellow, brown or red one drifted down to catch in the blackening bramble or form another layer on the path. The acrid smell of late autumn was in the air: somewhere someone must be burning rubbish; in the stillness the mournful descant of the chaffinch sounded unnaturally clear. A rustle in the undergrowth interrupted my quiet steps: a hedgehog perhaps, still searching for the last berries before his winter's sleep, but out a little early on his foraging; more likely a blackbird or thrush turning over the fallen leaves for grub or woodlice. The smell of bonfire was growing stronger and now I could hear the crackle of burning wood, see a drift of smoke over the trees to my right. I heard a scream, a shout, and suddenly realized how dangerously near the fire must be to the little house where Dorothea lived.

For a moment I hesitated, then ran to the joining of the ways and took the path to the Dower House. When I rounded the turn my worst fears were confirmed. The whole of the ground floor was alight, and smoke gushed from the upstairs windows: in one place the thatch was already smouldering. The woodcutter, Hobbs, was futilely filling buckets from the rainwater tub while his wife, her apron over her head, was indulging in hysteria.

I ran forward to address the man, a dreadful fear in my heart.

'Lady Dorothea – where is she?'

He glanced over his shoulder, not ceasing in his task. 'God knows: not in there at least. Little bitch set it off, though!'

I wasted a few moments calling her name, but there was only the roar of the flames, crackling of wood, and a sudden report as some bottle exploded, so I picked up my skirts and ran for Riverwood to fetch help, faster than I had ever run before.

But I was only halfway down the path when a shrill voice called over the thudding of my heart and the sound of my footsteps.

'Let it burn!'

I halted, a sudden relief changing my knees to water, and turned to find Dorothea standing a few yards behind me on the path. She was heavily cloaked, but the gauze mask was still a simpering blank.

'Thank God you're safe!' and I took a step towards her. But it was only one step, for beneath her cloak she brought out an old-fashioned double-barrelled shotgun and levelled it at my breast. Behind the expressionless mask the eyes were bright and malevolent.

'Yes, Esther Tregorran, it's loaded.' She walked one pace forward. 'And now I'm going to kill you.'

31

In that moment I was conscious of at least two missed heartbeats, and for a moment I forgot how to breathe; then my heart started again, but this time it was hammering in my chest and I gasped for breath.

'I don't understand! Why – what – the fire –'

She laughed, a high, erratic laugh, half shriek, half snigger. 'A diversion, my dear; Nan is usually drunk these days, well before noon . . . . I did not like that place, anyway, and now that I am going to the big house with James . . . . That is why I have been able to escape from them so much recently – each thought I was with the other, and did not bother to inquire further – and that is how I found out about *you*!' She spat out the last word and I could see her thumb move to the hammers of the gun, the joint whitening. 'You and George, you and Tom Fallon, you and that servant – and you and James! Behaving like a whore with them all, enticing and teasing and kissing . . . .'

Too late I remembered the figure in the lane with its weird song that day I had been surprised asleep by Sir George; the proxy salute I had given Jeremy before he rode to London; my affectionate farewells to Tom; last, and most important to Dorothea, that time when Jack had leaned from his horse to scoop me up in his arms and kiss me – now I recalled the little scream from the wood behind us, the sense of something flittering in the trees. So on all those occasions I had been observed by Dorothea, escaping by guile to feed her insane jealousy, spying and seeking and misinterpreting it all. All, that is, except my reaction to Jack.

'But you're wrong! I wasn't –'

'I know what I saw! Lying will do you no good, and you do not wish to die with a falsehood on your lips, do you?'

'I'm not lying! Dorothea, please –!'

'And do not dare to call me by my first name! I am Lady Jestyn now, and you had better remember it, slut!' She raised the shotgun to her shoulder.

'Wait!' I said desperately. 'I can explain . . . . Listen: I am going away. I know you and Sir James are to set up home together at Riverwood and I have no intention whatsoever of trying to come between you. Look!' I fumbled in my reticule and brought out a letter. 'I am going far away: I had written this letter –'

'You are going away for ever. I shall say it was an accident; you were a thief – no, I shall say I thought you were a deer, a roe deer in the wood and I wanted some sport. Or a poacher, perhaps . . . . So, say your prayers, Esther, and quickly!' and she raised the gun to her shoulder, took a sight, and her fingers curled round the trigger as she pulled the hammers back with her right thumb.

I could only stare helplessly at the wavering mouths of the barrels, not believing that this was really happening. I did not even hear the footsteps behind me but saw Dorothea's eyes widen behind her mask and focus on a spot over my shoulder. A moment later a pair of hands grasped me firmly and moved me aside.

'What's all this about?' asked Jack quietly.

All at once everything was changed: his voice was so normal, so conversational in tone that the tension leaked away like air from a punctured bladder and I was conscious of a sweat of relief on my forehead.

He took another step forward: now we stood in a rough triangle, each some five feet from the others. The gun in Dorothea's hands had wavered, but now she took a step back, both increasing her distance and widening the range of fire.

Jack continued as if he still did not notice anything amiss, ignoring me, but his quiet, firm voice had the same effect on both of us, I think: a sudden return to normality.

'I expected you would attend the funeral, my dear: several of our acquaintances were asking after your welfare. I said that you had some trifling indisposition, but that you would accept their condolences at the funeral luncheon. But I see that you have not changed: come, let me escort you up to the house.' He offered his arm, and I watched her out of the corner of my eye and saw the barrels of the gun begin to waver and droop.

'I can't – go back. It's burned. My little house – I didn't like it . . . .'

'No matter. There are dresses at Riverwood and I will fetch Mrs Hobbs to attend you. Come now, we shall be late.'

She giggled, a dreadful sound. 'She's drunk, always drunk . . . . No, I won't have her. *You* can help me! Yes, it must be you! Remember how you would send away my maid on our honeymoon? I spent so long dressing with you to help that sometimes it was noon before we . . . .' She giggled again, and this time I could not look at Jack.

'My dear, we are wasting time!' He spoke impatiently, naturally, as though they were discussing all this at ease in their own rooms. 'I recall you have a most suitable black velvet dress and –'

Somewhere a jay clattered noisily through the branches and there were thudding feet upon the path. From the direction of the Dower House Hobbs came running, only to pull up short when he saw Dorothea.

'Bloody hell! You little . . . . Don't use that thing, for Gawd's sake, it's lethal! It's not been fired –'

A shot rang out and Hobbs fell writhing to the path, his hand clasped convulsively to his right shoulder, whence a bright red stain crept down the cloth of his jacket.

'There's nothing wrong with this gun, see? And it *has* been fired: I just showed you.' The voice was that of a child. 'I found it in the shed, and the powder and shot, so don't you dare tell me it does not work!'

'It's rusted . . . the other barrel . . . shot out . . . .' His voice was barely audible. 'Sir James, stop her, for the love of Christ!'

'That's enough, Dorothea!' Jack's voice was now full of authority. 'If you are not careful you will do some real damage: that thing is not a toy! Now then, give it to me –' He moved forward but she swung the gun to her shoulder again and he stopped. 'Don't be foolish: you must give it up –'

I intervened, hoping desperately to distract her, for the weapon now pointed at Jack.

'Won't your baby need feeding? He must be hungry, for it's past one o'clock . . . .'

But her gaze was still directed at Jack, though there seemed a sudden change of mood. 'Baby? Baby is dead. Baby has been dead for many years . . . . George's baby. He gave me a disease and Baby died. Poor Baby . . . .'

Jack groaned, and now his face was no longer impassive. 'George? My *brother*?'

'Yes, your loving brother! He said he wished to console me for your absence. At first he was nice, gave me pretty presents, but when I told him I was pregnant he laughed in my face and told me it was my fault for being a whore and that you would put me away when you found out. He said he was damned if he would marry any girl to ensure the succession, but that the only way you would do it was with his bastard.' She sighed, and we listened to her as if we were frozen into a tableau. 'I could not bear for you to divorce me, not to love me any more, so I thought you would never know if I took the medicine from the old woman to make the baby come at the right time . . . . When I knew it was dead, knew it would have been dead anyway because of what – illness – he had given me, I swore that one day I would pay him back. Only sometimes I forgot what had happened . . . . But when I saw him try to rape Esther, I remembered and sang him a song to remind him. Later, I killed him. So he could not do it to anyone else, you understand.'

'*You* killed George?'

'Yes, James. It was the anniversary of the baby, you see: it seemed the right day to do it.'

'The twenty-second,' I said suddenly. They looked at me: I think they had forgotten I was there. 'The morning your mother was taken ill, Ja– Sir James. She asked what date it was when she heard of Sir George's death, then said: "How right: how very just. Ten years . . . Now I know. God forgive." '

'But how . . . ?'

'It was really very easy, James. I went to him pretending to be her.' She nodded in my direction. 'I wrote him a note and went to the house when it was dark. He let me in and the wind blew out his candle so he did not see who it was until he led me over to the fire. Then I took off my mask and threw it in the fire and opened my cloak and took off my shift and pressed myself against him. He fell down all choking and was dead. It was easy.'

'Oh 'Thea, 'Thea!' said Jack softly. 'You silly girl . . . .'

'That's the first time you have called me that for ten

673

years,' she said, and her voice was quite normal. 'James, I –'

I will never know if all life could have been different from that moment, if perhaps they could have found a kind of loving relationship again . . . . But it was not to be, for at that moment Hobbs, who had obviously been gathering his strength, lurched to his feet and stumbled towards her.

'Give us that gun!'

Immediately everything, the whole atmosphere, changed. She whirled to face him and, incidentally, me.

'Keep back! I have not finished!' Her voice cracked. 'I had almost forgotten!' He halted, and sank to his knees, the effort starting the bleeding in his shoulder afresh. She turned to face Jack again, and now her voice was full of cunning. 'I know what you have been trying to do – make me forget! But you will not, you will not! That slut –' she jerked her head at me '– she is your mistress, is she not?'

'Of course not,' said Jack, and 'No!' I said, in the same breath.

'You're lying, both of you!' She was almost hysterical now. 'I not only saw you embrace her when you went away –'

'I made him!' I said breathlessly.

'And did you make him kiss you in his room the other night? Did you persuade him to bed you as well?'

Too late I remembered our silhouettes on the uncurtained window, the candle behind us shining out into the night –

'Yes, yes! He was drunk and I was jealous of you: I wanted him at any price.'

The gun swung round to threaten me. 'Then I shall kill you, and James and I will be free –'

'Stop!' came Jack's voice, and I knew in a heart-stopping moment that he was going to play gentleman and tell her he was to blame – and she had a loaded gun. Suddenly all doubts and fears dropped away: I did love him enough

674

to sacrifice myself. It was a wonderful feeling, like knowing God . . . .

'Dorothea,' I said calmly, reasonably – and was able to stand back mentally and admire that same calm and reason – 'Dorothea – or Lady Jestyn, perhaps I should say – your husband is about to make a gentlemanly idiot of himself by denying he was drunk the other night: some men are like that, you know; they would rather confess to anything than be thought incapable of holding their liquor: something to do with pride, I think –'

'Zoe! Don't be stupid! She must realize how much I –'

'No, Sir James,' I interrupted, my fingers crossed convulsively behind my back. 'It is very gallant of you, but you were better to tell your wife the truth. Tell her now I have been throwing myself at you ever since we met; tell her how I hoped you would forget her and turn to me; tell her how I persuaded you to drink that night in order that you would –'

'Zoe!'

'Tell her of the miniature of her you carry always with you; tell her of the times you called out her name in your delirium –'

'Be *quiet!*' And this time he meant it. 'Dorothea, it is indeed time I told you the truth. I love –'

'He loves you!' I moved towards her. 'Don't risk losing your chance of happiness.' But I was speaking to him, as well as to her, for I knew, in a wild moment of irrational joy, that he had been going to say he loved me. I had waited for ever for this, and now –

'But he defends you?' Her voice was uncertain, querying, but she had not noticed his use of my real name.

'Of course: he is a Jestyn. So are you. You both are gentry. Not me; so why fear what a paid companion can do? I am a quick tumble when the blood is hot, you and your kind are for ever. Don't envy me, pity such as I; he is yours, Lady Jestyn, so you can put down that gun and have me dismissed, whipped if you like, but don't risk losing his affection for a stupid whim.'

But she was changing again. The words I had used twisted in her mind to an insult.

'Do not dare call me stupid! You are the reason for all this, and I shall not listen to any more! Say your prayers, slut!' and again I found myself staring down the twin barrels of the shotgun.

I knew I should pray, and indeed a few words ran like mice on a wheel through my caged mind. 'Thank-you-Lord-for-everything-please-take-care-of-Jack-thank-you-Lord . . . .'

I watched her knuckles whiten on the trigger – then everything happened at once.

Hobbs lurched to his feet again, Jack yelled: 'If you so much as hurt a hair of her head I'll never come near you again!' and launched himself into the space between us. And Dorothea pulled the trigger –

With the hideous explosion came a surprised thought: 'Dying doesn't hurt after all . . .' then the echo of a scream and a blackness that fell like a slow curtain and took with it the brightly lighted stage and all the actors and the sight and the smell and the taste and the feel and the sound . . . .

But it was Dorothea who died.

Hobbs had been quite right about the gun: the second barrel held some obstruction and the charge had no way but to recoil back into the face of the firer. She can have known nothing, for the load was strong enough to blow out her brains, and she must have died still believing that Jack loved her. I hope so, for they say God is merciful to the maimed, the simple-minded. All this I found out later, for there was a conspiracy of silence from the survivors when I woke from the concussion I had suffered when Jack's wild leap had cannoned me into a tree stronger than my head.

I came round in my own bed, an anxious Toby at my side and a weeping Kate rubbing my hands, telling me that Sir James had sent instructions for me not to speak a word until I felt better, adding that he knew I remembered nothing of what had happened. I therefore kept my mouth shut while she told me of the terrible accident, of the mysterious fire at the Dower House, the fighting of the flames, the unforeseen explosion of ammunition left carelessly by poachers and the dreadful death by chance of Lady Dorothea, who was standing near. I heard, too, of the hastily convened inquest, the verdict of accidental death, the departure of Mr and Mrs Hobbs to visit their relations in the North.

On the second evening, against the doctor's orders and Kate's instructions, I dressed and made my way shakily downstairs, only too conscious of my throbbing head. If Jack had been there, no doubt I should not have been allowed to stir, but he had posted to London as soon as the result of the inquest was known, to see his solicitors; the funeral was to be only for family, two days hence. So, time was on my side, but there was still one thing I had to do before I packed my things and left, for this latter I was still determined to do. He had left a message that he would see me when he returned, but by that time I meant to put many miles between me and Riverwood.

In those long hours upstairs in bed, nursing my aching head, I had had plenty of time to think. I loved him, and I believed now that he loved me, or he would never have risked that wild leap towards the gun, but I had no place in his life now. If he had not been Sir James, if we had still been on the road, I should have fought for his favours like any other travelling doxy, with no punches pulled. But Sir James Edward Jestyn, Bart was not Jack-of-the-road, and the landed gentleman with 'Loyalty above All' as his family motto and a family tree branched and twigged from root to tip with illustrious ancestors had nothing in common with a bastard of doubtful morals whose coat of arms (if she had had one) would have consisted of quartered: a book, a unicorn, a dog and a naked lady, crossed by a bar sinister and surmounted with the one word 'Survival'. If he really, *really* needed me, he would find me . . . .

There was still one thing to do before I evaded Kate's ministrations and went upstairs to pack: a letter to write, and my last respects to pay to the dead wife of the man I loved. I left the letter where he would be sure to find it, by his pipe rack, and made my way through the long wing to the main house. The bier was in the big hall, hothouse lilies at head and feet and candles in the four corners. The coffin had been sealed, for her injuries and disfigurements had made this imperative, and the flickering light shone calm and peaceful on the velvet-draped coffin. There was one wreath at the head, and on it a card. 'To Dorothea: "Sing a requiem . . . such rest to her as to peace-parted souls." James.'

I wondered how many of those who read it would recognize the words spoken at another grief-mad girl's funeral and recognized how they had been twisted out of context, defying convention . . . . I had learned from Kate that the little ten-year-dead baby was to be disinterred from his unmarked grave and laid to rest with Dorothea, on Jack's orders, so I said a prayer for them both and for the widower too, that he might find his own kind of peace.

The following morning, waiting till Kate was occupied in the kitchen, and hoping that Tom Fallon would not take it into his head to pay his projected visit until I was out of the way, I stole downstairs with Toby, and my possessions – only those I had come with, plus my sandalwood treasure box – to an arranged meeting with Young Bob and the pony cart in the lane leading to the village. He had been bribed heavily, both to keep his mouth shut and to be there on time, and the fact that he was, and alone, prompted another grateful guinea. As we jogged down the lanes on the first stage of my journey to the Plough on the Evesham–Cheltenham road where I would catch the Oxford coach, I took to wondering how Jack would react when he returned and found me gone. I cast my mind over the letter I had written the previous night, trying at the same time to envisage its reception at his hands. I had thanked him formally for his kindness, but said that I could no longer trespass on his hospitality, now that the reason for my employment was removed. I asked him not to try to trace me, and that I should return to visit my friends in a year or two when everyone was settled and comfortable again. I asked him to remind me to Tom and Kate, and to trust the latter to make an excellent housekeeper. I assured him I was in sufficient funds (true), had another post to go to (false), had excellent prospects and was in good spirits (lies!). I ended by wishing him health and prosperity, signed myself 'Zoe', then spoiled the whole effect, I realized in the cold light of morning, by writing an emotional postscript that owed more to midnight than to common sense: 'I shall never forget our life on the road together – I was happier with you than I shall ever be with anyone else.' How I wished now I had scratched it out, torn the offending words off the page, never written what was in my heart!

My journey back to Miss Thoroughgood's was smooth and uneventful, and Jessie welcomed me with quiet friendliness. At first she was a little suspicious of Toby.

'We're no' used to dogs . . . .'

'Very well-behaved,' I assured her. 'Never notice he's there.'

'We had working dogs with the cattle, now,' mused Jessie. 'And I mind that one of the girls saw a rat in the barn the other day –'

'Rats!' I said to Toby, and he immediately responded by baring his teeth, growling, and digging up the grass on the lawn with short, impatient thrusts of his back legs. So he was welcome, too.

Miss T was fading fast, kept to a barely conscious level by the laudanum the doctor had prescribed, and the entire running of the place had devolved on Jessie, who had been hard put to it to keep going. Luckily there were only a dozen or so scholars left, for she had refused to take any more when Miss T's illness was obviously terminal and of these remaining all but six were fully trained and ready for posts. It meant more work for everyone, for the place still had to be run on a self-sufficiency basis, but my coming did at least take some of the burden from Jessie as I could supervise the girls and finish the training, leaving her free to attend to the more urgent business. I swallowed my sorrows, which lay like an indigestible lump under the surface ready to rise and remind me if I would let them, and helped also with the nursing, wrote letters, placed the girls, helped to pack away furniture and crockery that would not now be needed any more; and at night, when my body lay at rest but my mind had free rein, I wet my pillows with tears, for every thinking moment was filled with thoughts of Jack and I longed, hopelessly it seemed, that he would care enough to come and find me.

Miss Thoroughgood died at the beginning of January and after the funeral, while Jessie and the four remaining girls put the house to rights before looking for a buyer, I took the long journey north in response to Annie's invitation to spend some time with her and Matthew. She had promised me a surprise in her letter, and it was the happiest I could have imagined for them both. There in the parlour, laughing and crowing in their cradles, were bonny, healthy twin girls, some five months old. They were fair and placid and plump, much like Annie herself; I say plump and not fat, for in a way that was the bigger surprise of the two: Annie in her happiness had shed stones of weight and the fat lady of my remembrance existed no more. She would never be thin but she bid fair to become unnoticeable in a crowd; while I regretted the passing of the old Annie, I nevertheless could not help appreciating how much she was now in her element caring for her babes and a noticeably happier Matthew. She had her brother's youngest staying with them, too, but she mentioned that the former was courting the widow next door on the hill, and that they expected, come spring, that there would be another wedding. While Annie's energy and devotion seemed to increase in direct opposition to every pound of weight lost, Matthew was noticeably putting it on. The business was thriving and he talked of taking on an apprentice. Annie confided that they were going to 'have another go', nodding at the twins, 'for Matt's fair set on having "& Son" up over the door . . . .'

I was made one of the family at once, even before I had explained away the last few years, and we gossiped and nattered like the housewives round the Fish-Stones on market day. Annie's nephews came round for Toby whenever they could, putting him through his tricks and taking him on the Moss to chase uncatchable rabbits, and a month slipped by so pleasantly that Jessie's letter telling me she had a buyer for the house came as a surprise. They were loath to let me go, and I had to promise another visit as soon as I could manage it: they even offered me a home with them if I could not find a suitable position, and I had to promise I would consider it if the need arose. Matthew had secretly made me the most beautiful pair of red slippers, recalling my wish once for red clogs, waving aside my thanks with a 'Nay, lass, we've never forgot, my good lady and I, how it was you helped to bring us together; 'sides, "shoes in hand save soles in holes" and if you wait while you need 'em nearest cobbler may be t'other side of the river . . . .'

I went back to the seminary with my heart full and Annie's farewell words ringing in my ears: 'Grown you may think you are, miss, but you're still behaving like a child when it comes to Jack: you'll neither be happy till you both stop playing prince and goosegirl and remember you're man and woman like any other . . . .'

Annie had been less surprised than I thought she would be to hear of Jack's transformation into a landed gentleman: to her he would always be Jack-of-the-road, none altered in the basic respects that made him what he was, and for the first time I began to wonder myself if I

were not making too much of his elevation into Sir James.
At the time it had seemed entirely right to leave, for I was
still thinking of him as Dorothea's husband, as a landlord
and master, as the rather stern and remote government
official, and there had been few glimpses of the Jack I
remembered. But were not the circumstances against
reminders of those earlier days? An invalid mother, a
dissolute brother, an ailing wife, an exacting job, dangerous
as well as tying, and finally the full responsibility of an
almost bankrupt estate . . . . No wonder the happy-go-
lucky Jack I had known was not in evidence. Too late,
now, my mind went increasingly back to those shared
days on the road: riding the lanes in a sleepy summer
haze, learning our lines together by candlelight, guzzling
Annie's famous stews, lying at nights in the van those
few feet apart; laughing, quarrelling, working, talking,
performing; yes, and loving too.

On that long journey back I remembered, too, Kat
Petulengro's words when she had read our palms at St
Bartholomew's: 'one love for you and two lesser affaires'
– Jack, Nick and John? She had told me of Riverwood:
'silks and swans', and she had warned me of Dorothea –
at least her words could now be interpreted that way: 'A
woman will try and sunder you, but fire will cleanse . . . .'
But the last thing she had said had been to warn me
against a second flight. I had left Jack once because of the
threat from Oliver, and now I had left him a second
time . . . . I was almost tempted to look at my own palm
– but like reading one's own cards in the tarot, that could
only make ill luck worse.

The winter passed, some way or another. The rest of
February was bitter, and well into March. Jessie had
found a wealthy tradesman with three daughters to buy
the Seminary as a country retreat, and he was going to
take most of the better furniture as well and was willing
to engage the two remaining girls as the nucleus of his

staff. The new home for Miss T's brother and Mabs was to be a small comfortable house overlooking the Chess valley, one of three in a row near Latimer. Once the weather became more clement Jessie was busy redecorating and moving the bits of furniture she would take with her, assisted by her sister's eldest two girls, who would have the advantage of Jessie's careful tutelage, eventually finding posts themselves – and there were plenty of her younger relatives to take their places later on. So far I had not been so lucky; once the news of Miss T's death had been printed in one London paper and two local ones, the offer of posts had been few and far between, and I had not advertised, believing that chance should play her part. And singularly loath to participate she had been, so far.

One sunny morning during Lent, while Mr Thoroughgood snoozed in his study and the others had gone up to the new house with Toby to hang some curtains, I sat in the parlour trying to decide whether to accept one of the only two offers of employment that had been received, or take advantage of Jessie's offer to live with them in the guest room until something else turned up. I was sitting at the small round table, the two letters open in front of me and at my elbow a bowl of late snowdrops that clever Mabs had found in the hedge. The first letter, from a Lady Hobbs, requested the services of a second kitchen maid; the second was from a widow with an invalid son who wanted a companion-help. This latter would need 'some light nursing' and I suspected there was more to that than the letter stated; however, it was better than being a kitchen maid, and I had almost decided to write a letter of acceptance when the girl from Amersham, who was helping out during our packing up, tapped at the door.

'Please, miss, there's a gemmum in the hall.' Vaguely I had heard sounds at the front door, but had thought it was the others returning.

'Who is it?'

'Dunno, miss: bit of a toff, if you asks me. Nose in the air, like.'

Having been so well trained myself, I became impatient of the careless attitude of servants in general – but I must remember she was only a village girl. Patiently I asked her to return and ask his business, and whom he wished to see.

Her face lighted up. 'Asked for you personal, miss!'

Who could it be? Not the new owner, surely? He was not due to take over till after Easter, but perhaps he had paid a courtesy visit to see how things were going. I had met him once, but was surprised he remembered my name. However, in Jessie's absence I supposed I could cope.

'Show him in then, Tabby.'

I was turned away from the door as he entered, poking the fire to a brighter blaze for the winds of March were far from gentle, and so the full impact of my visitor only struck me from the feet up as I turned and rose, the poker still in my hand, which promptly clattered back into the hearth.

Black, highly polished boots; fawn breeches; an olive-drab coat with silver buttons, and a green and brown striped waistcoat; snowy linen; dark hair neatly tied back with a back velvet ribbon; a fashionable round hat with tilted brim which, together with doeskin gloves, he was laying on the round table next to his silver-tipped riding whip. Face thinner, paler, and no smile.

Without conscious thought I dropped a bob-curtsey, my heart thumping in my ribs, my breath choking me.

'Well?' he said. 'Thought better of it yet?'

'How – how did you find me?' I squeaked, then tried to pull myself together. 'I asked you not to – I said I would come visiting some time when –'

'Oh, don't be silly, Zoe!' and he strode forward and attempted to take me in his arms, but somehow I slipped away from his embrace and put the table between us, fixing my gaze nervously on the bunch of snowdrops, counting them, counting the green stripes, anything rather than look at him. Why, when all my thoughts, all my dreams, had been full of him whenever I would let them? Why, when I had prayed unconsciously for this meeting for so long? At the time I acted on instinct, but afterwards I tried to rationalize my extraordinary behaviour and came up with the following truths: one, no woman, unless she is uncommonly beautiful, likes to be caught out in a dusty overall and with a smudge on her nose –

'You've got a smudge on your nose,' he said.

– Two, she does not like attention called to the fact if she has. Three: no woman likes to be taken for granted – there must be at least a token resistance. Four: he was a terrifying sight in his best-Sir-James, which only served to emphasize the gulf that existed between us. Five –

'What's the matter? When Annie wrote –'

'She told you where I was, then?'

Five: no one likes her beloved to call merely because someone else reminds him she exists, when he could not be bothered to find out for himself earlier. It had been *five* months . . . .

'No: I already knew. I found a note in my mother's bureau, giving the address of the Seminary.'

Six: five months was a *very* long time . . . .

'I would have tried to get here sooner, but there has been a great deal to do, and the government have kept me working . . . .'

Seven: excuses should be the first concern, not an afterthought. 'Why did Annie write, then?'

'To tell me you were pining away!' He grinned, and I suddenly caught a glimpse of the old Jack. 'Don't look too bad to me; in fact, I think you've put on a little weight. Suits you.'

'No, I haven't!' I said crossly, aware that I had. Eight: no woman likes to be told she is putting on weight. 'She had no right to tell you such – such untruths!' Then I forgot I was so angry with him and started to tell him about the twins and how she had *lost* weight but he

685

interrupted me, for which he got his ninth mental black mark.

'Bother Annie: it's us I want to talk about. Are you ready to come back?'

A quarter of an hour ago I would have given almost anything in the world to hear him ask that, and what's more I would have had my bags packed in five minutes, but somehow we had got off on the wrong footing. The five months without each other had increased my longing, but had also brought with them a kind of constraint; he was not the same, neither was I, and we could not suddenly pick up our old relationship when so much had changed around us. I objected to being treated in such an arbitrary fashion, too, as though the fault for my absence lay entirely with me. And where was the romantic, on-bended-knees approach? If one was asking someone to become one's mistress, what harm was there in being tactful and diplomatic about it? I was *not* a sack of goods to be bundled up on a horse and carted away! I was *not* a Toby, to be called to heel! I was *not* a petulant child to be indulged because I could not make up my mind –

'No! I'm not. Ever.'

Then he scowled, terrifyingly. 'You're being stupid –'

Ten: stupid I was not! Some of the others I might be, stupid: no! Eleven-twelve-thirteen . . . . Unlucky thirteen.

'I am *not* stupid! You're not the only man in the world, you know –'

'And you're not the only woman! To hell with you then!' And he snatched up his hat and jammed it on his head, to the detriment of the brim, picked up whip and gloves, strode over to the door and flung it open –

And tripped up on the mat.

I should never have laughed; it was more of a nervous titter, really, but it was the last straw as far as he was concerned. Jack would perhaps have laughed too after a moment, but Sir James was on his dignity. The front door slammed and a moment later I saw a tall man on a tall grey horse ride away, through a blur of self-blaming tears.

*

The day for removal was fixed for Easter Saturday. The first week of April went back to winter but as Lent passed the weather indulged itself again and was fair and almost unseasonably warm. Suddenly all the birds were courting, building, singing; toads were making their way to the nearest ponds; great furry bees hunted the meadows and hedgerows for early flowers and blossom, and the fields were of a sudden full of knock-kneed lambs. From hidden corners pale primroses lifted their faces to the sun, their thin, evocative scent a delight on the air. Hawthorn bristled with baby leaves and the chestnut buds were swelling to burst in their sticky coats.

All the household reflected the same bustle, goodwill and burgeoning hope – all except me. Ever since I had seen Jack ride out of my life I had been tortured with self-recriminations, doubts, fears; why had I been such a fool? Why had I behaved so stupidly, so childishly? Why, when everything I had ever wanted had been handed to me on a plate, did I have to dash it to the ground as if it were a worthless offering? Once or twice I had thought of writing to him, of apologizing for my behaviour, but that would be to invite the sort of answer I would not want to hear – or worse, no answer at all. No: I must face up to the fact that I had made a complete and utter mess of the whole thing and did not deserve any more chances. Easy to say, damned hard to reconcile oneself to, and I am sure Jessie and the others found me bad enough company in those busy days before we were all packed up, though I did my best to work myself into the ground in an effort to forget. At last came the day we were to leave: two loads had already trundled off down the lane, through the beech woods and down into the valley of the Chess below, and Jessie, Mabs and I were bringing up the rear, together with the crockery and linen used this morning, and the inevitable small items that everyone had forgotten till this moment. Jessie was to drive the trap and I helped Mabs up to sit behind where she chuckled down at me, mouthing the words of the action skipping rhyme I was trying to teach her:

> Pick a lily, pluck a goose;
> Smooth the rough, bind the loose.
> Wash fine glass, break a plate;
> Run a mile, jump a gate.
> Groom the horse, walk the hound;
> Hush the babe, and once more round . . . .

But she got stuck every time after the first couple of lines; perhaps it would be easier if I tried to fit it to a tune for her, for these she could hold –

'Esther,' said Jessie anxiously: 'I canna see the potato bucket anywhere.' As usual when she was flustered, her Scottish accent grew more pronounced.

'By the back door: sorry, I forgot!' and dashing back I retrieved it and handed it up to Mabs. I could see there was little enough room left in the trap, and I told Jessie I would walk, it would take very little longer than the ride, and it was a beautiful morning. So the trap continued down the lane and I stepped down into the ditch to look more closely at the speckled blue of the thrushes' eggs in the hedge, eggs whose blue was no clearer today than the sky. I found myself humming 'Over the hills and far away . . .' and reckoned the tune matched well to the rhyme I was teaching Mabs. Behind me another, heavier vehicle was squeaking its way up the lane: the axles need greasing, I thought automatically and then patient Toby suddenly darted from my side with an excited yelp and pelted off down the road to meet it.

After that I did not need the tune I had been humming, echoed as it was by a pipe, full of missed notes; I did not turn, I could not run, for suddenly I knew this was the moment I had been waiting for all my life . . . . For five years, anyway, almost to the day.

'I always seem to be rescuing you from ditches,' said Jack. 'You'll muddy your shoes.'

'It's dry,' I said. 'Not like last time. But it *is* April . . . .
No robin, though, but there are thrushes' eggs.'

'There was a time in between: on the way back from
Malvern, when you fell off the horse . . . .'

I could not look up at him, perched high on the caravan
steps, for the sun seemed of a sudden to be shining straight
in my eyes. But I could look at the extraordinary horse
between the shafts. 'It's Mumps!'

'In disgrace: this is his punishment.'

He didn't look to be in disfavour; as I regarded him he
turned his long-nosed faced in my direction, and if ever a
horse looked happy . . . .

'Why, whatever did he do?'

'I suppose Tom told you Daisy was in foal? To the most
expensive Arab in the county? Well, it appears that the
trusted Mumps pre-empted him, with the disgusting
Daisy's full approval. I've never seen Tom in such a
taking . . . .'

'Oh, *Mumps*!' But I could not keep the laughter out of
my voice as I went forward to stroke his nose. 'What's it
like?'

'The foal? Depends whether you are an optimist or a
pessimist, I suppose. If you're the latter it's a parody of
Daisy; if the former, it's a definite improvement on its sire!
Whichever way, it's yours, Tom says: make a nice child's
pony in a year or two . . . . What robin?'

Mumps definitely winked.

And now I found the sun had shifted enough to let me
look up at Jack. His eyes were as bright and promising as
the sky. He had bought a new red neckerchief, but there
were the old boots, the darned grey woollen stockings,
cord breeches, tattered shirt, waistcoat with the button
missing, and the disreputable bottle-green coat with the
full collar and poacher's pockets. We had been talking
nonsense for the last five minutes, and we both knew it,
but it was comfortable nonsense, as comfortable, well worn
and familiar as the clothes he wore. As if I had never
known differently I had slipped back into the old badinage

which was part of the Jack I remembered, the Jack who would talk about anything and anyone, and make one feel easy and relaxed whether one was privileged child, boy, woman; companion, friend, lover . . . .

He knew what I was thinking. 'You wouldn't come for Sir James, so I thought maybe your old Jack would do the trick. If this doesn't work I'm just going to have to tie you up in that new rope. Toby's ready to go,' and he nodded to my treacherous dog, who was already up on the van steps, head against Jack's knee, grinning idiotically with his tongue hanging out. 'Shows sense, more than some I could mention . . . .'

I was afraid that if I said what I felt at that moment I should cry. If I told him how much his effort to please me had made me happy, how I appreciated the time and trouble he had taken, he would only dismiss it as sentimental tarradiddle . . . .

'My box is in the back of the trap,' I said, pointing down the road to where Jessie had drawn up against the hedge and was staring back at us.

'Good: you stay there, and I'll go and fetch it,' and off he strode down the lane, whistling tunelessly between his teeth.

'Oh, Toby!' I exclaimed, uncertain whether to laugh or cry, so I did a little of both.

Jack was back in a remarkably short time, my box on his shoulder. 'Hope there's nothing breakable,' he said, as he tossed it into the back of the van. 'Now, up you go and change first. Mrs Jessie and Mr Thoroughgood will be back within the hour. I found a very pretty dress in your closet after you'd gone, one Kate said you had never worn – the same colour as those yellow daffodils over there – and I think I've brought the right size in stockings and shoes to go with it. Never knew you women had such different shapes: you should have seen me trying to guess your feet with my fingers and the length of your legs with a piece of string. Well, come on then: what on earth are you waiting for now?'

'I – I don't understand . . . .'

'Thick as two short planks, as I suppose Annie would say. It's now a quarter before eleven and the wedding service is at noon; after that we're going to forget the world for a while and Play the Jack – take that as you will – till you've got used to the idea of being not only Jack's wife, but the new Lady Jestyn, too.'

'Wedding?' I said, grasping at the first word, afraid to go further, afraid I hadn't heard what I knew I had.

'Toby,' said Jack, 'it appears I'm marrying an idiot. *Where* did you say you found her?'

'Jack,' I said. 'My very dear Jack . . . . Will you believe me when I say that I had no idea you meant marriage? You know I'm not fit to be the wife of a baronet; I'm a nobody. I should say and do the wrong things, make you ashamed of me . . . .'

'That's not what my mother thought; just before she became worse she told me to be wiser the second time around, "choose someone like Esther," she said; so I told her I had you in mind anyway, and she thoroughly approved.' Now at last he was being serious, coming forward to stand so near I had to tip my head to look up at him. 'I wouldn't ask you if I didn't think it would be all right. I made such a mess of my first marriage – don't you think I would be very careful before I tried it again? If it had only been an attraction I would have let it pass, but you've grown into me until you are a part of my life: when something exciting or nice or different happens I want you to be there so I can say: "What did you think of that, Zoe?" As for being the wife of a baronet – I'm not a duke or an earl, you know.' His finger traced the outline of my mouth. 'At first it will be a little like acting for you, I suppose, like when you were Desdemona to my Othello, remember? But with a different ending, of course . . . I'm just a man like any other, Zoe, and I can't think of any other woman I'd rather have to share my life and bear our children. Come to think of it, that fiasco of a night on Ditchling Heath was when I first knew you could be the one. Remember when I held you in my arms and kissed you after I had made you tell me the story of your life?' I remembered only too well: remembered, too, the shame and mortification of being treated at the end of my first grown-up moment as a naughty child . . . . 'Oh, I know what you are going to say: why didn't I tell you then about Dorothea, and make you my mistress? The answer is, I suppose, that you were still an innocent – besides, you would probably have said "yes", little fool! and I thought you should have a chance to find someone suitable – and free – for yourself. I suppose I could ask you now just to be my mistress, as you obviously expected, but that's not what *I* want. I want you, just you, always you, and legally you.' He laughed, a little shakily. 'There: that's probably the longest unrehearsed speech you've ever heard me make . . . . Cat got your tongue?'

'It – it's just the "Lady" bit . . . .'

'Idiot!' He bent and kissed the tip of my nose. 'Remember that very first night of all when we were round the fire, and the young Sprat that you were then asked me who I was? Jack o' Lent, Jack Sauce, Jack o' Legs, Jack-out-of-Doors, Jack of all trades, Jack-in-the-pulpit, Jack at a Pinch, Jack Straw, Jack Brag, Cousin Jack, Jack-in-the-Box, Jack Frost, Jack o' Lantern . . . .' Even as he spoke, infinitesimal changes of expression, of voice, of position, betrayed the showman Jack I remembered so well, 'And wasn't I all of these, some time or another, and more? Just think to yourself that the Jestyn part of me is part of the recital, too – and only a part. James Jestyn is part of all the others, and they are part of him . . . .

'If you insist, I shall go down on my knees, but I warn you I should probably laugh! Dear Sprat, Zoe, Gemini and Esther: you are a woman of many parts, too: won't one of you say yes?'

A well-paid priest married us without any question at noon in the little church down the road, and by nightfall we were camped snug off the road to Aylesbury. I went into his arms that night as naturally and eagerly as though I had been born to it, and it was good, so very good!

I do not remember what the weather was like during those carefree days, nor what we ate, where we went. We seemed quiet only when we slept for there was so much to ask, so much to say, so much to catch up on, so many endearments to exchange.

He told me of his government service that had started by accident in America and how when he returned home and discovered Dorothea's defection he had volunteered for more, angry and disillusioned, both to escape from all that Riverwood now meant to him, and to keep George's creditors from the door and ensure, in his pride, that his fallen wife wanted for nothing. His travelling the road with us was all part of his job too, for it was the perfect disguise for collecting information up and down the country from his various contacts – Chloe of Marlborough was one, and Signor Grappelli was working for Italian intelligence. From our travels Jack had observed attitudes, noted subversive elements, heard of support for a regency, possible approval of the action of the French revolutionaries, and the ordinary, everyday grumbles of ordinary, everyday people – which as long as they stayed grumbles and found no common voice were harmless enough. In winter he travelled the Continent, often in disguise, for the same purpose, his gift for languages fitting him better than most for the task. He told me, too, that he would have to return to France before long, stopping my mouth with kisses when I protested.

'I shall come back, my love, I shall always come back: but they will need me for a while longer, I fear, for things do not look too good out there . . . .'

We talked about Riverwood, about the estate, of how we were going to have to manage on a very limited income until everything started to become productive again as the farmers took fresh heart and we could afford better stock. We discussed what needed to be done in the village of

Crum Potting, also Jack's responsibility: the hovels pulled down and new cottages built; a school; work for all those who wished. Riverwood was sadly in need of repair and redecoration: painting, papering, plastering within; glazing, pointing, guttering without. The roof leaked in several places; there was woodworm, dry and damp rot as well.

'It'll be one room at a time,' said Jack. 'And no luxuries.'

Ten days later we camped on the side of Cleeve Hill. To the north was Bredon, to the northwest the Malverns, the land beyond a blue haze of hills; below us the Severn was a silver snake lazing its way to the sea. After supper, when the world around us had darkened, I walked apart a little way and gazed up the valley. A small wind blew from the southwest bringing with it the hint of rain and the moon wore a deep halo. Below me lights flickered in cottage windows and a slow, plodding lantern could have been man or horse in the deep lanes. Somewhere a restless lamb woke from a bad dream, complained, and was answered by another and another until the reassuring bleat of their dams quietened them. Under my feet, the cropped grass smelled of crushed thyme. We were in a world of our own, divorced by distance and our mutual absorption in each other from the hurly-burly of that other life that awaited us below. But we could not escape for ever; down there was a whole lifetime of living to do, good, bad or, as most living tended to be, just plain indifferent. There was a house to repair, a home to live in, children to raise, responsibilities to be shared, joys and sorrows to be welcomed or endured.

I glanced back at our camp. The fire flickered and crackled, smoke rising straight to the level of the van, then twisting and bending and dwindling into the night as it met the scoop of wind that slid over the roof. Jack was leaning back against the van steps staring into the fire, his pipe drawing companionably. The only sounds apart from those of the night were Mumps cropping the short, sweet grass and a scrunch! as Toby cracked a bone, eyes alternately shut in happy concentration and swivelling between Jack and me to make sure we had not strayed too far.

Somewhere, I thought, however many years passed, those with the ears to hear would catch our echo; hear the creak of axles and grate of wheels down some quiet lane, the brush of leaves on a van roof; half-recognize a faltering tune on a careless pipe, a snatch of laughter, a dog's bark . . . . For surely Jack and Toby and I, perhaps Annie and certainly Tom and Daisy would be Playing the Jack down the centuries, for our lives, like the lives of all those who had lived intensely and lovingly, must have left their mark on the very air of the roads, the fields, the hills we had trod . . . .

Listen for us, you who come after: we shall be there, just out of sight down the turn in the road . . . .

Jack came up behind me and putting his arms about my waist, pulled me back against him and kissed my left ear.

'Where would you like to go tomorrow?'

I wanted to say: 'Anywhere, as long as we keep on running and I'm with you,' but I knew the time had come for me to make the first decision of our future together, the decision I knew he wanted me to make. I put my hands over his where they had crept up to the curve of my breast, and I could feel the pulsing of my heart through his fingers.

'Let's go home,' I said.